Vol. 9

Vol. 9

Published by NRM Books.

ISBN: 978-1-965179-12-3

CREDITS
Cover Art by: Nathan Reese Maher

COPYRIGHT

The Ghastly Gothic Tomes are protected under the copyright laws of the United States of America. Any reproductions or unauthorized use of the contents herein including, but not limited to, artwork and text is prohibited without written permission from the author. Novels, poems, plays and short stories published herein are part of the public domain.

Copyright 1st Edition October 14th, 2024, all rights reserved.

Table of Contents

"Villette"
by Charlotte Brontë
Published 1850, p. 2-501

"The House of the Seven Gables"
by Nathaniel Hawthorne
Published 1851, p. 502-725

Villette

By Charlotte Brontë

CHAPTER I.

BRETTON.

My godmother lived in a handsome house in the clean and ancient town of Bretton. Her husband's family had been residents there for generations, and bore, indeed, the name of their birthplace—Bretton of Bretton: whether by coincidence, or because some remote ancestor had been a personage of sufficient importance to leave his name to his neighbourhood, I know not.

When I was a girl I went to Bretton about twice a year, and well I liked the visit. The house and its inmates specially suited me. The large peaceful rooms, the well-arranged furniture, the clear wide windows, the balcony outside, looking down on a fine antique street, where Sundays and holidays seemed always to abide—so quiet was its atmosphere, so clean its pavement—these things pleased me well.

One child in a household of grown people is usually made very much of, and in a quiet way I was a good deal taken notice of by Mrs. Bretton, who had been left a widow, with one son, before I knew her; her husband, a physician, having died while she was yet a young and handsome woman.

She was not young, as I remember her, but she was still handsome, tall, well-made, and though dark for an Englishwoman, yet wearing always the clearness of health in her brunette cheek, and its vivacity in a pair of fine, cheerful black eyes. People esteemed it a grievous pity that she had not conferred her complexion on her son, whose eyes were blue—though, even in boyhood, very piercing—and the colour of his long hair such as friends did not venture to specify, except as the sun shone on it, when they called it golden. He inherited the lines of his mother's features, however; also her good teeth, her stature (or the promise of her stature, for he was not yet full-grown), and, what was better, her health without flaw, and her spirits of that tone and equality which are better than a fortune

Villette

to the possessor.

In the autumn of the year – – I was staying at Bretton; my godmother having come in person to claim me of the kinsfolk with whom was at that time fixed my permanent residence. I believe she then plainly saw events coming, whose very shadow I scarce guessed; yet of which the faint suspicion sufficed to impart unsettled sadness, and made me glad to change scene and society.

Time always flowed smoothly for me at my godmother's side; not with tumultuous swiftness, but blandly, like the gliding of a full river through a plain. My visits to her resembled the sojourn of Christian and Hopeful beside a certain pleasant stream, with "green trees on each bank, and meadows beautified with lilies all the year round." The charm of variety there was not, nor the excitement of incident; but I liked peace so well, and sought stimulus so little, that when the latter came I almost felt it a disturbance, and wished rather it had still held aloof.

One day a letter was received of which the contents evidently caused Mrs. Bretton surprise and some concern. I thought at first it was from home, and trembled, expecting I know not what disastrous communication: to me, however, no reference was made, and the cloud seemed to pass.

The next day, on my return from a long walk, I found, as I entered my bedroom, an unexpected change. In addition to my own French bed in its shady recess, appeared in a corner a small crib, draped with white; and in addition to my mahogany chest of drawers, I saw a tiny rosewood chest. I stood still, gazed, and considered.

"Of what are these things the signs and tokens?" I asked. The answer was obvious. "A second guest is coming: Mrs. Bretton expects other visitors."

On descending to dinner, explanations ensued. A little girl, I was told, would shortly be my companion: the daughter of a friend and distant relation of the late Dr. Bretton's. This little girl, it was added, had recently lost her mother; though, indeed, Mrs. Bretton ere long subjoined, the loss was not so great as might at first appear. Mrs. Home (Home it seems was the name) had been a very pretty, but a giddy, careless woman, who had neglected her child, and disappointed and disheartened her husband. So far from congenial had the union proved, that separation at last ensued—separation by mutual consent, not after any legal process. Soon after this event, the lady having over-exerted herself at a ball, caught cold, took a fever, and died after a very brief illness. Her husband, naturally a man of very sensitive feelings, and shocked inexpressibly by too sudden communication of the news, could hardly, it seems, now be persuaded but that some over-severity on his part—some deficiency in patience and indulgence—had contributed to hasten her end. He had brooded over this idea till his spirits were seriously affected; the medical men insisted on travelling being tried as a remedy, and meanwhile Mrs. Bretton had offered to take charge of his little girl. "And I hope," added my godmother in conclusion, "the child will not be like her mamma; as silly and frivolous a little flirt as ever sensible man was weak enough to marry. For," said she, "Mr. Home is a sensible man in his way, though not very practical: he is fond of science, and lives half his life in a laboratory trying experiments—a thing his butterfly wife could neither comprehend nor endure; and indeed" confessed my godmother, "I should not have liked it myself."

In answer to a question of mine, she further informed me that her late husband used to say, Mr. Home had derived this scientific turn from a maternal uncle, a French savant; for he came, it seems; of mixed French and Scottish origin, and had connections now living in France, of whom more than one wrote de before his name, and called himself noble.

That same evening at nine o'clock, a servant was despatched to meet the coach by which our little visitor was expected. Mrs. Bretton and I sat alone in the drawing-room waiting her coming; John Graham Bretton being absent on a visit to one of his schoolfellows who lived in the country. My godmother read the evening paper while she waited; I sewed. It was a wet night; the rain lashed the panes, and the wind sounded angry and restless.

"Poor child!" said Mrs. Bretton from time to time. "What weather for her journey! I wish she were safe here."

A little before ten the door-bell announced Warren's return. No sooner was the door opened than I ran down into the hall; there lay a trunk and some band-boxes, beside them stood a person like a nurse-girl, and at the foot of the staircase was Warren with a shawled bundle in his arms.

"Is that the child?" I asked.

"Yes, miss."

I would have opened the shawl, and tried to get a peep at the face, but it was hastily turned from me to Warren's shoulder.

"Put me down, please," said a small voice when Warren opened the drawing-room door, "and take off this shawl," continued the speaker, extracting with its minute hand the pin, and with a sort of fastidious haste doffing the clumsy wrapping. The creature which now appeared made a deft attempt to fold the shawl; but the drapery was much too heavy and large to be sustained or wielded by those hands and arms. "Give it to Harriet, please," was then the direction, "and she can put it away." This said, it turned and fixed its eyes on Mrs. Bretton.

"Come here, little dear," said that lady. "Come and let me see if you are cold and damp: come and let me warm you at the fire."

The child advanced promptly. Relieved of her wrapping, she appeared exceedingly tiny; but was a neat, completely-fashioned little figure, light, slight, and straight. Seated on my godmother's ample lap, she looked a mere doll; her neck, delicate as wax, her head of silky curls, increased, I thought, the resemblance.

Mrs. Bretton talked in little fond phrases as she chafed the child's hands, arms, and feet; first she was considered with a wistful gaze, but soon a smile answered her. Mrs. Bretton was not generally a caressing woman: even with her deeply-cherished son, her manner was rarely sentimental, often the reverse; but when the small stranger smiled at her, she kissed it, asking, "What is my little one's name?"

"Missy."

"But besides Missy?"

"Polly, papa calls her."

"Will Polly be content to live with me?"

"Not always; but till papa comes home. Papa is gone away." She shook her head expressively.

"He will return to Polly, or send for her."

"Will he, ma'am? Do you know he will?"

"I think so."

"But Harriet thinks not: at least not for a long while. He is ill."

Her eyes filled. She drew her hand from Mrs. Bretton's and made a movement to leave her lap; it was at first resisted, but she said—"Please, I wish to go: I can sit on a stool."

She was allowed to slip down from the knee, and taking a footstool, she carried it to a corner where the shade was deep, and there seated herself. Mrs. Bretton, though a commanding, and in grave matters even a peremptory woman, was often passive in trifles: she allowed the child her way. She said to me, "Take no notice at present." But I did take notice: I watched Polly rest her small elbow on her small knee, her head on her hand; I observed her draw a square inch or two of pocket-handkerchief from the doll-pocket of her doll-skirt, and then I heard her weep. Other children in grief or pain cry aloud, without shame or restraint; but this being wept: the tiniest occasional sniff testified to her emotion. Mrs. Bretton did not hear it: which was quite as well. Ere long, a voice, issuing from the corner, demanded—"May the bell be rung for Harriet!"

I rang; the nurse was summoned and came.

"Harriet, I must be put to bed," said her little mistress. "You must ask where my bed is."

Harriet signified that she had already made that inquiry.

"Ask if you sleep with me, Harriet."

"No, Missy," said the nurse: "you are to share this young lady's room," designating me.

Missy did not leave her seat, but I saw her eyes seek me. After some minutes' silent scrutiny, she emerged from her corner.

"I wish you, ma'am, good night," said she to Mrs. Bretton; but she passed me mute.

"Good-night, Polly," I said.

"No need to say good-night, since we sleep in the same chamber," was the reply, with which she vanished from the drawing-room. We heard Harriet propose to carry her up-stairs.

Villette

"No need," was again her answer — "no need, no need:" and her small step toiled wearily up the staircase.

On going to bed an hour afterwards, I found her still wide awake. She had arranged her pillows so as to support her little person in a sitting posture: her hands, placed one within the other, rested quietly on the sheet, with an old-fashioned calm most unchildlike. I abstained from speaking to her for some time, but just before extinguishing the light, I recommended her to lie down.

"By and by," was the answer.

"But you will take cold, Missy."

She took some tiny article of raiment from the chair at her crib side, and with it covered her shoulders. I suffered her to do as she pleased. Listening awhile in the darkness, I was aware that she still wept, — wept under restraint, quietly and cautiously.

On awaking with daylight, a trickling of water caught my ear. Behold! there she was risen and mounted on a stool near the washstand, with pains and difficulty inclining the ewer (which she could not lift) so as to pour its contents into the basin. It was curious to watch her as she washed and dressed, so small, busy, and noiseless. Evidently she was little accustomed to perform her own toilet; and the buttons, strings, hooks and eyes, offered difficulties which she encountered with a perseverance good to witness. She folded her night-dress, she smoothed the drapery of her couch quite neatly; withdrawing into a corner, where the sweep of the white curtain concealed her, she became still. I half rose, and advanced my head to see how she was occupied. On her knees, with her forehead bent on her hands, I perceived that she was praying.

Her nurse tapped at the door. She started up.

"I am dressed, Harriet," said she; "I have dressed myself, but I do not feel neat. Make me neat!"

"Why did you dress yourself, Missy?"

"Hush! speak low, Harriet, for fear of waking the girl" (meaning me, who now lay with my eyes shut). "I dressed myself to learn, against the time you leave me."

"Do you want me to go?"

"When you are cross, I have many a time wanted you to go, but not now. Tie my sash straight; make my hair smooth, please."

"Your sash is straight enough. What a particular little body you are!"

"It must be tied again. Please to tie it."

"There, then. When I am gone you must get that young lady to dress you."

"On no account."

"Why? She is a very nice young lady. I hope you mean to behave prettily to her, Missy, and not show your airs."

"She shall dress me on no account."

"Comical little thing!"

"You are not passing the comb straight through my hair, Harriet; the line will be crooked."

"Ay, you are ill to please. Does that suit?"

"Pretty well. Where should I go now that I am dressed?"

"I will take you into the breakfast-room."

"Come, then."

They proceeded to the door. She stopped.

"Oh! Harriet, I wish this was papa's house! I don't know these people."

"Be a good child, Missy."

"I am good, but I ache here;" putting her hand to her heart, and moaning while she reiterated, "Papa! papa!"

I roused myself and started up, to check this scene while it was yet within bounds.

"Say good-morning to the young lady," dictated Harriet. She said, "Good-morning," and then followed her nurse from the room. Harriet temporarily left that same day, to go to her own friends, who lived in the neighbourhood.

On descending, I found Paulina (the child called herself Polly, but her full name was Paulina Mary) seated at the breakfast-table, by Mrs. Bretton's side; a mug of milk stood before her, a morsel of bread filled her hand, which lay passive on the table-cloth: she was not eating.

"How we shall conciliate this little creature," said Mrs. Bretton to me, "I don't know: she tastes nothing, and by her looks, she has not slept."

I expressed my confidence in the effects of time and kindness.

"If she were to take a fancy to anybody in the house, she would soon settle; but not till then," replied Mrs. Bretton.

CHAPTER II.
PAULINA.

Some days elapsed, and it appeared she was not likely to take much of a fancy to anybody in the house. She was not exactly naughty or wilful: she was far from disobedient; but an object less conducive to comfort—to tranquillity even—than she presented, it was scarcely possible to have before one's eyes. She moped: no grown person could have performed that uncheering business better; no furrowed face of adult exile, longing for Europe at Europe's antipodes, ever bore more legibly the signs of home sickness than did her infant visage. She seemed growing old and unearthly. I, Lucy Snowe, plead guiltless of that curse, an overheated and discursive imagination; but whenever, opening a room-door, I found her seated in a corner alone, her head in her pigmy hand, that room seemed to me not inhabited, but haunted.

And again, when of moonlight nights, on waking, I beheld her figure, white and conspicuous in its night-dress, kneeling upright in bed, and praying like some Catholic or Methodist enthusiast—some precocious fanatic or untimely saint—I scarcely know what thoughts I had; but they ran risk of being hardly more rational and healthy than that child's mind must have been.

I seldom caught a word of her prayers, for they were whispered low: sometimes, indeed, they were not whispered at all, but put up unuttered; such rare sentences as reached my ear still bore the burden, "Papa; my dear papa!" This, I perceived, was a one-idea'd nature; betraying that monomaniac tendency I have ever thought the most unfortunate with which man or woman can be cursed.

What might have been the end of this fretting, had it continued unchecked, can only be conjectured: it received, however, a sudden turn.

One afternoon, Mrs. Bretton, coaxing her from her usual station in a corner, had lifted her into the window-seat, and, by way of occupying her attention, told her to watch the passengers and count how many ladies should go down the street in a given time. She had sat listlessly, hardly looking, and not counting, when—my eye being fixed on hers—I witnessed in its iris and pupil a startling transfiguration. These sudden, dangerous natures—sensitive as they are called—offer many a curious spectacle to those whom a cooler temperament has secured from participation in their angular vagaries. The fixed and heavy gaze swum, trembled, then glittered in fire; the small, overcast brow cleared; the trivial and dejected features lit up; the sad countenance vanished, and in its place appeared a sudden eagerness, an intense expectancy. "It is!" were her words.

Like a bird or a shaft, or any other swift thing, she was gone from the room. How she got the house-door open I cannot tell; probably it might be ajar; perhaps Warren was in the way and obeyed her behest, which would be impetuous enough. I — watching calmly from the window — saw her, in her black frock and tiny braided apron (to pinafores she had an antipathy), dart half the length of the street; and, as I was on the point of turning, and quietly announcing to Mrs. Bretton that the child was run out mad, and ought instantly to be pursued, I saw her caught up, and rapt at once from my cool observation, and from the wondering stare of the passengers. A gentleman had done this good turn, and now, covering her with his cloak, advanced to restore her to the house whence he had seen her issue.

I concluded he would leave her in a servant's charge and withdraw; but he entered: having tarried a little while below, he came up-stairs.

His reception immediately explained that he was known to Mrs. Bretton. She recognised him; she greeted him, and yet she was fluttered, surprised, taken unawares. Her look and manner were even expostulatory; and in reply to these, rather than her words, he said, — "I could not help it, madam: I found it impossible to leave the country without seeing with my own eyes how she settled."

"But you will unsettle her."

"I hope not. And how is papa's little Polly?"

This question he addressed to Paulina, as he sat down and placed her gently on the ground before him.

"How is Polly's papa?" was the reply, as she leaned on his knee, and gazed up into his face.

It was not a noisy, not a wordy scene: for that I was thankful; but it was a scene of feeling too brimful, and which, because the cup did not foam up high or furiously overflow, only oppressed one the more. On all occasions of vehement, unrestrained expansion, a sense of disdain or ridicule comes to the weary spectator's relief; whereas I have ever felt most burdensome that sort of sensibility which bends of its own will, a giant slave under the sway of good sense.

Mr. Home was a stern-featured—perhaps I should rather say, a hard-featured man: his forehead was knotty, and his cheekbones were marked and prominent. The character of his face was quite Scotch; but there was feeling in his eye, and emotion in his now agitated countenance. His northern accent in speaking harmonised with his physiognomy. He was at once proud-looking and homely-looking. He laid his hand on the child's uplifted head. She said—"Kiss Polly."

He kissed her. I wished she would utter some hysterical cry, so that I might get relief and be at ease. She made wonderfully little noise: she seemed to have got what she wanted—all she wanted, and to be in a trance of content. Neither in mien nor in features was this creature like her sire, and yet she was of his strain: her mind had been filled from his, as the cup from the flagon.

Indisputably, Mr. Home owned manly self-control, however he might secretly feel on some matters. "Polly," he said, looking down on his little girl, "go into the hall; you will see papa's great-coat lying on a chair; put your hand into the pockets, you will find a pocket-handkerchief there; bring it to me."

She obeyed; went and returned deftly and nimbly. He was talking to Mrs. Bretton when she came back, and she waited with the handkerchief in her hand. It was a picture, in its way, to see her, with her tiny stature, and trim, neat shape, standing at his knee. Seeing that he continued to talk, apparently unconscious of her return, she took his hand, opened the unresisting fingers, insinuated into them the handkerchief, and closed them upon it one by one. He still seemed not to see or to feel her; but by-and-by, he lifted her to his knee; she nestled against him, and though neither looked at nor spoke to the other for an hour following, I suppose both were satisfied.

During tea, the minute thing's movements and behaviour gave, as usual, full occupation to the eye. First she directed Warren, as he placed the chairs.

"Put papa's chair here, and mine near it, between papa and Mrs. Bretton: I must hand his tea."

She took her own seat, and beckoned with her hand to her

Villette

father.

"Be near me, as if we were at home, papa."

And again, as she intercepted his cup in passing, and would stir the sugar, and put in the cream herself, "I always did it for you at home; papa: nobody could do it as well, not even your own self."

Throughout the meal she continued her attentions: rather absurd they were. The sugar-tongs were too wide for one of her hands, and she had to use both in wielding them; the weight of the silver cream-ewer, the bread-and-butter plates, the very cup and saucer, tasked her insufficient strength and dexterity; but she would lift this, hand that, and luckily contrived through it all to break nothing. Candidly speaking, I thought her a little busy-body; but her father, blind like other parents, seemed perfectly content to let her wait on him, and even wonderfully soothed by her offices.

"She is my comfort!" he could not help saying to Mrs. Bretton. That lady had her own "comfort" and nonpareil on a much larger scale, and, for the moment, absent; so she sympathised with his foible.

This second "comfort" came on the stage in the course of the evening. I knew this day had been fixed for his return, and was aware that Mrs. Bretton had been expecting him through all its hours. We were seated round the fire, after tea, when Graham joined our circle: I should rather say, broke it up—for, of course, his arrival made a bustle; and then, as Mr. Graham was fasting, there was refreshment to be provided. He and Mr. Home met as old acquaintance; of the little girl he took no notice for a time.

His meal over, and numerous questions from his mother answered, he turned from the table to the hearth. Opposite where he had placed himself was seated Mr. Home, and at his elbow, the child. When I say child I use an inappropriate and undescriptive term—a term suggesting any picture rather than that of the demure little person in a mourning frock and white chemisette, that might just have fitted a good-sized doll—perched now on a high chair beside a stand, whereon was her toy work-box of white varnished wood, and holding in her hands a shred of a handkerchief, which she was professing to hem, and at which she bored perseveringly with a needle, that in her fingers seemed almost a skewer, pricking herself ever and anon, marking the cambric with a track of minute red dots; occasionally starting when the perverse weapon—swerving from her control—inflicted a deeper stab than usual; but still silent, diligent, absorbed, womanly.

Graham was at that time a handsome, faithless-looking youth of sixteen. I say faithless-looking, not because he was really of a very perfidious disposition, but because the epithet strikes me as proper to describe the fair, Celtic (not Saxon) character of his good looks; his waved light auburn hair, his supple symmetry, his smile frequent, and destitute neither of fascination nor of subtlety (in no bad sense). A spoiled, whimsical boy he was in those days.

"Mother," he said, after eyeing the little figure before him in silence for some time, and when the temporary absence of Mr. Home from the room relieved him from the half-laughing bashfulness, which was all he knew of timidity—-"Mother, I see a young lady in the present society to whom I have not been introduced."

"Mr. Home's little girl, I suppose you mean," said his mother.

"Indeed, ma'am," replied her son, "I consider your expression of the least ceremonious: Miss Home I should certainly have said, in venturing to speak of the gentlewoman to whom I allude."

"Now, Graham, I will not have that child teased. Don't flatter yourself that I shall suffer you to make her your butt."

"Miss Home," pursued Graham, undeterred by his mother's remonstrance, "might I have the honour to introduce myself, since no one else seems willing to render you and me that service? Your slave, John Graham Bretton."

She looked at him; he rose and bowed quite gravely. She deliberately put down thimble, scissors, work; descended with precaution from her perch, and curtsying with unspeakable seriousness, said, "How do you do?"

"I have the honour to be in fair health, only in some measure fatigued with a hurried journey. I hope, ma'am, I see you well?"

"Tor-rer-ably well," was the ambitious reply of the little woman and she now essayed to regain her former elevation, but finding this could not be done without some climbing and straining—a sacrifice of decorum not to be thought of—and being utterly disdainful of aid in the presence of a strange young gentleman, she relinquished the high chair for a low stool: towards that low stool Graham drew in his chair.

"I hope, ma'am, the present residence, my mother's house, appears to you a convenient place of abode?"

"Not par-tic-er-er-ly; I want to go home."

"A natural and laudable desire, ma'am; but one which, notwithstanding, I shall do my best to oppose. I reckon on being able to get out of you a little of that precious commodity called amusement, which mamma and Mistress Snowe there fail to yield me."

"I shall have to go with papa soon: I shall not stay long at your mother's."

"Yes, yes; you will stay with me, I am sure. I have a pony on which you shall ride, and no end of books with pictures to show you."

"Are you going to live here now?"

"I am. Does that please you? Do you like me?"

"No."

"Why?"

"I think you queer."

"My face, ma'am?"

"Your face and all about you: You have long red hair."

"Auburn hair, if you please: mamma calls it auburn, or golden, and so do all her friends. But even with my 'long red hair'" (and he waved his mane with a sort of triumph—tawny he himself well knew that it was, and he was proud of the leonine hue), "I cannot possibly be queerer than is your ladyship."

"You call me queer?"

"Certainly."

(After a pause) "I think I shall go to bed."

"A little thing like you ought to have been in bed many hours since; but you probably sat up in the expectation of seeing me?"

"No, indeed."

"You certainly wished to enjoy the pleasure of my society. You knew I was coming home, and would wait to have a look at me."

"I sat up for papa, and not for you."

"Very good, Miss Home. I am going to be a favourite: preferred before papa soon, I daresay."

She wished Mrs. Bretton and myself good-night; she seemed hesitating whether Graham's deserts entitled him to the same attention, when he caught her up with one hand, and with that one hand held her poised aloft above his head. She saw herself thus lifted up on high, in the glass over the fireplace. The suddenness, the freedom, the disrespect of the action were too much.

"For shame, Mr. Graham!" was her indignant cry, "put me down!"—and when again on her feet, "I wonder what you would think of me if I were to treat you in that way, lifting you with my hand" (raising that mighty member) "as Warren lifts the little cat."

So saying, she departed.

CHAPTER III.

THE PLAYMATES.

Mr. Home stayed two days. During his visit he could not be prevailed on to go out: he sat all day long by the fireside, sometimes silent, sometimes receiving and answering Mrs. Bretton's chat, which was just of the proper sort for a man in his morbid mood—not over-sympathetic, yet not too uncongenial, sensible; and even with a touch of the motherly—she was sufficiently his senior to be permitted this touch.

As to Paulina, the child was at once happy and mute, busy and watchful. Her father frequently lifted her to his knee; she would sit there till she felt or fancied he grew restless; then it was—"Papa, put me down; I shall tire you with my weight."

And the mighty burden slid to the rug, and establishing itself on carpet or stool just at "papa's" feet, the white work-box and the scarlet-speckled handkerchief came into play. This handkerchief, it seems, was intended as a keepsake for "papa," and must be finished before his departure; consequently the demand on the sempstress's industry (she accomplished about a score of stitches in half-an-hour) was stringent.

The evening, by restoring Graham to the maternal roof (his days were passed at school), brought us an accession of animation—a quality not diminished by the nature of the scenes pretty sure to be enacted between him and Miss Paulina.

A distant and haughty demeanour had been the result of the indignity put upon her the first evening of his arrival: her usual answer, when he addressed her, was—"I can't attend to you; I have other things to think about." Being implored to state what things:

"Business."

Graham would endeavour to seduce her attention by opening his desk and displaying its multifarious contents: seals, bright sticks of wax, pen-knives, with a miscellany of engravings—some of them gaily coloured—which he had amassed from time to time. Nor was this powerful temptation wholly unavailing: her eyes, furtively raised from her work, cast many a peep towards the writing-table, rich in scattered pictures. An etching of a child playing with a Blenheim spaniel happened to flutter to the floor.

"Pretty little dog!" said she, delighted.

Graham prudently took no notice. Ere long, stealing from her corner, she approached to examine the treasure more closely. The dog's great eyes and long ears, and the child's hat and feathers, were irresistible.

"Nice picture!" was her favourable criticism.

"Well—you may have it," said Graham.

She seemed to hesitate. The wish to possess was strong, but to accept would be a compromise of dignity. No. She put it down and turned away.

"You won't have it, then, Polly?"

"I would rather not, thank you."

"Shall I tell you what I will do with the picture if you refuse it?"

She half turned to listen.

"Cut it into strips for lighting the taper."

"No!"

"But I shall."

"Please—don't."

Graham waxed inexorable on hearing the pleading tone; he took the scissors from his mother's work-basket.

"Here goes!" said he, making a menacing flourish. "Right through Fido's head, and splitting little Harry's nose."

"No! No! NO!"

"Then come to me. Come quickly, or it is done."

She hesitated, lingered, but complied.

"Now, will you have it?" he asked, as she stood before him.

"Please."

Villette

"But I shall want payment."

"How much?"

"A kiss."

"Give the picture first into my hand."

Polly, as she said this, looked rather faithless in her turn. Graham gave it. She absconded a debtor, darted to her father, and took refuge on his knee. Graham rose in mimic wrath and followed. She buried her face in Mr. Home's waistcoat.

"Papa—papa—send him away!"

"I'll not be sent away," said Graham.

With face still averted, she held out her hand to keep him off.

"Then, I shall kiss the hand," said he; but that moment it became a miniature fist, and dealt him payment in a small coin that was not kisses.

Graham—not failing in his way to be as wily as his little playmate—retreated apparently quite discomfited; he flung himself on a sofa, and resting his head against the cushion, lay like one in pain. Polly, finding him silent, presently peeped at him. His eyes and face were covered with his hands. She turned on her father's knee, and gazed at her foe anxiously and long. Graham groaned.

"Papa, what is the matter?" she whispered.

"You had better ask him, Polly."

"Is he hurt?" (groan second.)

"He makes a noise as if he were," said Mr. Home.

"Mother," suggested Graham, feebly, "I think you had better send for the doctor. Oh my eye!" (renewed silence, broken only by sighs from Graham.)

"If I were to become blind——?" suggested this last.

His chastiser could not bear the suggestion. She was beside him directly.

19

"Let me see your eye: I did not mean to touch it, only your mouth; and I did not think I hit so very hard."

Silence answered her. Her features worked,—"I am sorry; I am sorry!"

Then succeeded emotion, faltering; weeping.

"Have done trying that child, Graham," said Mrs. Bretton.

"It is all nonsense, my pet," cried Mr. Home.

And Graham once more snatched her aloft, and she again punished him; and while she pulled his lion's locks, termed him—"The naughtiest, rudest, worst, untruest person that ever was."

On the morning of Mr. Home's departure, he and his daughter had some conversation in a window-recess by themselves; I heard part of it.

"Couldn't I pack my box and go with you, papa?" she whispered earnestly.

He shook his head.

"Should I be a trouble to you?"

"Yes, Polly."

"Because I am little?"

"Because you are little and tender. It is only great, strong people that should travel. But don't look sad, my little girl; it breaks my heart. Papa, will soon come back to his Polly."

"Indeed, indeed, I am not sad, scarcely at all."

"Polly would be sorry to give papa pain; would she not?"

"Sorrier than sorry."

"Then Polly must be cheerful: not cry at parting; not fret afterwards. She must look forward to meeting again, and try to be happy meanwhile. Can she do this?"

"She will try."

Villette

"I see she will. Farewell, then. It is time to go."

"Now? — just now?

"Just now."

She held up quivering lips. Her father sobbed, but she, I remarked, did not. Having put her down, he shook hands with the rest present, and departed.

When the street-door closed, she dropped on her knees at a chair with a cry — "Papa!"

It was low and long; a sort of "Why hast thou forsaken me?" During an ensuing space of some minutes, I perceived she endured agony. She went through, in that brief interval of her infant life, emotions such as some never feel; it was in her constitution: she would have more of such instants if she lived. Nobody spoke. Mrs. Bretton, being a mother, shed a tear or two. Graham, who was writing, lifted up his eyes and gazed at her. I, Lucy Snowe, was calm.

The little creature, thus left unharassed, did for herself what none other could do — contended with an intolerable feeling; and, ere long, in some degree, repressed it. That day she would accept solace from none; nor the next day: she grew more passive afterwards.

On the third evening, as she sat on the floor, worn and quiet, Graham, coming in, took her up gently, without a word. She did not resist: she rather nestled in his arms, as if weary. When he sat down, she laid her head against him; in a few minutes she slept; he carried her upstairs to bed. I was not surprised that, the next morning, the first thing she demanded was, "Where is Mr. Graham?"

It happened that Graham was not coming to the breakfast-table; he had some exercises to write for that morning's class, and had requested his mother to send a cup of tea into the study. Polly volunteered to carry it: she must be busy about something, look after somebody. The cup was entrusted to her; for, if restless, she was also careful. As the study was opposite the breakfast-room, the doors facing across the passage, my eye followed her.

"What are you doing?" she asked, pausing on the threshold.

"Writing," said Graham.

"Why don't you come to take breakfast with your mamma?"

"Too busy."

"Do you want any breakfast?"

"Of course."

"There, then."

And she deposited the cup on the carpet, like a jailor putting a prisoner's pitcher of water through his cell-door, and retreated. Presently she returned.

"What will you have besides tea—what to eat?"

"Anything good. Bring me something particularly nice; that's a kind little woman."

She came back to Mrs. Bretton.

"Please, ma'am, send your boy something good."

"You shall choose for him, Polly; what shall my boy have?"

She selected a portion of whatever was best on the table; and, ere long, came back with a whispered request for some marmalade, which was not there. Having got it, however, (for Mrs. Bretton refused the pair nothing), Graham was shortly after heard lauding her to the skies; promising that, when he had a house of his own, she should be his housekeeper, and perhaps—if she showed any culinary genius—his cook; and, as she did not return, and I went to look after her, I found Graham and her breakfasting tête-à-tête—she standing at his elbow, and sharing his fare: excepting the marmalade, which she delicately refused to touch, lest, I suppose, it should appear that she had procured it as much on her own account as his. She constantly evinced these nice perceptions and delicate instincts.

The league of acquaintanceship thus struck up was not hastily dissolved; on the contrary, it appeared that time and circumstances served rather to cement than loosen it. Ill-assimilated as the two were in age, sex, pursuits, &c., they somehow found a great deal to say to each other. As to Paulina, I observed that her little character never properly came out, except with young Bretton. As she got settled, and accustomed to the house, she proved tractable enough with Mrs. Bretton; but she would sit on a stool at that lady's feet all day long,

Villette

learning her task, or sewing, or drawing figures with a pencil on a slate, and never kindling once to originality, or showing a single gleam of the peculiarities of her nature. I ceased to watch her under such circumstances: she was not interesting. But the moment Graham's knock sounded of an evening, a change occurred; she was instantly at the head of the staircase. Usually her welcome was a reprimand or a threat.

"You have not wiped your shoes properly on the mat. I shall tell your mamma."

"Little busybody! Are you there?"

"Yes—and you can't reach me: I am higher up than you" (peeping between the rails of the banister; she could not look over them).

"Polly!"

"My dear boy!" (such was one of her terms for him, adopted in imitation of his mother.)

"I am fit to faint with fatigue," declared Graham, leaning against the passage-wall in seeming exhaustion. "Dr. Digby" (the headmaster) "has quite knocked me up with overwork. Just come down and help me to carry up my books."

"Ah! you're cunning!"

"Not at all, Polly—it is positive fact. I'm as weak as a rush. Come down."

"Your eyes are quiet like the cat's, but you'll spring."

"Spring? Nothing of the kind: it isn't in me. Come down."

"Perhaps I may—if you'll promise not to touch—not to snatch me up, and not to whirl me round."

"I? I couldn't do it!" (sinking into a chair.)

"Then put the books down on the first step, and go three yards off."

This being done, she descended warily, and not taking her eyes from the feeble Graham. Of course her approach always galvanized him to new and spasmodic life: the game of romps was sure to be exacted. Sometimes she would be angry;

sometimes the matter was allowed to pass smoothly, and we could hear her say as she led him up-stairs: "Now, my dear boy, come and take your tea—I am sure you must want something."

It was sufficiently comical to observe her as she sat beside Graham, while he took that meal. In his absence she was a still personage, but with him the most officious, fidgety little body possible. I often wished she would mind herself and be tranquil; but no—herself was forgotten in him: he could not be sufficiently well waited on, nor carefully enough looked after; he was more than the Grand Turk in her estimation. She would gradually assemble the various plates before him, and, when one would suppose all he could possibly desire was within his reach, she would find out something else: "Ma'am," she would whisper to Mrs. Bretton,—"perhaps your son would like a little cake—sweet cake, you know—there is some in there" (pointing to the sideboard cupboard). Mrs. Bretton, as a rule, disapproved of sweet cake at tea, but still the request was urged,—"One little piece—only for him—as he goes to school: girls—such as me and Miss Snowe—don't need treats, but he would like it."

Graham did like it very well, and almost always got it. To do him justice, he would have shared his prize with her to whom he owed it; but that was never allowed: to insist, was to ruffle her for the evening. To stand by his knee, and monopolize his talk and notice, was the reward she wanted—not a share of the cake.

With curious readiness did she adapt herself to such themes as interested him. One would have thought the child had no mind or life of her own, but must necessarily live, move, and have her being in another: now that her father was taken from her, she nestled to Graham, and seemed to feel by his feelings: to exist in his existence. She learned the names of all his schoolfellows in a trice: she got by heart their characters as given from his lips: a single description of an individual seemed to suffice. She never forgot, or confused identities: she would talk with him the whole evening about people she had never seen, and appear completely to realise their aspect, manners, and dispositions. Some she learned to mimic: an under-master, who was an aversion of young Bretton's, had, it seems, some peculiarities, which she caught up in a moment from Graham's representation, and rehearsed for his amusement; this, however, Mrs. Bretton disapproved and forbade.

The pair seldom quarrelled; yet once a rupture occurred, in which her feelings received a severe shock.

Villette

One day Graham, on the occasion of his birthday, had some friends—lads of his own age—to dine with him. Paulina took much interest in the coming of these friends; she had frequently heard of them; they were amongst those of whom Graham oftenest spoke. After dinner, the young gentlemen were left by themselves in the dining-room, where they soon became very merry and made a good deal of noise. Chancing to pass through the hall, I found Paulina sitting alone on the lowest step of the staircase, her eyes fixed on the glossy panels of the dining-room door, where the reflection of the hall-lamp was shining; her little brow knit in anxious meditation.

"What are you thinking about, Polly?"

"Nothing particular; only I wish that door was clear glass—that I might see through it. The boys seem very cheerful, and I want to go to them: I want to be with Graham, and watch his friends."

"What hinders you from going?"

"I feel afraid: but may I try, do you think? May I knock at the door, and ask to be let in?"

I thought perhaps they might not object to have her as a playmate, and therefore encouraged the attempt.

She knocked—too faintly at first to be heard, but on a second essay the door unclosed; Graham's head appeared; he looked in high spirits, but impatient.

"What do you want, you little monkey?"

"To come to you."

"Do you indeed? As if I would be troubled with you! Away to mamma and Mistress Snowe, and tell them to put you to bed." The auburn head and bright flushed face vanished,—the door shut peremptorily. She was stunned.

"Why does he speak so? He never spoke so before," she said in consternation. "What have I done?"

"Nothing, Polly; but Graham is busy with his school-friends."

"And he likes them better than me! He turns me away now they are here!"

I had some thoughts of consoling her, and of improving the occasion by inculcating some of those maxims of philosophy whereof I had ever a tolerable stock ready for application. She stopped me, however, by putting her fingers in her ears at the first words I uttered, and then lying down on the mat with her face against the flags; nor could either Warren or the cook root her from that position: she was allowed to lie, therefore, till she chose to rise of her own accord.

Graham forgot his impatience the same evening, and would have accosted her as usual when his friends were gone, but she wrenched herself from his hand; her eye quite flashed; she would not bid him good-night; she would not look in his face. The next day he treated her with indifference, and she grew like a bit of marble. The day after, he teased her to know what was the matter; her lips would not unclose. Of course he could not feel real anger on his side: the match was too unequal in every way; he tried soothing and coaxing. "Why was she so angry? What had he done?" By-and-by tears answered him; he petted her, and they were friends. But she was one on whom such incidents were not lost: I remarked that never after this rebuff did she seek him, or follow him, or in any way solicit his notice. I told her once to carry a book or some other article to Graham when he was shut up in his study.

"I shall wait till he comes out," said she, proudly; "I don't choose to give him the trouble of rising to open the door."

Young Bretton had a favourite pony on which he often rode out; from the window she always watched his departure and return. It was her ambition to be permitted to have a ride round the courtyard on this pony; but far be it from her to ask such a favour. One day she descended to the yard to watch him dismount; as she leaned against the gate, the longing wish for the indulgence of a ride glittered in her eye.

"Come, Polly, will you have a canter?" asked Graham, half carelessly.

I suppose she thought he was too careless.

"No, thank you," said she, turning away with the utmost coolness.

"You'd better," pursued he. "You will like it, I am sure."

"Don't think I should care a fig about it," was the response.

"That is not true. You told Lucy Snowe you longed to have a ride."

"Lucy Snowe is a tatter-box," I heard her say (her imperfect articulation was the least precocious thing she had about her); and with this; she walked into the house.

Graham, coming in soon after, observed to his mother,— "Mamma, I believe that creature is a changeling: she is a perfect cabinet of oddities; but I should be dull without her: she amuses me a great deal more than you or Lucy Snowe."

"Miss Snowe," said Paulina to me (she had now got into the habit of occasionally chatting with me when we were alone in our room at night), "do you know on what day in the week I like Graham best?"

"How can I possibly know anything so strange? Is there one day out of the seven when he is otherwise than on the other six?"

"To be sure! Can't you see? Don't you know? I find him the most excellent on a Sunday; then we have him the whole day, and he is quiet, and, in the evening, so kind."

This observation was not altogether groundless: going to church, &c., kept Graham quiet on the Sunday, and the evening he generally dedicated to a serene, though rather indolent sort of enjoyment by the parlour fireside. He would take possession of the couch, and then he would call Polly.

Graham was a boy not quite as other boys are; all his delight did not lie in action: he was capable of some intervals of contemplation; he could take a pleasure too in reading, nor was his selection of books wholly indiscriminate: there were glimmerings of characteristic preference, and even of instinctive taste in the choice. He rarely, it is true, remarked on what he read, but I have seen him sit and think of it.

Polly, being near him, kneeling on a little cushion or the carpet, a conversation would begin in murmurs, not inaudible, though subdued. I caught a snatch of their tenor now and then; and, in truth, some influence better and finer than that of every day, seemed to soothe Graham at such times into no ungentle mood.

"Have you learned any hymns this week, Polly?"

"I have learned a very pretty one, four verses long. Shall I say it?"

"Speak nicely, then: don't be in a hurry."

The hymn being rehearsed, or rather half-chanted, in a little singing voice, Graham would take exceptions at the manner, and proceed to give a lesson in recitation. She was quick in learning, apt in imitating; and, besides, her pleasure was to please Graham: she proved a ready scholar. To the hymn would succeed some reading—perhaps a chapter in the Bible; correction was seldom required here, for the child could read any simple narrative chapter very well; and, when the subject was such as she could understand and take an interest in, her expression and emphasis were something remarkable. Joseph cast into the pit; the calling of Samuel; Daniel in the lions' den; —these were favourite passages: of the first especially she seemed perfectly to feel the pathos.

"Poor Jacob!" she would sometimes say, with quivering lips. "How he loved his son Joseph! As much," she once added—"as much, Graham, as I love you: if you were to die" (and she re-opened the book, sought the verse, and read), "I should refuse to be comforted, and go down into the grave to you mourning."

With these words she gathered Graham in her little arms, drawing his long-tressed head towards her. The action, I remember, struck me as strangely rash; exciting the feeling one might experience on seeing an animal dangerous by nature, and but half-tamed by art, too heedlessly fondled. Not that I feared Graham would hurt, or very roughly check her; but I thought she ran risk of incurring such a careless, impatient repulse, as would be worse almost to her than a blow. On the whole, however, these demonstrations were borne passively: sometimes even a sort of complacent wonder at her earnest partiality would smile not unkindly in his eyes. Once he said:— "You like me almost as well as if you were my little sister, Polly."

"Oh! I do like you," said she; "I do like you very much."

I was not long allowed the amusement of this study of character. She had scarcely been at Bretton two months, when a letter came from Mr. Home, signifying that he was now settled amongst his maternal kinsfolk on the Continent; that, as England was become wholly distasteful to him, he had no thoughts of returning hither, perhaps, for years; and that he wished his little girl to join him immediately.

Villette

"I wonder how she will take this news?" said Mrs. Bretton, when she had read the letter. I wondered, too, and I took upon myself to communicate it.

Repairing to the drawing-room — in which calm and decorated apartment she was fond of being alone, and where she could be implicitly trusted, for she fingered nothing, or rather soiled nothing she fingered — I found her seated, like a little Odalisque, on a couch, half shaded by the drooping draperies of the window near. She seemed happy; all her appliances for occupation were about her; the white wood workbox, a shred or two of muslin, an end or two of ribbon collected for conversion into doll-millinery. The doll, duly night-capped and night-gowned, lay in its cradle; she was rocking it to sleep, with an air of the most perfect faith in its possession of sentient and somnolent faculties; her eyes, at the same time, being engaged with a picture-book, which lay open on her lap.

"Miss Snowe," said she in a whisper, "this is a wonderful book. Candace" (the doll, christened by Graham; for, indeed, its begrimed complexion gave it much of an Ethiopian aspect) — "Candace is asleep now, and I may tell you about it; only we must both speak low, lest she should waken. This book was given me by Graham; it tells about distant countries, a long, long way from England, which no traveller can reach without sailing thousands of miles over the sea. Wild men live in these countries, Miss Snowe, who wear clothes different from ours: indeed, some of them wear scarcely any clothes, for the sake of being cool, you know; for they have very hot weather. Here is a picture of thousands gathered in a desolate place — a plain, spread with sand — round a man in black, — a good, good Englishman — a missionary, who is preaching to them under a palm-tree." (She showed a little coloured cut to that effect.) "And here are pictures" (she went on) "more stranger" (grammar was occasionally forgotten) "than that. There is the wonderful Great Wall of China; here is a Chinese lady, with a foot littler than mine. There is a wild horse of Tartary; and here, most strange of all — is a land of ice and snow, without green fields, woods, or gardens. In this land, they found some mammoth bones: there are no mammoths now. You don't know what it was; but I can tell you, because Graham told me. A mighty, goblin creature, as high as this room, and as long as the hall; but not a fierce, flesh-eating thing, Graham thinks. He believes, if I met one in a forest, it would not kill me, unless I came quite in its way; when it would trample me down amongst the bushes, as I might tread on a grasshopper in a hayfield without knowing it."

Thus she rambled on.

"Polly," I interrupted, "should you like to travel?"

"Not just yet," was the prudent answer; "but perhaps in twenty years, when I am grown a woman, as tall as Mrs. Bretton, I may travel with Graham. We intend going to Switzerland, and climbing Mount Blanck; and some day we shall sail over to South America, and walk to the top of Kim-kim-borazo."

"But how would you like to travel now, if your papa was with you?"

Her reply—not given till after a pause—evinced one of those unexpected turns of temper peculiar to her.

"Where is the good of talking in that silly way?" said she. "Why do you mention papa? What is papa to you? I was just beginning to be happy, and not think about him so much; and there it will be all to do over again!"

Her lip trembled. I hastened to disclose the fact of a letter having been received, and to mention the directions given that she and Harriet should immediately rejoin this dear papa. "Now, Polly, are you not glad?" I added.

She made no answer. She dropped her book and ceased to rock her doll; she gazed at me with gravity and earnestness.

"Shall not you like to go to papa?"

"Of course," she said at last in that trenchant manner she usually employed in speaking to me; and which was quite different from that she used with Mrs. Bretton, and different again from the one dedicated to Graham. I wished to ascertain more of what she thought but no: she would converse no more. Hastening to Mrs. Bretton, she questioned her, and received the confirmation of my news. The weight and importance of these tidings kept her perfectly serious the whole day. In the evening, at the moment Graham's entrance was heard below, I found her at my side. She began to arrange a locket-ribbon about my neck, she displaced and replaced the comb in my hair; while thus busied, Graham entered.

"Tell him by-and-by," she whispered; "tell him I am going."

In the course of tea-time I made the desired communication.

Villette

Graham, it chanced, was at that time greatly preoccupied about some school-prize, for which he was competing. The news had to be told twice before it took proper hold of his attention, and even then he dwelt on it but momently.

"Polly going? What a pity! Dear little Mousie, I shall be sorry to lose her: she must come to us again, mamma."

And hastily swallowing his tea, he took a candle and a small table to himself and his books, and was soon buried in study.

"Little Mousie" crept to his side, and lay down on the carpet at his feet, her face to the floor; mute and motionless she kept that post and position till bed-time. Once I saw Graham—wholly unconscious of her proximity—push her with his restless foot. She receded an inch or two. A minute after one little hand stole out from beneath her face, to which it had been pressed, and softly caressed the heedless foot. When summoned by her nurse she rose and departed very obediently, having bid us all a subdued good-night.

I will not say that I dreaded going to bed, an hour later; yet I certainly went with an unquiet anticipation that I should find that child in no peaceful sleep. The forewarning of my instinct was but fulfilled, when I discovered her, all cold and vigilant, perched like a white bird on the outside of the bed. I scarcely knew how to accost her; she was not to be managed like another child. She, however, accosted me. As I closed the door, and put the light on the dressing-table, she turned to me with these words:—"I cannot—cannot sleep; and in this way I cannot—cannot live!"

I asked what ailed her.

"Dedful miz-er-y!" said she, with her piteous lisp.

"Shall I call Mrs. Bretton?"

"That is downright silly," was her impatient reply; and, indeed, I well knew that if she had heard Mrs. Bretton's foot approach, she would have nestled quiet as a mouse under the bedclothes. Whilst lavishing her eccentricities regardlessly before me—for whom she professed scarcely the semblance of affection—she never showed my godmother one glimpse of her inner self: for her, she was nothing but a docile, somewhat quaint little maiden. I examined her; her cheek was crimson; her dilated eye was both troubled and glowing, and painfully restless: in this state it was obvious she must not be left till morning. I guessed how the case stood.

"Would you like to bid Graham good-night again?" I asked. "He is not gone to his room yet."

She at once stretched out her little arms to be lifted. Folding a shawl round her, I carried her back to the drawing-room. Graham was just coming out.

"She cannot sleep without seeing and speaking to you once more," I said. "She does not like the thought of leaving you."

"I've spoilt her," said he, taking her from me with good humour, and kissing her little hot face and burning lips. "Polly, you care for me more than for papa, now—"

"I do care for you, but you care nothing for me," was her whisper.

She was assured to the contrary, again kissed, restored to me, and I carried her away; but, alas! not soothed.

When I thought she could listen to me, I said—"Paulina, you should not grieve that Graham does not care for you so much as you care for him. It must be so."

Her lifted and questioning eyes asked why.

"Because he is a boy and you are a girl; he is sixteen and you are only six; his nature is strong and gay, and yours is otherwise."

"But I love him so much; he should love me a little."

"He does. He is fond of you. You are his favourite."

"Am I Graham's favourite?"

"Yes, more than any little child I know."

The assurance soothed her; she smiled in her anguish.

"But," I continued, "don't fret, and don't expect too much of him, or else he will feel you to be troublesome, and then it is all over."

"All over!" she echoed softly; "then I'll be good. I'll try to be good, Lucy Snowe."

Villette

I put her to bed.

"Will he forgive me this one time?" she asked, as I undressed myself. I assured her that he would; that as yet he was by no means alienated; that she had only to be careful for the future.

"There is no future," said she: "I am going. Shall I ever — ever — see him again, after I leave England?"

I returned an encouraging response. The candle being extinguished, a still half-hour elapsed. I thought her asleep, when the little white shape once more lifted itself in the crib, and the small voice asked — "Do you like Graham, Miss Snowe?"

"Like him! Yes, a little."

"Only a little! Do you like him as I do?"

"I think not. No: not as you do."

"Do you like him much?"

"I told you I liked him a little. Where is the use of caring for him so very much: he is full of faults."

"Is he?"

"All boys are."

"More than girls?"

"Very likely. Wise people say it is folly to think anybody perfect; and as to likes and dislikes, we should be friendly to all, and worship none."

"Are you a wise person?"

"I mean to try to be so. Go to sleep."

"I cannot go to sleep. Have you no pain just here" (laying her elfish hand on her elfish breast,) "when you think you shall have to leave Graham; for your home is not here?"

"Surely, Polly," said I, "you should not feel so much pain when you are very soon going to rejoin your father. Have you forgotten him? Do you no longer wish to be his little companion?"

Dead silence succeeded this question.

"Child, lie down and sleep," I urged.

"My bed is cold," said she. "I can't warm it."

I saw the little thing shiver. "Come to me," I said, wishing, yet scarcely hoping, that she would comply: for she was a most strange, capricious, little creature, and especially whimsical with me. She came, however, instantly, like a small ghost gliding over the carpet. I took her in. She was chill: I warmed her in my arms. She trembled nervously; I soothed her. Thus tranquillized and cherished she at last slumbered.

"A very unique child," thought I, as I viewed her sleeping countenance by the fitful moonlight, and cautiously and softly wiped her glittering eyelids and her wet cheeks with my handkerchief. "How will she get through this world, or battle with this life? How will she bear the shocks and repulses, the humiliations and desolations, which books, and my own reason, tell me are prepared for all flesh?"

She departed the next day; trembling like a leaf when she took leave, but exercising self-command.

CHAPTER IV.

MISS MARCHMONT.

On quitting Bretton, which I did a few weeks after Paulina's departure—little thinking then I was never again to visit it; never more to tread its calm old streets—I betook myself home, having been absent six months. It will be conjectured that I was of course glad to return to the bosom of my kindred. Well! the amiable conjecture does no harm, and may therefore be safely left uncontradicted. Far from saying nay, indeed, I will permit the reader to picture me, for the next eight years, as a bark slumbering through halcyon weather, in a harbour still as glass—the steersman stretched on the little deck, his face up to heaven, his eyes closed: buried, if you will, in a long prayer. A great many women and girls are supposed to pass their lives something in that fashion; why not I with the rest?

Picture me then idle, basking, plump, and happy, stretched on a cushioned deck, warmed with constant sunshine, rocked by breezes indolently soft. However, it cannot be concealed that, in that case, I must somehow have fallen overboard, or that there must have been wreck at last. I too well remember a time—a long time—of cold, of danger, of contention. To this hour, when I have the nightmare, it repeats the rush and saltness of briny waves in my throat, and their icy pressure on my lungs. I even know there was a storm, and that not of one hour nor one day. For many days and nights neither sun nor stars appeared; we cast with our own hands the tackling out of the ship; a heavy tempest lay on us; all hope that we should be saved was taken away. In fine, the ship was lost, the crew perished.

As far as I recollect, I complained to no one about these troubles. Indeed, to whom could I complain? Of Mrs. Bretton I had long lost sight. Impediments, raised by others, had, years ago, come in the way of our intercourse, and cut it off. Besides, time had brought changes for her, too: the handsome property of which she was left guardian for her son, and which had been chiefly invested in some joint-stock undertaking, had melted, it was said, to a fraction of its original amount. Graham, I learned from incidental rumours, had adopted a profession; both he and his mother were gone from Bretton, and were understood to be now in London. Thus, there remained no possibility of dependence on others; to myself alone could I look. I know not that I was of a self-reliant or active nature; but self-reliance and exertion were forced upon me by circumstances, as they are upon thousands besides; and when Miss Marchmont, a maiden lady of our neighbourhood, sent for me, I obeyed her behest, in the hope that she might assign me some task I could undertake.

Miss Marchmont was a woman of fortune, and lived in a handsome residence; but she was a rheumatic cripple, impotent, foot and hand, and had been so for twenty years. She always sat upstairs: her drawing-room adjoined her bed-room. I had often heard of Miss Marchmont, and of her peculiarities (she had the character of being very eccentric), but till now had never seen her. I found her a furrowed, grey-haired woman, grave with solitude, stern with long affliction, irritable also, and perhaps exacting. It seemed that a maid, or rather companion, who had waited on her for some years, was about to be married; and she, hearing of my bereaved lot, had sent for me, with the idea that I might supply this person's place. She made the proposal to me after tea, as she and I sat alone by her fireside.

"It will not be an easy life;" said she candidly, "for I require a good deal of attention, and you will be much confined; yet, perhaps, contrasted with the existence you have lately led, it may appear tolerable."

I reflected. Of course it ought to appear tolerable, I argued inwardly; but somehow, by some strange fatality, it would not. To live here, in this close room, the watcher of suffering—sometimes, perhaps, the butt of temper—through all that was to come of my youth; while all that was gone had passed, to say the least, not blissfully! My heart sunk one moment, then it revived; for though I forced myself to realise evils, I think I was too prosaic to idealise, and consequently to exaggerate them.

"My doubt is whether I should have strength for the undertaking," I observed.

"That is my own scruple," said she; "for you look a worn-out creature."

So I did. I saw myself in the glass, in my mourning-dress, a faded, hollow-eyed vision. Yet I thought little of the wan spectacle. The blight, I believed, was chiefly external: I still felt life at life's sources.

"What else have you in view—anything?"

"Nothing clear as yet: but I may find something."

"So you imagine: perhaps you are right. Try your own

Villette

method, then; and if it does not succeed, test mine. The chance I have offered shall be left open to you for three months."

This was kind. I told her so, and expressed my gratitude. While I was speaking, a paroxysm of pain came on. I ministered to her; made the necessary applications, according to her directions, and, by the time she was relieved, a sort of intimacy was already formed between us. I, for my part, had learned from the manner in which she bore this attack, that she was a firm, patient woman (patient under physical pain, though sometimes perhaps excitable under long mental canker); and she, from the good-will with which I succoured her, discovered that she could influence my sympathies (such as they were). She sent for me the next day; for five or six successive days she claimed my company. Closer acquaintance, while it developed both faults and eccentricities, opened, at the same time, a view of a character I could respect. Stern and even morose as she sometimes was, I could wait on her and sit beside her with that calm which always blesses us when we are sensible that our manners, presence, contact, please and soothe the persons we serve. Even when she scolded me—which she did, now and then, very tartly—it was in such a way as did not humiliate, and left no sting; it was rather like an irascible mother rating her daughter, than a harsh mistress lecturing a dependant: lecture, indeed, she could not, though she could occasionally storm. Moreover, a vein of reason ever ran through her passion: she was logical even when fierce. Ere long a growing sense of attachment began to present the thought of staying with her as companion in quite a new light; in another week I had agreed to remain.

Two hot, close rooms thus became my world; and a crippled old woman, my mistress, my friend, my all. Her service was my duty—her pain, my suffering—her relief, my hope—her anger, my punishment—her regard, my reward. I forgot that there were fields, woods, rivers, seas, an ever-changing sky outside the steam-dimmed lattice of this sick chamber; I was almost content to forget it. All within me became narrowed to my lot. Tame and still by habit, disciplined by destiny, I demanded no walks in the fresh air; my appetite needed no more than the tiny messes served for the invalid. In addition, she gave me the originality of her character to study: the steadiness of her virtues, I will add, the power of her passions, to admire; the truth of her feelings to trust. All these things she had, and for these things I clung to her.

For these things I would have crawled on with her for twenty years, if for twenty years longer her life of endurance had been protracted. But another decree was written. It seemed I must be stimulated into action. I must be goaded, driven, stung, forced to energy. My little morsel of human affection, which I prized as if it were a solid pearl, must melt in my fingers and slip thence like a dissolving hailstone. My small adopted duty must be snatched from my easily contented conscience. I had wanted to compromise with Fate: to escape occasional great agonies by submitting to a whole life of privation and small pains. Fate would not so be pacified; nor would Providence sanction this shrinking sloth and cowardly indolence.

One February night—I remember it well—there came a voice near Miss Marchmont's house, heard by every inmate, but translated, perhaps, only by one. After a calm winter, storms were ushering in the spring. I had put Miss Marchmont to bed; I sat at the fireside sewing. The wind was wailing at the windows; it had wailed all day; but, as night deepened, it took a new tone—an accent keen, piercing, almost articulate to the ear; a plaint, piteous and disconsolate to the nerves, trilled in every gust.

"Oh, hush! hush!" I said in my disturbed mind, dropping my work, and making a vain effort to stop my ears against that subtle, searching cry. I had heard that very voice ere this, and compulsory observation had forced on me a theory as to what it boded. Three times in the course of my life, events had taught me that these strange accents in the storm—this restless, hopeless cry—denote a coming state of the atmosphere unpropitious to life. Epidemic diseases, I believed, were often heralded by a gasping, sobbing, tormented, long-lamenting east wind. Hence, I inferred, arose the legend of the Banshee. I fancied, too, I had noticed—but was not philosopher enough to know whether there was any connection between the circumstances—that we often at the same time hear of disturbed volcanic action in distant parts of the world; of rivers suddenly rushing above their banks; and of strange high tides flowing furiously in on low sea-coasts. "Our globe," I had said to myself, "seems at such periods torn and disordered; the feeble amongst us wither in her distempered breath, rushing hot from steaming volcanoes."

I listened and trembled; Miss Marchmont slept.

About midnight, the storm in one half-hour fell to a dead calm. The fire, which had been burning dead, glowed up vividly. I felt the air change, and become keen. Raising blind and curtain, I looked out, and saw in the stars the keen sparkle of a sharp frost.

Turning away, the object that met my eyes was Miss Marchmont awake, lifting her head from the pillow, and regarding me with unusual earnestness.

"Is it a fine night?" she asked.

I replied in the affirmative.

"I thought so," she said; "for I feel so strong, so well. Raise me. I feel young to-night," she continued: "young, light-hearted, and happy. What if my complaint be about to take a turn, and I am yet destined to enjoy health? It would be a miracle!"

"And these are not the days of miracles," I thought to myself, and wondered to hear her talk so. She went on directing her conversation to the past, and seeming to recall its incidents, scenes, and personages, with singular vividness.

"I love Memory to-night," she said: "I prize her as my best friend. She is just now giving me a deep delight: she is bringing back to my heart, in warm and beautiful life, realities — not mere empty ideas, but what were once realities, and that I long have thought decayed, dissolved, mixed in with grave-mould. I possess just now the hours, the thoughts, the hopes of my youth. I renew the love of my life — its only love — almost its only affection; for I am not a particularly good woman: I am not amiable. Yet I have had my feelings, strong and concentrated; and these feelings had their object; which, in its single self, was dear to me, as to the majority of men and women, are all the unnumbered points on which they dissipate their regard. While I loved, and while I was loved, what an existence I enjoyed! What a glorious year I can recall — how bright it comes back to me! What a living spring — what a warm, glad summer — what soft moonlight, silvering the autumn evenings — what strength of hope under the ice-bound waters and frost-hoar fields of that year's winter! Through that year my heart lived with Frank's heart. O my noble Frank — my faithful Frank — my good Frank! so much better than myself — his standard in all things so much higher! This I can now see and say: if few women have suffered as I did in his loss, few have enjoyed what I did in his love. It was a far better kind of love than common; I had no doubts about it or him: it was such a love as honoured, protected, and elevated, no less than it gladdened her to whom it was given. Let me now ask, just at this moment, when my mind is so strangely clear, — let me reflect why it was taken from me? For what crime was I condemned, after twelve months of bliss, to undergo thirty years of sorrow?

"I do not know," she continued after a pause: "I cannot—cannot see the reason; yet at this hour I can say with sincerity, what I never tried to say before, Inscrutable God, Thy will be done! And at this moment I can believe that death will restore me to Frank. I never believed it till now."

"He is dead, then?" I inquired in a low voice.

"My dear girl," she said, "one happy Christmas Eve I dressed and decorated myself, expecting my lover, very soon to be my husband, would come that night to visit me. I sat down to wait. Once more I see that moment—I see the snow twilight stealing through the window over which the curtain was not dropped, for I designed to watch him ride up the white walk; I see and feel the soft firelight warming me, playing on my silk dress, and fitfully showing me my own young figure in a glass. I see the moon of a calm winter night, float full, clear, and cold, over the inky mass of shrubbery, and the silvered turf of my grounds. I wait, with some impatience in my pulse, but no doubt in my breast. The flames had died in the fire, but it was a bright mass yet; the moon was mounting high, but she was still visible from the lattice; the clock neared ten; he rarely tarried later than this, but once or twice he had been delayed so long.

"Would he for once fail me? No—not even for once; and now he was coming—and coming fast—to atone for lost time. 'Frank! you furious rider,' I said inwardly, listening gladly, yet anxiously, to his approaching gallop, 'you shall be rebuked for this: I will tell you it is my neck you are putting in peril; for whatever is yours is, in a dearer and tenderer sense, mine.' There he was: I saw him; but I think tears were in my eyes, my sight was so confused. I saw the horse; I heard it stamp—I saw at least a mass; I heard a clamour. Was it a horse? or what heavy, dragging thing was it, crossing, strangely dark, the lawn. How could I name that thing in the moonlight before me? or how could I utter the feeling which rose in my soul?

"I could only run out. A great animal—truly, Frank's black horse—stood trembling, panting, snorting before the door; a man held it, Frank, as I thought.

"'What is the matter?' I demanded. Thomas, my own servant, answered by saying sharply, 'Go into the house, madam.' And then calling to another servant, who came hurrying from the kitchen as if summoned by some instinct, 'Ruth, take missis into the house directly.' But I was kneeling down in the snow, beside something that lay there—something that I had seen dragged along the ground—something that sighed, that groaned on my breast, as I lifted and drew it to me. He was not dead; he was not quite unconscious. I had him carried in; I refused to be ordered about and thrust from him. I was quite collected enough, not only to be my own mistress but the mistress of others. They had begun by trying to treat me like a child, as they always do with people struck by God's hand; but I gave place to none except the surgeon; and when he had done what he could, I took my dying Frank to myself. He had strength to fold me in his arms; he had power to speak my name; he heard me as I prayed over him very softly; he felt me as I tenderly and fondly comforted him.

"'Maria,' he said, 'I am dying in Paradise.' He spent his last breath in faithful words for me. When the dawn of Christmas morning broke, my Frank was with God.

"And that," she went on, "happened thirty years ago. I have suffered since. I doubt if I have made the best use of all my calamities. Soft, amiable natures they would have refined to saintliness; of strong, evil spirits they would have made demons; as for me, I have only been a woe-struck and selfish woman."

"You have done much good," I said; for she was noted for her liberal almsgiving.

"I have not withheld money, you mean, where it could assuage affliction. What of that? It cost me no effort or pang to give. But I think from this day I am about to enter a better frame of mind, to prepare myself for reunion with Frank. You see I still think of Frank more than of God; and unless it be counted that in thus loving the creature so much, so long, and so exclusively, I have not at least blasphemed the Creator, small is my chance of salvation. What do you think, Lucy, of these things? Be my chaplain, and tell me."

This question I could not answer: I had no words. It seemed as if she thought I had answered it.

"Very right, my child. We should acknowledge God merciful, but not always for us comprehensible. We should accept our own lot, whatever it be, and try to render happy that of others. Should we not? Well, to-morrow I will begin by trying to make you happy. I will endeavour to do something for you, Lucy: something that will benefit you when I am dead. My head aches now with talking too much; still I am happy. Go to bed.

The clock strikes two. How late you sit up; or rather how late I, in my selfishness, keep you up. But go now; have no more anxiety for me; I feel I shall rest well."

She composed herself as if to slumber. I, too, retired to my crib in a closet within her room. The night passed in quietness; quietly her doom must at last have come: peacefully and painlessly: in the morning she was found without life, nearly cold, but all calm and undisturbed. Her previous excitement of spirits and change of mood had been the prelude of a fit; one stroke sufficed to sever the thread of an existence so long fretted by affliction.

CHAPTER V.

TURNING A NEW LEAF.

My mistress being dead, and I once more alone, I had to look out for a new place. About this time I might be a little — a very little — shaken in nerves. I grant I was not looking well, but, on the contrary, thin, haggard, and hollow-eyed; like a sitter-up at night, like an overwrought servant, or a placeless person in debt. In debt, however, I was not; nor quite poor; for though Miss Marchmont had not had time to benefit me, as, on that last night, she said she intended, yet, after the funeral, my wages were duly paid by her second cousin, the heir, an avaricious-looking man, with pinched nose and narrow temples, who, indeed, I heard long afterwards, turned out a thorough miser: a direct contrast to his generous kinswoman, and a foil to her memory, blessed to this day by the poor and needy. The possessor, then, of fifteen pounds; of health, though worn, not broken, and of a spirit in similar condition; I might still; in comparison with many people, be regarded as occupying an enviable position. An embarrassing one it was, however, at the same time; as I felt with some acuteness on a certain day, of which the corresponding one in the next week was to see my departure from my present abode, while with another I was not provided.

In this dilemma I went, as a last and sole resource, to see and consult an old servant of our family; once my nurse, now housekeeper at a grand mansion not far from Miss Marchmont's. I spent some hours with her; she comforted, but knew not how to advise me. Still all inward darkness, I left her about twilight; a walk of two miles lay before me; it was a clear, frosty night. In spite of my solitude, my poverty, and my perplexity, my heart, nourished and nerved with the vigour of a youth that had not yet counted twenty-three summers, beat light and not feebly. Not feebly, I am sure, or I should have trembled in that lonely walk, which lay through still fields, and passed neither village nor farmhouse, nor cottage: I should have quailed in the absence of moonlight, for it was by the leading of stars only I traced the dim path; I should have quailed still more in the unwonted presence of that which to-night shone in the north, a moving mystery — the Aurora Borealis. But this solemn stranger influenced me otherwise than through my fears. Some new power it seemed to bring. I drew in energy with the keen, low breeze that blew on its path. A bold thought was sent to my mind; my mind was made strong to receive it.

"Leave this wilderness," it was said to me, "and go out hence."

"Where?" was the query.

I had not very far to look; gazing from this country parish in that flat, rich middle of England—I mentally saw within reach what I had never yet beheld with my bodily eyes: I saw London.

The next day I returned to the hall, and asking once more to see the housekeeper, I communicated to her my plan.

Mrs. Barrett was a grave, judicious woman, though she knew little more of the world than myself; but grave and judicious as she was, she did not charge me with being out of my senses; and, indeed, I had a staid manner of my own which ere now had been as good to me as cloak and hood of hodden grey, since under its favour I had been enabled to achieve with impunity, and even approbation, deeds that, if attempted with an excited and unsettled air, would in some minds have stamped me as a dreamer and zealot.

The housekeeper was slowly propounding some difficulties, while she prepared orange-rind for marmalade, when a child ran past the window and came bounding into the room. It was a pretty child, and as it danced, laughing, up to me—for we were not strangers (nor, indeed, was its mother—a young married daughter of the house—a stranger)—I took it on my knee.

Different as were our social positions now, this child's mother and I had been schoolfellows, when I was a girl of ten and she a young lady of sixteen; and I remembered her, good-looking, but dull, in a lower class than mine.

I was admiring the boy's handsome dark eyes, when the mother, young Mrs. Leigh, entered. What a beautiful and kind-looking woman was the good-natured and comely, but unintellectual, girl become! Wifehood and maternity had changed her thus, as I have since seen them change others even less promising than she. Me she had forgotten. I was changed too, though not, I fear, for the better. I made no attempt to recall myself to her memory; why should I? She came for her son to accompany her in a walk, and behind her followed a nurse, carrying an infant. I only mention the incident because, in addressing the nurse, Mrs. Leigh spoke French (very bad French, by the way, and with an incorrigibly bad accent, again forcibly reminding me of our school-days): and I found the woman was a foreigner. The little boy chattered volubly in

Villette

French too. When the whole party were withdrawn, Mrs. Barrett remarked that her young lady had brought that foreign nurse home with her two years ago, on her return from a Continental excursion; that she was treated almost as well as a governess, and had nothing to do but walk out with the baby and chatter French with Master Charles; "and," added Mrs. Barrett, "she says there are many Englishwomen in foreign families as well placed as she."

I stored up this piece of casual information, as careful housewives store seemingly worthless shreds and fragments for which their prescient minds anticipate a possible use some day. Before I left my old friend, she gave me the address of a respectable old-fashioned inn in the City, which, she said, my uncles used to frequent in former days.

In going to London, I ran less risk and evinced less enterprise than the reader may think. In fact, the distance was only fifty miles. My means would suffice both to take me there, to keep me a few days, and also to bring me back if I found no inducement to stay. I regarded it as a brief holiday, permitted for once to work-weary faculties, rather than as an adventure of life and death. There is nothing like taking all you do at a moderate estimate: it keeps mind and body tranquil; whereas grandiloquent notions are apt to hurry both into fever.

Fifty miles were then a day's journey (for I speak of a time gone by: my hair, which, till a late period, withstood the frosts of time, lies now, at last white, under a white cap, like snow beneath snow). About nine o'clock of a wet February night I reached London.

My reader, I know, is one who would not thank me for an elaborate reproduction of poetic first impressions; and it is well, inasmuch as I had neither time nor mood to cherish such; arriving as I did late, on a dark, raw, and rainy evening, in a Babylon and a wilderness, of which the vastness and the strangeness tried to the utmost any powers of clear thought and steady self-possession with which, in the absence of more brilliant faculties, Nature might have gifted me.

When I left the coach, the strange speech of the cabmen and others waiting round, seemed to me odd as a foreign tongue. I had never before heard the English language chopped up in that way. However, I managed to understand and to be understood, so far as to get myself and trunk safely conveyed to the old inn whereof I had the address. How difficult, how oppressive, how puzzling seemed my flight! In London for the first time; at an inn for the first time; tired with travelling; confused with darkness; palsied with cold; unfurnished with either experience or advice to tell me how to act, and yet—to act obliged.

Into the hands of common sense I confided the matter. Common sense, however, was as chilled and bewildered as all my other faculties, and it was only under the spur of an inexorable necessity that she spasmodically executed her trust. Thus urged, she paid the porter: considering the crisis, I did not blame her too much that she was hugely cheated; she asked the waiter for a room; she timorously called for the chambermaid; what is far more, she bore, without being wholly overcome, a highly supercilious style of demeanour from that young lady, when she appeared.

I recollect this same chambermaid was a pattern of town prettiness and smartness. So trim her waist, her cap, her dress— I wondered how they had all been manufactured. Her speech had an accent which in its mincing glibness seemed to rebuke mine as by authority; her spruce attire flaunted an easy scorn to my plain country garb.

"Well, it can't be helped," I thought, "and then the scene is new, and the circumstances; I shall gain good."

Maintaining a very quiet manner towards this arrogant little maid, and subsequently observing the same towards the parsonic-looking, black-coated, white-neckclothed waiter, I got civility from them ere long. I believe at first they thought I was a servant; but in a little while they changed their minds, and hovered in a doubtful state between patronage and politeness.

I kept up well till I had partaken of some refreshment, warmed myself by a fire, and was fairly shut into my own room; but, as I sat down by the bed and rested my head and arms on the pillow, a terrible oppression overcame me. All at once my position rose on me like a ghost. Anomalous, desolate, almost blank of hope it stood. What was I doing here alone in great London? What should I do on the morrow? What prospects had I in life? What friends had I on earth? Whence did I come? Whither should I go? What should I do?

I wet the pillow, my arms, and my hair, with rushing tears. A dark interval of most bitter thought followed this burst; but I did not regret the step taken, nor wish to retract it. A strong, vague persuasion that it was better to go forward than backward, and that I could go forward—that a way, however

Villette

narrow and difficult, would in time open—predominated over other feelings: its influence hushed them so far, that at last I became sufficiently tranquil to be able to say my prayers and seek my couch. I had just extinguished my candle and lain down, when a deep, low, mighty tone swung through the night. At first I knew it not; but it was uttered twelve times, and at the twelfth colossal hum and trembling knell, I said: "I lie in the shadow of St. Paul's."

CHAPTER VI.

LONDON.

The next day was the first of March, and when I awoke, rose, and opened my curtain, I saw the risen sun struggling through fog. Above my head, above the house-tops, co-elevate almost with the clouds, I saw a solemn, orbed mass, dark blue and dim—THE DOME. While I looked, my inner self moved; my spirit shook its always-fettered wings half loose; I had a sudden feeling as if I, who never yet truly lived, were at last about to taste life. In that morning my soul grew as fast as Jonah's gourd.

"I did well to come," I said, proceeding to dress with speed and care. "I like the spirit of this great London which I feel around me. Who but a coward would pass his whole life in hamlets; and for ever abandon his faculties to the eating rust of obscurity?"

Being dressed, I went down; not travel-worn and exhausted, but tidy and refreshed. When the waiter came in with my breakfast, I managed to accost him sedately, yet cheerfully; we had ten minutes' discourse, in the course of which we became usefully known to each other.

He was a grey-haired, elderly man; and, it seemed, had lived in his present place twenty years. Having ascertained this, I was sure he must remember my two uncles, Charles and Wilmot, who, fifteen, years ago, were frequent visitors here. I mentioned their names; he recalled them perfectly, and with respect. Having intimated my connection, my position in his eyes was henceforth clear, and on a right footing. He said I was like my uncle Charles: I suppose he spoke truth, because Mrs. Barrett was accustomed to say the same thing. A ready and obliging courtesy now replaced his former uncomfortably doubtful manner; henceforth I need no longer be at a loss for a civil answer to a sensible question.

The street on which my little sitting-room window looked was narrow, perfectly quiet, and not dirty: the few passengers were just such as one sees in provincial towns: here was nothing formidable; I felt sure I might venture out alone.

Having breakfasted, out I went. Elation and pleasure were in my heart: to walk alone in London seemed of itself an adventure. Presently I found myself in Paternoster Row—classic ground this. I entered a bookseller's shop, kept by one Jones: I

Villette

bought a little book—a piece of extravagance I could ill afford; but I thought I would one day give or send it to Mrs. Barrett. Mr. Jones, a dried-in man of business, stood behind his desk: he seemed one of the greatest, and I one of the happiest of beings.

Prodigious was the amount of life I lived that morning. Finding myself before St. Paul's, I went in; I mounted to the dome: I saw thence London, with its river, and its bridges, and its churches; I saw antique Westminster, and the green Temple Gardens, with sun upon them, and a glad, blue sky, of early spring above; and between them and it, not too dense, a cloud of haze.

Descending, I went wandering whither chance might lead, in a still ecstasy of freedom and enjoyment; and I got—I know not how—I got into the heart of city life. I saw and felt London at last: I got into the Strand; I went up Cornhill; I mixed with the life passing along; I dared the perils of crossings. To do this, and to do it utterly alone, gave me, perhaps an irrational, but a real pleasure. Since those days, I have seen the West End, the parks, the fine squares; but I love the city far better. The city seems so much more in earnest: its business, its rush, its roar, are such serious things, sights, and sounds. The city is getting its living— the West End but enjoying its pleasure. At the West End you may be amused, but in the city you are deeply excited.

Faint, at last, and hungry (it was years since I had felt such healthy hunger), I returned, about two o'clock, to my dark, old, and quiet inn. I dined on two dishes—a plain joint and vegetables; both seemed excellent: how much better than the small, dainty messes Miss Marchmont's cook used to send up to my kind, dead mistress and me, and to the discussion of which we could not bring half an appetite between us! Delightfully tired, I lay down, on three chairs for an hour (the room did not boast a sofa). I slept, then I woke and thought for two hours.

My state of mind, and all accompanying circumstances, were just now such as most to favour the adoption of a new, resolute, and daring—perhaps desperate—line of action. I had nothing to lose. Unutterable loathing of a desolate existence past, forbade return. If I failed in what I now designed to undertake, who, save myself, would suffer? If I died far away from—home, I was going to say, but I had no home—from England, then, who would weep?

I might suffer; I was inured to suffering: death itself had not, I thought, those terrors for me which it has for the softly reared. I had, ere this, looked on the thought of death with a quiet eye.

Prepared, then, for any consequences, I formed a project.

That same evening I obtained from my friend, the waiter, information respecting, the sailing of vessels for a certain continental port, Boue-Marine. No time, I found, was to be lost: that very night I must take my berth. I might, indeed, have waited till the morning before going on board, but would not run the risk of being too late.

"Better take your berth at once, ma'am," counselled the waiter. I agreed with him, and having discharged my bill, and acknowledged my friend's services at a rate which I now know was princely, and which in his eyes must have seemed absurd — and indeed, while pocketing the cash, he smiled a faint smile which intimated his opinion of the donor's savoir-faire — he proceeded to call a coach. To the driver he also recommended me, giving at the same time an injunction about taking me, I think, to the wharf, and not leaving me to the watermen; which that functionary promised to observe, but failed in keeping his promise: on the contrary, he offered me up as an oblation, served me as a dripping roast, making me alight in the midst of a throng of watermen.

This was an uncomfortable crisis. It was a dark night. The coachman instantly drove off as soon as he had got his fare: the watermen commenced a struggle for me and my trunk. Their oaths I hear at this moment: they shook my philosophy more than did the night, or the isolation, or the strangeness of the scene. One laid hands on my trunk. I looked on and waited quietly; but when another laid hands on me, I spoke up, shook off his touch, stepped at once into a boat, desired austerely that the trunk should be placed beside me — "Just there," — which was instantly done; for the owner of the boat I had chosen became now an ally: I was rowed off.

Black was the river as a torrent of ink; lights glanced on it from the piles of building round, ships rocked on its bosom. They rowed me up to several vessels; I read by lantern-light their names painted in great white letters on a dark ground. "The Ocean," "The Phoenix," "The Consort," "The Dolphin," were passed in turns; but "The Vivid" was my ship, and it seemed she lay further down.

Down the sable flood we glided, I thought of the Styx, and of Charon rowing some solitary soul to the Land of Shades. Amidst the strange scene, with a chilly wind blowing in my face and midnight clouds dropping rain above my head; with two rude rowers for companions, whose insane oaths still tortured my ear, I asked myself if I was wretched or terrified. I was neither. Often in my life have I been far more so under comparatively safe circumstances. "How is this?" said I. "Methinks I am animated and alert, instead of being depressed and apprehensive?" I could not tell how it was.

"THE VIVID" started out, white and glaring, from the black night at last.—"Here you are!" said the waterman, and instantly demanded six shillings.

"You ask too much," I said. He drew off from the vessel and swore he would not embark me till I paid it. A young man, the steward as I found afterwards, was looking over the ship's side; he grinned a smile in anticipation of the coming contest; to disappoint him, I paid the money. Three times that afternoon I had given crowns where I should have given shillings; but I consoled myself with the reflection, "It is the price of experience."

"They've cheated you!" said the steward exultingly when I got on board. I answered phlegmatically that "I knew it," and went below.

A stout, handsome, and showy woman was in the ladies' cabin. I asked to be shown my berth; she looked hard at me, muttered something about its being unusual for passengers to come on board at that hour, and seemed disposed to be less than civil. What a face she had—so comely—so insolent and so selfish!

"Now that I am on board, I shall certainly stay here," was my answer. "I will trouble you to show me my berth."

She complied, but sullenly. I took off my bonnet, arranged my things, and lay down. Some difficulties had been passed through; a sort of victory was won: my homeless, anchorless, unsupported mind had again leisure for a brief repose. Till the "Vivid" arrived in harbour, no further action would be required of me; but then…. Oh! I could not look forward. Harassed, exhausted, I lay in a half-trance.

The stewardess talked all night; not to me but to the young steward, her son and her very picture. He passed in and out of the cabin continually: they disputed, they quarrelled, they made it up again twenty times in the course of the night. She professed to be writing a letter home—she said to her father; she read passages of it aloud, heeding me no more than a stock—perhaps she believed me asleep. Several of these passages appeared to comprise family secrets, and bore special reference to one "Charlotte," a younger sister who, from the bearing of the epistle, seemed to be on the brink of perpetrating a romantic and imprudent match; loud was the protest of this elder lady against the distasteful union. The dutiful son laughed his mother's correspondence to scorn. She defended it, and raved at him. They were a strange pair. She might be thirty-nine or forty, and was buxom and blooming as a girl of twenty. Hard, loud, vain and vulgar, her mind and body alike seemed brazen and imperishable. I should think, from her childhood, she must have lived in public stations; and in her youth might very likely have been a barmaid.

Towards morning her discourse ran on a new theme: "the Watsons," a certain expected family-party of passengers, known to her, it appeared, and by her much esteemed on account of the handsome profit realized in their fees. She said, "It was as good as a little fortune to her whenever this family crossed."

At dawn all were astir, and by sunrise the passengers came on board. Boisterous was the welcome given by the stewardess to the "Watsons," and great was the bustle made in their honour. They were four in number, two males and two females. Besides them, there was but one other passenger—a young lady, whom a gentlemanly, though languid-looking man escorted. The two groups offered a marked contrast. The Watsons were doubtless rich people, for they had the confidence of conscious wealth in their bearing; the women—youthful both of them, and one perfectly handsome, as far as physical beauty went—were dressed richly, gaily, and absurdly out of character for the circumstances. Their bonnets with bright flowers, their velvet cloaks and silk dresses, seemed better suited for park or promenade than for a damp packet deck. The men were of low stature, plain, fat, and vulgar; the oldest, plainest, greasiest, broadest, I soon found was the husband—the bridegroom I suppose, for she was very young—of the beautiful girl. Deep was my amazement at this discovery; and deeper still when I perceived that, instead of being desperately wretched in such a union, she was gay even to giddiness. "Her laughter," I reflected, "must be the mere frenzy of despair." And even while this thought was crossing my mind, as I stood leaning quiet and solitary against the ship's side, she came tripping up to me, an utter stranger, with a camp-stool in her hand, and smiling a smile of which the levity puzzled and startled me, though it showed a perfect set of perfect teeth, she offered me the accommodation of this piece of furniture. I declined it of course, with all the courtesy I could put into my manner; she danced off heedless and lightsome. She must have been good-natured; but what had made her marry that individual, who was at least as much like an oil-barrel as a man?

The other lady passenger, with the gentleman-companion, was quite a girl, pretty and fair: her simple print dress, untrimmed straw-bonnet and large shawl, gracefully worn, formed a costume plain to quakerism: yet, for her, becoming enough. Before the gentleman quitted her, I observed him throwing a glance of scrutiny over all the passengers, as if to ascertain in what company his charge would be left. With a most dissatisfied air did his eye turn from the ladies with the gay flowers; he looked at me, and then he spoke to his daughter, niece, or whatever she was: she also glanced in my direction, and slightly curled her short, pretty lip. It might be myself, or it might be my homely mourning habit, that elicited this mark of contempt; more likely, both. A bell rang; her father (I afterwards knew that it was her father) kissed her, and returned to land. The packet sailed.

Foreigners say that it is only English girls who can thus be trusted to travel alone, and deep is their wonder at the daring confidence of English parents and guardians. As for the "jeunes Meess," by some their intrepidity is pronounced masculine and "inconvenant," others regard them as the passive victims of an educational and theological system which wantonly dispenses with proper "surveillance." Whether this particular young lady was of the sort that can the most safely be left unwatched, I do not know: or, rather did not then know; but it soon appeared that the dignity of solitude was not to her taste. She paced the deck once or twice backwards and forwards; she looked with a little sour air of disdain at the flaunting silks and velvets, and the bears which thereon danced attendance, and eventually she approached me and spoke.

"Are you fond of a sea-voyage?" was her question.

I explained that my fondness for a sea-voyage had yet to undergo the test of experience; I had never made one.

"Oh, how charming!" cried she. "I quite envy you the novelty: first impressions, you know, are so pleasant. Now I have made so many, I quite forget the first: I am quite blasée about the sea and all that."

I could not help smiling.

"Why do you laugh at me?" she inquired, with a frank testiness that pleased me better than her other talk.

"Because you are so young to be blasée about anything."

"I am seventeen" (a little piqued).

"You hardly look sixteen. Do you like travelling alone?"

"Bah! I care nothing about it. I have crossed the Channel ten times, alone; but then I take care never to be long alone: I always make friends."

"You will scarcely make many friends this voyage, I think" (glancing at the Watson-group, who were now laughing and making a great deal of noise on deck).

"Not of those odious men and women," said she: "such people should be steerage passengers. Are you going to school?"

"No."

"Where are you going?"

"I have not the least idea—beyond, at least, the port of Boue-Marine."

She stared, then carelessly ran on:

"I am going to school. Oh, the number of foreign schools I have been at in my life! And yet I am quite an ignoramus. I know nothing—nothing in the world—I assure you; except that I play and dance beautifully,—and French and German of course I know, to speak; but I can't read or write them very well. Do you know they wanted me to translate a page of an easy German book into English the other day, and I couldn't do it. Papa was so mortified: he says it looks as if M. de Bassompierre—my godpapa, who pays all my school-bills—had thrown away all his money. And then, in matters of information—in history, geography, arithmetic, and so on, I am quite a baby; and I write English so badly—such spelling and grammar, they tell me. Into the bargain I have quite forgotten my religion; they call me a Protestant, you know, but really I am not sure whether I am one or not: I don't well know the difference between Romanism and Protestantism. However, I don't in the least care for that. I was a Lutheran once at Bonn—dear Bonn!—charming Bonn!—where there were so many handsome students. Every nice girl in our school had an admirer; they knew our hours for walking out, and almost always passed us on the promenade: 'Schönes Mädchen,' we used to hear them say. I was excessively happy at Bonn!"

"And where are you now?" I inquired.

"Oh! at—chose," said she.

Now, Miss Ginevra Fanshawe (such was this young person's name) only substituted this word "chose" in temporary oblivion of the real name. It was a habit she had: "chose" came in at every turn in her conversation—the convenient substitute for any missing word in any language she might chance at the time to be speaking. French girls often do the like; from them she had caught the custom. "Chose," however, I found in this instance, stood for Villette—the great capital of the great kingdom of Labassecour.

"Do you like Villette?" I asked.

"Pretty well. The natives, you know, are intensely stupid and vulgar; but there are some nice English families."

"Are you in a school?"

"Yes."

"A good one?"

"Oh, no! horrid: but I go out every Sunday, and care nothing about the maîtresses or the professeurs, or the élèves, and send lessons au diable (one daren't say that in English, you know, but it sounds quite right in French); and thus I get on charmingly…. You are laughing at me again?"

"No—I am only smiling at my own thoughts."

"What are they?" (Without waiting for an answer)—"Now, do tell me where you are going."

"Where Fate may lead me. My business is to earn a living where I can find it."

"To earn!" (in consternation) "are you poor, then?"

"As poor as Job."

(After a pause) "Bah! how unpleasant! But I know what it is to be poor: they are poor enough at home—papa and mamma, and all of them. Papa is called Captain Fanshawe; he is an officer on half-pay, but well-descended, and some of our connections are great enough; but my uncle and godpapa De Bassompierre, who lives in France, is the only one that helps us: he educates us girls. I have five sisters and three brothers. By-and-by we are to marry—rather elderly gentlemen, I suppose, with cash: papa and mamma manage that. My sister Augusta is married now to a man much older-looking than papa. Augusta is very beautiful—not in my style—but dark; her husband, Mr. Davies, had the yellow fever in India, and he is still the colour of a guinea; but then he is rich, and Augusta has her carriage and establishment, and we all think she has done perfectly well. Now, this is better than 'earning a living,' as you say. By the way, are you clever?"

"No—not at all."

"You can play, sing, speak three or four languages?"

"By no means."

"Still I think you are clever" (a pause and a yawn).

"Shall you be sea-sick?"

"Shall you?"

"Oh, immensely! as soon as ever we get in sight of the sea: I begin, indeed, to feel it already. I shall go below; and won't I order about that fat odious stewardess! Heureusement je sais faire aller mon monde."

Down she went.

It was not long before the other passengers followed her: throughout the afternoon I remained on deck alone. When I recall the tranquil, and even happy mood in which I passed those hours, and remember, at the same time, the position in which I was placed; its hazardous—some would have said its hopeless—character; I feel that, as—

"Stone walls do not a prison make,

Nor iron bars—a cage,"

so peril, loneliness, an uncertain future, are not oppressive evils, so long as the frame is healthy and the faculties are employed; so long, especially, as Liberty lends us her wings, and Hope guides us by her star.

Villette

I was not sick till long after we passed Margate, and deep was the pleasure I drank in with the sea-breeze; divine the delight I drew from the heaving Channel waves, from the sea-birds on their ridges, from the white sails on their dark distance, from the quiet yet beclouded sky, overhanging all. In my reverie, methought I saw the continent of Europe, like a wide dream-land, far away. Sunshine lay on it, making the long coast one line of gold; tiniest tracery of clustered town and snow-gleaming tower, of woods deep massed, of heights serrated, of smooth pasturage and veiny stream, embossed the metal-bright prospect. For background, spread a sky, solemn and dark blue, and — grand with imperial promise, soft with tints of enchantment — strode from north to south a God-bent bow, an arch of hope.

Cancel the whole of that, if you please, reader — or rather let it stand, and draw thence a moral — an alliterative, text-hand copy —

Day-dreams are delusions of the demon.

Becoming excessively sick, I faltered down into the cabin.

Miss Fanshawe's berth chanced to be next mine; and, I am sorry to say, she tormented me with an unsparing selfishness during the whole time of our mutual distress. Nothing could exceed her impatience and fretfulness. The Watsons, who were very sick too, and on whom the stewardess attended with shameless partiality, were stoics compared with her. Many a time since have I noticed, in persons of Ginevra Fanshawe's light, careless temperament, and fair, fragile style of beauty, an entire incapacity to endure: they seem to sour in adversity, like small beer in thunder. The man who takes such a woman for his wife, ought to be prepared to guarantee her an existence all sunshine. Indignant at last with her teasing peevishness, I curtly requested her "to hold her tongue." The rebuff did her good, and it was observable that she liked me no worse for it.

As dark night drew on, the sea roughened: larger waves swayed strong against the vessel's side. It was strange to reflect that blackness and water were round us, and to feel the ship ploughing straight on her pathless way, despite noise, billow, and rising gale. Articles of furniture began to fall about, and it became needful to lash them to their places; the passengers grew sicker than ever; Miss Fanshawe declared, with groans, that she must die.

"Not just yet, honey," said the stewardess. "We're just in

port." Accordingly, in another quarter of an hour, a calm fell upon us all; and about midnight the voyage ended.

I was sorry: yes, I was sorry. My resting-time was past; my difficulties—my stringent difficulties—recommenced. When I went on deck, the cold air and black scowl of the night seemed to rebuke me for my presumption in being where I was: the lights of the foreign sea-port town, glimmering round the foreign harbour, met me like unnumbered threatening eyes. Friends came on board to welcome the Watsons; a whole family of friends surrounded and bore away Miss Fanshawe; I—but I dared not for one moment dwell on a comparison of positions.

Yet where should I go? I must go somewhere. Necessity dare not be nice. As I gave the stewardess her fee—and she seemed surprised at receiving a coin of more value than, from such a quarter, her coarse calculations had probably reckoned on—I said, "Be kind enough to direct me to some quiet, respectable inn, where I can go for the night."

She not only gave me the required direction, but called a commissionaire, and bid him take charge of me, and—not my trunk, for that was gone to the custom-house.

I followed this man along a rudely-paved street, lit now by a fitful gleam of moonlight; he brought me to the inn. I offered him sixpence, which he refused to take; supposing it not enough, I changed it for a shilling; but this also he declined, speaking rather sharply, in a language to me unknown. A waiter, coming forward into the lamp-lit inn-passage, reminded me, in broken English, that my money was foreign money, not current here. I gave him a sovereign to change. This little matter settled, I asked for a bedroom; supper I could not take: I was still sea-sick and unnerved, and trembling all over. How deeply glad I was when the door of a very small chamber at length closed on me and my exhaustion. Again I might rest: though the cloud of doubt would be as thick to-morrow as ever; the necessity for exertion more urgent, the peril (of destitution) nearer, the conflict (for existence) more severe.

CHAPTER VII.

VILLETTE.

I awoke next morning with courage revived and spirits refreshed: physical debility no longer enervated my judgment; my mind felt prompt and clear.

Just as I finished dressing, a tap came to the door: I said, "Come in," expecting the chambermaid, whereas a rough man walked in and said, —

"Gif me your keys, Meess."

"Why?" I asked.

"Gif!" said he impatiently; and as he half-snatched them from my hand, he added, "All right! haf your tronc soon."

Fortunately it did turn out all right: he was from the custom-house. Where to go to get some breakfast I could not tell; but I proceeded, not without hesitation, to descend.

I now observed, what I had not noticed in my extreme weariness last night, viz. that this inn was, in fact, a large hotel; and as I slowly descended the broad staircase, halting on each step (for I was in wonderfully little haste to get down), I gazed at the high ceiling above me, at the painted walls around, at the wide windows which filled the house with light, at the veined marble I trod (for the steps were all of marble, though uncarpeted and not very clean), and contrasting all this with the dimensions of the closet assigned to me as a chamber, with the extreme modesty of its appointments, I fell into a philosophizing mood.

Much I marvelled at the sagacity evinced by waiters and chamber-maids in proportioning the accommodation to the guest. How could inn-servants and ship-stewardesses everywhere tell at a glance that I, for instance, was an individual of no social significance, and little burdened by cash? They did know it evidently: I saw quite well that they all, in a moment's calculation, estimated me at about the same fractional value. The fact seemed to me curious and pregnant: I would not disguise from myself what it indicated, yet managed to keep up my spirits pretty well under its pressure.

Having at last landed in a great hall, full of skylight glare, I made my way somehow to what proved to be the coffee-room. It cannot be denied that on entering this room I trembled somewhat; felt uncertain, solitary, wretched; wished to Heaven I knew whether I was doing right or wrong; felt convinced that it was the last, but could not help myself. Acting in the spirit and with the calm of a fatalist, I sat down at a small table, to which a waiter presently brought me some breakfast; and I partook of that meal in a frame of mind not greatly calculated to favour digestion. There were many other people breakfasting at other tables in the room; I should have felt rather more happy if amongst them all I could have seen any women; however, there was not one—all present were men. But nobody seemed to think I was doing anything strange; one or two gentlemen glanced at me occasionally, but none stared obtrusively: I suppose if there was anything eccentric in the business, they accounted for it by this word "Anglaise!"

Breakfast over, I must again move—in what direction? "Go to Villette," said an inward voice; prompted doubtless by the recollection of this slight sentence uttered carelessly and at random by Miss Fanshawe, as she bid me good-by: "I wish you would come to Madame Beck's; she has some marmots whom you might look after; she wants an English gouvernante, or was wanting one two months ago."

Who Madame Beck was, where she lived, I knew not; I had asked, but the question passed unheard: Miss Fanshawe, hurried away by her friends, left it unanswered. I presumed Villette to be her residence—to Villette I would go. The distance was forty miles. I knew I was catching at straws; but in the wide and weltering deep where I found myself, I would have caught at cobwebs. Having inquired about the means of travelling to Villette, and secured a seat in the diligence, I departed on the strength of this outline—this shadow of a project. Before you pronounce on the rashness of the proceeding, reader, look back to the point whence I started; consider the desert I had left, note how little I perilled: mine was the game where the player cannot lose and may win.

Of an artistic temperament, I deny that I am; yet I must possess something of the artist's faculty of making the most of present pleasure: that is to say, when it is of the kind to my taste. I enjoyed that day, though we travelled slowly, though it was cold, though it rained. Somewhat bare, flat, and treeless was the route along which our journey lay; and slimy canals crept, like half-torpid green snakes, beside the road; and formal pollard willows edged level fields, tilled like kitchen-garden beds. The sky, too, was monotonously gray; the atmosphere was stagnant and humid; yet amidst all these deadening influences, my fancy budded fresh and my heart basked in sunshine. These feelings, however, were well kept in check by the secret but ceaseless consciousness of anxiety lying in wait on enjoyment, like a tiger crouched in a jungle. The breathing of that beast of prey was in my ear always; his fierce heart panted close against mine; he never stirred in his lair but I felt him: I knew he waited only for sun-down to bound ravenous from his ambush.

I had hoped we might reach Villette ere night set in, and that thus I might escape the deeper embarrassment which obscurity seems to throw round a first arrival at an unknown bourne; but, what with our slow progress and long stoppages—what with a thick fog and small, dense rain—darkness, that might almost be felt, had settled on the city by the time we gained its suburbs.

I know we passed through a gate where soldiers were stationed—so much I could see by lamplight; then, having left behind us the miry Chaussée, we rattled over a pavement of strangely rough and flinty surface. At a bureau, the diligence stopped, and the passengers alighted. My first business was to get my trunk; a small matter enough, but important to me. Understanding that it was best not to be importunate or over-eager about luggage, but to wait and watch quietly the delivery of other boxes till I saw my own, and then promptly claim and secure it, I stood apart; my eye fixed on that part of the vehicle in which I had seen my little portmanteau safely stowed, and upon which piles of additional bags and boxes were now heaped. One by one, I saw these removed, lowered, and seized on.

I was sure mine ought to be by this time visible: it was not. I had tied on the direction-card with a piece of green ribbon, that I might know it at a glance: not a fringe or fragment of green was perceptible. Every package was removed; every tin-case and brown-paper parcel; the oilcloth cover was lifted; I saw with distinct vision that not an umbrella, cloak, cane, hat-box or band-box remained.

And my portmanteau, with my few clothes and little pocket-book enclasping the remnant of my fifteen pounds, where were they?

I ask this question now, but I could not ask it then. I could say nothing whatever; not possessing a phrase of speaking French: and it was French, and French only, the whole world seemed now gabbling around me. What should I do?

Villette

Approaching the conductor, I just laid my hand on his arm, pointed to a trunk, thence to the diligence-roof, and tried to express a question with my eyes. He misunderstood me, seized the trunk indicated, and was about to hoist it on the vehicle.

"Let that alone—will you?" said a voice in good English; then, in correction, "Qu'est-ce que vous faîtes donc? Cette malle est à moi."

But I had heard the Fatherland accents; they rejoiced my heart; I turned: "Sir," said I, appealing to the stranger, without, in my distress, noticing what he was like, "I cannot speak French. May I entreat you to ask this man what he has done with my trunk?"

Without discriminating, for the moment, what sort of face it was to which my eyes were raised and on which they were fixed, I felt in its expression half-surprise at my appeal and half-doubt of the wisdom of interference.

"Do ask him; I would do as much for you," said I.

I don't know whether he smiled, but he said in a gentlemanly tone—that is to say, a tone not hard nor terrifying,—"What sort of trunk was yours?"

I described it, including in my description the green ribbon. And forthwith he took the conductor under hand, and I felt, through all the storm of French which followed, that he raked him fore and aft. Presently he returned to me.

"The fellow avers he was overloaded, and confesses that he removed your trunk after you saw it put on, and has left it behind at Boue-Marine with other parcels; he has promised, however, to forward it to-morrow; the day after, therefore, you will find it safe at this bureau."

"Thank you," said I: but my heart sank.

Meantime what should I do? Perhaps this English gentleman saw the failure of courage in my face; he inquired kindly, "Have you any friends in this city?"

"No, and I don't know where to go."

There was a little pause, in the course of which, as he turned more fully to the light of a lamp above him, I saw that he was a young, distinguished, and handsome man; he might be a lord,

62

Villette

for anything I knew: nature had made him good enough for a prince, I thought. His face was very pleasant; he looked high but not arrogant, manly but not overbearing. I was turning away, in the deep consciousness of all absence of claim to look for further help from such a one as he.

"Was all your money in your trunk?" he asked, stopping me.

How thankful was I to be able to answer with truth—"No. I have enough in my purse" (for I had near twenty francs) "to keep me at a quiet inn till the day after to-morrow; but I am quite a stranger in Villette, and don't know the streets and the inns."

"I can give you the address of such an inn as you want," said he; "and it is not far off: with my direction you will easily find it."

He tore a leaf from his pocket-book, wrote a few words and gave it to me. I did think him kind; and as to distrusting him, or his advice, or his address, I should almost as soon have thought of distrusting the Bible. There was goodness in his countenance, and honour in his bright eyes.

"Your shortest way will be to follow the Boulevard and cross the park," he continued; "but it is too late and too dark for a woman to go through the park alone; I will step with you thus far."

He moved on, and I followed him, through the darkness and the small soaking rain. The Boulevard was all deserted, its path miry, the water dripping from its trees; the park was black as midnight. In the double gloom of trees and fog, I could not see my guide; I could only follow his tread. Not the least fear had I: I believe I would have followed that frank tread, through continual night, to the world's end.

"Now," said he, when the park was traversed, "you will go along this broad street till you come to steps; two lamps will show you where they are: these steps you will descend: a narrower street lies below; following that, at the bottom you will find your inn. They speak English there, so your difficulties are now pretty well over. Good-night."

"Good-night, sir," said I: "accept my sincerest thanks." And we parted.

The remembrance of his countenance, which I am sure wore

a light not unbenignant to the friendless — the sound in my ear of his voice, which spoke a nature chivalric to the needy and feeble, as well as the youthful and fair — were a sort of cordial to me long after. He was a true young English gentleman.

On I went, hurrying fast through a magnificent street and square, with the grandest houses round, and amidst them the huge outline of more than one overbearing pile; which might be palace or church — I could not tell. Just as I passed a portico, two mustachioed men came suddenly from behind the pillars; they were smoking cigars: their dress implied pretensions to the rank of gentlemen, but, poor things! they were very plebeian in soul. They spoke with insolence, and, fast as I walked, they kept pace with me a long way. At last I met a sort of patrol, and my dreaded hunters were turned from the pursuit; but they had driven me beyond my reckoning: when I could collect my faculties, I no longer knew where I was; the staircase I must long since have passed. Puzzled, out of breath, all my pulses throbbing in inevitable agitation, I knew not where to turn. It was terrible to think of again encountering those bearded, sneering simpletons; yet the ground must be retraced, and the steps sought out.

I came at last to an old and worn flight, and, taking it for granted that this must be the one indicated, I descended them. The street into which they led was indeed narrow, but it contained no inn. On I wandered. In a very quiet and comparatively clean and well-paved street, I saw a light burning over the door of a rather large house, loftier by a story than those round it. This might be the inn at last. I hastened on: my knees now trembled under me: I was getting quite exhausted.

No inn was this. A brass-plate embellished the great porte-cochère: "Pensionnat de Demoiselles" was the inscription; and beneath, a name, "Madame Beck."

I started. About a hundred thoughts volleyed through my mind in a moment. Yet I planned nothing, and considered nothing: I had not time. Providence said, "Stop here; this is your inn." Fate took me in her strong hand; mastered my will; directed my actions: I rang the door-bell.

While I waited, I would not reflect. I fixedly looked at the street-stones, where the door-lamp shone, and counted them and noted their shapes, and the glitter of wet on their angles. I rang again. They opened at last. A bonne in a smart cap stood before me.

Villette

"May I see Madame Beck?" I inquired.

I believe if I had spoken French she would not have admitted me; but, as I spoke English, she concluded I was a foreign teacher come on business connected with the pensionnat, and, even at that late hour, she let me in, without a word of reluctance, or a moment of hesitation.

The next moment I sat in a cold, glittering salon, with porcelain stove, unlit, and gilded ornaments, and polished floor. A pendule on the mantel-piece struck nine o'clock.

A quarter of an hour passed. How fast beat every pulse in my frame! How I turned cold and hot by turns! I sat with my eyes fixed on the door—a great white folding-door, with gilt mouldings: I watched to see a leaf move and open. All had been quiet: not a mouse had stirred; the white doors were closed and motionless.

"You ayre Engliss?" said a voice at my elbow. I almost bounded, so unexpected was the sound; so certain had I been of solitude.

No ghost stood beside me, nor anything of spectral aspect; merely a motherly, dumpy little woman, in a large shawl, a wrapping-gown, and a clean, trim nightcap.

I said I was English, and immediately, without further prelude, we fell to a most remarkable conversation. Madame Beck (for Madame Beck it was—she had entered by a little door behind me, and, being shod with the shoes of silence, I had heard neither her entrance nor approach)—Madame Beck had exhausted her command of insular speech when she said, "You ayre Engliss," and she now proceeded to work away volubly in her own tongue. I answered in mine. She partly understood me, but as I did not at all understand her—though we made together an awful clamour (anything like Madame's gift of utterance I had not hitherto heard or imagined)—we achieved little progress. She rang, ere long, for aid; which arrived in the shape of a "maîtresse," who had been partly educated in an Irish convent, and was esteemed a perfect adept in the English language. A bluff little personage this maîtresse was—Labassecourienne from top to toe: and how she did slaughter the speech of Albion! However, I told her a plain tale, which she translated. I told her how I had left my own country, intent on extending my knowledge, and gaining my bread; how I was ready to turn my hand to any useful thing, provided it was not wrong or degrading; how I would be a child's-nurse, or a lady's-maid, and would not refuse even housework adapted to my strength. Madame heard this; and, questioning her countenance, I almost thought the tale won her ear:

"Il n'y a que les Anglaises pour ces sortes d'entreprises," said she: "sont-elles donc intrépides ces femmes là!"

She asked my name, my age; she sat and looked at me — not pityingly, not with interest: never a gleam of sympathy, or a shade of compassion, crossed her countenance during the interview. I felt she was not one to be led an inch by her feelings: grave and considerate, she gazed, consulting her judgment and studying my narrative. A bell rang.

"Voilà pour la prière du soir!" said she, and rose. Through her interpreter, she desired me to depart now, and come back on the morrow; but this did not suit me: I could not bear to return to the perils of darkness and the street. With energy, yet with a collected and controlled manner, I said, addressing herself personally, and not the maîtresse: "Be assured, madame, that by instantly securing my services, your interests will be served and not injured: you will find me one who will wish to give, in her labour, a full equivalent for her wages; and if you hire me, it will be better that I should stay here this night: having no acquaintance in Villette, and not possessing the language of the country, how can I secure a lodging?"

"It is true," said she; "but at least you can give a reference?"

"None."

She inquired after my luggage: I told her when it would arrive. She mused. At that moment a man's step was heard in the vestibule, hastily proceeding to the outer door. (I shall go on with this part of my tale as if I had understood all that passed; for though it was then scarce intelligible to me, I heard it translated afterwards).

"Who goes out now?" demanded Madame Beck, listening to the tread.

"M. Paul," replied the teacher. "He came this evening to give a reading to the first class."

"The very man I should at this moment most wish to see. Call him."

The teacher ran to the salon door. M. Paul was summoned.

Villette

He entered: a small, dark and spare man, in spectacles.

"Mon cousin," began Madame, "I want your opinion. We know your skill in physiognomy; use it now. Read that countenance."

The little man fixed on me his spectacles: A resolute compression of the lips, and gathering of the brow, seemed to say that he meant to see through me, and that a veil would be no veil for him.

"I read it," he pronounced.

"Et qu'en dites vous?"

"Mais—bien des choses," was the oracular answer.

"Bad or good?"

"Of each kind, without doubt," pursued the diviner.

"May one trust her word?"

"Are you negotiating a matter of importance?"

"She wishes me to engage her as bonne or gouvernante; tells a tale full of integrity, but gives no reference."

"She is a stranger?"

"An Englishwoman, as one may see."

"She speaks French?"

"Not a word."

"She understands it?"

"No."

"One may then speak plainly in her presence?"

"Doubtless."

He gazed steadily. "Do you need her services?"

"I could do with them. You know I am disgusted with Madame Svini."

Still he scrutinized. The judgment, when it at last came, was as indefinite as what had gone before it.

"Engage her. If good predominates in that nature, the action will bring its own reward; if evil—eh bien! ma cousine, ce sera toujours une bonne œuvre." And with a bow and a "bon soir," this vague arbiter of my destiny vanished.

And Madame did engage me that very night—by God's blessing I was spared the necessity of passing forth again into the lonesome, dreary, hostile street.

CHAPTER VIII.

MADAME BECK.

Being delivered into the charge of the maîtresse, I was led through a long narrow passage into a foreign kitchen, very clean but very strange. It seemed to contain no means of cooking—neither fireplace nor oven; I did not understand that the great black furnace which filled one corner, was an efficient substitute for these. Surely pride was not already beginning its whispers in my heart; yet I felt a sense of relief when, instead of being left in the kitchen, as I half anticipated, I was led forward to a small inner room termed a "cabinet." A cook in a jacket, a short petticoat and sabots, brought my supper: to wit—some meat, nature unknown, served in an odd and acid, but pleasant sauce; some chopped potatoes, made savoury with, I know not what: vinegar and sugar, I think: a tartine, or slice of bread and butter, and a baked pear. Being hungry, I ate and was grateful.

After the "prière du soir," Madame herself came to have another look at me. She desired me to follow her up-stairs. Through a series of the queerest little dormitories—which, I heard afterwards, had once been nuns' cells: for the premises were in part of ancient date—and through the oratory—a long, low, gloomy room, where a crucifix hung, pale, against the wall, and two tapers kept dim vigils—she conducted me to an apartment where three children were asleep in three tiny beds. A heated stove made the air of this room oppressive; and, to mend matters, it was scented with an odour rather strong than delicate: a perfume, indeed, altogether surprising and unexpected under the circumstances, being like the combination of smoke with some spirituous essence—a smell, in short, of whisky.

Beside a table, on which flared the remnant of a candle guttering to waste in the socket, a coarse woman, heterogeneously clad in a broad striped showy silk dress, and a stuff apron, sat in a chair fast asleep. To complete the picture, and leave no doubt as to the state of matters, a bottle and an empty glass stood at the sleeping beauty's elbow.

Madame contemplated this remarkable tableau with great calm; she neither smiled nor scowled; no impress of anger, disgust, or surprise, ruffled the equality of her grave aspect; she did not even wake the woman! Serenely pointing to a fourth bed, she intimated that it was to be mine; then, having extinguished the candle and substituted for it a night-lamp, she

Villette

glided through an inner door, which she left ajar—the entrance to her own chamber, a large, well-furnished apartment; as was discernible through the aperture.

My devotions that night were all thanksgiving. Strangely had I been led since morning—unexpectedly had I been provided for. Scarcely could I believe that not forty-eight hours had elapsed since I left London, under no other guardianship than that which protects the passenger-bird—with no prospect but the dubious cloud-tracery of hope.

I was a light sleeper; in the dead of night I suddenly awoke. All was hushed, but a white figure stood in the room—Madame in her night-dress. Moving without perceptible sound, she visited the three children in the three beds; she approached me: I feigned sleep, and she studied me long. A small pantomime ensued, curious enough. I daresay she sat a quarter of an hour on the edge of my bed, gazing at my face. She then drew nearer, bent close over me; slightly raised my cap, and turned back the border so as to expose my hair; she looked at my hand lying on the bedclothes. This done, she turned to the chair where my clothes lay: it was at the foot of the bed. Hearing her touch and lift them, I opened my eyes with precaution, for I own I felt curious to see how far her taste for research would lead her. It led her a good way: every article did she inspect. I divined her motive for this proceeding, viz. the wish to form from the garments a judgment respecting the wearer, her station, means, neatness, &c. The end was not bad, but the means were hardly fair or justifiable. In my dress was a pocket; she fairly turned it inside out: she counted the money in my purse; she opened a little memorandum-book, coolly perused its contents, and took from between the leaves a small plaited lock of Miss Marchmont's grey hair. To a bunch of three keys, being those of my trunk, desk, and work-box, she accorded special attention: with these, indeed, she withdrew a moment to her own room. I softly rose in my bed and followed her with my eye: these keys, reader, were not brought back till they had left on the toilet of the adjoining room the impress of their wards in wax. All being thus done decently and in order, my property was returned to its place, my clothes were carefully refolded. Of what nature were the conclusions deduced from this scrutiny? Were they favourable or otherwise? Vain question. Madame's face of stone (for of stone in its present night aspect it looked: it had been human, and, as I said before, motherly, in the salon) betrayed no response.

Her duty done—I felt that in her eyes this business was a duty—she rose, noiseless as a shadow: she moved towards her own chamber; at the door, she turned, fixing her eye on the heroine of the bottle, who still slept and loudly snored. Mrs. Svini (I presume this was Mrs. Svini, Anglicé or Hibernicé, Sweeny) — Mrs. Sweeny's doom was in Madame Beck's eye — an immutable purpose that eye spoke: Madame's visitations for shortcomings might be slow, but they were sure. All this was very un-English: truly I was in a foreign land.

The morrow made me further acquainted with Mrs. Sweeny. It seems she had introduced herself to her present employer as an English lady in reduced circumstances: a native, indeed, of Middlesex, professing to speak the English tongue with the purest metropolitan accent. Madame — reliant on her own infallible expedients for finding out the truth in time — had a singular intrepidity in hiring service off-hand (as indeed seemed abundantly proved in my own case). She received Mrs. Sweeny as nursery-governess to her three children. I need hardly explain to the reader that this lady was in effect a native of Ireland; her station I do not pretend to fix: she boldly declared that she had "had the bringing-up of the son and daughter of a marquis." I think myself, she might possibly have been a hanger-on, nurse, fosterer, or washerwoman, in some Irish family: she spoke a smothered tongue, curiously overlaid with mincing cockney inflections. By some means or other she had acquired, and now held in possession, a wardrobe of rather suspicious splendour — gowns of stiff and costly silk, fitting her indifferently, and apparently made for other proportions than those they now adorned; caps with real lace borders, and — the chief item in the inventory, the spell by which she struck a certain awe through the household, quelling the otherwise scornfully disposed teachers and servants, and, so long as her broad shoulders wore the folds of that majestic drapery, even influencing Madame herself — a real Indian shawl — "un véritable cachemire," as Madame Beck said, with unmixed reverence and amaze. I feel quite sure that without this "cachemire" she would not have kept her footing in the pensionnat for two days: by virtue of it, and it only, she maintained the same a month.

But when Mrs. Sweeny knew that I was come to fill her shoes, then it was that she declared herself — then did she rise on Madame Beck in her full power — then come down on me with her concentrated weight. Madame bore this revelation and visitation so well, so stoically, that I for very shame could not support it otherwise than with composure. For one little moment Madame Beck absented herself from the room; ten minutes after, an agent of the police stood in the midst of us. Mrs. Sweeny and her effects were removed. Madame's brow had not been ruffled during the scene—her lips had not dropped one sharply-accented word.

This brisk little affair of the dismissal was all settled before breakfast: order to march given, policeman called, mutineer expelled; "chambre d'enfans" fumigated and cleansed, windows thrown open, and every trace of the accomplished Mrs. Sweeny—even to the fine essence and spiritual fragrance which gave token so subtle and so fatal of the head and front of her offending—was annihilated from the Rue Fossette: all this, I say, was done between the moment of Madame Beck's issuing like Aurora from her chamber, and that in which she coolly sat down to pour out her first cup of coffee.

About noon, I was summoned to dress Madame. (It appeared my place was to be a hybrid between gouvernante and lady's-maid.) Till noon, she haunted the house in her wrapping-gown, shawl, and soundless slippers. How would the lady-chief of an English school approve this custom?

The dressing of her hair puzzled me; she had plenty of it: auburn, unmixed with grey: though she was forty years old. Seeing my embarrassment, she said, "You have not been a femme-de-chambre in your own country?" And taking the brush from my hand, and setting me aside, not ungently or disrespectfully, she arranged it herself. In performing other offices of the toilet, she half-directed, half-aided me, without the least display of temper or impatience. N.B.—That was the first and last time I was required to dress her. Henceforth, on Rosine, the portress, devolved that duty.

When attired, Madame Beck appeared a personage of a figure rather short and stout, yet still graceful in its own peculiar way; that is, with the grace resulting from proportion of parts. Her complexion was fresh and sanguine, not too rubicund; her eye, blue and serene; her dark silk dress fitted her as a French sempstress alone can make a dress fit; she looked well, though a little bourgeoise; as bourgeoise, indeed, she was. I know not what of harmony pervaded her whole person; and yet her face offered contrast, too: its features were by no means such as are usually seen in conjunction with a complexion of such blended freshness and repose: their outline was stern: her forehead was high but narrow; it expressed capacity and some benevolence, but no expanse; nor did her peaceful yet watchful eye ever know the fire which is kindled in the heart or the softness which flows thence. Her mouth was hard: it could be a little grim; her lips were thin. For sensibility and genius, with all their tenderness and temerity, I felt somehow that Madame

Villette

would be the right sort of Minos in petticoats.

In the long run, I found she was something else in petticoats too. Her name was Modeste Maria Beck, née Kint: it ought to have been Ignacia. She was a charitable woman, and did a great deal of good. There never was a mistress whose rule was milder. I was told that she never once remonstrated with the intolerable Mrs. Sweeny, despite her tipsiness, disorder, and general neglect; yet Mrs. Sweeny had to go the moment her departure became convenient. I was told, too, that neither masters nor teachers were found fault with in that establishment; yet both masters and teachers were often changed: they vanished and others filled their places, none could well explain how.

The establishment was both a pensionnat and an externat: the externes or day-pupils exceeded one hundred in number; the boarders were about a score. Madame must have possessed high administrative powers: she ruled all these, together with four teachers, eight masters, six servants, and three children, managing at the same time to perfection the pupils' parents and friends; and that without apparent effort; without bustle, fatigue, fever, or any symptom of undue excitement: occupied she always was—busy, rarely. It is true that Madame had her own system for managing and regulating this mass of machinery; and a very pretty system it was: the reader has seen a specimen of it, in that small affair of turning my pocket inside out, and reading my private memoranda. "Surveillance," "espionage,"—these were her watchwords.

Still, Madame knew what honesty was, and liked it—that is, when it did not obtrude its clumsy scruples in the way of her will and interest. She had a respect for "Angleterre;" and as to "les Anglaises," she would have the women of no other country about her own children, if she could help it.

Often in the evening, after she had been plotting and counter-plotting, spying and receiving the reports of spies all day, she would come up to my room—a trace of real weariness on her brow—and she would sit down and listen while the children said their little prayers to me in English: the Lord's Prayer, and the hymn beginning "Gentle Jesus," these little Catholics were permitted to repeat at my knee; and, when I had put them to bed, she would talk to me (I soon gained enough French to be able to understand, and even answer her) about England and Englishwomen, and the reasons for what she was pleased to term their superior intelligence, and more real and reliable probity. Very good sense she often showed; very sound opinions she often broached: she seemed to know that keeping girls in distrustful restraint, in blind ignorance, and under a surveillance that left them no moment and no corner for retirement, was not the best way to make them grow up honest and modest women; but she averred that ruinous consequences would ensue if any other method were tried with continental children: they were so accustomed to restraint, that relaxation, however guarded, would be misunderstood and fatally presumed on. She was sick, she would declare, of the means she had to use, but use them she must; and after discoursing, often with dignity and delicacy, to me, she would move away on her "souliers de silence," and glide ghost-like through the house, watching and spying everywhere, peering through every keyhole, listening behind every door.

After all, Madame's system was not bad — let me do her justice. Nothing could be better than all her arrangements for the physical well-being of her scholars. No minds were overtasked: the lessons were well distributed and made incomparably easy to the learner; there was a liberty of amusement, and a provision for exercise which kept the girls healthy; the food was abundant and good: neither pale nor puny faces were anywhere to be seen in the Rue Fossette. She never grudged a holiday; she allowed plenty of time for sleeping, dressing, washing, eating; her method in all these matters was easy, liberal, salutary, and rational: many an austere English school-mistress would do vastly well to imitate her — and I believe many would be glad to do so, if exacting English parents would let them.

As Madame Beck ruled by espionage, she of course had her staff of spies: she perfectly knew the quality of the tools she used, and while she would not scruple to handle the dirtiest for a dirty occasion — flinging this sort from her like refuse rind, after the orange has been duly squeezed — I have known her fastidious in seeking pure metal for clean uses; and when once a bloodless and rustless instrument was found, she was careful of the prize, keeping it in silk and cotton-wool. Yet, woe be to that man or woman who relied on her one inch beyond the point where it was her interest to be trustworthy: interest was the master-key of Madame's nature — the mainspring of her motives — the alpha and omega of her life. I have seen her feelings appealed to, and I have smiled in half-pity, half-scorn at the appellants. None ever gained her ear through that channel, or swayed her purpose by that means. On the contrary, to attempt to touch her heart was the surest way to rouse her antipathy, and to make of her a secret foe. It proved to her that she had no heart to be touched: it reminded her where she was

Villette

impotent and dead. Never was the distinction between charity and mercy better exemplified than in her. While devoid of sympathy, she had a sufficiency of rational benevolence: she would give in the readiest manner to people she had never seen—rather, however, to classes than to individuals. "Pour les pauvres," she opened her purse freely—against the poor man, as a rule, she kept it closed. In philanthropic schemes for the benefit of society at large she took a cheerful part; no private sorrow touched her: no force or mass of suffering concentrated in one heart had power to pierce hers. Not the agony in Gethsemane, not the death on Calvary, could have wrung from her eyes one tear.

I say again, Madame was a very great and a very capable woman. That school offered her for her powers too limited a sphere; she ought to have swayed a nation: she should have been the leader of a turbulent legislative assembly. Nobody could have browbeaten her, none irritated her nerves, exhausted her patience, or over-reached her astuteness. In her own single person, she could have comprised the duties of a first minister and a superintendent of police. Wise, firm, faithless; secret, crafty, passionless; watchful and inscrutable; acute and insensate—withal perfectly decorous—what more could be desired?

The sensible reader will not suppose that I gained all the knowledge here condensed for his benefit in one month, or in one half-year. No! what I saw at first was the thriving outside of a large and flourishing educational establishment. Here was a great house, full of healthy, lively girls, all well-dressed and many of them handsome, gaining knowledge by a marvellously easy method, without painful exertion or useless waste of spirits; not, perhaps, making very rapid progress in anything; taking it easy, but still always employed, and never oppressed. Here was a corps of teachers and masters, more stringently tasked, as all the real head-labour was to be done by them, in order to save the pupils, yet having their duties so arranged that they relieved each other in quick succession whenever the work was severe: here, in short, was a foreign school; of which the life, movement, and variety made it a complete and most charming contrast to many English institutions of the same kind.

Behind the house was a large garden, and, in summer, the pupils almost lived out of doors amongst the rose-bushes and the fruit-trees. Under the vast and vine-draped berceau, Madame would take her seat on summer afternoons, and send for the classes, in turns, to sit round her and sew and read.

Meantime, masters came and went, delivering short and lively lectures, rather than lessons, and the pupils made notes of their instructions, or did not make them—just as inclination prompted; secure that, in case of neglect, they could copy the notes of their companions. Besides the regular monthly jours de sortie, the Catholic fête-days brought a succession of holidays all the year round; and sometimes on a bright summer morning, or soft summer evening; the boarders were taken out for a long walk into the country, regaled with gaufres and vin blanc, or new milk and pain bis, or pistolets au beurre (rolls) and coffee. All this seemed very pleasant, and Madame appeared goodness itself; and the teachers not so bad but they might be worse; and the pupils, perhaps, a little noisy and rough, but types of health and glee.

Thus did the view appear, seen through the enchantment of distance; but there came a time when distance was to melt for me—when I was to be called down from my watch-tower of the nursery, whence I had hitherto made my observations, and was to be compelled into closer intercourse with this little world of the Rue Fossette.

I was one day sitting up-stairs, as usual, hearing the children their English lessons, and at the same time turning a silk dress for Madame, when she came sauntering into the room with that absorbed air and brow of hard thought she sometimes wore, and which made her look so little genial. Dropping into a seat opposite mine, she remained some minutes silent. Désirée, the eldest girl, was reading to me some little essay of Mrs. Barbauld's, and I was making her translate currently from English to French as she proceeded, by way of ascertaining that she comprehended what she read: Madame listened.

Presently, without preface or prelude, she said, almost in the tone of one making an accusation, "Meess, in England you were a governess?"

"No, Madame," said I smiling, "you are mistaken."

"Is this your first essay at teaching—this attempt with my children?"

I assured her it was. Again she became silent; but looking up, as I took a pin from the cushion, I found myself an object of study: she held me under her eye; she seemed turning me round in her thoughts—measuring my fitness for a purpose, weighing my value in a plan. Madame had, ere this, scrutinized all I had, and I believe she esteemed herself cognizant of much that I was;

Villette

but from that day, for the space of about a fortnight, she tried me by new tests. She listened at the nursery door when I was shut in with the children; she followed me at a cautious distance when I walked out with them, stealing within ear-shot whenever the trees of park or boulevard afforded a sufficient screen: a strict preliminary process having thus been observed, she made a move forward.

One morning, coming on me abruptly, and with the semblance of hurry, she said she found herself placed in a little dilemma. Mr. Wilson, the English master, had failed to come at his hour, she feared he was ill; the pupils were waiting in classe; there was no one to give a lesson; should I, for once, object to giving a short dictation exercise, just that the pupils might not have it to say they had missed their English lesson?

"In classe, Madame?" I asked.

"Yes, in classe: in the second division."

"Where there are sixty pupils," said I; for I knew the number, and with my usual base habit of cowardice, I shrank into my sloth like a snail into its shell, and alleged incapacity and impracticability as a pretext to escape action. If left to myself, I should infallibly have let this chance slip. Inadventurous, unstirred by impulses of practical ambition, I was capable of sitting twenty years teaching infants the hornbook, turning silk dresses and making children's frocks. Not that true contentment dignified this infatuated resignation: my work had neither charm for my taste, nor hold on my interest; but it seemed to me a great thing to be without heavy anxiety, and relieved from intimate trial: the negation of severe suffering was the nearest approach to happiness I expected to know. Besides, I seemed to hold two lives—the life of thought, and that of reality; and, provided the former was nourished with a sufficiency of the strange necromantic joys of fancy, the privileges of the latter might remain limited to daily bread, hourly work, and a roof of shelter.

"Come," said Madame, as I stooped more busily than ever over the cutting-out of a child's pinafore, "leave that work."

"But Fifine wants it, Madame."

"Fifine must want it, then, for I want you."

And as Madame Beck did really want and was resolved to have me—as she had long been dissatisfied with the English master, with his shortcomings in punctuality, and his careless method of tuition—as, too, she did not lack resolution and practical activity, whether I lacked them or not—she, without more ado, made me relinquish thimble and needle; my hand was taken into hers, and I was conducted down-stairs. When we reached the carré, a large square hall between the dwelling-house and the pensionnat, she paused, dropped my hand, faced, and scrutinized me. I was flushed, and tremulous from head to foot: tell it not in Gath, I believe I was crying. In fact, the difficulties before me were far from being wholly imaginary; some of them were real enough; and not the least substantial lay in my want of mastery over the medium through which I should be obliged to teach. I had, indeed, studied French closely since my arrival in Villette; learning its practice by day, and its theory in every leisure moment at night, to as late an hour as the rule of the house would allow candle-light; but I was far from yet being able to trust my powers of correct oral expression.

"Dîtes donc," said Madame sternly, "vous sentez vous réellement trop faible?"

I might have said "Yes," and gone back to nursery obscurity, and there, perhaps, mouldered for the rest of my life; but looking up at Madame, I saw in her countenance a something that made me think twice ere I decided. At that instant she did not wear a woman's aspect, but rather a man's. Power of a particular kind strongly limned itself in all her traits, and that power was not my kind of power: neither sympathy, nor congeniality, nor submission, were the emotions it awakened. I stood—not soothed, nor won, nor overwhelmed. It seemed as if a challenge of strength between opposing gifts was given, and I suddenly felt all the dishonour of my diffidence—all the pusillanimity of my slackness to aspire.

"Will you," she said, "go backward or forward?" indicating with her hand, first, the small door of communication with the dwelling-house, and then the great double portals of the classes or schoolrooms.

"En avant," I said.

"But," pursued she, cooling as I warmed, and continuing the hard look, from very antipathy to which I drew strength and determination, "can you face the classes, or are you over-excited?"

She sneered slightly in saying this: nervous excitability was not much to Madame's taste.

"I am no more excited than this stone," I said, tapping the flag with my toe: "or than you," I added, returning her look.

"Bon! But let me tell you these are not quiet, decorous, English girls you are going to encounter. Ce sont des Labassecouriennes, rondes, franches, brusques, et tant soit peu rebelles."

I said: "I know; and I know, too, that though I have studied French hard since I came here, yet I still speak it with far too much hesitation — too little accuracy to be able to command their respect I shall make blunders that will lay me open to the scorn of the most ignorant. Still I mean to give the lesson."

"They always throw over timid teachers," said she.

"I know that too, Madame; I have heard how they rebelled against and persecuted Miss Turner" — a poor friendless English teacher, whom Madame had employed, and lightly discarded; and to whose piteous history I was no stranger.

"C'est vrai," said she, coolly. "Miss Turner had no more command over them than a servant from the kitchen would have had. She was weak and wavering; she had neither tact nor intelligence, decision nor dignity. Miss Turner would not do for these girls at all."

I made no reply, but advanced to the closed schoolroom door.

"You will not expect aid from me, or from any one," said Madame. "That would at once set you down as incompetent for your office."

I opened the door, let her pass with courtesy, and followed her. There were three schoolrooms, all large. That dedicated to the second division, where I was to figure, was considerably the largest, and accommodated an assemblage more numerous, more turbulent, and infinitely more unmanageable than the other two. In after days, when I knew the ground better, I used to think sometimes (if such a comparison may be permitted), that the quiet, polished, tame first division was to the robust, riotous, demonstrative second division, what the English House of Lords is to the House of Commons.

The first glance informed me that many of the pupils were more than girls — quite young women; I knew that some of them were of noble family (as nobility goes in Labassecour), and I was well convinced that not one amongst them was ignorant of my position in Madame's household. As I mounted the estràde (a low platform, raised a step above the flooring), where stood the teacher's chair and desk, I beheld opposite to me a row of eyes and brows that threatened stormy weather—eyes full of an insolent light, and brows hard and unblushing as marble. The continental "female" is quite a different being to the insular "female" of the same age and class: I never saw such eyes and brows in England. Madame Beck introduced me in one cool phrase, sailed from the room, and left me alone in my glory.

I shall never forget that first lesson, nor all the under-current of life and character it opened up to me. Then first did I begin rightly to see the wide difference that lies between the novelist's and poet's ideal "jeune fille" and the said "jeune fille" as she really is.

It seems that three titled belles in the first row had sat down predetermined that a bonne d'enfants should not give them lessons in English. They knew they had succeeded in expelling obnoxious teachers before now; they knew that Madame would at any time throw overboard a professeur or maitresse who became unpopular with the school—that she never assisted a weak official to retain his place—that if he had not strength to fight, or tact to win his way, down he went: looking at "Miss Snowe," they promised themselves an easy victory.

Mesdemoiselles Blanche, Virginie, and Angélique opened the campaign by a series of titterings and whisperings; these soon swelled into murmurs and short laughs, which the remoter benches caught up and echoed more loudly. This growing revolt of sixty against one, soon became oppressive enough; my command of French being so limited, and exercised under such cruel constraint.

Could I but have spoken in my own tongue, I felt as if I might have gained a hearing; for, in the first place, though I knew I looked a poor creature, and in many respects actually was so, yet nature had given me a voice that could make itself heard, if lifted in excitement or deepened by emotion. In the second place, while I had no flow, only a hesitating trickle of language, in ordinary circumstances, yet—under stimulus such as was now rife through the mutinous mass—I could, in English, have rolled out readily phrases stigmatizing their proceedings as such proceedings deserved to be stigmatized; and then with some sarcasm, flavoured with contemptuous bitterness for the ringleaders, and relieved with easy banter for the weaker but less knavish followers, it seemed to me that one

Villette

might possibly get command over this wild herd, and bring them into training, at least. All I could now do was to walk up to Blanche—Mademoiselle de Melcy, a young baronne—the eldest, tallest, handsomest, and most vicious—stand before her desk, take from under her hand her exercise-book, remount the estrade, deliberately read the composition, which I found very stupid, and, as deliberately, and in the face of the whole school, tear the blotted page in two.

This action availed to draw attention and check noise. One girl alone, quite in the background, persevered in the riot with undiminished energy. I looked at her attentively. She had a pale face, hair like night, broad strong eyebrows, decided features, and a dark, mutinous, sinister eye: I noted that she sat close by a little door, which door, I was well aware, opened into a small closet where books were kept. She was standing up for the purpose of conducting her clamour with freer energies. I measured her stature and calculated her strength. She seemed both tall and wiry; but, so the conflict were brief and the attack unexpected, I thought I might manage her.

Advancing up the room, looking as cool and careless as I possibly could, in short, ayant l'air de rien, I slightly pushed the door and found it was ajar. In an instant, and with sharpness, I had turned on her. In another instant she occupied the closet, the door was shut, and the key in my pocket.

It so happened that this girl, Dolores by name, and a Catalonian by race, was the sort of character at once dreaded and hated by all her associates; the act of summary justice above noted proved popular: there was not one present but, in her heart, liked to see it done. They were stilled for a moment; then a smile—not a laugh—passed from desk to desk: then—when I had gravely and tranquilly returned to the estrade, courteously requested silence, and commenced a dictation as if nothing at all had happened—the pens travelled peacefully over the pages, and the remainder of the lesson passed in order and industry.

"C'est bien," said Madame Beck, when I came out of class, hot and a little exhausted. "Ca ira."

She had been listening and peeping through a spy-hole the whole time.

From that day I ceased to be nursery governess, and became English teacher. Madame raised my salary; but she got thrice the work out of me she had extracted from Mr. Wilson, at half the expense.

CHAPTER IX.

ISIDORE.

My time was now well and profitably filled up. What with teaching others and studying closely myself, I had hardly a spare moment. It was pleasant. I felt I was getting on; not lying the stagnant prey of mould and rust, but polishing my faculties and whetting them to a keen edge with constant use. Experience of a certain kind lay before me, on no narrow scale. Villette is a cosmopolitan city, and in this school were girls of almost every European nation, and likewise of very varied rank in life. Equality is much practised in Labassecour; though not republican in form, it is nearly so in substance, and at the desks of Madame Beck's establishment the young countess and the young bourgeoise sat side by side. Nor could you always by outward indications decide which was noble and which plebeian; except that, indeed, the latter had often franker and more courteous manners, while the former bore away the bell for a delicately-balanced combination of insolence and deceit. In the former there was often quick French blood mixed with the marsh-phlegm: I regret to say that the effect of this vivacious fluid chiefly appeared in the oilier glibness with which flattery and fiction ran from the tongue, and in a manner lighter and livelier, but quite heartless and insincere.

To do all parties justice, the honest aboriginal Labassecouriennes had an hypocrisy of their own, too; but it was of a coarse order, such as could deceive few. Whenever a lie was necessary for their occasions, they brought it out with a careless ease and breadth altogether untroubled by the rebuke of conscience. Not a soul in Madame Beck's house, from the scullion to the directress herself, but was above being ashamed of a lie; they thought nothing of it: to invent might not be precisely a virtue, but it was the most venial of faults. "J'ai menti plusieurs fois," formed an item of every girl's and woman's monthly confession: the priest heard unshocked, and absolved unreluctant. If they had missed going to mass, or read a chapter of a novel, that was another thing: these were crimes whereof rebuke and penance were the unfailing weed.

While yet but half-conscious of this state of things, and unlearned in its results, I got on in my new sphere very well. After the first few difficult lessons, given amidst peril and on the edge of a moral volcano that rumbled under my feet and sent sparks and hot fumes into my eyes, the eruptive spirit seemed to subside, as far as I was concerned. My mind was a

Villette

good deal bent on success: I could not bear the thought of being baffled by mere undisciplined disaffection and wanton indocility, in this first attempt to get on in life. Many hours of the night I used to lie awake, thinking what plan I had best adopt to get a reliable hold on these mutineers, to bring this stiff-necked tribe under permanent influence. In the first place, I saw plainly that aid in no shape was to be expected from Madame: her righteous plan was to maintain an unbroken popularity with the pupils, at any and every cost of justice or comfort to the teachers. For a teacher to seek her alliance in any crisis of insubordination was equivalent to securing her own expulsion. In intercourse with her pupils, Madame only took to herself what was pleasant, amiable, and recommendatory; rigidly requiring of her lieutenants sufficiency for every annoying crisis, where to act with adequate promptitude was to be unpopular. Thus, I must look only to myself.

Imprimis—it was clear as the day that this swinish multitude were not to be driven by force. They were to be humoured, borne with very patiently: a courteous though sedate manner impressed them; a very rare flash of raillery did good. Severe or continuous mental application they could not, or would not, bear: heavy demand on the memory, the reason, the attention, they rejected point-blank. Where an English girl of not more than average capacity and docility would quietly take a theme and bind herself to the task of comprehension and mastery, a Labassecourienne would laugh in your face, and throw it back to you with the phrase,—"Dieu, que c'est difficile! Je n'en veux pas. Cela m'ennuie trop."

A teacher who understood her business would take it back at once, without hesitation, contest, or expostulation—proceed with even exaggerated care to smoothe every difficulty, to reduce it to the level of their understandings, return it to them thus modified, and lay on the lash of sarcasm with unsparing hand. They would feel the sting, perhaps wince a little under it; but they bore no malice against this sort of attack, provided the sneer was not sour, but hearty, and that it held well up to them, in a clear, light, and bold type, so that she who ran might read, their incapacity, ignorance, and sloth. They would riot for three additional lines to a lesson; but I never knew them rebel against a wound given to their self-respect: the little they had of that quality was trained to be crushed, and it rather liked the pressure of a firm heel than otherwise.

By degrees, as I acquired fluency and freedom in their language, and could make such application of its more nervous idioms as suited their case, the elder and more intelligent girls began rather to like me in their way: I noticed that whenever a pupil had been roused to feel in her soul the stirring of worthy emulation, or the quickening of honest shame, from that date she was won. If I could but once make their (usually large) ears burn under their thick glossy hair, all was comparatively well. By-and-by bouquets began to be laid on my desk in the morning; by way of acknowledgment for this little foreign attention, I used sometimes to walk with a select few during recreation. In the course of conversation it befel once or twice that I made an unpremeditated attempt to rectify some of their singularly distorted notions of principle; especially I expressed my ideas of the evil and baseness of a lie. In an unguarded moment, I chanced to say that, of the two errors; I considered falsehood worse than an occasional lapse in church-attendance. The poor girls were tutored to report in Catholic ears whatever the Protestant teacher said. An edifying consequence ensued. Something—an unseen, an indefinite, a nameless—something stole between myself and these my best pupils: the bouquets continued to be offered, but conversation thenceforth became impracticable. As I paced the alleys or sat in the berceau, a girl never came to my right hand but a teacher, as if by magic, appeared at my left. Also, wonderful to relate, Madame's shoes of silence brought her continually to my back, as quick, as noiseless and unexpected, as some wandering zephyr.

The opinion of my Catholic acquaintance concerning my spiritual prospects was somewhat naïvely expressed to me on one occasion. A pensionnaire, to whom I had rendered some little service, exclaimed one day as she sat beside me: "Mademoiselle, what a pity you are a Protestant!"

"Why, Isabelle?"

"Parceque, quand vous serez morte—vous brûlerez tout de suite dans l'Enfer."

"Croyez-vous?"

"Certainement que j'y crois: tout le monde le sait; et d'ailleurs le prêtre me l'a dit."

Isabelle was an odd, blunt little creature. She added, sotto voce: "Pour assurer votre salut là-haut, on ferait bien de vous brûler toute vive ici-bas."

I laughed, as, indeed, it was impossible to do otherwise.

Has the reader forgotten Miss Ginevra Fanshawe? If so, I

Villette

must be allowed to re-introduce that young lady as a thriving pupil of Madame Beck's; for such she was. On her arrival in the Rue Fossette, two or three days after my sudden settlement there, she encountered me with very little surprise. She must have had good blood in her veins, for never was any duchess more perfectly, radically, unaffectedly nonchalante than she: a weak, transient amaze was all she knew of the sensation of wonder. Most of her other faculties seemed to be in the same flimsy condition: her liking and disliking, her love and hate, were mere cobweb and gossamer; but she had one thing about her that seemed strong and durable enough, and that was — her selfishness.

She was not proud; and — bonne d'enfants as I was — she would forthwith have made of me a sort of friend and confidant. She teased me with a thousand vapid complaints about school-quarrels and household economy: the cookery was not to her taste; the people about her, teachers and pupils, she held to be despicable, because they were foreigners. I bore with her abuse of the Friday's salt fish and hard eggs — with her invective against the soup, the bread, the coffee — with some patience for a time; but at last, wearied by iteration, I turned crusty, and put her to rights: a thing I ought to have done in the very beginning, for a salutary setting down always agreed with her.

Much longer had I to endure her demands on me in the way of work. Her wardrobe, so far as concerned articles of external wear, was well and elegantly supplied; but there were other habiliments not so carefully provided: what she had, needed frequent repair. She hated needle-drudgery herself, and she would bring her hose, &c. to me in heaps, to be mended. A compliance of some weeks threatening to result in the establishment of an intolerable bore — I at last distinctly told her she must make up her mind to mend her own garments. She cried on receiving this information, and accused me of having ceased to be her friend; but I held by my decision, and let the hysterics pass as they could.

Notwithstanding these foibles, and various others needless to mention — but by no means of a refined or elevating character — how pretty she was! How charming she looked, when she came down on a sunny Sunday morning, well-dressed and well-humoured, robed in pale lilac silk, and with her fair long curls reposing on her white shoulders. Sunday was a holiday which she always passed with friends resident in town; and amongst these friends she speedily gave me to understand was one who would fain become something more.

By glimpses and hints it was shown me, and by the general buoyancy of her look and manner it was ere long proved, that ardent admiration—perhaps genuine love—was at her command. She called her suitor "Isidore:" this, however, she intimated was not his real name, but one by which it pleased her to baptize him—his own, she hinted, not being "very pretty." Once, when she had been bragging about the vehemence of "Isidore's" attachment, I asked if she loved him in return.

"Comme cela," said she: "he is handsome, and he loves me to distraction, so that I am well amused. Ca suffit."

Finding that she carried the thing on longer than, from her very fickle tastes, I had anticipated, I one day took it upon me to make serious inquiries as to whether the gentleman was such as her parents, and especially her uncle—on whom, it appeared, she was dependent—would be likely to approve. She allowed that this was very doubtful, as she did not believe "Isidore" had much money.

"Do you encourage him?" I asked.

"Furieusement sometimes," said she.

"Without being certain that you will be permitted to marry him?"

"Oh, how dowdyish you are! I don't want to be married. I am too young."

"But if he loves you as much as you say, and yet it comes to nothing in the end, he will be made miserable."

"Of course he will break his heart. I should be shocked and, disappointed if he didn't."

"I wonder whether this M. Isidore is a fool?" said I.

"He is, about me; but he is wise in other things, à ce qu'on dit. Mrs. Cholmondeley considers him extremely clever: she says he will push his way by his talents; all I know is, that he does little more than sigh in my presence, and that I can wind him round my little finger."

Wishing to get a more definite idea of this love-stricken M. Isidore; whose position seemed to me of the least secure, I requested her to favour me with a personal description; but she could not describe: she had neither words nor the power of putting them together so as to make graphic phrases. She even seemed not properly to have noticed him: nothing of his looks, of the changes in his countenance, had touched her heart or dwelt in her memory—that he was "beau, mais plutôt bel homme que joli garçon," was all she could assert. My patience would often have failed, and my interest flagged, in listening to her, but for one thing. All the hints she dropped, all the details she gave, went unconsciously to prove, to my thinking, that M. Isidore's homage was offered with great delicacy and respect. I informed her very plainly that I believed him much too good for her, and intimated with equal plainness my impression that she was but a vain coquette. She laughed, shook her curls from her eyes, and danced away as if I had paid her a compliment.

Miss Ginevra's school-studies were little better than nominal; there were but three things she practised in earnest, viz. music, singing, and dancing; also embroidering the fine cambric handkerchiefs which she could not afford to buy ready worked: such mere trifles as lessons in history, geography, grammar, and arithmetic, she left undone, or got others to do for her. Very much of her time was spent in visiting. Madame, aware that her stay at school was now limited to a certain period, which would not be extended whether she made progress or not, allowed her great licence in this particular. Mrs. Cholmondeley—her chaperon—a gay, fashionable lady, invited her whenever she had company at her own house, and sometimes took her to evening-parties at the houses of her acquaintance. Ginevra perfectly approved this mode of procedure: it had but one inconvenience; she was obliged to be well dressed, and she had not money to buy variety of dresses. All her thoughts turned on this difficulty; her whole soul was occupied with expedients for effecting its solution. It was wonderful to witness the activity of her otherwise indolent mind on this point, and to see the much-daring intrepidity to which she was spurred by a sense of necessity, and the wish to shine.

She begged boldly of Mrs. Cholmondeley—boldly, I say: not with an air of reluctant shame, but in this strain:—

"My darling Mrs. C., I have nothing in the world fit to wear for your party next week; you must give me a book-muslin dress, and then a ceinture bleu celeste: do—there's an angel! will you?"

The "darling Mrs. C." yielded at first; but finding that applications increased as they were complied with, she was soon obliged, like all Miss Fanshawe's friends, to oppose resistance to encroachment. After a while I heard no more of Mrs. Cholmondeley's presents; but still, visiting went on, and the absolutely necessary dresses continued to be supplied: also many little expensive etcetera—gloves, bouquets, even trinkets. These things, contrary to her custom, and even nature—for she was not secretive—were most sedulously kept out of sight for a time; but one evening, when she was going to a large party for which particular care and elegance of costume were demanded, she could not resist coming to my chamber to show herself in all her splendour.

Beautiful she looked: so young, so fresh, and with a delicacy of skin and flexibility of shape altogether English, and not found in the list of continental female charms. Her dress was new, costly, and perfect. I saw at a glance that it lacked none of those finishing details which cost so much, and give to the general effect such an air of tasteful completeness.

I viewed her from top to toe. She turned airily round that I might survey her on all sides. Conscious of her charms, she was in her best humour: her rather small blue eyes sparkled gleefully. She was going to bestow on me a kiss, in her school-girl fashion of showing her delights but I said, "Steady! Let us be Steady, and know what we are about, and find out the meaning of our magnificence"—and so put her off at arm's length, to undergo cooler inspection.

"Shall I do?" was her question.

"Do?" said I. "There are different ways of doing; and, by my word, I don't understand yours."

"But how do I look?"

"You look well dressed."

She thought the praise not warm enough, and proceeded to direct attention to the various decorative points of her attire. "Look at this parure," said she. "The brooch, the ear-rings, the bracelets: no one in the school has such a set—not Madame herself."

"I see them all." (Pause.) "Did M. de Bassompierre give you those jewels?"

"My uncle knows nothing about them."

"Were they presents from Mrs. Cholmondeley?"

"Not they, indeed. Mrs. Cholmondeley is a mean, stingy creature; she never gives me anything now."

I did not choose to ask any further questions, but turned abruptly away.

"Now, old Crusty—old Diogenes" (these were her familiar terms for me when we disagreed), "what is the matter now?"

"Take yourself away. I have no pleasure in looking at you or your parure."

For an instant, she seemed taken by surprise.

"What now, Mother Wisdom? I have not got into debt for it—that is, not for the jewels, nor the gloves, nor the bouquet. My dress is certainly not paid for, but uncle de Bassompierre will pay it in the bill: he never notices items, but just looks at the total; and he is so rich, one need not care about a few guineas more or less."

"Will you go? I want to shut the door.... Ginevra, people may tell you you are very handsome in that ball-attire; but, in my eyes, you will never look so pretty as you did in the gingham gown and plain straw bonnet you wore when I first saw you."

"Other people have not your puritanical tastes," was her angry reply. "And, besides, I see no right you have to sermonize me."

"Certainly! I have little right; and you, perhaps, have still less to come flourishing and fluttering into my chamber—a mere jay in borrowed plumes. I have not the least respect for your feathers, Miss Fanshawe; and especially the peacock's eyes you call a parure: very pretty things, if you had bought them with money which was your own, and which you could well spare, but not at all pretty under present circumstances."

"On est là pour Mademoiselle Fanshawe!" was announced by the portress, and away she tripped.

This semi-mystery of the parure was not solved till two or three days afterwards, when she came to make a voluntary confession.

"You need not be sulky with me," she began, "in the idea that I am running somebody, papa or M. de Bassompierre, deeply into debt. I assure you nothing remains unpaid for, but the few dresses I have lately had: all the rest is settled."

"There," I thought, "lies the mystery; considering that they were not given you by Mrs. Cholmondeley, and that your own means are limited to a few shillings, of which I know you to be excessively careful."

"Ecoutez!" she went on, drawing near and speaking in her most confidential and coaxing tone; for my "sulkiness" was inconvenient to her: she liked me to be in a talking and listening mood, even if I only talked to chide and listened to rail. "Ecoutez, chère grogneuse! I will tell you all how and about it; and you will then see, not only how right the whole thing is, but how cleverly managed. In the first place, I must go out. Papa himself said that he wished me to see something of the world; he particularly remarked to Mrs. Cholmondeley, that, though I was a sweet creature enough, I had rather a bread-and-butter-eating, school-girl air; of which it was his special desire that I should get rid, by an introduction to society here, before I make my regular début in England. Well, then, if I go out, I must dress. Mrs. Cholmondeley is turned shabby, and will give nothing more; it would be too hard upon uncle to make him pay for all the things I need: that you can't deny — that agrees with your own preachments. Well, but SOMEBODY who heard me (quite by chance, I assure you) complaining to Mrs. Cholmondeley of my distressed circumstances, and what straits I was put to for an ornament or two — somebody, far from grudging one a present, was quite delighted at the idea of being permitted to offer some trifle. You should have seen what a blanc-bec he looked when he first spoke of it: how he hesitated and blushed, and positively trembled from fear of a repulse."

"That will do, Miss Fanshawe. I suppose I am to understand that M. Isidore is the benefactor: that it is from him you have accepted that costly parure; that he supplies your bouquets and your gloves?"

"You express yourself so disagreeably," said she, "one hardly knows how to answer; what I mean to say is, that I occasionally allow Isidore the pleasure and honour of expressing his homage by the offer of a trifle."

"It comes to the same thing…. Now, Ginevra, to speak the plain truth, I don't very well understand these matters; but I believe you are doing very wrong — seriously wrong. Perhaps,

Villette

however, you now feel certain that you will be able to marry M. Isidore; your parents and uncle have given their consent, and, for your part, you love him entirely?"

"Mais pas du tout!" (she always had recourse to French when about to say something specially heartless and perverse). "Je suis sa reine, mais il n'est pas mon roi."

"Excuse me, I must believe this language is mere nonsense and coquetry. There is nothing great about you, yet you are above profiting by the good nature and purse of a man to whom you feel absolute indifference. You love M. Isidore far more than you think, or will avow."

"No. I danced with a young officer the other night, whom I love a thousand times more than he. I often wonder why I feel so very cold to Isidore, for everybody says he is handsome, and other ladies admire him; but, somehow, he bores me: let me see now how it is...."

And she seemed to make an effort to reflect. In this I encouraged her.

"Yes!" I said, "try to get a clear idea of the state of your mind. To me it seems in a great mess—chaotic as a rag-bag."

"It is something in this fashion," she cried out ere long: "the man is too romantic and devoted, and he expects something more of me than I find it convenient to be. He thinks I am perfect: furnished with all sorts of sterling qualities and solid virtues, such as I never had, nor intend to have. Now, one can't help, in his presence, rather trying to justify his good opinion; and it does so tire one to be goody, and to talk sense,—for he really thinks I am sensible. I am far more at my ease with you, old lady—you, you dear crosspatch—who take me at my lowest, and know me to be coquettish, and ignorant, and flirting, and fickle, and silly, and selfish, and all the other sweet things you and I have agreed to be a part of my character."

"This is all very well," I said, making a strenuous effort to preserve that gravity and severity which ran risk of being shaken by this whimsical candour, "but it does not alter that wretched business of the presents. Pack them up, Ginevra, like a good, honest girl, and send them back."

"Indeed, I won't," said she, stoutly.

"Then you are deceiving M. Isidore. It stands to reason that by accepting his presents you give him to understand he will one day receive an equivalent, in your regard…"

"But he won't," she interrupted: "he has his equivalent now, in the pleasure of seeing me wear them—quite enough for him: he is only bourgeois."

This phrase, in its senseless arrogance, quite cured me of the temporary weakness which had made me relax my tone and aspect. She rattled on:

"My present business is to enjoy youth, and not to think of fettering myself, by promise or vow, to this man or that. When first I saw Isidore, I believed he would help me to enjoy it I believed he would be content with my being a pretty girl; and that we should meet and part and flutter about like two butterflies, and be happy. Lo, and behold! I find him at times as grave as a judge, and deep-feeling and thoughtful. Bah! Les penseurs, les hommes profonds et passionnés ne sont pas à mon goût. Le Colonel Alfred de Hamal suits me far better. Va pour les beaux fats et les jolis fripons! Vive les joies et les plaisirs! A bas les grandes passions et les sévères vertus!"

She looked for an answer to this tirade. I gave none.

"J'aime mon beau Colonel," she went on: "je n'aimerai jamais son rival. Je ne serai jamais femme de bourgeois, moi!"

I now signified that it was imperatively necessary my apartment should be relieved of the honour of her presence: she went away laughing.

CHAPTER X.

DR JOHN.

Madame Beck was a most consistent character; forbearing with all the world, and tender to no part of it. Her own children drew her into no deviation from the even tenor of her stoic calm. She was solicitous about her family, vigilant for their interests and physical well-being; but she never seemed to know the wish to take her little children upon her lap, to press their rosy lips with her own, to gather them in a genial embrace, to shower on them softly the benignant caress, the loving word.

I have watched her sometimes sitting in the garden, viewing the little bees afar off, as they walked in a distant alley with Trinette, their bonne; in her mien spoke care and prudence. I know she often pondered anxiously what she called "leur avenir;" but if the youngest, a puny and delicate but engaging child, chancing to spy her, broke from its nurse, and toddling down the walk, came all eager and laughing and panting to clasp her knee, Madame would just calmly put out one hand, so as to prevent inconvenient concussion from the child's sudden onset: "Prends garde, mon enfant!" she would say unmoved, patiently permit it to stand near her a few moments, and then, without smile or kiss, or endearing syllable, rise and lead it back to Trinette.

Her demeanour to the eldest girl was equally characteristic in another way. This was a vicious child. "Quelle peste que cette Désirée! Quel poison que cet enfant là!" were the expressions dedicated to her, alike in kitchen and in schoolroom. Amongst her other endowments she boasted an exquisite skill in the art, of provocation, sometimes driving her bonne and the servants almost wild. She would steal to their attics, open their drawers and boxes, wantonly tear their best caps and soil their best shawls; she would watch her opportunity to get at the buffet of the salle-à-manger, where she would smash articles of porcelain or glass — or to the cupboard of the storeroom, where she would plunder the preserves, drink the sweet wine, break jars and bottles, and so contrive as to throw the onus of suspicion on the cook and the kitchen-maid. All this when Madame saw, and of which when she received report, her sole observation, uttered with matchless serenity, was:

"Désirée a besoin d'une surveillance toute particulière." Accordingly she kept this promising olive-branch a good deal at her side. Never once, I believe, did she tell her faithfully of her faults, explain the evil of such habits, and show the results which must thence ensue. Surveillance must work the whole cure. It failed of course. Désirée was kept in some measure from the servants, but she teased and pillaged her mamma instead. Whatever belonging to Madame's work-table or toilet she could lay her hands on, she stole and hid. Madame saw all this, but she still pretended not to see: she had not rectitude of soul to confront the child with her vices. When an article disappeared whose value rendered restitution necessary, she would profess to think that Désirée had taken it away in play, and beg her to restore it. Désirée was not to be so cheated: she had learned to bring falsehood to the aid of theft, and would deny having touched the brooch, ring, or scissors. Carrying on the hollow system, the mother would calmly assume an air of belief, and afterwards ceaselessly watch and dog the child till she tracked her: to her hiding-places — some hole in the garden-wall — some chink or cranny in garret or out-house. This done, Madame would send Désirée out for a walk with her bonne, and profit by her absence to rob the robber. Désirée proved herself the true daughter of her astute parent, by never suffering either her countenance or manner to betray the least sign of mortification on discovering the loss.

The second child, Fifine, was said to be like its dead father. Certainly, though the mother had given it her healthy frame, her blue eye and ruddy cheek, not from her was derived its moral being. It was an honest, gleeful little soul: a passionate, warm-tempered, bustling creature it was too, and of the sort likely to blunder often into perils and difficulties. One day it bethought itself to fall from top to bottom of a steep flight of stone steps; and when Madame, hearing the noise (she always heard every noise), issued from the salle-à-manger and picked it up, she said quietly, — "Cet enfant a un os de cassé."

At first we hoped this was not the case. It was, however, but too true: one little plump arm hung powerless.

"Let Meess" (meaning me) "take her," said Madame; "et qu'on aille tout de suite chercher un fiacre."

In a fiacre she promptly, but with admirable coolness and self-possession, departed to fetch a surgeon.

It appeared she did not find the family-surgeon at home; but that mattered not: she sought until she laid her hand on a substitute to her mind, and brought him back with her. Meantime I had cut the child's sleeve from its arm, undressed and put it to bed.

Villette

We none of us, I suppose (by we I mean the bonne, the cook, the portress, and myself, all which personages were now gathered in the small and heated chamber), looked very scrutinizingly at the new doctor when he came into the room. I, at least, was taken up with endeavouring to soothe Fifine; whose cries (for she had good lungs) were appalling to hear. These cries redoubled in intensity as the stranger approached her bed; when he took her up, "Let alone!" she cried passionately, in her broken English (for she spoke English as did the other children). "I will not you: I will Dr. Pillule!"

"And Dr. Pillule is my very good friend," was the answer, in perfect English; "but he is busy at a place three leagues off, and I am come in his stead. So now, when we get a little calmer, we must commence business; and we will soon have that unlucky little arm bandaged and in right order."

Hereupon he called for a glass of eau sucrée, fed her with some teaspoonfuls of the sweet liquid (Fifine was a frank gourmande; anybody could win her heart through her palate), promised her more when the operation should be over, and promptly went to work. Some assistance being needed, he demanded it of the cook, a robust, strong-armed woman; but she, the portress, and the nurse instantly fled. I did not like to touch that small, tortured limb, but thinking there was no alternative, my hand was already extended to do what was requisite. I was anticipated; Madame Beck had put out her own hand: hers was steady while mine trembled.

"Ca vaudra mieux," said the doctor, turning from me to her.

He showed wisdom in his choice. Mine would have been feigned stoicism, forced fortitude. Hers was neither forced nor feigned.

"Merci, Madame; très bien, fort bien!" said the operator when he had finished. "Voilà un sang-froid bien opportun, et qui vaut mille élans de sensibilité déplacée."

He was pleased with her firmness, she with his compliment. It was likely, too, that his whole general appearance, his voice, mien, and manner, wrought impressions in his favour. Indeed, when you looked well at him, and when a lamp was brought in—for it was evening and now waxing dusk—you saw that, unless Madame Beck had been less than woman, it could not well be otherwise. This young doctor (he was young) had no common aspect. His stature looked imposingly tall in that little chamber, and amidst that group of Dutch-made women; his profile was clear, fine and expressive: perhaps his eye glanced from face to face rather too vividly, too quickly, and too often; but it had a most pleasant character, and so had his mouth; his chin was full, cleft, Grecian, and perfect. As to his smile, one could not in a hurry make up one's mind as to the descriptive epithet it merited; there was something in it that pleased, but something too that brought surging up into the mind all one's foibles and weak points: all that could lay one open to a laugh. Yet Fifine liked this doubtful smile, and thought the owner genial: much as he had hurt her, she held out her hand to bid him a friendly good-night. He patted the little hand kindly, and then he and Madame went down-stairs together; she talking in her highest tide of spirits and volubility, he listening with an air of good-natured amenity, dashed with that unconscious roguish archness I find it difficult to describe.

I noticed that though he spoke French well, he spoke English better; he had, too, an English complexion, eyes, and form. I noticed more. As he passed me in leaving the room, turning his face in my direction one moment—not to address me, but to speak to Madame, yet so standing, that I almost necessarily looked up at him—a recollection which had been struggling to form in my memory, since the first moment I heard his voice, started up perfected. This was the very gentleman to whom I had spoken at the bureau; who had helped me in the matter of the trunk; who had been my guide through the dark, wet park. Listening, as he passed down the long vestibule out into the street, I recognised his very tread: it was the same firm and equal stride I had followed under the dripping trees.

It was to be concluded that this young surgeon-physician's first visit to the Rue Fossette would be the last. The respectable Dr. Pillule being expected home the next day, there appeared no reason why his temporary substitute should again represent him; but the Fates had written their decree to the contrary.

Dr. Pillule had been summoned to see a rich old hypochondriac at the antique university town of Bouquin-Moisi, and upon his prescribing change of air and travel as remedies, he was retained to accompany the timid patient on a tour of some weeks; it but remained, therefore, for the new doctor to continue his attendance at the Rue Fossette.

I often saw him when he came; for Madame would not trust the little invalid to Trinette, but required me to spend much of my time in the nursery. I think he was skilful. Fifine recovered rapidly under his care, yet even her convalescence did not hasten his dismissal. Destiny and Madame Beck seemed in league, and both had ruled that he should make deliberate acquaintance with the vestibule, the private staircase and upper chambers of the Rue Fossette.

No sooner did Fifine emerge from his hands than Désirée declared herself ill. That possessed child had a genius for simulation, and captivated by the attentions and indulgences of a sick-room, she came to the conclusion that an illness would perfectly accommodate her tastes, and took her bed accordingly. She acted well, and her mother still better; for while the whole case was transparent to Madame Beck as the day, she treated it with an astonishingly well-assured air of gravity and good faith.

What surprised me was, that Dr. John (so the young Englishman had taught Fifine to call him, and we all took from her the habit of addressing him by this name, till it became an established custom, and he was known by no other in the Rue Fossette) — that Dr. John consented tacitly to adopt Madame's tactics, and to fall in with her manœuvres. He betrayed, indeed, a period of comic doubt, cast one or two rapid glances from the child to the mother, indulged in an interval of self-consultation, but finally resigned himself with a good grace to play his part in the farce. Désirée eat like a raven, gambolled day and night in her bed, pitched tents with the sheets and blankets, lounged like a Turk amidst pillows and bolsters, diverted herself with throwing her shoes at her bonne and grimacing at her sisters — over-flowed, in short, with unmerited health and evil spirits; only languishing when her mamma and the physician paid their diurnal visit. Madame Beck, I knew, was glad, at any price, to have her daughter in bed out of the way of mischief; but I wondered that Dr. John did not tire of the business.

Every day, on this mere pretext of a motive, he gave punctual attendance; Madame always received him with the same empressement, the same sunshine for himself, the same admirably counterfeited air of concern for her child. Dr. John wrote harmless prescriptions for the patient, and viewed her mother with a shrewdly sparkling eye. Madame caught his rallying looks without resenting them — she had too much good sense for that. Supple as the young doctor seemed, one could not despise him — this pliant part was evidently not adopted in the design to curry favour with his employer: while he liked his office at the pensionnat, and lingered strangely about the Rue Fossette, he was independent, almost careless in his carriage there; and yet, too, he was often thoughtful and preoccupied.

It was not perhaps my business to observe the mystery of his bearing, or search out its origin or aim; but, placed as I was, I could hardly help it. He laid himself open to my observation, according to my presence in the room just that degree of notice and consequence a person of my exterior habitually expects: that is to say, about what is given to unobtrusive articles of furniture, chairs of ordinary joiner's work, and carpets of no striking pattern. Often, while waiting for Madame, he would muse, smile, watch, or listen like a man who thinks himself alone. I, meantime, was free to puzzle over his countenance and movements, and wonder what could be the meaning of that peculiar interest and attachment—all mixed up with doubt and strangeness, and inexplicably ruled by some presiding spell—which wedded him to this demi-convent, secluded in the built-up core of a capital. He, I believe, never remembered that I had eyes in my head, much less a brain behind them.

Nor would he ever have found this out, but that one day, while he sat in the sunshine and I was observing the colouring of his hair, whiskers, and complexion—the whole being of such a tone as a strong light brings out with somewhat perilous force (indeed I recollect I was driven to compare his beamy head in my thoughts to that of the "golden image" which Nebuchadnezzar the king had set up), an idea new, sudden, and startling, riveted my attention with an over-mastering strength and power of attraction. I know not to this day how I looked at him: the force of surprise, and also of conviction, made me forget myself; and I only recovered wonted consciousness when I saw that his notice was arrested, and that it had caught my movement in a clear little oval mirror fixed in the side of the window recess—by the aid of which reflector Madame often secretly spied persons walking in the garden below. Though of so gay and sanguine a temperament, he was not without a certain nervous sensitiveness which made him ill at ease under a direct, inquiring gaze. On surprising me thus, he turned and said, in a tone which, though courteous, had just so much dryness in it as to mark a shade of annoyance, as well as to give to what was said the character of rebuke, "Mademoiselle does not spare me: I am not vain enough to fancy that it is my merits which attract her attention; it must then be some defect. Dare I ask—what?"

I was confounded, as the reader may suppose, yet not with an irrecoverable confusion; being conscious that it was from no emotion of incautious admiration, nor yet in a spirit of unjustifiable inquisitiveness, that I had incurred this reproof. I might have cleared myself on the spot, but would not. I did not speak. I was not in the habit of speaking to him. Suffering him, then, to think what he chose and accuse me of what he would, I resumed some work I had dropped, and kept my head bent over it during the remainder of his stay. There is a perverse mood of the mind which is rather soothed than irritated by misconstruction; and in quarters where we can never be rightly known, we take pleasure, I think, in being consummately ignored. What honest man, on being casually taken for a housebreaker, does not feel rather tickled than vexed at the mistake?

CHAPTER XI.
THE PORTRESS'S CABINET.

It was summer and very hot. Georgette, the youngest of Madame Beck's children, took a fever. Désirée, suddenly cured of her ailments, was, together with Fifine, packed off to Bonne-Maman, in the country, by way of precaution against infection. Medical aid was now really needed, and Madame, choosing to ignore the return of Dr. Pillule, who had been at home a week, conjured his English rival to continue his visits. One or two of the pensionnaires complained of headache, and in other respects seemed slightly to participate in Georgette's ailment. "Now, at last," I thought, "Dr. Pillule must be recalled: the prudent directress will never venture to permit the attendance of so young a man on the pupils."

The directress was very prudent, but she could also be intrepidly venturous. She actually introduced Dr. John to the school-division of the premises, and established him in attendance on the proud and handsome Blanche de Melcy, and the vain, flirting Angélique, her friend. Dr. John, I thought, testified a certain gratification at this mark of confidence; and if discretion of bearing could have justified the step, it would by him have been amply justified. Here, however, in this land of convents and confessionals, such a presence as his was not to be suffered with impunity in a "pensionnat de demoiselles." The school gossiped, the kitchen whispered, the town caught the rumour, parents wrote letters and paid visits of remonstrance. Madame, had she been weak, would now have been lost: a dozen rival educational houses were ready to improve this false step—if false step it were—to her ruin; but Madame was not weak, and little Jesuit though she might be, yet I clapped the hands of my heart, and with its voice cried "brava!" as I watched her able bearing, her skilled management, her temper and her firmness on this occasion.

She met the alarmed parents with a good-humoured, easy grace for nobody matched her in, I know not whether to say the possession or the assumption of a certain "rondeur et franchise de bonne femme;" which on various occasions gained the point aimed at with instant and complete success, where severe gravity and serious reasoning would probably have failed.

"Ce pauvre Docteur Jean!" she would say, chuckling and rubbing joyously her fat little white hands; "ce cher jeune homme! le meilleur créature du monde!" and go on to explain

Villette

how she happened to be employing him for her own children, who were so fond of him they would scream themselves into fits at the thought of another doctor; how, where she had confidence for her own, she thought it natural to repose trust for others, and au reste, it was only the most temporary expedient in the world; Blanche and Angélique had the migraine; Dr. John had written a prescription; voilà tout!

The parents' mouths were closed. Blanche and Angélique saved her all remaining trouble by chanting loud duets in their physician's praise; the other pupils echoed them, unanimously declaring that when they were ill they would have Dr. John and nobody else; and Madame laughed, and the parents laughed too. The Labassecouriens must have a large organ of philoprogenitiveness: at least the indulgence of offspring is carried by them to excessive lengths; the law of most households being the children's will. Madame now got credit for having acted on this occasion in a spirit of motherly partiality: she came off with flying colours; people liked her as a directress better than ever.

To this day I never fully understood why she thus risked her interest for the sake of Dr. John. What people said, of course I know well: the whole house—pupils, teachers, servants included—affirmed that she was going to marry him. So they had settled it; difference of age seemed to make no obstacle in their eyes: it was to be so.

It must be admitted that appearances did not wholly discountenance this idea; Madame seemed so bent on retaining his services, so oblivious of her former protégé, Pillule. She made, too, such a point of personally receiving his visits, and was so unfailingly cheerful, blithe, and benignant in her manner to him. Moreover, she paid, about this time, marked attention to dress: the morning dishabille, the nightcap and shawl, were discarded; Dr. John's early visits always found her with auburn braids all nicely arranged, silk dress trimly fitted on, neat laced brodequins in lieu of slippers: in short the whole toilette complete as a model, and fresh as a flower. I scarcely think, however, that her intention in this went further than just to show a very handsome man that she was not quite a plain woman; and plain she was not. Without beauty of feature or elegance of form, she pleased. Without youth and its gay graces, she cheered. One never tired of seeing her: she was never monotonous, or insipid, or colourless, or flat. Her unfaded hair, her eye with its temperate blue light, her cheek with its wholesome fruit-like bloom—these things pleased in moderation, but with constancy.

Had she, indeed, floating visions of adopting Dr. John as a husband, taking him to her well-furnished home, endowing him with her savings, which were said to amount to a moderate competency, and making him comfortable for the rest of his life? Did Dr. John suspect her of such visions? I have met him coming out of her presence with a mischievous half-smile about his lips, and in his eyes a look as of masculine vanity elate and tickled. With all his good looks and good-nature, he was not perfect; he must have been very imperfect if he roguishly encouraged aims he never intended to be successful. But did he not intend them to be successful? People said he had no money, that he was wholly dependent upon his profession. Madame — though perhaps some fourteen years his senior — was yet the sort of woman never to grow old, never to wither, never to break down. They certainly were on good terms. He perhaps was not in love; but how many people ever do love, or at least marry for love, in this world. We waited the end.

For what he waited, I do not know, nor for what he watched; but the peculiarity of his manner, his expectant, vigilant, absorbed, eager look, never wore off: it rather intensified. He had never been quite within the compass of my penetration, and I think he ranged farther and farther beyond it.

One morning little Georgette had been more feverish and consequently more peevish; she was crying, and would not be pacified. I thought a particular draught ordered, disagreed with her, and I doubted whether it ought to be continued; I waited impatiently for the doctor's coming in order to consult him.

The door-bell rang, he was admitted; I felt sure of this, for I heard his voice addressing the portress. It was his custom to mount straight to the nursery, taking about three degrees of the staircase at once, and coming upon us like a cheerful surprise. Five minutes elapsed — ten — and I saw and heard nothing of him. What could he be doing? Possibly waiting in the corridor below. Little Georgette still piped her plaintive wail, appealing to me by her familiar term, "Minnie, Minnie, me very poorly!" till my heart ached. I descended to ascertain why he did not come. The corridor was empty. Whither was he vanished? Was he with Madame in the salle-à-manger? Impossible: I had left her but a short time since, dressing in her own chamber. I listened. Three pupils were just then hard at work practising in three proximate rooms — the dining-room and the greater and lesser drawing-rooms, between which and the corridor there was but the portress's cabinet communicating with the salons, and intended originally for a boudoir. Farther off, at a fourth instrument in the oratory, a whole class of a dozen or more were taking a singing lesson, and just then joining in a "barcarole" (I think they called it), whereof I yet remember these words "fraîchë," "brisë," and "Venisë." Under these circumstances, what could I hear? A great deal, certainly; had it only been to the purpose.

Yes; I heard a giddy treble laugh in the above-mentioned little cabinet, close by the door of which I stood—that door half-unclosed; a man's voice in a soft, deep, pleading tone, uttered some words, whereof I only caught the adjuration, "For God's sake!" Then, after a second's pause, forth issued Dr. John, his eye full shining, but not with either joy or triumph; his fair English cheek high-coloured; a baffled, tortured, anxious, and yet a tender meaning on his brow.

The open door served me as a screen; but had I been full in his way, I believe he would have passed without seeing me. Some mortification, some strong vexation had hold of his soul: or rather, to write my impressions now as I received them at the time I should say some sorrow, some sense of injustice. I did not so much think his pride was hurt, as that his affections had been wounded—cruelly wounded, it seemed to me. But who was the torturer? What being in that house had him so much in her power? Madame I believed to be in her chamber; the room whence he had stepped was dedicated to the portress's sole use; and she, Rosine Matou, an unprincipled though pretty little French grisette, airy, fickle, dressy, vain, and mercenary—it was not, surely, to her hand he owed the ordeal through which he seemed to have passed?

But while I pondered, her voice, clear, though somewhat sharp, broke out in a lightsome French song, trilling through the door still ajar: I glanced in, doubting my senses. There at the table she sat in a smart dress of "jaconas rose," trimming a tiny blond cap: not a living thing save herself was in the room, except indeed some gold fish in a glass globe, some flowers in pots, and a broad July sunbeam.

Here was a problem: but I must go up-stairs to ask about the medicine.

Dr. John sat in a chair at Georgette's bedside; Madame stood before him; the little patient had been examined and soothed, and now lay composed in her crib. Madame Beck, as I entered, was discussing the physician's own health, remarking on some real or fancied change in his looks, charging him with over-work, and recommending rest and change of air. He listened good-naturedly, but with laughing indifference, telling her that she was "trop bonne," and that he felt perfectly well. Madame appealed to me—Dr. John following her movement with a slow glance which seemed to express languid surprise at reference being made to a quarter so insignificant.

"What do you think, Miss Lucie?" asked Madame. "Is he not paler and thinner?"

It was very seldom that I uttered more than monosyllables in Dr. John's presence; he was the kind of person with whom I was likely ever to remain the neutral, passive thing he thought me. Now, however, I took licence to answer in a phrase: and a phrase I purposely made quite significant.

"He looks ill at this moment; but perhaps it is owing to some temporary cause: Dr. John may have been vexed or harassed." I cannot tell how he took this speech, as I never sought his face for information. Georgette here began to ask me in her broken English if she might have a glass of eau sucrée. I answered her in English. For the first time, I fancy, he noticed that I spoke his language; hitherto he had always taken me for a foreigner, addressing me as "Mademoiselle," and giving in French the requisite directions about the children's treatment. He seemed on the point of making a remark; but thinking better of it, held his tongue.

Madame recommenced advising him; he shook his head, laughing, rose and bid her good-morning, with courtesy, but still with the regardless air of one whom too much unsolicited attention was surfeiting and spoiling.

When he was gone, Madame dropped into the chair he had just left; she rested her chin in her hand; all that was animated and amiable vanished from her face: she looked stony and stern, almost mortified and morose. She sighed; a single, but a deep sigh. A loud bell rang for morning-school. She got up; as she passed a dressing-table with a glass upon it, she looked at her reflected image. One single white hair streaked her nut-brown tresses; she plucked it out with a shudder. In the full summer daylight, her face, though it still had the colour, could plainly be seen to have lost the texture of youth; and then, where were youth's contours? Ah, Madame! wise as you were, even you knew weakness. Never had I pitied Madame before, but my heart softened towards her, when she turned darkly from the glass. A calamity had come upon her. That hag Disappointment was greeting her with a grisly "All-hail," and her soul rejected the intimacy.

But Rosine! My bewilderment there surpasses description. I embraced five opportunities of passing her cabinet that day, with a view to contemplating her charms, and finding out the secret of their influence. She was pretty, young, and wore a well-made dress. All very good points, and, I suppose, amply sufficient to account, in any philosophic mind, for any amount of agony and distraction in a young man, like Dr. John. Still, I could not help forming half a wish that the said doctor were my brother; or at least that he had a sister or a mother who would kindly sermonize him. I say half a wish; I broke it, and flung it away before it became a whole one, discovering in good time its exquisite folly. "Somebody," I argued, "might as well sermonize Madame about her young physician: and what good would that do?"

I believe Madame sermonized herself. She did not behave weakly, or make herself in any shape ridiculous. It is true she had neither strong feelings to overcome, nor tender feelings by which to be miserably pained. It is true likewise that she had an important avocation, a real business to fill her time, divert her thoughts, and divide her interest. It is especially true that she possessed a genuine good sense which is not given to all women nor to all men; and by dint of these combined advantages she behaved wisely—she behaved well. Brava! once more, Madame Beck. I saw you matched against an Apollyon of a predilection; you fought a good fight, and you overcame!

CHAPTER XII.

THE CASKET.

Behind the house at the Rue Fossette there was a garden — large, considering that it lay in the heart of a city, and to my recollection at this day it seems pleasant: but time, like distance, lends to certain scenes an influence so softening; and where all is stone around, blank wall and hot pavement, how precious seems one shrub, how lovely an enclosed and planted spot of ground!

There went a tradition that Madame Beck's house had in old days been a convent. That in years gone by — how long gone by I cannot tell, but I think some centuries — before the city had over-spread this quarter, and when it was tilled ground and avenue, and such deep and leafy seclusion as ought to embosom a religious house — that something had happened on this site which, rousing fear and inflicting horror, had left to the place the inheritance of a ghost-story. A vague tale went of a black and white nun, sometimes, on some night or nights of the year, seen in some part of this vicinage. The ghost must have been built out some ages ago, for there were houses all round now; but certain convent-relics, in the shape of old and huge fruit-trees, yet consecrated the spot; and, at the foot of one — a Methuselah of a pear-tree, dead, all but a few boughs which still faithfully renewed their perfumed snow in spring, and their honey-sweet pendants in autumn — you saw, in scraping away the mossy earth between the half-bared roots, a glimpse of slab, smooth, hard, and black. The legend went, unconfirmed and unaccredited, but still propagated, that this was the portal of a vault, imprisoning deep beneath that ground, on whose surface grass grew and flowers bloomed, the bones of a girl whom a monkish conclave of the drear middle ages had here buried alive for some sin against her vow. Her shadow it was that tremblers had feared, through long generations after her poor frame was dust; her black robe and white veil that, for timid eyes, moonlight and shade had mocked, as they fluctuated in the night-wind through the garden-thicket.

Independently of romantic rubbish, however, that old garden had its charms. On summer mornings I used to rise early, to enjoy them alone; on summer evenings, to linger solitary, to keep tryste with the rising moon, or taste one kiss of the evening breeze, or fancy rather than feel the freshness of dew descending. The turf was verdant, the gravelled walks were white; sun-bright nasturtiums clustered beautiful about the roots of the doddered orchard giants. There was a large berceau, above which spread the shade of an acacia; there was a smaller, more sequestered bower, nestled in the vines which ran all along a high and grey wall, and gathered their tendrils in a knot of beauty, and hung their clusters in loving profusion about the favoured spot where jasmine and ivy met and married them.

Doubtless at high noon, in the broad, vulgar middle of the day, when Madame Beck's large school turned out rampant, and externes and pensionnaires were spread abroad, vying with the denizens of the boys' college close at hand, in the brazen exercise of their lungs and limbs—doubtless then the garden was a trite, trodden-down place enough. But at sunset or the hour of salut, when the externes were gone home, and the boarders quiet at their studies; pleasant was it then to stray down the peaceful alleys, and hear the bells of St. Jean Baptiste peal out with their sweet, soft, exalted sound.

I was walking thus one evening, and had been detained farther within the verge of twilight than usual, by the still-deepening calm, the mellow coolness, the fragrant breathing with which flowers no sunshine could win now answered the persuasion of the dew. I saw by a light in the oratory window that the Catholic household were then gathered to evening prayer—a rite, from attendance on which, I now and then, as a Protestant, exempted myself.

"One moment longer," whispered solitude and the summer moon, "stay with us: all is truly quiet now; for another quarter of an hour your presence will not be missed: the day's heat and bustle have tired you; enjoy these precious minutes."

The windowless backs of houses built in this garden, and in particular the whole of one side, was skirted by the rear of a long line of premises—being the boarding-houses of the neighbouring college. This rear, however, was all blank stone, with the exception of certain attic loopholes high up, opening from the sleeping-rooms of the women-servants, and also one casement in a lower story said to mark the chamber or study of a master. But, though thus secure, an alley, which ran parallel with the very high wall on that side the garden, was forbidden to be entered by the pupils. It was called indeed "l'allée défendue," and any girl setting foot there would have rendered herself liable to as severe a penalty as the mild rules of Madame Beck's establishment permitted. Teachers might indeed go there with impunity; but as the walk was narrow, and the neglected shrubs were grown very thick and close on each side, weaving overhead a roof of branch and leaf which the sun's rays penetrated but in rare chequers, this alley was seldom entered even during day, and after dusk was carefully shunned.

From the first I was tempted to make an exception to this rule of avoidance: the seclusion, the very gloom of the walk attracted me. For a long time the fear of seeming singular scared me away; but by degrees, as people became accustomed to me and my habits, and to such shades of peculiarity as were engrained in my nature — shades, certainly not striking enough to interest, and perhaps not prominent enough to offend, but born in and with me, and no more to be parted with than my identity — by slow degrees I became a frequenter of this strait and narrow path. I made myself gardener of some tintless flowers that grew between its closely-ranked shrubs; I cleared away the relics of past autumns, choking up a rustic seat at the far end. Borrowing of Goton, the cuisinière, a pail of water and a scrubbing-brush, I made this seat clean. Madame saw me at work and smiled approbation: whether sincerely or not I don't know; but she seemed sincere.

"Voyez-vous," cried she, "comme elle est propre, cette demoiselle Lucie? Vous aimez donc cette allée, meess?"

"Yes," I said, "it is quiet and shady."

"C'est juste," cried she with an air of bonté; and she kindly recommended me to confine myself to it as much as I chose, saying, that as I was not charged with the surveillance, I need not trouble myself to walk with the pupils: only I might permit her children to come there, to talk English with me.

On the night in question, I was sitting on the hidden seat reclaimed from fungi and mould, listening to what seemed the far-off sounds of the city. Far off, in truth, they were not: this school was in the city's centre; hence, it was but five minutes' walk to the park, scarce ten to buildings of palatial splendour. Quite near were wide streets brightly lit, teeming at this moment with life: carriages were rolling through them to balls or to the opera. The same hour which tolled curfew for our convent, which extinguished each lamp, and dropped the curtain round each couch, rang for the gay city about us the summons to festal enjoyment. Of this contrast I thought not, however: gay instincts my nature had few; ball or opera I had never seen; and though often I had heard them described, and even wished to see them, it was not the wish of one who hopes to partake a pleasure if she could only reach it — who feels fitted to shine in some bright distant sphere, could she but thither win

Villette

her way; it was no yearning to attain, no hunger to taste; only the calm desire to look on a new thing.

A moon was in the sky, not a full moon, but a young crescent. I saw her through a space in the boughs overhead. She and the stars, visible beside her, were no strangers where all else was strange: my childhood knew them. I had seen that golden sign with the dark globe in its curve leaning back on azure, beside an old thorn at the top of an old field, in Old England, in long past days, just as it now leaned back beside a stately spire in this continental capital.

Oh, my childhood! I had feelings: passive as I lived, little as I spoke, cold as I looked, when I thought of past days, I could feel. About the present, it was better to be stoical; about the future—such a future as mine—to be dead. And in catalepsy and a dead trance, I studiously held the quick of my nature.

At that time, I well remember whatever could excite—certain accidents of the weather, for instance, were almost dreaded by me, because they woke the being I was always lulling, and stirred up a craving cry I could not satisfy. One night a thunder-storm broke; a sort of hurricane shook us in our beds: the Catholics rose in panic and prayed to their saints. As for me, the tempest took hold of me with tyranny: I was roughly roused and obliged to live. I got up and dressed myself, and creeping outside the casement close by my bed, sat on its ledge, with my feet on the roof of a lower adjoining building. It was wet, it was wild, it was pitch-dark. Within the dormitory they gathered round the night-lamp in consternation, praying loud. I could not go in: too resistless was the delight of staying with the wild hour, black and full of thunder, pealing out such an ode as language never delivered to man—too terribly glorious, the spectacle of clouds, split and pierced by white and blinding bolts.

I did long, achingly, then and for four and twenty hours afterwards, for something to fetch me out of my present existence, and lead me upwards and onwards. This longing, and all of a similar kind, it was necessary to knock on the head; which I did, figuratively, after the manner of Jael to Sisera, driving a nail through their temples. Unlike Sisera, they did not die: they were but transiently stunned, and at intervals would turn on the nail with a rebellious wrench: then did the temples bleed, and the brain thrill to its core.

To-night, I was not so mutinous, nor so miserable. My Sisera lay quiet in the tent, slumbering; and if his pain ached through his slumbers, something like an angel — the ideal — knelt near, dropping balm on the soothed temples, holding before the sealed eyes a magic glass, of which the sweet, solemn visions were repeated in dreams, and shedding a reflex from her moonlight wings and robe over the transfixed sleeper, over the tent threshold, over all the landscape lying without. Jael, the stern woman; sat apart, relenting somewhat over her captive; but more prone to dwell on the faithful expectation of Heber coming home. By which words I mean that the cool peace and dewy sweetness of the night filled me with a mood of hope: not hope on any definite point, but a general sense of encouragement and heart-ease.

Should not such a mood, so sweet, so tranquil, so unwonted, have been the harbinger of good? Alas, no good came of it! I Presently the rude Real burst coarsely in — all evil grovelling and repellent as she too often is.

Amid the intense stillness of that pile of stone overlooking the walk, the trees, the high wall, I heard a sound; a casement [all the windows here are casements, opening on hinges] creaked. Ere I had time to look up and mark where, in which story, or by whom unclosed, a tree overhead shook, as if struck by a missile; some object dropped prone at my feet.

Nine was striking by St. Jean Baptiste's clock; day was fading, but it was not dark: the crescent moon aided little, but the deep gilding of that point in heaven where the sun beamed last, and the crystalline clearness of a wide space above, sustained the summer twilight; even in my dark walk I could, by approaching an opening, have managed to read print of a small type. Easy was it to see then that the missile was a box, a small box of white and coloured ivory; its loose lid opened in my hand; violets lay within, violets smothering a closely folded bit of pink paper, a note, superscribed, "Pour la robe grise." I wore indeed a dress of French grey.

Good. Was this a billet-doux? A thing I had heard of, but hitherto had not had the honour of seeing or handling. Was it this sort of commodity I held between my finger and thumb at this moment?

Scarcely: I did not dream it for a moment. Suitor or admirer my very thoughts had not conceived. All the teachers had dreams of some lover; one (but she was naturally of a credulous turn) believed in a future husband. All the pupils above fourteen knew of some prospective bridegroom; two or three were already affianced by their parents, and had been so from

Villette

childhood: but into the realm of feelings and hopes which such prospects open, my speculations, far less my presumptions, had never once had warrant to intrude. If the other teachers went into town, or took a walk on the boulevards, or only attended mass, they were very certain (according to the accounts brought back) to meet with some individual of the "opposite sex," whose rapt, earnest gaze assured them of their power to strike and to attract. I can't say that my experience tallied with theirs, in this respect. I went to church and I took walks, and am very well convinced that nobody minded me. There was not a girl or woman in the Rue Fossette who could not, and did not testify to having received an admiring beam from our young doctor's blue eyes at one time or other. I am obliged, however humbling it may sound, to except myself: as far as I was concerned, those blue eyes were guiltless, and calm as the sky, to whose tint theirs seemed akin. So it came to pass that I heard the others talk, wondered often at their gaiety, security, and self-satisfaction, but did not trouble myself to look up and gaze along the path they seemed so certain of treading. This then was no billet-doux; and it was in settled conviction to the contrary that I quietly opened it. Thus it ran—I translate:—

"Angel of my dreams! A thousand, thousand thanks for the promise kept: scarcely did I venture to hope its fulfilment. I believed you, indeed, to be half in jest; and then you seemed to think the enterprise beset with such danger—the hour so untimely, the alley so strictly secluded—often, you said, haunted by that dragon, the English teacher—*une véritable bégueule Britannique à ce que vous dites—espèce de monstre, brusque et rude comme un vieux caporal de grenadiers, et revêche comme une religieuse*" (the reader will excuse my modesty in allowing this flattering sketch of my amiable self to retain the slight veil of the original tongue). "You are aware," went on this precious effusion, "that little Gustave, on account of his illness, has been removed to a master's chamber—that favoured chamber, whose lattice overlooks your prison-ground. There, I, the best uncle in the world, am admitted to visit him. How tremblingly I approached the window and glanced into your Eden—an Eden for me, though a desert for you!—how I feared to behold vacancy, or the dragon aforesaid! How my heart palpitated with delight when, through apertures in the envious boughs, I at once caught the gleam of your graceful straw-hat, and the waving of your grey dress—dress that I should recognise amongst a thousand. But why, my angel, will you not look up? Cruel, to deny me one ray of those adorable eyes!—how a single glance would have revived me! I write this in fiery haste; while the physician examines Gustave, I snatch an opportunity to enclose it in a small casket, together with a bouquet of flowers, the sweetest that blow—yet less sweet than thee, my Peri—my all-charming! ever thine-thou well knowest whom!"

"I wish I did know whom," was my comment; and the wish bore even closer reference to the person addressed in this choice document, than to the writer thereof. Perhaps it was from the fiancé of one of the engaged pupils; and, in that case, there was no great harm done or intended—only a small irregularity. Several of the girls, the majority, indeed, had brothers or cousins at the neighbouring college. But "la robe grise, le chapeau de paille," here surely was a clue—a very confusing one. The straw-hat was an ordinary garden head-screen, common to a score besides myself. The grey dress hardly gave more definite indication. Madame Beck herself ordinarily wore a grey dress just now; another teacher, and three of the pensionnaires, had had grey dresses purchased of the same shade and fabric as mine: it was a sort of every-day wear which happened at that time to be in vogue.

Meanwhile, as I pondered, I knew I must go in. Lights, moving in the dormitory, announced that prayers were over, and the pupils going to bed. Another half-hour and all doors would be locked—all lights extinguished. The front door yet stood open, to admit into the heated house the coolness of the summer night; from the portress's cabinet close by shone a lamp, showing the long vestibule with the two-leaved drawing-room doors on one side, the great street-door closing the vista.

All at once, quick rang the bell—quick, but not loud—a cautious tinkle—a sort of warning metal whisper. Rosine darted from her cabinet and ran to open. The person she admitted stood with her two minutes in parley: there seemed a demur, a delay. Rosine came to the garden door, lamp in hand; she stood on the steps, lifting her lamp, looking round vaguely.

"Quel conte!" she cried, with a coquettish laugh. "Personne n'y a été."

"Let me pass," pleaded a voice I knew: "I ask but five minutes;" and a familiar shape, tall and grand (as we of the Rue Fossette all thought it), issued from the house, and strode down amongst the beds and walks. It was sacrilege—the intrusion of a man into that spot, at that hour; but he knew himself privileged, and perhaps he trusted to the friendly night. He wandered down the alleys, looking on this side and on that—he was lost in the shrubs, trampling flowers and breaking branches in his search—he penetrated at last the "forbidden walk." There I met

Villette

him, like some ghost, I suppose.

"Dr. John! it is found."

He did not ask by whom, for with his quick eye he perceived that I held it in my hand.

"Do not betray her," he said, looking at me as if I were indeed a dragon.

"Were I ever so disposed to treachery, I cannot betray what I do not know," was my answer. "Read the note, and you will see how little it reveals."

"Perhaps you have read it," I thought to myself; and yet I could not believe he wrote it: that could hardly be his style: besides, I was fool enough to think there would be a degree of hardship in his calling me such names. His own look vindicated him; he grew hot, and coloured as he read.

"This is indeed too much: this is cruel, this is humiliating," were the words that fell from him.

I thought it was cruel, when I saw his countenance so moved. No matter whether he was to blame or not; somebody, it seemed to me, must be more to blame.

"What shall you do about it?" he inquired of me. "Shall you tell Madame Beck what you have found, and cause a stir—an esclandre?"

I thought I ought to tell, and said so; adding that I did not believe there would be either stir or esclandre: Madame was much too prudent to make a noise about an affair of that sort connected with her establishment.

He stood looking down and meditating. He was both too proud and too honourable to entreat my secresy on a point which duty evidently commanded me to communicate. I wished to do right, yet loathed to grieve or injure him. Just then Rosine glanced out through the open door; she could not see us, though between the trees I could plainly see her: her dress was grey, like mine. This circumstance, taken in connection with prior transactions, suggested to me that perhaps the case, however deplorable, was one in which I was under no obligation whatever to concern myself. Accordingly, I said,—"If you can assure me that none of Madame Beck's pupils are implicated in this business, I shall be very happy to stand aloof from all interference. Take the casket, the bouquet, and the billet; for my part, I gladly forget the whole affair."

"Look there!" he whispered suddenly, as his hand closed on what I offered, and at the same time he pointed through the boughs.

I looked. Behold Madame, in shawl, wrapping-gown, and slippers, softly descending the steps, and stealing like a cat round the garden: in two minutes she would have been upon Dr. John. If she were like a cat, however, he, quite as much, resembled a leopard: nothing could be lighter than his tread when he chose. He watched, and as she turned a corner, he took the garden at two noiseless bounds. She reappeared, and he was gone. Rosine helped him, instantly interposing the door between him and his huntress. I, too, might have got away, but I preferred to meet Madame openly.

Though it was my frequent and well-known custom to spend twilight in the garden, yet, never till now, had I remained so late. Full sure was I that Madame had missed—was come in search of me, and designed now to pounce on the defaulter unawares. I expected a reprimand. No. Madame was all goodness. She tendered not even a remonstrance; she testified no shade of surprise. With that consummate tact of hers, in which I believe she was never surpassed by living thing, she even professed merely to have issued forth to taste "la brise du soir."

"Quelle belle nuit!" cried she, looking up at the stars—the moon was now gone down behind the broad tower of Jean Baptiste. "Qu'il fait bon? que l'air est frais!"

And, instead of sending me in, she detained me to take a few turns with her down the principal alley. When at last we both re-entered, she leaned affably on my shoulder by way of support in mounting the front-door steps; at parting, her cheek was presented to my lips, and "Bon soir, my bonne amie; dormez bien!" was her kindly adieu for the night.

I caught myself smiling as I lay awake and thoughtful on my couch—smiling at Madame. The unction, the suavity of her behaviour offered, for one who knew her, a sure token that suspicion of some kind was busy in her brain. From some aperture or summit of observation, through parted bough or open window, she had doubtless caught a glimpse, remote or near, deceptive or instructive, of that night's transactions. Finely accomplished as she was in the art of surveillance, it was next to impossible that a casket could be thrown into her garden, or an interloper could cross her walks to seek it, without that she, in shaken branch, passing shade, unwonted footfall, or stilly murmur (and though Dr. John had spoken very low in the few words he dropped me, yet the hum of his man's voice pervaded, I thought, the whole conventual ground) — without, I say, that she should have caught intimation of things extraordinary transpiring on her premises. What things, she might by no means see, or at that time be able to discover; but a delicious little ravelled plot lay tempting her to disentanglement; and in the midst, folded round and round in cobwebs, had she not secured "Meess Lucie" clumsily involved, like the foolish fly she was?

CHAPTER XIII.

A SNEEZE OUT OF SEASON.

I had occasion to smile—nay, to laugh, at Madame again, within the space of four and twenty hours after the little scene treated of in the last chapter.

Villette owns a climate as variable, though not so humid, as that of any English town. A night of high wind followed upon that soft sunset, and all the next day was one of dry storm—dark, beclouded, yet rainless,—the streets were dim with sand and dust, whirled from the boulevards. I know not that even lovely weather would have tempted me to spend the evening-time of study and recreation where I had spent it yesterday. My alley, and, indeed, all the walks and shrubs in the garden, had acquired a new, but not a pleasant interest; their seclusion was now become precarious; their calm—insecure. That casement which rained billets, had vulgarized the once dear nook it overlooked; and elsewhere, the eyes of the flowers had gained vision, and the knots in the tree-boles listened like secret ears. Some plants there were, indeed, trodden down by Dr. John in his search, and his hasty and heedless progress, which I wished to prop up, water, and revive; some footmarks, too, he had left on the beds: but these, in spite of the strong wind, I found a moment's leisure to efface very early in the morning, ere common eyes had discovered them. With a pensive sort of content, I sat down to my desk and my German, while the pupils settled to their evening lessons; and the other teachers took up their needlework.

The scene of the "etude du soir" was always the refectory, a much smaller apartment than any of the three classes or schoolrooms; for here none, save the boarders, were ever admitted, and these numbered only a score. Two lamps hung from the ceiling over the two tables; these were lit at dusk, and their kindling was the signal for school-books being set aside, a grave demeanour assumed, general silence enforced, and then commenced "la lecture pieuse." This said "lecture pieuse" was, I soon found, mainly designed as a wholesome mortification of the Intellect, a useful humiliation of the Reason; and such a dose for Common Sense as she might digest at her leisure, and thrive on as she best could.

The book brought out (it was never changed, but when finished, recommenced) was a venerable volume, old as the hills—grey as the Hôtel de Ville.

Villette

I would have given two francs for the chance of getting that book once into my hands, turning over the sacred yellow leaves, ascertaining the title, and perusing with my own eyes the enormous figments which, as an unworthy heretic, it was only permitted me to drink in with my bewildered ears. This book contained legends of the saints. Good God! (I speak the words reverently) what legends they were. What gasconading rascals those saints must have been, if they first boasted these exploits or invented these miracles. These legends, however, were no more than monkish extravagances, over which one laughed inwardly; there were, besides, priestly matters, and the priestcraft of the book was far worse than its monkery. The ears burned on each side of my head as I listened, perforce, to tales of moral martyrdom inflicted by Rome; the dread boasts of confessors, who had wickedly abused their office, trampling to deep degradation high-born ladies, making of countesses and princesses the most tormented slaves under the sun. Stories like that of Conrad and Elizabeth of Hungary, recurred again and again, with all its dreadful viciousness, sickening tyranny and black impiety: tales that were nightmares of oppression, privation, and agony.

I sat out this "lecture pieuse" for some nights as well as I could, and as quietly too; only once breaking off the points of my scissors by involuntarily sticking them somewhat deep in the worm-eaten board of the table before me. But, at last, it made me so burning hot, and my temples, and my heart, and my wrist throbbed so fast, and my sleep afterwards was so broken with excitement, that I could sit no longer. Prudence recommended henceforward a swift clearance of my person from the place, the moment that guilty old book was brought out. No Mause Headrigg ever felt a stronger call to take up her testimony against Sergeant Bothwell, than I—to speak my mind in this matter of the popish "lecture pieuse." However, I did manage somehow to curb and rein in; and though always, as soon as Rosine came to light the lamps, I shot from the room quickly, yet also I did it quietly; seizing that vantage moment given by the little bustle before the dead silence, and vanishing whilst the boarders put their books away.

When I vanished—it was into darkness; candles were not allowed to be carried about, and the teacher who forsook the refectory, had only the unlit hall, schoolroom, or bedroom, as a refuge. In winter I sought the long classes, and paced them fast to keep myself warm—fortunate if the moon shone, and if there were only stars, soon reconciled to their dim gleam, or even to the total eclipse of their absence. In summer it was never quite dark, and then I went up-stairs to my own quarter of the long dormitory, opened my own casement (that chamber was lit by five casements large as great doors), and leaning out, looked forth upon the city beyond the garden, and listened to band-music from the park or the palace-square, thinking meantime my own thoughts, living my own life, in my own still, shadow-world.

This evening, fugitive as usual before the Pope and his works, I mounted the staircase, approached the dormitory, and quietly opened the door, which was always kept carefully shut, and which, like every other door in this house, revolved noiselessly on well-oiled hinges. Before I saw, I felt that life was in the great room, usually void: not that there was either stir or breath, or rustle of sound, but Vacuum lacked, Solitude was not at home. All the white beds—the "lits d'ange," as they were poetically termed—lay visible at a glance; all were empty: no sleeper reposed therein. The sound of a drawer cautiously slid out struck my ear; stepping a little to one side, my vision took a free range, unimpeded by falling curtains. I now commanded my own bed and my own toilet, with a locked work-box upon it, and locked drawers underneath.

Very good. A dumpy, motherly little body, in decent shawl and the cleanest of possible nightcaps, stood before this toilet, hard at work apparently doing me the kindness of "tidying out" the "meuble." Open stood the lid of the work-box, open the top drawer; duly and impartially was each succeeding drawer opened in turn: not an article of their contents but was lifted and unfolded, not a paper but was glanced over, not a little box but was unlidded; and beautiful was the adroitness, exemplary the care with which the search was accomplished. Madame wrought at it like a true star, "unhasting yet unresting." I will not deny that it was with a secret glee I watched her. Had I been a gentleman I believe Madame would have found favour in my eyes, she was so handy, neat, thorough in all she did: some people's movements provoke the soul by their loose awkwardness, hers—satisfied by their trim compactness. I stood, in short, fascinated; but it was necessary to make an effort to break this spell, a retreat must be beaten. The searcher might have turned and caught me; there would have been nothing for it then but a scene, and she and I would have had to come all at once, with a sudden clash, to a thorough knowledge of each other: down would have gone conventionalities, away swept disguises, and I should have looked into her eyes, and she into mine—we should have known that we could work together no more, and parted in this life for ever.

Where was the use of tempting such a catastrophe? I was not

angry, and had no wish in the world to leave her. I could hardly get another employer whose yoke would be so light and so easy of carriage; and truly I liked Madame for her capital sense, whatever I might think of her principles: as to her system, it did me no harm; she might work me with it to her heart's content: nothing would come of the operation. Loverless and inexpectant of love, I was as safe from spies in my heart-poverty, as the beggar from thieves in his destitution of purse. I turned, then, and fled; descending the stairs with progress as swift and soundless as that of the spider, which at the same instant ran down the bannister.

How I laughed when I reached the schoolroom. I knew now she had certainly seen Dr. John in the garden; I knew what her thoughts were. The spectacle of a suspicious nature so far misled by its own inventions, tickled me much. Yet as the laugh died, a kind of wrath smote me, and then bitterness followed: it was the rock struck, and Meribah's waters gushing out. I never had felt so strange and contradictory an inward tumult as I felt for an hour that evening: soreness and laughter, and fire, and grief, shared my heart between them. I cried hot tears: not because Madame mistrusted me—I did not care twopence for her mistrust—but for other reasons. Complicated, disquieting thoughts broke up the whole repose of my nature. However, that turmoil subsided: next day I was again Lucy Snowe.

On revisiting my drawers, I found them all securely locked; the closest subsequent examination could not discover change or apparent disturbance in the position of one object. My few dresses were folded as I had left them; a certain little bunch of white violets that had once been silently presented to me by a stranger (a stranger to me, for we had never exchanged words), and which I had dried and kept for its sweet perfume between the folds of my best dress, lay there unstirred; my black silk scarf, my lace chemisette and collars, were unrumpled. Had she creased one solitary article, I own I should have felt much greater difficulty in forgiving her; but finding all straight and orderly, I said, "Let bygones be bygones. I am unharmed: why should I bear malice?"

A thing there was which puzzled myself, and I sought in my brain a key to that riddle almost as sedulously as Madame had sought a guide to useful knowledge in my toilet drawers. How was it that Dr. John, if he had not been accessory to the dropping of that casket into the garden, should have known that it was dropped, and appeared so promptly on the spot to seek it? So strong was the wish to clear up this point that I began to entertain this daring suggestion: "Why may I not, in case I should ever have the opportunity, ask Dr. John himself to explain this coincidence?"

And so long as Dr. John was absent, I really believed I had courage to test him with such a question.

Little Georgette was now convalescent; and her physician accordingly made his visits very rare: indeed, he would have ceased them altogether, had not Madame insisted on his giving an occasional call till the child should be quite well.

She came into the nursery one evening just after I had listened to Georgette's lisped and broken prayer, and had put her to bed. Taking the little one's hand, she said, "Cette enfant a toujours un peu de fièvre." And presently afterwards, looking at me with a quicker glance than was habitual to her quiet eye, "Le Docteur John l'a-t-il vue dernièrement? Non, n'est-ce pas?"

Of course she knew this better than any other person in the house. "Well," she continued, "I am going out, pour faire quelques courses en fiacre. I shall call on Dr. John, and send him to the child. I will that he sees her this evening; her cheeks are flushed, her pulse is quick; you will receive him—for my part, I shall be from home."

Now the child was well enough, only warm with the warmth of July; it was scarcely less needful to send for a priest to administer extreme unction than for a doctor to prescribe a dose; also Madame rarely made "courses," as she called them, in the evening: moreover, this was the first time she had chosen to absent herself on the occasion of a visit from Dr. John. The whole arrangement indicated some plan; this I saw, but without the least anxiety. "Ha! ha! Madame," laughed Light-heart the Beggar, "your crafty wits are on the wrong tack."

She departed, attired very smartly, in a shawl of price, and a certain chapeau vert tendre—hazardous, as to its tint, for any complexion less fresh than her own, but, to her, not unbecoming. I wondered what she intended: whether she really would send Dr. John or not; or whether indeed he would come: he might be engaged.

Madame had charged me not to let Georgette sleep till the doctor came; I had therefore sufficient occupation in telling her nursery tales and palavering the little language for her benefit. I affected Georgette; she was a sensitive and a loving child: to hold her in my lap, or carry her in my arms, was to me a treat. To-night she would have me lay my head on the pillow of her crib; she even put her little arms round my neck. Her clasp, and the nestling action with which she pressed her cheek to mine, made me almost cry with a tender pain. Feeling of no kind abounded in that house; this pure little drop from a pure little source was too sweet: it penetrated deep, and subdued the heart, and sent a gush to the eyes. Half an hour or an hour passed; Georgette murmured in her soft lisp that she was growing sleepy. "And you shall sleep," thought I, "malgré maman and médecin, if they are not here in ten minutes."

Hark! There was the ring, and there the tread, astonishing the staircase by the fleetness with which it left the steps behind. Rosine introduced Dr. John, and, with a freedom of manner not altogether peculiar to herself, but characteristic of the domestics of Villette generally, she stayed to hear what he had to say. Madame's presence would have awed her back to her own realm of the vestibule and the cabinet—for mine, or that of any other teacher or pupil, she cared not a jot. Smart, trim and pert, she stood, a hand in each pocket of her gay grisette apron, eyeing Dr. John with no more fear or shyness than if he had been a picture instead of a living gentleman.

"Le marmot n'a rien n'est ce pas?" said she, indicating Georgette with a jerk of her chin.

"Pas beaucoup," was the answer, as the doctor hastily scribbled with his pencil some harmless prescription.

"Eh bien!" pursued Rosine, approaching him quite near, while he put up his pencil. "And the box—did you get it? Monsieur went off like a coup-de-vent the other night; I had not time to ask him."

"I found it: yes."

"And who threw it, then?" continued Rosine, speaking quite freely the very words I should so much have wished to say, but had no address or courage to bring it out: how short some people make the road to a point which, for others, seems unattainable!

"That may be my secret," rejoined Dr. John briefly, but with no sort of hauteur: he seemed quite to understand the Rosine or grisette character.

"Mais enfin," continued she, nothing abashed, "monsieur knew it was thrown, since he came to seek it—how did he know?"

"I was attending a little patient in the college near," said he, "and saw it dropped out of his chamber window, and so came to pick it up."

How simple the whole explanation! The note had alluded to a physician as then examining "Gustave."

"Ah ça!" pursued Rosine; "il n'y a donc rien là-dessous: pas de mystère, pas d'amourette, par exemple?"

"Pas plus que sur ma main," responded the doctor, showing his palm.

"Quel dommage!" responded the grisette: "et moi — à qui tout cela commençait à donner des idées."

"Vraiment! vous en êtes pour vos frais," was the doctor's cool rejoinder.

She pouted. The doctor could not help laughing at the sort of "moue" she made: when he laughed, he had something peculiarly good-natured and genial in his look. I saw his hand incline to his pocket.

"How many times have you opened the door for me within this last month?" he asked.

"Monsieur ought to have kept count of that," said Rosine, quite readily.

"As if I had not something better to do!" rejoined he; but I saw him give her a piece of gold, which she took unscrupulously, and then danced off to answer the door-bell, ringing just now every five minutes, as the various servants came to fetch the half-boarders.

The reader must not think too hardly of Rosine; on the whole, she was not a bad sort of person, and had no idea there could be any disgrace in grasping at whatever she could get, or any effrontery in chattering like a pie to the best gentleman in Christendom.

I had learnt something from the above scene besides what concerned the ivory box: viz., that not on the robe de jaconas, pink or grey, nor yet on the frilled and pocketed apron, lay the blame of breaking Dr. John's heart: these items of array were obviously guiltless as Georgette's little blue tunic. So much the better. But who then was the culprit? What was the ground—

Villette

what the origin—what the perfect explanation of the whole business? Some points had been cleared, but how many yet remained obscure as night!

"However," I said to myself, "it is no affair of yours;" and turning from the face on which I had been unconsciously dwelling with a questioning gaze, I looked through the window which commanded the garden below. Dr. John, meantime, standing by the bed-side, was slowly drawing on his gloves and watching his little patient, as her eyes closed and her rosy lips parted in coming sleep. I waited till he should depart as usual, with a quick bow and scarce articulate "good-night.". Just as he took his hat, my eyes, fixed on the tall houses bounding the garden, saw the one lattice, already commemorated, cautiously open; forth from the aperture projected a hand and a white handkerchief; both waved. I know not whether the signal was answered from some viewless quarter of our own dwelling; but immediately after there fluttered from the lattice a falling object, white and light—billet the second, of course.

"There!" I ejaculated involuntarily.

"Where?", asked Dr. John with energy, making direct for the window. "What, is it?"

"They have gone and done it again," was my reply. "A handkerchief waved and something fell:" and I pointed to the lattice, now closed and looking hypocritically blank.

"Go, at once; pick it up and bring it here," was his prompt direction; adding, "Nobody will take notice of you: I should be seen."

Straight I went. After some little search, I found a folded paper, lodged on the lower branch of a shrub; I seized and brought it direct to Dr. John. This time, I believe not even Rosine saw me.

He instantly tore the billet into small pieces, without reading it. "It is not in the least her fault, you must remember," he said, looking at me.

"Whose fault?" I asked. "Who is it?"

"You don't yet know, then?"

"Not in the least."

"Have you no guess?"

"None."

"If I knew you better, I might be tempted to risk some confidence, and thus secure you as guardian over a most innocent and excellent, but somewhat inexperienced being."

"As a duenna?" I asked.

"Yes," said he abstractedly. "What snares are round her!" he added, musingly: and now, certainly for the first time, he examined my face, anxious, doubtless, to see if any kindly expression there, would warrant him in recommending to my care and indulgence some ethereal creature, against whom powers of darkness were plotting. I felt no particular vocation to undertake the surveillance of ethereal creatures; but recalling the scene at the bureau, it seemed to me that I owed him a good turn: if I could help him then I would, and it lay not with me to decide how. With as little reluctance as might be, I intimated that "I was willing to do what I could towards taking care of any person in whom he might be interested.".

"I am no farther interested than as a spectator," said he, with a modesty, admirable, as I thought, to witness. "I happen to be acquainted with the rather worthless character of the person, who, from the house opposite, has now twice invaded the sanctity of this place; I have also met in society the object at whom these vulgar attempts are aimed. Her exquisite superiority and innate refinement ought, one would think, to scare impertinence from her very idea. It is not so, however; and innocent, unsuspicious as she is, I would guard her from evil if I could. In person, however, I can do nothing, I cannot come near her" — he paused.

"Well, I am willing to help you," said I, "only tell me how." And busily, in my own mind, I ran over the list of our inmates, seeking this paragon, this pearl of great price, this gem without flaw. "It must be Madame," I concluded. "She only, amongst us all, has the art even to seem superior: but as to being unsuspicious, inexperienced, &c., Dr. John need not distract himself about that. However, this is just his whim, and I will not contradict him; he shall be humoured: his angel shall be an angel."

"Just notify the quarter to which my care is to be directed," I continued gravely: chuckling, however, to myself over the thought of being set to chaperon Madame Beck or any of her pupils. Now Dr. John had a fine set of nerves, and he at once felt by instinct, what no more coarsely constituted mind would have detected; namely, that I was a little amused at him. The colour rose to his cheek; with half a smile he turned and took his hat—he was going. My heart smote me.

"I will—I will help you," said I eagerly. "I will do what you wish. I will watch over your angel; I will take care of her, only tell me who she is."

"But you must know," said he then with earnestness, yet speaking very low. "So spotless, so good, so unspeakably beautiful! impossible that one house should contain two like her. I allude, of course—"

Here the latch of Madame Beck's chamber-door (opening into the nursery) gave a sudden click, as if the hand holding it had been slightly convulsed; there was the suppressed explosion of an irrepressible sneeze. These little accidents will happen to the best of us. Madame—excellent woman! was then on duty. She had come home quietly, stolen up-stairs on tip-toe; she was in her chamber. If she had not sneezed, she would have heard all, and so should I; but that unlucky sternutation routed Dr. John. While he stood aghast, she came forward alert, composed, in the best yet most tranquil spirits: no novice to her habits but would have thought she had just come in, and scouted the idea of her ear having been glued to the key-hole for at least ten minutes. She affected to sneeze again, declared she was "enrhumée," and then proceeded volubly to recount her "courses en fiacre." The prayer-bell rang, and I left her with the doctor.

CHAPTER XIV.
THE FÊTE.

As soon as Georgette was well, Madame sent her away into the country. I was sorry; I loved the child, and her loss made me poorer than before. But I must not complain. I lived in a house full of robust life; I might have had companions, and I chose solitude. Each of the teachers in turn made me overtures of special intimacy; I tried them all. One I found to be an honest woman, but a narrow thinker, a coarse feeler, and an egotist. The second was a Parisienne, externally refined—at heart, corrupt—without a creed, without a principle, without an affection: having penetrated the outward crust of decorum in this character, you found a slough beneath. She had a wonderful passion for presents; and, in this point, the third teacher—a person otherwise characterless and insignificant—closely resembled her. This last-named had also one other distinctive property—that of avarice. In her reigned the love of money for its own sake. The sight of a piece of gold would bring into her eyes a green glisten, singular to witness. She once, as a mark of high favour, took me up-stairs, and, opening a secret door, showed me a hoard—a mass of coarse, large coin—about fifteen guineas, in five-franc pieces. She loved this hoard as a bird loves its eggs. These were her savings. She would come and talk to me about them with an infatuated and persevering dotage, strange to behold in a person not yet twenty-five.

The Parisienne, on the other hand, was prodigal and profligate (in disposition, that is: as to action, I do not know). That latter quality showed its snake-head to me but once, peeping out very cautiously. A curious kind of reptile it seemed, judging from the glimpse I got; its novelty whetted my curiosity: if it would have come out boldly, perhaps I might philosophically have stood my ground, and coolly surveyed the long thing from forked tongue to scaly tail-tip; but it merely rustled in the leaves of a bad novel; and, on encountering a hasty and ill-advised demonstration of wrath, recoiled and vanished, hissing. She hated me from that day.

This Parisienne was always in debt; her salary being anticipated, not only in dress, but in perfumes, cosmetics, confectionery, and condiments. What a cold, callous epicure she was in all things! I see her now. Thin in face and figure, sallow in complexion, regular in features, with perfect teeth, lips like a thread, a large, prominent chin, a well-opened, but frozen eye, of light at once craving and ingrate. She mortally hated work,

Villette

and loved what she called pleasure; being an insipid, heartless, brainless dissipation of time.

Madame Beck knew this woman's character perfectly well. She once talked to me about her, with an odd mixture of discrimination, indifference, and antipathy. I asked why she kept her in the establishment. She answered plainly, "because it suited her interest to do so;" and pointed out a fact I had already noticed, namely, that Mademoiselle St. Pierre possessed, in an almost unique degree, the power of keeping order amongst her undisciplined ranks of scholars. A certain petrifying influence accompanied and surrounded her: without passion, noise, or violence, she held them in check as a breezeless frost-air might still a brawling stream. She was of little use as far as communication of knowledge went, but for strict surveillance and maintenance of rules she was invaluable. "Je sais bien qu'elle n'a pas de principes, ni, peut-être, de moeurs," admitted Madame frankly; but added with philosophy, "son maintien en classe est toujours convenable et rempli même d'une certaine dignité: c'est tout ce qu'il faut. Ni les élèves ni les parents ne regardent plus loin; ni, par conséquent, moi non plus."

A strange, frolicsome, noisy little world was this school: great pains were taken to hide chains with flowers: a subtle essence of Romanism pervaded every arrangement: large sensual indulgence (so to speak) was permitted by way of counterpoise to jealous spiritual restraint. Each mind was being reared in slavery; but, to prevent reflection from dwelling on this fact, every pretext for physical recreation was seized and made the most of. There, as elsewhere, the CHURCH strove to bring up her children robust in body, feeble in soul, fat, ruddy, hale, joyous, ignorant, unthinking, unquestioning. "Eat, drink, and live!" she says. "Look after your bodies; leave your souls to me. I hold their cure—guide their course: I guarantee their final fate." A bargain, in which every true Catholic deems himself a gainer. Lucifer just offers the same terms: "All this power will I give thee, and the glory of it; for that is delivered unto me, and to whomsoever I will I give it. If thou, therefore, wilt worship me, all shall be thine!"

About this time—in the ripest glow of summer—Madame Beck's house became as merry a place as a school could well be. All day long the broad folding-doors and the two-leaved casements stood wide open: settled sunshine seemed naturalized in the atmosphere; clouds were far off, sailing away beyond sea, resting, no doubt, round islands such as England—that dear land of mists—but withdrawn wholly from the drier continent. We lived far more in the garden than under a roof: classes were held, and meals partaken of, in the "grand berceau." Moreover, there was a note of holiday preparation, which almost turned freedom into licence. The autumnal long vacation was but two months distant; but before that, a great day — an important ceremony — none other than the fête of Madame — awaited celebration.

The conduct of this fête devolved chiefly on Mademoiselle St. Pierre: Madame herself being supposed to stand aloof, disinterestedly unconscious of what might be going forward in her honour. Especially, she never knew, never in the least suspected, that a subscription was annually levied on the whole school for the purchase of a handsome present. The polite tact of the reader will please to leave out of the account a brief, secret consultation on this point in Madame's own chamber.

"What will you have this year?" was asked by her Parisian lieutenant.

"Oh, no matter! Let it alone. Let the poor children keep their francs," And Madame looked benign and modest.

The St. Pierre would here protrude her chin; she knew Madame by heart; she always called her airs of "bonté" — "des grimaces." She never even professed to respect them one instant.

"Vite!" she would say coldly. "Name the article. Shall it be jewellery or porcelain, haberdashery or silver?"

"Eh bien! Deux ou trois cuillers, et autant de fourchettes en argent."

And the result was a handsome case, containing 300 francs worth of plate.

The programme of the fête-day's proceedings comprised: Presentation of plate, collation in the garden, dramatic performance (with pupils and teachers for actors), a dance and supper. Very gorgeous seemed the effect of the whole to me, as I well remember. Zélie St. Pierre understood these things and managed them ably.

The play was the main point; a month's previous drilling being there required. The choice, too, of the actors required knowledge and care; then came lessons in elocution, in attitude, and then the fatigue of countless rehearsals. For all this, as may

Villette

well be supposed, St. Pierre did not suffice: other management, other accomplishments than hers were requisite here. They were supplied in the person of a master—M. Paul Emanuel, professor of literature. It was never my lot to be present at the histrionic lessons of M. Paul, but I often saw him as he crossed the carré (a square hall between the dwelling-house and school-house). I heard him, too, in the warm evenings, lecturing with open doors, and his name, with anecdotes of him, resounded in ones ears from all sides. Especially our former acquaintance, Miss Ginevra Fanshawe,—who had been selected to take a prominent part in the play—used, in bestowing upon me a large portion of her leisure, to lard her discourse with frequent allusions to his sayings and doings. She esteemed him hideously plain, and used to profess herself frightened almost into hysterics at the sound of his step or voice. A dark little man he certainly was; pungent and austere. Even to me he seemed a harsh apparition, with his close-shorn, black head, his broad, sallow brow, his thin cheek, his wide and quivering nostril, his thorough glance, and hurried bearing. Irritable he was; one heard that, as he apostrophized with vehemence the awkward squad under his orders. Sometimes he would break out on these raw amateur actresses with a passion of impatience at their falseness of conception, their coldness of emotion, their feebleness of delivery. "Ecoutez!" he would cry; and then his voice rang through the premises like a trumpet; and when, mimicking it, came the small pipe of a Ginevra, a Mathilde, or a Blanche, one understood why a hollow groan of scorn, or a fierce hiss of rage, rewarded the tame echo.

"Vous n'êtes donc que des poupées," I heard him thunder. "Vous n'avez pas de passions—vous autres. Vous ne sentez donc rien? Votre chair est de neige, votre sang de glace! Moi, je veux que tout cela s'allume, qu'il ait une vie, une âme!"

Vain resolve! And when he at last found it was vain, he suddenly broke the whole business down. Hitherto he had been teaching them a grand tragedy; he tore the tragedy in morsels, and came next day with a compact little comic trifle. To this they took more kindly; he presently knocked it all into their smooth round pates.

Mademoiselle St. Pierre always presided at M. Emanuel's lessons, and I was told that the polish of her manner, her seeming attention, her tact and grace, impressed that gentleman very favourably. She had, indeed, the art of pleasing, for a given time, whom she would; but the feeling would not last: in an hour it was dried like dew, vanished like gossamer.

The day preceding Madame's fête was as much a holiday as the fête itself. It was devoted to clearing out, cleaning, arranging and decorating the three schoolrooms. All within-doors was the gayest bustle; neither up-stairs nor down could a quiet, isolated person find rest for the sole of her foot; accordingly, for my part, I took refuge in the garden. The whole day did I wander or sit there alone, finding warmth in the sun, shelter among the trees, and a sort of companionship in my own thoughts. I well remember that I exchanged but two sentences that day with any living being: not that I felt solitary; I was glad to be quiet. For a looker-on, it sufficed to pass through the rooms once or twice, observe what changes were being wrought, how a green-room and a dressing-room were being contrived, a little stage with scenery erected, how M. Paul Emanuel, in conjunction with Mademoiselle St. Pierre, was directing all, and how an eager band of pupils, amongst them Ginevra Fanshawe, were working gaily under his control.

The great day arrived. The sun rose hot and unclouded, and hot and unclouded it burned on till evening. All the doors and all the windows were set open, which gave a pleasant sense of summer freedom—and freedom the most complete seemed indeed the order of the day. Teachers and pupils descended to breakfast in dressing-gowns and curl-papers: anticipating "avec délices" the toilette of the evening, they seemed to take a pleasure in indulging that forenoon in a luxury of slovenliness; like aldermen fasting in preparation for a feast. About nine o'clock A.M., an important functionary, the "coiffeur," arrived. Sacrilegious to state, he fixed his head-quarters in the oratory, and there, in presence of bénitier, candle, and crucifix, solemnised the mysteries of his art. Each girl was summoned in turn to pass through his hands; emerging from them with head as smooth as a shell, intersected by faultless white lines, and wreathed about with Grecian plaits that shone as if lacquered. I took my turn with the rest, and could hardly believe what the glass said when I applied to it for information afterwards; the lavished garlandry of woven brown hair amazed me—I feared it was not all my own, and it required several convincing pulls to give assurance to the contrary. I then acknowledged in the coiffeur a first-rate artist—one who certainly made the most of indifferent materials.

The oratory closed, the dormitory became the scene of ablutions, arrayings and bedizenings curiously elaborate. To me it was, and ever must be an enigma, how they contrived to spend so much time in doing so little. The operation seemed close, intricate, prolonged: the result simple. A clear white muslin dress, a blue sash (the Virgin's colours), a pair of white, or straw-colour kid gloves—such was the gala uniform, to the assumption whereof that houseful of teachers and pupils devoted three mortal hours. But though simple, it must be allowed the array was perfect—perfect in fashion, fit, and freshness; every head being also dressed with exquisite nicety, and a certain compact taste—suiting the full, firm comeliness of Labassecourien contours, though too stiff for any more flowing and flexible style of beauty—the general effect was, on the whole, commendable.

In beholding this diaphanous and snowy mass, I well remember feeling myself to be a mere shadowy spot on a field of light; the courage was not in me to put on a transparent white dress: something thin I must wear—the weather and rooms being too hot to give substantial fabrics sufferance, so I had sought through a dozen shops till I lit upon a crape-like material of purple-gray—the colour, in short, of dun mist, lying on a moor in bloom. My tailleuse had kindly made it as well as she could: because, as she judiciously observed, it was "si triste—si pen voyant," care in the fashion was the more imperative: it was well she took this view of the matter, for I, had no flower, no jewel to relieve it: and, what was more, I had no natural rose of complexion.

We become oblivious of these deficiencies in the uniform routine of daily drudgery, but they will force upon us their unwelcome blank on those bright occasions when beauty should shine.

However, in this same gown of shadow, I felt at home and at ease; an advantage I should not have enjoyed in anything more brilliant or striking. Madame Beck, too, kept me in countenance; her dress was almost as quiet as mine, except that she wore a bracelet, and a large brooch bright with gold and fine stones. We chanced to meet on the stairs, and she gave me a nod and smile of approbation. Not that she thought I was looking well— a point unlikely to engage her interest—but she considered me dressed "convenablement," "décemment," and la Convenance et la Décence were the two calm deities of Madame's worship. She even paused, laid on my shoulder her gloved hand, holding an embroidered and perfumed handkerchief, and confided to my ear a sarcasm on the other teachers (whom she had just been complimenting to their faces). "Nothing so absurd," she said, "as for des femmes mûres 'to dress themselves like girls of fifteen'—quant à la St. Pierre, elle a l'air d'une vieille coquette qui fait l'ingénue."

Being dressed at least a couple of hours before anybody else,

I felt a pleasure in betaking myself—not to the garden, where servants were busy propping up long tables, placing seats, and spreading cloths in readiness for the collation but to the schoolrooms, now empty, quiet, cool, and clean; their walls fresh stained, their planked floors fresh scoured and scarce dry; flowers fresh gathered adorning the recesses in pots, and draperies, fresh hung, beautifying the great windows.

Withdrawing to the first classe, a smaller and neater room than the others, and taking from the glazed bookcase, of which I kept the key, a volume whose title promised some interest, I sat down to read. The glass-door of this "classe," or schoolroom, opened into the large berceau; acacia-boughs caressed its panes, as they stretched across to meet a rose-bush blooming by the opposite lintel: in this rose-bush bees murmured busy and happy. I commenced reading. Just as the stilly hum, the embowering shade, the warm, lonely calm of my retreat were beginning to steal meaning from the page, vision from my eyes, and to lure me along the track of reverie, down into some deep dell of dreamland—just then, the sharpest ring of the street-door bell to which that much-tried instrument had ever thrilled, snatched me back to consciousness.

Now the bell had been ringing all the morning, as workmen, or servants, or coiffeurs, or tailleuses, went and came on their several errands. Moreover, there was good reason to expect it would ring all the afternoon, since about one hundred externes were yet to arrive in carriages or fiacres: nor could it be expected to rest during the evening, when parents and friends would gather thronging to the play. Under these circumstances, a ring—even a sharp ring—was a matter of course: yet this particular peal had an accent of its own, which chased my dream, and startled my book from my knee.

I was stooping to pick up this last, when—firm, fast, straight—right on through vestibule—along corridor, across carré, through first division, second division, grand salle—strode a step, quick, regular, intent. The closed door of the first classe—my sanctuary—offered no obstacle; it burst open, and a paletôt and a bonnet grec filled the void; also two eyes first vaguely struck upon, and then hungrily dived into me.

"C'est cela!" said a voice. "Je la connais: c'est l'Anglaise. Tant pis. Toute Anglaise, et, par conséquent, toute bégueule qu'elle soit—elle fera mon affaire, ou je saurai pourquoi."

Then, with a certain stern politeness (I suppose he thought I had not caught the drift of his previous uncivil mutterings), and in a jargon the most execrable that ever was heard, "Meess — —, play you must: I am planted there."

"What can I do for you, M. Paul Emanuel?" I inquired: for M. Paul Emanuel it was, and in a state of no little excitement.

"Play you must. I will not have you shrink, or frown, or make the prude. I read your skull that night you came; I see your moyens: play you can; play you must."

"But how, M. Paul? What do you mean?"

"There is no time to be lost," he went on, now speaking in French; "and let us thrust to the wall all reluctance, all excuses, all minauderies. You must take a part."

"In the vaudeville?"

"In the vaudeville. You have said it."

I gasped, horror-struck. What did the little man mean?

"Listen!" he said. "The case shall be stated, and you shall then answer me Yes, or No; and according to your answer shall I ever after estimate you."

The scarce-suppressed impetus of a most irritable nature glowed in his cheek, fed with sharp shafts his glances, a nature — the injudicious, the mawkish, the hesitating, the sullen, the affected, above all, the unyielding, might quickly render violent and implacable. Silence and attention was the best balm to apply: I listened.

"The whole matter is going to fail," he began. "Louise Vanderkelkov has fallen ill — at least so her ridiculous mother asserts; for my part, I feel sure she might play if she would: it is only good-will that lacks. She was charged with a rôle, as you know, or do not know — it is equal: without that rôle the play is stopped. There are now but a few hours in which to learn it: not a girl in this school would hear reason, and accept the task. Forsooth, it is not an interesting, not an amiable, part; their vile amour-propre — that base quality of which women have so much — would revolt from it. Englishwomen are either the best or the worst of their sex. Dieu sait que je les déteste comme la peste, ordinairement" (this between his recreant teeth). "I apply to an Englishwoman to rescue me. What is her answer — Yes, or No?"

A thousand objections rushed into my mind. The foreign language, the limited time, the public display… Inclination recoiled, Ability faltered, Self-respect (that "vile quality") trembled. "Non, non, non!" said all these; but looking up at M. Paul, and seeing in his vexed, fiery, and searching eye, a sort of appeal behind all its menace, my lips dropped the word "oui". For a moment his rigid countenance relaxed with a quiver of content: quickly bent up again, however, he went on,—

"Vite à l'ouvrage! Here is the book; here is your rôle: read." And I read. He did not commend; at some passages he scowled and stamped. He gave me a lesson: I diligently imitated. It was a disagreeable part—a man's—an empty-headed fop's. One could put into it neither heart nor soul: I hated it. The play—a mere trifle—ran chiefly on the efforts of a brace of rivals to gain the hand of a fair coquette. One lover was called the "Ours," a good and gallant but unpolished man, a sort of diamond in the rough; the other was a butterfly, a talker, and a traitor: and I was to be the butterfly, talker, and traitor.

I did my best—which was bad, I know: it provoked M. Paul; he fumed. Putting both hands to the work, I endeavoured to do better than my best; I presume he gave me credit for good intentions; he professed to be partially content. "Ca ira!" he cried; and as voices began sounding from the garden, and white dresses fluttering among the trees, he added: "You must withdraw: you must be alone to learn this. Come with me."

Without being allowed time or power to deliberate, I found myself in the same breath convoyed along as in a species of whirlwind, up-stairs, up two pair of stairs, nay, actually up three (for this fiery little man seemed as by instinct to know his way everywhere); to the solitary and lofty attic was I borne, put in and locked in, the key being, in the door, and that key he took with him and vanished.

The attic was no pleasant place: I believe he did not know how unpleasant it was, or he never would have locked me in with so little ceremony. In this summer weather, it was hot as Africa; as in winter, it was always cold as Greenland. Boxes and lumber filled it; old dresses draped its unstained wall—cobwebs its unswept ceiling. Well was it known to be tenanted by rats, by black beetles, and by cockroaches—nay, rumour affirmed that the ghostly Nun of the garden had once been seen here. A partial darkness obscured one end, across which, as for deeper mystery, an old russet curtain was drawn, by way of screen to a sombre band of winter cloaks, pendent each from its pin, like a malefactor from his gibbet. From amongst these cloaks, and

Villette

behind that curtain, the Nun was said to issue. I did not believe this, nor was I troubled by apprehension thereof; but I saw a very dark and large rat, with a long tail, come gliding out from that squalid alcove; and, moreover, my eye fell on many a black-beetle, dotting the floor. These objects discomposed me more, perhaps, than it would be wise to say, as also did the dust, lumber, and stifling heat of the place. The last inconvenience would soon have become intolerable, had I not found means to open and prop up the skylight, thus admitting some freshness. Underneath this aperture I pushed a large empty chest, and having mounted upon it a smaller box, and wiped from both the dust, I gathered my dress (my best, the reader must remember, and therefore a legitimate object of care) fastidiously around me, ascended this species of extempore throne, and being seated, commenced the acquisition of my task; while I learned, not forgetting to keep a sharp look-out on the black-beetles and cockroaches, of which, more even, I believe, than of the rats, I sat in mortal dread.

My impression at first was that I had undertaken what it really was impossible to perform, and I simply resolved to do my best and be resigned to fail. I soon found, however, that one part in so short a piece was not more than memory could master at a few hours' notice. I learned and learned on, first in a whisper, and then aloud. Perfectly secure from human audience, I acted my part before the garret-vermin. Entering into its emptiness, frivolity, and falsehood, with a spirit inspired by scorn and impatience, I took my revenge on this "fat," by making him as fatuitous as I possibly could.

In this exercise the afternoon passed: day began to glide into evening; and I, who had eaten nothing since breakfast, grew excessively hungry. Now I thought of the collation, which doubtless they were just then devouring in the garden far below. (I had seen in the vestibule a basketful of small pâtés à la crême, than which nothing in the whole range of cookery seemed to me better). A pâté, or a square of cake, it seemed to me would come very àpropos; and as my relish for those dainties increased, it began to appear somewhat hard that I should pass my holiday, fasting and in prison. Remote as was the attic from the street-door and vestibule, yet the ever-tinkling bell was faintly audible here; and also the ceaseless roll of wheels, on the tormented pavement. I knew that the house and garden were thronged, and that all was gay and glad below; here it began to grow dusk: the beetles were fading from my sight; I trembled lest they should steal on me a march, mount my throne unseen, and, unsuspected, invade my skirts. Impatient and apprehensive, I recommenced the rehearsal of

135

my part merely to kill time. Just as I was concluding, the long-delayed rattle of the key in the lock came to my ear—no unwelcome sound. M. Paul (I could just see through the dusk that it was M. Paul, for light enough still lingered to show the velvet blackness of his close-shorn head, and the sallow ivory of his brow) looked in.

"Brava!" cried he, holding the door open and remaining at the threshold. "J'ai tout entendu. C'est assez bien. Encore!"

A moment I hesitated.

"Encore!" said he sternly. "Et point de grimaces! A bas la timidité!"

Again I went through the part, but not half so well as I had spoken it alone.

"Enfin, elle sait," said he, half dissatisfied, "and one cannot be fastidious or exacting under the circumstances." Then he added, "You may yet have twenty minutes for preparation: au revoir!" And he was going.

"Monsieur," I called out, taking courage.

"Eh bien! Qu'est-ce que c'est, Mademoiselle?"

"J'ai bien faim."

"Comment, vous avez faim! Et la collation?"

"I know nothing about it. I have not seen it, shut up here."

"Ah! C'est vrai," cried he.

In a moment my throne was abdicated, the attic evacuated; an inverse repetition of the impetus which had brought me up into the attic, instantly took me down—down—down to the very kitchen. I thought I should have gone to the cellar. The cook was imperatively ordered to produce food, and I, as imperatively, was commanded to eat. To my great joy this food was limited to coffee and cake: I had feared wine and sweets, which I did not like. How he guessed that I should like a petit pâté à la crême I cannot tell; but he went out and procured me one from some quarter. With considerable willingness I ate and drank, keeping the petit pâté till the last, as a bonne bouche. M. Paul superintended my repast, and almost forced upon me more than I could swallow.

Villette

"A la bonne heure," he cried, when I signified that I really could take no more, and, with uplifted hands, implored to be spared the additional roll on which he had just spread butter. "You will set me down as a species of tyrant and Bluebeard, starving women in a garret; whereas, after all, I am no such thing. Now, Mademoiselle, do you feel courage and strength to appear?"

I said, I thought I did; though, in truth, I was perfectly confused, and could hardly tell how I felt: but this little man was of the order of beings who must not be opposed, unless you possessed an all-dominant force sufficient to crush him at once.

"Come then," said he, offering his hand.

I gave him mine, and he set off with a rapid walk, which obliged me to run at his side in order to keep pace. In the carré he stopped a moment: it was lit with large lamps; the wide doors of the classes were open, and so were the equally wide garden-doors; orange-trees in tubs, and tall flowers in pots, ornamented these portals on each side; groups of ladies and gentlemen in evening-dress stood and walked amongst the flowers. Within, the long vista of the school-rooms presented a thronging, undulating, murmuring, waving, streaming multitude, all rose, and blue, and half translucent white. There were lustres burning overhead; far off there was a stage, a solemn green curtain, a row of footlights.

"N'est-ce pas que c'est beau?" demanded my companion.

I should have said it was, but my heart got up into my throat. M. Paul discovered this, and gave me a side-scowl and a little shake for my pains.

"I will do my best, but I wish it was over," said I; then I asked: "Are we to walk through that crowd?"

"By no means: I manage matters better: we pass through the garden—here."

In an instant we were out of doors: the cool, calm night revived me somewhat. It was moonless, but the reflex from the many glowing windows lit the court brightly, and even the alleys—dimly. Heaven was cloudless, and grand with the quiver of its living fires. How soft are the nights of the Continent! How bland, balmy, safe! No sea-fog; no chilling damp: mistless as noon, and fresh as morning.

Having crossed court and garden, we reached the glass door of the first classe. It stood open, like all other doors that night; we passed, and then I was ushered into a small cabinet, dividing the first classe from the grand salle. This cabinet dazzled me, it was so full of light: it deafened me, it was clamorous with voices: it stifled me, it was so hot, choking, thronged.

"De l'ordre! Du silence!" cried M. Paul. "Is this chaos?", he demanded; and there was a hush. With a dozen words, and as many gestures, he turned out half the persons present, and obliged the remnant to fall into rank. Those left were all in costume: they were the performers, and this was the green-room. M. Paul introduced me. All stared and some tittered. It was a surprise: they had not expected the Englishwoman would play in a vaudeville. Ginevra Fanshawe, beautifully dressed for her part, and looking fascinatingly pretty, turned on me a pair of eyes as round as beads. In the highest spirit, unperturbed by fear or bashfulness, delighted indeed at the thought of shining off before hundreds—my entrance seemed to transfix her with amazement in the midst of her joy. She would have exclaimed, but M. Paul held her and all the rest in check.

Having surveyed and criticized the whole troop, he turned to me.

"You, too, must be dressed for your part."

"Dressed—dressed like a man!" exclaimed Zélie St. Pierre, darting forwards; adding with officiousness, "I will dress her myself."

To be dressed like a man did not please, and would not suit me. I had consented to take a man's name and part; as to his dress—halte là! No. I would keep my own dress, come what might. M. Paul might storm, might rage: I would keep my own dress. I said so, with a voice as resolute in intent, as it was low, and perhaps unsteady in utterance.

He did not immediately storm or rage, as I fully thought he would he stood silent. But Zélie again interposed.

"She will make a capital petit-maître. Here are the garments, all—all complete: somewhat too large, but—I will arrange all that. Come, chère amie—belle Anglaise!"

And she sneered, for I was not "belle." She seized my hand, she was drawing me away. M. Paul stood impassable—neutral.

Villette

"You must not resist," pursued St. Pierre—for resist I did. "You will spoil all, destroy the mirth of the piece, the enjoyment of the company, sacrifice everything to your amour-propre. This would be too bad—monsieur will never permit this?"

She sought his eye. I watched, likewise, for a glance. He gave her one, and then he gave me one. "Stop!" he said slowly, arresting St. Pierre, who continued her efforts to drag me after her. Everybody awaited the decision. He was not angry, not irritated; I perceived that, and took heart.

"You do not like these clothes?" he asked, pointing to the masculine vestments.

"I don't object to some of them, but I won't have them all."

"How must it be, then? How accept a man's part, and go on the stage dressed as a woman? This is an amateur affair, it is true—a vaudeville de pensionnat; certain modifications I might sanction, yet something you must have to announce you as of the nobler sex."

"And I will, Monsieur; but it must be arranged in my own way: nobody must meddle; the things must not be forced upon me. Just let me dress myself."

Monsieur, without another word, took the costume from St. Pierre, gave it to me, and permitted me to pass into the dressing-room. Once alone, I grew calm, and collectedly went to work. Retaining my woman's garb without the slightest retrenchment, I merely assumed, in addition, a little vest, a collar, and cravat, and a paletôt of small dimensions; the whole being the costume of a brother of one of the pupils. Having loosened my hair out of its braids, made up the long back-hair close, and brushed the front hair to one side, I took my hat and gloves in my hand and came out. M. Paul was waiting, and so were the others. He looked at me. "That may pass in a pensionnat," he pronounced. Then added, not unkindly, "Courage, mon ami! Un peu de sangfroid—un peu d'aplomb, M. Lucien, et tout ira bien."

St. Pierre sneered again, in her cold snaky manner.

I was irritable, because excited, and I could not help turning upon her and saying, that if she were not a lady and I a gentleman, I should feel disposed to call her out.

"After the play, after the play," said M. Paul. "I will then divide my pair of pistols between you, and we will settle the dispute according to form: it will only be the old quarrel of France and England."

But now the moment approached for the performance to commence. M. Paul, setting us before him, harangued us briefly, like a general addressing soldiers about to charge. I don't know what he said, except that he recommended each to penetrate herself with a sense of her personal insignificance. God knows I thought this advice superfluous for some of us. A bell tinkled. I and two more were ushered on to the stage. The bell tinkled again. I had to speak the very first words.

"Do not look at the crowd, nor think of it," whispered M. Paul in my ear. "Imagine yourself in the garret, acting to the rats."

He vanished. The curtain drew up—shrivelled to the ceiling: the bright lights, the long room, the gay throng, burst upon us. I thought of the black-beetles, the old boxes, the worm-eaten bureau. I said my say badly; but I said it. That first speech was the difficulty; it revealed to me this fact, that it was not the crowd I feared so much as my own voice. Foreigners and strangers, the crowd were nothing to me. Nor did I think of them. When my tongue once got free, and my voice took its true pitch, and found its natural tone, I thought of nothing but the personage I represented—and of M. Paul, who was listening, watching, prompting in the side-scenes.

By-and-by, feeling the right power come—the spring demanded gush and rise inwardly—I became sufficiently composed to notice my fellow-actors. Some of them played very well; especially Ginevra Fanshawe, who had to coquette between two suitors, and managed admirably: in fact she was in her element. I observed that she once or twice threw a certain marked fondness and pointed partiality into her manner towards me—the fop. With such emphasis and animation did she favour me, such glances did she dart out into the listening and applauding crowd, that to me—who knew her—it presently became evident she was acting at some one; and I followed her eye, her smile, her gesture, and ere long discovered that she had at least singled out a handsome and distinguished aim for her shafts; full in the path of those arrows—taller than other spectators, and therefore more sure to receive them—stood, in attitude quiet but intent, a well-known form—that of Dr. John.

The spectacle seemed somehow suggestive. There was language in Dr. John's look, though I cannot tell what he said; it animated me: I drew out of it a history; I put my idea into the part I performed; I threw it into my wooing of Ginevra. In the "Ours," or sincere lover, I saw Dr. John. Did I pity him, as erst? No, I hardened my heart, rivalled and out-rivalled him. I knew myself but a fop, but where he was outcast I could please. Now I know I acted as if wishful and resolute to win and conquer. Ginevra seconded me; between us we half-changed the nature of the rôle, gilding it from top to toe. Between the acts M. Paul, told us he knew not what possessed us, and half expostulated. "C'est peut-être plus beau que votre modèle," said he, "mais ce n'est pas juste." I know not what possessed me either; but somehow, my longing was to eclipse the "Ours," i.e., Dr. John. Ginevra was tender; how could I be otherwise than chivalric? Retaining the letter, I recklessly altered the spirit of the rôle. Without heart, without interest, I could not play it at all. It must be played — in went the yearned-for seasoning — thus favoured, I played it with relish.

What I felt that night, and what I did, I no more expected to feel and do, than to be lifted in a trance to the seventh heaven. Cold, reluctant, apprehensive, I had accepted a part to please another: ere long, warming, becoming interested, taking courage, I acted to please myself. Yet the next day, when I thought it over, I quite disapproved of these amateur performances; and though glad that I had obliged M. Paul, and tried my own strength for once, I took a firm resolution, never to be drawn into a similar affair. A keen relish for dramatic expression had revealed itself as part of my nature; to cherish and exercise this new-found faculty might gift me with a world of delight, but it would not do for a mere looker-on at life: the strength and longing must be put by; and I put them by, and fastened them in with the lock of a resolution which neither Time nor Temptation has since picked.

No sooner was the play over, and well over, than the choleric and arbitrary M. Paul underwent a metamorphosis. His hour of managerial responsibility past, he at once laid aside his magisterial austerity; in a moment he stood amongst us, vivacious, kind, and social, shook hands with us all round, thanked us separately, and announced his determination that each of us should in turn be his partner in the coming ball. On his claiming my promise, I told him I did not dance. "For once I must," was the answer; and if I had not slipped aside and kept out of his way, he would have compelled me to this second performance. But I had acted enough for one evening; it was time I retired into myself and my ordinary life. My dun-coloured dress did well enough under a paletôt on the stage, but would not suit a waltz or a quadrille. Withdrawing to a quiet nook, whence unobserved I could observe — the ball, its splendours and its pleasures, passed before me as a spectacle.

Again Ginevra Fanshawe was the belle, the fairest and the gayest present; she was selected to open the ball: very lovely she looked, very gracefully she danced, very joyously she smiled. Such scenes were her triumphs — she was the child of pleasure. Work or suffering found her listless and dejected, powerless and repining; but gaiety expanded her butterfly's wings, lit up their gold-dust and bright spots, made her flash like a gem, and flush like a flower. At all ordinary diet and plain beverage she would pout; but she fed on creams and ices like a humming-bird on honey-paste: sweet wine was her element, and sweet cake her daily bread. Ginevra lived her full life in a ball-room; elsewhere she drooped dispirited.

Think not, reader, that she thus bloomed and sparkled for the mere sake of M. Paul, her partner, or that she lavished her best graces that night for the edification of her companions only, or for that of the parents and grand-parents, who filled the carré, and lined the ball-room; under circumstances so insipid and limited, with motives so chilly and vapid, Ginevra would scarce have deigned to walk one quadrille, and weariness and fretfulness would have replaced animation and good-humour, but she knew of a leaven in the otherwise heavy festal mass which lighted the whole; she tasted a condiment which gave it zest; she perceived reasons justifying the display of her choicest attractions.

In the ball-room, indeed, not a single male spectator was to be seen who was not married and a father — M. Paul excepted — that gentleman, too, being the sole creature of his sex permitted to lead out a pupil to the dance; and this exceptional part was allowed him, partly as a matter of old-established custom (for he was a kinsman of Madame Beck's, and high in her confidence), partly because he would always have his own way and do as he pleased, and partly because — wilful, passionate, partial, as he might be — he was the soul of honour, and might be trusted with a regiment of the fairest and purest; in perfect security that under his leadership they would come to no harm. Many of the girls — it may be noted in parenthesis — were not pure-minded at all, very much otherwise; but they no more dare betray their natural coarseness in M. Paul's presence, than they dare tread purposely on his corns, laugh in his face during a stormy apostrophe, or speak above their breath while some crisis of irritability was covering his human visage with the mask of an intelligent tiger. M. Paul, then, might dance with whom he would — and woe be to the interference which put him out of step.

Others there were admitted as spectators—with (seeming) reluctance, through prayers, by influence, under restriction, by special and difficult exercise of Madame Beck's gracious good-nature, and whom she all the evening—with her own personal surveillance—kept far aloof at the remotest, drearest, coldest, darkest side of the carré—a small, forlorn band of "jeunes gens;" these being all of the best families, grown-up sons of mothers present, and whose sisters were pupils in the school. That whole evening was Madame on duty beside these "jeunes gens"—attentive to them as a mother, but strict with them as a dragon. There was a sort of cordon stretched before them, which they wearied her with prayers to be permitted to pass, and just to revive themselves by one dance with that "belle blonde," or that "jolie brune," or "cette jeune fille magnifique aux cheveux noirs comme le jais."

"Taisez-vous!" Madame would reply, heroically and inexorably. "Vous ne passerez pas à moins que ce ne soit sur mon cadavre, et vous ne danserez qu'avec la nonnette du jardin" (alluding to the legend). And she majestically walked to and fro along their disconsolate and impatient line, like a little Bonaparte in a mouse-coloured silk gown.

Madame knew something of the world; Madame knew much of human nature. I don't think that another directress in Villette would have dared to admit a "jeune homme" within her walls; but Madame knew that by granting such admission, on an occasion like the present, a bold stroke might be struck, and a great point gained.

In the first place, the parents were made accomplices to the deed, for it was only through their mediation it was brought about. Secondly: the admission of these rattlesnakes, so fascinating and so dangerous, served to draw out Madame precisely in her strongest character—that of a first-rate surveillante. Thirdly: their presence furnished a most piquant ingredient to the entertainment: the pupils knew it, and saw it, and the view of such golden apples shining afar off, animated them with a spirit no other circumstance could have kindled. The children's pleasure spread to the parents; life and mirth circulated quickly round the ball-room; the "jeunes gens" themselves, though restrained, were amused: for Madame never permitted them to feel dull—and thus Madame Beck's fête annually ensured a success unknown to the fête of any other directress in the land.

I observed that Dr. John was at first permitted to walk at large through the classes: there was about him a manly, responsible look, that redeemed his youth, and half-expiated his beauty; but as soon as the ball began, Madame ran up to him.

"Come, Wolf; come," said she, laughing: "you wear sheep's clothing, but you must quit the fold notwithstanding. Come; I have a fine menagerie of twenty here in the carré: let me place you amongst my collection."

"But first suffer me to have one dance with one pupil of my choice."

"Have you the face to ask such a thing? It is madness: it is impiety. Sortez, sortez, au plus vite."

She drove him before her, and soon had him enclosed within the cordon.

Ginevra being, I suppose, tired with dancing, sought me out in my retreat. She threw herself on the bench beside me, and (a demonstration I could very well have dispensed with) cast her arms round my neck.

"Lucy Snowe! Lucy Snowe!" she cried in a somewhat sobbing voice, half hysterical.

"What in the world is the matter?" I drily said.

"How do I look — how do I look to-night?" she demanded.

"As usual," said I; "preposterously vain."

"Caustic creature! You never have a kind word for me; but in spite of you, and all other envious detractors, I know I am beautiful; I feel it, I see it — for there is a great looking-glass in the dressing-room, where I can view my shape from head to foot. Will you go with me now, and let us two stand before it?"

"I will, Miss Fanshawe: you shall be humoured even to the top of your bent."

The dressing-room was very near, and we stepped in. Putting her arm through mine, she drew me to the mirror. Without resistance remonstrance, or remark, I stood and let her self-love have its feast and triumph: curious to see how much it could swallow — whether it was possible it could feed to satiety — whether any whisper of consideration for others could penetrate her heart, and moderate its vainglorious exultation.

Not at all. She turned me and herself round; she viewed us both on all sides; she smiled, she waved her curls, she retouched her sash, she spread her dress, and finally, letting go my arm, and curtseying with mock respect, she said: "I would not be you for a kingdom."

The remark was too naïve to rouse anger; I merely said: "Very good."

"And what would you give to be ME?" she inquired.

"Not a bad sixpence—strange as it may sound," I replied. "You are but a poor creature."

"You don't think so in your heart."

"No; for in my heart you have not the outline of a place: I only occasionally turn you over in my brain."

"Well, but," said she, in an expostulatory tone, "just listen to the difference of our positions, and then see how happy am I, and how miserable are you."

"Go on; I listen."

"In the first place: I am the daughter of a gentleman of family, and though my father is not rich, I have expectations from an uncle. Then, I am just eighteen, the finest age possible. I have had a continental education, and though I can't spell, I have abundant accomplishments. I am pretty; you can't deny that; I may have as many admirers as I choose. This very night I have been breaking the hearts of two gentlemen, and it is the dying look I had from one of them just now, which puts me in such spirits. I do so like to watch them turn red and pale, and scowl and dart fiery glances at each other, and languishing ones at me. There is me—happy ME; now for you, poor soul!

"I suppose you are nobody's daughter, since you took care of little children when you first came to Villette: you have no relations; you can't call yourself young at twenty-three; you have no attractive accomplishments—no beauty. As to admirers, you hardly know what they are; you can't even talk on the subject: you sit dumb when the other teachers quote their conquests. I believe you never were in love, and never will be: you don't know the feeling, and so much the better, for though you might have your own heart broken, no living heart will you ever break. Isn't it all true?"

"A good deal of it is true as gospel, and shrewd besides. There must be good in you, Ginevra, to speak so honestly; that snake, Zélie St. Pierre, could not utter what you have uttered. Still, Miss Fanshawe, hapless as I am, according to your showing, sixpence I would not give to purchase you, body and soul."

"Just because I am not clever, and that is all you think of. Nobody in the world but you cares for cleverness."

"On the contrary, I consider you are clever, in your way — very smart indeed. But you were talking of breaking hearts — that edifying amusement into the merits of which I don't quite enter; pray on whom does your vanity lead you to think you have done execution to-night?"

She approached her lips to my ear — "Isidore and Alfred de Hamal are both here," she whispered.

"Oh! they are? I should like to see them."

"There's a dear creature! your curiosity is roused at last. Follow me, I will point them out."

She proudly led the way — "But you cannot see them well from the classes," said she, turning, "Madame keeps them too far off. Let us cross the garden, enter by the corridor, and get close to them behind: we shall be scolded if we are seen, but never mind."

For once, I did not mind. Through the garden we went — penetrated into the corridor by a quiet private entrance, and approaching the carré, yet keeping in the corridor shade, commanded a near view of the band of "jeunes gens."

I believe I could have picked out the conquering de Hamal even undirected. He was a straight-nosed, very correct-featured little dandy. I say little dandy, though he was not beneath the middle standard in stature; but his lineaments were small, and so were his hands and feet; and he was pretty and smooth, and as trim as a doll: so nicely dressed, so nicely curled, so booted and gloved and cravated — he was charming indeed. I said so. "What, a dear personage!" cried I, and commended Ginevra's taste warmly; and asked her what she thought de Hamal might have done with the precious fragments of that heart she had broken — whether he kept them in a scent-vial, and conserved them in otto of roses? I observed, too, with deep rapture of approbation, that the colonel's hands were scarce larger than Miss Fanshawe's own, and suggested that this circumstance might be convenient, as he could wear her gloves at a pinch. On his dear curls, I told her I doated: and as to his low, Grecian brow, and exquisite classic headpiece, I confessed I had no language to do such perfections justice.

"And if he were your lover?" suggested the cruelly exultant Ginevra.

"Oh! heavens, what bliss!" said I; "but do not be inhuman, Miss Fanshawe: to put such thoughts into my head is like showing poor outcast Cain a far, glimpse of Paradise."

"You like him, then?"

"As I like sweets, and jams, and comfits, and conservatory flowers."

Ginevra admired my taste, for all these things were her adoration; she could then readily credit that they were mine too.

"Now for Isidore," I went on. I own I felt still more curious to see him than his rival; but Ginevra was absorbed in the latter.

"Alfred was admitted here to-night," said she, "through the influence of his aunt, Madame la Baronne de Dorlodot; and now, having seen him, can you not understand why I have been in such spirits all the evening, and acted so well, and danced with such life, and why I am now happy as a queen? Dieu! Dieu! It was such good fun to glance first at him and then at the other, and madden them both."

"But that other—where is he? Show me Isidore."

"I don't like."

"Why not?"

"I am ashamed of him."

"For what reason?"

"Because—because" (in a whisper) "he has such—such whiskers, orange—red—there now!"

"The murder is out," I subjoined. "Never mind, show him all

the same; I engage not to faint."

She looked round. Just then an English voice spoke behind her and me.

"You are both standing in a draught; you must leave this corridor."

"There is no draught, Dr. John," said I, turning.

"She takes cold so easily," he pursued, looking at Ginevra with extreme kindness. "She is delicate; she must be cared for: fetch her a shawl."

"Permit me to judge for myself," said Miss Fanshawe, with hauteur. "I want no shawl."

"Your dress is thin, you have been dancing, you are heated."

"Always preaching," retorted she; "always coddling and admonishing."

The answer Dr. John would have given did not come; that his heart was hurt became evident in his eye; darkened, and saddened, and pained, he turned a little aside, but was patient. I knew where there were plenty of shawls near at hand; I ran and fetched one.

"She shall wear this, if I have strength to make her," said I, folding it well round her muslin dress, covering carefully her neck and her arms. "Is that Isidore?" I asked, in a somewhat fierce whisper.

She pushed up her lip, smiled, and nodded.

"Is that Isidore?" I repeated, giving her a shake: I could have given her a dozen.

"C'est lui-même," said she. "How coarse he is, compared with the Colonel-Count! And then—oh ciel!—the whiskers!"

Dr. John now passed on.

"The Colonel-Count!" I echoed. "The doll—the puppet—the manikin—the poor inferior creature! A mere lackey for Dr. John his valet, his foot-boy! Is it possible that fine generous gentleman—handsome as a vision—offers you his honourable hand and gallant heart, and promises to protect your flimsy person and feckless mind through the storms and struggles of life—and you hang back—you scorn, you sting, you torture him! Have you power to do this? Who gave you that power? Where is it? Does it lie all in your beauty—your pink and white complexion, and your yellow hair? Does this bind his soul at your feet, and bend his neck under your yoke? Does this purchase for you his affection, his tenderness, his thoughts, his hopes, his interest, his noble, cordial love—and will you not have it? Do you scorn it? You are only dissembling: you are not in earnest: you love him; you long for him; but you trifle with his heart to make him more surely yours?"

"Bah! How you run on! I don't understand half you have said."

I had got her out into the garden ere this. I now set her down on a seat and told her she should not stir till she had avowed which she meant in the end to accept—the man or the monkey.

"Him you call the man," said she, "is bourgeois, sandy-haired, and answers to the name of John!—cela suffit: je n'en veux pas. Colonel de Hamal is a gentleman of excellent connections, perfect manners, sweet appearance, with pale interesting face, and hair and eyes like an Italian. Then too he is the most delightful company possible—a man quite in my way; not sensible and serious like the other; but one with whom I can talk on equal terms—who does not plague and bore, and harass me with depths, and heights, and passions, and talents for which I have no taste. There now. Don't hold me so fast."

I slackened my grasp, and she darted off. I did not care to pursue her.

Somehow I could not avoid returning once more in the direction of the corridor to get another glimpse of Dr. John; but I met him on the garden-steps, standing where the light from a window fell broad. His well-proportioned figure was not to be mistaken, for I doubt whether there was another in that assemblage his equal. He carried his hat in his hand; his uncovered head, his face and fine brow were most handsome and manly. His features were not delicate, not slight like those of a woman, nor were they cold, frivolous, and feeble; though well cut, they were not so chiselled, so frittered away, as to lose in expression or significance what they gained in unmeaning symmetry. Much feeling spoke in them at times, and more sat silent in his eye. Such at least were my thoughts of him: to me he seemed all this. An inexpressible sense of wonder occupied me, as I looked at this man, and reflected that he could not be slighted.

It was, not my intention to approach or address him in the garden, our terms of acquaintance not warranting such a step; I had only meant to view him in the crowd—myself unseen: coming upon him thus alone, I withdrew. But he was looking out for me, or rather for her who had been with me: therefore he descended the steps, and followed me down the alley.

"You know Miss Fanshawe? I have often wished to ask whether you knew her," said he.

"Yes: I know her."

"Intimately?"

"Quite as intimately as I wish."

"What have you done with her now?"

"Am I her keeper?" I felt inclined to ask; but I simply answered, "I have shaken her well, and would have shaken her better, but she escaped out of my hands and ran away."

"Would you favour me," he asked, "by watching over her this one evening, and observing that she does nothing imprudent—does not, for instance, run out into the night-air immediately after dancing?"

"I may, perhaps, look after her a little; since you wish it; but she likes her own way too well to submit readily to control."

"She is so young, so thoroughly artless," said he.

"To me she is an enigma," I responded.

"Is she?" he asked—much interested. "How?"

"It would be difficult to say how—difficult, at least, to tell you how."

"And why me?"

"I wonder she is not better pleased that you are so much her friend."

"But she has not the slightest idea how much I am her friend. That is precisely the point I cannot teach her. May I

Villette

inquire did she ever speak of me to you?"

"Under the name of 'Isidore' she has talked about you often; but I must add that it is only within the last ten minutes I have discovered that you and 'Isidore' are identical. It is only, Dr. John, within that brief space of time I have learned that Ginevra Fanshawe is the person, under this roof, in whom you have long been interested—that she is the magnet which attracts you to the Rue Fossette, that for her sake you venture into this garden, and seek out caskets dropped by rivals."

"You know all?"

"I know so much."

"For more than a year I have been accustomed to meet her in society. Mrs. Cholmondeley, her friend, is an acquaintance of mine; thus I see her every Sunday. But you observed that under the name of 'Isidore' she often spoke of me: may I—without inviting you to a breach of confidence—inquire what was the tone, what the feeling of her remarks? I feel somewhat anxious to know, being a little tormented with uncertainty as to how I stand with her."

"Oh, she varies: she shifts and changes like the wind."

"Still, you can gather some general idea—?"

"I can," thought I, "but it would not do to communicate that general idea to you. Besides, if I said she did not love you, I know you would not believe me."

"You are silent," he pursued. "I suppose you have no good news to impart. No matter. If she feels for me positive coldness and aversion, it is a sign I do not deserve her."

"Do you doubt yourself? Do you consider yourself the inferior of Colonel de Hamal?"

"I love Miss Fanshawe far more than de Hamal loves any human being, and would care for and guard her better than he. Respecting de Hamal, I fear she is under an illusion; the man's character is known to me, all his antecedents, all his scrapes. He is not worthy of your beautiful young friend."

"My 'beautiful young friend' ought to know that, and to know or feel who is worthy of her," said I. "If her beauty or her brains will not serve her so far, she merits the sharp lesson of experience."

"Are you not a little severe?"

"I am excessively severe — more severe than I choose to show you. You should hear the strictures with which I favour my 'beautiful young friend,' only that you would be unutterably shocked at my want of tender considerateness for her delicate nature."

"She is so lovely, one cannot but be loving towards her. You — every woman older than herself, must feel for such a simple, innocent, girlish fairy a sort of motherly or elder-sisterly fondness. Graceful angel! Does not your heart yearn towards her when she pours into your ear her pure, childlike confidences? How you are privileged!" And he sighed.

"I cut short these confidences somewhat abruptly now and then," said I. "But excuse me, Dr. John, may I change the theme for one instant? What a god-like person is that de Hamal! What a nose on his face — perfect! Model one in putty or clay, you could not make a better or straighter, or neater; and then, such classic lips and chin — and his bearing — sublime."

"De Hamal is an unutterable puppy, besides being a very white-livered hero."

"You, Dr. John, and every man of a less-refined mould than he, must feel for him a sort of admiring affection, such as Mars and the coarser deities may be supposed to have borne the young, graceful Apollo."

"An unprincipled, gambling little jackanapes!" said Dr. John curtly, "whom, with one hand, I could lift up by the waistband any day, and lay low in the kennel if I liked."

"The sweet seraph!" said I. "What a cruel idea! Are you not a little severe, Dr. John?"

And now I paused. For the second time that night I was going beyond myself — venturing out of what I looked on as my natural habits — speaking in an unpremeditated, impulsive strain, which startled me strangely when I halted to reflect. On rising that morning, had I anticipated that before night I should have acted the part of a gay lover in a vaudeville; and an hour after, frankly discussed with Dr. John the question of his hapless suit, and rallied him on his illusions? I had no more presaged such feats than I had looked forward to an ascent in a balloon, or a voyage to Cape Horn.

The Doctor and I, having paced down the walk, were now returning; the reflex from the window again lit his face: he smiled, but his eye was melancholy. How I wished that he could feel heart's-ease! How I grieved that he brooded over pain, and pain from such a cause! He, with his great advantages, he to love in vain! I did not then know that the pensiveness of reverse is the best phase for some minds; nor did I reflect that some herbs, "though scentless when entire, yield fragrance when they're bruised."

"Do not be sorrowful, do not grieve," I broke out. "If there is in Ginevra one spark of worthiness of your affection, she will—she must feel devotion in return. Be cheerful, be hopeful, Dr. John. Who should hope, if not you?"

In return for this speech I got—what, it must be supposed, I deserved—a look of surprise: I thought also of some disapprobation. We parted, and I went into the house very chill. The clocks struck and the bells tolled midnight; people were leaving fast: the fête was over; the lamps were fading. In another hour all the dwelling-house, and all the pensionnat, were dark and hushed. I too was in bed, but not asleep. To me it was not easy to sleep after a day of such excitement.

CHAPTER XV.
THE LONG VACATION.

Following Madame Beck's fête, with its three preceding weeks of relaxation, its brief twelve hours' burst of hilarity and dissipation, and its one subsequent day of utter languor, came a period of reaction; two months of real application, of close, hard study. These two months, being the last of the "année scolaire," were indeed the only genuine working months in the year. To them was procrastinated — into them concentrated, alike by professors, mistresses, and pupils — the main burden of preparation for the examinations preceding the distribution of prizes. Candidates for rewards had then to work in good earnest; masters and teachers had to set their shoulders to the wheel, to urge on the backward, and diligently aid and train the more promising. A showy demonstration — a telling exhibition — must be got up for public view, and all means were fair to this end.

I scarcely noted how the other teachers went to work; I had my own business to mind; and my task was not the least onerous, being to imbue some ninety sets of brains with a due tincture of what they considered a most complicated and difficult science, that of the English language; and to drill ninety tongues in what, for them, was an almost impossible pronunciation — the lisping and hissing dentals of the Isles.

The examination-day arrived. Awful day! Prepared for with anxious care, dressed for with silent despatch — nothing vaporous or fluttering now — no white gauze or azure streamers; the grave, close, compact was the order of the toilette. It seemed to me that I was this day, especially doomed — the main burden and trial falling on me alone of all the female teachers. The others were not expected to examine in the studies they taught; the professor of literature, M. Paul, taking upon himself this duty. He, this school autocrat, gathered all and sundry reins into the hollow of his one hand; he irefully rejected any colleague; he would not have help. Madame herself, who evidently rather wished to undertake the examination in geography — her favourite study, which she taught well — was forced to succumb, and be subordinate to her despotic kinsman's direction. The whole staff of instructors, male and female, he set aside, and stood on the examiner's estrade alone. It irked him that he was forced to make one exception to this rule. He could not manage English: he was obliged to leave that branch of education in the English teacher's hands; which he did, not without a flash of naïve jealousy.

A constant crusade against the "amour-propre" of every human being but himself, was the crotchet of this able, but fiery and grasping little man. He had a strong relish for public representation in his own person, but an extreme abhorrence of the like display in any other. He quelled, he kept down when he could; and when he could not, he fumed like a bottled storm.

On the evening preceding the examination-day, I was walking in the garden, as were the other teachers and all the boarders. M. Emanuel joined me in the "allée défendue;" his cigar was at his lips; his paletôt—a most characteristic garment of no particular shape—hung dark and menacing; the tassel of his bonnet grec sternly shadowed his left temple; his black whiskers curled like those of a wrathful cat; his blue eye had a cloud in its glitter.

"Ainsi," he began, abruptly fronting and arresting me, "vous allez trôner comme une reine; demain—trôner à mes côtés? Sans doute vous savourez d'avance les délices de l'autorité. Je crois voir en je ne sais quoi de rayonnante, petite ambitieuse!"

Now the fact was, he happened to be entirely mistaken. I did not—could not—estimate the admiration or the good opinion of tomorrow's audience at the same rate he did. Had that audience numbered as many personal friends and acquaintance for me as for him, I know not how it might have been: I speak of the case as it stood. On me school-triumphs shed but a cold lustre. I had wondered—and I wondered now—how it was that for him they seemed to shine as with hearth-warmth and hearth-glow. He cared for them perhaps too much; I, probably, too little. However, I had my own fancies as well as he. I liked, for instance, to see M. Emanuel jealous; it lit up his nature, and woke his spirit; it threw all sorts of queer lights and shadows over his dun face, and into his violet-azure eyes (he used to say that his black hair and blue eyes were "une de ses beautés"). There was a relish in his anger; it was artless, earnest, quite unreasonable, but never hypocritical. I uttered no disclaimer then of the complacency he attributed to me; I merely asked where the English examination came in—whether at the commencement or close of the day?

"I hesitate," said he, "whether at the very beginning, before many persons are come, and when your aspiring nature will not be gratified by a large audience, or quite at the close, when everybody is tired, and only a jaded and worn-out attention will be at your service."

"Que vous êtes dur, Monsieur!" I said, affecting dejection.

"One ought to be 'dur' with you. You are one of those beings who must be kept down. I know you! I know you! Other people in this house see you pass, and think that a colourless shadow has gone by. As for me, I scrutinized your face once, and it sufficed."

"You are satisfied that you understand me?"

Without answering directly, he went on, "Were you not gratified when you succeeded in that vaudeville? I watched you and saw a passionate ardour for triumph in your physiognomy. What fire shot into the glance! Not mere light, but flame: je me tiens pour averti."

"What feeling I had on that occasion, Monsieur—and pardon me, if I say, you immensely exaggerate both its quality and quantity—was quite abstract. I did not care for the vaudeville. I hated the part you assigned me. I had not the slightest sympathy with the audience below the stage. They are good people, doubtless, but do I know them? Are they anything to me? Can I care for being brought before their view again to-morrow? Will the examination be anything but a task to me—a task I wish well over?"

"Shall I take it out of your hands?"

"With all my heart; if you do not fear failure."

"But I should fail. I only know three phrases of English, and a few words: par exemple, de sonn, de mone, de stare—est-ce bien dit? My opinion is that it would be better to give up the thing altogether: to have no English examination, eh?"

"If Madame consents, I consent."

"Heartily?"

"Very heartily."

He smoked his cigar in silence. He turned suddenly.

"Donnez-moi la main," said he, and the spite and jealousy melted out of his face, and a generous kindliness shone there instead.

"Come, we will not be rivals, we will be friends," he

Villette

pursued. "The examination shall take place, and I will choose a good moment; and instead of vexing and hindering, as I felt half-inclined ten minutes ago—for I have my malevolent moods: I always had from childhood—I will aid you sincerely. After all, you are solitary and a stranger, and have your way to make and your bread to earn; it may be well that you should become known. We will be friends: do you agree?"

"Out of my heart, Monsieur. I am glad of a friend. I like that better than a triumph."

"Pauvrette!" said he, and turned away and left the alley.

The examination passed over well; M. Paul was as good as his word, and did his best to make my part easy. The next day came the distribution of prizes; that also passed; the school broke up; the pupils went home, and now began the long vacation.

That vacation! Shall I ever forget it? I think not. Madame Beck went, the first day of the holidays, to join her children at the sea-side; all the three teachers had parents or friends with whom they took refuge; every professor quitted the city; some went to Paris, some to Boue-Marine; M. Paul set forth on a pilgrimage to Rome; the house was left quite empty, but for me, a servant, and a poor deformed and imbecile pupil, a sort of crétin, whom her stepmother in a distant province would not allow to return home.

My heart almost died within me; miserable longings strained its chords. How long were the September days! How silent, how lifeless! How vast and void seemed the desolate premises! How gloomy the forsaken garden—grey now with the dust of a town summer departed. Looking forward at the commencement of those eight weeks, I hardly knew how I was to live to the end. My spirits had long been gradually sinking; now that the prop of employment was withdrawn, they went down fast. Even to look forward was not to hope: the dumb future spoke no comfort, offered no promise, gave no inducement to bear present evil in reliance on future good. A sorrowful indifference to existence often pressed on me—a despairing resignation to reach betimes the end of all things earthly. Alas! When I had full leisure to look on life as life must be looked on by such as me, I found it but a hopeless desert: tawny sands, with no green fields, no palm-tree, no well in view. The hopes which are dear to youth, which bear it up and lead it on, I knew not and dared not know. If they knocked at my heart sometimes, an inhospitable bar to admission must be inwardly drawn. When they turned away thus rejected, tears sad enough sometimes flowed: but it could not be helped: I dared not give such guests lodging. So mortally did I fear the sin and weakness of presumption.

Religious reader, you will preach to me a long sermon about what I have just written, and so will you, moralist: and you, stern sage: you, stoic, will frown; you, cynic, sneer; you, epicure, laugh. Well, each and all, take it your own way. I accept the sermon, frown, sneer, and laugh; perhaps you are all right: and perhaps, circumstanced like me, you would have been, like me, wrong. The first month was, indeed, a long, black, heavy month to me.

The crétin did not seem unhappy. I did my best to feed her well and keep her warm, and she only asked food and sunshine, or when that lacked, fire. Her weak faculties approved of inertion: her brain, her eyes, her ears, her heart slept content; they could not wake to work, so lethargy was their Paradise.

Three weeks of that vacation were hot, fair, and dry, but the fourth and fifth were tempestuous and wet. I do not know why that change in the atmosphere made a cruel impression on me, why the raging storm and beating rain crushed me with a deadlier paralysis than I had experienced while the air had remained serene; but so it was; and my nervous system could hardly support what it had for many days and nights to undergo in that huge empty house. How I used to pray to Heaven for consolation and support! With what dread force the conviction would grasp me that Fate was my permanent foe, never to be conciliated. I did not, in my heart, arraign the mercy or justice of God for this; I concluded it to be a part of his great plan that some must deeply suffer while they live, and I thrilled in the certainty that of this number, I was one.

It was some relief when an aunt of the crétin, a kind old woman, came one day, and took away my strange, deformed companion. The hapless creature had been at times a heavy charge; I could not take her out beyond the garden, and I could not leave her a minute alone: for her poor mind, like her body, was warped: its propensity was to evil. A vague bent to mischief, an aimless malevolence, made constant vigilance indispensable. As she very rarely spoke, and would sit for hours together moping and mowing, and distorting her features with indescribable grimaces, it was more like being prisoned with some strange tameless animal, than associating with a human being. Then there were personal attentions to be rendered which required the nerve of a hospital nurse; my resolution was so tried, it sometimes fell dead-sick. These duties should not have fallen on me; a servant, now absent, had rendered them hitherto, and in the hurry of holiday departure, no substitute to fill this office had been provided. This tax and trial were by no means the least I have known in life. Still, menial and distasteful as they were, my mental pain was far more wasting and wearing. Attendance on the crétin deprived me often of the power and inclination to swallow a meal, and sent me faint to the fresh air, and the well or fountain in the court; but this duty never wrung my heart, or brimmed my eyes, or scalded my cheek with tears hot as molten metal.

The crétin being gone, I was free to walk out. At first I lacked courage to venture very far from the Rue Fossette, but by degrees I sought the city gates, and passed them, and then went wandering away far along chaussées, through fields, beyond cemeteries, Catholic and Protestant, beyond farmsteads, to lanes and little woods, and I know not where. A goad thrust me on, a fever forbade me to rest; a want of companionship maintained in my soul the cravings of a most deadly famine. I often walked all day, through the burning noon and the arid afternoon, and the dusk evening, and came back with moonrise.

While wandering in solitude, I would sometimes picture the present probable position of others, my acquaintance. There was Madame Beck at a cheerful watering-place with her children, her mother, and a whole troop of friends who had sought the same scene of relaxation. Zélie St. Pierre was at Paris, with her relatives; the other teachers were at their homes. There was Ginevra Fanshawe, whom certain of her connections had carried on a pleasant tour southward. Ginevra seemed to me the happiest. She was on the route of beautiful scenery; these September suns shone for her on fertile plains, where harvest and vintage matured under their mellow beam. These gold and crystal moons rose on her vision over blue horizons waved in mounted lines.

But all this was nothing; I too felt those autumn suns and saw those harvest moons, and I almost wished to be covered in with earth and turf, deep out of their influence; for I could not live in their light, nor make them comrades, nor yield them affection. But Ginevra had a kind of spirit with her, empowered to give constant strength and comfort, to gladden daylight and embalm darkness; the best of the good genii that guard humanity curtained her with his wings, and canopied her head with his bending form. By True Love was Ginevra followed: never could she be alone. Was she insensible to this presence? It seemed to me impossible: I could not realize such deadness. I imagined her grateful in secret, loving now with reserve; but purposing one day to show how much she loved: I pictured her faithful hero half conscious of her coy fondness, and comforted by that consciousness: I conceived an electric chord of sympathy between them, a fine chain of mutual understanding, sustaining union through a separation of a hundred leagues — carrying, across mound and hollow, communication by prayer and wish. Ginevra gradually became with me a sort of heroine. One day, perceiving this growing illusion, I said, "I really believe my nerves are getting overstretched: my mind has suffered somewhat too much a malady is growing upon it — what shall I do? How shall I keep well?"

Indeed there was no way to keep well under the circumstances. At last a day and night of peculiarly agonizing depression were succeeded by physical illness, I took perforce to my bed. About this time the Indian summer closed and the equinoctial storms began; and for nine dark and wet days, of which the hours rushed on all turbulent, deaf, dishevelled — bewildered with sounding hurricane — I lay in a strange fever of the nerves and blood. Sleep went quite away. I used to rise in the night, look round for her, beseech her earnestly to return. A rattle of the window, a cry of the blast only replied — Sleep never came!

I err. She came once, but in anger. Impatient of my importunity she brought with her an avenging dream. By the clock of St. Jean Baptiste, that dream remained scarce fifteen minutes — a brief space, but sufficing to wring my whole frame with unknown anguish; to confer a nameless experience that had the hue, the mien, the terror, the very tone of a visitation from eternity. Between twelve and one that night a cup was forced to my lips, black, strong, strange, drawn from no well, but filled up seething from a bottomless and boundless sea. Suffering, brewed in temporal or calculable measure, and mixed for mortal lips, tastes not as this suffering tasted. Having drank and woke, I thought all was over: the end come and past by. Trembling fearfully — as consciousness returned — ready to cry out on some fellow-creature to help me, only that I knew no fellow-creature was near enough to catch the wild summons — Goton in her far distant attic could not hear — I rose on my knees in bed. Some fearful hours went over me: indescribably was I torn, racked and oppressed in mind. Amidst the horrors of that dream I think the worst lay here. Methought the well-loved dead, who had loved me well in life, met me elsewhere, alienated: galled was my inmost spirit with an unutterable sense of despair about the future. Motive there was none why I should try to recover or wish to live; and yet quite unendurable

Villette

was the pitiless and haughty voice in which Death challenged me to engage his unknown terrors. When I tried to pray I could only utter these words: "From my youth up Thy terrors have I suffered with a troubled mind."

Most true was it.

On bringing me my tea next morning Goton urged me to call in a doctor. I would not: I thought no doctor could cure me.

One evening — and I was not delirious: I was in my sane mind, I got up — I dressed myself, weak and shaking. The solitude and the stillness of the long dormitory could not be borne any longer; the ghastly white beds were turning into spectres — the coronal of each became a death's-head, huge and sun-bleached — dead dreams of an elder world and mightier race lay frozen in their wide gaping eyeholes. That evening more firmly than ever fastened into my soul the conviction that Fate was of stone, and Hope a false idol — blind, bloodless, and of granite core. I felt, too, that the trial God had appointed me was gaining its climax, and must now be turned by my own hands, hot, feeble, trembling as they were. It rained still, and blew; but with more clemency, I thought, than it had poured and raged all day. Twilight was falling, and I deemed its influence pitiful; from the lattice I saw coming night-clouds trailing low like banners drooping. It seemed to me that at this hour there was affection and sorrow in Heaven above for all pain suffered on earth beneath; the weight of my dreadful dream became alleviated — that insufferable thought of being no more loved — no more owned, half-yielded to hope of the contrary — I was sure this hope would shine clearer if I got out from under this house-roof, which was crushing as the slab of a tomb, and went outside the city to a certain quiet hill, a long way distant in the fields. Covered with a cloak (I could not be delirious, for I had sense and recollection to put on warm clothing), forth I set. The bells of a church arrested me in passing; they seemed to call me in to the salut, and I went in. Any solemn rite, any spectacle of sincere worship, any opening for appeal to God was as welcome to me then as bread to one in extremity of want. I knelt down with others on the stone pavement. It was an old solemn church, its pervading gloom not gilded but purpled by light shed through stained glass.

Few worshippers were assembled, and, the salut over, half of them departed. I discovered soon that those left remained to confess. I did not stir. Carefully every door of the church was shut; a holy quiet sank upon, and a solemn shade gathered about us. After a space, breathless and spent in prayer, a penitent approached the confessional. I watched. She whispered her avowal; her shrift was whispered back; she returned consoled. Another went, and another. A pale lady, kneeling near me, said in a low, kind voice: — "Go you now, I am not quite prepared."

Mechanically obedient, I rose and went. I knew what I was about; my mind had run over the intent with lightning-speed. To take this step could not make me more wretched than I was; it might soothe me.

The priest within the confessional never turned his eyes to regard me; he only quietly inclined his ear to my lips. He might be a good man, but this duty had become to him a sort of form: he went through it with the phlegm of custom. I hesitated; of the formula of confession I was ignorant: instead of commencing, then, with the prelude usual, I said: — "Mon père, je suis Protestante."

He directly turned. He was not a native priest: of that class, the cast of physiognomy is, almost invariably, grovelling: I saw by his profile and brow he was a Frenchman; though grey and advanced in years, he did not, I think, lack feeling or intelligence. He inquired, not unkindly, why, being a Protestant, I came to him?

I said I was perishing for a word of advice or an accent of comfort. I had been living for some weeks quite alone; I had been ill; I had a pressure of affliction on my mind of which it would hardly any longer endure the weight.

"Was it a sin, a crime?" he inquired, somewhat startled. I reassured him on this point, and, as well as I could, I showed him the mere outline of my experience.

He looked thoughtful, surprised, puzzled. "You take me unawares," said he. "I have not had such a case as yours before: ordinarily we know our routine, and are prepared; but this makes a great break in the common course of confession. I am hardly furnished with counsel fitting the circumstances."

Of course, I had not expected he would be; but the mere relief of communication in an ear which was human and sentient, yet consecrated — the mere pouring out of some portion of long accumulating, long pent-up pain into a vessel whence it could not be again diffused — had done me good. I was already solaced.

Villette

"Must I go, father?" I asked of him as he sat silent.

"My daughter," he said kindly — and I am sure he was a kind man: he had a compassionate eye — "for the present you had better go: but I assure you your words have struck me. Confession, like other things, is apt to become formal and trivial with habit. You have come and poured your heart out; a thing seldom done. I would fain think your case over, and take it with me to my oratory. Were you of our faith I should know what to say — a mind so tossed can find repose but in the bosom of retreat, and the punctual practice of piety. The world, it is well known, has no satisfaction for that class of natures. Holy men have bidden penitents like you to hasten their path upward by penance, self-denial, and difficult good works. Tears are given them here for meat and drink — bread of affliction and waters of affliction — their recompence comes hereafter. It is my own conviction that these impressions under which you are smarting are messengers from God to bring you back to the true Church. You were made for our faith: depend upon it our faith alone could heal and help you — Protestantism is altogether too dry, cold, prosaic for you. The further I look into this matter, the more plainly I see it is entirely out of the common order of things. On no account would I lose sight of you. Go, my daughter, for the present; but return to me again."

I rose and thanked him. I was withdrawing when he signed me to return.

"You must not come to this church," said he: "I see you are ill, and this church is too cold; you must come to my house: I live — —" (and he gave me his address). "Be there to-morrow morning at ten."

In reply to this appointment, I only bowed; and pulling down my veil, and gathering round me my cloak, I glided away.

Did I, do you suppose, reader, contemplate venturing again within that worthy priest's reach? As soon should I have thought of walking into a Babylonish furnace. That priest had arms which could influence me: he was naturally kind, with a sentimental French kindness, to whose softness I knew myself not wholly impervious. Without respecting some sorts of affection, there was hardly any sort having a fibre of root in reality, which I could rely on my force wholly to withstand. Had I gone to him, he would have shown me all that was tender, and comforting, and gentle, in the honest Popish superstition. Then he would have tried to kindle, blow and stir up in me the zeal of good works. I know not how it would all have ended. We all think ourselves strong in some points; we all know ourselves weak in many; the probabilities are that had I visited Numero 10, Rue des Mages, at the hour and day appointed, I might just now, instead of writing this heretic narrative, be counting my beads in the cell of a certain Carmelite convent on the Boulevard of Crécy, in Villette. There was something of Fénélon about that benign old priest; and whatever most of his brethren may be, and whatever I may think of his Church and creed (and I like neither), of himself I must ever retain a grateful recollection. He was kind when I needed kindness; he did me good. May Heaven bless him!

Twilight had passed into night, and the lamps were lit in the streets ere I issued from that sombre church. To turn back was now become possible to me; the wild longing to breathe this October wind on the little hill far without the city walls had ceased to be an imperative impulse, and was softened into a wish with which Reason could cope: she put it down, and I turned, as I thought, to the Rue Fossette. But I had become involved in a part of the city with which I was not familiar; it was the old part, and full of narrow streets of picturesque, ancient, and mouldering houses. I was much too weak to be very collected, and I was still too careless of my own welfare and safety to be cautious; I grew embarrassed; I got immeshed in a network of turns unknown. I was lost and had no resolution to ask guidance of any passenger.

If the storm had lulled a little at sunset, it made up now for lost time. Strong and horizontal thundered the current of the wind from north-west to south-east; it brought rain like spray, and sometimes a sharp hail, like shot: it was cold and pierced me to the vitals. I bent my head to meet it, but it beat me back. My heart did not fail at all in this conflict; I only wished that I had wings and could ascend the gale, spread and repose my pinions on its strength, career in its course, sweep where it swept. While wishing this, I suddenly felt colder where before I was cold, and more powerless where before I was weak. I tried to reach the porch of a great building near, but the mass of frontage and the giant spire turned black and vanished from my eyes. Instead of sinking on the steps as I intended, I seemed to pitch headlong down an abyss. I remember no more.

CHAPTER XVI.

AULD LANG SYNE.

Where my soul went during that swoon I cannot tell. Whatever she saw, or wherever she travelled in her trance on that strange night she kept her own secret; never whispering a word to Memory, and baffling imagination by an indissoluble silence. She may have gone upward, and come in sight of her eternal home, hoping for leave to rest now, and deeming that her painful union with matter was at last dissolved. While she so deemed, an angel may have warned her away from heaven's threshold, and, guiding her weeping down, have bound her, once more, all shuddering and unwilling, to that poor frame, cold and wasted, of whose companionship she was grown more than weary.

I know she re-entered her prison with pain, with reluctance, with a moan and a long shiver. The divorced mates, Spirit and Substance, were hard to re-unite: they greeted each other, not in an embrace, but a racking sort of struggle. The returning sense of sight came upon me, red, as if it swam in blood; suspended hearing rushed back loud, like thunder; consciousness revived in fear: I sat up appalled, wondering into what region, amongst what strange beings I was waking. At first I knew nothing I looked on: a wall was not a wall—a lamp not a lamp. I should have understood what we call a ghost, as well as I did the commonest object: which is another way of intimating that all my eye rested on struck it as spectral. But the faculties soon settled each in his place; the life-machine presently resumed its wonted and regular working.

Still, I knew not where I was; only in time I saw I had been removed from the spot where I fell: I lay on no portico-step; night and tempest were excluded by walls, windows, and ceiling. Into some house I had been carried—but what house?

I could only think of the pensionnat in the Rue Fossette. Still half-dreaming, I tried hard to discover in what room they had put me; whether the great dormitory, or one of the little dormitories. I was puzzled, because I could not make the glimpses of furniture I saw accord with my knowledge of any of these apartments. The empty white beds were wanting, and the long line of large windows. "Surely," thought I, "it is not to Madame Beck's own chamber they have carried me!" And here my eye fell on an easy-chair covered with blue damask. Other seats, cushioned to match, dawned on me by degrees; and at last I took in the complete fact of a pleasant parlour, with a wood fire on a clear-shining hearth, a carpet where arabesques of bright blue relieved a ground of shaded fawn; pale walls over which a slight but endless garland of azure forget-me-nots ran mazed and bewildered amongst myriad gold leaves and tendrils. A gilded mirror filled up the space between two windows, curtained amply with blue damask. In this mirror I saw myself laid, not in bed, but on a sofa. I looked spectral; my eyes larger and more hollow, my hair darker than was natural, by contrast with my thin and ashen face. It was obvious, not only from the furniture, but from the position of windows, doors, and fireplace, that this was an unknown room in an unknown house.

Hardly less plain was it that my brain was not yet settled; for, as I gazed at the blue arm-chair, it appeared to grow familiar; so did a certain scroll-couch, and not less so the round centre-table, with a blue-covering, bordered with autumn-tinted foliage; and, above all, two little footstools with worked covers, and a small ebony-framed chair, of which the seat and back were also worked with groups of brilliant flowers on a dark ground.

Struck with these things, I explored further. Strange to say, old acquaintance were all about me, and "auld lang syne" smiled out of every nook. There were two oval miniatures over the mantel-piece, of which I knew by heart the pearls about the high and powdered "heads;" the velvets circling the white throats; the swell of the full muslin kerchiefs: the pattern of the lace sleeve-ruffles. Upon the mantel-shelf there were two china vases, some relics of a diminutive tea-service, as smooth as enamel and as thin as egg-shell, and a white centre ornament, a classic group in alabaster, preserved under glass. Of all these things I could have told the peculiarities, numbered the flaws or cracks, like any clairvoyante. Above all, there was a pair of handscreens, with elaborate pencil-drawings finished like line engravings; these, my very eyes ached at beholding again, recalling hours when they had followed, stroke by stroke and touch by touch, a tedious, feeble, finical, school-girl pencil held in these fingers, now so skeleton-like.

Where was I? Not only in what spot of the world, but in what year of our Lord? For all these objects were of past days, and of a distant country. Ten years ago I bade them good-by; since my fourteenth year they and I had never met. I gasped audibly, "Where am I?"

A shape hitherto unnoticed, stirred, rose, came forward: a

shape inharmonious with the environment, serving only to complicate the riddle further. This was no more than a sort of native bonne, in a common-place bonne's cap and print-dress. She spoke neither French nor English, and I could get no intelligence from her, not understanding her phrases of dialect. But she bathed my temples and forehead with some cool and perfumed water, and then she heightened the cushion on which I reclined, made signs that I was not to speak, and resumed her post at the foot of the sofa.

She was busy knitting; her eyes thus drawn from me, I could gaze on her without interruption. I did mightily wonder how she came there, or what she could have to do among the scenes, or with the days of my girlhood. Still more I marvelled what those scenes and days could now have to do with me.

Too weak to scrutinize thoroughly the mystery, I tried to settle it by saying it was a mistake, a dream, a fever-fit; and yet I knew there could be no mistake, and that I was not sleeping, and I believed I was sane. I wished the room had not been so well lighted, that I might not so clearly have seen the little pictures, the ornaments, the screens, the worked chair. All these objects, as well as the blue-damask furniture, were, in fact, precisely the same, in every minutest detail, with those I so well remembered, and with which I had been so thoroughly intimate, in the drawing-room of my godmother's house at Bretton. Methought the apartment only was changed, being of different proportions and dimensions.

I thought of Bedreddin Hassan, transported in his sleep from Cairo to the gates of Damascus. Had a Genius stooped his dark wing down the storm to whose stress I had succumbed, and gathering me from the church-steps, and "rising high into the air," as the eastern tale said, had he borne me over land and ocean, and laid me quietly down beside a hearth of Old England? But no; I knew the fire of that hearth burned before its Lares no more—it went out long ago, and the household gods had been carried elsewhere.

The bonne turned again to survey me, and seeing my eyes wide open, and, I suppose, deeming their expression perturbed and excited, she put down her knitting. I saw her busied for a moment at a little stand; she poured out water, and measured drops from a phial: glass in hand, she approached me. What dark-tinged draught might she now be offering? what Genii-elixir or Magi-distillation?

It was too late to inquire—I had swallowed it passively, and at once. A tide of quiet thought now came gently caressing my brain; softer and softer rose the flow, with tepid undulations smoother than balm. The pain of weakness left my limbs, my muscles slept. I lost power to move; but, losing at the same time wish, it was no privation. That kind bonne placed a screen between me and the lamp; I saw her rise to do this, but do not remember seeing her resume her place: in the interval between the two acts, I "fell on sleep."

At waking, lo! all was again changed. The light of high day surrounded me; not, indeed, a warm, summer light, but the leaden gloom of raw and blustering autumn. I felt sure now that I was in the pensionnat—sure by the beating rain on the casement; sure by the "wuther" of wind amongst trees, denoting a garden outside; sure by the chill, the whiteness, the solitude, amidst which I lay. I say whiteness—for the dimity curtains, dropped before a French bed, bounded my view.

I lifted them; I looked out. My eye, prepared to take in the range of a long, large, and whitewashed chamber, blinked baffled, on encountering the limited area of a small cabinet—a cabinet with sea-green walls; also, instead of five wide and naked windows, there was one high lattice, shaded with muslin festoons: instead of two dozen little stands of painted wood, each holding a basin and an ewer, there was a toilette-table dressed, like a lady for a ball, in a white robe over a pink skirt; a polished and large glass crowned, and a pretty pin-cushion frilled with lace, adorned it. This toilette, together with a small, low, green and white chintz arm-chair, a washstand topped with a marble slab, and supplied with utensils of pale-green ware, sufficiently furnished the tiny chamber.

Reader; I felt alarmed! Why? you will ask. What was there in this simple and somewhat pretty sleeping-closet to startle the most timid? Merely this—These articles of furniture could not be real, solid arm-chairs, looking-glasses, and washstands—they must be the ghosts of such articles; or, if this were denied as too wild an hypothesis—and, confounded as I was, I did deny it— there remained but to conclude that I had myself passed into an abnormal state of mind; in short, that I was very ill and delirious: and even then, mine was the strangest figment with which delirium had ever harassed a victim.

I knew—I was obliged to know—the green chintz of that little chair; the little snug chair itself, the carved, shining-black, foliated frame of that glass; the smooth, milky-green of the china vessels on the stand; the very stand too, with its top of grey marble, splintered at one corner;—all these I was compelled to recognise and to hail, as last night I had, perforce, recognised and hailed the rosewood, the drapery, the porcelain, of the drawing-room.

Bretton! Bretton! and ten years ago shone reflected in that mirror. And why did Bretton and my fourteenth year haunt me thus? Why, if they came at all, did they not return complete? Why hovered before my distempered vision the mere furniture, while the rooms and the locality were gone? As to that pincushion made of crimson satin, ornamented with gold beads and frilled with thread-lace, I had the same right to know it as to know the screens — I had made it myself. Rising with a start from the bed, I took the cushion in my hand and examined it. There was the cipher "L. L. B." formed in gold beds, and surrounded with an oval wreath embroidered in white silk. These were the initials of my godmother's name — Louisa Lucy Bretton.

"Am I in England? Am I at Bretton?" I muttered; and hastily pulling up the blind with which the lattice was shrouded, I looked out to try and discover where I was; half-prepared to meet the calm, old, handsome buildings and clean grey pavement of St. Ann's Street, and to see at the end the towers of the minster: or, if otherwise, fully expectant of a town view somewhere, a rue in Villette, if not a street in a pleasant and ancient English city.

I looked, on the contrary, through a frame of leafage, clustering round the high lattice, and forth thence to a grassy mead-like level, a lawn-terrace with trees rising from the lower ground beyond — high forest-trees, such as I had not seen for many a day. They were now groaning under the gale of October, and between their trunks I traced the line of an avenue, where yellow leaves lay in heaps and drifts, or were whirled singly before the sweeping west wind. Whatever landscape might lie further must have been flat, and these tall beeches shut it out. The place seemed secluded, and was to me quite strange: I did not know it at all.

Once more I lay down. My bed stood in a little alcove; on turning my face to the wall, the room with its bewildering accompaniments became excluded. Excluded? No! For as I arranged my position in this hope, behold, on the green space between the divided and looped-up curtains, hung a broad, gilded picture-frame enclosing a portrait. It was drawn — well drawn, though but a sketch — in water-colours; a head, a boy's head, fresh, life-like, speaking, and animated. It seemed a youth of sixteen, fair-complexioned, with sanguine health in his cheek;

hair long, not dark, and with a sunny sheen; penetrating eyes, an arch mouth, and a gay smile. On the whole a most pleasant face to look at, especially for those claiming a right to that youth's affections—parents, for instance, or sisters. Any romantic little school-girl might almost have loved it in its frame. Those eyes looked as if when somewhat older they would flash a lightning-response to love: I cannot tell whether they kept in store the steady-beaming shine of faith. For whatever sentiment met him in form too facile, his lips menaced, beautifully but surely, caprice and light esteem.

Striving to take each new discovery as quietly as I could, I whispered to myself—

"Ah! that portrait used to hang in the breakfast-room, over the mantel-piece: somewhat too high, as I thought. I well remember how I used to mount a music-stool for the purpose of unhooking it, holding it in my hand, and searching into those bonny wells of eyes, whose glance under their hazel lashes seemed like a pencilled laugh; and well I liked to note the colouring of the cheek, and the expression of the mouth." I hardly believed fancy could improve on the curve of that mouth, or of the chin; even my ignorance knew that both were beautiful, and pondered perplexed over this doubt: "How it was that what charmed so much, could at the same time so keenly pain?" Once, by way of test, I took little Missy Home, and, lifting her in my arms, told her to look at the picture.

"Do you like it, Polly?" I asked. She never answered, but gazed long, and at last a darkness went trembling through her sensitive eye, as she said, "Put me down." So I put her down, saying to myself. "The child feels it too."

All these things do I now think over, adding, "He had his faults, yet scarce ever was a finer nature; liberal, suave, impressible." My reflections closed in an audibly pronounced word, "Graham!"

"Graham!" echoed a sudden voice at the bedside. "Do you want Graham?"

I looked. The plot was but thickening; the wonder but culminating. If it was strange to see that well-remembered pictured form on the wall, still stranger was it to turn and behold the equally well-remembered living form opposite—a woman, a lady, most real and substantial, tall, well-attired, wearing widow's silk, and such a cap as best became her matron and motherly braids of hair. Hers, too, was a good face;

too marked, perhaps, now for beauty, but not for sense or character. She was little changed; something sterner, something more robust—but she was my godmother: still the distinct vision of Mrs. Bretton.

I kept quiet, yet internally I was much agitated: my pulse fluttered, and the blood left my cheek, which turned cold.

"Madam, where am I?" I inquired.

"In a very safe asylum; well protected for the present; make your mind quite easy till you get a little better; you look ill this morning."

"I am so entirely bewildered, I do not know whether I can trust my senses at all, or whether they are misleading me in every particular: but you speak English, do you not, madam?"

"I should think you might hear that: it would puzzle me to hold a long discourse in French."

"You do not come from England?"

"I am lately arrived thence. Have you been long in this country? You seem to know my son?"

"Do, I, madam? Perhaps I do. Your son—the picture there?"

"That is his portrait as a youth. While looking at it, you pronounced his name."

"Graham Bretton?"

She nodded.

"I speak to Mrs. Bretton, formerly of Bretton, ——shire?"

"Quite right; and you, I am told, are an English teacher in a foreign school here: my son recognised you as such."

"How was I found, madam, and by whom?"

"My son shall tell you that by-and-by," said she; "but at present you are too confused and weak for conversation: try to eat some breakfast, and then sleep."

Notwithstanding all I had undergone—the bodily fatigue, the perturbation of spirits, the exposure to weather—it seemed that I was better: the fever, the real malady which had oppressed my frame, was abating; for, whereas during the last nine days I had taken no solid food, and suffered from continual thirst, this morning, on breakfast being offered, I experienced a craving for nourishment: an inward faintness which caused me eagerly to taste the tea this lady offered, and to eat the morsel of dry toast she allowed in accompaniment. It was only a morsel, but it sufficed; keeping up my strength till some two or three hours afterwards, when the bonne brought me a little cup of broth and a biscuit.

As evening began to darken, and the ceaseless blast still blew wild and cold, and the rain streamed on, deluge-like, I grew weary—very weary of my bed. The room, though pretty, was small: I felt it confining: I longed for a change. The increasing chill and gathering gloom, too, depressed me; I wanted to see—to feel firelight. Besides, I kept thinking of the son of that tall matron: when should I see him? Certainly not till I left my room.

At last the bonne came to make my bed for the night. She prepared to wrap me in a blanket and place me in the little chintz chair; but, declining these attentions, I proceeded to dress myself:

The business was just achieved, and I was sitting down to take breath, when Mrs. Bretton once more appeared.

"Dressed!" she exclaimed, smiling with that smile I so well knew—a pleasant smile, though not soft. "You are quite better then? Quite strong—eh?"

She spoke to me so much as of old she used to speak that I almost fancied she was beginning to know me. There was the same sort of patronage in her voice and manner that, as a girl, I had always experienced from her—a patronage I yielded to and even liked; it was not founded on conventional grounds of superior wealth or station (in the last particular there had never been any inequality; her degree was mine); but on natural reasons of physical advantage: it was the shelter the tree gives the herb. I put a request without further ceremony.

"Do let me go down-stairs, madam; I am so cold and dull here."

"I desire nothing better, if you are strong enough to bear the change," was her reply. "Come then; here is an arm." And she offered me hers: I took it, and we descended one flight of carpeted steps to a landing where a tall door, standing open, gave admission into the blue-damask room. How pleasant it was in its air of perfect domestic comfort! How warm in its amber lamp-light and vermilion fire-flush! To render the picture perfect, tea stood ready on the table—an English tea, whereof the whole shining service glanced at me familiarly; from the solid silver urn, of antique pattern, and the massive pot of the same metal, to the thin porcelain cups, dark with purple and gilding. I knew the very seed-cake of peculiar form, baked in a peculiar mould, which always had a place on the tea-table at Bretton. Graham liked it, and there it was as of yore—set before Graham's plate with the silver knife and fork beside it. Graham was then expected to tea: Graham was now, perhaps, in the house; ere many minutes I might see him.

"Sit down—sit down," said my conductress, as my step faltered a little in passing to the hearth. She seated me on the sofa, but I soon passed behind it, saying the fire was too hot; in its shade I found another seat which suited me better. Mrs. Bretton was never wont to make a fuss about any person or anything; without remonstrance she suffered me to have my own way. She made the tea, and she took up the newspaper. I liked to watch every action of my godmother; all her movements were so young: she must have been now above fifty, yet neither her sinews nor her spirit seemed yet touched by the rust of age. Though portly, she was alert, and though serene, she was at times impetuous—good health and an excellent temperament kept her green as in her spring.

While she read, I perceived she listened—listened for her son. She was not the woman ever to confess herself uneasy, but there was yet no lull in the weather, and if Graham were out in that hoarse wind—roaring still unsatisfied—I well knew his mother's heart would be out with him.

"Ten minutes behind his time," said she, looking at her watch; then, in another minute, a lifting of her eyes from the page, and a slight inclination of her head towards the door, denoted that she heard some sound. Presently her brow cleared; and then even my ear, less practised, caught the iron clash of a gate swung to, steps on gravel, lastly the door-bell. He was come. His mother filled the teapot from the urn, she drew nearer the hearth the stuffed and cushioned blue chair—her own chair by right, but I saw there was one who might with impunity usurp it. And when that one came up the stairs—which he soon did, after, I suppose, some such attention to the toilet as the wild and wet night rendered necessary, and strode straight in—

"Is it you, Graham?" said his mother, hiding a glad smile and speaking curtly.

"Who else should it be, mamma?" demanded the Unpunctual, possessing himself irreverently of the abdicated throne.

"Don't you deserve cold tea, for being late?"

"I shall not get my deserts, for the urn sings cheerily."

"Wheel yourself to the table, lazy boy: no seat will serve you but mine; if you had one spark of a sense of propriety, you would always leave that chair for the Old Lady."

"So I should; only the dear Old Lady persists in leaving it for me. How is your patient, mamma?"

"Will she come forward and speak for herself?" said Mrs. Bretton, turning to my corner; and at this invitation, forward I came. Graham courteously rose up to greet me. He stood tall on the hearth, a figure justifying his mother's unconcealed pride.

"So you are come down," said he; "you must be better then—much better. I scarcely expected we should meet thus, or here. I was alarmed last night, and if I had not been forced to hurry away to a dying patient, I certainly would not have left you; but my mother herself is something of a doctress, and Martha an excellent nurse. I saw the case was a fainting-fit, not necessarily dangerous. What brought it on, I have yet to learn, and all particulars; meantime, I trust you really do feel better?"

"Much better," I said calmly. "Much better, I thank you, Dr. John."

For, reader, this tall young man—this darling son—this host of mine—this Graham Bretton, was Dr. John: he, and no other; and, what is more, I ascertained this identity scarcely with surprise. What is more, when I heard Graham's step on the stairs, I knew what manner of figure would enter, and for whose aspect to prepare my eyes. The discovery was not of to-day, its dawn had penetrated my perceptions long since. Of course I remembered young Bretton well; and though ten years (from sixteen to twenty-six) may greatly change the boy as they mature him to the man, yet they could bring no such utter difference as would suffice wholly to blind my eyes, or baffle my memory. Dr. John Graham Bretton retained still an affinity to the youth of sixteen: he had his eyes; he had some of his features; to wit, all the excellently-moulded lower half of the face; I found him out soon. I first recognised him on that occasion, noted several chapters back, when my unguardedly-fixed attention had drawn on me the mortification of an implied rebuke. Subsequent observation confirmed, in every point, that early surmise. I traced in the gesture, the port, and the habits of his manhood, all his boy's promise. I heard in his now deep tones the accent of former days. Certain turns of phrase, peculiar to him of old, were peculiar to him still; and so was many a trick of eye and lip, many a smile, many a sudden ray levelled from the irid, under his well-charactered brow.

To say anything on the subject, to hint at my discovery, had not suited my habits of thought, or assimilated with my system of feeling. On the contrary, I had preferred to keep the matter to myself. I liked entering his presence covered with a cloud he had not seen through, while he stood before me under a ray of special illumination which shone all partial over his head, trembled about his feet, and cast light no farther.

Well I knew that to him it could make little difference, were I to come forward and announce, "This is Lucy Snowe!" So I kept back in my teacher's place; and as he never asked my name, so I never gave it. He heard me called "Miss," and "Miss Lucy;" he never heard the surname, "Snowe." As to spontaneous recognition—though I, perhaps, was still less changed than he—the idea never approached his mind, and why should I suggest it?

During tea, Dr. John was kind, as it was his nature to be; that meal over, and the tray carried out, he made a cosy arrangement of the cushions in a corner of the sofa, and obliged me to settle amongst them. He and his mother also drew to the fire, and ere we had sat ten minutes, I caught the eye of the latter fastened steadily upon me. Women are certainly quicker in some things than men.

"Well," she exclaimed, presently, "I have seldom seen a stronger likeness! Graham, have you observed it?"

"Observed what? What ails the Old Lady now? How you stare, mamma! One would think you had an attack of second sight."

"Tell me, Graham, of whom does that young lady remind you?" pointing to me.

"Mamma, you put her out of countenance. I often tell you

abruptness is your fault; remember, too, that to you she is a stranger, and does not know your ways."

"Now, when she looks down; now, when she turns sideways, who is she like, Graham?"

"Indeed, mamma, since you propound the riddle, I think you ought to solve it!"

"And you have known her some time, you say—ever since you first began to attend the school in the Rue Fossette:—yet you never mentioned to me that singular resemblance!"

"I could not mention a thing of which I never thought, and which I do not now acknowledge. What can you mean?"

"Stupid boy! look at her."

Graham did look: but this was not to be endured; I saw how it must end, so I thought it best to anticipate.

"Dr. John," I said, "has had so much to do and think of, since he and I shook hands at our last parting in St. Ann's Street, that, while I readily found out Mr. Graham Bretton, some months ago, it never occurred to me as possible that he should recognise Lucy Snowe."

"Lucy Snowe! I thought so! I knew it!" cried Mrs. Bretton. And she at once stepped across the hearth and kissed me. Some ladies would, perhaps, have made a great bustle upon such a discovery without being particularly glad of it; but it was not my godmother's habit to make a bustle, and she preferred all sentimental demonstrations in bas-relief. So she and I got over the surprise with few words and a single salute; yet I daresay she was pleased, and I know I was. While we renewed old acquaintance, Graham, sitting opposite, silently disposed of his paroxysm of astonishment.

"Mamma calls me a stupid boy, and I think I am so," at length he said; "for, upon my honour, often as I have seen you, I never once suspected this fact: and yet I perceive it all now. Lucy Snowe! To be sure! I recollect her perfectly, and there she sits; not a doubt of it. But," he added, "you surely have not known me as an old acquaintance all this time, and never mentioned it."

"That I have," was my answer.

Villette

Dr. John commented not. I supposed he regarded my silence as eccentric, but he was indulgent in refraining from censure. I daresay, too, he would have deemed it impertinent to have interrogated me very closely, to have asked me the why and wherefore of my reserve; and, though he might feel a little curious, the importance of the case was by no means such as to tempt curiosity to infringe on discretion.

For my part, I just ventured to inquire whether he remembered the circumstance of my once looking at him very fixedly; for the slight annoyance he had betrayed on that occasion still lingered sore on my mind.

"I think I do!" said he: "I think I was even cross with you."

"You considered me a little bold; perhaps?" I inquired.

"Not at all. Only, shy and retiring as your general manner was, I wondered what personal or facial enormity in me proved so magnetic to your usually averted eyes."

"You see how it was now?"

"Perfectly."

And here Mrs. Bretton broke in with many, many questions about past times; and for her satisfaction I had to recur to gone-by troubles, to explain causes of seeming estrangement, to touch on single-handed conflict with Life, with Death, with Grief, with Fate. Dr. John listened, saying little. He and she then told me of changes they had known: even with them all had not gone smoothly, and fortune had retrenched her once abundant gifts. But so courageous a mother, with such a champion in her son, was well fitted to fight a good fight with the world, and to prevail ultimately. Dr. John himself was one of those on whose birth benign planets have certainly smiled. Adversity might set against him her most sullen front: he was the man to beat her down with smiles. Strong and cheerful, and firm and courteous; not rash, yet valiant; he was the aspirant to woo Destiny herself, and to win from her stone eyeballs a beam almost loving.

In the profession he had adopted, his success was now quite decided. Within the last three months he had taken this house (a small château, they told me, about half a league without the Porte de Crécy); this country site being chosen for the sake of his mother's health, with which town air did not now agree. Hither he had invited Mrs. Bretton, and she, on leaving England, had brought with her such residue furniture of the former St. Ann's Street mansion as she had thought fit to keep unsold. Hence my bewilderment at the phantoms of chairs, and the wraiths of looking-glasses, tea-urns, and teacups.

As the clock struck eleven, Dr. John stopped his mother.

"Miss Snowe must retire now," he said; "she is beginning to look very pale. To-morrow I will venture to put some questions respecting the cause of her loss of health. She is much changed, indeed, since last July, when I saw her enact with no little spirit the part of a very killing fine gentleman. As to last night's catastrophe, I am sure thereby hangs a tale, but we will inquire no further this evening. Good-night, Miss Lucy."

And so he kindly led me to the door, and holding a wax-candle, lighted me up the one flight of stairs.

When I had said my prayers, and when I was undressed and laid down, I felt that I still had friends. Friends, not professing vehement attachment, not offering the tender solace of well-matched and congenial relationship; on whom, therefore, but moderate demand of affection was to be made, of whom but moderate expectation formed; but towards whom my heart softened instinctively, and yearned with an importunate gratitude, which I entreated Reason betimes to check.

"Do not let me think of them too often, too much, too fondly," I implored: "let me be content with a temperate draught of this living stream: let me not run athirst, and apply passionately to its welcome waters: let me not imagine in them a sweeter taste than earth's fountains know. Oh! would to God I may be enabled to feel enough sustained by an occasional, amicable intercourse, rare, brief, unengrossing and tranquil: quite tranquil!"

Still repeating this word, I turned to my pillow; and still repeating it, I steeped that pillow with tears.

CHAPTER XVII.

LA TERRASSE.

These struggles with the natural character, the strong native bent of the heart, may seem futile and fruitless, but in the end they do good. They tend, however slightly, to give the actions, the conduct, that turn which Reason approves, and which Feeling, perhaps, too often opposes: they certainly make a difference in the general tenour of a life, and enable it to be better regulated, more equable, quieter on the surface; and it is on the surface only the common gaze will fall. As to what lies below, leave that with God. Man, your equal, weak as you, and not fit to be your judge, may be shut out thence: take it to your Maker—show Him the secrets of the spirit He gave—ask Him how you are to bear the pains He has appointed—kneel in His presence, and pray with faith for light in darkness, for strength in piteous weakness, for patience in extreme need. Certainly, at some hour, though perhaps not your hour, the waiting waters will stir; in some shape, though perhaps not the shape you dreamed, which your heart loved, and for which it bled, the healing herald will descend, the cripple and the blind, and the dumb, and the possessed will be led to bathe. Herald, come quickly! Thousands lie round the pool, weeping and despairing, to see it, through slow years, stagnant. Long are the "times" of Heaven: the orbits of angel messengers seem wide to mortal vision; they may enring ages: the cycle of one departure and return may clasp unnumbered generations; and dust, kindling to brief suffering life, and through pain, passing back to dust, may meanwhile perish out of memory again, and yet again. To how many maimed and mourning millions is the first and sole angel visitant, him easterns call Azrael!

I tried to get up next morning, but while I was dressing, and at intervals drinking cold water from the carafe on my washstand, with design to brace up that trembling weakness which made dressing so difficult, in came Mrs. Bretton.

"Here is an absurdity!" was her morning accost. "Not so," she added, and dealing with me at once in her own brusque, energetic fashion—that fashion which I used formerly to enjoy seeing applied to her son, and by him vigorously resisted—in two minutes she consigned me captive to the French bed.

"There you lie till afternoon," said she. "My boy left orders before he went out that such should be the case, and I can assure you my son is master and must be obeyed. Presently you shall have breakfast."

Presently she brought that meal—brought it with her own active hands—not leaving me to servants. She seated herself on the bed while I ate. Now it is not everybody, even amongst our respected friends and esteemed acquaintance, whom we like to have near us, whom we like to watch us, to wait on us, to approach us with the proximity of a nurse to a patient. It is not every friend whose eye is a light in a sick room, whose presence is there a solace: but all this was Mrs. Bretton to me; all this she had ever been. Food or drink never pleased me so well as when it came through her hands. I do not remember the occasion when her entrance into a room had not made that room cheerier. Our natures own predilections and antipathies alike strange. There are people from whom we secretly shrink, whom we would personally avoid, though reason confesses that they are good people: there are others with faults of temper, &c., evident enough, beside whom we live content, as if the air about them did us good. My godmother's lively black eye and clear brunette cheek, her warm, prompt hand, her self-reliant mood, her decided bearing, were all beneficial to me as the atmosphere of some salubrious climate. Her son used to call her "the old lady;" it filled me with pleasant wonder to note how the alacrity and power of five-and-twenty still breathed from her and around her.

"I would bring my work here," she said, as she took from me the emptied teacup, "and sit with you the whole day, if that overbearing John Graham had not put his veto upon such a proceeding. 'Now, mamma,' he said, when he went out, 'take notice, you are not to knock up your god-daughter with gossip,' and he particularly desired me to keep close to my own quarters, and spare you my fine company. He says, Lucy, he thinks you have had a nervous fever, judging from your look,—is that so?"

I replied that I did not quite know what my ailment had been, but that I had certainly suffered a good deal especially in mind. Further, on this subject, I did not consider it advisable to dwell, for the details of what I had undergone belonged to a portion of my existence in which I never expected my godmother to take a share. Into what a new region would such a confidence have led that hale, serene nature! The difference between her and me might be figured by that between the stately ship cruising safe on smooth seas, with its full complement of crew, a captain gay and brave, and venturous and provident; and the life-boat, which most days of the year lies dry and solitary in an old, dark boat-house, only putting to sea when the billows run high in rough weather, when cloud encounters water, when danger and death divide between them the rule of the great deep. No, the "Louisa Bretton" never was out of harbour on such a night, and in such a scene: her crew could not conceive it; so the half-drowned life-boat man keeps his own counsel, and spins no yarns.

She left me, and I lay in bed content: it was good of Graham to remember me before he went out.

My day was lonely, but the prospect of coming evening abridged and cheered it. Then, too, I felt weak, and rest seemed welcome; and after the morning hours were gone by, — those hours which always bring, even to the necessarily unoccupied, a sense of business to be done, of tasks waiting fulfilment, a vague impression of obligation to be employed — when this stirring time was past, and the silent descent of afternoon hushed housemaid steps on the stairs and in the chambers, I then passed into a dreamy mood, not unpleasant.

My calm little room seemed somehow like a cave in the sea. There was no colour about it, except that white and pale green, suggestive of foam and deep water; the blanched cornice was adorned with shell-shaped ornaments, and there were white mouldings like dolphins in the ceiling-angles. Even that one touch of colour visible in the red satin pincushion bore affinity to coral; even that dark, shining glass might have mirrored a mermaid. When I closed my eyes, I heard a gale, subsiding at last, bearing upon the house-front like a settling swell upon a rock-base. I heard it drawn and withdrawn far, far off, like a tide retiring from a shore of the upper world — a world so high above that the rush of its largest waves, the dash of its fiercest breakers, could sound down in this submarine home, only like murmurs and a lullaby.

Amidst these dreams came evening, and then Martha brought a light; with her aid I was quickly dressed, and stronger now than in the morning, I made my way down to the blue saloon unassisted.

Dr. John, it appears, had concluded his round of professional calls earlier than usual; his form was the first object that met my eyes as I entered the parlour; he stood in that window-recess opposite the door, reading the close type of a newspaper by such dull light as closing day yet gave. The fire shone clear, but the lamp stood on the table unlit, and tea was not yet brought up.

As to Mrs. Bretton, my active godmother—who, I afterwards found, had been out in the open air all day—lay half-reclined in her deep-cushioned chair, actually lost in a nap. Her son seeing me, came forward. I noticed that he trod carefully, not to wake the sleeper; he also spoke low: his mellow voice never had any sharpness in it; modulated as at present, it was calculated rather to soothe than startle slumber.

"This is a quiet little château," he observed, after inviting me to sit near the casement. "I don't know whether you may have noticed it in your walks: though, indeed, from the chaussée it is not visible; just a mile beyond the Porte de Crécy, you turn down a lane which soon becomes an avenue, and that leads you on, through meadow and shade, to the very door of this house. It is not a modern place, but built somewhat in the old style of the Basse-Ville. It is rather a manoir than a château; they call it 'La Terrasse,' because its front rises from a broad turfed walk, whence steps lead down a grassy slope to the avenue. See yonder! The moon rises: she looks well through the tree-boles."

Where, indeed, does the moon not look well? What is the scene, confined or expansive, which her orb does not hallow? Rosy or fiery, she mounted now above a not distant bank; even while we watched her flushed ascent, she cleared to gold, and in very brief space, floated up stainless into a now calm sky. Did moonlight soften or sadden Dr. Bretton? Did it touch him with romance? I think it did. Albeit of no sighing mood, he sighed in watching it: sighed to himself quietly. No need to ponder the cause or the course of that sigh; I knew it was wakened by beauty; I knew it pursued Ginevra. Knowing this, the idea pressed upon me that it was in some sort my duty to speak the name he meditated. Of course he was ready for the subject: I saw in his countenance a teeming plenitude of comment, question and interest; a pressure of language and sentiment, only checked, I thought, by sense of embarrassment how to begin. To spare him this embarrassment was my best, indeed my sole use. I had but to utter the idol's name, and love's tender litany would flow out. I had just found a fitting phrase, "You know that Miss Fanshawe is gone on a tour with the Cholmondeleys," and was opening my lips to speak to it, when he scattered my plans by introducing another theme.

"The first thing this morning," said he, putting his sentiment in his pocket, turning from the moon, and sitting down, "I went to the Rue Fossette, and told the cuisinière that you were safe and in good hands. Do you know that I actually found that she had not yet discovered your absence from the house: she thought you safe in the great dormitory. With what care you

Villette

must have been waited on!"

"Oh! all that is very conceivable," said I. "Goton could do nothing for me but bring me a little tisane and a crust of bread, and I had rejected both so often during the past week, that the good woman got tired of useless journeys from the dwelling-house kitchen to the school-dormitory, and only came once a day at noon to make my bed. I believe, however, that she is a good-natured creature, and would have been delighted to cook me côtelettes de mouton, if I could have eaten them."

"What did Madame Beck mean by leaving you alone?"

"Madame Beck could not foresee that I should fall ill."

"Your nervous system bore a good share of the suffering?"

"I am not quite sure what my nervous system is, but I was dreadfully low-spirited."

"Which disables me from helping you by pill or potion. Medicine can give nobody good spirits. My art halts at the threshold of Hypochondria: she just looks in and sees a chamber of torture, but can neither say nor do much. Cheerful society would be of use; you should be as little alone as possible; you should take plenty of exercise."

Acquiescence and a pause followed these remarks. They sounded all right, I thought, and bore the safe sanction of custom, and the well-worn stamp of use.

"Miss Snowe," recommenced Dr. John—my health, nervous system included, being now, somewhat to my relief, discussed and done with—"is it permitted me to ask what your religion is? Are you a Catholic?"

I looked up in some surprise—"A Catholic? No! Why suggest such an idea?"

"The manner in which you were consigned to me last night made me doubt."

"I consigned to you? But, indeed, I forget. It yet remains for me to learn how I fell into your hands."

"Why, under circumstances that puzzled me. I had been in attendance all day yesterday on a case of singularly interesting and critical character; the disease being rare, and its treatment doubtful: I saw a similar and still finer case in a hospital in Paris; but that will not interest you. At last a mitigation of the patient's most urgent symptoms (acute pain is one of its accompaniments) liberated me, and I set out homeward. My shortest way lay through the Basse-Ville, and as the night was excessively dark, wild, and wet, I took it. In riding past an old church belonging to a community of Béguines, I saw by a lamp burning over the porch or deep arch of the entrance, a priest lifting some object in his arms. The lamp was bright enough to reveal the priest's features clearly, and I recognised him; he was a man I have often met by the sick beds of both rich and poor: and chiefly the latter. He is, I think, a good old man, far better than most of his class in this country; superior, indeed, in every way, better informed, as well as more devoted to duty. Our eyes met; he called on me to stop: what he supported was a woman, fainting or dying. I alighted.

"'This person is one of your countrywomen,' he said: 'save her, if she is not dead.'

"My countrywoman, on examination, turned out to be the English teacher at Madame Beck's pensionnat. She was perfectly unconscious, perfectly bloodless, and nearly cold.

"'What does it all mean?' was my inquiry.

"He communicated a curious account; that you had been to him that evening at confessional; that your exhausted and suffering appearance, coupled with some things you had said—"

"Things I had said? I wonder what things!"

"Awful crimes, no doubt; but he did not tell me what: there, you know, the seal of the confessional checked his garrulity, and my curiosity. Your confidences, however, had not made an enemy of the good father; it seems he was so struck, and felt so sorry that you should be out on such a night alone, that he had esteemed it a Christian duty to watch you when you quitted the church, and so to manage as not to lose sight of you, till you should have reached home. Perhaps the worthy man might, half unconsciously, have blent in this proceeding some little of the subtlety of his class: it might have been his resolve to learn the locality of your home—did you impart that in your confession?"

"I did not: on the contrary, I carefully avoided the shadow of any indication: and as to my confession, Dr. John, I suppose you will think me mad for taking such a step, but I could not help it:

Villette

I suppose it was all the fault of what you call my 'nervous system.' I cannot put the case into words, but my days and nights were grown intolerable: a cruel sense of desolation pained my mind: a feeling that would make its way, rush out, or kill me—like (and this you will understand, Dr. John) the current which passes through the heart, and which, if aneurism or any other morbid cause obstructs its natural channels, seeks abnormal outlet. I wanted companionship, I wanted friendship, I wanted counsel. I could find none of these in closet or chamber, so I went and sought them in church and confessional. As to what I said, it was no confidence, no narrative. I have done nothing wrong: my life has not been active enough for any dark deed, either of romance or reality: all I poured out was a dreary, desperate complaint."

"Lucy, you ought to travel for about six months: why, your calm nature is growing quite excitable! Confound Madame Beck! Has the little buxom widow no bowels, to condemn her best teacher to solitary confinement?"

"It was not Madame Beck's fault," said I; "it is no living being's fault, and I won't hear any one blamed."

"Who is in the wrong, then, Lucy?"

"Me—Dr. John—me; and a great abstraction on whose wide shoulders I like to lay the mountains of blame they were sculptured to bear: me and Fate."

"'Me' must take better care in future," said Dr. John—smiling, I suppose, at my bad grammar.

"Change of air—change of scene; those are my prescriptions," pursued the practical young doctor. "But to return to our muttons, Lucy. As yet, Père Silas, with all his tact (they say he is a Jesuit), is no wiser than you choose him to be; for, instead of returning to the Rue Fossette, your fevered wanderings—there must have been high fever—"

"No, Dr. John: the fever took its turn that night—now, don't make out that I was delirious, for I know differently."

"Good! you were as collected as myself at this moment, no doubt. Your wanderings had taken an opposite direction to the pensionnat. Near the Béguinage, amidst the stress of flood and gust, and in the perplexity of darkness, you had swooned and fallen. The priest came to your succour, and the physician, as we have seen, supervened. Between us we procured a fiacre and brought you here. Père Silas, old as he is, would carry you upstairs, and lay you on that couch himself. He would certainly have remained with you till suspended animation had been restored: and so should I, but, at that juncture, a hurried messenger arrived from the dying patient I had scarcely left—the last duties were called for—the physician's last visit and the priest's last rite; extreme unction could not be deferred. Père Silas and myself departed together, my mother was spending the evening abroad; we gave you in charge to Martha, leaving directions, which it seems she followed successfully. Now, are you a Catholic?"

"Not yet," said I, with a smile. "And never let Père Silas know where I live, or he will try to convert me; but give him my best and truest thanks when you see him, and if ever I get rich I will send him money for his charities. See, Dr. John, your mother wakes; you ought to ring for tea."

Which he did; and, as Mrs. Bretton sat up—astonished and indignant at herself for the indulgence to which she had succumbed, and fully prepared to deny that she had slept at all—her son came gaily to the attack.

"Hushaby, mamma! Sleep again. You look the picture of innocence in your slumbers."

"My slumbers, John Graham! What are you talking about? You know I never do sleep by day: it was the slightest doze possible."

"Exactly! a seraph's gentle lapse—a fairy's dream. Mamma, under such circumstances, you always remind me of Titania."

"That is because you, yourself, are so like Bottom."

"Miss Snowe—did you ever hear anything like mamma's wit? She is a most sprightly woman of her size and age."

"Keep your compliments to yourself, sir, and do not neglect your own size: which seems to me a good deal on the increase. Lucy, has he not rather the air of an incipient John Bull? He used to be slender as an eel, and now I fancy in him a sort of heavy dragoon bent—a beef-eater tendency. Graham, take notice! If you grow fat I disown you."

"As if you could not sooner disown your own personality! I am indispensable to the old lady's happiness, Lucy. She would pine away in green and yellow melancholy if she had not my six feet of iniquity to scold. It keeps her lively—it maintains the wholesome ferment of her spirits."

The two were now standing opposite to each other, one on each side the fire-place; their words were not very fond, but their mutual looks atoned for verbal deficiencies. At least, the best treasure of Mrs. Bretton's life was certainly casketed in her son's bosom; her dearest pulse throbbed in his heart. As to him, of course another love shared his feelings with filial love, and, no doubt, as the new passion was the latest born, so he assigned it in his emotions Benjamin's portion. Ginevra! Ginevra! Did Mrs. Bretton yet know at whose feet her own young idol had laid his homage? Would she approve that choice? I could not tell; but I could well guess that if she knew Miss Fanshawe's conduct towards Graham: her alternations between coldness and coaxing, and repulse and allurement; if she could at all suspect the pain with which she had tried him; if she could have seen, as I had seen, his fine spirits subdued and harassed, his inferior preferred before him, his subordinate made the instrument of his humiliation—then Mrs. Bretton would have pronounced Ginevra imbecile, or perverted, or both. Well—I thought so too.

That second evening passed as sweetly as the first—more sweetly indeed: we enjoyed a smoother interchange of thought; old troubles were not reverted to, acquaintance was better cemented; I felt happier, easier, more at home. That night—instead of crying myself asleep—I went down to dreamland by a pathway bordered with pleasant thoughts.

CHAPTER XVIII.

WE QUARREL.

During the first days of my stay at the Terrace, Graham never took a seat near me, or in his frequent pacing of the room approached the quarter where I sat, or looked pre-occupied, or more grave than usual, but I thought of Miss Fanshawe and expected her name to leap from his lips. I kept my ear and mind in perpetual readiness for the tender theme; my patience was ordered to be permanently under arms, and my sympathy desired to keep its cornucopia replenished and ready for outpouring. At last, and after a little inward struggle, which I saw and respected, he one day launched into the topic. It was introduced delicately; anonymously as it were.

"Your friend is spending her vacation in travelling, I hear?"

"Friend, forsooth!" thought I to myself: but it would not do to contradict; he must have his own way; I must own the soft impeachment: friend let it be. Still, by way of experiment, I could not help asking whom he meant?

He had taken a seat at my work-table; he now laid hands on a reel of thread which he proceeded recklessly to unwind.

"Ginevra—Miss Fanshawe, has accompanied the Cholmondeleys on a tour through the south of France?"

"She has."

"Do you and she correspond?"

"It will astonish you to hear that I never once thought of making application for that privilege."

"You have seen letters of her writing?"

"Yes; several to her uncle."

"They will not be deficient in wit and naïveté; there is so much sparkle, and so little art in her soul?"

"She writes comprehensively enough when she writes to M. de Bassompierre: he who runs may read." (In fact, Ginevra's epistles to her wealthy kinsman were commonly business documents, unequivocal applications for cash.)

Villette

"And her handwriting? It must be pretty, light, ladylike, I should think?"

It was, and I said so.

"I verily believe that all she does is well done," said Dr. John; and as I seemed in no hurry to chime in with this remark, he added "You, who know her, could you name a point in which she is deficient?"

"She does several things very well." ("Flirtation amongst the rest," subjoined I, in thought.)

"When do you suppose she will return to town?" he soon inquired.

"Pardon me, Dr. John, I must explain. You honour me too much in ascribing to me a degree of intimacy with Miss Fanshawe I have not the felicity to enjoy. I have never been the depositary of her plans and secrets. You will find her particular friends in another sphere than mine: amongst the Cholmondeleys, for instance."

He actually thought I was stung with a kind of jealous pain similar to his own!

"Excuse her," he said; "judge her indulgently; the glitter of fashion misleads her, but she will soon find out that these people are hollow, and will return to you with augmented attachment and confirmed trust. I know something of the Cholmondeleys: superficial, showy, selfish people; depend on it, at heart Ginevra values you beyond a score of such."

"You are very kind," I said briefly.

A disclaimer of the sentiments attributed to me burned on my lips, but I extinguished the flame. I submitted to be looked upon as the humiliated, cast-off, and now pining confidante of the distinguished Miss Fanshawe: but, reader, it was a hard submission.

"Yet, you see," continued Graham, "while I comfort you, I cannot take the same consolation to myself; I cannot hope she will do me justice. De Hamal is most worthless, yet I fear he pleases her: wretched delusion!"

My patience really gave way, and without notice: all at once. I suppose illness and weakness had worn it and made it brittle.

"Dr. Bretton," I broke out, "there is no delusion like your own. On all points but one you are a man, frank, healthful, right-thinking, clear-sighted: on this exceptional point you are but a slave. I declare, where Miss Fanshawe is concerned, you merit no respect; nor have you mine."

I got up, and left the room very much excited.

This little scene took place in the morning; I had to meet him again in the evening, and then I saw I had done mischief. He was not made of common clay, not put together out of vulgar materials; while the outlines of his nature had been shaped with breadth and vigour, the details embraced workmanship of almost feminine delicacy: finer, much finer, than you could be prepared to meet with; than you could believe inherent in him, even after years of acquaintance. Indeed, till some over-sharp contact with his nerves had betrayed, by its effects, their acute sensibility, this elaborate construction must be ignored; and the more especially because the sympathetic faculty was not prominent in him: to feel, and to seize quickly another's feelings, are separate properties; a few constructions possess both, some neither. Dr. John had the one in exquisite perfection; and because I have admitted that he was not endowed with the other in equal degree, the reader will considerately refrain from passing to an extreme, and pronouncing him _un_ sympathizing, unfeeling: on the contrary, he was a kind, generous man. Make your need known, his hand was open. Put your grief into words, he turned no deaf ear. Expect refinements of perception, miracles of intuition, and realize disappointment. This night, when Dr. John entered the room, and met the evening lamp, I saw well and at one glance his whole mechanism.

To one who had named him "slave," and, on any point, banned him from respect, he must now have peculiar feelings. That the epithet was well applied, and the ban just, might be; he put forth no denial that it was so: his mind even candidly revolved that unmanning possibility. He sought in this accusation the cause of that ill-success which had got so galling a hold on his mental peace: Amid the worry of a self-condemnatory soliloquy, his demeanour seemed grave, perhaps cold, both to me and his mother. And yet there was no bad feeling, no malice, no rancour, no littleness in his countenance, beautiful with a man's best beauty, even in its depression. When I placed his chair at the table, which I hastened to do, anticipating the servant, and when I handed him his tea, which I did with trembling care, he said: "Thank you, Lucy," in as kindly a tone of his full pleasant voice as ever my ear

Villette

welcomed.

For my part, there was only one plan to be pursued; I must expiate my culpable vehemence, or I must not sleep that night. This would not do at all; I could not stand it: I made no pretence of capacity to wage war on this footing. School solitude, conventual silence and stagnation, anything seemed preferable to living embroiled with Dr. John. As to Ginevra, she might take the silver wings of a dove, or any other fowl that flies, and mount straight up to the highest place, among the highest stars, where her lover's highest flight of fancy chose to fix the constellation of her charms: never more be it mine to dispute the arrangement. Long I tried to catch his eye. Again and again that eye just met mine; but, having nothing to say, it withdrew, and I was baffled. After tea, he sat, sad and quiet, reading a book. I wished I could have dared to go and sit near him, but it seemed that if I ventured to take that step, he would infallibly evince hostility and indignation. I longed to speak out, and I dared not whisper. His mother left the room; then, moved by insupportable regret, I just murmured the words "Dr. Bretton."

He looked up from his book; his eyes were not cold or malevolent, his mouth was not cynical; he was ready and willing to hear what I might have to say: his spirit was of vintage too mellow and generous to sour in one thunder-clap.

"Dr. Bretton, forgive my hasty words: do, do forgive them."

He smiled that moment I spoke. "Perhaps I deserved them, Lucy. If you don't respect me, I am sure it is because I am not respectable. I fear, I am an awkward fool: I must manage badly in some way, for where I wish to please, it seems I don't please."

"Of that you cannot be sure; and even if such be the case, is it the fault of your character, or of another's perceptions? But now, let me unsay what I said in anger. In one thing, and in all things, I deeply respect you. If you think scarcely enough of yourself, and too much of others, what is that but an excellence?"

"Can I think too much of Ginevra?"

"I believe you may; you believe you can't. Let us agree to differ. Let me be pardoned; that is what I ask."

"Do you think I cherish ill-will for one warm word?"

"I see you do not and cannot; but just say, 'Lucy, I forgive you!' Say that, to ease me of the heart-ache."

"Put away your heart-ache, as I will put away mine; for you wounded me a little, Lucy. Now, when the pain is gone, I more than forgive: I feel grateful, as to a sincere well-wisher."

"I am your sincere well-wisher: you are right."

Thus our quarrel ended.

Reader, if in the course of this work, you find that my opinion of Dr. John undergoes modification, excuse the seeming inconsistency. I give the feeling as at the time I felt it; I describe the view of character as it appeared when discovered.

He showed the fineness of his nature by being kinder to me after that misunderstanding than before. Nay, the very incident which, by my theory, must in some degree estrange me and him, changed, indeed, somewhat our relations; but not in the sense I painfully anticipated. An invisible, but a cold something, very slight, very transparent, but very chill: a sort of screen of ice had hitherto, all through our two lives, glazed the medium through which we exchanged intercourse. Those few warm words, though only warm with anger, breathed on that frail frost-work of reserve; about this time, it gave note of dissolution. I think from that day, so long as we continued friends, he never in discourse stood on topics of ceremony with me. He seemed to know that if he would but talk about himself, and about that in which he was most interested, my expectation would always be answered, my wish always satisfied. It follows, as a matter of course, that I continued to hear much of "Ginevra."

"Ginevra!" He thought her so fair, so good; he spoke so lovingly of her charms, her sweetness, her innocence, that, in spite of my plain prose knowledge of the reality, a kind of reflected glow began to settle on her idea, even for me. Still, reader, I am free to confess, that he often talked nonsense; but I strove to be unfailingly patient with him. I had had my lesson: I had learned how severe for me was the pain of crossing, or grieving, or disappointing him. In a strange and new sense, I grew most selfish, and quite powerless to deny myself the delight of indulging his mood, and being pliant to his will. He still seemed to me most absurd when he obstinately doubted, and desponded about his power to win in the end Miss Fanshawe's preference. The fancy became rooted in my own mind more stubbornly than ever, that she was only coquetting to goad him, and that, at heart, she coveted every one of his words and looks. Sometimes he harassed me, in spite of my resolution to bear and hear; in the midst of the indescribable gall-honey pleasure of thus bearing and hearing, he struck so on the flint of what firmness I owned, that it emitted fire once and again. I chanced to assert one day, with a view to stilling his impatience, that in my own mind, I felt positive Miss Fanshawe must intend eventually to accept him.

"Positive! It was easy to say so, but had I any grounds for such assurance?"

"The best grounds."

"Now, Lucy, do tell me what!"

"You know them as well as I; and, knowing them, Dr. John, it really amazes me that you should not repose the frankest confidence in her fidelity. To doubt, under the circumstances, is almost to insult."

"Now you are beginning to speak fast and to breathe short; but speak a little faster and breathe a little shorter, till you have given an explanation—a full explanation: I must have it."

"You shall, Dr. John. In some cases, you are a lavish, generous man: you are a worshipper ever ready with the votive offering should Père Silas ever convert you, you will give him abundance of alms for his poor, you will supply his altar with tapers, and the shrine of your favourite saint you will do your best to enrich: Ginevra, Dr. John—"

"Hush!" said he, "don't go on."

"Hush, I will not: and go on I will: Ginevra has had her hands filled from your hands more times than I can count. You have sought for her the costliest flowers; you have busied your brain in devising gifts the most delicate: such, one would have thought, as only a woman could have imagined; and in addition, Miss Fanshawe owns a set of ornaments, to purchase which your generosity must have verged on extravagance."

The modesty Ginevra herself had never evinced in this matter, now flushed all over the face of her admirer.

"Nonsense!" he said, destructively snipping a skein of silk with my scissors. "I offered them to please myself: I felt she did me a favour in accepting them."

"She did more than a favour, Dr. John: she pledged her very honour that she would make you some return; and if she cannot pay you in affection, she ought to hand out a business-like equivalent, in the shape of some rouleaux of gold pieces."

"But you don't understand her; she is far too disinterested to care for my gifts, and too simple-minded to know their value."

I laughed out: I had heard her adjudge to every jewel its price; and well I knew money-embarrassment, money-schemes; money's worth, and endeavours to realise supplies, had, young as she was, furnished the most frequent, and the favourite stimulus of her thoughts for years.

He pursued. "You should have seen her whenever I have laid on her lap some trifle; so cool, so unmoved: no eagerness to take, not even pleasure in contemplating. Just from amiable reluctance to grieve me, she would permit the bouquet to lie beside her, and perhaps consent to bear it away. Or, if I achieved the fastening of a bracelet on her ivory arm, however pretty the trinket might be (and I always carefully chose what seemed to me pretty, and what of course was not valueless), the glitter never dazzled her bright eyes: she would hardly cast one look on my gift."

"Then, of course, not valuing it, she would unloose, and return it to you?"

"No; for such a repulse she was too good-natured. She would consent to seem to forget what I had done, and retain the offering with lady-like quiet and easy oblivion. Under such circumstances, how can a man build on acceptance of his presents as a favourable symptom? For my part, were I to offer her all I have, and she to take it, such is her incapacity to be swayed by sordid considerations, I should not venture to believe the transaction advanced me one step."

"Dr. John," I began, "Love is blind;" but just then a blue subtle ray sped sideways from Dr. John's eye: it reminded me of old days, it reminded me of his picture: it half led me to think that part, at least, of his professed persuasion of Miss Fanshawe's naïveté was assumed; it led me dubiously to conjecture that perhaps, in spite of his passion for her beauty, his appreciation of her foibles might possibly be less mistaken, more clear-sighted, than from his general language was presumable. After all it might be only a chance look, or at best the token of a merely momentary impression. Chance or intentional real or imaginary, it closed the conversation.

CHAPTER XIX.

THE CLEOPATRA.

My stay at La Terrasse was prolonged a fortnight beyond the close of the vacation. Mrs. Bretton's kind management procured me this respite. Her son having one day delivered the dictum that "Lucy was not yet strong enough to go back to that den of a pensionnat," she at once drove over to the Rue Fossette, had an interview with the directress, and procured the indulgence, on the plea of prolonged rest and change being necessary to perfect recovery. Hereupon, however, followed an attention I could very well have dispensed with, viz. — a polite call from Madame Beck.

That lady — one fine day — actually came out in a fiacre as far as the château. I suppose she had resolved within herself to see what manner of place Dr. John inhabited. Apparently, the pleasant site and neat interior surpassed her expectations; she eulogized all she saw, pronounced the blue salon "une pièce magnifique," profusely congratulated me on the acquisition of friends, "tellement dignes, aimables, et respectables," turned also a neat compliment in my favour, and, upon Dr. John coming in, ran up to him with the utmost buoyancy, opening at the same time such a fire of rapid language, all sparkling with felicitations and protestations about his "château," — "madame sa mère, la digne châtelaine:" also his looks; which, indeed, were very flourishing, and at the moment additionally embellished by the good-natured but amused smile with which he always listened to Madame's fluent and florid French. In short, Madame shone in her very best phase that day, and came in and went out quite a living catherine-wheel of compliments, delight, and affability. Half purposely, and half to ask some question about school-business, I followed her to the carriage, and looked in after she was seated and the door closed. In that brief fraction of time what a change had been wrought! An instant ago, all sparkles and jests, she now sat sterner than a judge and graver than a sage. Strange little woman!

I went back and teased Dr. John about Madame's devotion to him. How he laughed! What fun shone in his eyes as he recalled some of her fine speeches, and repeated them, imitating her voluble delivery! He had an acute sense of humour, and was the finest company in the world — when he could forget Miss Fanshawe.

To "sit in sunshine calm and sweet" is said to be excellent for weak people; it gives them vital force. When little Georgette Beck was recovering from her illness, I used to take her in my arms and walk with her in the garden by the hour together, beneath a certain wall hung with grapes, which the Southern sun was ripening: that sun cherished her little pale frame quite as effectually as it mellowed and swelled the clustering fruit.

There are human tempers, bland, glowing, and genial, within whose influence it is as good for the poor in spirit to live, as it is for the feeble in frame to bask in the glow of noon. Of the number of these choice natures were certainly both Dr. Bretton's and his mother's. They liked to communicate happiness, as some like to occasion misery: they did it instinctively; without fuss, and apparently with little consciousness; the means to give pleasure rose spontaneously in their minds. Every day while I stayed with them, some little plan was proposed which resulted in beneficial enjoyment. Fully occupied as was Dr. John's time, he still made it in his way to accompany us in each brief excursion. I can hardly tell how he managed his engagements; they were numerous, yet by dint of system, he classed them in an order which left him a daily period of liberty. I often saw him hard-worked, yet seldom over-driven, and never irritated, confused, or oppressed. What he did was accomplished with the ease and grace of all-sufficing strength; with the bountiful cheerfulness of high and unbroken energies. Under his guidance I saw, in that one happy fortnight, more of Villette, its environs, and its inhabitants, than I had seen in the whole eight months of my previous residence. He took me to places of interest in the town, of whose names I had not before so much as heard; with willingness and spirit he communicated much noteworthy information. He never seemed to think it a trouble to talk to me, and, I am sure, it was never a task to me to listen. It was not his way to treat subjects coldly and vaguely; he rarely generalized, never prosed. He seemed to like nice details almost as much as I liked them myself: he seemed observant of character: and not superficially observant, either. These points gave the quality of interest to his discourse; and the fact of his speaking direct from his own resources, and not borrowing or stealing from books—here a dry fact, and there a trite phrase, and elsewhere a hackneyed opinion—ensured a freshness, as welcome as it was rare. Before my eyes, too, his disposition seemed to unfold another phase; to pass to a fresh day: to rise in new and nobler dawn.

His mother possessed a good development of benevolence, but he owned a better and larger. I found, on accompanying him to the Basse-Ville—the poor and crowded quarter of the city—that his errands there were as much those of the

Villette

philanthropist as the physician. I understood presently that cheerfully, habitually, and in single-minded unconsciousness of any special merit distinguishing his deeds—he was achieving, amongst a very wretched population, a world of active good. The lower orders liked him well; his poor patients in the hospitals welcomed him with a sort of enthusiasm.

But stop—I must not, from the faithful narrator, degenerate into the partial eulogist. Well, full well, do I know that Dr. John was not perfect, any more than I am perfect. Human fallibility leavened him throughout: there was no hour, and scarcely a moment of the time I spent with him that in act or speech, or look, he did not betray something that was not of a god. A god could not have the cruel vanity of Dr. John, nor his sometime levity. No immortal could have resembled him in his occasional temporary oblivion of all but the present—in his passing passion for that present; shown not coarsely, by devoting it to material indulgence, but selfishly, by extracting from it whatever it could yield of nutriment to his masculine self-love: his delight was to feed that ravenous sentiment, without thought of the price of provender, or care for the cost of keeping it sleek and high-pampered.

The reader is requested to note a seeming contradiction in the two views which have been given of Graham Bretton—the public and private—the out-door and the in-door view. In the first, the public, he is shown oblivious of self; as modest in the display of his energies, as earnest in their exercise. In the second, the fireside picture, there is expressed consciousness of what he has and what he is; pleasure in homage, some recklessness in exciting, some vanity in receiving the same. Both portraits are correct.

It was hardly possible to oblige Dr. John quietly and in secret. When you thought that the fabrication of some trifle dedicated to his use had been achieved unnoticed, and that, like other men, he would use it when placed ready for his use, and never ask whence it came, he amazed you by a smilingly-uttered observation or two, proving that his eye had been on the work from commencement to close: that he had noted the design, traced its progress, and marked its completion. It pleased him to be thus served, and he let his pleasure beam in his eye and play about his mouth.

This would have been all very well, if he had not added to such kindly and unobtrusive evidence a certain wilfulness in discharging what he called debts. When his mother worked for him, he paid her by showering about her his bright animal spirits, with even more affluence than his gay, taunting, teasing, loving wont. If Lucy Snowe were discovered to have put her hand to such work, he planned, in recompence, some pleasant recreation.

I often felt amazed at his perfect knowledge of Villette; a knowledge not merely confined to its open streets, but penetrating to all its galleries, salles, and cabinets: of every door which shut in an object worth seeing, of every museum, of every hall, sacred to art or science, he seemed to possess the "Open! Sesame." I never had a head for science, but an ignorant, blind, fond instinct inclined me to art. I liked to visit the picture-galleries, and I dearly liked to be left there alone. In company, a wretched idiosyncracy forbade me to see much or to feel anything. In unfamiliar company, where it was necessary to maintain a flow of talk on the subjects in presence, half an hour would knock me up, with a combined pressure of physical lassitude and entire mental incapacity. I never yet saw the well-reared child, much less the educated adult, who could not put me to shame, by the sustained intelligence of its demeanour under the ordeal of a conversable, sociable visitation of pictures, historical sights or buildings, or any lions of public interest. Dr. Bretton was a cicerone after my own heart; he would take me betimes, ere the galleries were filled, leave me there for two or three hours, and call for me when his own engagements were discharged. Meantime, I was happy; happy, not always in admiring, but in examining, questioning, and forming conclusions. In the commencement of these visits, there was some misunderstanding and consequent struggle between Will and Power. The former faculty exacted approbation of that which it was considered orthodox to admire; the latter groaned forth its utter inability to pay the tax; it was then self-sneered at, spurred up, goaded on to refine its taste, and whet its zest. The more it was chidden, however, the more it wouldn't praise. Discovering gradually that a wonderful sense of fatigue resulted from these conscientious efforts, I began to reflect whether I might not dispense with that great labour, and concluded eventually that I might, and so sank supine into a luxury of calm before ninety-nine out of a hundred of the exhibited frames.

It seemed to me that an original and good picture was just as scarce as an original and good book; nor did I, in the end, tremble to say to myself, standing before certain chef-d'œuvres bearing great names, "These are not a whit like nature. Nature's daylight never had that colour: never was made so turbid, either by storm or cloud, as it is laid out there, under a sky of indigo: and that indigo is not ether; and those dark weeds plastered upon it are not trees." Several very well executed and complacent-looking fat women struck me as by no means the goddesses they appeared to consider themselves. Many scores of marvellously-finished little Flemish pictures, and also of sketches, excellent for fashion-books displaying varied costumes in the handsomest materials, gave evidence of laudable industry whimsically applied. And yet there were fragments of truth here and there which satisfied the conscience, and gleams of light that cheered the vision. Nature's power here broke through in a mountain snow-storm; and there her glory in a sunny southern day. An expression in this portrait proved clear insight into character; a face in that historical painting, by its vivid filial likeness, startlingly reminded you that genius gave it birth. These exceptions I loved: they grew dear as friends.

One day, at a quiet early hour, I found myself nearly alone in a certain gallery, wherein one particular picture of portentous size, set up in the best light, having a cordon of protection stretched before it, and a cushioned bench duly set in front for the accommodation of worshipping connoisseurs, who, having gazed themselves off their feet, might be fain to complete the business sitting: this picture, I say, seemed to consider itself the queen of the collection.

It represented a woman, considerably larger, I thought, than the life. I calculated that this lady, put into a scale of magnitude, suitable for the reception of a commodity of bulk, would infallibly turn from fourteen to sixteen stone. She was, indeed, extremely well fed: very much butcher's meat—to say nothing of bread, vegetables, and liquids—must she have consumed to attain that breadth and height, that wealth of muscle, that affluence of flesh. She lay half-reclined on a couch: why, it would be difficult to say; broad daylight blazed round her; she appeared in hearty health, strong enough to do the work of two plain cooks; she could not plead a weak spine; she ought to have been standing, or at least sitting bolt upright. She, had no business to lounge away the noon on a sofa. She ought likewise to have worn decent garments; a gown covering her properly, which was not the case: out of abundance of material—seven-and-twenty yards, I should say, of drapery—she managed to make inefficient raiment. Then, for the wretched untidiness surrounding her, there could be no excuse. Pots and pans—perhaps I ought to say vases and goblets—were rolled here and there on the foreground; a perfect rubbish of flowers was mixed amongst them, and an absurd and disorderly mass of curtain upholstery smothered the couch and cumbered the floor. On referring to the catalogue, I found that this notable production bore the name "Cleopatra."

Well, I was sitting wondering at it (as the bench was there, I thought I might as well take advantage of its accommodation), and thinking that while some of the details—as roses, gold cups, jewels, &c., were very prettily painted, it was on the whole an enormous piece of claptrap; the room, almost vacant when I entered, began to fill. Scarcely noticing this circumstance (as, indeed, it did not matter to me) I retained my seat; rather to rest myself than with a view to studying this huge, dark-complexioned gipsy-queen; of whom, indeed, I soon tired, and betook myself for refreshment to the contemplation of some exquisite little pictures of still life: wild-flowers, wild-fruit, mossy wood-nests, casketing eggs that looked like pearls seen through clear green sea-water; all hung modestly beneath that coarse and preposterous canvas.

Suddenly a light tap visited my shoulder. Starting, turning, I met a face bent to encounter mine; a frowning, almost a shocked face it was.

"Que faites-vous ici?" said a voice.

"Mais, Monsieur, je m'amuse."

"Vous vous amusez! et à quoi, s'il vous plait? Mais d'abord, faites-moi le plaisir de vous lever; prenez mon bras, et allons de l'autre côté."

I did precisely as I was bid. M. Paul Emanuel (it was he) returned from Rome, and now a travelled man, was not likely to be less tolerant of insubordination now, than before this added distinction laurelled his temples.

"Permit me to conduct you to your party," said he, as we crossed the room.

"I have no party."

"You are not alone?"

"Yes, Monsieur."

"Did you come here unaccompanied?"

"No, Monsieur. Dr. Bretton brought me here."

"Dr. Bretton and Madame his mother, of course?"

"No; only Dr. Bretton."

"And he told you to look at that picture?"

"By no means; I found it out for myself."

M. Paul's hair was shorn close as raven down, or I think it would have bristled on his head. Beginning now to perceive his drift, I had a certain pleasure in keeping cool, and working him up.

"Astounding insular audacity!" cried the Professor. "Singulières femmes que ces Anglaises!"

"What is the matter, Monsieur?"

"Matter! How dare you, a young person, sit coolly down, with the self-possession of a garçon, and look at that picture?"

"It is a very ugly picture, but I cannot at all see why I should not look at it."

"Bon! bon! Speak no more of it. But you ought not to be here alone."

"If, however, I have no society—no party, as you say? And then, what does it signify whether I am alone, or accompanied? nobody meddles with me."

"Taisez-vous, et asseyez-vous là—là!"—setting down a chair with emphasis in a particularly dull corner, before a series of most specially dreary "cadres."

"Mais, Monsieur?"

"Mais, Mademoiselle, asseyez-vous, et ne bougez pas—entendez-vous?—jusqu'à ce qu'on vienne vous chercher, ou que je vous donne la permission."

"Quel triste coin!" cried I, "et quelles laids tableaux!"

And "laids," indeed, they were; being a set of four, denominated in the catalogue "La vie d'une femme." They were painted rather in a remarkable style—flat, dead, pale, and formal. The first represented a "Jeune Fille," coming out of a church-door, a missal in her hand, her dress very prim, her eyes cast down, her mouth pursed up—the image of a most villanous little precocious she-hypocrite. The second, a "Mariée," with a long white veil, kneeling at a prie-dieu in her chamber, holding her hands plastered together, finger to finger, and showing the whites of her eyes in a most exasperating manner. The third, a "Jeune Mère," hanging disconsolate over a clayey and puffy baby with a face like an unwholesome full moon. The fourth, a "Veuve," being a black woman, holding by the hand a black little girl, and the twain studiously surveying an elegant French monument, set up in a corner of some Père la Chaise. All these four "Anges" were grim and grey as burglars, and cold and vapid as ghosts. What women to live with! insincere, ill-humoured, bloodless, brainless nonentities! As bad in their way as the indolent gipsy-giantess, the Cleopatra, in hers.

It was impossible to keep one's attention long confined to these master-pieces, and so, by degrees, I veered round, and surveyed the gallery.

A perfect crowd of spectators was by this time gathered round the Lioness, from whose vicinage I had been banished; nearly half this crowd were ladies, but M. Paul afterwards told me, these were "des dames," and it was quite proper for them to contemplate what no "demoiselle" ought to glance at. I assured him plainly I could not agree in this doctrine, and did not see the sense of it; whereupon, with his usual absolutism, he merely requested my silence, and also, in the same breath, denounced my mingled rashness and ignorance. A more despotic little man than M. Paul never filled a professor's chair. I noticed, by the way, that he looked at the picture himself quite at his ease, and for a very long while: he did not, however, neglect to glance from time to time my way, in order, I suppose, to make sure that I was obeying orders, and not breaking bounds. By-and-by, he again accosted me.

"Had I not been ill?" he wished to know: "he understood I had."

"Yes, but I was now quite well."

"Where had I spent the vacation?"

"Chiefly in the Rue Fossette; partly with Madame Bretton."

"He had heard that I was left alone in the Rue Fossette; was that so?"

"Not quite alone: Marie Broc" (the crétin) "was with me."

He shrugged his shoulders; varied and contradictory

Villette

expressions played rapidly over his countenance. Marie Broc was well known to M. Paul; he never gave a lesson in the third division (containing the least advanced pupils), that she did not occasion in him a sharp conflict between antagonistic impressions. Her personal appearance, her repulsive manners, her often unmanageable disposition, irritated his temper, and inspired him with strong antipathy; a feeling he was too apt to conceive when his taste was offended or his will thwarted. On the other hand, her misfortunes, constituted a strong claim on his forbearance and compassion—such a claim as it was not in his nature to deny; hence resulted almost daily drawn battles between impatience and disgust on the one hand, pity and a sense of justice on the other; in which, to his credit be it said, it was very seldom that the former feelings prevailed: when they did, however, M. Paul showed a phase of character which had its terrors. His passions were strong, his aversions and attachments alike vivid; the force he exerted in holding both in check by no means mitigated an observer's sense of their vehemence. With such tendencies, it may well be supposed he often excited in ordinary minds fear and dislike; yet it was an error to fear him: nothing drove him so nearly frantic as the tremor of an apprehensive and distrustful spirit; nothing soothed him like confidence tempered with gentleness. To evince these sentiments, however, required a thorough comprehension of his nature; and his nature was of an order rarely comprehended.

"How did you get on with Marie Broc?" he asked, after some minutes' silence.

"Monsieur, I did my best; but it was terrible to be alone with her!"

"You have, then, a weak heart! You lack courage; and, perhaps, charity. Yours are not the qualities which might constitute a Sister of Mercy."

[He was a religious little man, in his way: the self-denying and self-sacrificing part of the Catholic religion commanded the homage of his soul.]

"I don't know, indeed: I took as good care of her as I could; but when her aunt came to fetch her away, it was a great relief."

"Ah! you are an egotist. There are women who have nursed hospitals-full of similar unfortunates. You could not do that?"

"Could Monsieur do it himself?"

"Women who are worthy the name ought infinitely to surpass; our coarse, fallible, self-indulgent sex, in the power to perform such duties."

"I washed her, I kept her clean, I fed her, I tried to amuse her; but she made mouths at me instead of speaking."

"You think you did great things?"

"No; but as great as I could do."

"Then limited are your powers, for in tending one idiot you fell sick."

"Not with that, Monsieur; I had a nervous fever: my mind was ill."

"Vraiment! Vous valez peu de chose. You are not cast in an heroic mould; your courage will not avail to sustain you in solitude; it merely gives you the temerity to gaze with sang-froid at pictures of Cleopatra."

It would have been easy to show anger at the teasing, hostile tone of the little man. I had never been angry with him yet, however, and had no present disposition to begin.

"Cleopatra!" I repeated, quietly. "Monsieur, too, has been looking at Cleopatra; what does he think of her?"

"Cela ne vaut rien," he responded. "Une femme superbe—une taille d'impératrice, des formes de Junon, mais une personne dont je ne voudrais ni pour femme, ni pour fille, ni pour sœur. Aussi vous ne jeterez plus un seul coup d'oeil de sa côté."

"But I have looked at her a great many times while Monsieur has been talking: I can see her quite well from this corner."

"Turn to the wall and study your four pictures of a woman's life."

"Excuse me, M. Paul; they are too hideous: but if you admire them, allow me to vacate my seat and leave you to their contemplation."

"Mademoiselle," he said, grimacing a half-smile, or what he intended for a smile, though it was but a grim and hurried manifestation. "You nurslings of Protestantism astonish me.

Villette

You unguarded Englishwomen walk calmly amidst red-hot ploughshares and escape burning. I believe, if some of you were thrown into Nebuchadnezzar's hottest furnace you would issue forth untraversed by the smell of fire."

"Will Monsieur have the goodness to move an inch to one side?"

"How! At what are you gazing now? You are not recognising an acquaintance amongst that group of jeunes gens?"

"I think so—Yes, I see there a person I know."

In fact, I had caught a glimpse of a head too pretty to belong to any other than the redoubted Colonel de Hamal. What a very finished, highly polished little pate it was! What a figure, so trim and natty! What womanish feet and hands! How daintily he held a glass to one of his optics! with what admiration he gazed upon the Cleopatra! and then, how engagingly he tittered and whispered a friend at his elbow! Oh, the man of sense! Oh, the refined gentleman of superior taste and tact! I observed him for about ten minutes, and perceived that he was exceedingly taken with this dusk and portly Venus of the Nile. So much was I interested in his bearing, so absorbed in divining his character by his looks and movements, I temporarily forgot M. Paul; in the interim a group came between that gentleman and me; or possibly his scruples might have received another and worse shock from my present abstraction, causing him to withdraw voluntarily: at any rate, when I again looked round, he was gone.

My eye, pursuant of the search, met not him, but another and dissimilar figure, well seen amidst the crowd, for the height as well as the port lent each its distinction. This way came Dr. John, in visage, in shape, in hue, as unlike the dark, acerb, and caustic little professor, as the fruit of the Hesperides might be unlike the sloe in the wild thicket; as the high-couraged but tractable Arabian is unlike the rude and stubborn "sheltie." He was looking for me, but had not yet explored the corner where the schoolmaster had just put me. I remained quiet; yet another minute I would watch.

He approached de Hamal; he paused near him; I thought he had a pleasure in looking over his head; Dr. Bretton, too, gazed on the Cleopatra. I doubt if it were to his taste: he did not simper like the little Count; his mouth looked fastidious, his eye cool; without demonstration he stepped aside, leaving room for others to approach. I saw now that he was waiting, and, rising, I joined him.

We took one turn round the gallery; with Graham it was very pleasant to take such a turn. I always liked dearly to hear what he had to say about either pictures or books; because without pretending to be a connoisseur, he always spoke his thought, and that was sure to be fresh: very often it was also just and pithy. It was pleasant also to tell him some things he did not know—he listened so kindly, so teachably; unformalized by scruples lest so to bend his bright handsome head, to gather a woman's rather obscure and stammering explanation, should imperil the dignity of his manhood. And when he communicated information in return, it was with a lucid intelligence that left all his words clear graven on the memory; no explanation of his giving, no fact of his narrating, did I ever forget.

As we left the gallery, I asked him what he thought of the Cleopatra (after making him laugh by telling him how Professor Emanuel had sent me to the right about, and taking him to see the sweet series of pictures recommended to my attention.)

"Pooh!" said he. "My mother is a better-looking woman. I heard some French fops, yonder, designating her as 'le type du voluptueux;' if so, I can only say, 'le voluptueux' is little to my liking. Compare that mulatto with Ginevra!"

CHAPTER XX.

THE CONCERT.

One morning, Mrs. Bretton, coming promptly into my room, desired me to open my drawers and show her my dresses; which I did, without a word.

"That will do," said she, when she had turned them over. "You must have a new one."

She went out. She returned presently with a dressmaker. She had me measured. "I mean," said she, "to follow my own taste, and to have my own way in this little matter."

Two days after came home — a pink dress!

"That is not for me," I said, hurriedly, feeling that I would almost as soon clothe myself in the costume of a Chinese lady of rank.

"We shall see whether it is for you or not," rejoined my godmother, adding with her resistless decision: "Mark my words. You will wear it this very evening."

I thought I should not; I thought no human force should avail to put me into it. A pink dress! I knew it not. It knew not me. I had not proved it.

My godmother went on to decree that I was to go with her and Graham to a concert that same night: which concert, she explained, was a grand affair to be held in the large salle, or hall, of the principal musical society. The most advanced of the pupils of the Conservatoire were to perform: it was to be followed by a lottery "au bénéfice des pauvres;" and to crown all, the King, Queen, and Prince of Labassecour were to be present. Graham, in sending tickets, had enjoined attention to costume as a compliment due to royalty: he also recommended punctual readiness by seven o'clock.

About six, I was ushered upstairs. Without any force at all, I found myself led and influenced by another's will, unconsulted, unpersuaded, quietly overruled. In short, the pink dress went on, softened by some drapery of black lace. I was pronounced to be en grande tenue, and requested to look in the glass. I did so with some fear and trembling; with more fear and trembling, I turned away. Seven o'clock struck; Dr. Bretton was come; my godmother and I went down. She was clad in brown velvet; as I walked in her shadow, how I envied her those folds of grave, dark majesty! Graham stood in the drawing-room doorway.

"I do hope he will not think I have been decking myself out to draw attention," was my uneasy aspiration.

"Here, Lucy, are some flowers," said he, giving me a bouquet. He took no further notice of my dress than was conveyed in a kind smile and satisfied nod, which calmed at once my sense of shame and fear of ridicule. For the rest; the dress was made with extreme simplicity, guiltless of flounce or furbelow; it was but the light fabric and bright tint which scared me, and since Graham found in it nothing absurd, my own eye consented soon to become reconciled.

I suppose people who go every night to places of public amusement, can hardly enter into the fresh gala feeling with which an opera or a concert is enjoyed by those for whom it is a rarity: I am not sure that I expected great pleasure from the concert, having but a very vague notion of its nature, but I liked the drive there well. The snug comfort of the close carriage on a cold though fine night, the pleasure of setting out with companions so cheerful and friendly, the sight of the stars glinting fitfully through the trees as we rolled along the avenue; then the freer burst of the night-sky when we issued forth to the open chaussée, the passage through the city gates, the lights there burning, the guards there posted, the pretence of inspection, to which we there submitted, and which amused us so much—all these small matters had for me, in their novelty, a peculiarly exhilarating charm. How much of it lay in the atmosphere of friendship diffused about me, I know not: Dr. John and his mother were both in their finest mood, contending animatedly with each other the whole way, and as frankly kind to me as if I had been of their kin.

Our way lay through some of the best streets of Villette, streets brightly lit, and far more lively now than at high noon. How brilliant seemed the shops! How glad, gay, and abundant flowed the tide of life along the broad pavement! While I looked, the thought of the Rue Fossette came across me—of the walled-in garden and school-house, and of the dark, vast "classes," where, as at this very hour, it was my wont to wander all solitary, gazing at the stars through the high, blindless windows, and listening to the distant voice of the reader in the refectory, monotonously exercised upon the "lecture pieuse." Thus must I soon again listen and wander; and this shadow of the future stole with timely sobriety across the radiant present.

Villette

By this time we had got into a current of carriages all tending in one direction, and soon the front of a great illuminated building blazed before us. Of what I should see within this building, I had, as before intimated, but an imperfect idea; for no place of public entertainment had it ever been my lot to enter yet.

We alighted under a portico where there was a great bustle and a great crowd, but I do not distinctly remember further details, until I found myself mounting a majestic staircase wide and easy of ascent, deeply and softly carpeted with crimson, leading up to great doors closed solemnly, and whose panels were also crimson-clothed.

I hardly noticed by what magic these doors were made to roll back—Dr. John managed these points; roll back they did, however, and within was disclosed a hall—grand, wide, and high, whose sweeping circular walls, and domed hollow ceiling, seemed to me all dead gold (thus with nice art was it stained), relieved by cornicing, fluting, and garlandry, either bright, like gold burnished, or snow-white, like alabaster, or white and gold mingled in wreaths of gilded leaves and spotless lilies: wherever drapery hung, wherever carpets were spread, or cushions placed, the sole colour employed was deep crimson. Pendent from the dome, flamed a mass that dazzled me—a mass, I thought, of rock-crystal, sparkling with facets, streaming with drops, ablaze with stars, and gorgeously tinged with dews of gems dissolved, or fragments of rainbows shivered. It was only the chandelier, reader, but for me it seemed the work of eastern genii: I almost looked to see if a huge, dark, cloudy hand—that of the Slave of the Lamp—were not hovering in the lustrous and perfumed atmosphere of the cupola, guarding its wondrous treasure.

We moved on—I was not at all conscious whither—but at some turn we suddenly encountered another party approaching from the opposite direction. I just now see that group, as it flashed—upon me for one moment. A handsome middle-aged lady in dark velvet; a gentleman who might be her son—the best face, the finest figure, I thought, I had ever seen; a third person in a pink dress and black lace mantle.

I noted them all—the third person as well as the other two—and for the fraction of a moment believed them all strangers, thus receiving an impartial impression of their appearance. But the impression was hardly felt and not fixed, before the consciousness that I faced a great mirror, filling a compartment between two pillars, dispelled it: the party was our own party.

Thus for the first, and perhaps only time in my life, I enjoyed the "giftie" of seeing myself as others see me. No need to dwell on the result. It brought a jar of discord, a pang of regret; it was not flattering, yet, after all, I ought to be thankful; it might have been worse.

At last, we were seated in places commanding a good general view of that vast and dazzling, but warm and cheerful hall. Already it was filled, and filled with a splendid assemblage. I do not know that the women were very beautiful, but their dresses were so perfect; and foreigners, even such as are ungraceful in domestic privacy, seem to possess the art of appearing graceful in public: however blunt and boisterous those every-day and home movements connected with peignoir and papillotes, there is a slide, a bend, a carriage of the head and arms, a mien of the mouth and eyes, kept nicely in reserve for gala use—always brought out with the grande toilette, and duly put on with the "parure."

Some fine forms there were here and there, models of a peculiar style of beauty; a style, I think, never seen in England; a solid, firm-set, sculptural style. These shapes have no angles: a caryatid in marble is almost as flexible; a Phidian goddess is not more perfect in a certain still and stately sort. They have such features as the Dutch painters give to their madonnas: low-country classic features, regular but round, straight but stolid; and for their depth of expressionless calm, of passionless peace, a polar snow-field could alone offer a type. Women of this order need no ornament, and they seldom wear any; the smooth hair, closely braided, supplies a sufficient contrast to the smoother cheek and brow; the dress cannot be too simple; the rounded arm and perfect neck require neither bracelet nor chain.

With one of these beauties I once had the honour and rapture to be perfectly acquainted: the inert force of the deep, settled love she bore herself, was wonderful; it could only be surpassed by her proud impotency to care for any other living thing. Of blood, her cool veins conducted no flow; placid lymph filled and almost obstructed her arteries.

Such a Juno as I have described sat full in our view—a sort of mark for all eyes, and quite conscious that so she was, but proof to the magnetic influence of gaze or glance: cold, rounded, blonde, and beauteous as the white column, capitaled with gilding, which rose at her side.

Observing that Dr. John's attention was much drawn towards her, I entreated him in a low voice "for the love of heaven to shield well his heart. You need not fall in love with that lady," I said, "because, I tell you beforehand, you might die at her feet, and she would not love you again."

"Very well," said he, "and how do you know that the spectacle of her grand insensibility might not with me be the strongest stimulus to homage? The sting of desperation is, I think, a wonderful irritant to my emotions: but" (shrugging his shoulders) "you know nothing about these things; I'll address myself to my mother. Mamma, I'm in a dangerous way."

"As if that interested me!" said Mrs. Bretton.

"Alas! the cruelty of my lot!" responded her son. "Never man had a more unsentimental mother than mine: she never seems to think that such a calamity can befall her as a daughter-in-law."

"If I don't, it is not for want of having that same calamity held over my head: you have threatened me with it for the last ten years. 'Mamma, I am going to be married soon!' was the cry before you were well out of jackets."

"But, mother, one of these days it will be realized. All of a sudden, when you think you are most secure, I shall go forth like Jacob or Esau, or any other patriarch, and take me a wife: perhaps of these which are of the daughters of the land."

"At your peril, John Graham! that is all."

"This mother of mine means me to be an old bachelor. What a jealous old lady it is! But now just look at that splendid creature in the pale blue satin dress, and hair of paler brown, with 'reflets satinés' as those of her robe. Would you not feel proud, mamma, if I were to bring that goddess home some day, and introduce her to you as Mrs. Bretton, junior?"

"You will bring no goddess to La Terrasse: that little château will not contain two mistresses; especially if the second be of the height, bulk, and circumference of that mighty doll in wood and wax, and kid and satin."

"Mamma, she would fill your blue chair so admirably!"

"Fill my chair? I defy the foreign usurper! a rueful chair should it be for her: but hush, John Graham! Hold your tongue, and use your eyes."

During the above skirmish, the hall, which, I had thought, seemed full at the entrance, continued to admit party after party, until the semicircle before the stage presented one dense mass of heads, sloping from floor to ceiling. The stage, too, or rather the wide temporary platform, larger than any stage, desert half an hour since, was now overflowing with life; round two grand pianos, placed about the centre, a white flock of young girls, the pupils of the Conservatoire, had noiselessly poured. I had noticed their gathering, while Graham and his mother were engaged in discussing the belle in blue satin, and had watched with interest the process of arraying and marshalling them. Two gentlemen, in each of whom I recognised an acquaintance, officered this virgin troop. One, an artistic-looking man, bearded, and with long hair, was a noted pianiste, and also the first music-teacher in Villette; he attended twice a week at Madame Beck's pensionnat, to give lessons to the few pupils whose parents were rich enough to allow their daughters the privilege of his instructions; his name was M. Josef Emanuel, and he was half-brother to M. Paul: which potent personage was now visible in the person of the second gentleman.

M. Paul amused me; I smiled to myself as I watched him, he seemed so thoroughly in his element — standing conspicuous in presence of a wide and grand assemblage, arranging, restraining, over-aweing about one hundred young ladies. He was, too, so perfectly in earnest — so energetic, so intent, and, above all, so absolute: and yet what business had he there? What had he to do with music or the Conservatoire — he who could hardly distinguish one note from another? I knew that it was his love of display and authority which had brought him there — a love not offensive, only because so naive. It presently became obvious that his brother, M. Josef, was as much under his control as were the girls themselves. Never was such a little hawk of a man as that M. Paul! Ere long, some noted singers and musicians dawned upon the platform: as these stars rose, the comet-like professor set. Insufferable to him were all notorieties and celebrities: where he could not outshine, he fled.

And now all was prepared: but one compartment of the hall waited to be filled — a compartment covered with crimson, like the grand staircase and doors, furnished with stuffed and cushioned benches, ranged on each side of two regal chairs, placed solemnly under a canopy.

A signal was given, the doors rolled back, the assembly stood up, the orchestra burst out, and, to the welcome of a choral burst, enter the King, the Queen, the Court of

Villette

Labassecour.

Till then, I had never set eyes on living king or queen; it may consequently be conjectured how I strained my powers of vision to take in these specimens of European royalty. By whomsoever majesty is beheld for the first time, there will always be experienced a vague surprise bordering on disappointment, that the same does not appear seated, en permanence, on a throne, bonneted with a crown, and furnished, as to the hand, with a sceptre. Looking out for a king and queen, and seeing only a middle-aged soldier and a rather young lady, I felt half cheated, half pleased.

Well do I recall that King—a man of fifty, a little bowed, a little grey: there was no face in all that assembly which resembled his. I had never read, never been told anything of his nature or his habits; and at first the strong hieroglyphics graven as with iron stylet on his brow, round his eyes, beside his mouth, puzzled and baffled instinct. Ere long, however, if I did not know, at least I felt, the meaning of those characters written without hand. There sat a silent sufferer—a nervous, melancholy man. Those eyes had looked on the visits of a certain ghost—had long waited the comings and goings of that strangest spectre, Hypochondria. Perhaps he saw her now on that stage, over against him, amidst all that brilliant throng. Hypochondria has that wont, to rise in the midst of thousands—dark as Doom, pale as Malady, and well-nigh strong as Death. Her comrade and victim thinks to be happy one moment—"Not so," says she; "I come." And she freezes the blood in his heart, and beclouds the light in his eye.

Some might say it was the foreign crown pressing the King's brows which bent them to that peculiar and painful fold; some might quote the effects of early bereavement. Something there might be of both these; but these are embittered by that darkest foe of humanity—constitutional melancholy. The Queen, his wife, knew this: it seemed to me, the reflection of her husband's grief lay, a subduing shadow, on her own benignant face. A mild, thoughtful, graceful woman that princess seemed; not beautiful, not at all like the women of solid charms and marble feelings described a page or two since. Hers was a somewhat slender shape; her features, though distinguished enough, were too suggestive of reigning dynasties and royal lines to give unqualified pleasure. The expression clothing that profile was agreeable in the present instance; but you could not avoid connecting it with remembered effigies, where similar lines appeared, under phase ignoble; feeble, or sensual, or cunning, as the case might be. The Queen's eye, however, was her own;

and pity, goodness, sweet sympathy, blessed it with divinest light. She moved no sovereign, but a lady—kind, loving, elegant. Her little son, the Prince of Labassecour, and young Duc de Dindonneau, accompanied her: he leaned on his mother's knee; and, ever and anon, in the course of that evening, I saw her observant of the monarch at her side, conscious of his beclouded abstraction, and desirous to rouse him from it by drawing his attention to their son. She often bent her head to listen to the boy's remarks, and would then smilingly repeat them to his sire. The moody King started, listened, smiled, but invariably relapsed as soon as his good angel ceased speaking. Full mournful and significant was that spectacle! Not the less so because, both for the aristocracy and the honest bourgeoisie of Labassecour, its peculiarity seemed to be wholly invisible: I could not discover that one soul present was either struck or touched.

With the King and Queen had entered their court, comprising two or three foreign ambassadors; and with them came the elite of the foreigners then resident in Villette. These took possession of the crimson benches; the ladies were seated; most of the men remained standing: their sable rank, lining the background, looked like a dark foil to the splendour displayed in front. Nor was this splendour without varying light and shade and gradation: the middle distance was filled with matrons in velvets and satins, in plumes and gems; the benches in the foreground, to the Queen's right hand, seemed devoted exclusively to young girls, the flower—perhaps, I should rather say, the bud—of Villette aristocracy. Here were no jewels, no head-dresses, no velvet pile or silken sheen: purity, simplicity, and aërial grace reigned in that virgin band. Young heads simply braided, and fair forms (I was going to write sylph forms, but that would have been quite untrue: several of these "jeunes filles," who had not numbered more than sixteen or seventeen years, boasted contours as robust and solid as those of a stout Englishwoman of five-and-twenty)—fair forms robed in white, or pale rose, or placid blue, suggested thoughts of heaven and angels. I knew a couple, at least, of these "rose et blanche" specimens of humanity. Here was a pair of Madame Beck's late pupils—Mesdemoiselles Mathilde and Angélique: pupils who, during their last year at school, ought to have been in the first class, but whose brains never got them beyond the second division. In English, they had been under my own charge, and hard work it was to get them to translate rationally a page of The Vicar of Wakefield. Also during three months I had one of them for my vis-à-vis at table, and the quantity of household bread, butter, and stewed fruit, she would habitually consume at "second déjeuner" was a real world's wonder—to be exceeded only by the fact of her actually pocketing slices she could not eat. Here be truths—wholesome truths, too.

I knew another of these seraphs—the prettiest, or, at any rate, the least demure and hypocritical looking of the lot: she was seated by the daughter of an English peer, also an honest, though haughty-looking girl: both had entered in the suite of the British embassy. She (i.e. my acquaintance) had a slight, pliant figure, not at all like the forms of the foreign damsels: her hair, too, was not close-braided, like a shell or a skull-cap of satin; it looked like hair, and waved from her head, long, curled, and flowing. She chatted away volubly, and seemed full of a light-headed sort of satisfaction with herself and her position. I did not look at Dr. Bretton; but I knew that he, too, saw Ginevra Fanshawe: he had become so quiet, he answered so briefly his mother's remarks, he so often suppressed a sigh. Why should he sigh? He had confessed a taste for the pursuit of love under difficulties; here was full gratification for that taste. His ladylove beamed upon him from a sphere above his own: he could not come near her; he was not certain that he could win from her a look. I watched to see if she would so far favour him. Our seat was not far from the crimson benches; we must inevitably be seen thence, by eyes so quick and roving as Miss Fanshawe's, and very soon those optics of hers were upon us: at least, upon Dr. and Mrs. Bretton. I kept rather in the shade and out of sight, not wishing to be immediately recognised: she looked quite steadily at Dr. John, and then she raised a glass to examine his mother; a minute or two afterwards she laughingly whispered her neighbour; upon the performance commencing, her rambling attention was attracted to the platform.

On the concert I need not dwell; the reader would not care to have my impressions thereanent: and, indeed, it would not be worth while to record them, as they were the impressions of an ignorance crasse. The young ladies of the Conservatoire, being very much frightened, made rather a tremulous exhibition on the two grand pianos. M. Josef Emanuel stood by them while they played; but he had not the tact or influence of his kinsman, who, under similar circumstances, would certainly have compelled pupils of his to demean themselves with heroism and self-possession. M. Paul would have placed the hysteric débutantes between two fires—terror of the audience, and terror of himself—and would have inspired them with the courage of desperation, by making the latter terror incomparably the greater: M. Josef could not do this.

Following the white muslin pianistes, came a fine, full-grown, sulky lady in white satin. She sang. Her singing just affected me like the tricks of a conjuror: I wondered how she did it—how she made her voice run up and down, and cut such marvellous capers; but a simple Scotch melody, played by a rude street minstrel, has often moved me more deeply.

Afterwards stepped forth a gentleman, who, bending his body a good deal in the direction of the King and Queen, and frequently approaching his white-gloved hand to the region of his heart, vented a bitter outcry against a certain "fausse Isabelle." I thought he seemed especially to solicit the Queen's sympathy; but, unless I am egregiously mistaken, her Majesty lent her attention rather with the calm of courtesy than the earnestness of interest. This gentleman's state of mind was very harrowing, and I was glad when he wound up his musical exposition of the same.

Some rousing choruses struck me as the best part of the evening's entertainment. There were present deputies from all the best provincial choral societies; genuine, barrel-shaped, native Labassecouriens. These worthies gave voice without mincing the matter their hearty exertions had at least this good result—the ear drank thence a satisfying sense of power.

Through the whole performance—timid instrumental duets, conceited vocal solos, sonorous, brass-lunged choruses—my attention gave but one eye and one ear to the stage, the other being permanently retained in the service of Dr. Bretton: I could not forget him, nor cease to question how he was feeling, what he was thinking, whether he was amused or the contrary. At last he spoke.

"And how do you like it all, Lucy? You are very quiet," he said, in his own cheerful tone.

"I am quiet," I said, "because I am so very, very much interested: not merely with the music, but with everything about me."

He then proceeded to make some further remarks, with so much equanimity and composure that I began to think he had really not seen what I had seen, and I whispered—"Miss Fanshawe is here: have you noticed her?"

"Oh, yes! and I observed that you noticed her too."

"Is she come with Mrs. Cholmondeley, do you think?"

"Mrs. Cholmondeley is there with a very grand party. Yes;

Villette

Ginevra was in her train; and Mrs. Cholmondeley was in Lady — —'s train, who was in the Queen's train. If this were not one of the compact little minor European courts, whose very formalities are little more imposing than familiarities, and whose gala grandeur is but homeliness in Sunday array, it would sound all very fine."

"Ginevra saw you, I think?"

"So do I think so. I have had my eye on her several times since you withdrew yours; and I have had the honour of witnessing a little spectacle which you were spared."

I did not ask what; I waited voluntary information, which was presently given.

"Miss Fanshawe," he said, "has a companion with her — a lady of rank. I happen to know Lady Sara by sight; her noble mother has called me in professionally. She is a proud girl, but not in the least insolent, and I doubt whether Ginevra will have gained ground in her estimation by making a butt of her neighbours."

"What neighbours?"

"Merely myself and my mother. As to me it is all very natural: nothing, I suppose, can be fairer game than the young bourgeois doctor; but my mother! I never saw her ridiculed before. Do you know, the curling lip, and sarcastically levelled glass thus directed, gave me a most curious sensation?"

"Think nothing of it, Dr. John: it is not worth while. If Ginevra were in a giddy mood, as she is eminently to-night, she would make no scruple of laughing at that mild, pensive Queen, or that melancholy King. She is not actuated by malevolence, but sheer, heedless folly. To a feather-brained school-girl nothing is sacred."

"But you forget: I have not been accustomed to look on Miss Fanshawe in the light of a feather-brained school-girl. Was she not my divinity — the angel of my career?"

"Hem! There was your mistake."

"To speak the honest truth, without any false rant or assumed romance, there actually was a moment, six months ago, when I thought her divine. Do you remember our conversation about the presents? I was not quite open with you in discussing that subject: the warmth with which you took it up amused me. By way of having the full benefit of your lights, I allowed you to think me more in the dark than I really was. It was that test of the presents which first proved Ginevra mortal. Still her beauty retained its fascination: three days—three hours ago, I was very much her slave. As she passed me to-night, triumphant in beauty, my emotions did her homage; but for one luckless sneer, I should yet be the humblest of her servants. She might have scoffed at me, and, while wounding, she would not soon have alienated me: through myself, she could not in ten years have done what, in a moment, she has done through my mother."

He held his peace awhile. Never before had I seen so much fire, and so little sunshine in Dr. John's blue eye as just now.

"Lucy," he recommenced, "look well at my mother, and say, without fear or favour, in what light she now appears to you."

"As she always does—an English, middle-class gentlewoman; well, though gravely dressed, habitually independent of pretence, constitutionally composed and cheerful."

"So she seems to me—bless her! The merry may laugh with mamma, but the weak only will laugh at her. She shall not be ridiculed, with my consent, at least; nor without my—my scorn—my antipathy—my—"

He stopped: and it was time—for he was getting excited—more it seemed than the occasion warranted. I did not then know that he had witnessed double cause for dissatisfaction with Miss Fanshawe. The glow of his complexion, the expansion of his nostril, the bold curve which disdain gave his well-cut under lip, showed him in a new and striking phase. Yet the rare passion of the constitutionally suave and serene, is not a pleasant spectacle; nor did I like the sort of vindictive thrill which passed through his strong young frame.

"Do I frighten you, Lucy?" he asked.

"I cannot tell why you are so very angry."

"For this reason," he muttered in my ear. "Ginevra is neither a pure angel, nor a pure-minded woman."

"Nonsense! you exaggerate: she has no great harm in her."

"Too much for me. I can see where you are blind. Now dismiss the subject. Let me amuse myself by teasing mamma: I will assert that she is flagging. Mamma, pray rouse yourself."

"John, I will certainly rouse you if you are not better conducted. Will you and Lucy be silent, that I may hear the singing?"

They were then thundering in a chorus, under cover of which all the previous dialogue had taken place.

"You hear the singing, mamma! Now, I will wager my studs, which are genuine, against your paste brooch—"

"My paste brooch, Graham? Profane boy! you know that it is a stone of value."

"Oh! that is one of your superstitions: you were cheated in the business."

"I am cheated in fewer things than you imagine. How do you happen to be acquainted with young ladies of the court, John? I have observed two of them pay you no small attention during the last half-hour."

"I wish you would not observe them."

"Why not? Because one of them satirically levels her eyeglass at me? She is a pretty, silly girl: but are you apprehensive that her titter will discomfit the old lady?"

"The sensible, admirable old lady! Mother, you are better to me than ten wives yet."

"Don't be demonstrative, John, or I shall faint, and you will have to carry me out; and if that burden were laid upon you, you would reverse your last speech, and exclaim, 'Mother, ten wives could hardly be worse to me than you are!'"

The concert over, the Lottery "au bénéfice des pauvres" came next: the interval between was one of general relaxation, and the pleasantest imaginable stir and commotion. The white flock was cleared from the platform; a busy throng of gentlemen crowded it instead, making arrangements for the drawing; and amongst these—the busiest of all—re-appeared that certain well-known form, not tall but active, alive with the energy and movement of three tall men. How M. Paul did work! How he issued directions, and, at the same time, set his own shoulder to the wheel! Half-a-dozen assistants were at his beck to remove the pianos, &c.; no matter, he must add to their strength his own. The redundancy of his alertness was half-vexing, half-ludicrous: in my mind I both disapproved and derided most of this fuss. Yet, in the midst of prejudice and annoyance, I could not, while watching, avoid perceiving a certain not disagreeable naïveté in all he did and said; nor could I be blind to certain vigorous characteristics of his physiognomy, rendered conspicuous now by the contrast with a throng of tamer faces: the deep, intent keenness of his eye, the power of his forehead, pale, broad, and full—the mobility of his most flexible mouth. He lacked the calm of force, but its movement and its fire he signally possessed.

Meantime the whole hall was in a stir; most people rose and remained standing, for a change; some walked about, all talked and laughed. The crimson compartment presented a peculiarly animated scene. The long cloud of gentlemen, breaking into fragments, mixed with the rainbow line of ladies; two or three officer-like men approached the King and conversed with him. The Queen, leaving her chair, glided along the rank of young ladies, who all stood up as she passed; and to each in turn I saw her vouchsafe some token of kindness—a gracious word, look or smile. To the two pretty English girls, Lady Sara and Ginevra Fanshawe, she addressed several sentences; as she left them, both, and especially the latter, seemed to glow all over with gratification. They were afterwards accosted by several ladies, and a little circle of gentlemen gathered round them; amongst these—the nearest to Ginevra—stood the Count de Hamal.

"This room is stiflingly hot," said Dr. Bretton, rising with sudden impatience. "Lucy—mother—will you come a moment to the fresh air?"

"Go with him, Lucy," said Mrs. Bretton. "I would rather keep my seat."

Willingly would I have kept mine also, but Graham's desire must take precedence of my own; I accompanied him.

We found the night-air keen; or at least I did: he did not seem to feel it; but it was very still, and the star-sown sky spread cloudless. I was wrapped in a fur shawl. We took some turns on the pavement; in passing under a lamp, Graham encountered my eye.

"You look pensive, Lucy: is it on my account?"

"I was only fearing that you were grieved."

"Not at all: so be of good cheer—as I am. Whenever I die, Lucy, my persuasion is that it will not be of heart-complaint. I may be stung, I may seem to droop for a time, but no pain or malady of sentiment has yet gone through my whole system. You have always seen me cheerful at home?"

"Generally."

"I am glad she laughed at my mother. I would not give the old lady for a dozen beauties. That sneer did me all the good in the world. Thank you, Miss Fanshawe!" And he lifted his hat from his waved locks, and made a mock reverence.

"Yes," he said, "I thank her. She has made me feel that nine parts in ten of my heart have always been sound as a bell, and the tenth bled from a mere puncture: a lancet-prick that will heal in a trice."

"You are angry just now, heated and indignant; you will think and feel differently to-morrow."

"I heated and indignant! You don't know me. On the contrary, the heat is gone: I am as cool as the night—which, by the way, may be too cool for you. We will go back."

"Dr. John, this is a sudden change."

"Not it: or if it be, there are good reasons for it—two good reasons: I have told you one. But now let us re-enter."

We did not easily regain our seats; the lottery was begun, and all was excited confusion; crowds blocked the sort of corridor along which we had to pass: it was necessary to pause for a time. Happening to glance round—indeed I half fancied I heard my name pronounced—I saw quite near, the ubiquitous, the inevitable M. Paul. He was looking at me gravely and intently: at me, or rather at my pink dress—sardonic comment on which gleamed in his eye. Now it was his habit to indulge in strictures on the dress, both of the teachers and pupils, at Madame Beck's—a habit which the former, at least, held to be an offensive impertinence: as yet I had not suffered from it—my sombre daily attire not being calculated to attract notice. I was in no mood to permit any new encroachment to-night: rather than accept his banter, I would ignore his presence, and accordingly steadily turned my face to the sleeve of Dr. John's coat; finding in that same black sleeve a prospect more redolent of pleasure and comfort, more genial, more friendly, I thought, than was offered by the dark little Professor's unlovely visage. Dr. John seemed unconsciously to sanction the preference by looking down and saying in his kind voice, "Ay, keep close to my side, Lucy: these crowding burghers are no respecters of persons."

I could not, however, be true to myself. Yielding to some influence, mesmeric or otherwise—an influence unwelcome, displeasing, but effective—I again glanced round to see if M. Paul was gone. No, there he stood on the same spot, looking still, but with a changed eye; he had penetrated my thought, and read my wish to shun him. The mocking but not ill-humoured gaze was turned to a swarthy frown, and when I bowed, with a view to conciliation, I got only the stiffest and sternest of nods in return.

"Whom have you made angry, Lucy?" whispered Dr. Bretton, smiling. "Who is that savage-looking friend of yours?"

"One of the professors at Madame Beck's: a very cross little man."

"He looks mighty cross just now: what have you done to him? What is it all about? Ah, Lucy, Lucy! tell me the meaning of this."

"No mystery, I assure you. M. Emanuel is very exigent, and because I looked at your coat-sleeve, instead of curtseying and dipping to him, he thinks I have failed in respect."

"The little—" began Dr. John: I know not what more he would have added, for at that moment I was nearly thrown down amongst the feet of the crowd. M. Paul had rudely pushed past, and was elbowing his way with such utter disregard to the convenience and security of all around, that a very uncomfortable pressure was the consequence.

"I think he is what he himself would call 'méchant,'" said Dr. Bretton. I thought so, too.

Slowly and with difficulty we made our way along the passage, and at last regained our seats. The drawing of the lottery lasted nearly an hour; it was an animating and amusing scene; and as we each held tickets, we shared in the alternations of hope and fear raised by each turn of the wheel. Two little girls, of five and six years old, drew the numbers: and the prizes were duly proclaimed from the platform. These prizes were numerous, though of small value. It so fell out that Dr. John and I each gained one: mine was a cigar-case, his a lady's head-dress — a most airy sort of blue and silver turban, with a streamer of plumage on one side, like a snowy cloud. He was excessively anxious to make an exchange; but I could not be brought to hear reason, and to this day I keep my cigar-case: it serves, when I look at it, to remind me of old times, and one happy evening.

Dr. John, for his part, held his turban at arm's length between his finger and thumb, and looked at it with a mixture of reverence and embarrassment highly provocative of laughter. The contemplation over, he was about coolly to deposit the delicate fabric on the ground between his feet; he seemed to have no shadow of an idea of the treatment or stowage it ought to receive: if his mother had not come to the rescue, I think he would finally have crushed it under his arm like an opera-hat; she restored it to the band-box whence it had issued.

Graham was quite cheerful all the evening, and his cheerfulness seemed natural and unforced. His demeanour, his look, is not easily described; there was something in it peculiar, and, in its way, original. I read in it no common mastery of the passions, and a fund of deep and healthy strength which, without any exhausting effort, bore down Disappointment and extracted her fang. His manner, now, reminded me of qualities I had noticed in him when professionally engaged amongst the poor, the guilty, and the suffering, in the Basse-Ville: he looked at once determined, enduring, and sweet-tempered. Who could help liking him? He betrayed no weakness which harassed all your feelings with considerations as to how its faltering must be propped; from him broke no irritability which startled calm and quenched mirth; his lips let fall no caustic that burned to the bone; his eye shot no morose shafts that went cold, and rusty, and venomed through your heart: beside him was rest and refuge — around him, fostering sunshine.

And yet he had neither forgiven nor forgotten Miss Fanshawe. Once angered, I doubt if Dr. Bretton were to be soon propitiated — once alienated, whether he were ever to be reclaimed. He looked at her more than once; not stealthily or humbly, but with a movement of hardy, open observation. De Hamal was now a fixture beside her; Mrs. Cholmondeley sat near, and they and she were wholly absorbed in the discourse, mirth, and excitement, with which the crimson seats were as much astir as any plebeian part of the hall. In the course of some apparently animated discussion, Ginevra once or twice lifted her hand and arm; a handsome bracelet gleamed upon the latter. I saw that its gleam flickered in Dr. John's eye—quickening therein a derisive, ireful sparkle; he laughed: — —

"I think," he said, "I will lay my turban on my wonted altar of offerings; there, at any rate, it would be certain to find favour: no grisette has a more facile faculty of acceptance. Strange! for after all, I know she is a girl of family."

"But you don't know her education, Dr. John," said I. "Tossed about all her life from one foreign school to another, she may justly proffer the plea of ignorance in extenuation of most of her faults. And then, from what she says, I believe her father and mother were brought up much as she has been brought up."

"I always understood she had no fortune; and once I had pleasure in the thought," said he.

"She tells me," I answered, "that they are poor at home; she always speaks quite candidly on such points: you never find her lying, as these foreigners will often lie. Her parents have a large family: they occupy such a station and possess such connections as, in their opinion, demand display; stringent necessity of circumstances and inherent thoughtlessness of disposition combined, have engendered reckless unscrupulousness as to how they obtain the means of sustaining a good appearance. This is the state of things, and the only state of things, she has seen from childhood upwards."

"I believe it—and I thought to mould her to something better: but, Lucy, to speak the plain truth, I have felt a new thing to-night, in looking at her and de Hamal. I felt it before noticing the impertinence directed at my mother. I saw a look interchanged between them immediately after their entrance, which threw a most unwelcome light on my mind."

"How do you mean? You have been long aware of the flirtation they keep up?"

"Ay, flirtation! That might be an innocent girlish wile to lure on the true lover; but what I refer to was not flirtation: it was a look marking mutual and secret understanding—it was neither girlish nor innocent. No woman, were she as beautiful as Aphrodite, who could give or receive such a glance, shall ever be sought in marriage by me: I would rather wed a paysanne in a short petticoat and high cap—and be sure that she was honest."

I could not help smiling. I felt sure he now exaggerated the case: Ginevra, I was certain, was honest enough, with all her giddiness. I told him so. He shook his head, and said he would not be the man to trust her with his honour.

"The only thing," said I, "with which you may safely trust her. She would unscrupulously damage a husband's purse and property, recklessly try his patience and temper: I don't think she would breathe, or let another breathe, on his honour."

"You are becoming her advocate," said he. "Do you wish me to resume my old chains?"

"No: I am glad to see you free, and trust that free you will long remain. Yet be, at the same time, just."

"I am so: just as Rhadamanthus, Lucy. When once I am thoroughly estranged, I cannot help being severe. But look! the King and Queen are rising. I like that Queen: she has a sweet countenance. Mamma, too, is excessively tired; we shall never get the old lady home if we stay longer."

"I tired, John?" cried Mrs. Bretton, looking at least as animated and as wide-awake as her son. "I would undertake to sit you out yet: leave us both here till morning, and we should see which would look the most jaded by sunrise."

"I should not like to try the experiment; for, in truth, mamma, you are the most unfading of evergreens and the freshest of matrons. It must then be on the plea of your son's delicate nerves and fragile constitution that I found a petition for our speedy adjournment."

"Indolent young man! You wish you were in bed, no doubt; and I suppose you must be humoured. There is Lucy, too, looking quite done up. For shame, Lucy! At your age, a week of evenings-out would not have made me a shade paler. Come away, both of you; and you may laugh at the old lady as much as you please, but, for my part, I shall take charge of the bandbox and turban."

Which she did accordingly. I offered to relieve her, but was shaken off with kindly contempt: my godmother opined that I had enough to do to take care of myself. Not standing on ceremony now, in the midst of the gay "confusion worse confounded" succeeding to the King and Queen's departure, Mrs. Bretton preceded us, and promptly made us a lane through the crowd. Graham followed, apostrophizing his mother as the most flourishing grisette it had ever been his good fortune to see charged with carriage of a bandbox; he also desired me to mark her affection for the sky-blue turban, and announced his conviction that she intended one day to wear it.

The night was now very cold and very dark, but with little delay we found the carriage. Soon we were packed in it, as warm and as snug as at a fire-side; and the drive home was, I think, still pleasanter than the drive to the concert. Pleasant it was, even though the coachman—having spent in the shop of a "marchand de vin" a portion of the time we passed at the concert—drove us along the dark and solitary chaussée far past the turn leading down to La Terrasse; we, who were occupied in talking and laughing, not noticing the aberration till, at last, Mrs. Bretton intimated that, though she had always thought the château a retired spot, she did not know it was situated at the world's end, as she declared seemed now to be the case, for she believed we had been an hour and a half en route, and had not yet taken the turn down the avenue.

Then Graham looked out, and perceiving only dim-spread fields, with unfamiliar rows of pollards and limes ranged along their else invisible sunk-fences, began to conjecture how matters were, and calling a halt and descending, he mounted the box and took the reins himself. Thanks to him, we arrived safe at home about an hour and a half beyond our time.

Martha had not forgotten us; a cheerful fire was burning, and a neat supper spread in the dining-room: we were glad of both. The winter dawn was actually breaking before we gained our chambers. I took off my pink dress and lace mantle with happier feelings than I had experienced in putting them on. Not all, perhaps, who had shone brightly arrayed at that concert could say the same; for not all had been satisfied with friendship—with its calm comfort and modest hope.

CHAPTER XXI.

REACTION.

Yet three days, and then I must go back to the pensionnat. I almost numbered the moments of these days upon the clock; fain would I have retarded their flight; but they glided by while I watched them: they were already gone while I yet feared their departure.

"Lucy will not leave us to-day," said Mrs. Bretton, coaxingly at breakfast; "she knows we can procure a second respite."

"I would not ask for one if I might have it for a word," said I. "I long to get the good-by over, and to be settled in the Rue Fossette again. I must go this morning: I must go directly; my trunk is packed and corded."

It appeared; however, that my going depended upon Graham; he had said he would accompany me, and it so fell out that he was engaged all day, and only returned home at dusk. Then ensued a little combat of words. Mrs. Bretton and her son pressed me to remain one night more. I could have cried, so irritated and eager was I to be gone. I longed to leave them as the criminal on the scaffold longs for the axe to descend: that is, I wished the pang over. How much I wished it, they could not tell. On these points, mine was a state of mind out of their experience.

It was dark when Dr. John handed me from the carriage at Madame Beck's door. The lamp above was lit; it rained a November drizzle, as it had rained all day: the lamplight gleamed on the wet pavement. Just such a night was it as that on which, not a year ago, I had first stopped at this very threshold; just similar was the scene. I remembered the very shapes of the paving-stones which I had noted with idle eye, while, with a thick-beating heart, I waited the unclosing of that door at which I stood—a solitary and a supplicant. On that night, too, I had briefly met him who now stood with me. Had I ever reminded him of that rencontre, or explained it? I had not, nor ever felt the inclination to do so: it was a pleasant thought, laid by in my own mind, and best kept there.

Graham rung the bell. The door was instantly opened, for it was just that period of the evening when the half-boarders took their departure—consequently, Rosine was on the alert.

"Don't come in," said I to him; but he stepped a moment into the well-lighted vestibule. I had not wished him to see that "the water stood in my eyes," for his was too kind a nature ever to be needlessly shown such signs of sorrow. He always wished to heal — to relieve — when, physician as he was, neither cure nor alleviation were, perhaps, in his power.

"Keep up your courage, Lucy. Think of my mother and myself as true friends. We will not forget you."

"Nor will I forget you, Dr. John."

My trunk was now brought in. We had shaken hands; he had turned to go, but he was not satisfied: he had not done or said enough to content his generous impulses.

"Lucy," — stepping after me — "shall you feel very solitary here?"

"At first I shall."

"Well, my mother will soon call to see you; and, meantime, I'll tell you what I'll do. I'll write — just any cheerful nonsense that comes into my head — shall I?"

"Good, gallant heart!" thought I to myself; but I shook my head, smiling, and said, "Never think of it: impose on yourself no such task. You write to me! — you'll not have time."

"Oh! I will find or make time. Good-by!"

He was gone. The heavy door crashed to: the axe had fallen — the pang was experienced.

Allowing myself no time to think or feel — swallowing tears as if they had been wine — I passed to Madame's sitting-room to pay the necessary visit of ceremony and respect. She received me with perfectly well-acted cordiality — was even demonstrative, though brief, in her welcome. In ten minutes I was dismissed. From the salle-à-manger I proceeded to the refectory, where pupils and teachers were now assembled for evening study: again I had a welcome, and one not, I think, quite hollow. That over, I was free to repair to the dormitory.

"And will Graham really write?" I questioned, as I sank tired on the edge of the bed.

Reason, coming stealthily up to me through the twilight of

that long, dim chamber, whispered sedately—"He may write once. So kind is his nature, it may stimulate him for once to make the effort. But it cannot be continued—it may not be repeated. Great were that folly which should build on such a promise—insane that credulity which should mistake the transitory rain-pool, holding in its hollow one draught, for the perennial spring yielding the supply of seasons."

I bent my head: I sat thinking an hour longer. Reason still whispered me, laying on my shoulder a withered hand, and frostily touching my ear with the chill blue lips of eld.

"If," muttered she, "if he should write, what then? Do you meditate pleasure in replying? Ah, fool! I warn you! Brief be your answer. Hope no delight of heart—no indulgence of intellect: grant no expansion to feeling—give holiday to no single faculty: dally with no friendly exchange: foster no genial intercommunion...."

"But I have talked to Graham and you did not chide," I pleaded.

"No," said she, "I needed not. Talk for you is good discipline. You converse imperfectly. While you speak, there can be no oblivion of inferiority—no encouragement to delusion: pain, privation, penury stamp your language...."

"But," I again broke in, "where the bodily presence is weak and the speech contemptible, surely there cannot be error in making written language the medium of better utterance than faltering lips can achieve?"

Reason only answered, "At your peril you cherish that idea, or suffer its influence to animate any writing of yours!"

"But if I feel, may I never express?"

"Never!" declared Reason.

I groaned under her bitter sternness. Never—never—oh, hard word! This hag, this Reason, would not let me look up, or smile, or hope: she could not rest unless I were altogether crushed, cowed, broken-in, and broken-down. According to her, I was born only to work for a piece of bread, to await the pains of death, and steadily through all life to despond. Reason might be right; yet no wonder we are glad at times to defy her, to rush from under her rod and give a truant hour to Imagination—her soft, bright foe, our sweet Help, our divine Hope. We shall and must break bounds at intervals, despite the terrible revenge that awaits our return. Reason is vindictive as a devil: for me she was always envenomed as a step-mother. If I have obeyed her it has chiefly been with the obedience of fear, not of love. Long ago I should have died of her ill-usage her stint, her chill, her barren board, her icy bed, her savage, ceaseless blows; but for that kinder Power who holds my secret and sworn allegiance. Often has Reason turned me out by night, in mid-winter, on cold snow, flinging for sustenance the gnawed bone dogs had forsaken: sternly has she vowed her stores held nothing more for me—harshly denied my right to ask better things…. Then, looking up, have I seen in the sky a head amidst circling stars, of which the midmost and the brightest lent a ray sympathetic and attent. A spirit, softer and better than Human Reason, has descended with quiet flight to the waste—bringing all round her a sphere of air borrowed of eternal summer; bringing perfume of flowers which cannot fade—fragrance of trees whose fruit is life; bringing breezes pure from a world whose day needs no sun to lighten it. My hunger has this good angel appeased with food, sweet and strange, gathered amongst gleaning angels, garnering their dew-white harvest in the first fresh hour of a heavenly day; tenderly has she assuaged the insufferable fears which weep away life itself—kindly given rest to deadly weariness—generously lent hope and impulse to paralyzed despair. Divine, compassionate, succourable influence! When I bend the knee to other than God, it shall be at thy white and winged feet, beautiful on mountain or on plain. Temples have been reared to the Sun—altars dedicated to the Moon. Oh, greater glory! To thee neither hands build, nor lips consecrate: but hearts, through ages, are faithful to thy worship. A dwelling thou hast, too wide for walls, too high for dome—a temple whose floors are space—rites whose mysteries transpire in presence, to the kindling, the harmony of worlds!

Sovereign complete! thou hadst, for endurance, thy great army of martyrs; for achievement, thy chosen band of worthies. Deity unquestioned, thine essence foils decay!

This daughter of Heaven remembered me to-night; she saw me weep, and she came with comfort: "Sleep," she said. "Sleep, sweetly—I gild thy dreams!"

She kept her word, and watched me through a night's rest; but at dawn Reason relieved the guard. I awoke with a sort of start; the rain was dashing against the panes, and the wind uttering a peevish cry at intervals; the night-lamp was dying on the black circular stand in the middle of the dormitory: day had already broken. How I pity those whom mental pain stuns instead of rousing! This morning the pang of waking snatched me out of bed like a hand with a giant's gripe. How quickly I dressed in the cold of the raw dawn! How deeply I drank of the ice-cold water in my carafe! This was always my cordial, to which, like other dram-drinkers, I had eager recourse when unsettled by chagrin.

Ere long the bell rang its réveillée to the whole school. Being dressed, I descended alone to the refectory, where the stove was lit and the air was warm; through the rest of the house it was cold, with the nipping severity of a continental winter: though now but the beginning of November, a north wind had thus early brought a wintry blight over Europe: I remember the black stoves pleased me little when I first came; but now I began to associate with them a sense of comfort, and liked them, as in England we like a fireside.

Sitting down before this dark comforter, I presently fell into a deep argument with myself on life and its chances, on destiny and her decrees. My mind, calmer and stronger now than last night, made for itself some imperious rules, prohibiting under deadly penalties all weak retrospect of happiness past; commanding a patient journeying through the wilderness of the present, enjoining a reliance on faith—a watching of the cloud and pillar which subdue while they guide, and awe while they illumine—hushing the impulse to fond idolatry, checking the longing out-look for a far-off promised land whose rivers are, perhaps, never to be reached save in dying dreams, whose sweet pastures are to be viewed but from the desolate and sepulchral summit of a Nebo.

By degrees, a composite feeling of blended strength and pain wound itself wirily round my heart, sustained, or at least restrained, its throbbings, and made me fit for the day's work. I lifted my head.

As I said before, I was sitting near the stove, let into the wall beneath the refectory and the carré, and thus sufficing to heat both apartments. Piercing the same wall, and close beside the stove, was a window, looking also into the carré; as I looked up a cap-tassel, a brow, two eyes, filled a pane of that window; the fixed gaze of those two eyes hit right against my own glance: they were watching me. I had not till that moment known that tears were on my cheek, but I felt them now.

This was a strange house, where no corner was sacred from intrusion, where not a tear could be shed, nor a thought pondered, but a spy was at hand to note and to divine. And this new, this out-door, this male spy, what business had brought him to the premises at this unwonted hour? What possible right had he to intrude on me thus? No other professor would have dared to cross the carré before the class-bell rang. M. Emanuel took no account of hours nor of claims: there was some book of reference in the first-class library which he had occasion to consult; he had come to seek it: on his way he passed the refectory. It was very much his habit to wear eyes before, behind, and on each side of him: he had seen me through the little window — he now opened the refectory door, and there he stood.

"Mademoiselle, vous êtes triste."

"Monsieur, j'en ai bien le droit."

"Vous êtes malade de cœur et d'humeur," he pursued. "You are at once mournful and mutinous. I see on your cheek two tears which I know are hot as two sparks, and salt as two crystals of the sea. While I speak you eye me strangely. Shall I tell you of what I am reminded while watching you?"

"Monsieur, I shall be called away to prayers shortly; my time for conversation is very scant and brief at this hour — excuse — —"

"I excuse everything," he interrupted; "my mood is so meek, neither rebuff nor, perhaps, insult could ruffle it. You remind me, then, of a young she wild creature, new caught, untamed, viewing with a mixture of fire and fear the first entrance of the breaker-in."

Unwarrantable accost! — rash and rude if addressed to a pupil; to a teacher inadmissible. He thought to provoke a warm reply; I had seen him vex the passionate to explosion before now. In me his malice should find no gratification; I sat silent.

"You look," said he, "like one who would snatch at a draught of sweet poison, and spurn wholesome bitters with disgust."

"Indeed, I never liked bitters; nor do I believe them wholesome. And to whatever is sweet, be it poison or food, you cannot, at least, deny its own delicious quality — sweetness. Better, perhaps, to die quickly a pleasant death, than drag on long a charmless life."

"Yet," said he, "you should take your bitter dose duly and

Villette

daily, if I had the power to administer it; and, as to the well-beloved poison, I would, perhaps, break the very cup which held it."

I sharply turned my head away, partly because his presence utterly displeased me, and partly because I wished to shun questions: lest, in my present mood, the effort of answering should overmaster self-command.

"Come," said he, more softly, "tell me the truth—you grieve at being parted from friends—is it not so?"

The insinuating softness was not more acceptable than the inquisitorial curiosity. I was silent. He came into the room, sat down on the bench about two yards from me, and persevered long, and, for him, patiently, in attempts to draw me into conversation—attempts necessarily unavailing, because I could not talk. At last I entreated to be let alone. In uttering the request, my voice faltered, my head sank on my arms and the table. I wept bitterly, though quietly. He sat a while longer. I did not look up nor speak, till the closing door and his retreating step told me that he was gone. These tears proved a relief.

I had time to bathe my eyes before breakfast, and I suppose I appeared at that meal as serene as any other person: not, however, quite as jocund-looking as the young lady who placed herself in the seat opposite mine, fixed on me a pair of somewhat small eyes twinkling gleefully, and frankly stretched across the table a white hand to be shaken. Miss Fanshawe's travels, gaieties, and flirtations agreed with her mightily; she had become quite plump, her cheeks looked as round as apples. I had seen her last in elegant evening attire. I don't know that she looked less charming now in her school-dress, a kind of careless peignoir of a dark-blue material, dimly and dingily plaided with black. I even think this dusky wrapper gave her charms a triumph; enhancing by contrast the fairness of her skin, the freshness of her bloom, the golden beauty of her tresses.

"I am glad you are come back, Timon," said she. Timon was one of her dozen names for me. "You don't know how often I have wanted you in this dismal hole."

"Oh, have you? Then, of course, if you wanted me, you have something for me to do: stockings to mend, perhaps." I never gave Ginevra a minute's or a farthing's credit for disinterestedness.

"Crabbed and crusty as ever!" said she. "I expected as much: it would not be you if you did not snub one. But now, come, grand-mother, I hope you like coffee as much, and pistolets as little as ever: are you disposed to barter?"

"Take your own way."

This way consisted in a habit she had of making me convenient. She did not like the morning cup of coffee; its school brewage not being strong or sweet enough to suit her palate; and she had an excellent appetite, like any other healthy school-girl, for the morning pistolets or rolls, which were new-baked and very good, and of which a certain allowance was served to each. This allowance being more than I needed, I gave half to Ginevra; never varying in my preference, though many others used to covet the superfluity; and she in return would sometimes give me a portion of her coffee. This morning I was glad of the draught; hunger I had none, and with thirst I was parched. I don't know why I chose to give my bread rather to Ginevra than to another; nor why, if two had to share the convenience of one drinking-vessel, as sometimes happened—for instance, when we took a long walk into the country, and halted for refreshment at a farm—I always contrived that she should be my convive, and rather liked to let her take the lion's share, whether of the white beer, the sweet wine, or the new milk: so it was, however, and she knew it; and, therefore, while we wrangled daily, we were never alienated.

After breakfast my custom was to withdraw to the first classe, and sit and read, or think (oftenest the latter) there alone, till the nine-o'clock bell threw open all doors, admitted the gathered rush of externes and demi-pensionnaires, and gave the signal for entrance on that bustle and business to which, till five P.M., there was no relax.

I was just seated this morning, when a tap came to the door.

"Pardon, Mademoiselle," said a pensionnaire, entering gently; and having taken from her desk some necessary book or paper, she withdrew on tip-toe, murmuring as she passed me, "Que mademoiselle est appliquée!"

Appliquée, indeed! The means of application were spread before me, but I was doing nothing; and had done nothing, and meant to do nothing. Thus does the world give us credit for merits we have not. Madame Beck herself deemed me a regular bas-bleu, and often and solemnly used to warn me not to study too much, lest "the blood should all go to my head." Indeed, everybody in the Rue Fossette held a superstition that "Meess Lucie" was learned; with the notable exception of M. Emanuel, who, by means peculiar to himself, and quite inscrutable to me, had obtained a not inaccurate inkling of my real qualifications, and used to take quiet opportunities of chuckling in my ear his malign glee over their scant measure. For my part, I never troubled myself about this penury. I dearly like to think my own thoughts; I had great pleasure in reading a few books, but not many: preferring always those on whose style or sentiment the writer's individual nature was plainly stamped; flagging inevitably over characterless books, however clever and meritorious: perceiving well that, as far as my own mind was concerned, God had limited its powers and, its action—thankful, I trust, for the gift bestowed, but unambitious of higher endowments, not restlessly eager after higher culture.

The polite pupil was scarcely gone, when, unceremoniously, without tap, in burst a second intruder. Had I been blind I should have known who this was. A constitutional reserve of manner had by this time told with wholesome and, for me, commodious effect, on the manners of my co-inmates; rarely did I now suffer from rude or intrusive treatment. When I first came, it would happen once and again that a blunt German would clap me on the shoulder, and ask me to run a race; or a riotous Labassecourienne seize me by the arm and drag me towards the playground: urgent proposals to take a swing at the "Pas de Géant," or to join in a certain romping hide-and-seek game called "Un, deux, trois," were formerly also of hourly occurrence; but all these little attentions had ceased some time ago—ceased, too, without my finding it necessary to be at the trouble of point-blank cutting them short. I had now no familiar demonstration to dread or endure, save from one quarter; and as that was English I could bear it. Ginevra Fanshawe made no scruple of—at times—catching me as I was crossing the carré, whirling me round in a compulsory waltz, and heartily enjoying the mental and physical discomfiture her proceeding induced. Ginevra Fanshawe it was who now broke in upon "my learned leisure." She carried a huge music-book under her arm.

"Go to your practising," said I to her at once: "away with you to the little salon!"

"Not till I have had a talk with you, chère amie. I know where you have been spending your vacation, and how you have commenced sacrificing to the graces, and enjoying life like any other belle. I saw you at the concert the other night, dressed, actually, like anybody else. Who is your tailleuse?"

"Tittle-tattle: how prettily it begins! My tailleuse! — a fiddlestick! Come, sheer off, Ginevra. I really don't want your company."

"But when I want yours so much, ange farouche, what does a little reluctance on your part signify? Dieu merci! we know how to manœuvre with our gifted compatriote — the learned 'ourse Britannique.' And so, Ourson, you know Isidore?"

"I know John Bretton."

"Oh, hush!" (putting her fingers in her ears) "you crack my tympanums with your rude Anglicisms. But, how is our well-beloved John? Do tell me about him. The poor man must be in a sad way. What did he say to my behaviour the other night? Wasn't I cruel?"

"Do you think I noticed you?"

"It was a delightful evening. Oh, that divine de Hamal! And then to watch the other sulking and dying in the distance; and the old lady — my future mamma-in-law! But I am afraid I and Lady Sara were a little rude in quizzing her."

"Lady Sara never quizzed her at all; and for what you did, don't make yourself in the least uneasy: Mrs. Bretton will survive your sneer."

"She may: old ladies are tough; but that poor son of hers! Do tell me what he said: I saw he was terribly cut up."

"He said you looked as if at heart you were already Madame de Hamal."

"Did he?" she cried with delight. "He noticed that? How charming! I thought he would be mad with jealousy."

"Ginevra, have you seriously done with Dr. Bretton? Do you want him to give you up?"

"Oh! you know he can't do that: but wasn't he mad?"

"Quite mad," I assented; "as mad as a March hare."

"Well, and how ever did you get him home?"

"How ever, indeed! Have you no pity on his poor mother and me? Fancy us holding him tight down in the carriage, and he raving between us, fit to drive everybody delirious. The very coachman went wrong, somehow, and we lost our way."

"You don't say so? You are laughing at me. Now, Lucy Snowe—"

"I assure you it is fact—and fact, also, that Dr. Bretton would not stay in the carriage: he broke from us, and would ride outside."

"And afterwards?"

"Afterwards—when he did reach home—the scene transcends description."

"Oh, but describe it—you know it is such fun!"

"Fun for you, Miss Fanshawe? but" (with stern gravity) "you know the proverb—'What is sport to one may be death to another.'"

"Go on, there's a darling Timon."

"Conscientiously, I cannot, unless you assure me you have some heart."

"I have—such an immensity, you don't know!"

"Good! In that case, you will be able to conceive Dr. Graham Bretton rejecting his supper in the first instance—the chicken, the sweetbread prepared for his refreshment, left on the table untouched. Then——but it is of no use dwelling at length on the harrowing details. Suffice it to say, that never, in the most stormy fits and moments of his infancy, had his mother such work to tuck the sheets about him as she had that night."

"He wouldn't lie still?"

"He wouldn't lie still: there it was. The sheets might be tucked in, but the thing was to keep them tucked in."

"And what did he say?"

"Say! Can't you imagine him demanding his divine Ginevra, anathematizing that demon, de Hamal—raving about golden locks, blue eyes, white arms, glittering bracelets?"

"No, did he? He saw the bracelet?"

"Saw the bracelet? Yes, as plain as I saw it: and, perhaps, for the first time, he saw also the brand-mark with which its pressure has encircled your arm. Ginevra" (rising, and changing my tone), "come, we will have an end of this. Go away to your practising."

And I opened the door.

"But you have not told me all."

"You had better not wait until I do tell you all. Such extra communicativeness could give you no pleasure. March!"

"Cross thing!" said she; but she obeyed: and, indeed, the first classe was my territory, and she could not there legally resist a notice of quittance from me.

Yet, to speak the truth, never had I been less dissatisfied with her than I was then. There was pleasure in thinking of the contrast between the reality and my description—to remember Dr. John enjoying the drive home, eating his supper with relish, and retiring to rest with Christian composure. It was only when I saw him really unhappy that I felt really vexed with the fair, frail cause of his suffering.

A fortnight passed; I was getting once more inured to the harness of school, and lapsing from the passionate pain of change to the palsy of custom. One afternoon, in crossing the carré, on my way to the first classe, where I was expected to assist at a lesson of "style and literature," I saw, standing by one of the long and large windows, Rosine, the portress. Her attitude, as usual, was quite nonchalante. She always "stood at ease;" one of her hands rested in her apron-pocket, the other at this moment held to her eyes a letter, whereof Mademoiselle coolly perused the address, and deliberately studied the seal.

A letter! The shape of a letter similar to that had haunted my brain in its very core for seven days past. I had dreamed of a letter last night. Strong magnetism drew me to that letter now; yet, whether I should have ventured to demand of Rosine so much as a glance at that white envelope, with the spot of red wax in the middle, I know not. No; I think I should have sneaked past in terror of a rebuff from Disappointment: my heart throbbed now as if I already heard the tramp of her approach. Nervous mistake! It was the rapid step of the Professor of Literature measuring the corridor. I fled before him. Could I but be seated quietly at my desk before his arrival, with the class under my orders all in disciplined readiness, he would,

Villette

perhaps, exempt me from notice; but, if caught lingering in the carré, I should be sure to come in for a special harangue. I had time to get seated, to enforce perfect silence, to take out my work, and to commence it amidst the profoundest and best trained hush, ere M. Emanuel entered with his vehement burst of latch and panel, and his deep, redundant bow, prophetic of choler.

As usual he broke upon us like a clap of thunder; but instead of flashing lightning-wise from the door to the estrade, his career halted midway at my desk. Setting his face towards me and the window, his back to the pupils and the room, he gave me a look—such a look as might have licensed me to stand straight up and demand what he meant—a look of scowling distrust.

"Voilà! pour vous," said he, drawing his hand from his waist-coat, and placing on my desk a letter—the very letter I had seen in Rosine's hand—the letter whose face of enamelled white and single Cyclop's-eye of vermilion-red had printed themselves so clear and perfect on the retina of an inward vision. I knew it, I felt it to be the letter of my hope, the fruition of my wish, the release from my doubt, the ransom from my terror. This letter M. Paul, with his unwarrantably interfering habits, had taken from the portress, and now delivered it himself.

I might have been angry, but had not a second for the sensation. Yes: I held in my hand not a slight note, but an envelope, which must, at least, contain a sheet: it felt not flimsy, but firm, substantial, satisfying. And here was the direction, "Miss Lucy Snowe," in a clean, clear, equal, decided hand; and here was the seal, round, full, deftly dropped by untremulous fingers, stamped with the well-cut impress of initials, "J. G. B." I experienced a happy feeling—a glad emotion which went warm to my heart, and ran lively through all my veins. For once a hope was realized. I held in my hand a morsel of real solid joy: not a dream, not an image of the brain, not one of those shadowy chances imagination pictures, and on which humanity starves but cannot live; not a mess of that manna I drearily eulogized awhile ago—which, indeed, at first melts on the lips with an unspeakable and preternatural sweetness, but which, in the end, our souls full surely loathe; longing deliriously for natural and earth-grown food, wildly praying Heaven's Spirits to reclaim their own spirit-dew and essence—an aliment divine, but for mortals deadly. It was neither sweet hail nor small coriander-seed—neither slight wafer, nor luscious honey, I had lighted on; it was the wild, savoury mess of the hunter, nourishing and salubrious meat, forest-fed or desert-reared, fresh, healthful, and life-sustaining. It was what the old dying patriarch demanded of his son Esau, promising in requital the blessing of his last breath. It was a godsend; and I inwardly thanked the God who had vouchsafed it. Outwardly I only thanked man, crying, "Thank you, thank you, Monsieur!"

Monsieur curled his lip, gave me a vicious glance of the eye, and strode to his estrade. M. Paul was not at all a good little man, though he had good points.

Did I read my letter there and then? Did I consume the venison at once and with haste, as if Esau's shaft flew every day?

I knew better. The cover with its address — the seal, with its three clear letters — was bounty and abundance for the present. I stole from the room, I procured the key of the great dormitory, which was kept locked by day. I went to my bureau; with a sort of haste and trembling lest Madame should creep up-stairs and spy me, I opened a drawer, unlocked a box, and took out a case, and — having feasted my eyes with one more look, and approached the seal with a mixture of awe and shame and delight, to my lips — I folded the untasted treasure, yet all fair and inviolate, in silver paper, committed it to the case, shut up box and drawer, reclosed, relocked the dormitory, and returned to class, feeling as if fairy tales were true, and fairy gifts no dream. Strange, sweet insanity! And this letter, the source of my joy, I had not yet read: did not yet know the number of its lines.

When I re-entered the schoolroom, behold M. Paul raging like a pestilence! Some pupil had not spoken audibly or distinctly enough to suit his ear and taste, and now she and others were weeping, and he was raving from his estrade, almost livid. Curious to mention, as I appeared, he fell on me.

"Was I the mistress of these girls? Did I profess to teach them the conduct befitting ladies? — and did I permit and, he doubted not, encourage them to strangle their mother-tongue in their throats, to mince and mash it between their teeth, as if they had some base cause to be ashamed of the words they uttered? Was this modesty? He knew better. It was a vile pseudo sentiment — the offspring or the forerunner of evil. Rather than submit to this mopping and mowing, this mincing and grimacing, this, grinding of a noble tongue, this general affectation and sickening stubbornness of the pupils of the first class, he would throw them up for a set of insupportable petites maîtresses, and confine himself to teaching the ABC to the babies of the third division."

What could I say to all this? Really nothing; and I hoped he would allow me to be silent. The storm recommenced.

"Every answer to his queries was then refused? It seemed to be considered in that place — that conceited boudoir of a first classe, with its pretentious book-cases, its green-baized desks, its rubbish of flower-stands, its trash of framed pictures and maps, and its foreign surveillante, forsooth! — it seemed to be the fashion to think there that the Professor of Literature was not worthy of a reply! These were new ideas; imported, he did not doubt, straight from 'la Grande Bretagne:' they savoured of island insolence and arrogance."

Lull the second — the girls, not one of whom was ever known to weep a tear for the rebukes of any other master, now all melting like snow-statues before the intemperate heat of M. Emanuel: I not yet much shaken, sitting down, and venturing to resume my work.

Something — either in my continued silence or in the movement of my hand, stitching — transported M. Emanuel beyond the last boundary of patience; he actually sprang from his estrade. The stove stood near my desk, he attacked it; the little iron door was nearly dashed from its hinges, the fuel was made to fly.

"Est-ce que vous avez l'intention de m'insulter?" said he to me, in a low, furious voice, as he thus outraged, under pretence of arranging the fire.

It was time to soothe him a little if possible.

"Mais, Monsieur," said I, "I would not insult you for the world. I remember too well that you once said we should be friends."

I did not intend my voice to falter, but it did: more, I think, through the agitation of late delight than in any spasm of present fear. Still there certainly was something in M. Paul's anger — a kind of passion of emotion — that specially tended to draw tears. I was not unhappy, nor much afraid, yet I wept.

"Allons, allons!" said he presently, looking round and seeing the deluge universal. "Decidedly I am a monster and a ruffian. I have only one pocket-handkerchief," he added, "but if I had twenty, I would offer you each one. Your teacher shall be your representative. Here, Miss Lucy."

And he took forth and held out to me a clean silk handkerchief. Now a person who did not know M. Paul, who was unused to him and his impulses, would naturally have bungled at this offer—declined accepting the same—et cetera. But I too plainly felt this would never do: the slightest hesitation would have been fatal to the incipient treaty of peace. I rose and met the handkerchief half-way, received it with decorum, wiped therewith my eyes, and, resuming my seat, and retaining the flag of truce in my hand and on my lap, took especial care during the remainder of the lesson to touch neither needle nor thimble, scissors nor muslin. Many a jealous glance did M. Paul cast at these implements; he hated them mortally, considering sewing a source of distraction from the attention due to himself. A very eloquent lesson he gave, and very kind and friendly was he to the close. Ere he had done, the clouds were dispersed and the sun shining out—tears were exchanged for smiles.

In quitting the room he paused once more at my desk.

"And your letter?" said he, this time not quite fiercely.

"I have not yet read it, Monsieur."

"Ah! it is too good to read at once; you save it, as, when I was a boy, I used to save a peach whose bloom was very ripe?"

The guess came so near the truth, I could not prevent a suddenly-rising warmth in my face from revealing as much.

"You promise yourself a pleasant moment," said he, "in reading that letter; you will open it when alone—n'est-ce pas? Ah! a smile answers. Well, well! one should not be too harsh; 'la jeunesse n'a qu'un temps.'"

"Monsieur, Monsieur!" I cried, or rather whispered after him, as he turned to go, "do not leave me under a mistake. This is merely a friend's letter. Without reading it, I can vouch for that."

"Je conçois, je conçois: on sait ce que c'est qu'un ami. Bonjour, Mademoiselle!"

"But, Monsieur, here is your handkerchief."

"Keep it, keep it, till the letter is read, then bring it me; I shall read the billet's tenor in your eyes."

Villette

When he was gone, the pupils having already poured out of the schoolroom into the berceau, and thence into the garden and court to take their customary recreation before the five-o'clock dinner, I stood a moment thinking, and absently twisting the handkerchief round my arm. For some reason—gladdened, I think, by a sudden return of the golden glimmer of childhood, roused by an unwonted renewal of its buoyancy, made merry by the liberty of the closing hour, and, above all, solaced at heart by the joyous consciousness of that treasure in the case, box, drawer up-stairs,—I fell to playing with the handkerchief as if it were a ball, casting it into the air and catching it—as it fell. The game was stopped by another hand than mine—a hand emerging from a paletôt-sleeve and stretched over my shoulder; it caught the extemporised plaything and bore it away with these sullen words:

"Je vois bien que vous vous moquez de moi et de mes effets."

Really that little man was dreadful: a mere sprite of caprice and, ubiquity: one never knew either his whim or his whereabout.

CHAPTER XXII.

THE LETTER.

When all was still in the house; when dinner was over and the noisy recreation-hour past; when darkness had set in, and the quiet lamp of study was lit in the refectory; when the externes were gone home, the clashing door and clamorous bell hushed for the evening; when Madame was safely settled in the salle-à-manger in company with her mother and some friends; I then glided to the kitchen, begged a bougie for one half-hour for a particular occasion, found acceptance of my petition at the hands of my friend Goton, who answered, "Mais certainement, chou-chou, vous en aurez deux, si vous voulez;" and, light in hand, I mounted noiseless to the dormitory.

Great was my chagrin to find in that apartment a pupil gone to bed indisposed,—greater when I recognised, amid the muslin nightcap borders, the "figure chiffonnée" of Mistress Ginevra Fanshawe; supine at this moment, it is true—but certain to wake and overwhelm me with chatter when the interruption would be least acceptable: indeed, as I watched her, a slight twinkling of the eyelids warned me that the present appearance of repose might be but a ruse, assumed to cover sly vigilance over "Timon's" movements; she was not to be trusted. And I had so wished to be alone, just to read my precious letter in peace.

Well, I must go to the classes. Having sought and found my prize in its casket, I descended. Ill-luck pursued me. The classes were undergoing sweeping and purification by candle-light, according to hebdomadal custom: benches were piled on desks, the air was dim with dust, damp coffee-grounds (used by Labassecourien housemaids instead of tea-leaves) darkened the floor; all was hopeless confusion. Baffled, but not beaten, I withdrew, bent as resolutely as ever on finding solitude somewhere.

Taking a key whereof I knew the repository, I mounted three staircases in succession, reached a dark, narrow, silent landing, opened a worm-eaten door, and dived into the deep, black, cold garret. Here none would follow me—none interrupt—not Madame herself. I shut the garret-door; I placed my light on a doddered and mouldy chest of drawers; I put on a shawl, for the air was ice-cold; I took my letter; trembling with sweet impatience, I broke its seal.

"Will it be long—will it be short?" thought I, passing my hand across my eyes to dissipate the silvery dimness of a suave, south-wind shower.

It was long.

"Will it be cool?—will it be kind?"

It was kind.

To my checked, bridled, disciplined expectation, it seemed very kind: to my longing and famished thought it seemed, perhaps, kinder than it was.

So little had I hoped, so much had I feared; there was a fulness of delight in this taste of fruition—such, perhaps, as many a human being passes through life without ever knowing. The poor English teacher in the frosty garret, reading by a dim candle guttering in the wintry air, a letter simply good-natured—nothing more; though that good-nature then seemed to me godlike—was happier than most queens in palaces.

Of course, happiness of such shallow origin could be but brief; yet, while it lasted it was genuine and exquisite: a bubble—but a sweet bubble—of real honey-dew. Dr. John had written to me at length; he had written to me with pleasure; he had written with benignant mood, dwelling with sunny satisfaction on scenes that had passed before his eyes and mine, — on places we had visited together — on conversations we had held — on all the little subject-matter, in short, of the last few halcyon weeks. But the cordial core of the delight was, a conviction the blithe, genial language generously imparted, that it had been poured out not merely to content me — but to gratify himself. A gratification he might never more desire, never more seek — an hypothesis in every point of view approaching the certain; but that concerned the future. This present moment had no pain, no blot, no want; full, pure, perfect, it deeply blessed me. A passing seraph seemed to have rested beside me, leaned towards my heart, and reposed on its throb a softening, cooling, healing, hallowing wing. Dr. John, you pained me afterwards: forgiven be every ill — freely forgiven — for the sake of that one dear remembered good!

Are there wicked things, not human, which envy human bliss? Are there evil influences haunting the air, and poisoning it for man? What was near me?

Something in that vast solitary garret sounded strangely. Most surely and certainly I heard, as it seemed, a stealthy foot on that floor: a sort of gliding out from the direction of the black recess haunted by the malefactor cloaks. I turned: my light was dim; the room was long — but as I live! I saw in the middle of that ghostly chamber a figure all black and white; the skirts straight, narrow, black; the head bandaged, veiled, white.

Say what you will, reader — tell me I was nervous or mad; affirm that I was unsettled by the excitement of that letter; declare that I dreamed; this I vow — I saw there — in that room — on that night — an image like — a NUN.

I cried out; I sickened. Had the shape approached me I might have swooned. It receded: I made for the door. How I descended all the stairs I know not. By instinct I shunned the refectory, and shaped my course to Madame's sitting-room: I burst in. I said —

"There is something in the grenier; I have been there: I saw something. Go and look at it, all of you!"

I said, "All of you;" for the room seemed to me full of people, though in truth there were but four present: Madame Beck; her mother, Madame Kint, who was out of health, and now staying with her on a visit; her brother, M. Victor Kint, and another gentleman, who, when I entered the room, was conversing with the old lady, and had his back towards the door.

My mortal fear and faintness must have made me deadly pale. I felt cold and shaking. They all rose in consternation; they surrounded me. I urged them to go to the grenier; the sight of the gentlemen did me good and gave me courage: it seemed as if there were some help and hope, with men at hand. I turned to the door, beckoning them to follow. They wanted to stop me, but I said they must come this way: they must see what I had seen—something strange, standing in the middle of the garret. And, now, I remembered my letter, left on the drawers with the light. This precious letter! Flesh or spirit must be defied for its sake. I flew up-stairs, hastening the faster as I knew I was followed: they were obliged to come.

Lo! when I reached the garret-door, all within was dark as a pit: the light was out. Happily some one—Madame, I think, with her usual calm sense—had brought a lamp from the room; speedily, therefore, as they came up, a ray pierced the opaque blackness. There stood the bougie quenched on the drawers; but where was the letter? And I looked for that now, and not for the nun.

"My letter! my letter!" I panted and plained, almost beside myself. I groped on the floor, wringing my hands wildly. Cruel, cruel doom! To have my bit of comfort preternaturally snatched from me, ere I had well tasted its virtue!

I don't know what the others were doing; I could not watch them: they asked me questions I did not answer; they ransacked all corners; they prattled about this and that disarrangement of cloaks, a breach or crack in the sky-light—I know not what. "Something or somebody has been here," was sagely averred.

"Oh! they have taken my letter!" cried the grovelling, groping, monomaniac.

"What letter, Lucy? My dear girl, what letter?" asked a known voice in my ear. Could I believe that ear? No: and I looked up. Could I trust my eyes? Had I recognised the tone? Did I now look on the face of the writer of that very letter? Was this gentleman near me in this dim garret, John Graham—Dr. Bretton himself?

Yes: it was. He had been called in that very evening to prescribe for some access of illness in old Madame Kint; he was the second gentleman present in the salle-à-manger when I entered.

Villette

"Was it my letter, Lucy?"

"Your own: yours—the letter you wrote to me. I had come here to read it quietly. I could not find another spot where it was possible to have it to myself. I had saved it all day—never opened it till this evening: it was scarcely glanced over: I cannot bear to lose it. Oh, my letter!"

"Hush! don't cry and distress yourself so cruelly. What is it worth? Hush! Come out of this cold room; they are going to send for the police now to examine further: we need not stay here—come, we will go down."

A warm hand, taking my cold fingers, led me down to a room where there was a fire. Dr. John and I sat before the stove. He talked to me and soothed me with unutterable goodness, promising me twenty letters for the one lost. If there are words and wrongs like knives, whose deep-inflicted lacerations never heal—cutting injuries and insults of serrated and poison-dripping edge—so, too, there are consolations of tone too fine for the ear not fondly and for ever to retain their echo: caressing kindnesses—loved, lingered over through a whole life, recalled with unfaded tenderness, and answering the call with undimmed shine, out of that raven cloud foreshadowing Death himself. I have been told since that Dr. Bretton was not nearly so perfect as I thought him: that his actual character lacked the depth, height, compass, and endurance it possessed in my creed. I don't know: he was as good to me as the well is to the parched wayfarer—as the sun to the shivering jailbird. I remember him heroic. Heroic at this moment will I hold him to be.

He asked me, smiling, why I cared for his letter so very much. I thought, but did not say, that I prized it like the blood in my veins. I only answered that I had so few letters to care for.

"I am sure you did not read it," said he; "or you would think nothing of it!"

"I read it, but only once. I want to read it again. I am sorry it is lost." And I could not help weeping afresh.

"Lucy, Lucy, my poor little god-sister (if there be such a relationship), here—here is your letter. Why is it not better worth such tears, and such tenderly exaggerating faith?"

Curious, characteristic manœuvre! His quick eye had seen the letter on the floor where I sought it; his hand, as quick, had snatched it up. He had hidden it in his waistcoat pocket. If my trouble had wrought with a whit less stress and reality, I doubt whether he would ever have acknowledged or restored it. Tears of temperature one degree cooler than those I shed would only have amused Dr. John.

Pleasure at regaining made me forget merited reproach for the teasing torment; my joy was great; it could not be concealed: yet I think it broke out more in countenance than language. I said little.

"Are you satisfied now?" asked Dr. John.

I replied that I was—satisfied and happy.

"Well then," he proceeded, "how do you feel physically? Are you growing calmer? Not much: for you tremble like a leaf still."

It seemed to me, however, that I was sufficiently calm: at least I felt no longer terrified. I expressed myself composed.

"You are able, consequently, to tell me what you saw? Your account was quite vague, do you know? You looked white as the wall; but you only spoke of 'something,' not defining what. Was it a man? Was it an animal? What was it?"

"I never will tell exactly what I saw," said I, "unless some one else sees it too, and then I will give corroborative testimony; but otherwise, I shall be discredited and accused of dreaming."

"Tell me," said Dr. Bretton; "I will hear it in my professional character: I look on you now from a professional point of view, and I read, perhaps, all you would conceal—in your eye, which is curiously vivid and restless: in your cheek, which the blood has forsaken; in your hand, which you cannot steady. Come, Lucy, speak and tell me."

"You would laugh—?"

"If you don't tell me you shall have no more letters."

"You are laughing now."

"I will again take away that single epistle: being mine, I think I have a right to reclaim it."

I felt raillery in his words: it made me grave and quiet; but I

Villette

folded up the letter and covered it from sight.

"You may hide it, but I can possess it any moment I choose. You don't know my skill in sleight of hand; I might practise as a conjuror if I liked. Mamma says sometimes, too, that I have a harmonizing property of tongue and eye; but you never saw that in me—did you, Lucy?"

"Indeed—indeed—when you were a mere boy I used to see both: far more then than now—for now you are strong, and strength dispenses with subtlety. But still,—Dr. John, you have what they call in this country 'un air fin,' that nobody can mistake. Madame Beck saw it, and—"

"And liked it," said he, laughing, "because she has it herself. But, Lucy, give me that letter—you don't really care for it."

To this provocative speech I made no answer. Graham in mirthful mood must not be humoured too far. Just now there was a new sort of smile playing about his lips—very sweet, but it grieved me somehow—a new sort of light sparkling in his eyes: not hostile, but not reassuring. I rose to go—I bid him good-night a little sadly.

His sensitiveness—that peculiar, apprehensive, detective faculty of his—felt in a moment the unspoken complaint—the scarce-thought reproach. He asked quietly if I was offended. I shook my head as implying a negative.

"Permit me, then, to speak a little seriously to you before you go. You are in a highly nervous state. I feel sure from what is apparent in your look and manner, however well controlled, that whilst alone this evening in that dismal, perishing sepulchral garret—that dungeon under the leads, smelling of damp and mould, rank with phthisis and catarrh: a place you never ought to enter—that you saw, or thought you saw, some appearance peculiarly calculated to impress the imagination. I know that you are not, nor ever were, subject to material terrors, fears of robbers, &c.—I am not so sure that a visitation, bearing a spectral character, would not shake your very mind. Be calm now. This is all a matter of the nerves, I see: but just specify the vision."

"You will tell nobody?"

"Nobody—most certainly. You may trust me as implicitly as you did Père Silas. Indeed, the doctor is perhaps the safer confessor of the two, though he has not grey hair."

"You will not laugh?"

"Perhaps I may, to do you good: but not in scorn. Lucy, I feel as a friend towards you, though your timid nature is slow to trust."

He now looked like a friend: that indescribable smile and sparkle were gone; those formidable arched curves of lip, nostril, eyebrow, were depressed; repose marked his attitude—attention sobered his aspect. Won to confidence, I told him exactly what I had seen: ere now I had narrated to him the legend of the house—whiling away with that narrative an hour of a certain mild October afternoon, when he and I rode through Bois l'Etang.

He sat and thought, and while he thought, we heard them all coming down-stairs.

"Are they going to interrupt?" said he, glancing at the door with an annoyed expression.

"They will not come here," I answered; for we were in the little salon where Madame never sat in the evening, and where it was by mere chance that heat was still lingering in the stove. They passed the door and went on to the salle-à-manger.

"Now," he pursued, "they will talk about thieves, burglars, and so on: let them do so—mind you say nothing, and keep your resolution of describing your nun to nobody. She may appear to you again: don't start."

"You think then," I said, with secret horror, "she came out of my brain, and is now gone in there, and may glide out again at an hour and a day when I look not for her?"

"I think it a case of spectral illusion: I fear, following on and resulting from long-continued mental conflict."

"Oh, Doctor John—I shudder at the thought of being liable to such an illusion! It seemed so real. Is there no cure?—no preventive?"

"Happiness is the cure—a cheerful mind the preventive: cultivate both."

No mockery in this world ever sounds to me so hollow as that of being told to cultivate happiness. What does such advice mean? Happiness is not a potato, to be planted in mould, and

Villette

tilled with manure. Happiness is a glory shining far down upon us out of Heaven. She is a divine dew which the soul, on certain of its summer mornings, feels dropping upon it from the amaranth bloom and golden fruitage of Paradise.

"Cultivate happiness!" I said briefly to the doctor: "do you cultivate happiness? How do you manage?"

"I am a cheerful fellow by nature: and then ill-luck has never dogged me. Adversity gave me and my mother one passing scowl and brush, but we defied her, or rather laughed at her, and she went by.".

"There is no cultivation in all this."

"I do not give way to melancholy."

"Yes: I have seen you subdued by that feeling."

"About Ginevra Fanshawe—eh?"

"Did she not sometimes make you miserable?"

"Pooh! stuff! nonsense! You see I am better now."

If a laughing eye with a lively light, and a face bright with beaming and healthy energy, could attest that he was better, better he certainly was.

"You do not look much amiss, or greatly out of condition," I allowed.

"And why, Lucy, can't you look and feel as I do—buoyant, courageous, and fit to defy all the nuns and flirts in Christendom? I would give gold on the spot just to see you snap your fingers. Try the manœuvre."

"If I were to bring Miss Fanshawe into your presence just now?"

"I vow, Lucy, she should not move me: or, she should move me but by one thing—true, yes, and passionate love. I would accord forgiveness at no less a price."

"Indeed! a smile of hers would have been a fortune to you a while since."

"Transformed, Lucy: transformed! Remember, you once

called me a slave! but I am a free man now!"

He stood up: in the port of his head, the carriage of his figure, in his beaming eye and mien, there revealed itself a liberty which was more than ease—a mood which was disdain of his past bondage.

"Miss Fanshawe," he pursued, "has led me through a phase of feeling which is over: I have entered another condition, and am now much disposed to exact love for love—passion for passion—and good measure of it, too."

"Ah, Doctor! Doctor! you said it was your nature to pursue Love under difficulties—to be charmed by a proud insensibility!".

He laughed, and answered, "My nature varies: the mood of one hour is sometimes the mockery of the next. Well, Lucy" (drawing on his gloves), "will the Nun come again to-night, think you?"

"I don't think she will."

"Give her my compliments, if she does—Dr. John's compliments—and entreat her to have the goodness to wait a visit from him. Lucy, was she a pretty nun? Had she a pretty face? You have not told me that yet; and that is the really important point."

"She had a white cloth over her face," said I, "but her eyes glittered."

"Confusion to her goblin trappings!" cried he, irreverently: "but at least she had handsome eyes—bright and soft."

"Cold and fixed," was the reply.

"No, no, we'll none of her: she shall not haunt you, Lucy. Give her that shake of the hand, if she comes again. Will she stand that, do you think?"

I thought it too kind and cordial for a ghost to stand: and so was the smile which matched it, and accompanied his "Good-night."

And had there been anything in the garret? What did they discover? I believe, on the closest examination, their discoveries amounted to very little. They talked, at first, of the cloaks being disturbed; but Madame Beck told me afterwards she thought they hung much as usual: and as for the broken pane in the skylight, she affirmed that aperture was rarely without one or more panes broken or cracked: and besides, a heavy hail-storm had fallen a few days ago. Madame questioned me very closely as to what I had seen, but I only described an obscure figure clothed in black: I took care not to breathe the word "nun," certain that this word would at once suggest to her mind an idea of romance and unreality. She charged me to say nothing on the subject to any servant, pupil, or teacher, and highly commended my discretion in coming to her private salle-à-manger, instead of carrying the tale of horror to the school refectory. Thus the subject dropped. I was left secretly and sadly to wonder, in my own mind, whether that strange thing was of this world, or of a realm beyond the grave; or whether indeed it was only the child of malady, and I of that malady the prey.

CHAPTER XXIII.

VASHTI.

To wonder sadly, did I say? No: a new influence began to act upon my life, and sadness, for a certain space, was held at bay. Conceive a dell, deep-hollowed in forest secresy; it lies in dimness and mist: its turf is dank, its herbage pale and humid. A storm or an axe makes a wide gap amongst the oak-trees; the breeze sweeps in; the sun looks down; the sad, cold dell becomes a deep cup of lustre; high summer pours her blue glory and her golden light out of that beauteous sky, which till now the starved hollow never saw.

A new creed became mine — a belief in happiness.

It was three weeks since the adventure of the garret, and I possessed in that case, box, drawer up-stairs, casketed with that first letter, four companions like to it, traced by the same firm pen, sealed with the same clear seal, full of the same vital comfort. Vital comfort it seemed to me then: I read them in after years; they were kind letters enough — pleasing letters, because composed by one well pleased; in the two last there were three or four closing lines half-gay, half-tender, "by feeling touched, but not subdued." Time, dear reader, mellowed them to a beverage of this mild quality; but when I first tasted their elixir, fresh from the fount so honoured, it seemed juice of a divine vintage: a draught which Hebe might fill, and the very gods approve.

Does the reader, remembering what was said some pages back, care to ask how I answered these letters: whether under the dry, stinting check of Reason, or according to the full, liberal impulse of Feeling?

To speak truth, I compromised matters; I served two masters: I bowed down in the houses of Rimmon, and lifted the heart at another shrine. I wrote to these letters two answers — one for my own relief, the other for Graham's perusal.

To begin with: Feeling and I turned Reason out of doors, drew against her bar and bolt, then we sat down, spread our paper, dipped in the ink an eager pen, and, with deep enjoyment, poured out our sincere heart. When we had done — when two sheets were covered with the language of a strongly-adherent affection, a rooted and active gratitude — (once, for all, in this parenthesis, I disclaim, with the utmost scorn, every sneaking suspicion of what are called "warmer feelings:" women do not entertain these "warmer feelings" where, from the commencement, through the whole progress of an acquaintance, they have never once been cheated of the conviction that, to do so would be to commit a mortal absurdity: nobody ever launches into Love unless he has seen or dreamed the rising of Hope's star over Love's troubled waters) — when, then, I had given expression to a closely-clinging and deeply-honouring attachment — an attachment that wanted to attract to itself and take to its own lot all that was painful in the destiny of its object; that would, if it could, have absorbed and conducted away all storms and lightnings from an existence viewed with a passion of solicitude — then, just at that moment, the doors of my heart would shake, bolt and bar would yield, Reason would leap in vigorous and revengeful, snatch the full sheets, read, sneer, erase, tear up, re-write, fold, seal, direct, and send a terse, curt missive of a page. She did right.

I did not live on letters only: I was visited, I was looked after; once a week I was taken out to La Terrasse; always I was made much of. Dr. Bretton failed not to tell me why he was so kind: "To keep away the nun," he said; "he was determined to dispute with her her prey. He had taken," he declared, "a thorough dislike to her, chiefly on account of that white face-cloth, and those cold grey eyes: the moment he heard of those odious particulars," he affirmed, "consummate disgust had incited him to oppose her; he was determined to try whether he or she was the cleverest, and he only wished she would once more look in upon me when he was present:" but that she never did. In short, he regarded me scientifically in the light of a patient, and at once exercised his professional skill, and gratified his natural benevolence, by a course of cordial and attentive treatment.

One evening, the first in December, I was walking by myself in the carré; it was six o'clock; the classe-doors were closed; but within, the pupils, rampant in the licence of evening recreation, were counterfeiting a miniature chaos. The carré was quite dark, except a red light shining under and about the stove; the wide glass-doors and the long windows were frosted over; a crystal sparkle of starlight, here and there spangling this blanched winter veil, and breaking with scattered brilliance the paleness of its embroidery, proved it a clear night, though moonless. That I should dare to remain thus alone in darkness, showed that my nerves were regaining a healthy tone: I thought of the nun, but hardly feared her; though the staircase was behind me, leading up, through blind, black night, from landing to landing, to the haunted grenier. Yet I own my heart quaked, my pulse leaped, when I suddenly heard breathing and rustling, and turning, saw in the deep shadow of the steps a deeper shadow still—a shape that moved and descended. It paused a while at the classe-door, and then it glided before me. Simultaneously came a clangor of the distant door-bell. Life-like sounds bring life-like feelings: this shape was too round and low for my gaunt nun: it was only Madame Beck on duty.

"Mademoiselle Lucy!" cried Rosine, bursting in, lamp in hand, from the corridor, "on est là pour vous au salon."

Madame saw me, I saw Madame, Rosine saw us both: there was no mutual recognition. I made straight for the salon. There I found what I own I anticipated I should find—Dr. Bretton; but he was in evening-dress.

"The carriage is at the door," said he; "my mother has sent it to take you to the theatre; she was going herself, but an arrival has prevented her: she immediately said, 'Take Lucy in my place.' Will you go?"

"Just now? I am not dressed," cried I, glancing despairingly at my dark merino.

"You have half an hour to dress. I should have given you notice, but I only determined on going since five o'clock, when I heard there was to be a genuine regale in the presence of a great actress."

And he mentioned a name that thrilled me—a name that, in those days, could thrill Europe. It is hushed now: its once restless echoes are all still; she who bore it went years ago to her rest: night and oblivion long since closed above her; but then her day—a day of Sirius—stood at its full height, light and fervour.

"I'll go; I will be ready in ten minutes," I vowed. And away I flew, never once checked, reader, by the thought which perhaps at this moment checks you: namely, that to go anywhere with Graham and without Mrs. Bretton could be objectionable. I could not have conceived, much less have expressed to Graham, such thought—such scruple—without risk of exciting a tyrannous self-contempt: of kindling an inward fire of shame so quenchless, and so devouring, that I think it would soon have licked up the very life in my veins. Besides, my godmother, knowing her son, and knowing me, would as soon have thought of chaperoning a sister with a brother, as of keeping anxious guard over our incomings and outgoings.

Villette

The present was no occasion for showy array; my dun mist crape would suffice, and I sought the same in the great oak-wardrobe in the dormitory, where hung no less than forty dresses. But there had been changes and reforms, and some innovating hand had pruned this same crowded wardrobe, and carried divers garments to the grenier—my crape amongst the rest. I must fetch it. I got the key, and went aloft fearless, almost thoughtless. I unlocked the door, I plunged in. The reader may believe it or not, but when I thus suddenly entered, that garret was not wholly dark as it should have been: from one point there shone a solemn light, like a star, but broader. So plainly it shone, that it revealed the deep alcove with a portion of the tarnished scarlet curtain drawn over it. Instantly, silently, before my eyes, it vanished; so did the curtain and alcove: all that end of the garret became black as night. I ventured no research; I had not time nor will; snatching my dress, which hung on the wall, happily near the door, I rushed out, relocked the door with convulsed haste, and darted downwards to the dormitory.

But I trembled too much to dress myself: impossible to arrange hair or fasten hooks-and-eyes with such fingers, so I called Rosine and bribed her to help me. Rosine liked a bribe, so she did her best, smoothed and plaited my hair as well as a coiffeur would have done, placed the lace collar mathematically straight, tied the neck-ribbon accurately—in short, did her work like the neat-handed Phillis she could be when she chose. Having given me my handkerchief and gloves, she took the candle and lighted me down-stairs. After all, I had forgotten my shawl; she ran back to fetch it; and I stood with Dr. John in the vestibule, waiting.

"What is this, Lucy?" said he, looking down at me narrowly. "Here is the old excitement. Ha! the nun again?"

But I utterly denied the charge: I was vexed to be suspected of a second illusion. He was sceptical.

"She has been, as sure as I live," said he; "her figure crossing your eyes leaves on them a peculiar gleam and expression not to be mistaken."

"She has not been," I persisted: for, indeed, I could deny her apparition with truth.

"The old symptoms are there," he affirmed: "a particular pale, and what the Scotch call a 'raised' look."

He was so obstinate, I thought it better to tell him what I

really had seen. Of course with him it was held to be another effect of the same cause: it was all optical illusion—nervous malady, and so on. Not one bit did I believe him; but I dared not contradict: doctors are so self-opinionated, so immovable in their dry, materialist views.

Rosine brought the shawl, and I was bundled into the carriage.

The theatre was full—crammed to its roof: royal and noble were there: palace and hotel had emptied their inmates into those tiers so thronged and so hushed. Deeply did I feel myself privileged in having a place before that stage; I longed to see a being of whose powers I had heard reports which made me conceive peculiar anticipations. I wondered if she would justify her renown: with strange curiosity, with feelings severe and austere, yet of riveted interest, I waited. She was a study of such nature as had not encountered my eyes yet: a great and new planet she was: but in what shape? I waited her rising.

She rose at nine that December night: above the horizon I saw her come. She could shine yet with pale grandeur and steady might; but that star verged already on its judgment-day. Seen near, it was a chaos—hollow, half-consumed: an orb perished or perishing—half lava, half glow.

I had heard this woman termed "plain," and I expected bony harshness and grimness—something large, angular, sallow. What I saw was the shadow of a royal Vashti: a queen, fair as the day once, turned pale now like twilight, and wasted like wax in flame.

For a while—a long while—I thought it was only a woman, though an unique woman, who moved in might and grace before this multitude. By-and-by I recognised my mistake. Behold! I found upon her something neither of woman nor of man: in each of her eyes sat a devil. These evil forces bore her through the tragedy, kept up her feeble strength—for she was but a frail creature; and as the action rose and the stir deepened, how wildly they shook her with their passions of the pit! They wrote HELL on her straight, haughty brow. They tuned her voice to the note of torment. They writhed her regal face to a demoniac mask. Hate and Murder and Madness incarnate she stood.

It was a marvellous sight: a mighty revelation.

It was a spectacle low, horrible, immoral.

Villette

Swordsmen thrust through, and dying in their blood on the arena sand; bulls goring horses disembowelled, made a meeker vision for the public — a milder condiment for a people's palate — than Vashti torn by seven devils: devils which cried sore and rent the tenement they haunted, but still refused to be exorcised.

Suffering had struck that stage empress; and she stood before her audience neither yielding to, nor enduring, nor, in finite measure, resenting it: she stood locked in struggle, rigid in resistance. She stood, not dressed, but draped in pale antique folds, long and regular like sculpture. A background and entourage and flooring of deepest crimson threw her out, white like alabaster — like silver: rather, be it said, like Death.

Where was the artist of the Cleopatra? Let him come and sit down and study this different vision. Let him seek here the mighty brawn, the muscle, the abounding blood, the full-fed flesh he worshipped: let all materialists draw nigh and look on.

I have said that she does not resent her grief. No; the weakness of that word would make it a lie. To her, what hurts becomes immediately embodied: she looks on it as a thing that can be attacked, worried down, torn in shreds. Scarcely a substance herself, she grapples to conflict with abstractions. Before calamity she is a tigress; she rends her woes, shivers them in convulsed abhorrence. Pain, for her, has no result in good: tears water no harvest of wisdom: on sickness, on death itself, she looks with the eye of a rebel. Wicked, perhaps, she is, but also she is strong; and her strength has conquered Beauty, has overcome Grace, and bound both at her side, captives peerlessly fair, and docile as fair. Even in the uttermost frenzy of energy is each maenad movement royally, imperially, incedingly upborne. Her hair, flying loose in revel or war, is still an angel's hair, and glorious under a halo. Fallen, insurgent, banished, she remembers the heaven where she rebelled. Heaven's light, following her exile, pierces its confines, and discloses their forlorn remoteness.

Place now the Cleopatra, or any other slug, before her as an obstacle, and see her cut through the pulpy mass as the scimitar of Saladin clove the down cushion. Let Paul Peter Rubens wake from the dead, let him rise out of his cerements, and bring into this presence all the army of his fat women; the magian power or prophet-virtue gifting that slight rod of Moses, could, at one waft, release and re-mingle a sea spell-parted, whelming the heavy host with the down-rush of overthrown sea-ramparts.

Vashti was not good, I was told; and I have said she did not look good: though a spirit, she was a spirit out of Tophet. Well, if so much of unholy force can arise from below, may not an equal efflux of sacred essence descend one day from above?

What thought Dr. Graham of this being?

For long intervals I forgot to look how he demeaned himself, or to question what he thought. The strong magnetism of genius drew my heart out of its wonted orbit; the sunflower turned from the south to a fierce light, not solar—a rushing, red, cometary light—hot on vision and to sensation. I had seen acting before, but never anything like this: never anything which astonished Hope and hushed Desire; which outstripped Impulse and paled Conception; which, instead of merely irritating imagination with the thought of what might be done, at the same time fevering the nerves because it was not done, disclosed power like a deep, swollen winter river, thundering in cataract, and bearing the soul, like a leaf, on the steep and steelly sweep of its descent.

Miss Fanshawe, with her usual ripeness of judgment, pronounced Dr. Bretton a serious, impassioned man, too grave and too impressible. Not in such light did I ever see him: no such faults could I lay to his charge. His natural attitude was not the meditative, nor his natural mood the sentimental; impressionable he was as dimpling water, but, almost as water, unimpressible: the breeze, the sun, moved him—metal could not grave, nor fire brand.

Dr. John could think and think well, but he was rather a man of action than of thought; he could feel, and feel vividly in his way, but his heart had no chord for enthusiasm: to bright, soft, sweet influences his eyes and lips gave bright, soft, sweet welcome, beautiful to see as dyes of rose and silver, pearl and purple, imbuing summer clouds; for what belonged to storm, what was wild and intense, dangerous, sudden, and flaming, he had no sympathy, and held with it no communion. When I took time and regained inclination to glance at him, it amused and enlightened me to discover that he was watching that sinister and sovereign Vashti, not with wonder, nor worship, nor yet dismay, but simply with intense curiosity. Her agony did not pain him, her wild moan—worse than a shriek—did not much move him; her fury revolted him somewhat, but not to the point of horror. Cool young Briton! The pale cliffs of his own England do not look down on the tides of the Channel more calmly than he watched the Pythian inspiration of that night.

Villette

Looking at his face, I longed to know his exact opinions, and at last I put a question tending to elicit them. At the sound of my voice he awoke as if out of a dream; for he had been thinking, and very intently thinking, his own thoughts, after his own manner. "How did he like Vashti?" I wished to know.

"Hm-m-m," was the first scarce articulate but expressive answer; and then such a strange smile went wandering round his lips, a smile so critical, so almost callous! I suppose that for natures of that order his sympathies were callous. In a few terse phrases he told me his opinion of, and feeling towards, the actress: he judged her as a woman, not an artist: it was a branding judgment.

That night was already marked in my book of life, not with white, but with a deep-red cross. But I had not done with it yet; and other memoranda were destined to be set down in characters of tint indelible.

Towards midnight, when the deepening tragedy blackened to the death-scene, and all held their breath, and even Graham bit his under-lip, and knit his brow, and sat still and struck— when the whole theatre was hushed, when the vision of all eyes centred in one point, when all ears listened towards one quarter—nothing being seen but the white form sunk on a seat, quivering in conflict with her last, her worst-hated, her visibly-conquering foe—nothing heard but her throes, her gaspings, breathing yet of mutiny, panting still defiance; when, as it seemed, an inordinate will, convulsing a perishing mortal frame, bent it to battle with doom and death, fought every inch of ground, sold every drop of blood, resisted to the latest the rape of every faculty, would see, would hear, would breathe, would live, up to, within, well-nigh beyond the moment when death says to all sense and all being—"Thus far and no farther!"—

Just then a stir, pregnant with omen, rustled behind the scenes—feet ran, voices spoke. What was it? demanded the whole house. A flame, a smell of smoke replied.

"Fire!" rang through the gallery. "Fire!" was repeated, re-echoed, yelled forth: and then, and faster than pen can set it down, came panic, rushing, crushing—a blind, selfish, cruel chaos.

And Dr. John? Reader, I see him yet, with his look of comely courage and cordial calm.

"Lucy will sit still, I know," said he, glancing down at me with the same serene goodness, the same repose of firmness that I have seen in him when sitting at his side amid the secure peace of his mother's hearth. Yes, thus adjured, I think I would have sat still under a rocking crag: but, indeed, to sit still in actual circumstances was my instinct; and at the price of my very life, I would not have moved to give him trouble, thwart his will, or make demands on his attention. We were in the stalls, and for a few minutes there was a most terrible, ruthless pressure about us.

"How terrified are the women!" said he; "but if the men were not almost equally so, order might be maintained. This is a sorry scene: I see fifty selfish brutes at this moment, each of whom, if I were near, I could conscientiously knock down. I see some women braver than some men. There is one yonder—Good God!"

While Graham was speaking, a young girl who had been very quietly and steadily clinging to a gentleman before us, was suddenly struck from her protector's arms by a big, butcherly intruder, and hurled under the feet of the crowd. Scarce two seconds lasted her disappearance. Graham rushed forwards; he and the gentleman, a powerful man though grey-haired, united their strength to thrust back the throng; her head and long hair fell back over his shoulder: she seemed unconscious.

"Trust her with me; I am a medical man," said Dr. John.

"If you have no lady with you, be it so," was the answer. "Hold her, and I will force a passage: we must get her to the air."

"I have a lady," said Graham; "but she will be neither hindrance nor incumbrance."

He summoned me with his eye: we were separated. Resolute, however, to rejoin him, I penetrated the living barrier, creeping under where I could not get between or over.

"Fasten on me, and don't leave go," he said; and I obeyed him.

Our pioneer proved strong and adroit; he opened the dense mass like a wedge; with patience and toil he at last bored through the flesh-and-blood rock—so solid, hot, and suffocating—and brought us to the fresh, freezing night.

Villette

"You are an Englishman!" said he, turning shortly on Dr. Bretton, when we got into the street.

"An Englishman. And I speak to a countryman?" was the reply.

"Right. Be good enough to stand here two minutes, whilst I find my carriage."

"Papa, I am not hurt," said a girlish voice; "am I with papa?"

"You are with a friend, and your father is close at hand."

"Tell him I am not hurt, except just in my shoulder. Oh, my shoulder! They trod just here."

"Dislocation, perhaps!" muttered the Doctor: "let us hope there is no worse injury done. Lucy, lend a hand one instant."

And I assisted while he made some arrangement of drapery and position for the ease of his suffering burden. She suppressed a moan, and lay in his arms quietly and patiently.

"She is very light," said Graham, "like a child!" and he asked in my ear, "Is she a child, Lucy? Did you notice her age?"

"I am not a child—I am a person of seventeen," responded the patient, demurely and with dignity. Then, directly after: "Tell papa to come; I get anxious."

The carriage drove up; her father relieved Graham; but in the exchange from one bearer to another she was hurt, and moaned again.

"My darling!" said the father, tenderly; then turning to Graham, "You said, sir, you are a medical man?"

"I am: Dr. Bretton, of La Terrasse."

"Good. Will you step into my carriage?"

"My own carriage is here: I will seek it, and accompany you."

"Be pleased, then, to follow us." And he named his address: "The Hôtel Crécy, in the Rue Crécy."

We followed; the carriage drove fast; myself and Graham

were silent. This seemed like an adventure.

Some little time being lost in seeking our own equipage, we reached the hotel perhaps about ten minutes after these strangers. It was an hotel in the foreign sense: a collection of dwelling-houses, not an inn—a vast, lofty pile, with a huge arch to its street-door, leading through a vaulted covered way, into a square all built round.

We alighted, passed up a wide, handsome public staircase, and stopped at Numéro 2 on the second landing; the first floor comprising the abode of I know not what "prince Russe," as Graham informed me. On ringing the bell at a second great door, we were admitted to a suite of very handsome apartments. Announced by a servant in livery, we entered a drawing-room whose hearth glowed with an English fire, and whose walls gleamed with foreign mirrors. Near the hearth appeared a little group: a slight form sunk in a deep arm-chair, one or two women busy about it, the iron-grey gentleman anxiously looking on.

"Where is Harriet? I wish Harriet would come to me," said the girlish voice, faintly.

"Where is Mrs. Hurst?" demanded the gentleman impatiently and somewhat sternly of the man-servant who had admitted us.

"I am sorry to say she is gone out of town, sir; my young lady gave her leave till to-morrow."

"Yes—I did—I did. She is gone to see her sister; I said she might go: I remember now," interposed the young lady; "but I am so sorry, for Manon and Louison cannot understand a word I say, and they hurt me without meaning to do so."

Dr. John and the gentleman now interchanged greetings; and while they passed a few minutes in consultation, I approached the easy-chair, and seeing what the faint and sinking girl wished to have done, I did it for her.

I was still occupied in the arrangement, when Graham drew near; he was no less skilled in surgery than medicine, and, on examination, found that no further advice than his own was necessary to the treatment of the present case. He ordered her to be carried to her chamber, and whispered to me:—"Go with the women, Lucy; they seem but dull; you can at least direct their movements, and thus spare her some pain. She must be touched

Villette

very tenderly."

The chamber was a room shadowy with pale-blue hangings, vaporous with curtainings and veilings of muslin; the bed seemed to me like snow-drift and mist—spotless, soft, and gauzy. Making the women stand apart, I undressed their mistress, without their well-meaning but clumsy aid. I was not in a sufficiently collected mood to note with separate distinctness every detail of the attire I removed, but I received a general impression of refinement, delicacy, and perfect personal cultivation; which, in a period of after-thought, offered in my reflections a singular contrast to notes retained of Miss Ginevra Fanshawe's appointments.

The girl was herself a small, delicate creature, but made like a model. As I folded back her plentiful yet fine hair, so shining and soft, and so exquisitely tended, I had under my observation a young, pale, weary, but high-bred face. The brow was smooth and clear; the eyebrows were distinct, but soft, and melting to a mere trace at the temples; the eyes were a rich gift of nature—fine and full, large, deep, seeming to hold dominion over the slighter subordinate features—capable, probably, of much significance at another hour and under other circumstances than the present, but now languid and suffering. Her skin was perfectly fair, the neck and hands veined finely like the petals of a flower; a thin glazing of the ice of pride polished this delicate exterior, and her lip wore a curl—I doubt not inherent and unconscious, but which, if I had seen it first with the accompaniments of health and state, would have struck me as unwarranted, and proving in the little lady a quite mistaken view of life and her own consequence.

Her demeanour under the Doctor's hands at first excited a smile; it was not puerile—rather, on the whole, patient and firm—but yet, once or twice she addressed him with suddenness and sharpness, saying that he hurt her, and must contrive to give her less pain; I saw her large eyes, too, settle on his face like the solemn eyes of some pretty, wondering child. I know not whether Graham felt this examination: if he did, he was cautious not to check or discomfort it by any retaliatory look. I think he performed his work with extreme care and gentleness, sparing her what pain he could; and she acknowledged as much, when he had done, by the words:— "Thank you, Doctor, and good-night," very gratefully pronounced as she uttered them, however, it was with a repetition of the serious, direct gaze, I thought, peculiar in its gravity and intentness.

The injuries, it seems, were not dangerous: an assurance which her father received with a smile that almost made one his friend—it was so glad and gratified. He now expressed his obligations to Graham with as much earnestness as was befitting an Englishman addressing one who has served him, but is yet a stranger; he also begged him to call the next day.

"Papa," said a voice from the veiled couch, "thank the lady, too; is she there?"

I opened the curtain with a smile, and looked in at her. She lay now at comparative ease; she looked pretty, though pale; her face was delicately designed, and if at first sight it appeared proud, I believe custom might prove it to be soft.

"I thank the lady very sincerely," said her father: "I fancy she has been very good to my child. I think we scarcely dare tell Mrs. Hurst who has been her substitute and done her work; she will feel at once ashamed and jealous."

And thus, in the most friendly spirit, parting greetings were interchanged; and refreshment having been hospitably offered, but by us, as it was late, refused, we withdrew from the Hôtel Crécy.

On our way back we repassed the theatre. All was silence and darkness: the roaring, rushing crowd all vanished and gone—the damps, as well as the incipient fire, extinct and forgotten. Next morning's papers explained that it was but some loose drapery on which a spark had fallen, and which had blazed up and been quenched in a moment.

CHAPTER XXIV.

M. DE BASSOMPIERRE.

Those who live in retirement, whose lives have fallen amid the seclusion of schools or of other walled-in and guarded dwellings, are liable to be suddenly and for a long while dropped out of the memory of their friends, the denizens of a freer world. Unaccountably, perhaps, and close upon some space of unusually frequent intercourse — some congeries of rather exciting little circumstances, whose natural sequel would rather seem to be the quickening than the suspension of communication — there falls a stilly pause, a wordless silence, a long blank of oblivion. Unbroken always is this blank; alike entire and unexplained. The letter, the message once frequent, are cut off; the visit, formerly periodical, ceases to occur; the book, paper, or other token that indicated remembrance, comes no more.

Always there are excellent reasons for these lapses, if the hermit but knew them. Though he is stagnant in his cell, his connections without are whirling in the very vortex of life. That void interval which passes for him so slowly that the very clocks seem at a stand, and the wingless hours plod by in the likeness of tired tramps prone to rest at milestones — that same interval, perhaps, teems with events, and pants with hurry for his friends.

The hermit — if he be a sensible hermit — will swallow his own thoughts, and lock up his own emotions during these weeks of inward winter. He will know that Destiny designed him to imitate, on occasion, the dormouse, and he will be conformable: make a tidy ball of himself, creep into a hole of life's wall, and submit decently to the drift which blows in and soon blocks him up, preserving him in ice for the season.

Let him say, "It is quite right: it ought to be so, since so it is." And, perhaps, one day his snow-sepulchre will open, spring's softness will return, the sun and south-wind will reach him; the budding of hedges, and carolling of birds, and singing of liberated streams, will call him to kindly resurrection. Perhaps this may be the case, perhaps not: the frost may get into his heart and never thaw more; when spring comes, a crow or a pie may pick out of the wall only his dormouse-bones. Well, even in that case, all will be right: it is to be supposed he knew from the first he was mortal, and must one day go the way of all flesh, "As well soon as syne."

Villette

Following that eventful evening at the theatre, came for me seven weeks as bare as seven sheets of blank paper: no word was written on one of them; not a visit, not a token.

About the middle of that time I entertained fancies that something had happened to my friends at La Terrasse. The mid-blank is always a beclouded point for the solitary: his nerves ache with the strain of long expectancy; the doubts hitherto repelled gather now to a mass and — strong in accumulation — roll back upon him with a force which savours of vindictiveness. Night, too, becomes an unkindly time, and sleep and his nature cannot agree: strange starts and struggles harass his couch: the sinister band of bad dreams, with horror of calamity, and sick dread of entire desertion at their head, join the league against him. Poor wretch! He does his best to bear up, but he is a poor, pallid, wasting wretch, despite that best.

Towards the last of these long seven weeks I admitted, what through the other six I had jealously excluded — the conviction that these blanks were inevitable: the result of circumstances, the fiat of fate, a part of my life's lot and — above all — a matter about whose origin no question must ever be asked, for whose painful sequence no murmur ever uttered. Of course I did not blame myself for suffering: I thank God I had a truer sense of justice than to fall into any imbecile extravagance of self-accusation; and as to blaming others for silence, in my reason I well knew them blameless, and in my heart acknowledged them so: but it was a rough and heavy road to travel, and I longed for better days.

I tried different expedients to sustain and fill existence: I commenced an elaborate piece of lace-work, I studied German pretty hard, I undertook a course of regular reading of the driest and thickest books in the library; in all my efforts I was as orthodox as I knew how to be. Was there error somewhere? Very likely. I only know the result was as if I had gnawed a file to satisfy hunger, or drank brine to quench thirst.

My hour of torment was the post-hour. Unfortunately, I knew it too well, and tried as vainly as assiduously to cheat myself of that knowledge; dreading the rack of expectation, and the sick collapse of disappointment which daily preceded and followed upon that well-recognised ring.

I suppose animals kept in cages, and so scantily fed as to be always upon the verge of famine, await their food as I awaited a letter. Oh! — to speak truth, and drop that tone of a false calm which long to sustain, outwears nature's endurance — I

Villette

underwent in those seven weeks bitter fears and pains, strange inward trials, miserable defections of hope, intolerable encroachments of despair. This last came so near me sometimes that her breath went right through me. I used to feel it like a baleful air or sigh, penetrate deep, and make motion pause at my heart, or proceed only under unspeakable oppression. The letter — the well-beloved letter — would not come; and it was all of sweetness in life I had to look for.

In the very extremity of want, I had recourse again, and yet again, to the little packet in the case — the five letters. How splendid that month seemed whose skies had beheld the rising of these five stars! It was always at night I visited them, and not daring to ask every evening for a candle in the kitchen, I bought a wax taper and matches to light it, and at the study-hour stole up to the dormitory and feasted on my crust from the Barmecide's loaf. It did not nourish me: I pined on it, and got as thin as a shadow: otherwise I was not ill.

Reading there somewhat late one evening, and feeling that the power to read was leaving me — for the letters from incessant perusal were losing all sap and significance: my gold was withering to leaves before my eyes, and I was sorrowing over the disillusion — suddenly a quick tripping foot ran up the stairs. I knew Ginevra Fanshawe's step: she had dined in town that afternoon; she was now returned, and would come here to replace her shawl, &c. in the wardrobe.

Yes: in she came, dressed in bright silk, with her shawl falling from her shoulders, and her curls, half-uncurled in the damp of night, drooping careless and heavy upon her neck. I had hardly time to recasket my treasures and lock them up when she was at my side her humour seemed none of the best.

"It has been a stupid evening: they are stupid people," she began.

"Who? Mrs. Cholmondeley? I thought you always found her house charming?"

"I have not been to Mrs. Cholmondeley's."

"Indeed! Have you made new acquaintance?"

"My uncle de Bassompierre is come."

"Your uncle de Bassompierre! Are you not glad? — I thought he was a favourite."

"You thought wrong: the man is odious; I hate him."

"Because he is a foreigner? or for what other reason of equal weight?"

"He is not a foreigner. The man is English enough, goodness knows; and had an English name till three or four years ago; but his mother was a foreigner, a de Bassompierre, and some of her family are dead and have left him estates, a title, and this name: he is quite a great man now."

"Do you hate him for that reason?"

"Don't I know what mamma says about him? He is not my own uncle, but married mamma's sister. Mamma detests him; she says he killed aunt Ginevra with unkindness: he looks like a bear. Such a dismal evening!" she went on. "I'll go no more to his big hotel. Fancy me walking into a room alone, and a great man fifty years old coming forwards, and after a few minutes' conversation actually turning his back upon me, and then abruptly going out of the room. Such odd ways! I daresay his conscience smote him, for they all say at home I am the picture of aunt Ginevra. Mamma often declares the likeness is quite ridiculous."

"Were you the only visitor?"

"The only visitor? Yes; then there was missy, my cousin: little spoiled, pampered thing."

"M. de Bassompierre has a daughter?"

"Yes, yes: don't tease one with questions. Oh, dear! I am so tired."

She yawned. Throwing herself without ceremony on my bed she added, "It seems Mademoiselle was nearly crushed to a jelly in a hubbub at the theatre some weeks ago."

"Ah! indeed. And they live at a large hotel in the Rue Crécy?"

"Justement. How do you know?"

"I have been there."

"Oh, you have? Really! You go everywhere in these days. I suppose Mother Bretton took you. She and Esculapius have the

Villette

entrée of the de Bassompierre apartments: it seems 'my son John' attended missy on the occasion of her accident—Accident? Bah! All affectation! I don't think she was squeezed more than she richly deserves for her airs. And now there is quite an intimacy struck up: I heard something about 'auld lang syne,' and what not. Oh, how stupid they all were!"

"All! You said you were the only visitor."

"Did I? You see one forgets to particularize an old woman and her boy."

"Dr. and Mrs. Bretton were at M. de Bassompierre's this evening?"

"Ay, ay! as large as life; and missy played the hostess. What a conceited doll it is!"

Soured and listless, Miss Fanshawe was beginning to disclose the causes of her prostrate condition. There had been a retrenchment of incense, a diversion or a total withholding of homage and attention coquetry had failed of effect, vanity had undergone mortification. She lay fuming in the vapours.

"Is Miss de Bassompierre quite well now?" I asked.

"As well as you or I, no doubt; but she is an affected little thing, and gave herself invalid airs to attract medical notice. And to see the old dowager making her recline on a couch, and 'my son John' prohibiting excitement, etcetera—faugh! the scene was quite sickening."

"It would not have been so if the object of attention had been changed: if you had taken Miss de Bassompierre's place."

"Indeed! I hate 'my son John!'"

"'My son John!'—whom do you indicate by that name? Dr. Bretton's mother never calls him so."

"Then she ought. A clownish, bearish John he is."

"You violate the truth in saying so; and as the whole of my patience is now spun off the distaff, I peremptorily desire you to rise from that bed, and vacate this room."

"Passionate thing! Your face is the colour of a coquelicot. I wonder what always makes you so mighty testy à l'endroit du gros Jean? 'John Anderson, my Joe, John!' Oh, the distinguished name!"

Thrilling with exasperation, to which it would have been sheer folly to have given vent—for there was no contending with that unsubstantial feather, that mealy-winged moth—I extinguished my taper, locked my bureau, and left her, since she would not leave me. Small-beer as she was, she had turned insufferably acid.

The morrow was Thursday and a half-holiday. Breakfast was over; I had withdrawn to the first classe. The dreaded hour, the post-hour, was nearing, and I sat waiting it, much as a ghost-seer might wait his spectre. Less than ever was a letter probable; still, strive as I would, I could not forget that it was possible. As the moments lessened, a restlessness and fear almost beyond the average assailed me. It was a day of winter east wind, and I had now for some time entered into that dreary fellowship with the winds and their changes, so little known, so incomprehensible to the healthy. The north and east owned a terrific influence, making all pain more poignant, all sorrow sadder. The south could calm, the west sometimes cheer: unless, indeed, they brought on their wings the burden of thunder-clouds, under the weight and warmth of which all energy died.

Bitter and dark as was this January day, I remember leaving the classe, and running down without bonnet to the bottom of the long garden, and then lingering amongst the stripped shrubs, in the forlorn hope that the postman's ring might occur while I was out of hearing, and I might thus be spared the thrill which some particular nerve or nerves, almost gnawed through with the unremitting tooth of a fixed idea, were becoming wholly unfit to support. I lingered as long as I dared without fear of attracting attention by my absence. I muffled my head in my apron, and stopped my ears in terror of the torturing clang, sure to be followed by such blank silence, such barren vacuum for me. At last I ventured to re-enter the first classe, where, as it was not yet nine o'clock, no pupils had been admitted. The first thing seen was a white object on my black desk, a white, flat object. The post had, indeed, arrived; by me unheard. Rosine had visited my cell, and, like some angel, had left behind her a bright token of her presence. That shining thing on the desk was indeed a letter, a real letter; I saw so much at the distance of three yards, and as I had but one correspondent on earth, from that one it must come. He remembered me yet. How deep a pulse of gratitude sent new life through my heart.

Drawing near, bending and looking on the letter, in

trembling but almost certain hope of seeing a known hand, it was my lot to find, on the contrary, an autograph for the moment deemed unknown—a pale female scrawl, instead of a firm, masculine character. I then thought fate was too hard for me, and I said, audibly, "This is cruel."

But I got over that pain also. Life is still life, whatever its pangs: our eyes and ears and their use remain with us, though the prospect of what pleases be wholly withdrawn, and the sound of what consoles be quite silenced.

I opened the billet: by this time I had recognised its handwriting as perfectly familiar. It was dated "La Terrasse," and it ran thus:—

"DEAR LUCY,—It occurs to me to inquire what you have been doing with yourself for the last month or two? Not that I suspect you would have the least difficulty in giving an account of your proceedings. I daresay you have been just as busy and as happy as ourselves at La Terrasse. As to Graham, his professional connection extends daily: he is so much sought after, so much engaged, that I tell him he will grow quite conceited. Like a right good mother, as I am, I do my best to keep him down: no flattery does he get from me, as you know. And yet, Lucy, he is a fine fellow: his mother's heart dances at the sight of him. After being hurried here and there the whole day, and passing the ordeal of fifty sorts of tempers, and combating a hundred caprices, and sometimes witnessing cruel sufferings—perhaps, occasionally, as I tell him, inflicting them—at night he still comes home to me in such kindly, pleasant mood, that really, I seem to live in a sort of moral antipodes, and on these January evenings my day rises when other people's night sets in.

"Still he needs keeping in order, and correcting, and repressing, and I do him that good service; but the boy is so elastic there is no such thing as vexing him thoroughly. When I think I have at last driven him to the sullens, he turns on me with jokes for retaliation: but you know him and all his iniquities, and I am but an elderly simpleton to make him the subject of this epistle.

"As for me, I have had my old Bretton agent here on a visit, and have been plunged overhead and ears in business matters. I do so wish to regain for Graham at least some part of what his father left him. He laughs to scorn my anxiety on this point, bidding me look and see how he can provide for himself and me too, and asking what the old lady can possibly want that she has not; hinting about sky-blue turbans; accusing me of an ambition to wear diamonds, keep livery servants, have an hotel, and lead the fashion amongst the English clan in Villette.

"Talking of sky-blue turbans, I wish you had been with us the other evening. He had come in really tired, and after I had given him his tea, he threw himself into my chair with his customary presumption. To my great delight, he dropped asleep. (You know how he teases me about being drowsy; I, who never, by any chance, close an eye by daylight.) While he slept, I thought he looked very bonny, Lucy: fool as I am to be so proud of him; but who can help it? Show me his peer. Look where I will, I see nothing like him in Villette. Well, I took it into my head to play him a trick: so I brought out the sky-blue turban, and handling it with gingerly precaution, I managed to invest his brows with this grand adornment. I assure you it did not at all misbecome him; he looked quite Eastern, except that he is so fair. Nobody, however, can accuse him of having red hair now—it is genuine chestnut—a dark, glossy chestnut; and when I put my large cashmere about him, there was as fine a young bey, dey, or pacha improvised as you would wish to see.

"It was good entertainment; but only half-enjoyed, since I was alone: you should have been there.

"In due time my lord awoke: the looking-glass above the fireplace soon intimated to him his plight: as you may imagine, I now live under threat and dread of vengeance.

"But to come to the gist of my letter. I know Thursday is a half-holiday in the Rue Fossette: be ready, then, by five in the afternoon, at which hour I will send the carriage to take you out to La Terrasse. Be sure to come: you may meet some old acquaintance. Good-by, my wise, dear, grave little god-daughter.—Very truly yours,

"LOUISA BRETTON."

Now, a letter like that sets one to rights! I might still be sad after reading that letter, but I was more composed; not exactly cheered, perhaps, but relieved. My friends, at least, were well and happy: no accident had occurred to Graham; no illness had seized his mother—calamities that had so long been my dream and thought. Their feelings for me too were—as they had been. Yet, how strange it was to look on Mrs. Bretton's seven weeks and contrast them with my seven weeks! Also, how very wise it is in people placed in an exceptional position to hold their tongues and not rashly declare how such position galls them!

Villette

The world can understand well enough the process of perishing for want of food: perhaps few persons can enter into or follow out that of going mad from solitary confinement. They see the long-buried prisoner disinterred, a maniac or an idiot! — how his senses left him — how his nerves, first inflamed, underwent nameless agony, and then sunk to palsy — is a subject too intricate for examination, too abstract for popular comprehension. Speak of it! you might almost as well stand up in an European market-place, and propound dark sayings in that language and mood wherein Nebuchadnezzar, the imperial hypochondriac, communed with his baffled Chaldeans. And long, long may the minds to whom such themes are no mystery — by whom their bearings are sympathetically seized — be few in number, and rare of rencounter. Long may it be generally thought that physical privations alone merit compassion, and that the rest is a figment. When the world was younger and haler than now, moral trials were a deeper mystery still: perhaps in all the land of Israel there was but one Saul — certainly but one David to soothe or comprehend him.

The keen, still cold of the morning was succeeded, later in the day, by a sharp breathing from Russian wastes: the cold zone sighed over the temperate zone, and froze it fast. A heavy firmament, dull, and thick with snow, sailed up from the north, and settled over expectant Europe. Towards afternoon began the descent. I feared no carriage would come, the white tempest raged so dense and wild. But trust my godmother! Once having asked, she would have her guest. About six o'clock I was lifted from the carriage over the already blocked-up front steps of the château, and put in at the door of La Terrasse.

Running through the vestibule, and up-stairs to the drawing-room, there I found Mrs. Bretton — a summer-day in her own person. Had I been twice as cold as I was, her kind kiss and cordial clasp would have warmed me. Inured now for so long a time to rooms with bare boards, black benches, desks, and stoves, the blue saloon seemed to me gorgeous. In its Christmas-like fire alone there was a clear and crimson splendour which quite dazzled me.

When my godmother had held my hand for a little while, and chatted with me, and scolded me for having become thinner than when she last saw me, she professed to discover that the snow-wind had disordered my hair, and sent me up-stairs to make it neat and remove my shawl.

Repairing to my own little sea-green room, there also I found a bright fire, and candles too were lit: a tall waxlight stood on each side the great looking-glass; but between the candles, and before the glass, appeared something dressing itself—an airy, fairy thing—small, slight, white—a winter spirit.

I declare, for one moment I thought of Graham and his spectral illusions. With distrustful eye I noted the details of this new vision. It wore white, sprinkled slightly with drops of scarlet; its girdle was red; it had something in its hair leafy, yet shining—a little wreath with an evergreen gloss. Spectral or not, here truly was nothing frightful, and I advanced.

Turning quick upon me, a large eye, under long lashes, flashed over me, the intruder: the lashes were as dark as long, and they softened with their pencilling the orb they guarded.

"Ah! you are come!" she breathed out, in a soft, quiet voice, and she smiled slowly, and gazed intently.

I knew her now. Having only once seen that sort of face, with that cast of fine and delicate featuring, I could not but know her.

"Miss de Bassompierre," I pronounced.

"No," was the reply, "not Miss de Bassompierre for you!" I did not inquire who then she might be, but waited voluntary information.

"You are changed, but still you are yourself," she said, approaching nearer. "I remember you well—your countenance, the colour of your hair, the outline of your face…."

I had moved to the fire, and she stood opposite, and gazed into me; and as she gazed, her face became gradually more and more expressive of thought and feeling, till at last a dimness quenched her clear vision.

"It makes me almost cry to look so far back," said she: "but as to being sorry, or sentimental, don't think it: on the contrary, I am quite pleased and glad."

Interested, yet altogether at fault, I knew not what to say. At last I stammered, "I think I never met you till that night, some weeks ago, when you were hurt…?"

She smiled. "You have forgotten then that I have sat on your knee, been lifted in your arms, even shared your pillow? You no longer remember the night when I came crying, like a naughty little child as I was, to your bedside, and you took me in. You have no memory for the comfort and protection by which you soothed an acute distress? Go back to Bretton. Remember Mr. Home."

At last I saw it all. "And you are little Polly?"

"I am Paulina Mary Home de Bassompierre."

How time can change! Little Polly wore in her pale, small features, her fairy symmetry, her varying expression, a certain promise of interest and grace; but Paulina Mary was become beautiful—not with the beauty that strikes the eye like a rose—orbed, ruddy, and replete; not with the plump, and pink, and flaxen attributes of her blond cousin Ginevra; but her seventeen years had brought her a refined and tender charm which did not lie in complexion, though hers was fair and clear; nor in outline, though her features were sweet, and her limbs perfectly turned; but, I think, rather in a subdued glow from the soul outward. This was not an opaque vase, of material however costly, but a lamp chastely lucent, guarding from extinction, yet not hiding from worship, a flame vital and vestal. In speaking of her attractions, I would not exaggerate language; but, indeed, they seemed to me very real and engaging. What though all was on a small scale, it was the perfume which gave this white violet distinction, and made it superior to the broadest camelia—the fullest dahlia that ever bloomed.

"Ah! and you remember the old time at Bretton?"

"Better," said she, "better, perhaps, than you. I remember it with minute distinctness: not only the time, but the days of the time, and the hours of the days."

"You must have forgotten some things?"

"Very little, I imagine."

"You were then a little creature of quick feelings: you must, long ere this, have outgrown the impressions with which joy and grief, affection and bereavement, stamped your mind ten years ago."

"You think I have forgotten whom I liked, and in what degree I liked them when a child?"

"The sharpness must be gone—the point, the poignancy—the deep imprint must be softened away and effaced?"

"I have a good memory for those days."

She looked as if she had. Her eyes were the eyes of one who can remember; one whose childhood does not fade like a dream, nor whose youth vanish like a sunbeam. She would not take life, loosely and incoherently, in parts, and let one season slip as she entered on another: she would retain and add; often review from the commencement, and so grow in harmony and consistency as she grew in years. Still I could not quite admit the conviction that all the pictures which now crowded upon me were vivid and visible to her. Her fond attachments, her sports and contests with a well-loved playmate, the patient, true devotion of her child's heart, her fears, her delicate reserves, her little trials, the last piercing pain of separation.... I retraced these things, and shook my head incredulous. She persisted. "The child of seven years lives yet in the girl of seventeen," said she.

"You used to be excessively fond of Mrs. Bretton," I remarked, intending to test her. She set me right at once.

"Not excessively fond," said she; "I liked her: I respected her as I should do now: she seems to me very little altered."

"She is not much changed," I assented.

We were silent a few minutes. Glancing round the room she said, "There are several things here that used to be at Bretton! I remember that pincushion and that looking-glass."

Evidently she was not deceived in her estimate of her own memory; not, at least, so far.

"You think, then, you would have known Mrs. Bretton?" I went on.

"I perfectly remembered her; the turn of her features, her olive complexion, and black hair, her height, her walk, her voice."

"Dr. Bretton, of course," I pursued, "would be out of the question: and, indeed, as I saw your first interview with him, I am aware that he appeared to you as a stranger."

"That first night I was puzzled," she answered.

"How did the recognition between him and your father come about?"

Villette

"They exchanged cards. The names Graham Bretton and Home de Bassompierre gave rise to questions and explanations. That was on the second day; but before then I was beginning to know something."

"How—know something?"

"Why," she said, "how strange it is that most people seem so slow to feel the truth—not to see, but feel! When Dr. Bretton had visited me a few times, and sat near and talked to me; when I had observed the look in his eyes, the expression about his mouth, the form of his chin, the carriage of his head, and all that we do observe in persons who approach us—how could I avoid being led by association to think of Graham Bretton? Graham was slighter than he, and not grown so tall, and had a smoother face, and longer and lighter hair, and spoke—not so deeply—more like a girl; but yet he is Graham, just as I am little Polly, or you are Lucy Snowe."

I thought the same, but I wondered to find my thoughts hers: there are certain things in which we so rarely meet with our double that it seems a miracle when that chance befalls.

"You and Graham were once playmates."

"And do you remember that?" she questioned in her turn.

"No doubt he will remember it also," said I.

"I have not asked him: few things would surprise me so much as to find that he did. I suppose his disposition is still gay and careless?"

"Was it so formerly? Did it so strike you? Do you thus remember him?"

"I scarcely remember him in any other light. Sometimes he was studious; sometimes he was merry: but whether busy with his books or disposed for play, it was chiefly the books or game he thought of; not much heeding those with whom he read or amused himself."

"Yet to you he was partial."

"Partial to me? Oh, no! he had other playmates—his schoolfellows; I was of little consequence to him, except on Sundays: yes, he was kind on Sundays. I remember walking with him hand-in-hand to St. Mary's, and his finding the places in my prayer-book; and how good and still he was on Sunday evenings! So mild for such a proud, lively boy; so patient with all my blunders in reading; and so wonderfully to be depended on, for he never spent those evenings from home: I had a constant fear that he would accept some invitation and forsake us; but he never did, nor seemed ever to wish to do it. Thus, of course, it can be no more. I suppose Sunday will now be Dr. Bretton's dining-out day…?"

"Children, come down!" here called Mrs. Bretton from below. Paulina would still have lingered, but I inclined to descend: we went down.

CHAPTER XXV.

THE LITTLE COUNTESS.

Cheerful as my godmother naturally was, and entertaining as, for our sakes, she made a point of being, there was no true enjoyment that evening at La Terrasse, till, through the wild howl of the winter-night, were heard the signal sounds of arrival. How often, while women and girls sit warm at snug fire-sides, their hearts and imaginations are doomed to divorce from the comfort surrounding their persons, forced out by night to wander through dark ways, to dare stress of weather, to contend with the snow-blast, to wait at lonely gates and stiles in wildest storms, watching and listening to see and hear the father, the son, the husband coming home.

Father and son came at last to the château: for the Count de Bassompierre that night accompanied Dr. Bretton. I know not which of our trio heard the horses first; the asperity, the violence of the weather warranted our running down into the hall to meet and greet the two riders as they came in; but they warned us to keep our distance: both were white — two mountains of snow; and indeed Mrs. Bretton, seeing their condition, ordered them instantly to the kitchen; prohibiting them, at their peril, from setting foot on her carpeted staircase till they had severally put off that mask of Old Christmas they now affected. Into the kitchen, however, we could not help following them: it was a large old Dutch kitchen, picturesque and pleasant. The little white Countess danced in a circle about her equally white sire, clapping her hands and crying, "Papa, papa, you look like an enormous Polar bear."

The bear shook himself, and the little sprite fled far from the frozen shower. Back she came, however, laughing, and eager to aid in removing the arctic disguise. The Count, at last issuing from his dreadnought, threatened to overwhelm her with it as with an avalanche.

"Come, then," said she, bending to invite the fall, and when it was playfully advanced above her head, bounding out of reach like some little chamois.

Her movements had the supple softness, the velvet grace of a kitten; her laugh was clearer than the ring of silver and crystal; as she took her sire's cold hands and rubbed them, and stood on tiptoe to reach his lips for a kiss, there seemed to shine round her a halo of loving delight. The grave and reverend seignor looked down on her as men do look on what is the apple of their eye.

"Mrs. Bretton," said he: "what am I to do with this daughter or daughterling of mine? She neither grows in wisdom nor in stature. Don't you find her pretty nearly as much the child as she was ten years ago?"

"She cannot be more the child than this great boy of mine," said Mrs. Bretton, who was in conflict with her son about some change of dress she deemed advisable, and which he resisted. He stood leaning against the Dutch dresser, laughing and keeping her at arm's length.

"Come, mamma," said he, "by way of compromise, and to secure for us inward as well as outward warmth, let us have a Christmas wassail-cup, and toast Old England here, on the hearth."

So, while the Count stood by the fire, and Paulina Mary still danced to and fro—happy in the liberty of the wide hall-like kitchen—Mrs. Bretton herself instructed Martha to spice and heat the wassail-bowl, and, pouring the draught into a Bretton flagon, it was served round, reaming hot, by means of a small silver vessel, which I recognised as Graham's christening-cup.

"Here's to Auld Lang Syne!" said the Count; holding the glancing cup on high. Then, looking at Mrs. Bretton.—

"We twa ha' paidlet i' the burn

    Fra morning sun till dine,

But seas between us braid ha' roared

    Sin' auld lang syne.

"And surely ye'll be your pint-stoup,

    And surely I'll be mine;

And we'll taste a cup o' kindness yet

    For auld lang syne."

"Scotch! Scotch!" cried Paulina; "papa is talking Scotch; and Scotch he is, partly. We are Home and de Bassompierre, Caledonian and Gallic."

"And is that a Scotch reel you are dancing, you Highland fairy?" asked her father. "Mrs. Bretton, there will be a green ring growing up in the middle of your kitchen shortly. I would not answer for her being quite cannie: she is a strange little mortal."

"Tell Lucy to dance with me, papa; there is Lucy Snowe."

Mr. Home (there was still quite as much about him of plain Mr. Home as of proud Count de Bassompierre) held his hand out to me, saying kindly, "he remembered me well; and, even had his own memory been less trustworthy, my name was so often on his daughter's lips, and he had listened to so many long tales about me, I should seem like an old acquaintance."

Every one now had tasted the wassail-cup except Paulina, whose pas de fée, ou de fantaisie, nobody thought of interrupting to offer so profanatory a draught; but she was not to be overlooked, nor baulked of her mortal privileges.

"Let me taste," said she to Graham, as he was putting the cup on the shelf of the dresser out of her reach.

Mrs. Bretton and Mr. Home were now engaged in conversation. Dr. John had not been unobservant of the fairy's dance; he had watched it, and he had liked it. To say nothing of the softness and beauty of the movements, eminently grateful to his grace-loving eye, that ease in his mother's house charmed him, for it set him at ease: again she seemed a child for him—again, almost his playmate. I wondered how he would speak to her; I had not yet seen him address her; his first words proved that the old days of "little Polly" had been recalled to his mind by this evening's child-like light-heartedness.

"Your ladyship wishes for the tankard?"

"I think I said so. I think I intimated as much."

"Couldn't consent to a step of the kind on any account. Sorry for it, but couldn't do it."

"Why? I am quite well now: it can't break my collar-bone again, or dislocate my shoulder. Is it wine?"

"No; nor dew."

"I don't want dew; I don't like dew: but what is it?"

"Ale—strong ale—old October; brewed, perhaps, when I was born."

"It must be curious: is it good?"

"Excessively good."

And he took it down, administered to himself a second dose of this mighty elixir, expressed in his mischievous eyes extreme contentment with the same, and solemnly replaced the cup on the shelf.

"I should like a little," said Paulina, looking up; "I never had any 'old October:' is it sweet?"

"Perilously sweet," said Graham.

She continued to look up exactly with the countenance of a child that longs for some prohibited dainty. At last the Doctor relented, took it down, and indulged himself in the gratification of letting her taste from his hand; his eyes, always expressive in the revelation of pleasurable feelings, luminously and smilingly avowed that it was a gratification; and he prolonged it by so regulating the position of the cup that only a drop at a time could reach the rosy, sipping lips by which its brim was courted.

"A little more—a little more," said she, petulantly touching his hand with the forefinger, to make him incline the cup more generously and yieldingly. "It smells of spice and sugar, but I can't taste it; your wrist is so stiff, and you are so stingy."

He indulged her, whispering, however, with gravity: "Don't tell my mother or Lucy; they wouldn't approve."

"Nor do I," said she, passing into another tone and manner as soon as she had fairly assayed the beverage, just as if it had acted upon her like some disenchanting draught, undoing the work of a wizard: "I find it anything but sweet; it is bitter and hot, and takes away my breath. Your old October was only desirable while forbidden. Thank you, no more."

And, with a slight bend—careless, but as graceful as her dance—she glided from him and rejoined her father.

I think she had spoken truth: the child of seven was in the girl of seventeen.

Villette

Graham looked after her a little baffled, a little puzzled; his eye was on her a good deal during the rest of the evening, but she did not seem to notice him.

As we ascended to the drawing-room for tea, she took her father's arm: her natural place seemed to be at his side; her eyes and her ears were dedicated to him. He and Mrs. Bretton were the chief talkers of our little party, and Paulina was their best listener, attending closely to all that was said, prompting the repetition of this or that trait or adventure.

"And where were you at such a time, papa? And what did you say then? And tell Mrs. Bretton what happened on that occasion." Thus she drew him out.

She did not again yield to any effervescence of glee; the infantine sparkle was exhaled for the night: she was soft, thoughtful, and docile. It was pretty to see her bid good-night; her manner to Graham was touched with dignity: in her very slight smile and quiet bow spoke the Countess, and Graham could not but look grave, and bend responsive. I saw he hardly knew how to blend together in his ideas the dancing fairy and delicate dame.

Next day, when we were all assembled round the breakfast-table, shivering and fresh from the morning's chill ablutions, Mrs. Bretton pronounced a decree that nobody, who was not forced by dire necessity, should quit her house that day.

Indeed, egress seemed next to impossible; the drift darkened the lower panes of the casement, and, on looking out, one saw the sky and air vexed and dim, the wind and snow in angry conflict. There was no fall now, but what had already descended was torn up from the earth, whirled round by brief shrieking gusts, and cast into a hundred fantastic forms.

The Countess seconded Mrs. Bretton.

"Papa shall not go out," said she, placing a seat for herself beside her father's arm-chair. "I will look after him. You won't go into town, will you, papa?"

"Ay, and No," was the answer. "If you and Mrs. Bretton are very good to me, Polly—kind, you know, and attentive; if you pet me in a very nice manner, and make much of me, I may possibly be induced to wait an hour after breakfast and see whether this razor-edged wind settles. But, you see, you give me no breakfast; you offer me nothing: you let me starve."

"Quick! please, Mrs. Bretton, and pour out the coffee," entreated Paulina, "whilst I take care of the Count de Bassompierre in other respects: since he grew into a Count, he has needed so much attention."

She separated and prepared a roll.

"There, papa, are your 'pistolets' charged," said she. "And there is some marmalade, just the same sort of marmalade we used to have at Bretton, and which you said was as good as if it had been conserved in Scotland—"

"And which your little ladyship used to beg for my boy—do you remember that?" interposed Mrs. Bretton. "Have you forgotten how you would come to my elbow and touch my sleeve with the whisper, 'Please, ma'am, something good for Graham—a little marmalade, or honey, or jam?'"

"No, mamma," broke in Dr. John, laughing, yet reddening; "it surely was not so: I could not have cared for these things."

"Did he or did he not, Paulina?"

"He liked them," asserted Paulina.

"Never blush for it, John," said Mr. Home, encouragingly. "I like them myself yet, and always did. And Polly showed her sense in catering for a friend's material comforts: it was I who put her into the way of such good manners—nor do I let her forget them. Polly, offer me a small slice of that tongue."

"There, papa: but remember you are only waited upon with this assiduity; on condition of being persuadable, and reconciling yourself to La Terrasse for the day."

"Mrs. Bretton," said the Count, "I want to get rid of my daughter—to send her to school. Do you know of any good school?"

"There is Lucy's place—Madame Beck's."

"Miss Snowe is in a school?"

"I am a teacher," I said, and was rather glad of the opportunity of saying this. For a little while I had been feeling as if placed in a false position. Mrs. Bretton and son knew my circumstances; but the Count and his daughter did not. They might choose to vary by some shades their hitherto cordial manner towards me, when aware of my grade in society. I spoke then readily: but a swarm of thoughts I had not anticipated nor invoked, rose dim at the words, making me sigh involuntarily. Mr. Home did not lift his eyes from his breakfast-plate for about two minutes, nor did he speak; perhaps he had not caught the words—perhaps he thought that on a confession of that nature, politeness would interdict comment: the Scotch are proverbially proud; and homely as was Mr. Home in look, simple in habits and tastes, I have all along intimated that he was not without his share of the national quality. Was his a pseudo pride? was it real dignity? I leave the question undecided in its wide sense. Where it concerned me individually I can only answer: then, and always, he showed himself a true-hearted gentleman.

By nature he was a feeler and a thinker; over his emotions and his reflections spread a mellowing of melancholy; more than a mellowing: in trouble and bereavement it became a cloud. He did not know much about Lucy Snowe; what he knew, he did not very accurately comprehend: indeed his misconceptions of my character often made me smile; but he saw my walk in life lay rather on the shady side of the hill: he gave me credit for doing my endeavour to keep the course honestly straight; he would have helped me if he could: having no opportunity of helping, he still wished me well. When he did look at me, his eye was kind; when he did speak, his voice was benevolent.

"Yours," said he, "is an arduous calling. I wish you health and strength to win in it—success."

His fair little daughter did not take the information quite so composedly: she fixed on me a pair of eyes wide with wonder—almost with dismay.

"Are you a teacher?" cried she. Then, having paused on the unpalatable idea, "Well, I never knew what you were, nor ever thought of asking: for me, you were always Lucy Snowe."

"And what am I now?" I could not forbear inquiring.

"Yourself, of course. But do you really teach here, in Villette?"

"I really do."

"And do you like it?"

"Not always."

"And why do you go on with it?"

Her father looked at, and, I feared, was going to check her; but he only said, "Proceed, Polly, proceed with that catechism—prove yourself the little wiseacre you are. If Miss Snowe were to blush and look confused, I should have to bid you hold your tongue; and you and I would sit out the present meal in some disgrace; but she only smiles, so push her hard, multiply the cross-questions. Well, Miss Snowe, why do you go on with it?"

"Chiefly, I fear, for the sake of the money I get."

"Not then from motives of pure philanthropy? Polly and I were clinging to that hypothesis as the most lenient way of accounting for your eccentricity."

"No—no, sir. Rather for the roof of shelter I am thus enabled to keep over my head; and for the comfort of mind it gives me to think that while I can work for myself, I am spared the pain of being a burden to anybody."

"Papa, say what you will, I pity Lucy."

"Take up that pity, Miss de Bassompierre; take it up in both hands, as you might a little callow gosling squattering out of bounds without leave; put it back in the warm nest of a heart whence it issued, and receive in your ear this whisper. If my Polly ever came to know by experience the uncertain nature of this world's goods, I should like her to act as Lucy acts: to work for herself, that she might burden neither kith nor kin."

"Yes, papa," said she, pensively and tractably. "But poor Lucy! I thought she was a rich lady, and had rich friends."

"You thought like a little simpleton. I never thought so. When I had time to consider Lucy's manner and aspect, which was not often, I saw she was one who had to guard and not be guarded; to act and not be served: and this lot has, I imagine, helped her to an experience for which, if she live long enough to realize its full benefit, she may yet bless Providence. But this school," he pursued, changing his tone from grave to gay: "would Madame Beck admit my Polly, do you think, Miss Lucy?"

I said, there needed but to try Madame; it would soon be seen: she was fond of English pupils. "If you, sir," I added, "will

Villette

but take Miss de Bassompierre in your carriage this very afternoon, I think I can answer for it that Rosine, the portress, will not be very slow in answering your ring; and Madame, I am sure, will put on her best pair of gloves to come into the salon to receive you."

"In that case," responded Mr. Home, "I see no sort of necessity there is for delay. Mrs. Hurst can send what she calls her young lady's 'things' after her; Polly can settle down to her horn-book before night; and you, Miss Lucy, I trust, will not disdain to cast an occasional eye upon her, and let me know, from time to time, how she gets on. I hope you approve of the arrangement, Countess de Bassompierre?"

The Countess hemmed and hesitated. "I thought," said she, "I thought I had finished my education—"

"That only proves how much we may be mistaken in our thoughts. I hold a far different opinion, as most of these will who have been auditors of your profound knowledge of life this morning. Ah, my little girl, thou hast much to learn; and papa ought to have taught thee more than he has done! Come, there is nothing for it but to try Madame Beck; and the weather seems settling, and I have finished my breakfast—"

"But, papa!"

"Well?"

"I see an obstacle."

"I don't at all."

"It is enormous, papa; it can never be got over; it is as large as you in your greatcoat, and the snowdrift on the top."

"And, like that snowdrift, capable of melting?"

"No! it is of too—too solid flesh: it is just your own self. Miss Lucy, warn Madame Beck not to listen to any overtures about taking me, because, in the end, it would turn out that she would have to take papa too: as he is so teasing, I will just tell tales about him. Mrs. Bretton and all of you listen: About five years ago, when I was twelve years old, he took it into his head that he was spoiling me; that I was growing unfitted for the world, and I don't know what, and nothing would serve or satisfy him, but I must go to school. I cried, and so on; but M. de Bassompierre proved hard-hearted, quite firm and flinty, and to school I went. What was the result? In the most admirable manner, papa came to school likewise: every other day he called to see me. Madame Aigredoux grumbled, but it was of no use; and so, at last, papa and I were both, in a manner, expelled. Lucy can just tell Madame Beck this little trait: it is only fair to let her know what she has to expect."

Mrs. Bretton asked Mr. Home what he had to say in answer to this statement. As he made no defence, judgment was given against him, and Paulina triumphed.

But she had other moods besides the arch and naïve. After breakfast; when the two elders withdrew—I suppose to talk over certain of Mrs. Bretton's business matters—and the Countess, Dr. Bretton, and I, were for a short time alone together—all the child left her; with us, more nearly her companions in age, she rose at once to the little lady: her very face seemed to alter; that play of feature, and candour of look, which, when she spoke to her father, made it quite dimpled and round, yielded to an aspect more thoughtful, and lines distincter and less mobile.

No doubt Graham noted the change as well as I. He stood for some minutes near the window, looking out at the snow; presently he approached the hearth, and entered into conversation, but not quite with his usual ease: fit topics did not seem to rise to his lips; he chose them fastidiously, hesitatingly, and consequently infelicitously: he spoke vaguely of Villette— its inhabitants, its notable sights and buildings. He was answered by Miss de Bassompierre in quite womanly sort; with intelligence, with a manner not indeed wholly disindividualized: a tone, a glance, a gesture, here and there, rather animated and quick than measured and stately, still recalled little Polly; but yet there was so fine and even a polish, so calm and courteous a grace, gilding and sustaining these peculiarities, that a less sensitive man than Graham would not have ventured to seize upon them as vantage points, leading to franker intimacy.

Yet while Dr. Bretton continued subdued, and, for him, sedate, he was still observant. Not one of those petty impulses and natural breaks escaped him. He did not miss one characteristic movement, one hesitation in language, or one lisp in utterance. At times, in speaking fast, she still lisped; but coloured whenever such lapse occurred, and in a painstaking, conscientious manner, quite as amusing as the slight error, repeated the word more distinctly.

Villette

Whenever she did this, Dr. Bretton smiled. Gradually, as they conversed, the restraint on each side slackened: might the conference have but been prolonged, I believe it would soon have become genial: already to Paulina's lip and cheek returned the wreathing, dimpling smile; she lisped once, and forgot to correct herself. And Dr. John, I know not how he changed, but change he did. He did not grow gayer—no raillery, no levity sparkled across his aspect—but his position seemed to become one of more pleasure to himself, and he spoke his augmented comfort in readier language, in tones more suave. Ten years ago this pair had always found abundance to say to each other; the intervening decade had not narrowed the experience or impoverished the intelligence of either: besides, there are certain natures of which the mutual influence is such, that the more they say, the more they have to say. For these out of association grows adhesion, and out of adhesion, amalgamation.

Graham, however, must go: his was a profession whose claims are neither to be ignored nor deferred. He left the room; but before he could leave the house there was a return. I am sure he came back—not for the paper, or card in his desk, which formed his ostensible errand—but to assure himself, by one more glance, that Paulina's aspect was really such as memory was bearing away: that he had not been viewing her somehow by a partial, artificial light, and making a fond mistake. No! he found the impression true—rather, indeed, he gained than lost by this return: he took away with him a parting look—shy, but very soft—as beautiful, as innocent, as any little fawn could lift out of its cover of fern, or any lamb from its meadow-bed.

Being left alone, Paulina and I kept silence for some time: we both took out some work, and plied a mute and diligent task. The white-wood workbox of old days was now replaced by one inlaid with precious mosaic, and furnished with implements of gold; the tiny and trembling fingers that could scarce guide the needle, though tiny still, were now swift and skilful: but there was the same busy knitting of the brow, the same little dainty mannerisms, the same quick turns and movements—now to replace a stray tress, and anon to shake from the silken skirt some imaginary atom of dust—some clinging fibre of thread.

That morning I was disposed for silence: the austere fury of the winter-day had on me an awing, hushing influence. That passion of January, so white and so bloodless, was not yet spent: the storm had raved itself hoarse, but seemed no nearer exhaustion. Had Ginevra Fanshawe been my companion in that drawing-room, she would not have suffered me to muse and listen undisturbed. The presence just gone from us would have been her theme; and how she would have rung the changes on one topic! how she would have pursued and pestered me with questions and surmises—worried and oppressed me with comments and confidences I did not want, and longed to avoid.

Paulina Mary cast once or twice towards me a quiet but penetrating glance of her dark, full eye; her lips half opened, as if to the impulse of coming utterance: but she saw and delicately respected my inclination for silence.

"This will not hold long," I thought to myself; for I was not accustomed to find in women or girls any power of self-control, or strength of self-denial. As far as I knew them, the chance of a gossip about their usually trivial secrets, their often very washy and paltry feelings, was a treat not to be readily foregone.

The little Countess promised an exception: she sewed till she was tired of sewing, and then she took a book.

As chance would have it, she had sought it in Dr. Bretton's own compartment of the bookcase; and it proved to be an old Bretton book—some illustrated work of natural history. Often had I seen her standing at Graham's side, resting that volume on his knee, and reading to his tuition; and, when the lesson was over, begging, as a treat, that he would tell her all about the pictures. I watched her keenly: here was a true test of that memory she had boasted; would her recollections now be faithful?

Faithful? It could not be doubted. As she turned the leaves, over her face passed gleam after gleam of expression, the least intelligent of which was a full greeting to the Past. And then she turned to the title-page, and looked at the name written in the schoolboy hand. She looked at it long; nor was she satisfied with merely looking: she gently passed over the characters the tips of her fingers, accompanying the action with an unconscious but tender smile, which converted the touch into a caress. Paulina loved the Past; but the peculiarity of this little scene was, that she said nothing: she could feel without pouring out her feelings in a flux of words.

She now occupied herself at the bookcase for nearly an hour; taking down volume after volume, and renewing her acquaintance with each. This done, she seated herself on a low stool, rested her cheek on her hand, and thought, and still was mute.

The sound of the front door opened below, a rush of cold

wind, and her father's voice speaking to Mrs. Bretton in the hall, startled her at last. She sprang up: she was down-stairs in one second.

"Papa! papa! you are not going out?"

"My pet, I must go into town."

"But it is too—too cold, papa."

And then I heard M. de Bassompierre showing to her how he was well provided against the weather; and how he was going to have the carriage, and to be quite snugly sheltered; and, in short, proving that she need not fear for his comfort.

"But you will promise to come back here this evening, before it is quite dark;—you and Dr. Bretton, both, in the carriage? It is not fit to ride."

"Well, if I see the Doctor, I will tell him a lady has laid on him her commands to take care of his precious health and come home early under my escort."

"Yes, you must say a lady; and he will think it is his mother, and be obedient. And, papa, mind to come soon, for I shall watch and listen."

The door closed, and the carriage rolled softly through the snow; and back returned the Countess, pensive and anxious.

She did listen, and watch, when evening closed; but it was in stillest sort: walking the drawing-room with quite noiseless step. She checked at intervals her velvet march; inclined her ear, and consulted the night sounds: I should rather say, the night silence; for now, at last, the wind was fallen. The sky, relieved of its avalanche, lay naked and pale: through the barren boughs of the avenue we could see it well, and note also the polar splendour of the new-year moon—an orb white as a world of ice. Nor was it late when we saw also the return of the carriage.

Paulina had no dance of welcome for this evening. It was with a sort of gravity that she took immediate possession of her father, as he entered the room; but she at once made him her entire property, led him to the seat of her choice, and, while softly showering round him honeyed words of commendation for being so good and coming home so soon, you would have thought it was entirely by the power of her little hands he was put into his chair, and settled and arranged; for the strong man seemed to take pleasure in wholly yielding himself to this dominion-potent only by love.

Graham did not appear till some minutes after the Count. Paulina half turned when his step was heard: they spoke, but only a word or two; their fingers met a moment, but obviously with slight contact. Paulina remained beside her father; Graham threw himself into a seat on the other side of the room.

It was well that Mrs. Bretton and Mr. Home had a great deal to say to each other—almost an inexhaustible fund of discourse in old recollections; otherwise, I think, our party would have been but a still one that evening.

After tea, Paulina's quick needle and pretty golden thimble were busily plied by the lamp-light, but her tongue rested, and her eyes seemed reluctant to raise often their lids, so smooth and so full-fringed. Graham, too, must have been tired with his day's work: he listened dutifully to his elders and betters, said very little himself, and followed with his eye the gilded glance of Paulina's thimble; as if it had been some bright moth on the wing, or the golden head of some darting little yellow serpent.

CHAPTER XXVI.

A BURIAL.

From this date my life did not want variety; I went out a good deal, with the entire consent of Madame Beck, who perfectly approved the grade of my acquaintance. That worthy directress had never from the first treated me otherwise than with respect; and when she found that I was liable to frequent invitations from a château and a great hotel, respect improved into distinction.

Not that she was fulsome about it: Madame, in all things worldly, was in nothing weak; there was measure and sense in her hottest pursuit of self-interest, calm and considerateness in her closest clutch of gain; without, then, laying herself open to my contempt as a time-server and a toadie, she marked with tact that she was pleased people connected with her establishment should frequent such associates as must cultivate and elevate, rather than those who might deteriorate and depress. She never praised either me or my friends; only once when she was sitting in the sun in the garden, a cup of coffee at her elbow and the Gazette in her hand, looking very comfortable, and I came up and asked leave of absence for the evening, she delivered herself in this gracious sort:—

"Oui, oui, ma bonne amie: je vous donne la permission de cœur et de gré. Votre travail dans ma maison a toujours été admirable, rempli de zèle et de discrétion: vous avez bien le droit de vous amuser. Sortez donc tant que vous voudrez. Quant à votre choix de connaissances, j'en suis contente; c'est sage, digne, laudable."

She closed her lips and resumed the Gazette.

The reader will not too gravely regard the little circumstance that about this time the triply-enclosed packet of five letters temporarily disappeared from my bureau. Blank dismay was naturally my first sensation on making the discovery; but in a moment I took heart of grace.

"Patience!" whispered I to myself. "Let me say nothing, but wait peaceably; they will come back again."

And they did come back: they had only been on a short visit to Madame's chamber; having passed their examination, they came back duly and truly: I found them all right the next day.

I wonder what she thought of my correspondence? What estimate did she form of Dr. John Bretton's epistolary powers? In what light did the often very pithy thoughts, the generally sound, and sometimes original opinions, set, without pretension, in an easily-flowing, spirited style, appear to her? How did she like that genial, half humorous vein, which to me gave such delight? What did she think of the few kind words scattered here and there—not thickly, as the diamonds were scattered in the valley of Sindbad, but sparely, as those gems lie in unfabled beds? Oh, Madame Beck! how seemed these things to you?

I think in Madame Beck's eyes the five letters found a certain favour. One day after she had borrowed them of me (in speaking of so suave a little woman, one ought to use suave terms), I caught her examining me with a steady contemplative gaze, a little puzzled, but not at all malevolent. It was during that brief space between lessons, when the pupils turned out into the court for a quarter of an hour's recreation; she and I remained in the first classe alone: when I met her eye, her thoughts forced themselves partially through her lips.

"Il y a," said she, "quelquechose de bien remarquable dans le caractère Anglais."

"How, Madame?"

She gave a little laugh, repeating the word "how" in English.

"Je ne saurais vous dire 'how;' mais, enfin, les Anglais ont des idées à eux, en amitié, en amour, en tout. Mais au moins il n'est pas besoin de les surveiller," she added, getting up and trotting away like the compact little pony she was.

"Then I hope," murmured I to myself, "you will graciously let alone my letters for the future."

Alas! something came rushing into my eyes, dimming utterly their vision, blotting from sight the schoolroom, the garden, the bright winter sun, as I remembered that never more would letters, such as she had read, come to me. I had seen the last of them. That goodly river on whose banks I had sojourned, of whose waves a few reviving drops had trickled to my lips, was bending to another course: it was leaving my little hut and field forlorn and sand-dry, pouring its wealth of waters far away. The change was right, just, natural; not a word could be said: but I loved my Rhine, my Nile; I had almost worshipped my Ganges, and I grieved that the grand tide should roll

Villette

estranged, should vanish like a false mirage. Though stoical, I was not quite a stoic; drops streamed fast on my hands, on my desk: I wept one sultry shower, heavy and brief.

But soon I said to myself, "The Hope I am bemoaning suffered and made me suffer much: it did not die till it was full time: following an agony so lingering, death ought to be welcome."

Welcome I endeavoured to make it. Indeed, long pain had made patience a habit. In the end I closed the eyes of my dead, covered its face, and composed its limbs with great calm.

The letters, however, must be put away, out of sight: people who have undergone bereavement always jealously gather together and lock away mementos: it is not supportable to be stabbed to the heart each moment by sharp revival of regret.

One vacant holiday afternoon (the Thursday) going to my treasure, with intent to consider its final disposal, I perceived — and this time with a strong impulse of displeasure — that it had been again tampered with: the packet was there, indeed, but the ribbon which secured it had been untied and retied; and by other symptoms I knew that my drawer had been visited.

This was a little too much. Madame Beck herself was the soul of discretion, besides having as strong a brain and sound a judgment as ever furnished a human head; that she should know the contents of my casket, was not pleasant, but might be borne. Little Jesuit inquisitress as she was, she could see things in a true light, and understand them in an unperverted sense; but the idea that she had ventured to communicate information, thus gained, to others; that she had, perhaps, amused herself with a companion over documents, in my eyes most sacred, shocked me cruelly. Yet, that such was the case I now saw reason to fear; I even guessed her confidant. Her kinsman, M. Paul Emanuel, had spent yesterday evening with her: she was much in the habit of consulting him, and of discussing with him matters she broached to no one else. This very morning, in class, that gentleman had favoured me with a glance which he seemed to have borrowed from Vashti, the actress; I had not at the moment comprehended that blue, yet lurid, flash out of his angry eye; but I read its meaning now. He, I believed, was not apt to regard what concerned me from a fair point of view, nor to judge me with tolerance and candour: I had always found him severe and suspicious: the thought that these letters, mere friendly letters as they were, had fallen once, and might fall again, into his hands, jarred my very soul.

What should I do to prevent this? In what corner of this strange house was it possible to find security or secrecy? Where could a key be a safeguard, or a padlock a barrier?

In the grenier? No, I did not like the grenier. Besides, most of the boxes and drawers there were mouldering, and did not lock. Rats, too, gnawed their way through the decayed wood; and mice made nests amongst the litter of their contents: my dear letters (most dear still, though Ichabod was written on their covers) might be consumed by vermin; certainly the writing would soon become obliterated by damp. No; the grenier would not do—but where then?

While pondering this problem, I sat in the dormitory window-seat. It was a fine frosty afternoon; the winter sun, already setting, gleamed pale on the tops of the garden-shrubs in the "allée défendue." One great old pear-tree—the nun's pear-tree—stood up a tall dryad skeleton, grey, gaunt, and stripped. A thought struck me—one of those queer fantastic thoughts that will sometimes strike solitary people. I put on my bonnet, cloak, and furs, and went out into the city.

Bending my steps to the old historical quarter of the town, whose hoar and overshadowed precincts I always sought by instinct in melancholy moods, I wandered on from street to street, till, having crossed a half deserted "place" or square, I found myself before a sort of broker's shop; an ancient place, full of ancient things. What I wanted was a metal box which might be soldered, or a thick glass jar or bottle which might be stoppered or sealed hermetically. Amongst miscellaneous heaps, I found and purchased the latter article.

I then made a little roll of my letters, wrapped them in oiled silk, bound them with twine, and, having put them in the bottle, got the old Jew broker to stopper, seal, and make it air-tight. While obeying my directions, he glanced at me now and then suspiciously from under his frost-white eyelashes. I believe he thought there was some evil deed on hand. In all this I had a dreary something—not pleasure—but a sad, lonely satisfaction. The impulse under which I acted, the mood controlling me, were similar to the impulse and the mood which had induced me to visit the confessional. With quick walking I regained the pensionnat just at dark, and in time for dinner.

At seven o'clock the moon rose. At half-past seven, when the pupils and teachers were at study, and Madame Beck was with her mother and children in the salle-à-manger, when the half-boarders were all gone home, and Rosine had left the vestibule,

Villette

and all was still—I shawled myself, and, taking the sealed jar, stole out through the first-classe door, into the berceau and thence into the "allée défendue."

Methusaleh, the pear-tree, stood at the further end of this walk, near my seat: he rose up, dim and gray, above the lower shrubs round him. Now Methusaleh, though so very old, was of sound timber still; only there was a hole, or rather a deep hollow, near his root. I knew there was such a hollow, hidden partly by ivy and creepers growing thick round; and there I meditated hiding my treasure. But I was not only going to hide a treasure—I meant also to bury a grief. That grief over which I had lately been weeping, as I wrapped it in its winding-sheet, must be interred.

Well, I cleared away the ivy, and found the hole; it was large enough to receive the jar, and I thrust it deep in. In a tool-shed at the bottom of the garden, lay the relics of building-materials, left by masons lately employed to repair a part of the premises. I fetched thence a slate and some mortar, put the slate on the hollow, secured it with cement, covered the hole with black mould, and, finally, replaced the ivy. This done, I rested, leaning against the tree; lingering, like any other mourner, beside a newly-sodded grave.

The air of the night was very still, but dim with a peculiar mist, which changed the moonlight into a luminous haze. In this air, or this mist, there was some quality—electrical, perhaps—which acted in strange sort upon me. I felt then as I had felt a year ago in England—on a night when the aurora borealis was streaming and sweeping round heaven, when, belated in lonely fields, I had paused to watch that mustering of an army with banners—that quivering of serried lances—that swift ascent of messengers from below the north star to the dark, high keystone of heaven's arch. I felt, not happy, far otherwise, but strong with reinforced strength.

If life be a war, it seemed my destiny to conduct it single-handed. I pondered now how to break up my winter-quarters—to leave an encampment where food and forage failed. Perhaps, to effect this change, another pitched battle must be fought with fortune; if so, I had a mind to the encounter: too poor to lose, God might destine me to gain. But what road was open?—what plan available?

On this question I was still pausing, when the moon, so dim hitherto, seemed to shine out somewhat brighter: a ray gleamed even white before me, and a shadow became distinct and marked. I looked more narrowly, to make out the cause of this well-defined contrast appearing a little suddenly in the obscure alley: whiter and blacker it grew on my eye: it took shape with instantaneous transformation. I stood about three yards from a tall, sable-robed, snowy-veiled woman.

Five minutes passed. I neither fled nor shrieked. She was there still. I spoke.

"Who are you? and why do you come to me?"

She stood mute. She had no face — no features: all below her brow was masked with a white cloth; but she had eyes, and they viewed me.

I felt, if not brave, yet a little desperate; and desperation will often suffice to fill the post and do the work of courage. I advanced one step. I stretched out my hand, for I meant to touch her. She seemed to recede. I drew nearer: her recession, still silent, became swift. A mass of shrubs, full-leaved evergreens, laurel and dense yew, intervened between me and what I followed. Having passed that obstacle, I looked and saw nothing. I waited. I said, — "If you have any errand to men, come back and deliver it." Nothing spoke or re-appeared.

This time there was no Dr. John to whom to have recourse: there was no one to whom I dared whisper the words, "I have again seen the nun."

Paulina Mary sought my frequent presence in the Rue Crécy. In the old Bretton days, though she had never professed herself fond of me, my society had soon become to her a sort of unconscious necessary. I used to notice that if I withdrew to my room, she would speedily come trotting after me, and opening the door and peeping in, say, with her little peremptory accent, —"Come down. Why do you sit here by yourself? You must come into the parlour."

In the same spirit she urged me now—"Leave the Rue Fossette," she said, "and come and live with us. Papa would give you far more than Madame Beck gives you."

Mr. Home himself offered me a handsome sum—thrice my present salary—if I would accept the office of companion to his daughter. I declined. I think I should have declined had I been poorer than I was, and with scantier fund of resource, more stinted narrowness of future prospect. I had not that vocation. I could teach; I could give lessons; but to be either a private governess or a companion was unnatural to me. Rather than fill the former post in any great house, I would deliberately have taken a housemaid's place, bought a strong pair of gloves, swept bedrooms and staircases, and cleaned stoves and locks, in peace and independence. Rather than be a companion, I would have made shirts and starved.

I was no bright lady's shadow—not Miss de Bassompierre's. Overcast enough it was my nature often to be; of a subdued habit I was: but the dimness and depression must both be voluntary—such as kept me docile at my desk, in the midst of my now well-accustomed pupils in Madame Beck's first classe; or alone, at my own bedside, in her dormitory, or in the alley and seat which were called mine, in her garden: my qualifications were not convertible, nor adaptable; they could not be made the foil of any gem, the adjunct of any beauty, the appendage of any greatness in Christendom. Madame Beck and I, without assimilating, understood each other well. I was not her companion, nor her children's governess; she left me free: she tied me to nothing—not to herself—not even to her interests: once, when she had for a fortnight been called from home by a near relation's illness, and on her return, all anxious and full of care about her establishment, lest something in her absence should have gone wrong finding that matters had proceeded much as usual, and that there was no evidence of glaring neglect—she made each of the teachers a present, in acknowledgment of steadiness. To my bedside she came at twelve o'clock at night, and told me she had no present for me: "I must make fidelity advantageous to the St. Pierre," said she; "if I attempt to make it advantageous to you, there will arise misunderstanding between us—perhaps separation. One thing, however, I can do to please you—leave you alone with your liberty: c'est-ce que je ferai." She kept her word. Every slight shackle she had ever laid on me, she, from that time, with quiet hand removed. Thus I had pleasure in voluntarily respecting her rules: gratification in devoting double time, in taking double pains with the pupils she committed to my charge.

As to Mary de Bassompierre, I visited her with pleasure, though I would not live with her. My visits soon taught me that it was unlikely even my occasional and voluntary society would long be indispensable to her. M. de Bassompierre, for his part, seemed impervious to this conjecture, blind to this possibility; unconscious as any child to the signs, the likelihoods, the fitful beginnings of what, when it drew to an end, he might not approve.

Whether or not he would cordially approve, I used to

speculate. Difficult to say. He was much taken up with scientific interests; keen, intent, and somewhat oppugnant in what concerned his favourite pursuits, but unsuspicious and trustful in the ordinary affairs of life. From all I could gather, he seemed to regard his "daughterling" as still but a child, and probably had not yet admitted the notion that others might look on her in a different light: he would speak of what should be done when "Polly" was a woman, when she should be grown up; and "Polly," standing beside his chair, would sometimes smile and take his honoured head between her little hands, and kiss his iron-grey locks; and, at other times, she would pout and toss her curls: but she never said, "Papa, I am grown up."

She had different moods for different people. With her father she really was still a child, or child-like, affectionate, merry, and playful. With me she was serious, and as womanly as thought and feeling could make her. With Mrs. Bretton she was docile and reliant, but not expansive. With Graham she was shy, at present very shy; at moments she tried to be cold; on occasion she endeavoured to shun him. His step made her start; his entrance hushed her; when he spoke, her answers failed of fluency; when he took leave, she remained self-vexed and disconcerted. Even her father noticed this demeanour in her.

"My little Polly," he said once, "you live too retired a life; if you grow to be a woman with these shy manners, you will hardly be fitted for society. You really make quite a stranger of Dr. Bretton: how is this? Don't you remember that, as a little girl, you used to be rather partial to him?"

"Rather, papa," echoed she, with her slightly dry, yet gentle and simple tone.

"And you don't like him now? What has he done?"

"Nothing. Y—e—s, I like him a little; but we are grown strange to each other."

"Then rub it off, Polly; rub the rust and the strangeness off. Talk away when he is here, and have no fear of him?"

"He does not talk much. Is he afraid of me, do you think, papa?"

"Oh, to be sure, what man would not be afraid of such a little silent lady?"

"Then tell him some day not to mind my being silent. Say

that it is my way, and that I have no unfriendly intention."

"Your way, you little chatter-box? So far from being your way, it is only your whim!"

"Well, I'll improve, papa."

And very pretty was the grace with which, the next day, she tried to keep her word. I saw her make the effort to converse affably with Dr. John on general topics. The attention called into her guest's face a pleasurable glow; he met her with caution, and replied to her in his softest tones, as if there was a kind of gossamer happiness hanging in the air which he feared to disturb by drawing too deep a breath. Certainly, in her timid yet earnest advance to friendship, it could not be denied that there was a most exquisite and fairy charm.

When the Doctor was gone, she approached her father's chair.

"Did I keep my word, papa? Did I behave better?"

"My Polly behaved like a queen. I shall become quite proud of her if this improvement continues. By-and-by we shall see her receiving my guests with quite a calm, grand manner. Miss Lucy and I will have to look about us, and polish up all our best airs and graces lest we should be thrown into the shade. Still, Polly, there is a little flutter, a little tendency to stammer now and then, and even, to lisp as you lisped when you were six years old."

"No, papa," interrupted she indignantly, "that can't be true."

"I appeal to Miss Lucy. Did she not, in answering Dr. Bretton's question as to whether she had ever seen the palace of the Prince of Bois l'Etang, say, 'yeth,' she had been there 'theveral' times?"

"Papa, you are satirical, you are méchant! I can pronounce all the letters of the alphabet as clearly as you can. But tell me this you are very particular in making me be civil to Dr. Bretton, do you like him yourself?"

"To be sure: for old acquaintance sake I like him: then he is a very good son to his mother; besides being a kind-hearted fellow and clever in his profession: yes, the callant is well enough."

"Callant! Ah, Scotchman! Papa, is it the Edinburgh or the Aberdeen accent you have?"

"Both, my pet, both: and doubtless the Glaswegian into the bargain. It is that which enables me to speak French so well: a gude Scots tongue always succeeds well at the French."

"The French! Scotch again: incorrigible papa. You, too, need schooling."

"Well, Polly, you must persuade Miss Snowe to undertake both you and me; to make you steady and womanly, and me refined and classical."

The light in which M. de Bassompierre evidently regarded "Miss Snowe," used to occasion me much inward edification. What contradictory attributes of character we sometimes find ascribed to us, according to the eye with which we are viewed! Madame Beck esteemed me learned and blue; Miss Fanshawe, caustic, ironic, and cynical; Mr. Home, a model teacher, the essence of the sedate and discreet: somewhat conventional, perhaps, too strict, limited, and scrupulous, but still the pink and pattern of governess-correctness; whilst another person, Professor Paul Emanuel, to wit, never lost an opportunity of intimating his opinion that mine was rather a fiery and rash nature—adventurous, indocile, and audacious. I smiled at them all. If any one knew me it was little Paulina Mary.

As I would not be Paulina's nominal and paid companion, genial and harmonious as I began to find her intercourse, she persuaded me to join her in some study, as a regular and settled means of sustaining communication: she proposed the German language, which, like myself, she found difficult of mastery. We agreed to take our lessons in the Rue Crécy of the same mistress; this arrangement threw us together for some hours of every week. M. de Bassompierre seemed quite pleased: it perfectly met his approbation, that Madame Minerva Gravity should associate a portion of her leisure with that of his fair and dear child.

That other self-elected judge of mine, the professor in the Rue Fossette, discovering by some surreptitious spying means, that I was no longer so stationary as hitherto, but went out regularly at certain hours of certain days, took it upon himself to place me under surveillance. People said M. Emanuel had been brought up amongst Jesuits. I should more readily have accredited this report had his manœuvres been better masked. As it was, I doubted it. Never was a more undisguised schemer,

Villette

a franker, looser intriguer. He would analyze his own machinations: elaborately contrive plots, and forthwith indulge in explanatory boasts of their skill. I know not whether I was more amused or provoked, by his stepping up to me one morning and whispering solemnly that he "had his eye on me: he at least would discharge the duty of a friend, and not leave me entirely to my own devices. My proceedings seemed at present very unsettled: he did not know what to make of them: he thought his cousin Beck very much to blame in suffering this sort of fluttering inconsistency in a teacher attached to her house. What had a person devoted to a serious calling, that of education, to do with Counts and Countesses, hotels and châteaux? To him, I seemed altogether 'en l'air.' On his faith, he believed I went out six days in the seven."

I said, "Monsieur exaggerated. I certainly had enjoyed the advantage of a little change lately, but not before it had become necessary; and the privilege was by no means exercised in excess."

"Necessary! How was it necessary? I was well enough, he supposed? Change necessary! He would recommend me to look at the Catholic 'religieuses,' and study their lives. They asked no change."

I am no judge of what expression crossed my face when he thus spoke, but it was one which provoked him: he accused me of being reckless, worldly, and epicurean; ambitious of greatness, and feverishly athirst for the pomps and vanities of life. It seems I had no "dévouement," no "récueillement" in my character; no spirit of grace, faith, sacrifice, or self-abasement. Feeling the inutility of answering these charges, I mutely continued the correction of a pile of English exercises.

"He could see in me nothing Christian: like many other Protestants, I revelled in the pride and self-will of paganism."

I slightly turned from him, nestling still closer under the wing of silence.

A vague sound grumbled between his teeth; it could not surely be a "juron:" he was too religious for that; but I am certain I heard the word sacré. Grievous to relate, the same word was repeated, with the unequivocal addition of mille something, when I passed him about two hours afterwards in the corridor, prepared to go and take my German lesson in the Rue Crécy. Never was a better little man, in some points, than M. Paul: never, in others, a more waspish little despot.

Our German mistress, Fräulein Anna Braun, was a worthy, hearty woman, of about forty-five; she ought, perhaps, to have lived in the days of Queen Elizabeth, as she habitually consumed, for her first and second breakfasts, beer and beef: also, her direct and downright Deutsch nature seemed to suffer a sensation of cruel restraint from what she called our English reserve; though we thought we were very cordial with her: but we did not slap her on the shoulder, and if we consented to kiss her cheek, it was done quietly, and without any explosive smack. These omissions oppressed and depressed her considerably; still, on the whole, we got on very well. Accustomed to instruct foreign girls, who hardly ever will think and study for themselves—who have no idea of grappling with a difficulty, and overcoming it by dint of reflection or application—our progress, which in truth was very leisurely, seemed to astound her. In her eyes, we were a pair of glacial prodigies, cold, proud, and preternatural.

The young Countess was a little proud, a little fastidious: and perhaps, with her native delicacy and beauty, she had a right to these feelings; but I think it was a total mistake to ascribe them to me. I never evaded the morning salute, which Paulina would slip when she could; nor was a certain little manner of still disdain a weapon known in my armoury of defence; whereas, Paulina always kept it clear, fine, and bright, and any rough German sally called forth at once its steely glisten.

Honest Anna Braun, in some measure, felt this difference; and while she half-feared, half-worshipped Paulina, as a sort of dainty nymph—an Undine—she took refuge with me, as a being all mortal, and of easier mood.

A book we liked well to read and translate was Schiller's Ballads; Paulina soon learned to read them beautifully; the Fräulein would listen to her with a broad smile of pleasure, and say her voice sounded like music. She translated them, too, with a facile flow of language, and in a strain of kindred and poetic fervour: her cheek would flush, her lips tremblingly smile, her beauteous eyes kindle or melt as she went on. She learnt the best by heart, and would often recite them when we were alone together. One she liked well was "Des Mädchens Klage:" that is, she liked well to repeat the words, she found plaintive melody in the sound; the sense she would criticise. She murmured, as we sat over the fire one evening:—

Du Heilige, rufe dein Kind zurück,

Villette

Ich habe genossen das irdische Glück,

Ich habe gelebt und geliebet!

"Lived and loved!" said she, "is that the summit of earthly happiness, the end of life—to love? I don't think it is. It may be the extreme of mortal misery, it may be sheer waste of time, and fruitless torture of feeling. If Schiller had said to be loved, he might have come nearer the truth. Is not that another thing, Lucy, to be loved?"

"I suppose it may be: but why consider the subject? What is love to you? What do you know about it?"

She crimsoned, half in irritation, half in shame.

"Now, Lucy," she said, "I won't take that from you. It may be well for papa to look on me as a baby: I rather prefer that he should thus view me; but you know and shall learn to acknowledge that I am verging on my nineteenth year."

"No matter if it were your twenty-ninth; we will anticipate no feelings by discussion and conversation; we will not talk about love."

"Indeed, indeed!" said she—all in hurry and heat—"you may think to check and hold me in, as much as you please; but I have talked about it, and heard about it too; and a great deal and lately, and disagreeably and detrimentally: and in a way you wouldn't approve."

And the vexed, triumphant, pretty, naughty being laughed. I could not discern what she meant, and I would not ask her: I was nonplussed. Seeing, however, the utmost innocence in her countenance—combined with some transient perverseness and petulance—I said at last,—

"Who talks to you disagreeably and detrimentally on such matters? Who that has near access to you would dare to do it?"

"Lucy," replied she more softly, "it is a person who makes me miserable sometimes; and I wish she would keep away—I don't want her."

"But who, Paulina, can it be? You puzzle me much."

"It is—it is my cousin Ginevra. Every time she has leave to visit Mrs. Cholmondeley she calls here, and whenever she finds me alone she begins to talk about her admirers. Love, indeed! You should hear all she has to say about love."

"Oh, I have heard it," said I, quite coolly; "and on the whole, perhaps it is as well you should have heard it too: it is not to be regretted, it is all right. Yet, surely, Ginevra's mind cannot influence yours. You can look over both her head and her heart."

"She does influence me very much. She has the art of disturbing my happiness and unsettling my opinions. She hurts me through the feelings and people dearest to me."

"What does she say, Paulina? Give me some idea. There may be counteraction of the damage done."

"The people I have longest and most esteemed are degraded by her. She does not spare Mrs. Bretton—she does not spare…. Graham."

"No, I daresay: and how does she mix up these with her sentiment and her….love? She does mix them, I suppose?"

"Lucy, she is insolent; and, I believe, false. You know Dr. Bretton. We both know him. He may be careless and proud; but when was he ever mean or slavish? Day after day she shows him to me kneeling at her feet, pursuing her like her shadow. She—repulsing him with insult, and he imploring her with infatuation. Lucy, is it true? Is any of it true?"

"It may be true that he once thought her handsome: does she give him out as still her suitor?"

"She says she might marry him any day: he only waits her consent."

"It is these tales which have caused that reserve in your manner towards Graham which your father noticed."

"They have certainly made me all doubtful about his character. As Ginevra speaks, they do not carry with them the sound of unmixed truth: I believe she exaggerates—perhaps invents—but I want to know how far."

"Suppose we bring Miss Fanshawe to some proof. Give her an opportunity of displaying the power she boasts."

"I could do that to-morrow. Papa has asked some gentlemen

to dinner, all savants. Graham, who, papa is beginning to discover, is a savant, too—skilled, they say, in more than one branch of science—is among the number. Now I should be miserable to sit at table unsupported, amidst such a party. I could not talk to Messieurs A— — and Z— —, the Parisian Academicians: all my new credit for manner would be put in peril. You and Mrs. Bretton must come for my sake; Ginevra, at a word, will join you."

"Yes; then I will carry a message of invitation, and she shall have the chance of justifying her character for veracity."

CHAPTER XXVII.
THE HÔTEL CRÉCY.

The morrow turned out a more lively and busy day than we — or than I, at least — had anticipated. It seems it was the birthday of one of the young princes of Labassecour — the eldest, I think, the Duc de Dindonneau, and a general holiday was given in his honour at the schools, and especially at the principal "Athénée," or college. The youth of that institution had also concocted, and were to present a loyal address; for which purpose they were to be assembled in the public building where the yearly examinations were conducted, and the prizes distributed. After the ceremony of presentation, an oration, or "discours," was to follow from one of the professors.

Several of M. de Bassompierre's friends — the savants — being more or less connected with the Athénée, they were expected to attend on this occasion; together with the worshipful municipality of Villette, M. le Chevalier Staas, the burgomaster, and the parents and kinsfolk of the Athenians in general. M. de Bassompierre was engaged by his friends to accompany them; his fair daughter would, of course, be of the party, and she wrote a little note to Ginevra and myself, bidding us come early that we might join her.

As Miss Fanshawe and I were dressing in the dormitory of the Rue Fossette, she (Miss F.) suddenly burst into a laugh.

"What now?" I asked; for she had suspended the operation of arranging her attire, and was gazing at me.

"It seems so odd," she replied, with her usual half-honest half-insolent unreserve, "that you and I should now be so much on a level, visiting in the same sphere; having the same connections."

"Why, yes," said I; "I had not much respect for the connections you chiefly frequented awhile ago: Mrs. Cholmondeley and Co. would never have suited me at all."

"Who are you, Miss Snowe?" she inquired, in a tone of such undisguised and unsophisticated curiosity, as made me laugh in my turn.

"You used to call yourself a nursery governess; when you first came here you really had the care of the children in this house: I have seen you carry little Georgette in your arms, like a bonne—few governesses would have condescended so far—and now Madame Beck treats you with more courtesy than she treats the Parisienne, St. Pierre; and that proud chit, my cousin, makes you her bosom friend!"

"Wonderful!" I agreed, much amused at her mystification. "Who am I indeed? Perhaps a personage in disguise. Pity I don't look the character."

"I wonder you are not more flattered by all this," she went on; "you take it with strange composure. If you really are the nobody I once thought you, you must be a cool hand."

"The nobody you once thought me!" I repeated, and my face grew a little hot; but I would not be angry: of what importance was a school-girl's crude use of the terms nobody and somebody? I confined myself, therefore, to the remark that I had merely met with civility; and asked "what she saw in civility to throw the recipient into a fever of confusion?"

"One can't help wondering at some things," she persisted.

"Wondering at marvels of your own manufacture. Are you ready at last?"

"Yes; let me take your arm."

"I would rather not: we will walk side by side."

When she took my arm, she always leaned upon me her whole weight; and, as I was not a gentleman, or her lover, I did not like it.

"There, again!" she cried. "I thought, by offering to take your arm, to intimate approbation of your dress and general appearance: I meant it as a compliment."

"You did? You meant, in short, to express that you are not ashamed to be seen in the street with me? That if Mrs. Cholmondeley should be fondling her lapdog at some window, or Colonel de Hamal picking his teeth in a balcony, and should catch a glimpse of us, you would not quite blush for your companion?"

"Yes," said she, with that directness which was her best point—which gave an honest plainness to her very fibs when she told them—which was, in short, the salt, the sole preservative ingredient of a character otherwise not formed to keep.

I delegated the trouble of commenting on this "yes" to my countenance; or rather, my under-lip voluntarily anticipated my tongue of course, reverence and solemnity were not the feelings expressed in the look I gave her.

"Scornful, sneering creature!" she went on, as we crossed a great square, and entered the quiet, pleasant park, our nearest way to the Rue Crécy. "Nobody in this world was ever such a Turk to me as you are!"

"You bring it on yourself: let me alone: have the sense to be quiet: I will let you alone."

"As if one could let you alone, when you are so peculiar and so mysterious!"

"The mystery and peculiarity being entirely the conception of your own brain — maggots — neither more nor less, be so good as to keep them out of my sight."

"But are you anybody?" persevered she, pushing her hand, in spite of me, under my arm; and that arm pressed itself with inhospitable closeness against my side, by way of keeping out the intruder.

"Yes," I said, "I am a rising character: once an old lady's companion, then a nursery-governess, now a school-teacher."

"Do — do tell me who you are? I'll not repeat it," she urged, adhering with ludicrous tenacity to the wise notion of an incognito she had got hold of; and she squeezed the arm of which she had now obtained full possession, and coaxed and conjured till I was obliged to pause in the park to laugh. Throughout our walk she rang the most fanciful changes on this theme; proving, by her obstinate credulity, or incredulity, her incapacity to conceive how any person not bolstered up by birth or wealth, not supported by some consciousness of name or connection, could maintain an attitude of reasonable integrity. As for me, it quite sufficed to my mental tranquillity that I was known where it imported that known I should be; the rest sat on me easily: pedigree, social position, and recondite intellectual acquisition, occupied about the same space and place in my interests and thoughts; they were my third-class lodgers — to whom could be assigned only the small sitting-room and the little back bedroom: even if the dining and

Villette

drawing-rooms stood empty, I never confessed it to them, as thinking minor accommodations better suited to their circumstances. The world, I soon learned, held a different estimate: and I make no doubt, the world is very right in its view, yet believe also that I am not quite wrong in mine.

There are people whom a lowered position degrades morally, to whom loss of connection costs loss of self-respect: are not these justified in placing the highest value on that station and association which is their safeguard from debasement? If a man feels that he would become contemptible in his own eyes were it generally known that his ancestry were simple and not gentle, poor and not rich, workers and not capitalists, would it be right severely to blame him for keeping these fatal facts out of sight—for starting, trembling, quailing at the chance which threatens exposure? The longer we live, the more our experience widens; the less prone are we to judge our neighbour's conduct, to question the world's wisdom: wherever an accumulation of small defences is found, whether surrounding the prude's virtue or the man of the world's respectability, there, be sure, it is needed.

We reached the Hôtel Crécy; Paulina was ready; Mrs. Bretton was with her; and, under her escort and that of M. de Bassompierre, we were soon conducted to the place of assembly, and seated in good seats, at a convenient distance from the Tribune. The youth of the Athénée were marshalled before us, the municipality and their bourgmestre were in places of honour, the young princes, with their tutors, occupied a conspicuous position, and the body of the building was crowded with the aristocracy and first burghers of the town.

Concerning the identity of the professor by whom the "discours" was to be delivered, I had as yet entertained neither care nor question. Some vague expectation I had that a savant would stand up and deliver a formal speech, half dogmatism to the Athenians, half flattery to the princes.

The Tribune was yet empty when we entered, but in ten minutes after it was filled; suddenly, in a second of time, a head, chest, and arms grew above the crimson desk. This head I knew: its colour, shape, port, expression, were familiar both to me and Miss Fanshawe; the blackness and closeness of cranium, the amplitude and paleness of brow, the blueness and fire of glance, were details so domesticated in the memory, and so knit with many a whimsical association, as almost by this their sudden apparition, to tickle fancy to a laugh. Indeed, I confess, for my part, I did laugh till I was warm; but then I bent my head, and made my handkerchief and a lowered veil the sole confidants of my mirth.

I think I was glad to see M. Paul; I think it was rather pleasant than otherwise, to behold him set up there, fierce and frank, dark and candid, testy and fearless, as when regnant on his estrade in class. His presence was such a surprise: I had not once thought of expecting him, though I knew he filled the chair of Belles Lettres in the college. With him in that Tribune, I felt sure that neither formalism nor flattery would be our doom; but for what was vouchsafed us, for what was poured suddenly, rapidly, continuously, on our heads — I own I was not prepared.

He spoke to the princes, the nobles, the magistrates, and the burghers, with just the same ease, with almost the same pointed, choleric earnestness, with which he was wont to harangue the three divisions of the Rue Fossette. The collegians he addressed, not as schoolboys, but as future citizens and embryo patriots. The times which have since come on Europe had not been foretold yet, and M. Emanuel's spirit seemed new to me. Who would have thought the flat and fat soil of Labassecour could yield political convictions and national feelings, such as were now strongly expressed? Of the bearing of his opinions I need here give no special indication; yet it may be permitted me to say that I believed the little man not more earnest than right in what he said: with all his fire he was severe and sensible; he trampled Utopian theories under his heel; he rejected wild dreams with scorn;—but when he looked in the face of tyranny—oh, then there opened a light in his eye worth seeing; and when he spoke of injustice, his voice gave no uncertain sound, but reminded me rather of the band-trumpet, ringing at twilight from the park.

I do not think his audience were generally susceptible of sharing his flame in its purity; but some of the college youth caught fire as he eloquently told them what should be their path and endeavour in their country's and in Europe's future. They gave him a long, loud, ringing cheer, as he concluded: with all his fierceness, he was their favourite professor.

As our party left the Hall, he stood at the entrance; he saw and knew me, and lifted his hat; he offered his hand in passing, and uttered the words "Qu'en dites vous?"—question eminently characteristic, and reminding me, even in this his moment of triumph, of that inquisitive restlessness, that absence of what I considered desirable self-control, which were amongst his faults. He should not have cared just then to ask what I thought, or what anybody thought, but he did care, and he was

Villette

too natural to conceal, too impulsive to repress his wish. Well! if I blamed his over-eagerness, I liked his naiveté. I would have praised him: I had plenty of praise in my heart; but, alas! no words on my lips. Who has words at the right moment? I stammered some lame expressions; but was truly glad when other people, coming up with profuse congratulations, covered my deficiency by their redundancy.

A gentleman introduced him to M. de Bassompierre; and the Count, who had likewise been highly gratified, asked him to join his friends (for the most part M. Emanuel's likewise), and to dine with them at the Hôtel Crécy. He declined dinner, for he was a man always somewhat shy at meeting the advances of the wealthy: there was a strength of sturdy independence in the stringing of his sinews—not obtrusive, but pleasant enough to discover as one advanced in knowledge of his character; he promised, however, to step in with his friend, M. A——, a French Academician, in the course of the evening.

At dinner that day, Ginevra and Paulina each looked, in her own way, very beautiful; the former, perhaps, boasted the advantage in material charms, but the latter shone pre-eminent for attractions more subtle and spiritual: for light and eloquence of eye, for grace of mien, for winning variety of expression. Ginevra's dress of deep crimson relieved well her light curls, and harmonized with her rose-like bloom. Paulina's attire—in fashion close, though faultlessly neat, but in texture clear and white—made the eye grateful for the delicate life of her complexion, for the soft animation of her countenance, for the tender depth of her eyes, for the brown shadow and bounteous flow of her hair—darker than that of her Saxon cousin, as were also her eyebrows, her eyelashes, her full irids, and large mobile pupils. Nature having traced all these details slightly, and with a careless hand, in Miss Fanshawe's case; and in Miss de Bassompierre's, wrought them to a high and delicate finish.

Paulina was awed by the savants, but not quite to mutism: she conversed modestly, diffidently; not without effort, but with so true a sweetness, so fine and penetrating a sense, that her father more than once suspended his own discourse to listen, and fixed on her an eye of proud delight. It was a polite Frenchman, M. Z——, a very learned, but quite a courtly man, who had drawn her into discourse. I was charmed with her French; it was faultless—the structure correct, the idioms true, the accent pure; Ginevra, who had lived half her life on the Continent, could do nothing like it not that words ever failed Miss Fanshawe, but real accuracy and purity she neither possessed, nor in any number of years would acquire. Here, too,

M. de Bassompierre was gratified; for, on the point of language, he was critical.

Another listener and observer there was; one who, detained by some exigency of his profession, had come in late to dinner. Both ladies were quietly scanned by Dr. Bretton, at the moment of taking his seat at the table; and that guarded survey was more than once renewed. His arrival roused Miss Fanshawe, who had hitherto appeared listless: she now became smiling and complacent, talked — though what she said was rarely to the purpose — or rather, was of a purpose somewhat mortifyingly below the standard of the occasion. Her light, disconnected prattle might have gratified Graham once; perhaps it pleased him still: perhaps it was only fancy which suggested the thought that, while his eye was filled and his ear fed, his taste, his keen zest, his lively intelligence, were not equally consulted and regaled. It is certain that, restless and exacting as seemed the demand on his attention, he yielded courteously all that was required: his manner showed neither pique nor coolness: Ginevra was his neighbour, and to her, during dinner, he almost exclusively confined his notice. She appeared satisfied, and passed to the drawing-room in very good spirits.

Yet, no sooner had we reached that place of refuge, than she again became flat and listless: throwing herself on a couch, she denounced both the "discours" and the dinner as stupid affairs, and inquired of her cousin how she could hear such a set of prosaic "gros-bonnets" as her father gathered about him. The moment the gentlemen were heard to move, her railings ceased: she started up, flew to the piano, and dashed at it with spirit. Dr. Bretton entering, one of the first, took up his station beside her. I thought he would not long maintain that post: there was a position near the hearth to which I expected to see him attracted: this position he only scanned with his eye; while he looked, others drew in. The grace and mind of Paulina charmed these thoughtful Frenchmen: the fineness of her beauty, the soft courtesy of her manner, her immature, but real and inbred tact, pleased their national taste; they clustered about her, not indeed to talk science; which would have rendered her dumb, but to touch on many subjects in letters, in arts, in actual life, on which it soon appeared that she had both read and reflected. I listened. I am sure that though Graham stood aloof, he listened too: his hearing as well as his vision was very fine, quick, discriminating. I knew he gathered the conversation; I felt that the mode in which it was sustained suited him exquisitely — pleased him almost to pain.

In Paulina there was more force, both of feeling and

character; than most people thought—than Graham himself imagined—than she would ever show to those who did not wish to see it. To speak truth, reader, there is no excellent beauty, no accomplished grace, no reliable refinement, without strength as excellent, as complete, as trustworthy. As well might you look for good fruit and blossom on a rootless and sapless tree, as for charms that will endure in a feeble and relaxed nature. For a little while, the blooming semblance of beauty may flourish round weakness; but it cannot bear a blast: it soon fades, even in serenest sunshine. Graham would have started had any suggestive spirit whispered of the sinew and the stamina sustaining that delicate nature; but I who had known her as a child, knew or guessed by what a good and strong root her graces held to the firm soil of reality.

While Dr. Bretton listened, and waited an opening in the magic circle, his glance restlessly sweeping the room at intervals, lighted by chance on me, where I sat in a quiet nook not far from my godmother and M. de Bassompierre, who, as usual, were engaged in what Mr. Home called "a two-handed crack:" what the Count would have interpreted as a tête-à-tête. Graham smiled recognition, crossed the room, asked me how I was, told me I looked pale. I also had my own smile at my own thought: it was now about three months since Dr. John had spoken to me—a lapse of which he was not even conscious. He sat down, and became silent. His wish was rather to look than converse. Ginevra and Paulina were now opposite to him: he could gaze his fill: he surveyed both forms—studied both faces.

Several new guests, ladies as well as gentlemen, had entered the room since dinner, dropping in for the evening conversation; and amongst the gentlemen, I may incidentally observe, I had already noticed by glimpses, a severe, dark, professorial outline, hovering aloof in an inner saloon, seen only in vista. M. Emanuel knew many of the gentlemen present, but I think was a stranger to most of the ladies, excepting myself; in looking towards the hearth, he could not but see me, and naturally made a movement to approach; seeing, however, Dr. Bretton also, he changed his mind and held back. If that had been all, there would have been no cause for quarrel; but not satisfied with holding back, he puckered up his eyebrows, protruded his lip, and looked so ugly that I averted my eyes from the displeasing spectacle. M. Joseph Emanuel had arrived, as well as his austere brother, and at this very moment was relieving Ginevra at the piano. What a master-touch succeeded her school-girl jingle! In what grand, grateful tones the instrument acknowledged the hand of the true artist!

"Lucy," began Dr. Bretton, breaking silence and smiling, as Ginevra glided before him, casting a glance as she passed by, "Miss Fanshawe is certainly a fine girl."

Of course I assented.

"Is there," he pursued, "another in the room as lovely?"

"I think there is not another as handsome."

"I agree with you, Lucy: you and I do often agree in opinion, in taste, I think; or at least in judgment."

"Do we?" I said, somewhat doubtfully.

"I believe if you had been a boy, Lucy, instead of a girl—my mother's god-son instead of her god-daughter, we should have been good friends: our opinions would have melted into each other."

He had assumed a bantering air: a light, half-caressing, half-ironic, shone aslant in his eye. Ah, Graham! I have given more than one solitary moment to thoughts and calculations of your estimate of Lucy Snowe: was it always kind or just? Had Lucy been intrinsically the same but possessing the additional advantages of wealth and station, would your manner to her, your value for her, have been quite what they actually were? And yet by these questions I would not seriously infer blame. No; you might sadden and trouble me sometimes; but then mine was a soon-depressed, an easily-deranged temperament—it fell if a cloud crossed the sun. Perhaps before the eye of severe equity I should stand more at fault than you.

Trying, then, to keep down the unreasonable pain which thrilled my heart, on thus being made to feel that while Graham could devote to others the most grave and earnest, the manliest interest, he had no more than light raillery for Lucy, the friend of lang syne, I inquired calmly,—"On what points are we so closely in accordance?"

"We each have an observant faculty. You, perhaps, don't give me credit for the possession; yet I have it."

"But you were speaking of tastes: we may see the same objects, yet estimate them differently?"

"Let us bring it to the test. Of course, you cannot but render homage to the merits of Miss Fanshawe: now, what do you

Villette

think of others in the room? — my mother, for instance; or the lions yonder, Messieurs A— — and Z— —; or, let us say, that pale little lady, Miss de Bassompierre?"

"You know what I think of your mother. I have not thought of Messieurs A— — and Z— —."

"And the other?"

"I think she is, as you say, a pale little lady — pale, certainly, just now, when she is fatigued with over-excitement."

"You don't remember her as a child?"

"I wonder, sometimes, whether you do."

"I had forgotten her; but it is noticeable, that circumstances, persons, even words and looks, that had slipped your memory, may, under certain conditions, certain aspects of your own or another's mind, revive."

"That is possible enough."

"Yet," he continued, "the revival is imperfect — needs confirmation, partakes so much of the dim character of a dream, or of the airy one of a fancy, that the testimony of a witness becomes necessary for corroboration. Were you not a guest at Bretton ten years ago, when Mr. Home brought his little girl, whom we then called 'little Polly,' to stay with mamma?"

"I was there the night she came, and also the morning she went away."

"Rather a peculiar child, was she not? I wonder how I treated her. Was I fond of children in those days? Was there anything gracious or kindly about me — great, reckless, schoolboy as I was? But you don't recollect me, of course?"

"You have seen your own picture at La Terrasse. It is like you personally. In manner, you were almost the same yesterday as to-day."

"But, Lucy, how is that? Such an oracle really whets my curiosity. What am I to-day? What was I the yesterday of ten years back?"

"Gracious to whatever pleased you — unkindly or cruel to nothing."

"There you are wrong; I think I was almost a brute to you, for instance."

"A brute! No, Graham: I should never have patiently endured brutality."

"This, however, I do remember: quiet Lucy Snowe tasted nothing of my grace."

"As little of your cruelty."

"Why, had I been Nero himself, I could not have tormented a being inoffensive as a shadow."

I smiled; but I also hushed a groan. Oh! — I just wished he would let me alone — cease allusion to me. These epithets — these attributes I put from me. His "quiet Lucy Snowe," his "inoffensive shadow," I gave him back; not with scorn, but with extreme weariness: theirs was the coldness and the pressure of lead; let him whelm me with no such weight. Happily, he was soon on another theme.

"On what terms were 'little Polly' and I? Unless my recollections deceive me, we were not foes —"

"You speak very vaguely. Do you think little Polly's memory, not more definite?"

"Oh! we don't talk of 'little Polly' now. Pray say, Miss de Bassompierre; and, of course, such a stately personage remembers nothing of Bretton. Look at her large eyes, Lucy; can they read a word in the page of memory? Are they the same which I used to direct to a horn-book? She does not know that I partly taught her to read."

"In the Bible on Sunday nights?"

"She has a calm, delicate, rather fine profile now: once what a little restless, anxious countenance was hers! What a thing is a child's preference — what a bubble! Would you believe it? that lady was fond of me!"

"I think she was in some measure fond of you," said I, moderately.

"You don't remember then? I had forgotten; but I remember now. She liked me the best of whatever there was at Bretton."

"You thought so."

"I quite well recall it. I wish I could tell her all I recall; or rather, I wish some one, you for instance, would go behind and whisper it all in her ear, and I could have the delight—here, as I sit—of watching her look under the intelligence. Could you manage that, think you, Lucy, and make me ever grateful?"

"Could I manage to make you ever grateful?" said I. "No, I could not." And I felt my fingers work and my hands interlock: I felt, too, an inward courage, warm and resistant. In this matter I was not disposed to gratify Dr. John: not at all. With now welcome force, I realized his entire misapprehension of my character and nature. He wanted always to give me a role not mine. Nature and I opposed him. He did not at all guess what I felt: he did not read my eyes, or face, or gestures; though, I doubt not, all spoke. Leaning towards me coaxingly, he said, softly, "Do content me, Lucy."

And I would have contented, or, at least, I would clearly have enlightened him, and taught him well never again to expect of me the part of officious soubrette in a love drama; when, following his, soft, eager, murmur, meeting almost his pleading, mellow—"Do content me, Lucy!" a sharp hiss pierced my ear on the other side.

"Petite chatte, doucerette, coquette!" sibillated the sudden boa-constrictor; "vous avez l'air bien triste, soumis, rêveur, mais vous ne l'êtes pas; c'est moi qui vous le dis: Sauvage! la flamme à l'âme, l'éclair aux yeux!"

"Oui; j'ai la flamme à l'âme, et je dois l'avoir!" retorted I, turning in just wrath: but Professor Emanuel had hissed his insult and was gone.

The worst of the matter was, that Dr. Bretton, whose ears, as I have said, were quick and fine, caught every word of this apostrophe; he put his handkerchief to his face, and laughed till he shook.

"Well done, Lucy," cried he; "capital! petite chatte, petite coquette! Oh, I must tell my mother! Is it true, Lucy, or half-true? I believe it is: you redden to the colour of Miss Fanshawe's gown. And really, by my word, now I examine him, that is the same little man who was so savage with you at the concert: the very same, and in his soul he is frantic at this moment because he sees me laughing. Oh! I must tease him."

And Graham, yielding to his bent for mischief, laughed, jested, and whispered on till I could bear no more, and my eyes filled.

Suddenly he was sobered: a vacant space appeared near Miss de Bassompierre; the circle surrounding her seemed about to dissolve. This movement was instantly caught by Graham's eye—ever-vigilant, even while laughing; he rose, took his courage in both hands, crossed the room, and made the advantage his own. Dr. John, throughout his whole life, was a man of luck—a man of success. And why? Because he had the eye to see his opportunity, the heart to prompt to well-timed action, the nerve to consummate a perfect work. And no tyrant-passion dragged him back; no enthusiasms, no foibles encumbered his way. How well he looked at this very moment! When Paulina looked up as he reached her side, her glance mingled at once with an encountering glance, animated, yet modest; his colour, as he spoke to her, became half a blush, half a glow. He stood in her presence brave and bashful: subdued and unobtrusive, yet decided in his purpose and devoted in his ardour. I gathered all this by one view. I did not prolong my observation—time failed me, had inclination served: the night wore late; Ginevra and I ought already to have been in the Rue Fossette. I rose, and bade good-night to my godmother and M. de Bassompierre.

I know not whether Professor Emanuel had noticed my reluctant acceptance of Dr. Bretton's badinage, or whether he perceived that I was pained, and that, on the whole, the evening had not been one flow of exultant enjoyment for the volatile, pleasure-loving Mademoiselle Lucie; but, as I was leaving the room, he stepped up and inquired whether I had any one to attend me to the Rue Fossette. The professor now spoke politely, and even deferentially, and he looked apologetic and repentant; but I could not recognise his civility at a word, nor meet his contrition with crude, premature oblivion. Never hitherto had I felt seriously disposed to resent his brusqueries, or freeze before his fierceness; what he had said to-night, however, I considered unwarranted: my extreme disapprobation of the proceeding must be marked, however slightly. I merely said:—"I am provided with attendance."

Which was true, as Ginevra and I were to be sent home in the carriage; and I passed him with the sliding obeisance with which he was wont to be saluted in classe by pupils crossing his estrade.

Having sought my shawl, I returned to the vestibule. M.

Villette

Emanuel stood there as if waiting. He observed that the night was fine.

"Is it?" I said, with a tone and manner whose consummate chariness and frostiness I could not but applaud. It was so seldom I could properly act out my own resolution to be reserved and cool where I had been grieved or hurt, that I felt almost proud of this one successful effort. That "Is it?" sounded just like the manner of other people. I had heard hundreds of such little minced, docked, dry phrases, from the pursed-up coral lips of a score of self-possessed, self-sufficing misses and mesdemoiselles. That M. Paul would not stand any prolonged experience of this sort of dialogue I knew; but he certainly merited a sample of the curt and arid. I believe he thought so himself, for he took the dose quietly. He looked at my shawl and objected to its lightness. I decidedly told him it was as heavy as I wished. Receding aloof, and standing apart, I leaned on the banister of the stairs, folded my shawl about me, and fixed my eyes on a dreary religious painting darkening the wall.

Ginevra was long in coming: tedious seemed her loitering. M. Paul was still there; my ear expected from his lips an angry tone. He came nearer. "Now for another hiss!" thought I: had not the action been too uncivil I could have stopped my ears with my fingers in terror of the thrill. Nothing happens as we expect: listen for a coo or a murmur; it is then you will hear a cry of prey or pain. Await a piercing shriek, an angry threat, and welcome an amicable greeting, a low kind whisper. M. Paul spoke gently:—"Friends," said he, "do not quarrel for a word. Tell me, was it I or ce grand fat d'Anglais" (so he profanely denominated Dr. Bretton), "who made your eyes so humid, and your cheeks so hot as they are even now?"

"I am not conscious of you, monsieur, or of any other having excited such emotion as you indicate," was my answer; and in giving it, I again surpassed my usual self, and achieved a neat, frosty falsehood.

"But what did I say?" he pursued; "tell me: I was angry: I have forgotten my words; what were they?"

"Such as it is best to forget!" said I, still quite calm and chill.

"Then it was my words which wounded you? Consider them unsaid: permit my retractation; accord my pardon."

"I am not angry, Monsieur."

"Then you are worse than angry—grieved. Forgive me, Miss Lucy."

"M. Emanuel, I do forgive you."

"Let me hear you say, in the voice natural to you, and not in that alien tone, 'Mon ami, je vous pardonne.'"

He made me smile. Who could help smiling at his wistfulness, his simplicity, his earnestness?

"Bon!" he cried. "Voilà que le jour va poindre! Dites donc, mon ami."

"Monsieur Paul, je vous pardonne."

"I will have no monsieur: speak the other word, or I shall not believe you sincere: another effort—mon ami, or else in English,—my friend!"

Now, "my friend" had rather another sound and significancy than "mon ami;" it did not breathe the same sense of domestic and intimate affection; "mon ami" I could not say to M. Paul; "my friend," I could, and did say without difficulty. This distinction existed not for him, however, and he was quite satisfied with the English phrase. He smiled. You should have seen him smile, reader; and you should have marked the difference between his countenance now, and that he wore half an hour ago. I cannot affirm that I had ever witnessed the smile of pleasure, or content, or kindness round M. Paul's lips, or in his eyes before. The ironic, the sarcastic, the disdainful, the passionately exultant, I had hundreds of times seen him express by what he called a smile, but any illuminated sign of milder or warmer feelings struck me as wholly new in his visage. It changed it as from a mask to a face: the deep lines left his features; the very complexion seemed clearer and fresher; that swart, sallow, southern darkness which spoke his Spanish blood, became displaced by a lighter hue. I know not that I have ever seen in any other human face an equal metamorphosis from a similar cause. He now took me to the carriage: at the same moment M. de Bassompierre came out with his niece.

In a pretty humour was Mistress Fanshawe; she had found the evening a grand failure: completely upset as to temper, she gave way to the most uncontrolled moroseness as soon as we were seated, and the carriage-door closed. Her invectives against Dr. Bretton had something venomous in them. Having found herself impotent either to charm or sting him, hatred was

Villette

her only resource; and this hatred she expressed in terms so unmeasured and proportion so monstrous, that, after listening for a while with assumed stoicism, my outraged sense of justice at last and suddenly caught fire. An explosion ensued: for I could be passionate, too; especially with my present fair but faulty associate, who never failed to stir the worst dregs of me. It was well that the carriage-wheels made a tremendous rattle over the flinty Choseville pavement, for I can assure the reader there was neither dead silence nor calm discussion within the vehicle. Half in earnest, half in seeming, I made it my business to storm down Ginevra. She had set out rampant from the Rue Crécy; it was necessary to tame her before we reached the Rue Fossette: to this end it was indispensable to show up her sterling value and high deserts; and this must be done in language of which the fidelity and homeliness might challenge comparison with the compliments of a John Knox to a Mary Stuart. This was the right discipline for Ginevra; it suited her. I am quite sure she went to bed that night all the better and more settled in mind and mood, and slept all the more sweetly for having undergone a sound moral drubbing.

CHAPTER XXVIII.

THE WATCHGUARD.

M. Paul Emanuel owned an acute sensitiveness to the annoyance of interruption, from whatsoever cause occurring, during his lessons: to pass through the classe under such circumstances was considered by the teachers and pupils of the school, individually and collectively, to be as much as a woman's or girl's life was worth.

Madame Beck herself, if forced to the enterprise, would "skurry" through, retrenching her skirts, and carefully coasting the formidable estrade, like a ship dreading breakers. As to Rosine, the portress—on whom, every half-hour, devolved the fearful duty of fetching pupils out of the very heart of one or other of the divisions to take their music-lessons in the oratory, the great or little saloon, the salle-à-manger, or some other piano-station—she would, upon her second or third attempt, frequently become almost tongue-tied from excess of consternation—a sentiment inspired by the unspeakable looks levelled at her through a pair of dart-dealing spectacles.

One morning I was sitting in the carré, at work upon a piece of embroidery which one of the pupils had commenced but delayed to finish, and while my fingers wrought at the frame, my ears regaled themselves with listening to the crescendos and cadences of a voice haranguing in the neighbouring classe, in tones that waxed momentarily more unquiet, more ominously varied. There was a good strong partition-wall between me and the gathering storm, as well as a facile means of flight through the glass-door to the court, in case it swept this way; so I am afraid I derived more amusement than alarm from these thickening symptoms. Poor Rosine was not safe: four times that blessed morning had she made the passage of peril; and now, for the fifth time, it became her dangerous duty to snatch, as it were, a brand from the burning—a pupil from under M. Paul's nose.

"Mon Dieu! Mon Dieu!" cried she. "Que vais-je devenir? Monsieur va me tuer, je suis sûre; car il est d'une colère!"

Nerved by the courage of desperation, she opened the door.

"Mademoiselle La Malle au piano!" was her cry.

Ere she could make good her retreat, or quite close the door,

Villette

this voice uttered itself:—

"Dès ce moment!—la classe est défendue. La première qui ouvrira cette porte, ou passera par cette division, sera pendue— fut-ce Madame Beck elle-même!"

Ten minutes had not succeeded the promulgation of this decree when Rosine's French pantoufles were again heard shuffling along the corridor.

"Mademoiselle," said she, "I would not for a five-franc piece go into that classe again just now: Monsieur's lunettes are really terrible; and here is a commissionaire come with a message from the Athénée. I have told Madame Beck I dare not deliver it, and she says I am to charge you with it."

"Me? No, that is rather too bad! It is not in my line of duty. Come, come, Rosine! bear your own burden. Be brave—charge once more!"

"I, Mademoiselle?—impossible! Five times I have crossed him this day. Madame must really hire a gendarme for this service. Ouf! Je n'en puis plus!"

"Bah! you are only a coward. What is the message?"

"Precisely of the kind with which Monsieur least likes to be pestered: an urgent summons to go directly to the Athénée, as there is an official visitor—inspector—I know not what— arrived, and Monsieur must meet him: you know how he hates a must."

Yes, I knew well enough. The restive little man detested spur or curb: against whatever was urgent or obligatory, he was sure to revolt. However, I accepted the responsibility—not, certainly, without fear, but fear blent with other sentiments, curiosity, amongst them. I opened the door, I entered, I closed it behind me as quickly and quietly as a rather unsteady hand would permit; for to be slow or bustling, to rattle a latch, or leave a door gaping wide, were aggravations of crime often more disastrous in result than the main crime itself. There I stood then, and there he sat; his humour was visibly bad—almost at its worst; he had been giving a lesson in arithmetic—for he gave lessons on any and every subject that struck his fancy—and arithmetic being a dry subject, invariably disagreed with him: not a pupil but trembled when he spoke of figures. He sat, bent above his desk: to look up at the sound of an entrance, at the occurrence of a direct breach of his will and law, was an effort he could not for the moment bring himself to make. It was quite as well: I thus gained time to walk up the long classe; and it suited my idiosyncracy far better to encounter the near burst of anger like his, than to bear its menace at a distance.

At his estrade I paused, just in front; of course I was not worthy of immediate attention: he proceeded with his lesson. Disdain would not do: he must hear and he must answer my message.

Not being quite tall enough to lift my head over his desk, elevated upon the estrade, and thus suffering eclipse in my present position, I ventured to peep round, with the design, at first, of merely getting a better view of his face, which had struck me when I entered as bearing a close and picturesque resemblance to that of a black and sallow tiger. Twice did I enjoy this side-view with impunity, advancing and receding unseen; the third time my eye had scarce dawned beyond the obscuration of the desk, when it was caught and transfixed through its very pupil—transfixed by the "lunettes." Rosine was right; these utensils had in them a blank and immutable terror, beyond the mobile wrath of the wearer's own unglazed eyes.

I now found the advantage of proximity: these short-sighted "lunettes" were useless for the inspection of a criminal under Monsieur's nose; accordingly, he doffed them, and he and I stood on more equal terms.

I am glad I was not really much afraid of him—that, indeed, close in his presence, I felt no terror at all; for upon his demanding cord and gibbet to execute the sentence recently pronounced, I was able to furnish him with a needleful of embroidering thread with such accommodating civility as could not but allay some portion at least of his surplus irritation. Of course I did not parade this courtesy before public view: I merely handed the thread round the angle of the desk, and attached it, ready noosed, to the barred back of the Professor's chair.

"Que me voulez-vous?" said he in a growl of which the music was wholly confined to his chest and throat, for he kept his teeth clenched; and seemed registering to himself an inward vow that nothing earthly should wring from him a smile.

My answer commenced uncompromisingly: "Monsieur," I said, "je veux l'impossible, des choses inouïes;" and thinking it best not to mince matters, but to administer the "douche" with decision, in a low but quick voice, I delivered the Athenian message, floridly exaggerating its urgency.

Of course, he would not hear a word of it. "He would not go; he would not leave his present class, let all the officials of Villette send for him. He would not put himself an inch out of his way at the bidding of king, cabinet, and chambers together."

I knew, however, that he must go; that, talk as he would, both his duty and interest commanded an immediate and literal compliance with the summons: I stood, therefore, waiting in silence, as if he had not yet spoken. He asked what more I wanted.

"Only Monsieur's answer to deliver to the commissionaire."

He waved an impatient negative.

I ventured to stretch my hand to the bonnet-grec which lay in grim repose on the window-sill. He followed this daring movement with his eye, no doubt in mixed pity and amazement at its presumption.

"Ah!" he muttered, "if it came to that—if Miss Lucy meddled with his bonnet-grec—she might just put it on herself, turn garçon for the occasion, and benevolently go to the Athénée in his stead."

With great respect, I laid the bonnet on the desk, where its tassel seemed to give me an awful nod.

"I'll write a note of apology—that will do!" said he, still bent on evasion.

Knowing well it would not do, I gently pushed the bonnet towards his hand. Thus impelled, it slid down the polished slope of the varnished and unbaized desk, carried before it the light steel-framed "lunettes," and, fearful to relate, they fell to the estrade. A score of times ere now had I seen them fall and receive no damage—this time, as Lucy Snowe's hapless luck would have it, they so fell that each clear pebble became a shivered and shapeless star.

Now, indeed, dismay seized me—dismay and regret. I knew the value of these "lunettes": M. Paul's sight was peculiar, not easily fitted, and these glasses suited him. I had heard him call them his treasures: as I picked them up, cracked and worthless, my hand trembled. Frightened through all my nerves I was to see the mischief I had done, but I think I was even more sorry than afraid. For some seconds I dared not look the bereaved Professor in the face; he was the first to speak.

"Là!" said he: "me voilà veuf de mes lunettes! I think Mademoiselle Lucy will now confess that the cord and gallows are amply earned; she trembles in anticipation of her doom. Ah, traitress! traitress! You are resolved to have me quite blind and helpless in your hands!"

I lifted my eyes: his face, instead of being irate, lowering, and furrowed, was overflowing with the smile, coloured with the bloom I had seen brightening it that evening at the Hotel Crécy. He was not angry—not even grieved. For the real injury he showed himself full of clemency; under the real provocation, patient as a saint. This event, which seemed so untoward—which I thought had ruined at once my chance of successful persuasion—proved my best help. Difficult of management so long as I had done him no harm, he became graciously pliant as soon as I stood in his presence a conscious and contrite offender.

Still gently railing at me as "une forte femme—une Anglaise terrible—une petite casse-tout"—he declared that he dared not but obey one who had given such an instance of her dangerous prowess; it was absolutely like the "grand Empereur smashing the vase to inspire dismay." So, at last, crowning himself with his bonnet-grec, and taking his ruined "lunettes" from my hand with a clasp of kind pardon and encouragement, he made his bow, and went off to the Athénée in first-rate humour and spirits.

After all this amiability, the reader will be sorry for my sake to hear that I was quarrelling with M. Paul again before night; yet so it was, and I could not help it.

It was his occasional custom—and a very laudable, acceptable custom, too—to arrive of an evening, always à l'improviste, unannounced, burst in on the silent hour of study, establish a sudden despotism over us and our occupations, cause books to be put away, work-bags to be brought out, and, drawing forth a single thick volume, or a handful of pamphlets, substitute for the besotted "lecture pieuse," drawled by a sleepy pupil, some tragedy made grand by grand reading, ardent by fiery action—some drama, whereof, for my part, I rarely studied the intrinsic merit; for M. Emanuel made it a vessel for an outpouring, and filled it with his native verve and passion like a cup with a vital brewage. Or else he would flash through our conventual darkness a reflex of a brighter world, show us a

Villette

glimpse of the current literature of the day, read us passages from some enchanting tale, or the last witty feuilleton which had awakened laughter in the saloons of Paris; taking care always to expunge, with the severest hand, whether from tragedy, melodrama, tale, or essay, whatever passage, phrase, or word, could be deemed unsuited to an audience of "jeunes filles." I noticed more than once, that where retrenchment without substitute would have left unmeaning vacancy, or introduced weakness, he could, and did, improvise whole paragraphs, no less vigorous than irreproachable; the dialogue—the description—he engrafted was often far better than that he pruned away.

Well, on the evening in question, we were sitting silent as nuns in a "retreat," the pupils studying, the teachers working. I remember my work; it was a slight matter of fancy, and it rather interested me; it had a purpose; I was not doing it merely to kill time; I meant it when finished as a gift; and the occasion of presentation being near, haste was requisite, and my fingers were busy.

We heard the sharp bell-peal which we all knew; then the rapid step familiar to each ear: the words "Voilà Monsieur!" had scarcely broken simultaneously from every lip, when the two-leaved door split (as split it always did for his admission—such a slow word as "open" is inefficient to describe his movements), and he stood in the midst of us.

There were two study tables, both long and flanked with benches; over the centre of each hung a lamp; beneath this lamp, on either side the table, sat a teacher; the girls were arranged to the right hand and the left; the eldest and most studious nearest the lamps or tropics; the idlers and little ones towards the north and south poles. Monsieur's habit was politely to hand a chair to some teacher, generally Zélie St. Pierre, the senior mistress; then to take her vacated seat; and thus avail himself of the full beam of Cancer or Capricorn, which, owing to his near sight, he needed.

As usual, Zélie rose with alacrity, smiling to the whole extent of her mouth, and the full display of her upper and under rows of teeth—that strange smile which passes from ear to ear, and is marked only by a sharp thin curve, which fails to spread over the countenance, and neither dimples the cheek nor lights the eye. I suppose Monsieur did not see her, or he had taken a whim that he would not notice her, for he was as capricious as women are said to be; then his "lunettes" (he had got another pair) served him as an excuse for all sorts of little oversights and shortcomings. Whatever might be his reason, he passed by Zélie, came to the other side of the table, and before I could start up to clear the way, whispered, "Ne bougez pas," and established himself between me and Miss Fanshawe, who always would be my neighbour, and have her elbow in my side, however often I declared to her, "Ginevra, I wish you were at Jericho."

It was easy to say, "Ne bougez pas;" but how could I help it? I must make him room, and I must request the pupils to recede that I might recede. It was very well for Ginevra to be gummed to me, "keeping herself warm," as she said, on the winter evenings, and harassing my very heart with her fidgetings and pokings, obliging me, indeed, sometimes to put an artful pin in my girdle by way of protection against her elbow; but I suppose M. Emanuel was not to be subjected to the same kind of treatment, so I swept away my working materials, to clear space for his book, and withdrew myself to make room for his person; not, however, leaving more than a yard of interval, just what any reasonable man would have regarded as a convenient, respectful allowance of bench. But M. Emanuel never was reasonable; flint and tinder that he was! he struck and took fire directly.

"Vous ne voulez pas de moi pour voisin," he growled: "vous vous donnez des airs de caste; vous me traitez en paria;" he scowled. "Soit! je vais arranger la chose!" And he set to work.

"Levez vous toutes, Mesdemoiselles!" cried he.

The girls rose. He made them all file off to the other table. He then placed me at one extremity of the long bench, and having duly and carefully brought me my work-basket, silk, scissors, all my implements, he fixed himself quite at the other end.

At this arrangement, highly absurd as it was, not a soul in the room dared to laugh; luckless for the giggler would have been the giggle. As for me, I took it with entire coolness. There I sat, isolated and cut off from human intercourse; I sat and minded my work, and was quiet, and not at all unhappy.

"Est ce assez de distance?" he demanded.

"Monsieur en est l'arbitre," said I.

"Vous savez bien que non. C'est vous qui avez crée ce vide immense: moi je n'y ai pas mis la main."

And with this assertion he commenced the reading.

For his misfortune he had chosen a French translation of what he called "un drame de Williams Shackspire; le faux dieu," he further announced, "de ces sots païens, les Anglais." How far otherwise he would have characterized him had his temper not been upset, I scarcely need intimate.

Of course, the translation being French, was very inefficient; nor did I make any particular effort to conceal the contempt which some of its forlorn lapses were calculated to excite. Not that it behoved or beseemed me to say anything: but one can occasionally look the opinion it is forbidden to embody in words. Monsieur's lunettes being on the alert, he gleaned up every stray look; I don't think he lost one: the consequence was, his eyes soon discarded a screen, that their blaze might sparkle free, and he waxed hotter at the north pole to which he had voluntarily exiled himself, than, considering the general temperature of the room, it would have been reasonable to become under the vertical ray of Cancer itself.

The reading over, it appeared problematic whether he would depart with his anger unexpressed, or whether he would give it vent. Suppression was not much in his habits; but still, what had been done to him definite enough to afford matter for overt reproof? I had not uttered a sound, and could not justly be deemed amenable to reprimand or penalty for having permitted a slightly freer action than usual to the muscles about my eyes and mouth.

The supper, consisting of bread, and milk diluted with tepid water, was brought in. In respectful consideration of the Professor's presence, the rolls and glasses were allowed to stand instead of being immediately handed round.

"Take your supper, ladies," said he, seeming to be occupied in making marginal notes to his "Williams Shackspire." They took it. I also accepted a roll and glass, but being now more than ever interested in my work, I kept my seat of punishment, and wrought while I munched my bread and sipped my beverage, the whole with easy sang-froid; with a certain snugness of composure, indeed, scarcely in my habits, and pleasantly novel to my feelings. It seemed as if the presence of a nature so restless, chafing, thorny as that of M. Paul absorbed all feverish and unsettling influences like a magnet, and left me none but such as were placid and harmonious.

He rose. "Will he go away without saying another word?"

Yes; he turned to the door.

No: he re-turned on his steps; but only, perhaps, to take his pencil-case, which had been left on the table.

He took it—shut the pencil in and out, broke its point against the wood, re-cut and pocketed it, and . . . walked promptly up to me.

The girls and teachers, gathered round the other table, were talking pretty freely: they always talked at meals; and, from the constant habit of speaking fast and loud at such times, did not now subdue their voices much.

M. Paul came and stood behind me. He asked at what I was working; and I said I was making a watchguard.

He asked, "For whom?" And I answered, "For a gentleman—one of my friends."

M. Paul stooped down and proceeded—as novel-writers say, and, as was literally true in his case—to "hiss" into my ear some poignant words.

He said that, of all the women he knew, I was the one who could make herself the most consummately unpleasant: I was she with whom it was least possible to live on friendly terms. I had a "caractère intraitable," and perverse to a miracle. How I managed it, or what possessed me, he, for his part, did not know; but with whatever pacific and amicable intentions a person accosted me—crac! I turned concord to discord, good-will to enmity. He was sure, he—M. Paul—wished me well enough; he had never done me any harm that he knew of; he might, at least, he supposed, claim a right to be regarded as a neutral acquaintance, guiltless of hostile sentiments: yet, how I behaved to him! With what pungent vivacities—what an impetus of mutiny—what a "fougue" of injustice!

Here I could not avoid opening my eyes somewhat wide, and even slipping in a slight interjectional observation: "Vivacities? Impetus? Fougue? I didn't know...."

"Chut! à l'instant! There! there I went—vive comme la poudre!" He was sorry—he was very sorry: for my sake he grieved over the hapless peculiarity. This "emportement," this "chaleur"—generous, perhaps, but excessive—would yet, he feared, do me a mischief. It was a pity: I was not—he believed, in his soul—wholly without good qualities: and would I but

Villette

hear reason, and be more sedate, more sober, less "en l'air," less "coquette," less taken by show, less prone to set an undue value on outside excellence—to make much of the attentions of people remarkable chiefly for so many feet of stature, "des couleurs de poupée," "un nez plus ou moins bien fait," and an enormous amount of fatuity—I might yet prove an useful, perhaps an exemplary character. But, as it was—And here, the little man's voice was for a minute choked.

I would have looked up at him, or held out my hand, or said a soothing word; but I was afraid, if I stirred, I should either laugh or cry; so odd, in all this, was the mixture of the touching and the absurd.

I thought he had nearly done: but no; he sat down that he might go on at his ease.

"While he, M. Paul, was on these painful topics, he would dare my anger for the sake of my good, and would venture to refer to a change he had noticed in my dress. He was free to confess that when he first knew me—or, rather, was in the habit of catching a passing glimpse of me from time to time—I satisfied him on this point: the gravity, the austere simplicity, obvious in this particular, were such as to inspire the highest hopes for my best interests. What fatal influence had impelled me lately to introduce flowers under the brim of my bonnet, to wear 'des cols brodés,' and even to appear on one occasion in a scarlet gown—he might indeed conjecture, but, for the present, would not openly declare."

Again I interrupted, and this time not without an accent at once indignant and horror-struck.

"Scarlet, Monsieur Paul? It was not scarlet! It was pink, and pale pink too, and further subdued by black lace."

"Pink or scarlet, yellow or crimson, pea-green or sky-blue, it was all one: these were all flaunting, giddy colours; and as to the lace I talked of, that was but a 'colifichet de plus.'" And he sighed over my degeneracy. "He could not, he was sorry to say, be so particular on this theme as he could wish: not possessing the exact names of these 'babioles,' he might run into small verbal errors which would not fail to lay him open to my sarcasm, and excite my unhappily sudden and passionate disposition. He would merely say, in general terms—and in these general terms he knew he was correct—that my costume had of late assumed 'des façons mondaines,' which it wounded him to see."

What "façons mondaines" he discovered in my present winter merino and plain white collar, I own it puzzled me to guess: and when I asked him, he said it was all made with too much attention to effect—and besides, "had I not a bow of ribbon at my neck?"

"And if you condemn a bow of ribbon for a lady, Monsieur, you would necessarily disapprove of a thing like this for a gentleman?"—holding up my bright little chainlet of silk and gold. His sole reply was a groan—I suppose over my levity.

After sitting some minutes in silence, and watching the progress of the chain, at which I now wrought more assiduously than ever, he inquired: "Whether what he had just said would have the effect of making me entirely detest him?"

I hardly remember what answer I made, or how it came about; I don't think I spoke at all, but I know we managed to bid good-night on friendly terms: and, even after M. Paul had reached the door, he turned back just to explain, "that he would not be understood to speak in entire condemnation of the scarlet dress" ("Pink! pink!" I threw in); "that he had no intention to deny it the merit of looking rather well" (the fact was, M. Emanuel's taste in colours decidedly leaned to the brilliant); "only he wished to counsel me, whenever I wore it, to do so in the same spirit as if its material were 'bure,' and its hue 'gris de poussière.'"

"And the flowers under my bonnet, Monsieur?" I asked. "They are very little ones—?"

"Keep them little, then," said he. "Permit them not to become full-blown."

"And the bow, Monsieur—the bit of ribbon?"

"Va pour le ruban!" was the propitious answer.

And so we settled it.

"Well done, Lucy Snowe!" cried I to myself; "you have come in for a pretty lecture—brought on yourself a 'rude savant,' and all through your wicked fondness for worldly vanities! Who would have thought it? You deemed yourself a melancholy sober-sides enough! Miss Fanshawe there regards you as a second Diogenes. M. de Bassompierre, the other day, politely turned the conversation when it ran on the wild gifts of the actress Vashti, because, as he kindly said, 'Miss Snowe looked

Villette

uncomfortable.' Dr. John Bretton knows you only as 'quiet Lucy' — 'a creature inoffensive as a shadow;' he has said, and you have heard him say it: 'Lucy's disadvantages spring from over-gravity in tastes and manner — want of colour in character and costume.' Such are your own and your friends' impressions; and behold! there starts up a little man, differing diametrically from all these, roundly charging you with being too airy and cheery — too volatile and versatile — too flowery and coloury. This harsh little man — this pitiless censor — gathers up all your poor scattered sins of vanity, your luckless chiffon of rose-colour, your small fringe of a wreath, your small scrap of ribbon, your silly bit of lace, and calls you to account for the lot, and for each item. You are well habituated to be passed by as a shadow in Life's sunshine: it is a new thing to see one testily lifting his hand to screen his eyes, because you tease him with an obtrusive ray."

CHAPTER XXIX.
MONSIEUR'S FÊTE.

I was up the next morning an hour before daybreak, and finished my guard, kneeling on the dormitory floor beside the centre stand, for the benefit of such expiring glimmer as the night-lamp afforded in its last watch.

All my materials—my whole stock of beads and silk—were used up before the chain assumed the length and richness I wished; I had wrought it double, as I knew, by the rule of contraries, that to, suit the particular taste whose gratification was in view, an effective appearance was quite indispensable. As a finish to the ornament, a little gold clasp was needed; fortunately I possessed it in the fastening of my sole necklace; I duly detached and re-attached it, then coiled compactly the completed guard; and enclosed it in a small box I had bought for its brilliancy, made of some tropic shell of the colour called "nacarat," and decked with a little coronal of sparkling blue stones. Within the lid of the box, I carefully graved with my scissors' point certain initials.

The reader will, perhaps, remember the description of Madame Beck's fête; nor will he have forgotten that at each anniversary, a handsome present was subscribed for and offered by the school. The observance of this day was a distinction accorded to none but Madame, and, in a modified form, to her kinsman and counsellor, M. Emanuel. In the latter case it was an honour spontaneously awarded, not plotted and contrived beforehand, and offered an additional proof, amongst many others, of the estimation in which—despite his partialities, prejudices, and irritabilities—the professor of literature was held by his pupils. No article of value was offered to him: he distinctly gave it to be understood, that he would accept neither plate nor jewellery. Yet he liked a slight tribute; the cost, the money-value, did not touch him: a diamond ring, a gold snuff-box, presented, with pomp, would have pleased him less than a flower, or a drawing, offered simply and with sincere feelings. Such was his nature. He was a man, not wise in his generation, yet could he claim a filial sympathy with "the dayspring on high."

M. Paul's fête fell on the first of March and a Thursday. It proved a fine sunny day; and being likewise the morning on which it was customary to attend mass; being also otherwise distinguished by the half-holiday which permitted the privilege of walking out, shopping, or paying visits in the afternoon: these combined considerations induced a general smartness and freshness of dress. Clean collars were in vogue; the ordinary dingy woollen classe-dress was exchanged for something lighter and clearer. Mademoiselle Zélie St. Pierre, on this particular Thursday, even assumed a "robe de soie," deemed in economical Labassecour an article of hazardous splendour and luxury; nay, it was remarked that she sent for a "coiffeur" to dress her hair that morning; there were pupils acute enough to discover that she had bedewed her handkerchief and her hands with a new and fashionable perfume. Poor Zélie! It was much her wont to declare about this time, that she was tired to death of a life of seclusion and labour; that she longed to have the means and leisure for relaxation; to have some one to work for her — a husband who would pay her debts (she was woefully encumbered with debt), supply her wardrobe, and leave her at liberty, as she said, to "goûter un peu les plaisirs." It had long been rumoured, that her eye was upon M. Emanuel. Monsieur Emanuel's eye was certainly often upon her. He would sit and watch her perseveringly for minutes together. I have seen him give her a quarter-of-an-hour's gaze, while the class was silently composing, and he sat throned on his estrade, unoccupied. Conscious always of this basilisk attention, she would writhe under it, half-flattered, half-puzzled, and Monsieur would follow her sensations, sometimes looking appallingly acute; for in some cases, he had the terrible unerring penetration of instinct, and pierced in its hiding-place the last lurking thought of the heart, and discerned under florid veilings the bare; barren places of the spirit: yes, and its perverted tendencies, and its hidden false curves — all that men and women would not have known — the twisted spine, the malformed limb that was born with them, and far worse, the stain or disfigurement they have perhaps brought on themselves. No calamity so accursed but M. Emanuel could pity and forgive, if it were acknowledged candidly; but where his questioning eyes met dishonest denial — where his ruthless researches found deceitful concealment — oh, then, he could be cruel, and I thought wicked! he would exultantly snatch the screen from poor shrinking wretches, passionately hurry them to the summit of the mount of exposure, and there show them all naked, all false — poor living lies — the spawn of that horrid Truth which cannot be looked on unveiled. He thought he did justice; for my part I doubt whether man has a right to do such justice on man: more than once in these his visitations, I have felt compelled to give tears to his victims, and not spared ire and keen reproach to himself. He deserved it; but it was difficult to shake him in his firm conviction that the work was righteous and needed.

Villette

Breakfast being over and mass attended, the school-bell rang and the rooms filled: a very pretty spectacle was presented in classe. Pupils and teachers sat neatly arrayed, orderly and expectant, each bearing in her hand the bouquet of felicitation — the prettiest spring-flowers all fresh, and filling the air with their fragrance: I only had no bouquet. I like to see flowers growing, but when they are gathered, they cease to please. I look on them as things rootless and perishable; their likeness to life makes me sad. I never offer flowers to those I love; I never wish to receive them from hands dear to me. Mademoiselle St. Pierre marked my empty hands — she could not believe I had been so remiss; with avidity her eye roved over and round me: surely I must have some solitary symbolic flower somewhere: some small knot of violets, something to win myself praise for taste, commendation for ingenuity. The unimaginative "Anglaise" proved better than the Parisienne's fears: she sat literally unprovided, as bare of bloom or leaf as the winter tree. This ascertained, Zélie smiled, well pleased.

"How wisely you have acted to keep your money, Miss Lucie," she said: "silly I have gone and thrown away two francs on a bouquet of hot-house flowers!"

And she showed with pride her splendid nosegay.

But hush! a step: the step. It came prompt, as usual, but with a promptitude, we felt disposed to flatter ourselves, inspired by other feelings than mere excitability of nerve and vehemence of intent. We thought our Professor's "foot-fall" (to speak romantically) had in it a friendly promise this morning; and so it had.

He entered in a mood which made him as good as a new sunbeam to the already well-lit first classe. The morning light playing amongst our plants and laughing on our walls, caught an added lustre from M. Paul's all-benignant salute. Like a true Frenchman (though I don't know why I should say so, for he was of strain neither French nor Labassecourien), he had dressed for the "situation" and the occasion. Not by the vague folds, sinister and conspirator-like, of his soot-dark paletôt were the outlines of his person obscured; on the contrary, his figure (such as it was, I don't boast of it) was well set off by a civilized coat and a silken vest quite pretty to behold. The defiant and pagan bonnet-grec had vanished: bare-headed, he came upon us, carrying a Christian hat in his gloved hand. The little man looked well, very well; there was a clearness of amity in his blue eye, and a glow of good feeling on his dark complexion, which passed perfectly in the place of beauty: one really did not care to

Villette

observe that his nose, though far from small, was of no particular shape, his cheek thin, his brow marked and square, his mouth no rose-bud: one accepted him as he was, and felt his presence the reverse of damping or insignificant.

He passed to his desk; he placed on the same his hat and gloves. "Bon jour, mes amies," said he, in a tone that somehow made amends to some amongst us for many a sharp snap and savage snarl: not a jocund, good-fellow tone, still less an unctuous priestly, accent, but a voice he had belonging to himself—a voice used when his heart passed the words to his lips. That same heart did speak sometimes; though an irritable, it was not an ossified organ: in its core was a place, tender beyond a man's tenderness; a place that humbled him to little children, that bound him to girls and women to whom, rebel as he would, he could not disown his affinity, nor quite deny that, on the whole, he was better with them than with his own sex.

"We all wish Monsieur a good day, and present to him our congratulations on the anniversary of his fête," said Mademoiselle Zélie, constituting herself spokeswoman of the assembly; and advancing with no more twists of affectation than were with her indispensable to the achievement of motion, she laid her costly bouquet before him. He bowed over it.

The long train of offerings followed: all the pupils, sweeping past with the gliding step foreigners practise, left their tributes as they went by. Each girl so dexterously adjusted her separate gift, that when the last bouquet was laid on the desk, it formed the apex to a blooming pyramid—a pyramid blooming, spreading, and towering with such exuberance as, in the end, to eclipse the hero behind it. This ceremony over, seats were resumed, and we sat in dead silence, expectant of a speech.

I suppose five minutes might have elapsed, and the hush remained unbroken; ten—and there was no sound.

Many present began, doubtless, to wonder for what Monsieur waited; as well they might. Voiceless and viewless, stirless and wordless, he kept his station behind the pile of flowers.

At last there issued forth a voice, rather deep, as if it spoke out of a hollow:—

"Est-ce là tout?"

Mademoiselle Zélie looked round.

"You have all presented your bouquets?" inquired she of the pupils.

Yes; they had all given their nosegays, from the eldest to the youngest, from the tallest to the most diminutive. The senior mistress signified as much.

"Est-ce là tout?" was reiterated in an intonation which, deep before, had now descended some notes lower.

"Monsieur," said Mademoiselle St. Pierre, rising, and this time speaking with her own sweet smile, "I have the honour to tell you that, with a single exception, every person in classe has offered her bouquet. For Meess Lucie, Monsieur will kindly make allowance; as a foreigner she probably did not know our customs, or did not appreciate their significance. Meess Lucie has regarded this ceremony as too frivolous to be honoured by her observance."

"Famous!" I muttered between my teeth: "you are no bad speaker, Zélie, when you begin."

The answer vouchsafed to Mademoiselle St Pierre from the estrade was given in the gesticulation of a hand from behind the pyramid. This manual action seemed to deprecate words, to enjoin silence.

A form, ere long, followed the hand. Monsieur emerged from his eclipse; and producing himself on the front of his estrade, and gazing straight and fixedly before him at a vast "mappe-monde" covering the wall opposite, he demanded a third time, and now in really tragic tones—

"Est-ce là tout?"

I might yet have made all right, by stepping forwards and slipping into his hand the ruddy little shell-box I at that moment held tight in my own. It was what I had fully purposed to do; but, first, the comic side of Monsieur's behaviour had tempted me to delay, and now, Mademoiselle St. Pierre's affected interference provoked contumacity. The reader not having hitherto had any cause to ascribe to Miss Snowe's character the most distant pretensions to perfection, will be scarcely surprised to learn that she felt too perverse to defend herself from any imputation the Parisienne might choose to insinuate and besides, M. Paul was so tragic, and took my defection so seriously, he deserved to be vexed. I kept, then, both my box and my countenance, and sat insensate as any stone.

Villette

"It is well!" dropped at length from the lips of M. Paul; and having uttered this phrase, the shadow of some great paroxysm—the swell of wrath, scorn, resolve—passed over his brow, rippled his lips, and lined his cheeks. Gulping down all further comment, he launched into his customary "discours."

I can't at all remember what this "discours" was; I did not listen to it: the gulping-down process, the abrupt dismissal of his mortification or vexation, had given me a sensation which half-counteracted the ludicrous effect of the reiterated "Est-ce là tout?"

Towards the close of the speech there came a pleasing diversion my attention was again amusingly arrested.

Owing to some little accidental movement—I think I dropped my thimble on the floor, and in stooping to regain it, hit the crown of my head against the sharp corner of my desk; which casualties (exasperating to me, by rights, if to anybody) naturally made a slight bustle—M. Paul became irritated, and dismissing his forced equanimity, and casting to the winds that dignity and self-control with which he never cared long to encumber himself, he broke forth into the strain best calculated to give him ease.

I don't know how, in the progress of his "discours", he had contrived to cross the Channel and land on British ground; but there I found him when I began to listen.

Casting a quick, cynical glance round the room—a glance which scathed, or was intended to scathe, as it crossed me—he fell with fury upon "les Anglaises."

Never have I heard English women handled as M. Paul that morning handled them: he spared nothing—neither their minds, morals, manners, nor personal appearance. I specially remember his abuse of their tall stature, their long necks, their thin arms, their slovenly dress, their pedantic education, their impious scepticism(!), their insufferable pride, their pretentious virtue: over which he ground his teeth malignantly, and looked as if, had he dared, he would have said singular things. Oh! he was spiteful, acrid, savage; and, as a natural consequence, detestably ugly.

"Little wicked venomous man!" thought I; "am I going to harass myself with fears of displeasing you, or hurting your feelings? No, indeed; you shall be indifferent to me, as the shabbiest bouquet in your pyramid."

I grieve to say I could not quite carry out this resolution. For some time the abuse of England and the English found and left me stolid: I bore it some fifteen minutes stoically enough; but this hissing cockatrice was determined to sting, and he said such things at last—fastening not only upon our women, but upon our greatest names and best men; sullying, the shield of Britannia, and dabbling the union jack in mud—that I was stung. With vicious relish he brought up the most spicy current continental historical falsehoods—than which nothing can be conceived more offensive. Zélie, and the whole class, became one grin of vindictive delight; for it is curious to discover how these clowns of Labassecour secretly hate England. At last, I struck a sharp stroke on my desk, opened my lips, and let loose this cry:—

"Vive l'Angleterre, l'Histoire et les Héros! A bas la France, la Fiction et les Faquins!"

The class was struck of a heap. I suppose they thought me mad. The Professor put up his handkerchief, and fiendishly smiled into its folds. Little monster of malice! He now thought he had got the victory, since he had made me angry. In a second he became good-humoured. With great blandness he resumed the subject of his flowers; talked poetically and symbolically of their sweetness, perfume, purity, etcetera; made Frenchified comparisons between the "jeunes filles" and the sweet blossoms before him; paid Mademoiselle St. Pierre a very full-blown compliment on the superiority of her bouquet; and ended by announcing that the first really fine, mild, and balmy morning in spring, he intended to take the whole class out to breakfast in the country. "Such of the class, at least," he added, with emphasis, "as he could count amongst the number of his friends."

"Donc je n'y serai pas," declared I, involuntarily.

"Soit!" was his response; and, gathering his flowers in his arms, he flashed out of classe; while I, consigning my work, scissors, thimble, and the neglected little box, to my desk, swept up-stairs. I don't know whether he felt hot and angry, but I am free to confess that I did.

Yet with a strange evanescent anger, I had not sat an hour on the edge of my bed, picturing and repicturing his look, manner, words ere I smiled at the whole scene. A little pang of regret I underwent that the box had not been offered. I had meant to gratify him. Fate would not have it so.

Villette

In the course of the afternoon, remembering that desks in classe were by no means inviolate repositories, and thinking that it was as well to secure the box, on account of the initials in the lid, P. C. D. E., for Paul Carl (or Carlos) David Emanuel—such was his full name—these foreigners must always have a string of baptismals—I descended to the schoolroom.

It slept in holiday repose. The day pupils were all gone home, the boarders were out walking, the teachers, except the surveillante of the week, were in town, visiting or shopping; the suite of divisions was vacant; so was the grande salle, with its huge solemn globe hanging in the midst, its pair of many-branched chandeliers, and its horizontal grand piano closed, silent, enjoying its mid-week Sabbath. I rather wondered to find the first classe door ajar; this room being usually locked when empty, and being then inaccessible to any save Madame Beck and myself, who possessed a duplicate key. I wondered still more, on approaching, to hear a vague movement as of life—a step, a chair stirred, a sound like the opening of a desk.

"It is only Madame Beck doing inspection duty," was the conclusion following a moment's reflection. The partially-opened door gave opportunity for assurance on this point. I looked. Behold! not the inspecting garb of Madame Beck—the shawl and the clean cap—but the coat, and the close-shorn, dark head of a man. This person occupied my chair; his olive hand held my desk open, his nose was lost to view amongst my papers. His back was towards me, but there could not be a moment's question about identity. Already was the attire of ceremony discarded: the cherished and ink-stained paletôt was resumed; the perverse bonnet-grec lay on the floor, as if just dropped from the hand, culpably busy.

Now I knew, and I had long known, that that hand of M. Emanuel's was on the most intimate terms with my desk; that it raised and lowered the lid, ransacked and arranged the contents, almost as familiarly as my own. The fact was not dubious, nor did he wish it to be so: he left signs of each visit palpable and unmistakable; hitherto, however, I had never caught him in the act: watch as I would, I could not detect the hours and moments of his coming. I saw the brownie's work in exercises left overnight full of faults, and found next morning carefully corrected: I profited by his capricious good-will in loans full welcome and refreshing. Between a sallow dictionary and worn-out grammar would magically grow a fresh interesting new work, or a classic, mellow and sweet in its ripe age. Out of my work-basket would laughingly peep a romance, under it would lurk the pamphlet, the magazine, whence last evening's reading had been extracted. Impossible to doubt the source whence these treasures flowed: had there been no other indication, one condemning and traitor peculiarity, common to them all, settled the question—they smelt of cigars. This was very shocking, of course: I thought so at first, and used to open the window with some bustle, to air my desk, and with fastidious finger and thumb, to hold the peccant brochures forth to the purifying breeze. I was cured of that formality suddenly. Monsieur caught me at it one day, understood the inference, instantly relieved my hand of its burden, and, in another moment, would have thrust the same into the glowing stove. It chanced to be a book, on the perusal of which I was bent; so for once I proved as decided and quicker than himself; recaptured the spoil, and—having saved this volume—never hazarded a second. With all this, I had never yet been able to arrest in his visits the freakish, friendly, cigar-loving phantom.

But now at last I had him: there he was—the very brownie himself; and there, curling from his lips, was the pale blue breath of his Indian darling: he was smoking into my desk: it might well betray him. Provoked at this particular, and yet pleased to surprise him—pleased, that is, with the mixed feeling of the housewife who discovers at last her strange elfin ally busy in the dairy at the untimely churn—I softly stole forward, stood behind him, bent with precaution over his shoulder.

My heart smote me to see that—after this morning's hostility, after my seeming remissness, after the puncture experienced by his feelings, and the ruffling undergone by his temper—he, all willing to forget and forgive, had brought me a couple of handsome volumes, of which the title and authorship were guarantees for interest. Now, as he sat bending above the desk, he was stirring up its contents; but with gentle and careful hand; disarranging indeed, but not harming. My heart smote me: as I bent over him, as he sat unconscious, doing me what good he could, and I daresay not feeling towards me unkindly, my morning's anger quite melted: I did not dislike Professor Emanuel.

I think he heard me breathe. He turned suddenly: his temperament was nervous, yet he never started, and seldom changed colour: there was something hardy about him.

"I thought you were gone into town with the other teachers," said he, taking a grim gripe of his self-possession, which half-escaped him—"It is as well you are not. Do you think I care for being caught? Not I. I often visit your desk."

"Monsieur, I know it."

"You find a brochure or tome now and then; but you don't read them, because they have passed under this?"—touching his cigar.

"They have, and are no better for the process; but I read them."

"Without pleasure?"

"Monsieur must not be contradicted."

"Do you like them, or any of them?—are they acceptable?"
"Monsieur has seen me reading them a hundred times, and knows I have not so many recreations as to undervalue those he provides."

"I mean well; and, if you see that I mean well, and derive some little amusement from my efforts, why can we not be friends?"

"A fatalist would say—because we cannot."

"This morning," he continued, "I awoke in a bright mood, and came into classe happy; you spoiled my day."

"No, Monsieur, only an hour or two of it, and that unintentionally."

"Unintentionally! No. It was my fête-day; everybody wished me happiness but you. The little children of the third division gave each her knot of violets, lisped each her congratulation:—you—nothing. Not a bud, leaf, whisper—not a glance. Was this unintentional?"

"I meant no harm."

"Then you really did not know our custom? You were unprepared? You would willingly have laid out a few centimes on a flower to give me pleasure, had you been aware that it was expected? Say so, and all is forgotten, and the pain soothed."

"I did know that it was expected: I was prepared; yet I laid out no centimes on flowers."

"It is well—you do right to be honest. I should almost have hated you had you flattered and lied. Better declare at once

'Paul Carl Emanuel — je te déteste, mon garçon!' — than smile an interest, look an affection, and be false and cold at heart. False and cold I don't think you are; but you have made a great mistake in life, that I believe; I think your judgment is warped — that you are indifferent where you ought to be grateful — and perhaps devoted and infatuated, where you ought to be cool as your name. Don't suppose that I wish you to have a passion for me, Mademoiselle; Dieu vous en garde! What do you start for? Because I said passion? Well, I say it again. There is such a word, and there is such a thing — though not within these walls, thank heaven! You are no child that one should not speak of what exists; but I only uttered the word — the thing, I assure you, is alien to my whole life and views. It died in the past — in the present it lies buried — its grave is deep-dug, well-heaped, and many winters old: in the future there will be a resurrection, as I believe to my souls consolation; but all will then be changed — form and feeling: the mortal will have put on immortality — it will rise, not for earth, but heaven. All I say to you, Miss Lucy Snowe, is — that you ought to treat Professor Paul Emanuel decently."

I could not, and did not contradict such a sentiment.

"Tell me," he pursued, "when it is your fête-day, and I will not grudge a few centimes for a small offering."

"You will be like me, Monsieur: this cost more than a few centimes, and I did not grudge its price."

And taking from the open desk the little box, I put it into his hand.

"It lay ready in my lap this morning," I continued; "and if Monsieur had been rather more patient, and Mademoiselle St. Pierre less interfering — perhaps I should say, too, if I had been calmer and wiser — I should have given it then."

He looked at the box: I saw its clear warm tint and bright azure circlet pleased his eyes. I told him to open it.

"My initials!" said he, indicating the letters in the lid. "Who told you I was called Carl David?"

"A little bird, Monsieur."

"Does it fly from me to you? Then one can tie a message under its wing when needful."

Villette

He took out the chain—a trifle indeed as to value, but glossy with silk and sparkling with beads. He liked that too—admired it artlessly, like a child.

"For me?"

"Yes, for you."

"This is the thing you were working at last night?"

"The same."

"You finished it this morning?"

"I did."

"You commenced it with the intention that it should be mine?"

"Undoubtedly."

"And offered on my fête-day?"

"Yes."

"This purpose continued as you wove it?"

Again I assented.

"Then it is not necessary that I should cut out any portion—saying, this part is not mine: it was plaited under the idea and for the adornment of another?"

"By no means. It is neither necessary, nor would it be just."

"This object is all mine?"

"That object is yours entirely."

Straightway Monsieur opened his paletôt, arranged the guard splendidly across his chest, displaying as much and suppressing as little as he could: for he had no notion of concealing what he admired and thought decorative. As to the box, he pronounced it a superb bonbonnière—he was fond of bonbons, by the way—and as he always liked to share with others what pleased himself, he would give his "dragées" as freely as he lent his books. Amongst the kind brownie's gifts left in my desk, I forgot to enumerate many a paper of chocolate comfits. His tastes in these matters were southern, and what we think infantine. His simple lunch consisted frequently of a "brioche," which, as often as not, he shared with some child of the third division.

"A présent c'est un fait accompli," said he, re-adjusting his paletôt; and we had no more words on the subject. After looking over the two volumes he had brought, and cutting away some pages with his penknife (he generally pruned before lending his books, especially if they were novels, and sometimes I was a little provoked at the severity of his censorship, the retrenchments interrupting the narrative), he rose, politely touched his bonnet-grec, and bade me a civil good-day.

"We are friends now," thought I, "till the next time we quarrel."

We might have quarrelled again that very same evening, but, wonderful to relate, failed, for once, to make the most of our opportunity.

Contrary to all expectation, M. Paul arrived at the study-hour. Having seen so much of him in the morning, we did not look for his presence at night. No sooner were we seated at lessons, however, than he appeared. I own I was glad to see him, so glad that I could not help greeting his arrival with a smile; and when he made his way to the same seat about which so serious a misunderstanding had formerly arisen, I took good care not to make too much room for him; he watched with a jealous, side-long look, to see whether I shrank away, but I did not, though the bench was a little crowded. I was losing the early impulse to recoil from M. Paul. Habituated to the paletôt and bonnet-grec, the neighbourhood of these garments seemed no longer uncomfortable or very formidable. I did not now sit restrained, "asphyxiée" (as he used to say) at his side; I stirred when I wished to stir, coughed when it was necessary, even yawned when I was tired—did, in short, what I pleased, blindly reliant upon his indulgence. Nor did my temerity, this evening at least, meet the punishment it perhaps merited; he was both indulgent and good-natured; not a cross glance shot from his eyes, not a hasty word left his lips. Till the very close of the evening, he did not indeed address me at all, yet I felt, somehow, that he was full of friendliness. Silence is of different kinds, and breathes different meanings; no words could inspire a pleasanter content than did M. Paul's worldless presence. When the tray came in, and the bustle of supper commenced, he just said, as he retired, that he wished me a good night and sweet dreams; and a good night and sweet dreams I had.

CHAPTER XXX.

M. PAUL.

Yet the reader is advised not to be in any hurry with his kindly conclusions, or to suppose, with an over-hasty charity, that from that day M. Paul became a changed character—easy to live with, and no longer apt to flash danger and discomfort round him.

No; he was naturally a little man of unreasonable moods. When over-wrought, which he often was, he became acutely irritable; and, besides, his veins were dark with a livid belladonna tincture, the essence of jealousy. I do not mean merely the tender jealousy of the heart, but that sterner, narrower sentiment whose seat is in the head.

I used to think, as I sat looking at M. Paul, while he was knitting his brow or protruding his lip over some exercise of mine, which had not as many faults as he wished (for he liked me to commit faults: a knot of blunders was sweet to him as a cluster of nuts), that he had points of resemblance to Napoleon Bonaparte. I think so still.

In a shameless disregard of magnanimity, he resembled the great Emperor. M. Paul would have quarrelled with twenty learned women, would have unblushingly carried on a system of petty bickering and recrimination with a whole capital of coteries, never troubling himself about loss or lack of dignity. He would have exiled fifty Madame de Staëls, if they had annoyed, offended, outrivalled, or opposed him.

I well remember a hot episode of his with a certain Madame Panache—a lady temporarily employed by Madame Beck to give lessons in history. She was clever—that is, she knew a good deal; and, besides, thoroughly possessed the art of making the most of what she knew; of words and confidence she held unlimited command. Her personal appearance was far from destitute of advantages; I believe many people would have pronounced her "a fine woman;" and yet there were points in her robust and ample attractions, as well as in her bustling and demonstrative presence, which, it appeared, the nice and capricious tastes of M. Paul could not away with. The sound of her voice, echoing through the carré, would put him into a strange taking; her long free step—almost stride—along the corridor, would often make him snatch up his papers and decamp on the instant.

With malicious intent he bethought himself, one day, to intrude on her class; as quick as lightning he gathered her method of instruction; it differed from a pet plan of his own. With little ceremony, and less courtesy, he pointed out what he termed her errors. Whether he expected submission and attention, I know not; he met an acrid opposition, accompanied by a round reprimand for his certainly unjustifiable interference.

Instead of withdrawing with dignity, as he might still have done, he threw down the gauntlet of defiance. Madame Panache, bellicose as a Penthesilea, picked it up in a minute. She snapped her fingers in the intermeddler's face; she rushed upon him with a storm of words. M. Emanuel was eloquent; but Madame Panache was voluble. A system of fierce antagonism ensued. Instead of laughing in his sleeve at his fair foe, with all her sore amour-propre and loud self-assertion, M. Paul detested her with intense seriousness; he honoured her with his earnest fury; he pursued her vindictively and implacably, refusing to rest peaceably in his bed, to derive due benefit from his meals, or even serenely to relish his cigar, till she was fairly rooted out of the establishment. The Professor conquered, but I cannot say that the laurels of this victory shadowed gracefully his temples. Once I ventured to hint as much. To my great surprise he allowed that I might be right, but averred that when brought into contact with either men or women of the coarse, self-complacent quality, whereof Madame Panache was a specimen, he had no control over his own passions; an unspeakable and active aversion impelled him to a war of extermination.

Three months afterwards, hearing that his vanquished foe had met with reverses, and was likely to be really distressed for want of employment, he forgot his hatred, and alike active in good and evil, he moved heaven and earth till he found her a place. Upon her coming to make up former differences, and thank him for his recent kindness, the old voice—a little loud— the old manner—a little forward—so acted upon him that in ten minutes he started up and bowed her, or rather himself, out of the room, in a transport of nervous irritation.

To pursue a somewhat audacious parallel, in a love of power, in an eager grasp after supremacy, M. Emanuel was like Bonaparte. He was a man not always to be submitted to. Sometimes it was needful to resist; it was right to stand still, to look up into his eyes and tell him that his requirements went beyond reason—that his absolutism verged on tyranny.

The dawnings, the first developments of peculiar talent

Villette

appearing within his range, and under his rule, curiously excited, even disturbed him. He watched its struggle into life with a scowl; he held back his hand — perhaps said, "Come on if you have strength," but would not aid the birth.

When the pang and peril of the first conflict were over, when the breath of life was drawn, when he saw the lungs expand and contract, when he felt the heart beat and discovered life in the eye, he did not yet offer to foster.

"Prove yourself true ere I cherish you," was his ordinance; and how difficult he made that proof! What thorns and briers, what flints, he strewed in the path of feet not inured to rough travel! He watched tearlessly — ordeals that he exacted should be passed through — fearlessly. He followed footprints that, as they approached the bourne, were sometimes marked in blood — followed them grimly, holding the austerest police-watch over the pain-pressed pilgrim. And when at last he allowed a rest, before slumber might close the eyelids, he opened those same lids wide, with pitiless finger and thumb, and gazed deep through the pupil and the irids into the brain, into the heart, to search if Vanity, or Pride, or Falsehood, in any of its subtlest forms, was discoverable in the furthest recess of existence. If, at last, he let the neophyte sleep, it was but a moment; he woke him suddenly up to apply new tests: he sent him on irksome errands when he was staggering with weariness; he tried the temper, the sense, and the health; and it was only when every severest test had been applied and endured, when the most corrosive aquafortis had been used, and failed to tarnish the ore, that he admitted it genuine, and, still in clouded silence, stamped it with his deep brand of approval.

I speak not ignorant of these evils.

Till the date at which the last chapter closes, M. Paul had not been my professor — he had not given me lessons, but about that time, accidentally hearing me one day acknowledge an ignorance of some branch of education (I think it was arithmetic), which would have disgraced a charity-school boy, as he very truly remarked, he took me in hand, examined me first, found me, I need not say, abundantly deficient, gave me some books and appointed me some tasks.

He did this at first with pleasure, indeed with unconcealed exultation, condescending to say that he believed I was "bonne et pas trop faible" (i.e. well enough disposed, and not wholly destitute of parts), but, owing he supposed to adverse circumstances, "as yet in a state of wretchedly imperfect mental development."

The beginning of all effort has indeed with me been marked by a preternatural imbecility. I never could, even in forming a common acquaintance, assert or prove a claim to average quickness. A depressing and difficult passage has prefaced every new page I have turned in life.

So long as this passage lasted, M. Paul was very kind, very good, very forbearing; he saw the sharp pain inflicted, and felt the weighty humiliation imposed by my own sense of incapacity; and words can hardly do justice to his tenderness and helpfulness. His own eyes would moisten, when tears of shame and effort clouded mine; burdened as he was with work, he would steal half his brief space of recreation to give to me.

But, strange grief! when that heavy and overcast dawn began at last to yield to day; when my faculties began to struggle themselves, free, and my time of energy and fulfilment came; when I voluntarily doubled, trebled, quadrupled the tasks he set, to please him as I thought, his kindness became sternness; the light changed in his eyes from a beam to a spark; he fretted, he opposed, he curbed me imperiously; the more I did, the harder I worked, the less he seemed content. Sarcasms of which the severity amazed and puzzled me, harassed my ears; then flowed out the bitterest inuendoes against the "pride of intellect." I was vaguely threatened with I know not what doom, if I ever trespassed the limits proper to my sex, and conceived a contraband appetite for unfeminine knowledge. Alas! I had no such appetite. What I loved, it joyed me by any effort to content; but the noble hunger for science in the abstract — the godlike thirst after discovery — these feelings were known to me but by briefest flashes.

Yet, when M. Paul sneered at me, I wanted to possess them more fully; his injustice stirred in me ambitious wishes — it imparted a strong stimulus — it gave wings to aspiration.

In the beginning, before I had penetrated to motives, that uncomprehended sneer of his made my heart ache, but by-and-by it only warmed the blood in my veins, and sent added action to my pulses. Whatever my powers — feminine or the contrary — God had given them, and I felt resolute to be ashamed of no faculty of his bestowal.

The combat was very sharp for a time. I seemed to have lost M. Paul's affection; he treated me strangely. In his most unjust moments he would insinuate that I had deceived him when I appeared, what he called "faible" — that is incompetent; he said I had feigned a false incapacity. Again, he would turn suddenly round and accuse me of the most far-fetched imitations and impossible plagiarisms, asserting that I had extracted the pith out of books I had not so much as heard of — and over the perusal of which I should infallibly have fallen down in a sleep as deep as that of Eutychus.

Once, upon his preferring such an accusation, I turned upon him — I rose against him. Gathering an armful of his books out of my desk, I filled my apron and poured them in a heap upon his estrade, at his feet.

"Take them away, M. Paul," I said, "and teach me no more. I never asked to be made learned, and you compel me to feel very profoundly that learning is not happiness."

And returning to my desk, I laid my head on my arms, nor would I speak to him for two days afterwards. He pained and chagrined me. His affection had been very sweet and dear — a pleasure new and incomparable: now that this seemed withdrawn, I cared not for his lessons.

The books, however, were not taken away; they were all restored with careful hand to their places, and he came as usual to teach me. He made his peace somehow — too readily, perhaps: I ought to have stood out longer, but when he looked kind and good, and held out his hand with amity, memory refused to reproduce with due force his oppressive moments. And then, reconcilement is always sweet!

On a certain morning a message came from my godmother, inviting me to attend some notable lecture to be delivered in the same public rooms before described. Dr. John had brought the message himself, and delivered it verbally to Rosine, who had not scrupled to follow the steps of M. Emanuel, then passing to the first classe, and, in his presence, stand "carrément" before my desk, hand in apron-pocket, and rehearse the same, saucily and aloud, concluding with the words, "Qu'il est vraiment beau, Mademoiselle, ce jeune docteur! Quels yeux — quel regard! Tenez! J'en ai le cœur tout ému!"

When she was gone, my professor demanded of me why I suffered "cette fille effrontée, cette créature sans pudeur," to address me in such terms.

I had no pacifying answer to give. The terms were precisely

such as Rosine—a young lady in whose skull the organs of reverence and reserve were not largely developed—was in the constant habit of using. Besides, what she said about the young doctor was true enough. Graham was handsome; he had fine eyes and a thrilling glance. An observation to that effect actually formed itself into sound on my lips.

"Elle ne dit que la vérité," I said.

"Ah! vous trouvez?"

"Mais, sans doute."

The lesson to which we had that day to submit was such as to make us very glad when it terminated. At its close, the released pupils rushed out, half-trembling, half-exultant. I, too, was going. A mandate to remain arrested me. I muttered that I wanted some fresh air sadly—the stove was in a glow, the classe over-heated. An inexorable voice merely recommended silence; and this salamander—for whom no room ever seemed too hot—sitting down between my desk and the stove—a situation in which he ought to have felt broiled, but did not—proceeded to confront me with—a Greek quotation!

In M. Emanuel's soul rankled a chronic suspicion that I knew both Greek and Latin. As monkeys are said to have the power of speech if they would but use it, and are reported to conceal this faculty in fear of its being turned to their detriment, so to me was ascribed a fund of knowledge which I was supposed criminally and craftily to conceal. The privileges of a "classical education," it was insinuated, had been mine; on flowers of Hymettus I had revelled; a golden store, hived in memory, now silently sustained my efforts, and privily nurtured my wits.

A hundred expedients did M. Paul employ to surprise my secret—to wheedle, to threaten, to startle it out of me. Sometimes he placed Greek and Latin books in my way, and then watched me, as Joan of Arc's jailors tempted her with the warrior's accoutrements, and lay in wait for the issue. Again he quoted I know not what authors and passages, and while rolling out their sweet and sounding lines (the classic tones fell musically from his lips—for he had a good voice—remarkable for compass, modulation, and matchless expression), he would fix on me a vigilant, piercing, and often malicious eye. It was evident he sometimes expected great demonstrations; they never occurred, however; not comprehending, of course I could neither be charmed nor annoyed.

Villette

Baffled—almost angry—he still clung to his fixed idea; my susceptibilities were pronounced marble—my face a mask. It appeared as if he could not be brought to accept the homely truth, and take me for what I was: men, and women too, must have delusion of some sort; if not made ready to their hand, they will invent exaggeration for themselves.

At moments I did wish that his suspicions had been better founded. There were times when I would have given my right hand to possess the treasures he ascribed to me. He deserved condign punishment for his testy crotchets. I could have gloried in bringing home to him his worst apprehensions astoundingly realized. I could have exulted to burst on his vision, confront and confound his "lunettes," one blaze of acquirements. Oh! why did nobody undertake to make me clever while I was young enough to learn, that I might, by one grand, sudden, inhuman revelation—one cold, cruel, overwhelming triumph—have for ever crushed the mocking spirit out of Paul Carl David Emanuel!

Alas! no such feat was in my power. To-day, as usual, his quotations fell ineffectual: he soon shifted his ground.

"Women of intellect" was his next theme: here he was at home. A "woman of intellect," it appeared, was a sort of "lusus naturae," a luckless accident, a thing for which there was neither place nor use in creation, wanted neither as wife nor worker. Beauty anticipated her in the first office. He believed in his soul that lovely, placid, and passive feminine mediocrity was the only pillow on which manly thought and sense could find rest for its aching temples; and as to work, male mind alone could work to any good practical result—hein?

This "hein?" was a note of interrogation intended to draw from me contradiction or objection. However, I only said—"Cela ne me regarde pas: je ne m'en soucie pas;" and presently added—"May I go, Monsieur? They have rung the bell for the second déjeuner" (i.e. luncheon).

"What of that? You are not hungry?"

"Indeed I was," I said; "I had had nothing since breakfast, at seven, and should have nothing till dinner, at five, if I missed this bell."

"Well, he was in the same plight, but I might share with him."

And he broke in two the "brioche" intended for his own refreshment, and gave me half. Truly his bark was worse than his bite; but the really formidable attack was yet to come. While eating his cake, I could not forbear expressing my secret wish that I really knew all of which he accused me.

"Did I sincerely feel myself to be an ignoramus?" he asked, in a softened tone.

If I had replied meekly by an unqualified affirmative, I believe he would have stretched out his hand, and we should have been friends on the spot, but I answered —

"Not exactly. I am ignorant, Monsieur, in the knowledge you ascribe to me, but I sometimes, not always, feel a knowledge of my own."

"What did I mean?" he inquired, sharply.

Unable to answer this question in a breath, I evaded it by change of subject. He had now finished his half of the brioche: feeling sure that on so trifling a fragment he could not have satisfied his appetite, as indeed I had not appeased mine, and inhaling the fragrance of baked apples afar from the refectory, I ventured to inquire whether he did not also perceive that agreeable odour. He confessed that he did. I said if he would let me out by the garden-door, and permit me just to run across the court, I would fetch him a plateful; and added that I believed they were excellent, as Goton had a very good method of baking, or rather stewing fruit, putting in a little spice, sugar, and a glass or two of vin blanc — might I go?

"Petite gourmande!" said he, smiling, "I have not forgotten how pleased you were with the pâté à la crême I once gave you, and you know very well, at this moment, that to fetch the apples for me will be the same as getting them for yourself. Go, then, but come back quickly."

And at last he liberated me on parole. My own plan was to go and return with speed and good faith, to put the plate in at the door, and then to vanish incontinent, leaving all consequences for future settlement.

That intolerably keen instinct of his seemed to have anticipated my scheme: he met me at the threshold, hurried me into the room, and fixed me in a minute in my former seat. Taking the plate of fruit from my hand, he divided the portion intended only for himself, and ordered me to eat my share. I

Villette

complied with no good grace, and vexed, I suppose, by my reluctance, he opened a masked and dangerous battery. All he had yet said, I could count as mere sound and fury, signifying nothing: not so of the present attack.

It consisted in an unreasonable proposition with which he had before afflicted me: namely, that on the next public examination-day I should engage—foreigner as I was—to take my place on the first form of first-class pupils, and with them improvise a composition in French, on any subject any spectator might dictate, without benefit of grammar or lexicon.

I knew what the result of such an experiment would be. I, to whom nature had denied the impromptu faculty; who, in public, was by nature a cypher; whose time of mental activity, even when alone, was not under the meridian sun; who needed the fresh silence of morning, or the recluse peace of evening, to win from the Creative Impulse one evidence of his presence, one proof of his force; I, with whom that Impulse was the most intractable, the most capricious, the most maddening of masters (him before me always excepted)—a deity which sometimes, under circumstances—apparently propitious, would not speak when questioned, would not hear when appealed to, would not, when sought, be found; but would stand, all cold, all indurated, all granite, a dark Baal with carven lips and blank eye-balls, and breast like the stone face of a tomb; and again, suddenly, at some turn, some sound, some long-trembling sob of the wind, at some rushing past of an unseen stream of electricity, the irrational demon would wake unsolicited, would stir strangely alive, would rush from its pedestal like a perturbed Dagon, calling to its votary for a sacrifice, whatever the hour—to its victim for some blood, or some breath, whatever the circumstance or scene—rousing its priest, treacherously promising vaticination, perhaps filling its temple with a strange hum of oracles, but sure to give half the significance to fateful winds, and grudging to the desperate listener even a miserable remnant—yielding it sordidly, as though each word had been a drop of the deathless ichor of its own dark veins. And this tyrant I was to compel into bondage, and make it improvise a theme, on a school estrade, between a Mathilde and a Coralie, under the eye of a Madame Beck, for the pleasure, and to the inspiration of a bourgeois of Labassecour!

Upon this argument M. Paul and I did battle more than once—strong battle, with confused noise of demand and rejection, exaction and repulse.

On this particular day I was soundly rated. "The obstinacy

of my whole sex," it seems, was concentrated in me; I had an "orgueil de diable." I feared to fail, forsooth! What did it matter whether I failed or not? Who was I that I should not fail, like my betters? It would do me good to fail. He wanted to see me worsted (I knew he did), and one minute he paused to take breath.

"Would I speak now, and be tractable?"

"Never would I be tractable in this matter. Law itself should not compel me. I would pay a fine, or undergo an imprisonment, rather than write for a show and to order, perched up on a platform."

"Could softer motives influence me? Would I yield for friendship's sake?"

"Not a whit, not a hair-breadth. No form of friendship under the sun had a right to exact such a concession. No true friendship would harass me thus."

He supposed then (with a sneer—M. Paul could sneer supremely, curling his lip, opening his nostrils, contracting his eyelids)—he supposed there was but one form of appeal to which I would listen, and of that form it was not for him to make use.

"Under certain persuasions, from certain quarters, je vous vois d'ici," said he, "eagerly subscribing to the sacrifice, passionately arming for the effort."

"Making a simpleton, a warning, and an example of myself, before a hundred and fifty of the 'papas' and 'mammas' of Villette."

And here, losing patience, I broke out afresh with a cry that I wanted to be liberated—to get out into the air—I was almost in a fever.

"Chut!" said the inexorable, "this was a mere pretext to run away; he was not hot, with the stove close at his back; how could I suffer, thoroughly screened by his person?"

"I did not understand his constitution. I knew nothing of the natural history of salamanders. For my own part, I was a phlegmatic islander, and sitting in an oven did not agree with me; at least, might I step to the well, and get a glass of water— the sweet apples had made me thirsty?"

"If that was all, he would do my errand."

He went to fetch the water. Of course, with a door only on the latch behind me, I lost not my opportunity. Ere his return, his half-worried prey had escaped.

CHAPTER XXXI.

THE DRYAD.

The spring was advancing, and the weather had turned suddenly warm. This change of temperature brought with it for me, as probably for many others, temporary decrease of strength. Slight exertion at this time left me overcome with fatigue—sleepless nights entailed languid days.

One Sunday afternoon, having walked the distance of half a league to the Protestant church, I came back weary and exhausted; and taking refuge in my solitary sanctuary, the first classe, I was glad to sit down, and to make of my desk a pillow for my arms and head.

Awhile I listened to the lullaby of bees humming in the berceau, and watched, through the glass door and the tender, lightly-strewn spring foliage, Madame Beck and a gay party of friends, whom she had entertained that day at dinner after morning mass, walking in the centre-alley under orchard boughs dressed at this season in blossom, and wearing a colouring as pure and warm as mountain-snow at sun-rise.

My principal attraction towards this group of guests lay, I remember, in one figure—that of a handsome young girl whom I had seen before as a visitor at Madame Beck's, and of whom I had been vaguely told that she was a "filleule," or god-daughter, of M. Emanuel's, and that between her mother, or aunt, or some other female relation of hers, and the Professor, had existed of old a special friendship. M. Paul was not of the holiday band to-day, but I had seen this young girl with him ere now, and as far as distant observation could enable me to judge, she seemed to enjoy him with the frank ease of a ward with an indulgent guardian. I had seen her run up to him, put her arm through his, and hang upon him. Once, when she did so, a curious sensation had struck through me—a disagreeable anticipatory sensation—one of the family of presentiments, I suppose—but I refused to analyze or dwell upon it. While watching this girl, Mademoiselle Sauveur by name, and following the gleam of her bright silk robe (she was always richly dressed, for she was said to be wealthy) through the flowers and the glancing leaves of tender emerald, my eyes became dazzled—they closed; my lassitude, the warmth of the day, the hum of bees and birds, all lulled me, and at last I slept.

Two hours stole over me. Ere I woke, the sun had declined

out of sight behind the towering houses, the garden and the room were grey, bees had gone homeward, and the flowers were closing; the party of guests, too, had vanished; each alley was void.

On waking, I felt much at ease—not chill, as I ought to have been after sitting so still for at least two hours; my cheek and arms were not benumbed by pressure against the hard desk. No wonder. Instead of the bare wood on which I had laid them, I found a thick shawl, carefully folded, substituted for support, and another shawl (both taken from the corridor where such things hung) wrapped warmly round me.

Who had done this? Who was my friend? Which of the teachers? Which of the pupils? None, except St. Pierre, was inimical to me; but which of them had the art, the thought, the habit, of benefiting thus tenderly? Which of them had a step so quiet, a hand so gentle, but I should have heard or felt her, if she had approached or touched me in a day-sleep?

As to Ginevra Fanshawe, that bright young creature was not gentle at all, and would certainly have pulled me out of my chair, if she had meddled in the matter. I said at last: "It is Madame Beck's doing; she has come in, seen me asleep, and thought I might take cold. She considers me a useful machine, answering well the purpose for which it was hired; so would not have me needlessly injured. And now," methought, "I'll take a walk; the evening is fresh, and not very chill."

So I opened the glass door and stepped into the berceau.

I went to my own alley: had it been dark, or even dusk, I should have hardly ventured there, for I had not yet forgotten the curious illusion of vision (if illusion it were) experienced in that place some months ago. But a ray of the setting sun burnished still the grey crown of Jean Baptiste; nor had all the birds of the garden yet vanished into their nests amongst the tufted shrubs and thick wall-ivy. I paced up and down, thinking almost the same thoughts I had pondered that night when I buried my glass jar—how I should make some advance in life, take another step towards an independent position; for this train of reflection, though not lately pursued, had never by me been wholly abandoned; and whenever a certain eye was averted from me, and a certain countenance grew dark with unkindness and injustice, into that track of speculation did I at once strike; so that, little by little, I had laid half a plan.

"Living costs little," said I to myself, "in this economical town of Villette, where people are more sensible than I understand they are in dear old England — infinitely less worried about appearance, and less emulous of display — where nobody is in the least ashamed to be quite as homely and saving as he finds convenient. House-rent, in a prudently chosen situation, need not be high. When I shall have saved one thousand francs, I will take a tenement with one large room, and two or three smaller ones, furnish the first with a few benches and desks, a black tableau, an estrade for myself; upon it a chair and table, with a sponge and some white chalks; begin with taking day-pupils, and so work my way upwards. Madame Beck's commencement was — as I have often heard her say — from no higher starting-point, and where is she now? All these premises and this garden are hers, bought with her money; she has a competency already secured for old age, and a flourishing establishment under her direction, which will furnish a career for her children.

"Courage, Lucy Snowe! With self-denial and economy now, and steady exertion by-and-by, an object in life need not fail you. Venture not to complain that such an object is too selfish, too limited, and lacks interest; be content to labour for independence until you have proved, by winning that prize, your right to look higher. But afterwards, is there nothing more for me in life — no true home — nothing to be dearer to me than myself, and by its paramount preciousness, to draw from me better things than I care to culture for myself only? Nothing, at whose feet I can willingly lay down the whole burden of human egotism, and gloriously take up the nobler charge of labouring and living for others? I suppose, Lucy Snowe, the orb of your life is not to be so rounded: for you, the crescent-phase must suffice. Very good. I see a huge mass of my fellow-creatures in no better circumstances. I see that a great many men, and more women, hold their span of life on conditions of denial and privation. I find no reason why I should be of the few favoured. I believe in some blending of hope and sunshine sweetening the worst lots. I believe that this life is not all; neither the beginning nor the end. I believe while I tremble; I trust while I weep."

So this subject is done with. It is right to look our life-accounts bravely in the face now and then, and settle them honestly. And he is a poor self-swindler who lies to himself while he reckons the items, and sets down under the head — happiness that which is misery. Call anguish — anguish, and despair — despair; write both down in strong characters with a resolute pen: you will the better pay your debt to Doom. Falsify: insert "privilege" where you should have written "pain;" and see if your mighty creditor will allow the fraud to pass, or accept the coin with which you would cheat him. Offer to the strongest—if the darkest angel of God's host—water, when he has asked blood—will he take it? Not a whole pale sea for one red drop. I settled another account.

Pausing before Methusaleh—the giant and patriarch of the garden—and leaning my brow against his knotty trunk, my foot rested on the stone sealing the small sepulchre at his root; and I recalled the passage of feeling therein buried; I recalled Dr. John; my warm affection for him; my faith in his excellence; my delight in his grace. What was become of that curious one-sided friendship which was half marble and half life; only on one hand truth, and on the other perhaps a jest?

Was this feeling dead? I do not know, but it was buried. Sometimes I thought the tomb unquiet, and dreamed strangely of disturbed earth, and of hair, still golden, and living, obtruded through coffin-chinks.

Had I been too hasty? I used to ask myself; and this question would occur with a cruel sharpness after some brief chance interview with Dr. John. He had still such kind looks, such a warm hand; his voice still kept so pleasant a tone for my name; I never liked "Lucy" so well as when he uttered it. But I learned in time that this benignity, this cordiality, this music, belonged in no shape to me: it was a part of himself; it was the honey of his temper; it was the balm of his mellow mood; he imparted it, as the ripe fruit rewards with sweetness the rifling bee; he diffused it about him, as sweet plants shed their perfume. Does the nectarine love either the bee or bird it feeds? Is the sweetbriar enamoured of the air?

"Good-night, Dr. John; you are good, you are beautiful; but you are not mine. Good-night, and God bless you!"

Thus I closed my musings. "Good-night" left my lips in sound; I heard the words spoken, and then I heard an echo—quite close.

"Good-night, Mademoiselle; or, rather, good-evening—the sun is scarce set; I hope you slept well?"

I started, but was only discomposed a moment; I knew the voice and speaker.

"Slept, Monsieur! When? where?"

"You may well inquire when—where. It seems you turn day

into night, and choose a desk for a pillow; rather hard lodging —?"

"It was softened for me, Monsieur, while I slept. That unseen, gift-bringing thing which haunts my desk, remembered me. No matter how I fell asleep; I awoke pillowed and covered."

"Did the shawls keep you warm?"

"Very warm. Do you ask thanks for them?"

"No. You looked pale in your slumbers: are you home-sick?"

"To be home-sick, one must have a home; which I have not."

"Then you have more need of a careful friend. I scarcely know any one, Miss Lucy, who needs a friend more absolutely than you; your very faults imperatively require it. You want so much checking, regulating, and keeping down."

This idea of "keeping down" never left M. Paul's head; the most habitual subjugation would, in my case, have failed to relieve him of it. No matter; what did it signify? I listened to him, and did not trouble myself to be too submissive; his occupation would have been gone had I left him nothing to "keep down."

"You need watching, and watching over," he pursued; "and it is well for you that I see this, and do my best to discharge both duties. I watch you and others pretty closely, pretty constantly, nearer and oftener than you or they think. Do you see that window with a light in it?"

He pointed to a lattice in one of the college boarding-houses.

"That," said he, "is a room I have hired, nominally for a study — virtually for a post of observation. There I sit and read for hours together: it is my way — my taste. My book is this garden; its contents are human nature — female human nature. I know you all by heart. Ah! I know you well — St. Pierre, the Parisienne — cette maîtresse-femme, my cousin Beck herself."

"It is not right, Monsieur."

"Comment? it is not right? By whose creed? Does some dogma of Calvin or Luther condemn it? What is that to me? I am no Protestant. My rich father (for, though I have known poverty, and once starved for a year in a garret in Rome—starved wretchedly, often on a meal a day, and sometimes not that—yet I was born to wealth)—my rich father was a good Catholic; and he gave me a priest and a Jesuit for a tutor. I retain his lessons; and to what discoveries, grand Dieu! have they not aided me!"

"Discoveries made by stealth seem to me dishonourable discoveries."

"Puritaine! I doubt it not. Yet see how my Jesuit's system works. You know the St. Pierre?"

"Partially."

He laughed. "You say right—'partially'; whereas I know her thoroughly; there is the difference. She played before me the amiable; offered me patte de velours; caressed, flattered, fawned on me. Now, I am accessible to a woman's flattery—accessible against my reason. Though never pretty, she was—when I first knew her—young, or knew how to look young. Like all her countrywomen, she had the art of dressing—she had a certain cool, easy, social assurance, which spared me the pain of embarrassment—"

"Monsieur, that must have been unnecessary. I never saw you embarrassed in my life."

"Mademoiselle, you know little of me; I can be embarrassed as a petite pensionnaire; there is a fund of modesty and diffidence in my nature—"

"Monsieur, I never saw it."

"Mademoiselle, it is there. You ought to have seen it."

"Monsieur, I have observed you in public—on platforms, in tribunes, before titles and crowned heads—and you were as easy as you are in the third division."

"Mademoiselle, neither titles nor crowned heads excite my modesty; and publicity is very much my element. I like it well, and breathe in it quite freely;—but—but, in short, here is the sentiment brought into action, at this very moment; however, I disdain to be worsted by it. If, Mademoiselle, I were a marrying man (which I am not; and you may spare yourself the trouble of any sneer you may be contemplating at the thought), and found it necessary to ask a lady whether she could look upon me in the light of a future husband, then would it be proved that I am as I say—modest."

I quite believed him now; and, in believing, I honoured him with a sincerity of esteem which made my heart ache.

"As to the St. Pierre," he went on, recovering himself, for his voice had altered a little, "she once intended to be Madame Emanuel; and I don't know whither I might have been led, but for yonder little lattice with the light. Ah, magic lattice! what miracles of discovery hast thou wrought! Yes," he pursued, "I have seen her rancours, her vanities, her levities—not only here, but elsewhere: I have witnessed what bucklers me against all her arts: I am safe from poor Zélie."

"And my pupils," he presently recommenced, "those blondes jeunes filles—so mild and meek—I have seen the most reserved—romp like boys, the demurest—snatch grapes from the walls, shake pears from the trees. When the English teacher came, I saw her, marked her early preference for this alley, noticed her taste for seclusion, watched her well, long before she and I came to speaking terms; do you recollect my once coming silently and offering you a little knot of white violets when we were strangers?"

"I recollect it. I dried the violets, kept them, and have them still."

"It pleased me when you took them peacefully and promptly, without prudery—that sentiment which I ever dread to excite, and which, when it is revealed in eye or gesture, I vindictively detest. To return. Not only did I watch you; but often—especially at eventide—another guardian angel was noiselessly hovering near: night after night my cousin Beck has stolen down yonder steps, and glidingly pursued your movements when you did not see her."

"But, Monsieur, you could not from the distance of that window see what passed in this garden at night?"

"By moonlight I possibly might with a glass—I use a glass—but the garden itself is open to me. In the shed, at the bottom, there is a door leading into a court, which communicates with the college; of that door I possess the key, and thus come and go at pleasure. This afternoon I came through it, and found you asleep in classe; again this evening I have availed myself of the same entrance."

Villette

I could not help saying, "If you were a wicked, designing man, how terrible would all this be!"

His attention seemed incapable of being arrested by this view of the subject: he lit his cigar, and while he puffed it, leaning against a tree, and looking at me in a cool, amused way he had when his humour was tranquil, I thought proper to go on sermonizing him: he often lectured me by the hour together—I did not see why I should not speak my mind for once. So I told him my impressions concerning his Jesuit-system.

"The knowledge it brings you is bought too dear, Monsieur; this coming and going by stealth degrades your own dignity."

"My dignity!" he cried, laughing; "when did you ever see me trouble my head about my dignity? It is you, Miss Lucy, who are 'digne.' How often, in your high insular presence, have I taken a pleasure in trampling upon, what you are pleased to call, my dignity; tearing it, scattering it to the winds, in those mad transports you witness with such hauteur, and which I know you think very like the ravings of a third-rate London actor."

"Monsieur, I tell you every glance you cast from that lattice is a wrong done to the best part of your own nature. To study the human heart thus, is to banquet secretly and sacrilegiously on Eve's apples. I wish you were a Protestant."

Indifferent to the wish, he smoked on. After a space of smiling yet thoughtful silence, he said, rather suddenly—"I have seen other things."

"What other things?"

Taking the weed from his lips, he threw the remnant amongst the shrubs, where, for a moment, it lay glowing in the gloom.

"Look, at it," said he: "is not that spark like an eye watching you and me?"

He took a turn down the walk; presently returning, he went on:—"I have seen, Miss Lucy, things to me unaccountable, that have made me watch all night for a solution, and I have not yet found it."

The tone was peculiar; my veins thrilled; he saw me shiver.

"Are you afraid? Whether is it of my words or that red jealous eye just winking itself out?"

"I am cold; the night grows dark and late, and the air is changed; it is time to go in."

"It is little past eight, but you shall go in soon. Answer me only this question."

Yet he paused ere he put it. The garden was truly growing dark; dusk had come on with clouds, and drops of rain began to patter through the trees. I hoped he would feel this, but, for the moment, he seemed too much absorbed to be sensible of the change.

"Mademoiselle, do you Protestants believe in the supernatural?"

"There is a difference of theory and belief on this point amongst Protestants as amongst other sects," I answered. "Why, Monsieur, do you ask such a question?"

"Why do you shrink and speak so faintly? Are you superstitious?"

"I am constitutionally nervous. I dislike the discussion of such subjects. I dislike it the more because—"

"You believe?"

"No: but it has happened to me to experience impressions—"

"Since you came here?"

"Yes; not many months ago."

"Here?—in this house?"

"Yes."

"Bon! I am glad of it. I knew it, somehow; before you told me. I was conscious of rapport between you and myself. You are patient, and I am choleric; you are quiet and pale, and I am tanned and fiery; you are a strict Protestant, and I am a sort of lay Jesuit: but we are alike—there is affinity between us. Do you see it, Mademoiselle, when you look in the glass? Do you observe that your forehead is shaped like mine—that your eyes

Villette

are cut like mine? Do you hear that you have some of my tones of voice? Do you know that you have many of my looks? I perceive all this, and believe that you were born under my star. Yes, you were born under my star! Tremble! for where that is the case with mortals, the threads of their destinies are difficult to disentangle; knottings and catchings occur—sudden breaks leave damage in the web. But these 'impressions,' as you say, with English caution. I, too, have had my 'impressions.'"

"Monsieur, tell me them."

"I desire no better, and intend no less. You know the legend of this house and garden?"

"I know it. Yes. They say that hundreds of years ago a nun was buried here alive at the foot of this very tree, beneath the ground which now bears us."

"And that in former days a nun's ghost used to come and go here."

"Monsieur, what if it comes and goes here still?"

"Something comes and goes here: there is a shape frequenting this house by night, different to any forms that show themselves by day. I have indisputably seen a something, more than once; and to me its conventual weeds were a strange sight, saying more than they can do to any other living being. A nun!"

"Monsieur, I, too, have seen it."

"I anticipated that. Whether this nun be flesh and blood, or something that remains when blood is dried, and flesh is wasted, her business is as much with you as with me, probably. Well, I mean to make it out; it has baffled me so far, but I mean to follow up the mystery. I mean—"

Instead of telling what he meant, he raised his head suddenly; I made the same movement in the same instant; we both looked to one point—the high tree shadowing the great berceau, and resting some of its boughs on the roof of the first classe. There had been a strange and inexplicable sound from that quarter, as if the arms of that tree had swayed of their own motion, and its weight of foliage had rushed and crushed against the massive trunk. Yes; there scarce stirred a breeze, and that heavy tree was convulsed, whilst the feathery shrubs stood still. For some minutes amongst the wood and leafage a rending and heaving went on. Dark as it was, it seemed to me that something more solid than either night-shadow, or branch-shadow, blackened out of the boles. At last the struggle ceased. What birth succeeded this travail? What Dryad was born of these throes? We watched fixedly. A sudden bell rang in the house—the prayer-bell. Instantly into our alley there came, out of the berceau, an apparition, all black and white. With a sort of angry rush-close, close past our faces—swept swiftly the very NUN herself! Never had I seen her so clearly. She looked tall of stature, and fierce of gesture. As she went, the wind rose sobbing; the rain poured wild and cold; the whole night seemed to feel her.

CHAPTER XXXII.

THE FIRST LETTER.

Where, it becomes time to inquire, was Paulina Mary? How fared my intercourse with the sumptuous Hôtel Crécy? That intercourse had, for an interval, been suspended by absence; M. and Miss de Bassompierre had been travelling, dividing some weeks between the provinces and capital of France. Chance apprised me of their return very shortly after it took place.

I was walking one mild afternoon on a quiet boulevard, wandering slowly on, enjoying the benign April sun, and some thoughts not unpleasing, when I saw before me a group of riders, stopping as if they had just encountered, and exchanging greetings in the midst of the broad, smooth, linden-bordered path; on one side a middle-aged gentleman and young lady, on the other—a young and handsome man. Very graceful was the lady's mien, choice her appointments, delicate and stately her whole aspect. Still, as I looked, I felt they were known to me, and, drawing a little nearer, I fully recognised them all: the Count Home de Bassompierre, his daughter, and Dr. Graham Bretton.

How animated was Graham's face! How true, how warm, yet how retiring the joy it expressed! This was the state of things, this the combination of circumstances, at once to attract and enchain, to subdue and excite Dr. John. The pearl he admired was in itself of great price and truest purity, but he was not the man who, in appreciating the gem, could forget its setting. Had he seen Paulina with the same youth, beauty, and grace, but on foot, alone, unguarded, and in simple attire, a dependent worker, a demi-grisette, he would have thought her a pretty little creature, and would have loved with his eye her movements and her mien, but it required other than this to conquer him as he was now vanquished, to bring him safe under dominion as now, without loss, and even with gain to his manly honour, one saw that he was reduced; there was about Dr. John all the man of the world; to satisfy himself did not suffice; society must approve—the world must admire what he did, or he counted his measures false and futile. In his victrix he required all that was here visible—the imprint of high cultivation, the consecration of a careful and authoritative protection, the adjuncts that Fashion decrees, Wealth purchases, and Taste adjusts; for these conditions his spirit stipulated ere it surrendered: they were here to the utmost fulfilled; and now, proud, impassioned, yet fearing, he did homage to Paulina as his sovereign. As for her, the smile of feeling, rather than of conscious power, slept soft in her eyes.

They parted. He passed me at speed, hardly feeling the earth he skimmed, and seeing nothing on either hand. He looked very handsome; mettle and purpose were roused in him fully.

"Papa, there is Lucy!" cried a musical, friendly voice. "Lucy, dear Lucy—do come here!"

I hastened to her. She threw back her veil, and stooped from her saddle to kiss me.

"I was coming to see you to-morrow," said she; "but now to-morrow you will come and see me."

She named the hour, and I promised compliance.

The morrow's evening found me with her—she and I shut into her own room. I had not seen her since that occasion when her claims were brought into comparison with those of Ginevra Fanshawe, and had so signally prevailed; she had much to tell me of her travels in the interval. A most animated, rapid speaker was she in such a tête-à-tête, a most lively describer; yet with her artless diction and clear soft voice, she never seemed to speak too fast or to say too much. My own attention I think would not soon have flagged, but by-and-by, she herself seemed to need some change of subject; she hastened to wind up her narrative briefly. Yet why she terminated with so concise an abridgment did not immediately appear; silence followed—a restless silence, not without symptoms of abstraction. Then, turning to me, in a diffident, half-appealing voice—"Lucy—"

"Well, I am at your side."

"Is my cousin Ginevra still at Madame Beck's?"

"Your cousin is still there; you must be longing to see her."

"No—not much."

"You want to invite her to spend another evening?"

"No… I suppose she still talks about being married?"

"Not to any one you care for."

"But of course she still thinks of Dr. Bretton? She cannot

Villette

have changed her mind on that point, because it was so fixed two months ago."

"Why, you know, it does not matter. You saw the terms on which they stood."

"There was a little misunderstanding that evening, certainly; does she seem unhappy?"

"Not she. To change the subject. Have you heard or seen nothing of, or from, Graham during your absence?"

"Papa had letters from him once or twice about business, I think. He undertook the management of some affair which required attention while we were away. Dr. Bretton seems to respect papa, and to have pleasure in obliging him."

"Yes: you met him yesterday on the boulevard; you would be able to judge from his aspect that his friends need not be painfully anxious about his health?"

"Papa seems to have thought with you. I could not help smiling. He is not particularly observant, you know, because he is often thinking of other things than what pass before his eyes; but he said, as Dr. Bretton rode away, 'Really it does a man good to see the spirit and energy of that boy.' He called Dr. Bretton a boy; I believe he almost thinks him so, just as he thinks me a little girl; he was not speaking to me, but dropped that remark to himself. Lucy...."

Again fell the appealing accent, and at the same instant she left her chair, and came and sat on the stool at my feet.

I liked her. It is not a declaration I have often made concerning my acquaintance, in the course of this book: the reader will bear with it for once. Intimate intercourse, close inspection, disclosed in Paulina only what was delicate, intelligent, and sincere; therefore my regard for her lay deep. An admiration more superficial might have been more demonstrative; mine, however, was quiet.

"What have you to ask of Lucy?" said I; "be brave, and speak out."

But there was no courage in her eye; as it met mine, it fell; and there was no coolness on her cheek — not a transient surface-blush, but a gathering inward excitement raised its tint and its temperature.

"Lucy, I do wish to know your thoughts of Dr. Bretton. Do, do give me your real opinion of his character, his disposition."

"His character stands high, and deservedly high."

"And his disposition? Tell me about his disposition," she urged; "you know him well."

"I know him pretty well."

"You know his home-side. You have seen him with his mother; speak of him as a son."

"He is a fine-hearted son; his mother's comfort and hope, her pride and pleasure."

She held my hand between hers, and at each favourable word gave it a little caressing stroke.

"In what other way is he good, Lucy?"

"Dr. Bretton is benevolent—humanely disposed towards all his race, Dr. Bretton would have benignity for the lowest savage, or the worst criminal."

"I heard some gentlemen, some of papa's friends, who were talking about him, say the same. They say many of the poor patients at the hospitals, who tremble before some pitiless and selfish surgeons, welcome him."

"They are right; I have witnessed as much. He once took me over a hospital; I saw how he was received: your father's friends are right."

The softest gratitude animated her eye as she lifted it a moment. She had yet more to say, but seemed hesitating about time and place. Dusk was beginning to reign; her parlour fire already glowed with twilight ruddiness; but I thought she wished the room dimmer, the hour later.

"How quiet and secluded we feel here!" I remarked, to reassure her.

"Do we? Yes; it is a still evening, and I shall not be called down to tea; papa is dining out."

Still holding my hand, she played with the fingers unconsciously, dressed them, now in her own rings, and now

Villette

circled them with a twine of her beautiful hair; she patted the palm against her hot cheek, and at last, having cleared a voice that was naturally liquid as a lark's, she said:—

"You must think it rather strange that I should talk so much about Dr. Bretton, ask so many questions, take such an interest, but—".

"Not at all strange; perfectly natural; you like him."

"And if I did," said she, with slight quickness, "is that a reason why I should talk? I suppose you think me weak, like my cousin Ginevra?"

"If I thought you one whit like Madame Ginevra, I would not sit here waiting for your communications. I would get up, walk at my ease about the room, and anticipate all you had to say by a round lecture. Go on."

"I mean to go on," retorted she; "what else do you suppose I mean to do?"

And she looked and spoke—the little Polly of Bretton—petulant, sensitive.

"If," said she, emphatically, "if I liked Dr. John till I was fit to die for liking him, that alone could not license me to be otherwise than dumb—dumb as the grave—dumb as you, Lucy Snowe—you know it—and you know you would despise me if I failed in self-control, and whined about some rickety liking that was all on my side."

"It is true I little respect women or girls who are loquacious either in boasting the triumphs, or bemoaning the mortifications, of feelings. But as to you, Paulina, speak, for I earnestly wish to hear you. Tell me all it will give you pleasure or relief to tell: I ask no more."

"Do you care for me, Lucy?"

"Yes, I do, Paulina."

"And I love you. I had an odd content in being with you even when I was a little, troublesome, disobedient girl; it was charming to me then to lavish on you my naughtiness and whims. Now you are acceptable to me, and I like to talk with and trust you. So listen, Lucy."

And she settled herself, resting against my arm—resting gently, not with honest Mistress Fanshawe's fatiguing and selfish weight.

"A few minutes since you asked whether we had not heard from Graham during our absence, and I said there were two letters for papa on business; this was true, but I did not tell you all."

"You evaded?"

"I shuffled and equivocated, you know. However, I am going to speak the truth now; it is getting darker; one can talk at one's ease. Papa often lets me open the letter-bag and give him out the contents. One morning, about three weeks ago, you don't know how surprised I was to find, amongst a dozen letters for M. de Bassompierre, a note addressed to Miss de Bassompierre. I spied it at once, amidst all the rest; the handwriting was not strange; it attracted me directly. I was going to say, 'Papa, here is another letter from Dr. Bretton;' but the 'Miss' struck me mute. I actually never received a letter from a gentleman before. Ought I to have shown it to papa, and let him open it and read it first? I could not for my life, Lucy. I know so well papa's ideas about me: he forgets my age; he thinks I am a mere school-girl; he is not aware that other people see I am grown up as tall as I shall be; so, with a curious mixture of feelings, some of them self-reproachful, and some so fluttering and strong, I cannot describe them, I gave papa his twelve letters—his herd of possessions—and kept back my one, my ewe-lamb. It lay in my lap during breakfast, looking up at me with an inexplicable meaning, making me feel myself a thing double-existent—a child to that dear papa, but no more a child to myself. After breakfast I carried my letter up-stairs, and having secured myself by turning the key in the door, I began to study the outside of my treasure: it was some minutes before I could get over the direction and penetrate the seal; one does not take a strong place of this kind by instant storm—one sits down awhile before it, as beleaguers say. Graham's hand is like himself, Lucy, and so is his seal—all clear, firm, and rounded—no slovenly splash of wax—a full, solid, steady drop—a distinct impress; no pointed turns harshly pricking the optic nerve, but a clean, mellow, pleasant manuscript, that soothes you as you read. It is like his face—just like the chiselling of his features: do you know his autograph?"

"I have seen it: go on."

"The seal was too beautiful to be broken, so I cut it round

Villette

with my scissors. On the point of reading the letter at last, I once more drew back voluntarily; it was too soon yet to drink that draught—the sparkle in the cup was so beautiful—I would watch it yet a minute. Then I remembered all at once that I had not said my prayers that morning. Having heard papa go down to breakfast a little earlier than usual, I had been afraid of keeping him waiting, and had hastened to join him as soon as dressed, thinking no harm to put off prayers till afterwards. Some people would say I ought to have served God first and then man; but I don't think heaven could be jealous of anything I might do for papa. I believe I am superstitious. A voice seemed now to say that another feeling than filial affection was in question—to urge me to pray before I dared to read what I so longed to read—to deny myself yet a moment, and remember first a great duty. I have had these impulses ever since I can remember. I put the letter down and said my prayers, adding, at the end, a strong entreaty that whatever happened, I might not be tempted or led to cause papa any sorrow, and might never, in caring for others, neglect him. The very thought of such a possibility, so pierced my heart that it made me cry. But still, Lucy, I felt that in time papa would have to be taught the truth, managed, and induced to hear reason.

"I read the letter. Lucy, life is said to be all disappointment. I was not disappointed. Ere I read, and while I read, my heart did more than throb—it trembled fast—every quiver seemed like the pant of an animal athirst, laid down at a well and drinking; and the well proved quite full, gloriously clear; it rose up munificently of its own impulse; I saw the sun through its gush, and not a mote, Lucy, no moss, no insect, no atom in the thrice-refined golden gurgle.

"Life," she went on, "is said to be full of pain to some. I have read biographies where the wayfarer seemed to journey on from suffering to suffering; where Hope flew before him fast, never alighting so near, or lingering so long, as to give his hand a chance of one realizing grasp. I have read of those who sowed in tears, and whose harvest, so far from being reaped in joy, perished by untimely blight, or was borne off by sudden whirlwind; and, alas! some of these met the winter with empty garners, and died of utter want in the darkest and coldest of the year."

"Was it their fault, Paulina, that they of whom you speak thus died?"

"Not always their fault. Some of them were good endeavouring people. I am not endeavouring, nor actively good, yet God has caused me to grow in sun, due moisture, and safe protection, sheltered, fostered, taught, by my dear father; and now — now — another comes. Graham loves me."

For some minutes we both paused on this climax.

"Does your father know?" I inquired, in a low voice.

"Graham spoke with deep respect of papa, but implied that he dared not approach that quarter as yet; he must first prove his worth: he added that he must have some light respecting myself and my own feelings ere he ventured to risk a step in the matter elsewhere."

"How did you reply?"

"I replied briefly, but I did not repulse him. Yet I almost trembled for fear of making the answer too cordial: Graham's tastes are so fastidious. I wrote it three times — chastening and subduing the phrases at every rescript; at last, having confected it till it seemed to me to resemble a morsel of ice flavoured with ever so slight a zest of fruit or sugar, I ventured to seal and despatch it."

"Excellent, Paulina! Your instinct is fine; you understand Dr. Bretton."

"But how must I manage about papa? There I am still in pain."

"Do not manage at all. Wait now. Only maintain no further correspondence till your father knows all, and gives his sanction."

"Will he ever give it?"

"Time will show. Wait."

"Dr. Bretton wrote one other letter, deeply grateful for my calm, brief note; but I anticipated your advice, by saying, that while my sentiments continued the same, I could not, without my father's knowledge, write again."

"You acted as you ought to have done; so Dr. Bretton will feel: it will increase his pride in you, his love for you, if either be capable of increase. Paulina, that gentle hoar-frost of yours, surrounding so much pure, fine flame, is a priceless privilege of nature."

"You see I feel Graham's disposition," said she. "I feel that no delicacy can be too exquisite for his treatment."

"It is perfectly proved that you comprehend him, and then — whatever Dr. Bretton's disposition, were he one who expected to be more nearly met — you would still act truthfully, openly, tenderly, with your father."

"Lucy, I trust I shall thus act always. Oh, it will be pain to wake papa from his dream, and tell him I am no more a little girl!"

"Be in no hurry to do so, Paulina. Leave the revelation to Time and your kind Fate. I also have noticed the gentleness of her cares for you: doubt not she will benignantly order the circumstances, and fitly appoint the hour. Yes: I have thought over your life just as you have yourself thought it over; I have made comparisons like those to which you adverted. We know not the future, but the past has been propitious.

"As a child I feared for you; nothing that has life was ever more susceptible than your nature in infancy: under harshness or neglect, neither your outward nor your inward self would have ripened to what they now are. Much pain, much fear, much struggle, would have troubled the very lines of your features, broken their regularity, would have harassed your nerves into the fever of habitual irritation; you would have lost in health and cheerfulness, in grace and sweetness. Providence has protected and cultured you, not only for your own sake, but I believe for Graham's. His star, too, was fortunate: to develop fully the best of his nature, a companion like you was needed: there you are, ready. You must be united. I knew it the first day I saw you together at La Terrasse. In all that mutually concerns you and Graham there seems to me promise, plan, harmony. I do not think the sunny youth of either will prove the forerunner of stormy age. I think it is deemed good that you two should live in peace and be happy — not as angels, but as few are happy amongst mortals. Some lives are thus blessed: it is God's will: it is the attesting trace and lingering evidence of Eden. Other lives run from the first another course. Other travellers encounter weather fitful and gusty, wild and variable — breast adverse winds, are belated and overtaken by the early closing winter night. Neither can this happen without the sanction of God; and I know that, amidst His boundless works, is somewhere stored the secret of this last fate's justice: I know that His treasures contain the proof as the promise of its mercy."

CHAPTER XXXIII.
M. PAUL KEEPS HIS PROMISE.

On the first of May, we had all—i.e. the twenty boarders and the four teachers—notice to rise at five o'clock of the morning, to be dressed and ready by six, to put ourselves under the command of M. le Professeur Emanuel, who was to head our march forth from Villette, for it was on this day he proposed to fulfil his promise of taking us to breakfast in the country. I, indeed, as the reader may perhaps remember, had not had the honour of an invitation when this excursion was first projected—rather the contrary; but on my now making allusion to this fact, and wishing to know how it was to be, my ear received a pull, of which I did not venture to challenge the repetition by raising, further difficulties.

"Je vous conseille de vous faire prier," said M. Emanuel, imperially menacing the other ear. One Napoleonic compliment, however, was enough, so I made up my mind to be of the party.

The morning broke calm as summer, with singing of birds in the garden, and a light dew-mist that promised heat. We all said it would be warm, and we all felt pleasure in folding away heavy garments, and in assuming the attire suiting a sunny season. The clean fresh print dress, and the light straw bonnet, each made and trimmed as the French workwoman alone can make and trim, so as to unite the utterly unpretending with the perfectly becoming, was the rule of costume. Nobody flaunted in faded silk; nobody wore a second-hand best article.

At six the bell rang merrily, and we poured down the staircase, through the carré, along the corridor, into the vestibule. There stood our Professor, wearing, not his savage-looking paletôt and severe bonnet-grec, but a young-looking belted blouse and cheerful straw hat. He had for us all the kindest good-morrow, and most of us for him had a thanksgiving smile. We were marshalled in order and soon started.

The streets were yet quiet, and the boulevards were fresh and peaceful as fields. I believe we were very happy as we walked along. This chief of ours had the secret of giving a certain impetus to happiness when he would; just as, in an opposite mood, he could give a thrill to fear.

Villette

He did not lead nor follow us, but walked along the line, giving a word to every one, talking much to his favourites, and not wholly neglecting even those he disliked. It was rather my wish, for a reason I had, to keep slightly aloof from notice, and being paired with Ginevra Fanshawe, bearing on my arm the dear pressure of that angel's not unsubstantial limb—(she continued in excellent case, and I can assure the reader it was no trifling business to bear the burden of her loveliness; many a time in the course of that warm day I wished to goodness there had been less of the charming commodity)—however, having her, as I said, I tried to make her useful by interposing her always between myself and M. Paul, shifting my place, according as I heard him coming up to the right hand or the left. My private motive for this manœuvre might be traced to the circumstance of the new print dress I wore, being pink in colour—a fact which, under our present convoy, made me feel something as I have felt, when, clad in a shawl with a red border, necessitated to traverse a meadow where pastured a bull.

For awhile, the shifting system, together with some modifications in the arrangement of a black silk scarf, answered my purpose; but, by-and-by, he found out, that whether he came to this side or to that, Miss Fanshawe was still his neighbour. The course of acquaintance between Ginevra and him had never run so smooth that his temper did not undergo a certain crisping process whenever he heard her English accent: nothing in their dispositions fitted; they jarred if they came in contact; he held her empty and affected; she deemed him bearish, meddling, repellent.

At last, when he had changed his place for about the sixth time, finding still the same untoward result to the experiment—he thrust his head forward, settled his eyes on mine, and demanded with impatience, "Qu'est-ce que c'est? Vous me jouez des tours?"

The words were hardly out of his mouth, however, ere, with his customary quickness, he seized the root of this proceeding: in vain I shook out the long fringe, and spread forth the broad end of my scarf. "A-h-h! c'est la robe rose!" broke from his lips, affecting me very much like the sudden and irate low of some lord of the meadow.

"It is only cotton," I alleged, hurriedly; "and cheaper, and washes better than any other colour."

"Et Mademoiselle Lucy est coquette comme dix

Parisiennes," he answered. "A-t-on jamais vu une Anglaise pareille. Regardez plutôt son chapeau, et ses gants, et ses brodequins!" These articles of dress were just like what my companions wore; certainly not one whit smarter—perhaps rather plainer than most—but Monsieur had now got hold of his text, and I began to chafe under the expected sermon. It went off, however, as mildly as the menace of a storm sometimes passes on a summer day. I got but one flash of sheet lightning in the shape of a single bantering smile from his eyes; and then he said, "Courage!—à vrai dire je ne suis pas fâché, peut-être même suis je content qu'on s'est fait si belle pour ma petite fête."

"Mais ma robe n'est pas belle, Monsieur—elle n'est que propre."

"J'aime la propreté," said he. In short, he was not to be dissatisfied; the sun of good humour was to triumph on this auspicious morning; it consumed scudding clouds ere they sullied its disk.

And now we were in the country, amongst what they called "les bois et les petits sentiers." These woods and lanes a month later would offer but a dusty and doubtful seclusion: now, however, in their May greenness and morning repose, they looked very pleasant.

We reached a certain well, planted round, in the taste of Labassecour, with an orderly circle of lime-trees: here a halt was called; on the green swell of ground surrounding this well, we were ordered to be seated, Monsieur taking his place in our midst, and suffering us to gather in a knot round him. Those who liked him more than they feared, came close, and these were chiefly little ones; those who feared more than they liked, kept somewhat aloof; those in whom much affection had given, even to what remained of fear, a pleasurable zest, observed the greatest distance.

He began to tell us a story. Well could he narrate: in such a diction as children love, and learned men emulate; a diction simple in its strength, and strong in its simplicity. There were beautiful touches in that little tale; sweet glimpses of feeling and hues of description that, while I listened, sunk into my mind, and since have never faded. He tinted a twilight scene—I hold it in memory still—such a picture I have never looked on from artist's pencil.

I have said, that, for myself, I had no impromptu faculty;

Villette

and perhaps that very deficiency made me marvel the more at one who possessed it in perfection. M. Emanuel was not a man to write books; but I have heard him lavish, with careless, unconscious prodigality, such mental wealth as books seldom boast; his mind was indeed my library, and whenever it was opened to me, I entered bliss. Intellectually imperfect as I was, I could read little; there were few bound and printed volumes that did not weary me—whose perusal did not fag and blind—but his tomes of thought were collyrium to the spirit's eyes; over their contents, inward sight grew clear and strong. I used to think what a delight it would be for one who loved him better than he loved himself, to gather and store up those handfuls of gold-dust, so recklessly flung to heaven's reckless winds.

His story done, he approached the little knoll where I and Ginevra sat apart. In his usual mode of demanding an opinion (he had not reticence to wait till it was voluntarily offered) he asked, "Were you interested?"

According to my wonted undemonstrative fashion, I simply answered—"Yes."

"Was it good?"

"Very good."

"Yet I could not write that down," said he.

"Why not, Monsieur?"

"I hate the mechanical labour; I hate to stoop and sit still. I could dictate it, though, with pleasure, to an amanuensis who suited me. Would Mademoiselle Lucy write for me if I asked her?"

"Monsieur would be too quick; he would urge me, and be angry if my pen did not keep pace with his lips."

"Try some day; let us see the monster I can make of myself under the circumstances. But just now, there is no question of dictation; I mean to make you useful in another office. Do you see yonder farm-house?"

"Surrounded with trees? Yes."

"There we are to breakfast; and while the good fermière makes the café au lait in a caldron, you and five others, whom I shall select, will spread with butter half a hundred rolls."

Having formed his troop into line once more, he marched us straight on the farm, which, on seeing our force, surrendered without capitulation.

Clean knives and plates, and fresh butter being provided, half-a-dozen of us, chosen by our Professor, set to work under his directions, to prepare for breakfast a huge basket of rolls, with which the baker had been ordered to provision the farm, in anticipation of our coming. Coffee and chocolate were already made hot; cream and new-laid eggs were added to the treat, and M. Emanuel, always generous, would have given a large order for "jambon" and "confitures" in addition, but that some of us, who presumed perhaps upon our influence, insisted that it would be a most reckless waste of victual. He railed at us for our pains, terming us "des ménagères avares;" but we let him talk, and managed the economy of the repast our own way.

With what a pleasant countenance he stood on the farm-kitchen hearth looking on! He was a man whom it made happy to see others happy; he liked to have movement, animation, abundance and enjoyment round him. We asked where he would sit. He told us, we knew well he was our slave, and we his tyrants, and that he dared not so much as choose a chair without our leave; so we set him the farmer's great chair at the head of the long table, and put him into it.

Well might we like him, with all his passions and hurricanes, when he could be so benignant and docile at times, as he was just now. Indeed, at the worst, it was only his nerves that were irritable, not his temper that was radically bad; soothe, comprehend, comfort him, and he was a lamb; he would not harm a fly. Only to the very stupid, perverse, or unsympathizing, was he in the slightest degree dangerous.

Mindful always of his religion, he made the youngest of the party say a little prayer before we began breakfast, crossing himself as devotedly as a woman. I had never seen him pray before, or make that pious sign; he did it so simply, with such child-like faith, I could not help smiling pleasurably as I watched; his eyes met my smile; he just stretched out his kind hand, saying, "Donnez-moi la main! I see we worship the same God, in the same spirit, though by different rites."

Most of M. Emanuel's brother Professors were emancipated free-thinkers, infidels, atheists; and many of them men whose lives would not bear scrutiny; he was more like a knight of old, religious in his way, and of spotless fame. Innocent childhood, beautiful youth were safe at his side. He had vivid passions, keen feelings, but his pure honour and his artless piety were the strong charm that kept the lions couchant.

That breakfast was a merry meal, and the merriment was not mere vacant clatter: M. Paul originated, led, controlled and heightened it; his social, lively temper played unfettered and unclouded; surrounded only by women and children there was nothing to cross and thwart him; he had his own way, and a pleasant way it was.

The meal over, the party were free to run and play in the meadows; a few stayed to help the farmer's wife to put away her earthenware. M. Paul called me from among these to come out and sit near him under a tree—whence he could view the troop gambolling, over a wide pasture—and read to him whilst he took his cigar. He sat on a rustic bench, and I at the tree-root. While I read (a pocket-classic—a Corneille—I did not like it, but he did, finding therein beauties I never could be brought to perceive), he listened with a sweetness of calm the more impressive from the impetuosity of his general nature; the deepest happiness filled his blue eye and smoothed his broad forehead. I, too, was happy—happy with the bright day, happier with his presence, happiest with his kindness.

He asked, by-and-by, if I would not rather run to my companions than sit there? I said, no; I felt content to be where he was. He asked whether, if I were his sister, I should always be content to stay with a brother such as he. I said, I believed I should; and I felt it. Again, he inquired whether, if he were to leave Villette, and go far away, I should be sorry; and I dropped Corneille, and made no reply.

"Petite sœur," said he; "how long could you remember me if we were separated?"

"That, Monsieur, I can never tell, because I do not know how long it will be before I shall cease to remember everything earthly."

"If I were to go beyond seas for two—three—five years, should you welcome me on my return?"

"Monsieur, how could I live in the interval?"

"Pourtant j'ai été pour vous bien dur, bien exigeant."

I hid my face with the book, for it was covered with tears. I asked him why he talked so; and he said he would talk so no more, and cheered me again with the kindest encouragement. Still, the gentleness with which he treated me during the rest of the day, went somehow to my heart. It was too tender. It was mournful. I would rather he had been abrupt, whimsical, and irate as was his wont.

When hot noon arrived — for the day turned out as we had anticipated, glowing as June — our shepherd collected his sheep from the pasture, and proceeded to lead us all softly home. But we had a whole league to walk, thus far from Villette was the farm where he had breakfasted; the children, especially, were tired with their play; the spirits of most flagged at the prospect of this mid-day walk over chaussées flinty, glaring, and dusty. This state of things had been foreseen and provided for. Just beyond the boundary of the farm we met two spacious vehicles coming to fetch us — such conveyances as are hired out purposely for the accommodation of school-parties; here, with good management, room was found for all, and in another hour M. Paul made safe consignment of his charge at the Rue Fossette. It had been a pleasant day: it would have been perfect, but for the breathing of melancholy which had dimmed its sunshine a moment.

That tarnish was renewed the same evening.

Just about sunset, I saw M. Emanuel come out of the front-door, accompanied by Madame Beck. They paced the centre-alley for nearly an hour, talking earnestly: he — looking grave, yet restless; she — wearing an amazed, expostulatory, dissuasive air.

I wondered what was under discussion; and when Madame Beck re-entered the house as it darkened, leaving her kinsman Paul yet lingering in the garden, I said to myself — "He called me 'petite sœur' this morning. If he were really my brother, how I should like to go to him just now, and ask what it is that presses on his mind. See how he leans against that tree, with his arms crossed and his brow bent. He wants consolation, I know: Madame does not console: she only remonstrates. What now — —?"

Starting from quiescence to action, M. Paul came striding erect and quick down the garden. The carré doors were yet open: I thought he was probably going to water the orange-trees in the tubs, after his occasional custom; on reaching the court, however, he took an abrupt turn and made for the berceau and the first-classe glass door. There, in that first classe I was, thence I had been watching him; but there I could not find courage to await his approach. He had turned so suddenly, he strode so fast, he looked so strange; the coward within me grew pale, shrank and—not waiting to listen to reason, and hearing the shrubs crush and the gravel crunch to his advance—she was gone on the wings of panic.

Nor did I pause till I had taken sanctuary in the oratory, now empty. Listening there with beating pulses, and an unaccountable, undefined apprehension, I heard him pass through all the schoolrooms, clashing the doors impatiently as he went; I heard him invade the refectory which the "lecture pieuse" was now holding under hallowed constraint; I heard him pronounce these words—"Où est Mademoiselle Lucie?"

And just as, summoning my courage, I was preparing to go down and do what, after all, I most wished to do in the world— viz., meet him—the wiry voice of St. Pierre replied glibly and falsely, "Elle est au lit." And he passed, with the stamp of vexation, into the corridor. There Madame Beck met, captured, chid, convoyed to the street-door, and finally dismissed him.

As that street-door closed, a sudden amazement at my own perverse proceeding struck like a blow upon me. I felt from the first it was me he wanted—me he was seeking—and had not I wanted him too? What, then, had carried me away? What had rapt me beyond his reach? He had something to tell: he was going to tell me that something: my ear strained its nerve to hear it, and I had made the confidence impossible. Yearning to listen and console, while I thought audience and solace beyond hope's reach—no sooner did opportunity suddenly and fully arrive, than I evaded it as I would have evaded the levelled shaft of mortality.

Well, my insane inconsistency had its reward. Instead of the comfort, the certain satisfaction, I might have won—could I but have put choking panic down, and stood firm two minutes— here was dead blank, dark doubt, and drear suspense.

I took my wages to my pillow, and passed the night counting them.

CHAPTER XXXIV.

MALEVOLA.

Madame Beck called me on Thursday afternoon, and asked whether I had any occupation to hinder me from going into town and executing some little commissions for her at the shops.

Being disengaged, and placing myself at her service, I was presently furnished with a list of the wools, silks, embroidering thread, etcetera, wanted in the pupils' work, and having equipped myself in a manner suiting the threatening aspect of a cloudy and sultry day, I was just drawing the spring-bolt of the street-door, in act to issue forth, when Madame's voice again summoned me to the salle-à-manger.

"Pardon, Meess Lucie!" cried she, in the seeming haste of an impromptu thought, "I have just recollected one more errand for you, if your good-nature will not deem itself over-burdened?"

Of course I "confounded myself" in asseverations to the contrary; and Madame, running into the little salon, brought thence a pretty basket, filled with fine hothouse fruit, rosy, perfect, and tempting, reposing amongst the dark green, wax-like leaves, and pale yellow stars of, I know not what, exotic plant.

"There," she said, "it is not heavy, and will not shame your neat toilette, as if it were a household, servant-like detail. Do me the favour to leave this little basket at the house of Madame Walravens, with my felicitations on her fête. She lives down in the old town, Numéro 3, Rue des Mages. I fear you will find the walk rather long, but you have the whole afternoon before you, and do not hurry; if you are not back in time for dinner, I will order a portion to be saved, or Goton, with whom you are a favourite, will have pleasure in tossing up some trifle, for your especial benefit. You shall not be forgotten, ma bonne Meess. And oh! please!" (calling me back once more) "be sure to insist on seeing Madame Walravens herself, and giving the basket into her own hands, in order that there may be no mistake, for she is rather a punctilious personage. Adieu! Au revoir!"

And at last I got away. The shop commissions took some time to execute, that choosing and matching of silks and wools being always a tedious business, but at last I got through my

Villette

list. The patterns for the slippers, the bell-ropes, the cabas were selected — the slides and tassels for the purses chosen — the whole "tripotage," in short, was off my mind; nothing but the fruit and the felicitations remained to be attended to.

I rather liked the prospect of a long walk, deep into the old and grim Basse-Ville; and I liked it no worse because the evening sky, over the city, was settling into a mass of black-blue metal, heated at the rim, and inflaming slowly to a heavy red.

I fear a high wind, because storm demands that exertion of strength and use of action I always yield with pain; but the sullen down-fall, the thick snow-descent, or dark rush of rain, ask only resignation — the quiet abandonment of garments and person to be drenched. In return, it sweeps a great capital clean before you; it makes you a quiet path through broad, grand streets; it petrifies a living city as if by eastern enchantment; it transforms a Villette into a Tadmor. Let, then, the rains fall, and the floods descend — only I must first get rid of this basket of fruit.

An unknown clock from an unknown tower (Jean Baptiste's voice was now too distant to be audible) was tolling the third quarter past five, when I reached that street and house whereof Madame Beck had given me the address. It was no street at all; it seemed rather to be part of a square: it was quiet, grass grew between the broad grey flags, the houses were large and looked very old — behind them rose the appearance of trees, indicating gardens at the back. Antiquity brooded above this region, business was banished thence. Rich men had once possessed this quarter, and once grandeur had made her seat here. That church, whose dark, half-ruinous turrets overlooked the square, was the venerable and formerly opulent shrine of the Magi. But wealth and greatness had long since stretched their gilded pinions and fled hence, leaving these their ancient nests, perhaps to house Penury for a time, or perhaps to stand cold and empty, mouldering untenanted in the course of winters.

As I crossed this deserted "place," on whose pavement drops almost as large as a five-franc piece were now slowly darkening, I saw, in its whole expanse, no symptom or evidence of life, except what was given in the figure of an infirm old priest, who went past, bending and propped on a staff — the type of eld and decay.

He had issued from the very house to which I was directed; and when I paused before the door just closed after him, and rang the bell, he turned to look at me. Nor did he soon avert his gaze; perhaps he thought me, with my basket of summer fruit, and my lack of the dignity age confers, an incongruous figure in such a scene. I know, had a young ruddy-faced bonne opened the door to admit me, I should have thought such a one little in harmony with her dwelling; but, when I found myself confronted by a very old woman, wearing a very antique peasant costume, a cap alike hideous and costly, with long flaps of native lace, a petticoat and jacket of cloth, and sabots more like little boats than shoes, it seemed all right, and soothingly in character.

The expression of her face was not quite so soothing as the cut of her costume; anything more cantankerous I have seldom seen; she would scarcely reply to my inquiry after Madame Walravens; I believe she would have snatched the basket of fruit from my hand, had not the old priest, hobbling up, checked her, and himself lent an ear to the message with which I was charged.

His apparent deafness rendered it a little difficult to make him fully understand that I must see Madame Walravens, and consign the fruit into her own hands. At last, however, he comprehended the fact that such were my orders, and that duty enjoined their literal fulfilment. Addressing the aged bonne, not in French, but in the aboriginal tongue of Labassecour, he persuaded her, at last, to let me cross the inhospitable threshold, and himself escorting me up-stairs, I was ushered into a sort of salon, and there left.

The room was large, and had a fine old ceiling, and almost church-like windows of coloured-glass; but it was desolate, and in the shadow of a coming storm, looked strangely lowering. Within—opened a smaller room; there, however, the blind of the single casement was closed; through the deep gloom few details of furniture were apparent. These few I amused myself by puzzling to make out; and, in particular, I was attracted by the outline of a picture on the wall.

By-and-by the picture seemed to give way: to my bewilderment, it shook, it sunk, it rolled back into nothing; its vanishing left an opening arched, leading into an arched passage, with a mystic winding stair; both passage and stair were of cold stone, uncarpeted and unpainted. Down this donjon stair descended a tap, tap, like a stick; soon there fell on the steps a shadow, and last of all, I was aware of a substance.

Yet, was it actual substance, this appearance approaching me? this obstruction, partially darkening the arch?

Villette

It drew near, and I saw it well. I began to comprehend where I was. Well might this old square be named quarter of the Magi—well might the three towers, overlooking it, own for godfathers three mystic sages of a dead and dark art. Hoar enchantment here prevailed; a spell had opened for me elf-land—that cell-like room, that vanishing picture, that arch and passage, and stair of stone, were all parts of a fairy tale. Distincter even than these scenic details stood the chief figure—Cunegonde, the sorceress! Malevola, the evil fairy. How was she?

She might be three feet high, but she had no shape; her skinny hands rested upon each other, and pressed the gold knob of a wand-like ivory staff. Her face was large, set, not upon her shoulders, but before her breast; she seemed to have no neck; I should have said there were a hundred years in her features, and more perhaps in her eyes—her malign, unfriendly eyes, with thick grey brows above, and livid lids all round. How severely they viewed me, with a sort of dull displeasure!

This being wore a gown of brocade, dyed bright blue, full-tinted as the gentianella flower, and covered with satin foliage in a large pattern; over the gown a costly shawl, gorgeously bordered, and so large for her, that its many-coloured fringe swept the floor. But her chief points were her jewels: she had long, clear earrings, blazing with a lustre which could not be borrowed or false; she had rings on her skeleton hands, with thick gold hoops, and stones—purple, green, and blood-red. Hunchbacked, dwarfish, and doting, she was adorned like a barbarian queen.

"Que me voulez-vous?" said she, hoarsely, with the voice rather of male than of female old age; and, indeed, a silver beard bristled her chin.

I delivered my basket and my message.

"Is that all?" she demanded.

"It is all," said I.

"Truly, it was well worth while," she answered. "Return to Madame Beck, and tell her I can buy fruit when I want it, et quant à ses félicitations, je m'en moque!" And this courteous dame turned her back.

Just as she turned, a peal of thunder broke, and a flash of lightning blazed broad over salon and boudoir. The tale of magic seemed to proceed with due accompaniment of the elements. The wanderer, decoyed into the enchanted castle, heard rising, outside, the spell-wakened tempest.

What, in all this, was I to think of Madame Beck? She owned strange acquaintance; she offered messages and gifts at an unique shrine, and inauspicious seemed the bearing of the uncouth thing she worshipped. There went that sullen Sidonia, tottering and trembling like palsy incarnate, tapping her ivory staff on the mosaic parquet, and muttering venomously as she vanished.

Down washed the rain, deep lowered the welkin; the clouds, ruddy a while ago, had now, through all their blackness, turned deadly pale, as if in terror. Notwithstanding my late boast about not fearing a shower, I hardly liked to go out under this waterspout. Then the gleams of lightning were very fierce, the thunder crashed very near; this storm had gathered immediately above Villette; it seemed to have burst at the zenith; it rushed down prone; the forked, slant bolts pierced athwart vertical torrents; red zigzags interlaced a descent blanched as white metal: and all broke from a sky heavily black in its swollen abundance.

Leaving Madame Walravens' inhospitable salon, I betook myself to her cold staircase; there was a seat on the landing — there I waited. Somebody came gliding along the gallery just above; it was the old priest.

"Indeed Mademoiselle shall not sit there," said he. "It would displeasure our benefactor if he knew a stranger was so treated in this house."

And he begged me so earnestly to return to the salon, that, without discourtesy, I could not but comply. The smaller room was better furnished and more habitable than the larger; thither he introduced me. Partially withdrawing the blind, he disclosed what seemed more like an oratory than a boudoir, a very solemn little chamber, looking as if it were a place rather dedicated to relics and remembrance, than designed for present use and comfort.

The good father sat down, as if to keep me company; but instead of conversing, he took out a book, fastened on the page his eyes, and employed his lips in whispering — what sounded like a prayer or litany. A yellow electric light from the sky gilded his bald head; his figure remained in shade — deep and purple; he sat still as sculpture; he seemed to forget me for his

Villette

prayers; he only looked up when a fiercer bolt, or a harsher, closer rattle told of nearing danger; even then, it was not in fear, but in seeming awe, he raised his eyes. I too was awe-struck; being, however, under no pressure of slavish terror, my thoughts and observations were free.

To speak truth, I was beginning to fancy that the old priest resembled that Père Silas, before whom I had knelt in the church of the Béguinage. The idea was vague, for I had seen my confessor only in dusk and in profile, yet still I seemed to trace a likeness: I thought also I recognized the voice. While I watched him, he betrayed, by one lifted look, that he felt my scrutiny; I turned to note the room; that too had its half mystic interest.

Beside a cross of curiously carved old ivory, yellow with time, and sloped above a dark-red prie-dieu, furnished duly, with rich missal and ebon rosary — hung the picture whose dim outline had drawn my eyes before — the picture which moved, fell away with the wall and let in phantoms. Imperfectly seen, I had taken it for a Madonna; revealed by clearer light, it proved to be a woman's portrait in a nun's dress. The face, though not beautiful, was pleasing; pale, young, and shaded with the dejection of grief or ill health. I say again it was not beautiful; it was not even intellectual; its very amiability was the amiability of a weak frame, inactive passions, acquiescent habits: yet I looked long at that picture, and could not choose but look.

The old priest, who at first had seemed to me so deaf and infirm, must yet have retained his faculties in tolerable preservation; absorbed in his book as he appeared, without once lifting his head, or, as far as I knew, turning his eyes, he perceived the point towards which my attention was drawn, and, in a slow distinct voice, dropped, concerning it, these four observations:—

"She was much beloved.

"She gave herself to God.

"She died young.

"She is still remembered, still wept."

"By that aged lady, Madame Walravens?" I inquired, fancying that I had discovered in the incurable grief of bereavement, a key to that same aged lady's desperate ill-humour.

The father shook his head with half a smile.

"No, no," said he; "a grand-dame's affection for her children's children may be great, and her sorrow for their loss, lively; but it is only the affianced lover, to whom Fate, Faith, and Death have trebly denied the bliss of union, who mourns what he has lost, as Justine Marie is still mourned."

I thought the father rather wished to be questioned, and therefore I inquired who had lost and who still mourned "Justine Marie." I got, in reply, quite a little romantic narrative, told not unimpressively, with the accompaniment of the now subsiding storm. I am bound to say it might have been made much more truly impressive, if there had been less French, Rousseau-like sentimentalizing and wire-drawing; and rather more healthful carelessness of effect. But the worthy father was obviously a Frenchman born and bred (I became more and more persuaded of his resemblance to my confessor) — he was a true son of Rome; when he did lift his eyes, he looked at me out of their corners, with more and sharper subtlety than, one would have thought, could survive the wear and tear of seventy years. Yet, I believe, he was a good old man.

The hero of his tale was some former pupil of his, whom he now called his benefactor, and who, it appears, had loved this pale Justine Marie, the daughter of rich parents, at a time when his own worldly prospects were such as to justify his aspiring to a well-dowered hand. The pupil's father — once a rich banker — had failed, died, and left behind him only debts and destitution. The son was then forbidden to think of Marie; especially that old witch of a grand-dame I had seen, Madame Walravens, opposed the match with all the violence of a temper which deformity made sometimes demoniac. The mild Marie had neither the treachery to be false, nor the force to be quite staunch to her lover; she gave up her first suitor, but, refusing to accept a second with a heavier purse, withdrew to a convent, and there died in her noviciate.

Lasting anguish, it seems, had taken possession of the faithful heart which worshipped her, and the truth of that love and grief had been shown in a manner which touched even me, as I listened.

Some years after Justine Marie's death, ruin had come on her house too: her father, by nominal calling a jeweller, but who also dealt a good deal on the Bourse, had been concerned in some financial transactions which entailed exposure and ruinous fines. He died of grief for the loss, and shame for the

Villette

infamy. His old hunchbacked mother and his bereaved wife were left penniless, and might have died too of want; but their lost daughter's once-despised, yet most true-hearted suitor, hearing of the condition of these ladies, came with singular devotedness to the rescue. He took on their insolent pride the revenge of the purest charity — housing, caring for, befriending them, so as no son could have done it more tenderly and efficiently. The mother — on the whole a good woman — died blessing him; the strange, godless, loveless, misanthrope grandmother lived still, entirely supported by this self-sacrificing man. Her, who had been the bane of his life, blighting his hope, and awarding him, for love and domestic happiness, long mourning and cheerless solitude, he treated with the respect a good son might offer a kind mother. He had brought her to this house, "and," continued the priest, while genuine tears rose to his eyes, "here, too, he shelters me, his old tutor, and Agnes, a superannuated servant of his father's family. To our sustenance, and to other charities, I know he devotes three-parts of his income, keeping only the fourth to provide himself with bread and the most modest accommodations. By this arrangement he has rendered it impossible to himself ever to marry: he has given himself to God and to his angel-bride as much as if he were a priest, like me."

The father had wiped away his tears before he uttered these last words, and in pronouncing them, he for one instant raised his eyes to mine. I caught this glance, despite its veiled character; the momentary gleam shot a meaning which struck me.

These Romanists are strange beings. Such a one among them — whom you know no more than the last Inca of Peru, or the first Emperor of China — knows you and all your concerns; and has his reasons for saying to you so and so, when you simply thought the communication sprang impromptu from the instant's impulse: his plan in bringing it about that you shall come on such a day, to such a place, under such and such circumstances, when the whole arrangement seems to your crude apprehension the ordinance of chance, or the sequel of exigency. Madame Beck's suddenly-recollected message and present, my artless embassy to the Place of the Magi, the old priest accidentally descending the steps and crossing the square, his interposition on my behalf with the bonne who would have sent me away, his reappearance on the staircase, my introduction to this room, the portrait, the narrative so affably volunteered — all these little incidents, taken as they fell out, seemed each independent of its successor; a handful of loose beads: but threaded through by that quick-shot and crafty glance of a Jesuit-eye, they dropped pendent in a long string, like that rosary on the prie-dieu. Where lay the link of junction, where the little clasp of this monastic necklace? I saw or felt union, but could not yet find the spot, or detect the means of connection.

Perhaps the musing-fit into which I had by this time fallen, appeared somewhat suspicious in its abstraction; he gently interrupted: "Mademoiselle," said he, "I trust you have not far to go through these inundated streets?"

"More than half a league."

"You live — —?"

"In the Rue Fossette."

"Not" (with animation), "not at the pensionnat of Madame Beck?"

"The same."

"Donc" (clapping his hands), "donc, vous devez connaître mon noble élève, mon Paul?"

"Monsieur Paul Emanuel, Professor of Literature?"

"He and none other."

A brief silence fell. The spring of junction seemed suddenly to have become palpable; I felt it yield to pressure.

"Was it of M. Paul you have been speaking?" I presently inquired. "Was he your pupil and the benefactor of Madame Walravens?"

"Yes, and of Agnes, the old servant: and moreover, (with a certain emphasis), he was and is the lover, true, constant and eternal, of that saint in heaven — Justine Marie."

"And who, father, are you?" I continued; and though I accentuated the question, its utterance was well nigh superfluous; I was ere this quite prepared for the answer which actually came.

"I, daughter, am Père Silas; that unworthy son of Holy Church whom you once honoured with a noble and touching

Villette

confidence, showing me the core of a heart, and the inner shrine of a mind whereof, in solemn truth, I coveted the direction, in behalf of the only true faith. Nor have I for a day lost sight of you, nor for an hour failed to take in you a rooted interest. Passed under the discipline of Rome, moulded by her high training, inoculated with her salutary doctrines, inspired by the zeal she alone gives—I realize what then might be your spiritual rank, your practical value; and I envy Heresy her prey."

This struck me as a special state of things—I half-realized myself in that condition also; passed under discipline, moulded, trained, inoculated, and so on. "Not so," thought I, but I restrained deprecation, and sat quietly enough.

"I suppose M. Paul does not live here?" I resumed, pursuing a theme which I thought more to the purpose than any wild renegade dreams.

"No; he only comes occasionally to worship his beloved saint, to make his confession to me, and to pay his respects to her he calls his mother. His own lodging consists but of two rooms: he has no servant, and yet he will not suffer Madame Walravens to dispose of those splendid jewels with which you see her adorned, and in which she takes a puerile pride as the ornaments of her youth, and the last relics of her son the jeweller's wealth."

"How often," murmured I to myself, "has this man, this M. Emanuel, seemed to me to lack magnanimity in trifles, yet how great he is in great things!"

I own I did not reckon amongst the proofs of his greatness, either the act of confession, or the saint-worship.

"How long is it since that lady died?" I inquired, looking at Justine Marie.

"Twenty years. She was somewhat older than M. Emanuel; he was then very young, for he is not much beyond forty."

"Does he yet weep her?"

"His heart will weep her always: the essence of Emanuel's nature is—constancy."

This was said with marked emphasis.

And now the sun broke out pallid and waterish; the rain yet

fell, but there was no more tempest: that hot firmament had cloven and poured out its lightnings. A longer delay would scarce leave daylight for my return, so I rose, thanked the father for his hospitality and his tale, was benignantly answered by a "pax vobiscum," which I made kindly welcome, because it seemed uttered with a true benevolence; but I liked less the mystic phrase accompanying it.

"Daughter, you shall be what you shall be!" an oracle that made me shrug my shoulders as soon as I had got outside the door. Few of us know what we are to come to certainly, but for all that had happened yet, I had good hopes of living and dying a sober-minded Protestant: there was a hollowness within, and a flourish around "Holy Church" which tempted me but moderately. I went on my way pondering many things. Whatever Romanism may be, there are good Romanists: this man, Emanuel, seemed of the best; touched with superstition, influenced by priestcraft, yet wondrous for fond faith, for pious devotion, for sacrifice of self, for charity unbounded. It remained to see how Rome, by her agents, handled such qualities; whether she cherished them for their own sake and for God's, or put them out to usury and made booty of the interest.

By the time I reached home, it was sundown. Goton had kindly saved me a portion of dinner, which indeed I needed. She called me into the little cabinet to partake of it, and there Madame Beck soon made her appearance, bringing me a glass of wine.

"Well," began she, chuckling, "and what sort of a reception did Madame Walravens give you? Elle est drôle, n'est-ce pas?"

I told her what had passed, delivering verbatim the courteous message with which I had been charged.

"Oh la singulière petite bossue!" laughed she. "Et figurez-vous qu'elle me déteste, parcequ'elle me croit amoureuse de mon cousin Paul; ce petit dévot qui n'ose pas bouger, à moins que son confesseur ne lui donne la permission! Au reste" (she went on), "if he wanted to marry ever so much—soit moi, soit une autre—he could not do it; he has too large a family already on his hands: Mère Walravens, Père Silas, Dame Agnes, and a whole troop of nameless paupers. There never was a man like him for laying on himself burdens greater than he can bear, voluntarily incurring needless responsibilities. Besides, he harbours a romantic idea about some pale-faced Marie Justine—personnage assez niaise à ce que je pense" (such was Madame's irreverent remark), "who has been an angel in heaven, or

Villette

elsewhere, this score of years, and to whom he means to go, free from all earthly ties, pure comme un lis, à ce qu'il dit. Oh, you would laugh could you but know half M. Emanuel's crotchets and eccentricities! But I hinder you from taking refreshment, ma bonne Meess, which you must need; eat your supper, drink your wine, oubliez les anges, les bossues, et surtout, les Professeurs — et bon soir!"

CHAPTER XXXV.

FRATERNITY.

"Oubliez les Professeurs." So said Madame Beck. Madame Beck was a wise woman, but she should not have uttered those words. To do so was a mistake. That night she should have left me calm—not excited, indifferent, not interested, isolated in my own estimation and that of others—not connected, even in idea, with this second person whom I was to forget.

Forget him? Ah! they took a sage plan to make me forget him—the wiseheads! They showed me how good he was; they made of my dear little man a stainless little hero. And then they had prated about his manner of loving. What means had I, before this day, of being certain whether he could love at all or not?

I had known him jealous, suspicious; I had seen about him certain tendernesses, fitfulnesses—a softness which came like a warm air, and a ruth which passed like early dew, dried in the heat of his irritabilities: this was all I had seen. And they, Père Silas and Modeste Maria Beck (that these two wrought in concert I could not doubt) opened up the adytum of his heart—showed me one grand love, the child of this southern nature's youth, born so strong and perfect, that it had laughed at Death himself, despised his mean rape of matter, clung to immortal spirit, and in victory and faith, had watched beside a tomb twenty years.

This had been done—not idly: this was not a mere hollow indulgence of sentiment; he had proven his fidelity by the consecration of his best energies to an unselfish purpose, and attested it by limitless personal sacrifices: for those once dear to her he prized—he had laid down vengeance, and taken up a cross.

Now, as for Justine Marie, I knew what she was as well as if I had seen her. I knew she was well enough; there were girls like her in Madame Beck's school—phlegmatics—pale, slow, inert, but kind-natured, neutral of evil, undistinguished for good.

If she wore angels' wings, I knew whose poet-fancy conferred them. If her forehead shone luminous with the reflex of a halo, I knew in the fire of whose irids that circlet of holy flame had generation.

Villette

Was I, then, to be frightened by Justine Marie? Was the picture of a pale dead nun to rise, an eternal barrier? And what of the charities which absorbed his worldly goods? What of his heart sworn to virginity?

Madame Beck—Père Silas—you should not have suggested these questions. They were at once the deepest puzzle, the strongest obstruction, and the keenest stimulus, I had ever felt. For a week of nights and days I fell asleep—I dreamt, and I woke upon these two questions. In the whole world there was no answer to them, except where one dark little man stood, sat, walked, lectured, under the head-piece of a bandit bonnet-grec, and within the girth of a sorry paletôt, much be-inked, and no little adust.

After that visit to the Rue des Mages, I did want to see him again. I felt as if—knowing what I now knew—his countenance would offer a page more lucid, more interesting than ever; I felt a longing to trace in it the imprint of that primitive devotedness, the signs of that half-knightly, half-saintly chivalry which the priest's narrative imputed to his nature. He had become my Christian hero: under that character I wanted to view him.

Nor was opportunity slow to favour; my new impressions underwent her test the next day. Yes: I was granted an interview with my "Christian hero"—an interview not very heroic, or sentimental, or biblical, but lively enough in its way.

About three o'clock of the afternoon, the peace of the first classe—safely established, as it seemed, under the serene sway of Madame Beck, who, in propria persona, was giving one of her orderly and useful lessons—this peace, I say, suffered a sudden fracture by the wild inburst of a paletôt.

Nobody at the moment was quieter than myself. Eased of responsibility by Madame Beck's presence, soothed by her uniform tones, pleased and edified with her clear exposition of the subject in hand (for she taught well), I sat bent over my desk, drawing—that is, copying an elaborate line engraving, tediously working up my copy to the finish of the original, for that was my practical notion of art; and, strange to say, I took extreme pleasure in the labour, and could even produce curiously finical Chinese facsimiles of steel or mezzotint plates—things about as valuable as so many achievements in worsted-work, but I thought pretty well of them in those days.

What was the matter? My drawing, my pencils, my precious copy, gathered into one crushed-up handful, perished from before my sight; I myself appeared to be shaken or emptied out of my chair, as a solitary and withered nutmeg might be emptied out of a spice-box by an excited cook. That chair and my desk, seized by the wild paletôt, one under each sleeve, were borne afar; in a second, I followed the furniture; in two minutes they and I were fixed in the centre of the grand salle—a vast adjoining room, seldom used save for dancing and choral singing-lessons—fixed with an emphasis which seemed to prohibit the remotest hope of our ever being permitted to stir thence again.

Having partially collected my scared wits, I found myself in the presence of two men, gentlemen, I suppose I should say—one dark, the other light—one having a stiff, half-military air, and wearing a braided surtout; the other partaking, in garb and bearing, more of the careless aspect of the student or artist class: both flourishing in full magnificence of moustaches, whiskers, and imperial. M. Emanuel stood a little apart from these; his countenance and eyes expressed strong choler; he held forth his hand with his tribune gesture.

"Mademoiselle," said he, "your business is to prove to these gentlemen that I am no liar. You will answer, to the best of your ability, such questions as they shall put. You will also write on such theme as they shall select. In their eyes, it appears, I hold the position of an unprincipled impostor. I write essays; and, with deliberate forgery, sign to them my pupils' names, and boast of them as their work. You will disprove this charge."

Grand ciel! Here was the show-trial, so long evaded, come on me like a thunder-clap. These two fine, braided, mustachioed, sneering personages, were none other than dandy professors of the college—Messieurs Boissec and Rochemorte—a pair of cold-blooded fops and pedants, sceptics, and scoffers. It seems that M. Paul had been rashly exhibiting something I had written—something, he had never once praised, or even mentioned, in my hearing, and which I deemed forgotten. The essay was not remarkable at all; it only seemed remarkable, compared with the average productions of foreign school-girls; in an English establishment it would have passed scarce noticed. Messieurs Boissec and Rochemorte had thought proper to question its genuineness, and insinuate a cheat; I was now to bear my testimony to the truth, and to be put to the torture of their examination.

A memorable scene ensued.

They began with classics. A dead blank. They went on to

Villette

French history. I hardly knew Mérovée from Pharamond. They tried me in various 'ologies, and still only got a shake of the head, and an unchanging "Je n'en sais rien."

After an expressive pause, they proceeded to matters of general information, broaching one or two subjects which I knew pretty well, and on which I had often reflected. M. Emanuel, who had hitherto stood looking on, dark as the winter-solstice, brightened up somewhat; he thought I should now show myself at least no fool.

He learned his error. Though answers to the questions surged up fast, my mind filling like a rising well, ideas were there, but not words. I either could not, or would not speak—I am not sure which: partly, I think, my nerves had got wrong, and partly my humour was crossed.

I heard one of my examiners—he of the braided surtout—whisper to his co-professor, "Est-elle donc idiote?"

"Yes," I thought, "an idiot she is, and always will be, for such as you."

But I suffered—suffered cruelly; I saw the damps gather on M. Paul's brow, and his eye spoke a passionate yet sad reproach. He would not believe in my total lack of popular cleverness; he thought I could be prompt if I would.

At last, to relieve him, the professors, and myself, I stammered out:

"Gentlemen, you had better let me go; you will get no good of me; as you say, I am an idiot."

I wish I could have spoken with calm and dignity, or I wish my sense had sufficed to make me hold my tongue; that traitor tongue tripped, faltered. Beholding the judges cast on M. Emanuel a hard look of triumph, and hearing the distressed tremor of my own voice, out I burst in a fit of choking tears. The emotion was far more of anger than grief; had I been a man and strong, I could have challenged that pair on the spot—but it was emotion, and I would rather have been scourged than betrayed it.

The incapables! Could they not see at once the crude hand of a novice in that composition they called a forgery? The subject was classical. When M. Paul dictated the trait on which the essay was to turn, I heard it for the first time; the matter was new to me, and I had no material for its treatment. But I got books, read up the facts, laboriously constructed a skeleton out of the dry bones of the real, and then clothed them, and tried to breathe into them life, and in this last aim I had pleasure. With me it was a difficult and anxious time till my facts were found, selected, and properly jointed; nor could I rest from research and effort till I was satisfied of correct anatomy; the strength of my inward repugnance to the idea of flaw or falsity sometimes enabled me to shun egregious blunders; but the knowledge was not there in my head, ready and mellow; it had not been sown in Spring, grown in Summer, harvested in Autumn, and garnered through Winter; whatever I wanted I must go out and gather fresh; glean of wild herbs my lapful, and shred them green into the pot. Messieurs Boissec and Rochemorte did not perceive this. They mistook my work for the work of a ripe scholar.

They would not yet let me go: I must sit down and write before them. As I dipped my pen in the ink with a shaking hand, and surveyed the white paper with eyes half-blinded and overflowing, one of my judges began mincingly to apologize for the pain he caused.

"Nous agissons dans l'intérêt de la vérité. Nous ne voulons pas vous blesser," said he.

Scorn gave me nerve. I only answered,—

"Dictate, Monsieur."

Rochemorte named this theme: "Human Justice."

Human Justice! What was I to make of it? Blank, cold abstraction, unsuggestive to me of one inspiring idea; and there stood M. Emanuel, sad as Saul, and stern as Joab, and there triumphed his accusers.

At these two I looked. I was gathering my courage to tell them that I would neither write nor speak another word for their satisfaction, that their theme did not suit, nor their presence inspire me, and that, notwithstanding, whoever threw the shadow of a doubt on M. Emanuel's honour, outraged that truth of which they had announced themselves the— champions: I meant to utter all this, I say, when suddenly, a light darted on memory.

Those two faces looking out of the forest of long hair, moustache, and whisker—those two cold yet bold, trustless yet presumptuous visages—were the same faces, the very same that, projected in full gaslight from behind the pillars of a portico, had half frightened me to death on the night of my desolate arrival in Villette. These, I felt morally certain, were the very heroes who had driven a friendless foreigner beyond her reckoning and her strength, chased her breathless over a whole quarter of the town.

"Pious mentors!" thought I. "Pure guides for youth! If 'Human Justice' were what she ought to be, you two would scarce hold your present post, or enjoy your present credit."

An idea once seized, I fell to work. "Human Justice" rushed before me in novel guise, a red, random beldame, with arms akimbo. I saw her in her house, the den of confusion: servants called to her for orders or help which she did not give; beggars stood at her door waiting and starving unnoticed; a swarm of children, sick and quarrelsome, crawled round her feet, and yelled in her ears appeals for notice, sympathy, cure, redress. The honest woman cared for none of these things. She had a warm seat of her own by the fire, she had her own solace in a short black pipe, and a bottle of Mrs. Sweeny's soothing syrup; she smoked and she sipped, and she enjoyed her paradise; and whenever a cry of the suffering souls about her pierced her ears too keenly—my jolly dame seized the poker or the hearth-brush: if the offender was weak, wronged, and sickly, she effectually settled him: if he was strong, lively, and violent, she only menaced, then plunged her hand in her deep pouch, and flung a liberal shower of sugar-plums.

Such was the sketch of "Human Justice," scratched hurriedly on paper, and placed at the service of Messrs. Boissec and Rochemorte. M. Emanuel read it over my shoulder. Waiting no comment, I curtsied to the trio, and withdrew.

After school that day, M. Paul and I again met. Of course the meeting did not at first run smooth; there was a crow to pluck with him; that forced examination could not be immediately digested. A crabbed dialogue terminated in my being called "une petite moqueuse et sans-cœur," and in Monsieur's temporary departure.

Not wishing him to go quite away, only desiring he should feel that such a transport as he had that day given way to, could not be indulged with perfect impunity, I was not sorry to see him, soon after, gardening in the berceau. He approached the glass door; I drew near also. We spoke of some flowers growing round it. By-and-by Monsieur laid down his spade; by-and-by he recommenced conversation, passed to other subjects, and at last touched a point of interest.

Conscious that his proceeding of that day was specially open to a charge of extravagance, M. Paul half apologized; he half regretted, too, the fitfulness of his moods at all times, yet he hinted that some allowance ought to be made for him. "But," said he, "I can hardly expect it at your hands, Miss Lucy; you know neither me, nor my position, nor my history."

His history. I took up the word at once; I pursued the idea.

"No, Monsieur," I rejoined. "Of course, as you say, I know neither your history, nor your position, nor your sacrifices, nor any of your sorrows, or trials, or affections, or fidelities. Oh, no! I know nothing about you; you are for me altogether a stranger."

"Hein?" he murmured, arching his brows in surprise.

"You know, Monsieur, I only see you in classe—stern, dogmatic, hasty, imperious. I only hear of you in town as active and wilful, quick to originate, hasty to lead, but slow to persuade, and hard to bend. A man like you, without ties, can have no attachments; without dependants, no duties. All we, with whom you come in contact, are machines, which you thrust here and there, inconsiderate of their feelings. You seek your recreations in public, by the light of the evening chandelier: this school and yonder college are your workshops, where you fabricate the ware called pupils. I don't so much as know where you live; it is natural to take it for granted that you have no home, and need none."

"I am judged," said he. "Your opinion of me is just what I thought it was. For you I am neither a man nor a Christian. You see me void of affection and religion, unattached by friend or family, unpiloted by principle or faith. It is well, Mademoiselle; such is our reward in this life."

"You are a philosopher, Monsieur; a cynic philosopher" (and I looked at his paletôt, of which he straightway brushed the dim sleeve with his hand), "despising the foibles of humanity—above its luxuries—independent of its comforts."

"Et vous, Mademoiselle? vous êtes proprette et douillette, et affreusement insensible, par-dessus le marché."

"But, in short, Monsieur, now I think of it, you must live

Villette

somewhere? Do tell me where; and what establishment of servants do you keep?"

With a fearful projection of the under-lip, implying an impetus of scorn the most decided, he broke out—

"Je vis dans un trou! I inhabit a den, Miss—a cavern, where you would not put your dainty nose. Once, with base shame of speaking the whole truth, I talked about my 'study' in that college: know now that this 'study' is my whole abode; my chamber is there and my drawing-room. As for my 'establishment of servants'" (mimicking my voice) "they number ten; les voilà."

And he grimly spread, close under my eyes, his ten fingers.

"I black my boots," pursued he savagely. "I brush my paletôt."

"No, Monsieur, it is too plain; you never do that," was my parenthesis.

"Je fais mon lit et mon ménage; I seek my dinner in a restaurant; my supper takes care, of itself; I pass days laborious and loveless; nights long and lonely; I am ferocious, and bearded and monkish; and nothing now living in this world loves me, except some old hearts worn like my own, and some few beings, impoverished, suffering, poor in purse and in spirit, whom the kingdoms of this world own not, but to whom a will and testament not to be disputed has bequeathed the kingdom of heaven."

"Ah, Monsieur; but I know!"

"What do you know? many things, I verily believe; yet not me, Lucy!"

"I know that you have a pleasant old house in a pleasant old square of the Basse-Ville—why don't you go and live there?"

"Hein?" muttered he again.

"I liked it much, Monsieur; with the steps ascending to the door, the grey flags in front, the nodding trees behind—real trees, not shrubs—trees dark, high, and of old growth. And the boudoir-oratoire—you should make that room your study; it is so quiet and solemn."

He eyed me closely; he half-smiled, half-coloured. "Where did you pick up all that? Who told you?" he asked.

"Nobody told me. Did I dream it, Monsieur, do you think?"

"Can I enter into your visions? Can I guess a woman's waking thoughts, much less her sleeping fantasies?"

"If I dreamt it, I saw in my dream human beings as well as a house. I saw a priest, old, bent, and grey, and a domestic—old, too, and picturesque; and a lady, splendid but strange; her head would scarce reach to my elbow—her magnificence might ransom a duke. She wore a gown bright as lapis-lazuli—a shawl worth a thousand francs: she was decked with ornaments so brilliant, I never saw any with such a beautiful sparkle; but her figure looked as if it had been broken in two and bent double; she seemed also to have outlived the common years of humanity, and to have attained those which are only labour and sorrow. She was become morose—almost malevolent; yet somebody, it appears, cared for her in her infirmities—somebody forgave her trespasses, hoping to have his trespasses forgiven. They lived together, these three people—the mistress, the chaplain, the servant—all old, all feeble, all sheltered under one kind wing."

He covered with his hand the upper part of his face, but did not conceal his mouth, where I saw hovering an expression I liked.

"I see you have entered into my secrets," said he, "but how was it done?"

So I told him how—the commission on which I had been sent, the storm which had detained me, the abruptness of the lady, the kindness of the priest.

"As I sat waiting for the rain to cease, Père Silas whiled away the time with a story," I said.

"A story! What story? Père Silas is no romancist."

"Shall I tell Monsieur the tale?"

"Yes: begin at the beginning. Let me hear some of Miss Lucy's French—her best or her worst—I don't much care which: let us have a good poignée of barbarisms, and a bounteous dose of the insular accent."

"Monsieur is not going to be gratified by a tale of ambitious proportions, and the spectacle of the narrator sticking fast in the midst. But I will tell him the title—the 'Priest's Pupil.'"

"Bah!" said he, the swarthy flush again dyeing his dark cheek. "The good old father could not have chosen a worse subject; it is his weak point. But what of the 'Priest's Pupil?'"

"Oh! many things."

"You may as well define what things. I mean to know."

"There was the pupil's youth, the pupil's manhood;—his avarice, his ingratitude, his implacability, his inconstancy. Such a bad pupil, Monsieur!—so thankless, cold-hearted, unchivalrous, unforgiving!"

"Et puis?" said he, taking a cigar.

"Et puis," I pursued, "he underwent calamities which one did not pity—bore them in a spirit one did not admire—endured wrongs for which one felt no sympathy; finally took the unchristian revenge of heaping coals of fire on his adversary's head."

"You have not told me all," said he.

"Nearly all, I think: I have indicated the heads of Père Silas's chapters."

"You have forgotten one—that which touched on the pupil's lack of affection—on his hard, cold, monkish heart."

"True; I remember now. Père Silas did say that his vocation was almost that of a priest—that his life was considered consecrated."

"By what bonds or duties?"

"By the ties of the past and the charities of the present."

"You have, then, the whole situation?"

"I have now told Monsieur all that was told me."

Some meditative minutes passed.

"Now, Mademoiselle Lucy, look at me, and with that truth

which I believe you never knowingly violate, answer me one question. Raise your eyes; rest them on mine; have no hesitation; fear not to trust me—I am a man to be trusted."

I raised my eyes.

"Knowing me thoroughly now—all my antecedents, all my responsibilities—having long known my faults, can you and I still be friends?"

"If Monsieur wants a friend in me, I shall be glad to have a friend in him."

"But a close friend I mean—intimate and real—kindred in all but blood. Will Miss Lucy be the sister of a very poor, fettered, burdened, encumbered man?"

I could not answer him in words, yet I suppose I did answer him; he took my hand, which found comfort, in the shelter of his. His friendship was not a doubtful, wavering benefit—a cold, distant hope—a sentiment so brittle as not to bear the weight of a finger: I at once felt (or thought I felt) its support like that of some rock.

"When I talk of friendship, I mean true friendship," he repeated emphatically; and I could hardly believe that words so earnest had blessed my ear; I hardly could credit the reality of that kind, anxious look he gave. If he really wished for my confidence and regard, and really would give me his—why, it seemed to me that life could offer nothing more or better. In that case, I was become strong and rich: in a moment I was made substantially happy. To ascertain the fact, to fix and seal it, I asked—

"Is Monsieur quite serious? Does he really think he needs me, and can take an interest in me as a sister?"

"Surely, surely," said he; "a lonely man like me, who has no sister, must be but too glad to find in some woman's heart a sister's pure affection."

"And dare I rely on Monsieur's regard? Dare I speak to him when I am so inclined?"

"My little sister must make her own experiments," said he; "I will give no promises. She must tease and try her wayward brother till she has drilled him into what she wishes. After all, he is no inductile material in some hands."

Villette

While he spoke, the tone of his voice, the light of his now affectionate eye, gave me such a pleasure as, certainly, I had never felt. I envied no girl her lover, no bride her bridegroom, no wife her husband; I was content with this my voluntary, self-offering friend. If he would but prove reliable, and he looked reliable, what, beyond his friendship, could I ever covet? But, if all melted like a dream, as once before had happened—?

"Qu'est-ce donc? What is it?" said he, as this thought threw its weight on my heart, its shadow on my countenance. I told him; and after a moment's pause, and a thoughtful smile, he showed me how an equal fear—lest I should weary of him, a man of moods so difficult and fitful—had haunted his mind for more than one day, or one month.

On hearing this, a quiet courage cheered me. I ventured a word of re-assurance. That word was not only tolerated; its repetition was courted. I grew quite happy—strangely happy—in making him secure, content, tranquil. Yesterday, I could not have believed that earth held, or life afforded, moments like the few I was now passing. Countless times it had been my lot to watch apprehended sorrow close darkly in; but to see unhoped-for happiness take form, find place, and grow more real as the seconds sped, was indeed a new experience.

"Lucy," said M. Paul, speaking low, and still holding my hand, "did you see a picture in the boudoir of the old house?"

"I did; a picture painted on a panel."

"The portrait of a nun?"

"Yes."

"You heard her history?"

"Yes."

"You remember what we saw that night in the berceau?"

"I shall never forget it."

"You did not connect the two ideas; that would be folly?"

"I thought of the apparition when I saw the portrait," said I; which was true enough.

"You did not, nor will you fancy," pursued he, "that a saint in heaven perturbs herself with rivalries of earth? Protestants are rarely superstitious; these morbid fancies will not beset you?"

"I know not what to think of this matter; but I believe a perfectly natural solution of this seeming mystery will one day be arrived at."

"Doubtless, doubtless. Besides, no good-living woman—much less a pure, happy spirit—would trouble amity like ours—n'est-il pas vrai?"

Ere I could answer, Fifine Beck burst in, rosy and abrupt, calling out that I was wanted. Her mother was going into town to call on some English family, who had applied for a prospectus: my services were needed as interpreter. The interruption was not unseasonable: sufficient for the day is always the evil; for this hour, its good sufficed. Yet I should have liked to ask M. Paul whether the "morbid fancies," against which he warned me, wrought in his own brain.

CHAPTER XXXVI.

THE APPLE OF DISCORD.

Besides Fifine Beck's mother, another power had a word to say to M. Paul and me, before that covenant of friendship could be ratified. We were under the surveillance of a sleepless eye: Rome watched jealously her son through that mystic lattice at which I had knelt once, and to which M. Emanuel drew nigh month by month—the sliding panel of the confessional.

"Why were you so glad to be friends with M. Paul?" asks the reader. "Had he not long been a friend to you? Had he not given proof on proof of a certain partiality in his feelings?"

Yes, he had; but still I liked to hear him say so earnestly—that he was my close, true friend; I liked his modest doubts, his tender deference—that trust which longed to rest, and was grateful when taught how. He had called me "sister." It was well. Yes; he might call me what he pleased, so long as he confided in me. I was willing to be his sister, on condition that he did not invite me to fill that relation to some future wife of his; and tacitly vowed as he was to celibacy, of this dilemma there seemed little danger.

Through most of the succeeding night I pondered that evening's interview. I wanted much the morning to break, and then listened for the bell to ring; and, after rising and dressing, I deemed prayers and breakfast slow, and all the hours lingering, till that arrived at last which brought me the lesson of literature. My wish was to get a more thorough comprehension of this fraternal alliance: to note with how much of the brother he would demean himself when we met again; to prove how much of the sister was in my own feelings; to discover whether I could summon a sister's courage, and he a brother's frankness.

He came. Life is so constructed, that the event does not, cannot, will not, match the expectation. That whole day he never accosted me. His lesson was given rather more quietly than usual, more mildly, and also more gravely. He was fatherly to his pupils, but he was not brotherly to me. Ere he left the classe, I expected a smile, if not a word; I got neither: to my portion fell one nod—hurried, shy.

This distance, I argued, is accidental—it is involuntary; patience, and it will vanish. It vanished not; it continued for days; it increased. I suppressed my surprise, and swallowed whatever other feelings began to surge.

Well might I ask when he offered fraternity — "Dare I rely on you?" Well might he, doubtless knowing himself, withhold all pledge. True, he had bid me make my own experiments — tease and try him. Vain injunction! Privilege nominal and unavailable! Some women might use it! Nothing in my powers or instinct placed me amongst this brave band. Left alone, I was passive; repulsed, I withdrew; forgotten — my lips would not utter, nor my eyes dart a reminder. It seemed there had been an error somewhere in my calculations, and I wanted for time to disclose it.

But the day came when, as usual, he was to give me a lesson. One evening in seven he had long generously bestowed on me, devoting it to the examination of what had been done in various studies during the past week, and to the preparation of work for the week in prospect. On these occasions my schoolroom was anywhere, wherever the pupils and the other teachers happened to be, or in their close vicinage, very often in the large second division, where it was easy to choose a quiet nook when the crowding day pupils were absent, and the few boarders gathered in a knot about the surveillante's estrade.

On the customary evening, hearing the customary hour strike, I collected my books and papers, my pen and ink, and sought the large division.

In classe there was no one, and it lay all in cool deep shadow; but through the open double doors was seen the carré, filled with pupils and with light; over hall and figures blushed the westering sun. It blushed so ruddily and vividly, that the hues of the walls and the variegated tints of the dresses seemed all fused in one warm glow. The girls were seated, working or studying; in the midst of their circle stood M. Emanuel, speaking good-humouredly to a teacher. His dark paletôt, his jetty hair, were tinged with many a reflex of crimson; his Spanish face, when he turned it momentarily, answered the sun's animated kiss with an animated smile. I took my place at a desk.

The orange-trees, and several plants, full and bright with bloom, basked also in the sun's laughing bounty; they had partaken it the whole day, and now asked water. M. Emanuel had a taste for gardening; he liked to tend and foster plants. I used to think that working amongst shrubs with a spade or a watering-pot soothed his nerves; it was a recreation to which he often had recourse; and now he looked to the orange-trees, the

Villette

geraniums, the gorgeous cactuses, and revived them all with the refreshment their drought needed. His lips meantime sustained his precious cigar, that (for him) first necessary and prime luxury of life; its blue wreaths curled prettily enough amongst the flowers, and in the evening light. He spoke no more to the pupils, nor to the mistresses, but gave many an endearing word to a small spanieless (if one may coin a word), that nominally belonged to the house, but virtually owned him as master, being fonder of him than any inmate. A delicate, silky, loving, and lovable little doggie she was, trotting at his side, looking with expressive, attached eyes into his face; and whenever he dropped his bonnet-grec or his handkerchief, which he occasionally did in play, crouching beside it with the air of a miniature lion guarding a kingdom's flag.

There were many plants, and as the amateur gardener fetched all the water from the well in the court, with his own active hands, his work spun on to some length. The great school-clock ticked on. Another hour struck. The carré and the youthful group lost the illusion of sunset. Day was drooping. My lesson, I perceived, must to-night be very short; but the orange-trees, the cacti, the camelias were all served now. Was it my turn?

Alas! in the garden were more plants to be looked after,— favourite rose-bushes, certain choice flowers; little Sylvie's glad bark and whine followed the receding paletôt down the alleys. I put up some of my books; I should not want them all; I sat and thought; and waited, involuntarily deprecating the creeping invasion of twilight.

Sylvie, gaily frisking, emerged into view once more, heralding the returning paletôt; the watering-pot was deposited beside the well; it had fulfilled its office; how glad I was! Monsieur washed his hands in a little stone bowl. There was no longer time for a lesson now; ere long the prayer-bell must ring; but still we should meet; he would speak; a chance would be offered of reading in his eyes the riddle of his shyness. His ablutions over, he stood, slowly re-arranging his cuffs, looking at the horn of a young moon, set pale in the opal sky, and glimmering faint on the oriel of Jean Baptiste. Sylvie watched the mood contemplative; its stillness irked her; she whined and jumped to break it. He looked down.

"Petite exigeante," said he; "you must not be forgotten one moment, it seems."

He stopped, lifted her in his arms, sauntered across the

court, within a yard of the line of windows near one of which I sat: he sauntered lingeringly, fondling the spaniel in his bosom, calling her tender names in a tender voice. On the front-door steps he turned; once again he looked at the moon, at the grey cathedral, over the remoter spires and house-roofs fading into a blue sea of night-mist; he tasted the sweet breath of dusk, and noted the folded bloom of the garden; he suddenly looked round; a keen beam out of his eye rased the white façade of the classes, swept the long line of croisées. I think he bowed; if he did, I had no time to return the courtesy. In a moment he was gone; the moonlit threshold lay pale and shadowless before the closed front door.

Gathering in my arms all that was spread on the desk before me, I carried back the unused heap to its place in the third classe. The prayer-bell rang; I obeyed its summons.

The morrow would not restore him to the Rue Fossette, that day being devoted entirely to his college. I got through my teaching; I got over the intermediate hours; I saw evening approaching, and armed myself for its heavy ennuis. Whether it was worse to stay with my co-inmates, or to sit alone, I had not considered; I naturally took up the latter alternative; if there was a hope of comfort for any moment, the heart or head of no human being in this house could yield it; only under the lid of my desk could it harbour, nestling between the leaves of some book, gilding a pencil-point, the nib of a pen, or tinging the black fluid in that ink-glass. With a heavy heart I opened my desk-lid; with a weary hand I turned up its contents.

One by one, well-accustomed books, volumes sewn in familiar covers, were taken out and put back hopeless: they had no charm; they could not comfort. Is this something new, this pamphlet in lilac? I had not seen it before, and I re-arranged my desk this very day—this very afternoon; the tract must have been introduced within the last hour, while we were at dinner.

I opened it. What was it? What would it say to me?

It was neither tale nor poem, neither essay nor history; it neither sung, nor related, not discussed. It was a theological work; it preached and it persuaded.

I lent to it my ear very willingly, for, small as it was, it possessed its own spell, and bound my attention at once. It preached Romanism; it persuaded to conversion. The voice of that sly little book was a honeyed voice; its accents were all unction and balm. Here roared no utterance of Rome's

Villette

thunders, no blasting of the breath of her displeasure. The Protestant was to turn Papist, not so much in fear of the heretic's hell, as on account of the comfort, the indulgence, the tenderness Holy Church offered: far be it from her to threaten or to coerce; her wish was to guide and win. She persecute? Oh dear no! not on any account!

This meek volume was not addressed to the hardened and worldly; it was not even strong meat for the strong: it was milk for babes: the mild effluence of a mother's love towards her tenderest and her youngest; intended wholly and solely for those whose head is to be reached through the heart. Its appeal was not to intellect; it sought to win the affectionate through their affections, the sympathizing through their sympathies: St. Vincent de Paul, gathering his orphans about him, never spoke more sweetly.

I remember one capital inducement to apostacy was held out in the fact that the Catholic who had lost dear friends by death could enjoy the unspeakable solace of praying them out of purgatory. The writer did not touch on the firmer peace of those whose belief dispenses with purgatory altogether: but I thought of this; and, on the whole, preferred the latter doctrine as the most consolatory. The little book amused, and did not painfully displease me. It was a canting, sentimental, shallow little book, yet something about it cheered my gloom and made me smile; I was amused with the gambols of this unlicked wolf-cub muffled in the fleece, and mimicking the bleat of a guileless lamb. Portions of it reminded me of certain Wesleyan Methodist tracts I had once read when a child; they were flavoured with about the same seasoning of excitation to fanaticism. He that had written it was no bad man, and while perpetually betraying the trained cunning—the cloven hoof of his system—I should pause before accusing himself of insincerity. His judgment, however, wanted surgical props; it was rickety.

I smiled then over this dose of maternal tenderness, coming from the ruddy old lady of the Seven Hills; smiled, too, at my own disinclination, not to say disability, to meet these melting favours. Glancing at the title-page, I found the name of "Père Silas." A fly-leaf bore in small, but clear and well-known pencil characters: "From P. C. D. E. to L—y." And when I saw this I laughed: but not in my former spirit. I was revived.

A mortal bewilderment cleared suddenly from my head and vision; the solution of the Sphinx-riddle was won; the conjunction of those two names, Père Silas and Paul Emanuel, gave the key to all. The penitent had been with his director;

permitted to withhold nothing; suffered to keep no corner of his heart sacred to God and to himself; the whole narrative of our late interview had been drawn from him; he had avowed the covenant of fraternity, and spoken of his adopted sister. How could such a covenant, such adoption, be sanctioned by the Church? Fraternal communion with a heretic! I seemed to hear Père Silas annulling the unholy pact; warning his penitent of its perils; entreating, enjoining reserve, nay, by the authority of his office, and in the name, and by the memory of all M. Emanuel held most dear and sacred, commanding the enforcement of that new system whose frost had pierced to the marrow of my bones.

These may not seem pleasant hypotheses; yet, by comparison, they were welcome. The vision of a ghostly troubler hovering in the background, was as nothing, matched with the fear of spontaneous change arising in M. Paul himself.

At this distance of time, I cannot be sure how far the above conjectures were self-suggested: or in what measure they owed their origin and confirmation to another quarter. Help was not wanting.

This evening there was no bright sunset: west and east were one cloud; no summer night-mist, blue, yet rose-tinged, softened the distance; a clammy fog from the marshes crept grey round Villette. To-night the watering-pot might rest in its niche by the well: a small rain had been drizzling all the afternoon, and still it fell fast and quietly. This was no weather for rambling in the wet alleys, under the dripping trees; and I started to hear Sylvie's sudden bark in the garden—her bark of welcome. Surely she was not accompanied and yet this glad, quick bark was never uttered, save in homage to one presence.

Through the glass door and the arching berceau, I commanded the deep vista of the allée défendue: thither rushed Sylvie, glistening through its gloom like a white guelder-rose. She ran to and fro, whining, springing, harassing little birds amongst the bushes. I watched five minutes; no fulfilment followed the omen. I returned to my books; Sylvie's sharp bark suddenly ceased. Again I looked up. She was standing not many yards distant, wagging her white feathery tail as fast as the muscle would work, and intently watching the operations of a spade, plied fast by an indefatigable hand. There was M. Emanuel, bent over the soil, digging in the wet mould amongst the rain-laden and streaming shrubs, working as hard as if his day's pittance were yet to earn by the literal sweat of his brow.

Villette

In this sign I read a ruffled mood. He would dig thus in frozen snow on the coldest winter day, when urged inwardly by painful emotion, whether of nervous excitation, or, sad thoughts of self-reproach. He would dig by the hour, with knit brow and set teeth, nor once lift his head, or open his lips.

Sylvie watched till she was tired. Again scampering devious, bounding here, rushing there, snuffing and sniffing everywhere; she at last discovered me in classe. Instantly she flew barking at the panes, as if to urge me forth to share her pleasure or her master's toil; she had seen me occasionally walking in that alley with M. Paul; and I doubt not, considered it my duty to join him now, wet as it was.

She made such a bustle that M. Paul at last looked up, and of course perceived why, and at whom she barked. He whistled to call her off; she only barked the louder. She seemed quite bent upon having the glass door opened. Tired, I suppose, with her importunity, he threw down his spade, approached, and pushed the door ajar. Sylvie burst in all impetuous, sprang to my lap, and with her paws at my neck, and her little nose and tongue somewhat overpoweringly busy about my face, mouth, and eyes, flourished her bushy tail over the desk, and scattered books and papers far and wide.

M. Emanuel advanced to still the clamour and repair the disarrangement. Having gathered up the books, he captured Sylvie, and stowed her away under his paletôt, where she nestled as quiet as a mouse, her head just peeping forth. She was very tiny, and had the prettiest little innocent face, the silkiest long ears, the finest dark eyes in the world. I never saw her, but I thought of Paulina de Bassompierre: forgive the association, reader, it would occur.

M. Paul petted and patted her; the endearments she received were not to be wondered at; she invited affection by her beauty and her vivacious life.

While caressing the spaniel, his eye roved over the papers and books just replaced; it settled on the religious tract. His lips moved; he half checked the impulse to speak. What! had he promised never to address me more? If so, his better nature pronounced the vow "more honoured in the breach than in the observance," for with a second effort, he spoke. — "You have not yet read the brochure, I presume? It is not sufficiently inviting?"

I replied that I had read it.

He waited, as if wishing me to give an opinion upon it unasked. Unasked, however, I was in no mood to do or say anything. If any concessions were to be made—if any advances were demanded—that was the affair of the very docile pupil of Père Silas, not mine. His eye settled upon me gently: there was mildness at the moment in its blue ray—there was solicitude—a shade of pathos; there were meanings composite and contrasted—reproach melting into remorse. At the moment probably, he would have been glad to see something emotional in me. I could not show it. In another minute, however, I should have betrayed confusion, had I not bethought myself to take some quill-pens from my desk, and begin soberly to mend them.

I knew that action would give a turn to his mood. He never liked to see me mend pens; my knife was always dull-edged—my hand, too, was unskilful; I hacked and chipped. On this occasion I cut my own finger—half on purpose. I wanted to restore him to his natural state, to set him at his ease, to get him to chide.

"Maladroit!" he cried at last, "she will make mincemeat of her hands."

He put Sylvie down, making her lie quiet beside his bonnet-grec, and, depriving me of the pens and penknife, proceeded to slice, nib, and point with the accuracy and celerity of a machine.

"Did I like the little book?" he now inquired.

Suppressing a yawn, I said I hardly knew.

"Had it moved me?"

"I thought it had made me a little sleepy."

(After a pause) "Allons donc! It was of no use taking that tone with him. Bad as I was—and he should be sorry to have to name all my faults at a breath—God and nature had given me 'trop de sensibilité et de sympathie' not to be profoundly affected by an appeal so touching."

"Indeed!" I responded, rousing myself quickly, "I was not affected at all—not a whit."

And in proof, I drew from my pocket a perfectly dry handkerchief, still clean and in its folds.

Villette

Hereupon I was made the object of a string of strictures rather piquant than polite. I listened with zest. After those two days of unnatural silence, it was better than music to hear M. Paul haranguing again just in his old fashion. I listened, and meantime solaced myself and Sylvie with the contents of a bonbonnière, which M. Emanuel's gifts kept well supplied with chocolate comfits: It pleased him to see even a small matter from his hand duly appreciated. He looked at me and the spaniel while we shared the spoil; he put up his penknife. Touching my hand with the bundle of new-cut quills, he said:—"Dites donc, petite sœur—speak frankly—what have you thought of me during the last two days?"

But of this question I would take no manner of notice; its purport made my eyes fill. I caressed Sylvie assiduously. M. Paul, leaning—over the desk, bent towards me:—"I called myself your brother," he said: "I hardly know what I am—brother—friend—I cannot tell. I know I think of you—I feel I wish, you well—but I must check myself; you are to be feared. My best friends point out danger, and whisper caution."

"You do right to listen to your friends. By all means be cautious."

"It is your religion—your strange, self-reliant, invulnerable creed, whose influence seems to clothe you in, I know not what, unblessed panoply. You are good—Père Silas calls you good, and loves you—but your terrible, proud, earnest Protestantism, there is the danger. It expresses itself by your eye at times; and again, it gives you certain tones and certain gestures that make my flesh creep. You are not demonstrative, and yet, just now—when you handled that tract—my God! I thought Lucifer smiled."

"Certainly I don't respect that tract—what then?"

"Not respect that tract? But it is the pure essence of faith, love, charity! I thought it would touch you: in its gentleness, I trusted that it could not fail. I laid it in your desk with a prayer: I must indeed be a sinner: Heaven will not hear the petitions that come warmest from my heart. You scorn my little offering. Oh, cela me fait mal!"

"Monsieur, I don't scorn it—at least, not as your gift. Monsieur, sit down; listen to me. I am not a heathen, I am not hard-hearted, I am not unchristian, I am not dangerous, as they tell you; I would not trouble your faith; you believe in God and Christ and the Bible, and so do I."

"But do you believe in the Bible? Do you receive Revelation? What limits are there to the wild, careless daring of your country and sect. Père Silas dropped dark hints."

By dint of persuasion, I made him half-define these hints; they amounted to crafty Jesuit-slanders. That night M. Paul and I talked seriously and closely. He pleaded, he argued. I could not argue—a fortunate incapacity; it needed but triumphant, logical opposition to effect all the director wished to be effected; but I could talk in my own way—the way M. Paul was used to—and of which he could follow the meanderings and fill the hiatus, and pardon the strange stammerings, strange to him no longer. At ease with him, I could defend my creed and faith in my own fashion; in some degree I could lull his prejudices. He was not satisfied when he went away, hardly was he appeased; but he was made thoroughly to feel that Protestants were not necessarily the irreverent Pagans his director had insinuated; he was made to comprehend something of their mode of honouring the Light, the Life, the Word; he was enabled partly to perceive that, while their veneration for things venerable was not quite like that cultivated in his Church, it had its own, perhaps, deeper power—its own more solemn awe.

I found that Père Silas (himself, I must repeat, not a bad man, though the advocate of a bad cause) had darkly stigmatized Protestants in general, and myself by inference, with strange names, had ascribed to us strange "isms;" Monsieur Emanuel revealed all this in his frank fashion, which knew not secretiveness, looking at me as he spoke with a kind, earnest fear, almost trembling lest there should be truth in the charges. Père Silas, it seems, had closely watched me, had ascertained that I went by turns, and indiscriminately, to the three Protestant Chapels of Villette—the French, German, and English—id est, the Presbyterian, Lutheran, Episcopalian. Such liberality argued in the father's eyes profound indifference— who tolerates all, he reasoned, can be attached to none. Now, it happened that I had often secretly wondered at the minute and unimportant character of the differences between these three sects—at the unity and identity of their vital doctrines: I saw nothing to hinder them from being one day fused into one grand Holy Alliance, and I respected them all, though I thought that in each there were faults of form, incumbrances, and trivialities. Just what I thought, that did I tell M. Emanuel, and explained to him that my own last appeal, the guide to which I looked, and the teacher which I owned, must always be the Bible itself, rather than any sect, of whatever name or nation.

He left me soothed, yet full of solicitude, breathing a wish, as strong as a prayer, that if I were wrong, Heaven would lead me right. I heard, poured forth on the threshold, some fervid murmurings to "Marie, Reine du Ciel," some deep aspiration that his hope might yet be mine.

Strange! I had no such feverish wish to turn him from the faith of his fathers. I thought Romanism wrong, a great mixed image of gold and clay; but it seemed to me that this Romanist held the purer elements of his creed with an innocency of heart which God must love.

The preceding conversation passed between eight and nine o'clock of the evening, in a schoolroom of the quiet Rue Fossette, opening on a sequestered garden. Probably about the same, or a somewhat later hour of the succeeding evening, its echoes, collected by holy obedience, were breathed verbatim in an attent ear, at the panel of a confessional, in the hoary church of the Magi. It ensued that Père Silas paid a visit to Madame Beck, and stirred by I know not what mixture of motives, persuaded her to let him undertake for a time the Englishwoman's spiritual direction.

Hereupon I was put through a course of reading—that is, I just glanced at the books lent me; they were too little in my way to be thoroughly read, marked, learned, or inwardly digested. And besides, I had a book up-stairs, under my pillow, whereof certain chapters satisfied my needs in the article of spiritual lore, furnishing such precept and example as, to my heart's core, I was convinced could not be improved on.

Then Père Silas showed me the fair side of Rome, her good works; and bade me judge the tree by its fruits.

In answer, I felt and I avowed that these works were not the fruits of Rome; they were but her abundant blossoming, but the fair promise she showed the world, that bloom when set, savoured not of charity; the apple full formed was ignorance, abasement, and bigotry. Out of men's afflictions and affections were forged the rivets of their servitude. Poverty was fed and clothed, and sheltered, to bind it by obligation to "the Church;" orphanage was reared and educated that it might grow up in the fold of "the Church;" sickness was tended that it might die after the formula and in the ordinance of "the Church;" and men were overwrought, and women most murderously sacrificed, and all laid down a world God made pleasant for his creatures' good, and took up a cross, monstrous in its galling weight, that they might serve Rome, prove her sanctity, confirm her power, and spread the reign of her tyrant "Church."

For man's good was little done; for God's glory, less. A thousand ways were opened with pain, with blood-sweats, with lavishing of life; mountains were cloven through their breasts, and rocks were split to their base; and all for what? That a Priesthood might march straight on and straight upward to an all-dominating eminence, whence they might at last stretch the sceptre of their Moloch "Church."

It will not be. God is not with Rome, and, were human sorrows still for the Son of God, would he not mourn over her cruelties and ambitions, as once he mourned over the crimes and woes of doomed Jerusalem!

Oh, lovers of power! Oh, mitred aspirants for this world's kingdoms! an hour will come, even to you, when it will be well for your hearts — pausing faint at each broken beat — that there is a Mercy beyond human compassions, a Love, stronger than this strong death which even you must face, and before it, fall; a Charity more potent than any sin, even yours; a Pity which redeems worlds — nay, absolves Priests.

My third temptation was held out in the pomp of Rome — the glory of her kingdom. I was taken to the churches on solemn occasions — days of fête and state; I was shown the Papal ritual and ceremonial. I looked at it.

Many people — men and women — no doubt far my superiors in a thousand ways, have felt this display impressive, have declared that though their Reason protested, their Imagination was subjugated. I cannot say the same. Neither full procession, nor high mass, nor swarming tapers, nor swinging censers, nor ecclesiastical millinery, nor celestial jewellery, touched my imagination a whit. What I saw struck me as tawdry, not grand; as grossly material, not poetically spiritual.

This I did not tell Père Silas; he was old, he looked venerable: through every abortive experiment, under every repeated disappointment, he remained personally kind to me, and I felt tender of hurting his feelings. But on the evening of a certain day when, from the balcony of a great house, I had been made to witness a huge mingled procession of the church and the army — priests with relics, and soldiers with weapons, an obese and aged archbishop, habited in cambric and lace, looking strangely like a grey daw in bird-of-paradise plumage, and a band of young girls fantastically robed and garlanded — then I spoke my mind to M. Paul.

"I did not like it," I told him; "I did not respect such

ceremonies; I wished to see no more."

And having relieved my conscience by this declaration, I was able to go on, and, speaking more currently and clearly than my wont, to show him that I had a mind to keep to my reformed creed; the more I saw of Popery the closer I clung to Protestantism; doubtless there were errors in every church, but I now perceived by contrast how severely pure was my own, compared with her whose painted and meretricious face had been unveiled for my admiration. I told him how we kept fewer forms between us and God; retaining, indeed, no more than, perhaps, the nature of mankind in the mass rendered necessary for due observance. I told him I could not look on flowers and tinsel, on wax-lights and embroidery, at such times and under such circumstances as should be devoted to lifting the secret vision to Him whose home is Infinity, and His being—Eternity. That when I thought of sin and sorrow, of earthly corruption, mortal depravity, weighty temporal woe—I could not care for chanting priests or mumming officials; that when the pains of existence and the terrors of dissolution pressed before me—when the mighty hope and measureless doubt of the future arose in view—then, even the scientific strain, or the prayer in a language learned and dead, harassed: with hindrance a heart which only longed to cry—"God be merciful to me, a sinner!"

When I had so spoken, so declared my faith, and so widely severed myself, from him I addressed—then, at last, came a tone accordant, an echo responsive, one sweet chord of harmony in two conflicting spirits.

"Whatever say priests or controversialists," murmured M. Emanuel, "God is good, and loves all the sincere. Believe, then, what you can; believe it as you can; one prayer, at least, we have in common; I also cry—'O Dieu, sois appaisé envers moi qui suis pécheur!'"

He leaned on the back of my chair. After some thought he again spoke:

"How seem in the eyes of that God who made all firmaments, from whose nostrils issued whatever of life is here, or in the stars shining yonder—how seem the differences of man? But as Time is not for God, nor Space, so neither is Measure, nor Comparison. We abase ourselves in our littleness, and we do right; yet it may be that the constancy of one heart, the truth and faith of one mind according to the light He has appointed, import as much to Him as the just motion of satellites about their planets, of planets about their suns, of suns around that mighty unseen centre incomprehensible, irrealizable, with strange mental effort only divined.

"God guide us all! God bless you, Lucy!"

CHAPTER XXXVII.

SUNSHINE.

It was very well for Paulina to decline further correspondence with Graham till her father had sanctioned the intercourse. But Dr. Bretton could not live within a league of the Hôtel Crécy, and not contrive to visit there often. Both lovers meant at first, I believe, to be distant; they kept their intention so far as demonstrative courtship went, but in feeling they soon drew very near.

All that was best in Graham sought Paulina; whatever in him was noble, awoke, and grew in her presence. With his past admiration of Miss Fanshawe, I suppose his intellect had little to do, but his whole intellect, and his highest tastes, came in question now. These, like all his faculties, were active, eager for nutriment, and alive to gratification when it came.

I cannot say that Paulina designedly led him to talk of books, or formally proposed to herself for a moment the task of winning him to reflection, or planned the improvement of his mind, or so much as fancied his mind could in any one respect be improved. She thought him very perfect; it was Graham himself, who, at first by the merest chance, mentioned some book he had been reading, and when in her response sounded a welcome harmony of sympathies, something, pleasant to his soul, he talked on, more and better perhaps than he had ever talked before on such subjects. She listened with delight, and answered with animation. In each successive answer, Graham heard a music waxing finer and finer to his sense; in each he found a suggestive, persuasive, magic accent that opened a scarce-known treasure-house within, showed him unsuspected power in his own mind, and what was better, latent goodness in his heart. Each liked the way in which the other talked; the voice, the diction, the expression pleased; each keenly relished the flavour of the other's wit; they met each other's meaning with strange quickness, their thoughts often matched like carefully-chosen pearls. Graham had wealth of mirth by nature; Paulina possessed no such inherent flow of animal spirits—unstimulated, she inclined to be thoughtful and pensive—but now she seemed merry as a lark; in her lover's genial presence, she glanced like some soft glad light. How beautiful she grew in her happiness, I can hardly express, but I wondered to see her. As to that gentle ice of hers—that reserve on which she had depended; where was it now? Ah! Graham would not long bear it; he brought with him a generous influence that soon thawed the timid, self-imposed restriction.

Now were the old Bretton days talked over; perhaps brokenly at first, with a sort of smiling diffidence, then with opening candour and still growing confidence. Graham had made for himself a better opportunity than that he had wished me to give; he had earned independence of the collateral help that disobliging Lucy had refused; all his reminiscences of "little Polly" found their proper expression in his own pleasant tones, by his own kind and handsome lips; how much better than if suggested by me.

More than once when we were alone, Paulina would tell me how wonderful and curious it was to discover the richness and accuracy of his memory in this matter. How, while he was looking at her, recollections would seem to be suddenly quickened in his mind. He reminded her that she had once gathered his head in her arms, caressed his leonine graces, and cried out, "Graham, I do like you!" He told her how she would set a footstool beside him, and climb by its aid to his knee. At this day he said he could recall the sensation of her little hands smoothing his cheek, or burying themselves in his thick mane. He remembered the touch of her small forefinger, placed half tremblingly, half curiously, in the cleft in his chin, the lisp, the look with which she would name it "a pretty dimple," then seek his eyes and question why they pierced so, telling him he had a "nice, strange face; far nicer, far stranger, than either his mamma or Lucy Snowe."

"Child as I was," remarked Paulina, "I wonder how I dared be so venturous. To me he seems now all sacred, his locks are inaccessible, and, Lucy, I feel a sort of fear, when I look at his firm, marble chin, at his straight Greek features. Women are called beautiful, Lucy; he is not like a woman, therefore I suppose he is not beautiful, but what is he, then? Do other people see him with my eyes? Do you admire him?"

"I'll tell you what I do, Paulina," was once my answer to her many questions. "I never see him. I looked at him twice or thrice about a year ago, before he recognised me, and then I shut my eyes; and if he were to cross their balls twelve times between each day's sunset and sunrise, except from memory, I should hardly know what shape had gone by."

"Lucy, what do you mean?" said she, under her breath.

"I mean that I value vision, and dread being struck stone blind."

It was best to answer her strongly at once, and to silence for ever the tender, passionate confidences which left her lips sweet honey, and sometimes dropped in my ear—molten lead. To me, she commented no more on her lover's beauty.

Yet speak of him she would; sometimes shyly, in quiet, brief phrases; sometimes with a tenderness of cadence, and music of voice exquisite in itself; but which chafed me at times miserably; and then, I know, I gave her stern looks and words; but cloudless happiness had dazzled her native clear sight, and she only thought Lucy—fitful.

"Spartan girl! Proud Lucy!" she would say, smiling at me. "Graham says you are the most peculiar, capricious little woman he knows; but yet you are excellent; we both think so."

"You both think you know not what," said I. "Have the goodness to make me as little the subject of your mutual talk and thoughts as possible. I have my sort of life apart from yours."

"But ours, Lucy, is a beautiful life, or it will be; and you shall share it."

"I shall share no man's or woman's life in this world, as you understand sharing. I think I have one friend of my own, but am not sure; and till I am sure, I live solitary."

"But solitude is sadness."

"Yes; it is sadness. Life, however; has worse than that. Deeper than melancholy, lies heart-break."

"Lucy, I wonder if anybody will ever comprehend you altogether."

There is, in lovers, a certain infatuation of egotism; they will have a witness of their happiness, cost that witness what it may. Paulina had forbidden letters, yet Dr. Bretton wrote; she had resolved against correspondence, yet she answered, were it only to chide. She showed me these letters; with something of the spoiled child's wilfulness, and of the heiress's imperiousness, she made me read them. As I read Graham's, I scarce wondered at her exaction, and understood her pride: they were fine letters—manly and fond—modest and gallant. Hers must have appeared to him beautiful. They had not been written to show her talents; still less, I think, to express her love. On the contrary, it appeared that she had proposed to herself the task of hiding that feeling, and bridling her lover's ardour. But how could such letters serve such a purpose? Graham was become dear as her life; he drew her like a powerful magnet. For her there was influence unspeakable in all he uttered, wrote, thought, or looked. With this unconfessed confession, her letters glowed; it kindled them, from greeting to adieu.

"I wish papa knew; I do wish papa knew!" began now to be her anxious murmur. "I wish, and yet I fear. I can hardly keep Graham back from telling him. There is nothing I long for more than to have this affair settled—to speak out candidly; and yet I dread the crisis. I know, I am certain, papa will be angry at the first; I fear he will dislike me almost; it will seem to him an untoward business; it will be a surprise, a shock: I can hardly foresee its whole effect on him."

The fact was—her father, long calm, was beginning to be a little stirred: long blind on one point, an importunate light was beginning to trespass on his eye.

To her, he said nothing; but when she was not looking at, or perhaps thinking of him, I saw him gaze and meditate on her.

One evening—Paulina was in her dressing-room, writing, I believe, to Graham; she had left me in the library, reading—M. de Bassompierre came in; he sat down: I was about to withdraw; he requested me to remain—gently, yet in a manner which showed he wished compliance. He had taken his seat near the window, at a distance from me; he opened a desk; he took from it what looked like a memorandum-book; of this book he studied a certain entry for several minutes.

"Miss Snowe," said he, laying it down, "do you know my little girl's age?"

"About eighteen, is it not, sir?"

"It seems so. This old pocket-book tells me she was born on the 5th of May, in the year 18—, eighteen years ago. It is strange; I had lost the just reckoning of her age. I thought of her as twelve—fourteen—an indefinite date; but she seemed a child."

"She is about eighteen," I repeated. "She is grown up; she will be no taller."

"My little jewel!" said M. de Bassompierre, in a tone which penetrated like some of his daughter's accents.

432

He sat very thoughtful.

"Sir, don't grieve," I said; for I knew his feelings, utterly unspoken as they were.

"She is the only pearl I have," he said; "and now others will find out that she is pure and of price: they will covet her."

I made no answer. Graham Bretton had dined with us that day; he had shone both in converse and looks: I know not what pride of bloom embellished his aspect and mellowed his intercourse. Under the stimulus of a high hope, something had unfolded in his whole manner which compelled attention. I think he had purposed on that day to indicate the origin of his endeavours, and the aim of his ambition. M. de Bassompierre had found himself forced, in a manner, to descry the direction and catch the character of his homage. Slow in remarking, he was logical in reasoning: having once seized the thread, it had guided him through a long labyrinth.

"Where is she?" he asked.

"She is up-stairs."

"What is she doing?"

"She is writing."

"She writes, does she? Does she receive letters?"

"None but such as she can show me. And — sir — she — they have long wanted to consult you."

"Pshaw! They don't think of me — an old father! I am in the way."

"Ah, M. de Bassompierre — not so — that can't be! But Paulina must speak for herself: and Dr. Bretton, too, must be his own advocate."

"It is a little late. Matters are advanced, it seems."

"Sir, till you approve, nothing is done — only they love each other."

"Only!" he echoed.

Invested by fate with the part of confidante and mediator, I was obliged to go on: "Hundreds of times has Dr. Bretton been on the point of appealing to you, sir; but, with all his high courage, he fears you mortally."

"He may well—he may well fear me. He has touched the best thing I have. Had he but let her alone, she would have remained a child for years yet. So. Are they engaged?"

"They could not become engaged without your permission."

"It is well for you, Miss Snowe, to talk and think with that propriety which always characterizes you; but this matter is a grief to me; my little girl was all I had: I have no more daughters and no son; Bretton might as well have looked elsewhere; there are scores of rich and pretty women who would not, I daresay, dislike him: he has looks, and conduct, and connection. Would nothing serve him but my Polly?"

"If he had never seen your 'Polly,' others might and would have pleased him—your niece, Miss Fanshawe, for instance."

"Ah! I would have given him Ginevra with all my heart; but Polly!—I can't let him have her. No—I can't. He is not her equal," he affirmed, rather gruffly. "In what particular is he her match? They talk of fortune! I am not an avaricious or interested man, but the world thinks of these things—and Polly will be rich."

"Yes, that is known," said I: "all Villette knows her as an heiress."

"Do they talk of my little girl in that light?"

"They do, sir."

He fell into deep thought. I ventured to say, "Would you, sir, think any one Paulina's match? Would you prefer any other to Dr. Bretton? Do you think higher rank or more wealth would make much difference in your feelings towards a future son-in-law?"

"You touch me there," said he.

"Look at the aristocracy of Villette—you would not like them, sir?"

"I should not—never a duc, baron, or vicomte of the lot."

"I am told many of these persons think about her, sir," I went on, gaining courage on finding that I met attention rather than repulse. "Other suitors will come, therefore, if Dr. Bretton is refused. Wherever you go, I suppose, aspirants will not be wanting. Independent of heiress-ship, it appears to me that Paulina charms most of those who see her."

"Does she? How? My little girl is not thought a beauty."

"Sir, Miss de Bassompierre is very beautiful."

"Nonsense!—begging your pardon, Miss Snowe, but I think you are too partial. I like Polly: I like all her ways and all her looks—but then I am her father; and even I never thought about beauty. She is amusing, fairy-like, interesting to me;—you must be mistaken in supposing her handsome?"

"She attracts, sir: she would attract without the advantages of your wealth and position."

"My wealth and position! Are these any bait to Graham? If I thought so——"

"Dr. Bretton knows these points perfectly, as you may be sure, M. de Bassompierre, and values them as any gentleman would—as you would yourself, under the same circumstances—but they are not his baits. He loves your daughter very much; he feels her finest qualities, and they influence him worthily."

"What! has my little pet 'fine qualities?'"

"Ah, sir! did you observe her that evening when so many men of eminence and learning dined here?"

"I certainly was rather struck and surprised with her manner that day; its womanliness made me smile."

"And did you see those accomplished Frenchmen gather round her in the drawing-room?"

"I did; but I thought it was by way of relaxation—as one might amuse one's self with a pretty infant."

"Sir, she demeaned herself with distinction; and I heard the French gentlemen say she was 'pétrie d'esprit et de graces.' Dr. Bretton thought the same."

"She is a good, dear child, that is certain; and I do believe she has some character. When I think of it, I was once ill; Polly nursed me; they thought I should die; she, I recollect, grew at once stronger and tenderer as I grew worse in health. And as I recovered, what a sunbeam she was in my sick-room! Yes; she played about my chair as noiselessly and as cheerful as light. And now she is sought in marriage! I don't want to part with her," said he, and he groaned.

"You have known Dr. and Mrs. Bretton so long," I suggested, "it would be less like separation to give her to him than to another."

He reflected rather gloomily.

"True. I have long known Louisa Bretton," he murmured. "She and I are indeed old, old friends; a sweet, kind girl she was when she was young. You talk of beauty, Miss Snowe! she was handsome, if you will—tall, straight, and blooming—not the mere child or elf my Polly seems to me: at eighteen, Louisa had a carriage and stature fit for a princess. She is a comely and a good woman now. The lad is like her; I have always thought so, and favoured and wished him well. Now he repays me by this robbery! My little treasure used to love her old father dearly and truly. It is all over now, doubtless—I am an incumbrance."

The door opened—his "little treasure" came in. She was dressed, so to speak, in evening beauty; that animation which sometimes comes with the close of day, warmed her eye and cheek; a tinge of summer crimson heightened her complexion; her curls fell full and long on her lily neck; her white dress suited the heat of June. Thinking me alone, she had brought in her hand the letter just written—brought it folded but unsealed. I was to read it. When she saw her father, her tripping step faltered a little, paused a moment—the colour in her cheek flowed rosy over her whole face.

"Polly," said M. de Bassompierre, in a low voice, with a grave smile, "do you blush at seeing papa? That is something new."

"I don't blush—I never do blush," affirmed she, while another eddy from the heart sent up its scarlet. "But I thought you were in the dining-room, and I wanted Lucy."

"You thought I was with John Graham Bretton, I suppose? But he has just been called out: he will be back soon, Polly. He can post your letter for you; it will save Matthieu a 'course,' as he calls it."

"I don't post letters," said she, rather pettishly.

"What do you do with them, then?—come here and tell me."

Both her mind and gesture seemed to hesitate a second—to say "Shall I come?"—but she approached.

"How long is it since you became a letter-writer, Polly? It only seems yesterday when you were at your pot-hooks, labouring away absolutely with both hands at the pen."

"Papa, they are not letters to send to the post in your letter-bag; they are only notes, which I give now and then into the person's hands, just to satisfy."

"The person! That means Miss Snowe, I suppose?"

"No, papa—not Lucy."

"Who then? Perhaps Mrs. Bretton?"

"No, papa—not Mrs. Bretton."

"Who, then, my little daughter? Tell papa the truth."

"Oh, papa!" she cried with earnestness, "I will—I will tell you the truth—all the truth; I am glad to tell you—glad, though I tremble."

She did tremble: growing excitement, kindling feeling, and also gathering courage, shook her.

"I hate to hide my actions from you, papa. I fear you and love you above everything but God. Read the letter; look at the address."

She laid it on his knee. He took it up and read it through; his hand shaking, his eyes glistening meantime.

He re-folded it, and viewed the writer with a strange, tender, mournful amaze.

"Can she write so—the little thing that stood at my knee but yesterday? Can she feel so?"

"Papa, is it wrong? Does it pain you?"

"There is nothing wrong in it, my innocent little Mary; but it pains me."

"But, papa, listen! You shall not be pained by me. I would give up everything—almost" (correcting herself); "I would die rather than make you unhappy; that would be too wicked!"

She shuddered.

"Does the letter not please you? Must it not go? Must it be torn? It shall, for your sake, if you order it."

"I order nothing."

"Order something, papa; express your wish; only don't hurt, don't grieve Graham. I cannot, cannot bear that. I love you, papa; but I love Graham too—because—because—it is impossible to help it."

"This splendid Graham is a young scamp, Polly—that is my present notion of him: it will surprise you to hear that, for my part, I do not love him one whit. Ah! years ago I saw something in that lad's eye I never quite fathomed—something his mother has not—a depth which warned a man not to wade into that stream too far; now, suddenly, I find myself taken over the crown of the head."

"Papa, you don't—you have not fallen in; you are safe on the bank; you can do as you please; your power is despotic; you can shut me up in a convent, and break Graham's heart to-morrow, if you choose to be so cruel. Now, autocrat, now czar, will you do this?"

"Off with him to Siberia, red whiskers and all; I say, I don't like him, Polly, and I wonder that you should."

"Papa," said she, "do you know you are very naughty? I never saw you look so disagreeable, so unjust, so almost vindictive before. There is an expression in your face which does not belong to you."

"Off with him!" pursued Mr. Home, who certainly did look sorely crossed and annoyed—even a little bitter; "but, I suppose, if he went, Polly would pack a bundle and run after him; her heart is fairly won—won, and weaned from her old father."

"Papa, I say it is naughty, it is decidedly wrong, to talk in

Villette

that way. I am not weaned from you, and no human being and no mortal influence can wean me."

"Be married, Polly! Espouse the red whiskers. Cease to be a daughter; go and be a wife!"

"Red whiskers! I wonder what you mean, papa. You should take care of prejudice. You sometimes say to me that all the Scotch, your countrymen, are the victims of prejudice. It is proved now, I think, when no distinction is to be made between red and deep nut-brown."

"Leave the prejudiced old Scotchman; go away."

She stood looking at him a minute. She wanted to show firmness, superiority to taunts; knowing her father's character, guessing his few foibles, she had expected the sort of scene which was now transpiring; it did not take her by surprise, and she desired to let it pass with dignity, reliant upon reaction. Her dignity stood her in no stead. Suddenly her soul melted in her eyes; she fell on his neck: — "I won't leave you, papa; I'll never leave you. I won't pain you! I'll never pain you!" was her cry.

"My lamb! my treasure!" murmured the loving though rugged sire. He said no more for the moment; indeed, those two words were hoarse.

The room was now darkening. I heard a movement, a step without. Thinking it might be a servant coming with candles, I gently opened, to prevent intrusion. In the ante-room stood no servant: a tall gentleman was placing his hat on the table, drawing off his gloves slowly — lingering, waiting, it seemed to me. He called me neither by sign nor word; yet his eye said: — "Lucy, come here." And I went.

Over his face a smile flowed, while he looked down on me: no temper, save his own, would have expressed by a smile the sort of agitation which now fevered him.

"M. de Bassompierre is there — is he not?" he inquired, pointing to the library.

"Yes."

"He noticed me at dinner? He understood me?"

"Yes, Graham."

"I am brought up for judgment, then, and so is she?"

"Mr. Home" (we now and always continued to term him Mr. Home at times) "is talking to his daughter."

"Ha! These are sharp moments, Lucy!"

He was quite stirred up; his young hand trembled; a vital (I was going to write mortal, but such words ill apply to one all living like him) — a vital suspense now held, now hurried, his breath: in all this trouble his smile never faded.

"Is he very angry, Lucy?"

"She is very faithful, Graham."

"What will be done unto me?"

"Graham, your star must be fortunate."

"Must it? Kind prophet! So cheered, I should be a faint heart indeed to quail. I think I find all women faithful, Lucy. I ought to love them, and I do. My mother is good; she is divine; and you are true as steel. Are you not?"

"Yes, Graham."

"Then give me thy hand, my little god-sister: it is a friendly little hand to me, and always has been. And now for the great venture. God be with the right. Lucy, say Amen!"

He turned, and waited till I said "Amen!" — which I did to please him: the old charm, in doing as he bid me, came back. I wished him success; and successful I knew he would be. He was born victor, as some are born vanquished.

"Follow me!" he said; and I followed him into Mr. Home's presence.

"Sir," he asked, "what is my sentence?"

The father looked at him: the daughter kept her face hid.

"Well, Bretton," said Mr. Home, "you have given me the usual reward of hospitality. I entertained you; you have taken my best. I was always glad to see you; you were glad to see the one precious thing I had. You spoke me fair; and, meantime, I will not say you robbed me, but I am bereaved, and what I have

Villette

lost, you, it seems, have won."

"Sir, I cannot repent."

"Repent! Not you! You triumph, no doubt: John Graham, you descended partly from a Highlander and a chief, and there is a trace of the Celt in all you look, speak, and think. You have his cunning and his charm. The red — (Well then, Polly, the fair) hair, the tongue of guile, and brain of wile, are all come down by inheritance."

"Sir, I feel honest enough," said Graham; and a genuine English blush covered his face with its warm witness of sincerity. "And yet," he added, "I won't deny that in some respects you accuse me justly. In your presence I have always had a thought which I dared not show you. I did truly regard you as the possessor of the most valuable thing the world owns for me. I wished for it: I tried for it. Sir, I ask for it now."

"John, you ask much."

"Very much, sir. It must come from your generosity, as a gift; from your justice, as a reward. I can never earn it."

"Ay! Listen to the Highland tongue!" said Mr. Home. "Look up, Polly! Answer this 'braw wooer;' send him away!"

She looked up. She shyly glanced at her eager, handsome suitor. She gazed tenderly on her furrowed sire.

"Papa, I love you both," said she; "I can take care of you both. I need not send Graham away — he can live here; he will be no inconvenience," she alleged with that simplicity of phraseology which at times was wont to make both her father and Graham smile. They smiled now.

"He will be a prodigious inconvenience to me," still persisted Mr. Home. "I don't want him, Polly, he is too tall; he is in my way. Tell him to march."

"You will get used to him, papa. He seemed exceedingly tall to me at first — like a tower when I looked up at him; but, on the whole, I would rather not have him otherwise."

"I object to him altogether, Polly; I can do without a son-in-law. I should never have requested the best man in the land to stand to me in that relation. Dismiss this gentleman."

"But he has known you so long, papa, and suits you so well."

"Suits me, forsooth! Yes; he has pretended to make my opinions and tastes his own. He has humoured me for good reasons. I think, Polly, you and I will bid him good-by."

"Till to-morrow only. Shake hands with Graham, papa."

"No: I think not: I am not friends with him. Don't think to coax me between you."

"Indeed, indeed, you are friends. Graham, stretch out your right hand. Papa, put out yours. Now, let them touch. Papa, don't be stiff; close your fingers; be pliant—there! But that is not a clasp—it is a grasp? Papa, you grasp like a vice. You crush Graham's hand to the bone; you hurt him!"

He must have hurt him; for he wore a massive ring, set round with brilliants, of which the sharp facets cut into Graham's flesh and drew blood: but pain only made Dr. John laugh, as anxiety had made him smile.

"Come with me into my study," at last said Mr. Home to the doctor. They went. Their intercourse was not long, but I suppose it was conclusive. The suitor had to undergo an interrogatory and a scrutiny on many things. Whether Dr. Bretton was at times guileful in look and language or not, there was a sound foundation below. His answers, I understood afterwards, evinced both wisdom and integrity. He had managed his affairs well. He had struggled through entanglements; his fortunes were in the way of retrieval; he proved himself in a position to marry.

Once more the father and lover appeared in the library. M. de Bassompierre shut the door; he pointed to his daughter.

"Take her," he said. "Take her, John Bretton: and may God deal with you as you deal with her!"

Not long after, perhaps a fortnight, I saw three persons, Count de Bassompierre, his daughter, and Dr. Graham Bretton, sitting on one seat, under a low-spreading and umbrageous tree, in the grounds of the palace at Bois l'Etang. They had come thither to enjoy a summer evening: outside the magnificent gates their carriage waited to take them home; the green sweeps of turf spread round them quiet and dim; the palace rose at a distance, white as a crag on Pentelicus; the evening star shone above it; a forest of flowering shrubs embalmed the climate of this spot; the hour was still and sweet; the scene, but for this group, was solitary.

Paulina sat between the two gentlemen: while they conversed, her little hands were busy at some work; I thought at first she was binding a nosegay. No; with the tiny pair of scissors, glittering in her lap, she had severed spoils from each manly head beside her, and was now occupied in plaiting together the grey lock and the golden wave. The plait woven — no silk-thread being at hand to bind it — a tress of her own hair was made to serve that purpose; she tied it like a knot, prisoned it in a locket, and laid it on her heart.

"Now," said she, "there is an amulet made, which has virtue to keep you two always friends. You can never quarrel so long as I wear this."

An amulet was indeed made, a spell framed which rendered enmity impossible. She was become a bond to both, an influence over each, a mutual concord. From them she drew her happiness, and what she borrowed, she, with interest, gave back.

"Is there, indeed, such happiness on earth?" I asked, as I watched the father, the daughter, the future husband, now united — all blessed and blessing.

Yes; it is so. Without any colouring of romance, or any exaggeration of fancy, it is so. Some real lives do — for some certain days or years — actually anticipate the happiness of Heaven; and, I believe, if such perfect happiness is once felt by good people (to the wicked it never comes), its sweet effect is never wholly lost. Whatever trials follow, whatever pains of sickness or shades of death, the glory precedent still shines through, cheering the keen anguish, and tinging the deep cloud.

I will go farther. I do believe there are some human beings so born, so reared, so guided from a soft cradle to a calm and late grave, that no excessive suffering penetrates their lot, and no tempestuous blackness overcasts their journey. And often, these are not pampered, selfish beings, but Nature's elect, harmonious and benign; men and women mild with charity, kind agents of God's kind attributes.

Let me not delay the happy truth. Graham Bretton and Paulina de Bassompierre were married, and such an agent did Dr. Bretton prove. He did not with time degenerate; his faults decayed, his virtues ripened; he rose in intellectual refinement, he won in moral profit: all dregs filtered away, the clear wine settled bright and tranquil. Bright, too, was the destiny of his sweet wife. She kept her husband's love, she aided in his progress—of his happiness she was the corner stone.

This pair was blessed indeed, for years brought them, with great prosperity, great goodness: they imparted with open hand, yet wisely. Doubtless they knew crosses, disappointments, difficulties; but these were well borne. More than once, too, they had to look on Him whose face flesh scarce can see and live: they had to pay their tribute to the King of Terrors. In the fulness of years, M. de Bassompierre was taken: in ripe old age departed Louisa Bretton. Once even there rose a cry in their halls, of Rachel weeping for her children; but others sprang healthy and blooming to replace the lost: Dr. Bretton saw himself live again in a son who inherited his looks and his disposition; he had stately daughters, too, like himself: these children he reared with a suave, yet a firm hand; they grew up according to inheritance and nurture.

In short, I do but speak the truth when I say that these two lives of Graham and Paulina were blessed, like that of Jacob's favoured son, with "blessings of Heaven above, blessings of the deep that lies under." It was so, for God saw that it was good.

CHAPTER XXXVIII.

CLOUD.

But it is not so for all. What then? His will be done, as done it surely will be, whether we humble ourselves to resignation or not. The impulse of creation forwards it; the strength of powers, seen and unseen, has its fulfilment in charge. Proof of a life to come must be given. In fire and in blood, if needful, must that proof be written. In fire and in blood do we trace the record throughout nature. In fire and in blood does it cross our own experience. Sufferer, faint not through terror of this burning evidence. Tired wayfarer, gird up thy loins; look upward, march onward. Pilgrims and brother mourners, join in friendly company. Dark through the wilderness of this world stretches the way for most of us: equal and steady be our tread; be our cross our banner. For staff we have His promise, whose "word is tried, whose way perfect:" for present hope His providence, "who gives the shield of salvation, whose gentleness makes great;" for final home His bosom, who "dwells in the height of Heaven;" for crowning prize a glory, exceeding and eternal. Let us so run that we may obtain: let us endure hardness as good soldiers; let us finish our course, and keep the faith, reliant in the issue to come off more than conquerors: "Art thou not from everlasting mine Holy One? WE SHALL NOT DIE!"

On a Thursday morning we were all assembled in classe, waiting for the lesson of literature. The hour was come; we expected the master.

The pupils of the first classe sat very still; the cleanly-written compositions prepared since the last lesson lay ready before them, neatly tied with ribbon, waiting to be gathered by the hand of the Professor as he made his rapid round of the desks. The month was July, the morning fine, the glass-door stood ajar, through it played a fresh breeze, and plants, growing at the lintel, waved, bent, looked in, seeming to whisper tidings.

M. Emanuel was not always quite punctual; we scarcely wondered at his being a little late, but we wondered when the door at last opened and, instead of him with his swiftness and his fire, there came quietly upon us the cautious Madame Beck.

She approached M. Paul's desk; she stood before it; she drew round her the light shawl covering her shoulders; beginning to speak in low, yet firm tones, and with a fixed gaze, she said, "This morning there will be no lesson of literature."

The second paragraph of her address followed, after about two minutes' pause.

"It is probable the lessons will be suspended for a week. I shall require at least that space of time to find an efficient substitute for M. Emanuel. Meanwhile, it shall be our study to fill the blanks usefully.

"Your Professor, ladies," she went on, "intends, if possible, duly to take leave of you. At the present moment he has not leisure for that ceremony. He is preparing for a long voyage. A very sudden and urgent summons of duty calls him to a great distance. He has decided to leave Europe for an indefinite time. Perhaps he may tell you more himself. Ladies, instead of the usual lesson with M. Emanuel, you will, this morning, read English with Mademoiselle Lucy."

She bent her head courteously, drew closer the folds of her shawl, and passed from the classe.

A great silence fell: then a murmur went round the room: I believe some pupils wept.

Some time elapsed. The noise, the whispering, the occasional sobbing increased. I became conscious of a relaxation of discipline, a sort of growing disorder, as if my girls felt that vigilance was withdrawn, and that surveillance had virtually left the classe. Habit and the sense of duty enabled me to rally quickly, to rise in my usual way, to speak in my usual tone, to enjoin, and finally to establish quiet. I made the English reading long and close. I kept them at it the whole morning. I remember feeling a sentiment of impatience towards the pupils who sobbed. Indeed, their emotion was not of much value: it was only an hysteric agitation. I told them so unsparingly. I half ridiculed them. I was severe. The truth was, I could not do with their tears, or that gasping sound; I could not bear it. A rather weak-minded, low-spirited pupil kept it up when the others had done; relentless necessity obliged and assisted me so to accost her, that she dared not carry on the demonstration, that she was forced to conquer the convulsion.

That girl would have had a right to hate me, except that, when school was over and her companions departing, I ordered her to stay, and when they were gone, I did what I had never done to one among them before — pressed her to my heart and kissed her cheek. But, this impulse yielded to, I speedily put her out of the classe, for, upon that poignant strain, she wept more bitterly than ever.

Villette

I filled with occupation every minute of that day, and should have liked to sit up all night if I might have kept a candle burning; the night, however, proved a bad time, and left bad effects, preparing me ill for the next day's ordeal of insufferable gossip. Of course this news fell under general discussion. Some little reserve had accompanied the first surprise: that soon wore off; every mouth opened; every tongue wagged; teachers, pupils, the very servants, mouthed the name of "Emanuel." He, whose connection with the school was contemporary with its commencement, thus suddenly to withdraw! All felt it strange.

They talked so much, so long, so often, that, out of the very multitude of their words and rumours, grew at last some intelligence. About the third day I heard it said that he was to sail in a week; then—that he was bound for the West Indies. I looked at Madame Beck's face, and into her eyes, for disproof or confirmation of this report; I perused her all over for information, but no part of her disclosed more than what was unperturbed and commonplace.

"This secession was an immense loss to her," she alleged. "She did not know how she should fill up the vacancy. She was so used to her kinsman, he had become her right hand; what should she do without him? She had opposed the step, but M. Paul had convinced her it was his duty."

She said all this in public, in classe, at the dinner-table, speaking audibly to Zélie St. Pierre.

"Why was it his duty?" I could have asked her that. I had impulses to take hold of her suddenly, as she calmly passed me in classe, to stretch out my hand and grasp her fast, and say, "Stop. Let us hear the conclusion of the whole matter. Why is it his duty to go into banishment?" But Madame always addressed some other teacher, and never looked at me, never seemed conscious I could have a care in the question.

The week wore on. Nothing more was said about M. Emanuel coming to bid us good-by; and none seemed anxious for his coming; none questioned whether or not he would come; none betrayed torment lest he should depart silent and unseen; incessantly did they talk, and never, in all their talk, touched on this vital point. As to Madame, she of course could see him, and say to him as much as she pleased. What should she care whether or not he appeared in the schoolroom?

The week consumed. We were told that he was going on such a day, that his destination was "Basseterre in

Guadaloupe:" the business which called him abroad related to a friend's interests, not his own: I thought as much.

"Basseterre in Guadaloupe." I had little sleep about this time, but whenever I did slumber, it followed infallibly that I was quickly roused with a start, while the words "Basseterre," "Guadaloupe," seemed pronounced over my pillow, or ran athwart the darkness round and before me, in zigzag characters of red or violet light.

For what I felt there was no help, and how could I help feeling? M. Emanuel had been very kind to me of late days; he had been growing hourly better and kinder. It was now a month since we had settled the theological difference, and in all that time there had been no quarrel. Nor had our peace been the cold daughter of divorce; we had not lived aloof; he had come oftener, he had talked with me more than before; he had spent hours with me, with temper soothed, with eye content, with manner home-like and mild. Kind subjects of conversation had grown between us; he had inquired into my plans of life, and I had communicated them; the school project pleased him; he made me repeat it more than once, though he called it an Alnaschar dream. The jar was over; the mutual understanding was settling and fixing; feelings of union and hope made themselves profoundly felt in the heart; affection and deep esteem and dawning trust had each fastened its bond.

What quiet lessons I had about this time! No more taunts on my "intellect," no more menaces of grating public shows! How sweetly, for the jealous gibe, and the more jealous, half-passionate eulogy, were substituted a mute, indulgent help, a fond guidance, and a tender forbearance which forgave but never praised. There were times when he would sit for many minutes and not speak at all; and when dusk or duty brought separation, he would leave with words like these, "Il est doux, le repos! Il est précieux le calme bonheur!"

One evening, not ten short days since, he joined me whilst walking in my alley. He took my hand. I looked up in his face. I thought he meant to arrest my attention.

"Bonne petite amie!" said he, softly; "douce consolatrice!" But through his touch, and with his words, a new feeling and a strange thought found a course. Could it be that he was becoming more than friend or brother? Did his look speak a kindness beyond fraternity or amity?

His eloquent look had more to say, his hand drew me

Villette

forward, his interpreting lips stirred. No. Not now. Here into the twilight alley broke an interruption: it came dual and ominous: we faced two bodeful forms—a woman's and a priest's—Madame Beck and Père Silas.

The aspect of the latter I shall never forget. On the first impulse it expressed a Jean-Jacques sensibility, stirred by the signs of affection just surprised; then, immediately, darkened over it the jaundice of ecclesiastical jealousy. He spoke to me with unction. He looked on his pupil with sternness. As to Madame Beck, she, of course, saw nothing—nothing; though her kinsman retained in her presence the hand of the heretic foreigner, not suffering withdrawal, but clasping it close and fast.

Following these incidents, that sudden announcement of departure had struck me at first as incredible. Indeed, it was only frequent repetition, and the credence of the hundred and fifty minds round me, which forced on me its full acceptance. As to that week of suspense, with its blank, yet burning days, which brought from him no word of explanation—I remember, but I cannot describe its passage.

The last day broke. Now would he visit us. Now he would come and speak his farewell, or he would vanish mute, and be seen by us nevermore.

This alternative seemed to be present in the mind of not a living creature in that school. All rose at the usual hour; all breakfasted as usual; all, without reference to, or apparent thought of their late Professor, betook themselves with wonted phlegm to their ordinary duties.

So oblivious was the house, so tame, so trained its proceedings, so inexpectant its aspect—I scarce knew how to breathe in an atmosphere thus stagnant, thus smothering. Would no one lend me a voice? Had no one a wish, no one a word, no one a prayer to which I could say—Amen?

I had seen them unanimous in demand for the merest trifle—a treat, a holiday, a lesson's remission; they could not, they would not now band to besiege Madame Beck, and insist on a last interview with a Master who had certainly been loved, at least by some—loved as they could love—but, oh! what is the love of the multitude?

I knew where he lived: I knew where he was to be heard of, or communicated with; the distance was scarce a stone's-throw:

had it been in the next room—unsummoned, I could make no use of my knowledge. To follow, to seek out, to remind, to recall—for these things I had no faculty.

M. Emanuel might have passed within reach of my arm: had he passed silent and unnoticing, silent and stirless should I have suffered him to go by.

Morning wasted. Afternoon came, and I thought all was over. My heart trembled in its place. My blood was troubled in its current. I was quite sick, and hardly knew how to keep at my post—or do my work. Yet the little world round me plodded on indifferent; all seemed jocund, free of care, or fear, or thought: the very pupils who, seven days since, had wept hysterically at a startling piece of news, appeared quite to have forgotten the news, its import, and their emotion.

A little before five o'clock, the hour of dismissal, Madame Beck sent for me to her chamber, to read over and translate some English letter she had received, and to write for her the answer. Before settling to this work, I observed that she softly closed the two doors of her chamber; she even shut and fastened the casement, though it was a hot day, and free circulation of air was usually regarded by her as indispensable. Why this precaution? A keen suspicion, an almost fierce distrust, suggested such question. Did she want to exclude sound? what sound?

I listened as I had never listened before; I listened like the evening and winter-wolf, snuffing the snow, scenting prey, and hearing far off the traveller's tramp. Yet I could both listen and write. About the middle of the letter I heard—what checked my pen—a tread in the vestibule. No door-bell had rung; Rosine—acting doubtless by orders—had anticipated such réveillée. Madame saw me halt. She coughed, made a bustle, spoke louder. The tread had passed on to the classes.

"Proceed," said Madame; but my hand was fettered, my ear enchained, my thoughts were carried off captive.

The classes formed another building; the hall parted them from the dwelling-house: despite distance and partition, I heard the sudden stir of numbers, a whole division rising at once.

"They are putting away work," said Madame.

It was indeed the hour to put away work, but why that sudden hush—that instant quell of the tumult?

Villette

"Wait, Madame—I will see what it is."

And I put down my pen and left her. Left her? No: she would not be left: powerless to detain me, she rose and followed, close as my shadow. I turned on the last step of the stair.

"Are you coming, too?" I asked.

"Yes," said she; meeting my glance with a peculiar aspect—a look, clouded, yet resolute.

We proceeded then, not together, but she walked in my steps.

He was come. Entering the first classe, I saw him. There, once more appeared the form most familiar. I doubt not they had tried to keep him away, but he was come.

The girls stood in a semicircle; he was passing round, giving his farewells, pressing each hand, touching with his lips each cheek. This last ceremony, foreign custom permitted at such a parting—so solemn, to last so long.

I felt it hard that Madame Beck should dog me thus; following and watching me close; my neck and shoulder shrunk in fever under her breath; I became terribly goaded.

He was approaching; the semicircle was almost travelled round; he came to the last pupil; he turned. But Madame was before me; she had stepped out suddenly; she seemed to magnify her proportions and amplify her drapery; she eclipsed me; I was hid. She knew my weakness and deficiency; she could calculate the degree of moral paralysis—the total default of self-assertion—with which, in a crisis, I could be struck. She hastened to her kinsman, she broke upon him volubly, she mastered his attention, she hurried him to the door—the glass-door opening on the garden. I think he looked round; could I but have caught his eye, courage, I think, would have rushed in to aid feeling, and there would have been a charge, and, perhaps, a rescue; but already the room was all confusion, the semicircle broken into groups, my figure was lost among thirty more conspicuous. Madame had her will; yes, she got him away, and he had not seen me; he thought me absent. Five o'clock struck, the loud dismissal-bell rang, the school separated, the room emptied.

There seems, to my memory, an entire darkness and

distraction in some certain minutes I then passed alone—a grief inexpressible over a loss unendurable. What should I do; oh! what should I do; when all my life's hope was thus torn by the roots out of my riven, outraged heart?

What I should have done, I know not, when a little child—the least child in the school—broke with its simplicity and its unconsciousness into the raging yet silent centre of that inward conflict.

"Mademoiselle," lisped the treble voice, "I am to give you that. M. Paul said I was to seek you all over the house, from the grenier to the cellar, and when I found you, to give you that."

And the child delivered a note; the little dove dropped on my knee, its olive leaf plucked off. I found neither address nor name, only these words:—

"It was not my intention to take leave of you when I said good-by to the rest, but I hoped to see you in classe. I was disappointed. The interview is deferred. Be ready for me. Ere I sail, I must see you at leisure, and speak with you at length. Be ready; my moments are numbered, and, just now, monopolized; besides, I have a private business on hand which I will not share with any, nor communicate—even to you.—PAUL."

"Be ready?" Then it must be this evening: was he not to go on the morrow? Yes; of that point I was certain. I had seen the date of his vessel's departure advertised. Oh! I would be ready, but could that longed-for meeting really be achieved? the time was so short, the schemers seemed so watchful, so active, so hostile; the way of access appeared strait as a gully, deep as a chasm—Apollyon straddled across it, breathing flames. Could my Greatheart overcome? Could my guide reach me?

Who might tell? Yet I began to take some courage, some comfort; it seemed to me that I felt a pulse of his heart beating yet true to the whole throb of mine.

I waited my champion. Apollyon came trailing his Hell behind him. I think if Eternity held torment, its form would not be fiery rack, nor its nature despair. I think that on a certain day amongst those days which never dawned, and will not set, an angel entered Hades—stood, shone, smiled, delivered a prophecy of conditional pardon, kindled a doubtful hope of bliss to come, not now, but at a day and hour unlooked for, revealed in his own glory and grandeur the height and compass of his promise: spoke thus—then towering, became a star, and

Villette

vanished into his own Heaven. His legacy was suspense—a worse boon than despair.

All that evening I waited, trusting in the dove-sent olive-leaf, yet in the midst of my trust, terribly fearing. My fear pressed heavy. Cold and peculiar, I knew it for the partner of a rarely-belied presentiment. The first hours seemed long and slow; in spirit I clung to the flying skirts of the last. They passed like drift cloud—like the wrack scudding before a storm.

They passed. All the long, hot summer day burned away like a Yule-log; the crimson of its close perished; I was left bent among the cool blue shades, over the pale and ashen gleams of its night.

Prayers were over; it was bed-time; my co-inmates were all retired. I still remained in the gloomy first classe, forgetting, or at least disregarding, rules I had never forgotten or disregarded before.

How long I paced that classe I cannot tell; I must have been afoot many hours; mechanically had I moved aside benches and desks, and had made for myself a path down its length. There I walked, and there, when certain that the whole household were abed, and quite out of hearing—there, I at last wept. Reliant on Night, confiding in Solitude, I kept my tears sealed, my sobs chained, no longer; they heaved my heart; they tore their way. In this house, what grief could be sacred?

Soon after eleven o'clock—a very late hour in the Rue Fossette—the door unclosed, quietly but not stealthily; a lamp's flame invaded the moonlight; Madame Beck entered, with the same composed air, as if coming on an ordinary occasion, at an ordinary season. Instead of at once addressing me, she went to her desk, took her keys, and seemed to seek something: she loitered over this feigned search long, too long. She was calm, too calm; my mood scarce endured the pretence; driven beyond common range, two hours since I had left behind me wonted respects and fears. Led by a touch, and ruled by a word, under usual circumstances, no yoke could now be borne—no curb obeyed.

"It is more than time for retirement," said Madame; "the rule of the house has already been transgressed too long."

Madame met no answer: I did not check my walk; when she came in my way, I put her out of it.

"Let me persuade you to calm, Meess; let me lead you to your chamber," said she, trying to speak softly.

"No!" I said; "neither you nor another shall persuade or lead me."

"Your bed shall be warmed. Goton is sitting up still. She shall make you comfortable: she shall give you a sedative."

"Madame," I broke out, "you are a sensualist. Under all your serenity, your peace, and your decorum, you are an undenied sensualist. Make your own bed warm and soft; take sedatives and meats, and drinks spiced and sweet, as much as you will. If you have any sorrow or disappointment—and, perhaps, you have—nay, I know you have—seek your own palliatives, in your own chosen resources. Leave me, however. Leave me, I say!"

"I must send another to watch you, Meess: I must send Goton."

"I forbid it. Let me alone. Keep your hand off me, and my life, and my troubles. Oh, Madame! in your hand there is both chill and poison. You envenom and you paralyze."

"What have I done, Meess? You must not marry Paul. He cannot marry."

"Dog in the manger!" I said: for I knew she secretly wanted him, and had always wanted him. She called him "insupportable:" she railed at him for a "dévot:" she did not love, but she wanted to marry, that she might bind him to her interest. Deep into some of Madame's secrets I had entered—I know not how: by an intuition or an inspiration which came to me—I know not whence. In the course of living with her too, I had slowly learned, that, unless with an inferior, she must ever be a rival. She was my rival, heart and soul, though secretly, under the smoothest bearing, and utterly unknown to all save her and myself.

Two minutes I stood over Madame, feeling that the whole woman was in my power, because in some moods, such as the present—in some stimulated states of perception, like that of this instant—her habitual disguise, her mask and her domino, were to me a mere network reticulated with holes; and I saw underneath a being heartless, self-indulgent, and ignoble. She quietly retreated from me: meek and self-possessed, though very uneasy, she said, "If I would not be persuaded to take rest, she must reluctantly leave me." Which she did incontinent, perhaps even more glad to get away, than I was to see her vanish.

This was the sole flash-eliciting, truth-extorting, rencontre which ever occurred between me and Madame Beck: this short night-scene was never repeated. It did not one whit change her manner to me. I do not know that she revenged it. I do not know that she hated me the worse for my fell candour. I think she bucklered herself with the secret philosophy of her strong mind, and resolved to forget what it irked her to remember. I know that to the end of our mutual lives there occurred no repetition of, no allusion to, that fiery passage.

That night passed: all nights — even the starless night before dissolution — must wear away. About six o'clock, the hour which called up the household, I went out to the court, and washed my face in its cold, fresh well-water. Entering by the carré, a piece of mirror-glass, set in an oaken cabinet, repeated my image. It said I was changed: my cheeks and lips were sodden white, my eyes were glassy, and my eyelids swollen and purple.

On rejoining my companions, I knew they all looked at me — my heart seemed discovered to them: I believed myself self-betrayed. Hideously certain did it seem that the very youngest of the school must guess why and for whom I despaired.

"Isabelle," the child whom I had once nursed in sickness, approached me. Would she, too, mock me!

"Que vous êtes pâle! Vous êtes donc bien malade, Mademoiselle!" said she, putting her finger in her mouth, and staring with a wistful stupidity which at the moment seemed to me more beautiful than the keenest intelligence.

Isabelle did not long stand alone in the recommendation of ignorance: before the day was over, I gathered cause of gratitude towards the whole blind household. The multitude have something else to do than to read hearts and interpret dark sayings. Who wills, may keep his own counsel — be his own secret's sovereign. In the course of that day, proof met me on proof, not only that the cause of my present sorrow was unguessed, but that my whole inner life for the last six months, was still mine only. It was not known — it had not been noted — that I held in peculiar value one life among all lives. Gossip had passed me by; curiosity had looked me over; both subtle influences, hovering always round, had never become centred upon me. A given organization may live in a full fever-hospital, and escape typhus. M. Emanuel had come and gone: I had been taught and sought; in season and out of season he had called me, and I had obeyed him: "M. Paul wants Miss Lucy"—"Miss Lucy is with M. Paul"—such had been the perpetual bulletin; and nobody commented, far less condemned. Nobody hinted, nobody jested. Madame Beck read the riddle: none else resolved it. What I now suffered was called illness—a headache: I accepted the baptism.

But what bodily illness was ever like this pain? This certainty that he was gone without a farewell—this cruel conviction that fate and pursuing furies—a woman's envy and a priest's bigotry—would suffer me to see him no more? What wonder that the second evening found me like the first—untamed, tortured, again pacing a solitary room in an unalterable passion of silent desolation?

Madame Beck did not herself summon me to bed that night—she did not come near me: she sent Ginevra Fanshawe—a more efficient agent for the purpose she could not have employed. Ginevra's first words—"Is your headache very bad to-night?" (for Ginevra, like the rest, thought I had a headache—an intolerable headache which made me frightfully white in the face, and insanely restless in the foot)—her first words, I say, inspired the impulse to flee anywhere, so that it were only out of reach. And soon, what followed—plaints about her own headaches—completed the business.

I went up-stairs. Presently I was in my bed—my miserable bed—haunted with quick scorpions. I had not been laid down five minutes, when another emissary arrived: Goton came, bringing me something to drink. I was consumed with thirst—I drank eagerly; the beverage was sweet, but I tasted a drug.

"Madame says it will make you sleep, chou-chou," said Goton, as she received back the emptied cup.

Ah! the sedative had been administered. In fact, they had given me a strong opiate. I was to be held quiet for one night.

The household came to bed, the night-light was lit, the dormitory hushed. Sleep soon reigned: over those pillows, sleep won an easy supremacy: contented sovereign over heads and hearts which did not ache—he passed by the unquiet.

The drug wrought. I know not whether Madame had overcharged or under-charged the dose; its result was not that

Villette

she intended. Instead of stupor, came excitement. I became alive to new thought—to reverie peculiar in colouring. A gathering call ran among the faculties, their bugles sang, their trumpets rang an untimely summons. Imagination was roused from her rest, and she came forth impetuous and venturous. With scorn she looked on Matter, her mate—"Rise!" she said. "Sluggard! this night I will have my will; nor shalt thou prevail."

"Look forth and view the night!" was her cry; and when I lifted the heavy blind from the casement close at hand—with her own royal gesture, she showed me a moon supreme, in an element deep and splendid.

To my gasping senses she made the glimmering gloom, the narrow limits, the oppressive heat of the dormitory, intolerable. She lured me to leave this den and follow her forth into dew, coolness, and glory.

She brought upon me a strange vision of Villette at midnight. Especially she showed the park, the summer-park, with its long alleys all silent, lone and safe; among these lay a huge stone basin—that basin I knew, and beside which I had often stood—deep-set in the tree-shadows, brimming with cool water, clear, with a green, leafy, rushy bed. What of all this? The park-gates were shut up, locked, sentinelled: the place could not be entered.

Could it not? A point worth considering; and while revolving it, I mechanically dressed. Utterly incapable of sleeping or lying still—excited from head to foot—what could I do better than dress?

The gates were locked, soldiers set before them: was there, then, no admission to the park?

The other day, in walking past, I had seen, without then attending to the circumstance, a gap in the paling—one stake broken down: I now saw this gap again in recollection—saw it very plainly—the narrow, irregular aperture visible between the stems of the lindens, planted orderly as a colonnade. A man could not have made his way through that aperture, nor could a stout woman, perhaps not Madame Beck; but I thought I might: I fancied I should like to try, and once within, at this hour the whole park would be mine—the moonlight, midnight park!

How soundly the dormitory slept! What deep slumbers! What quiet breathing! How very still the whole large house! What was the time? I felt restless to know. There stood a clock in the classe below: what hindered me from venturing down to consult it? By such a moon, its large white face and jet black figures must be vividly distinct.

As for hindrance to this step, there offered not so much as a creaking hinge or a clicking latch. On these hot July nights, close air could not be tolerated, and the chamber-door stood wide open. Will the dormitory-planks sustain my tread untraitorous? Yes. I know wherever a board is loose, and will avoid it. The oak staircase creaks somewhat as I descend, but not much: — I am in the carré.

The great classe-doors are close shut: they are bolted. On the other hand, the entrance to the corridor stands open. The classes seem to my thought, great dreary jails, buried far back beyond thoroughfares, and for me, filled with spectral and intolerable Memories, laid miserable amongst their straw and their manacles. The corridor offers a cheerful vista, leading to the high vestibule which opens direct upon the street.

Hush! — the clock strikes. Ghostly deep as is the stillness of this convent, it is only eleven. While my ear follows to silence the hum of the last stroke, I catch faintly from the built-out capital, a sound like bells or like a band — a sound where sweetness, where victory, where mourning blend. Oh, to approach this music nearer, to listen to it alone by the rushy basin! Let me go — oh, let me go! What hinders, what does not aid freedom?

There, in the corridor, hangs my garden-costume, my large hat, my shawl. There is no lock on the huge, heavy, porte-cochère; there is no key to seek: it fastens with a sort of spring-bolt, not to be opened from the outside, but which, from within, may be noiselessly withdrawn. Can I manage it? It yields to my hand, yields with propitious facility. I wonder as that portal seems almost spontaneously to unclose — I wonder as I cross the threshold and step on the paved street, wonder at the strange ease with which this prison has been forced. It seems as if I had been pioneered invisibly, as if some dissolving force had gone before me: for myself, I have scarce made an effort.

Quiet Rue Fossette! I find on this pavement that wanderer-wooing summer night of which I mused; I see its moon over me; I feel its dew in the air. But here I cannot stay; I am still too near old haunts: so close under the dungeon, I can hear the prisoners moan. This solemn peace is not what I seek, it is not what I can bear: to me the face of that sky bears the aspect of a world's death. The park also will be calm — I know, a mortal serenity

Villette

prevails everywhere — yet let me seek the park.

I took a route well known, and went up towards the palatial and royal Haute-Ville; thence the music I had heard certainly floated; it was hushed now, but it might re-waken. I went on: neither band nor bell music came to meet me; another sound replaced it, a sound like a strong tide, a great flow, deepening as I proceeded. Light broke, movement gathered, chimes pealed — to what was I coming? Entering on the level of a Grande Place, I found myself, with the suddenness of magic, plunged amidst a gay, living, joyous crowd.

Villette is one blaze, one broad illumination; the whole world seems abroad; moonlight and heaven are banished: the town, by her own flambeaux, beholds her own splendour — gay dresses, grand equipages, fine horses and gallant riders throng the bright streets. I see even scores of masks. It is a strange scene, stranger than dreams. But where is the park? — I ought to be near it. In the midst of this glare the park must be shadowy and calm — there, at least, are neither torches, lamps, nor crowd?

I was asking this question when an open carriage passed me filled with known faces. Through the deep throng it could pass but slowly; the spirited horses fretted in their curbed ardour. I saw the occupants of that carriage well: me they could not see, or, at least, not know, folded close in my large shawl, screened with my straw hat (in that motley crowd no dress was noticeably strange). I saw the Count de Bassompierre; I saw my godmother, handsomely apparelled, comely and cheerful; I saw, too, Paulina Mary, compassed with the triple halo of her beauty, her youth, and her happiness. In looking on her countenance of joy, and eyes of festal light, one scarce remembered to note the gala elegance of what she wore; I know only that the drapery floating about her was all white and light and bridal; seated opposite to her I saw Graham Bretton; it was in looking up at him her aspect had caught its lustre — the light repeated in her eyes beamed first out of his.

It gave me strange pleasure to follow these friends viewlessly, and I did follow them, as I thought, to the park. I watched them alight (carriages were inadmissible) amidst new and unanticipated splendours. Lo! the iron gateway, between the stone columns, was spanned by a flaming arch built of massed stars; and, following them cautiously beneath that arch, where were they, and where was I?

In a land of enchantment, a garden most gorgeous, a plain sprinkled with coloured meteors, a forest with sparks of purple and ruby and golden fire gemming the foliage; a region, not of trees and shadow, but of strangest architectural wealth—of altar and of temple, of pyramid, obelisk, and sphinx: incredible to say, the wonders and the symbols of Egypt teemed throughout the park of Villette.

No matter that in five minutes the secret was mine—the key of the mystery picked up, and its illusion unveiled—no matter that I quickly recognised the material of these solemn fragments—the timber, the paint, and the pasteboard—these inevitable discoveries failed to quite destroy the charm, or undermine the marvel of that night. No matter that I now seized the explanation of the whole great fête—a fête of which the conventual Rue Fossette had not tasted, though it had opened at dawn that morning, and was still in full vigour near midnight.

In past days there had been, said history, an awful crisis in the fate of Labassecour, involving I know not what peril to the rights and liberties of her gallant citizens. Rumours of wars there had been, if not wars themselves; a kind of struggling in the streets—a bustle—a running to and fro, some rearing of barricades, some burgher-rioting, some calling out of troops, much interchange of brickbats, and even a little of shot. Tradition held that patriots had fallen: in the old Basse-Ville was shown an enclosure, solemnly built in and set apart, holding, it was said, the sacred bones of martyrs. Be this as it may, a certain day in the year was still kept as a festival in honour of the said patriots and martyrs of somewhat apocryphal memory—the morning being given to a solemn Te Deum in St. Jean Baptiste, the evening devoted to spectacles, decorations, and illuminations, such as these I now saw.

While looking up at the image of a white ibis, fixed on a column—while fathoming the deep, torch-lit perspective of an avenue, at the close of which was couched a sphinx—I lost sight of the party which, from the middle of the great square, I had followed—or, rather, they vanished like a group of apparitions. On this whole scene was impressed a dream-like character: every shape was wavering, every movement floating, every voice echo-like—half-mocking, half-uncertain. Paulina and her friends being gone, I scarce could avouch that I had really seen them; nor did I miss them as guides through the chaos, far less regret them as protectors amidst the night.

That festal night would have been safe for a very child. Half the peasantry had come in from the outlying environs of Villette, and the decent burghers were all abroad and around, dressed in their best. My straw-hat passed amidst cap and

Villette

jacket, short petticoat, and long calico mantle, without, perhaps, attracting a glance; I only took the precaution to bind down the broad leaf gipsy-wise, with a supplementary ribbon — and then I felt safe as if masked.

Safe I passed down the avenues — safe I mixed with the crowd where it was deepest. To be still was not in my power, nor quietly to observe. I took a revel of the scene; I drank the elastic night-air — the swell of sound, the dubious light, now flashing, now fading. As to Happiness or Hope, they and I had shaken hands, but just now — I scorned Despair.

My vague aim, as I went, was to find the stone-basin, with its clear depth and green lining: of that coolness and verdure I thought, with the passionate thirst of unconscious fever. Amidst the glare, and hurry, and throng, and noise, I still secretly and chiefly longed to come on that circular mirror of crystal, and surprise the moon glassing therein her pearly front.

I knew my route, yet it seemed as if I was hindered from pursuing it direct: now a sight, and now a sound, called me aside, luring me down this alley and down that. Already I saw the thick-planted trees which framed this tremulous and rippled glass, when, choiring out of a glade to the right, broke such a sound as I thought might be heard if Heaven were to open — such a sound, perhaps, as was heard above the plain of Bethlehem, on the night of glad tidings.

The song, the sweet music, rose afar, but rushing swiftly on fast-strengthening pinions — there swept through these shades so full a storm of harmonies that, had no tree been near against which to lean, I think I must have dropped. Voices were there, it seemed to me, unnumbered; instruments varied and countless — bugle, horn, and trumpet I knew. The effect was as a sea breaking into song with all its waves.

The swaying tide swept this way, and then it fell back, and I followed its retreat. It led me towards a Byzantine building — a sort of kiosk near the park's centre. Round about stood crowded thousands, gathered to a grand concert in the open air. What I had heard was, I think, a wild Jäger chorus; the night, the space, the scene, and my own mood, had but enhanced the sounds and their impression.

Here were assembled ladies, looking by this light most beautiful: some of their dresses were gauzy, and some had the sheen of satin, the flowers and the blond trembled, and the veils waved about their decorated bonnets, as that host-like chorus, with its greatly-gathering sound, sundered the air above them. Most of these ladies occupied the little light park-chairs, and behind and beside them stood guardian gentlemen. The outer ranks of the crowd were made up of citizens, plebeians and police.

In this outer rank I took my place. I rather liked to find myself the silent, unknown, consequently unaccosted neighbour of the short petticoat and the sabot; and only the distant gazer at the silk robe, the velvet mantle, and the plumed chapeau. Amidst so much life and joy, too, it suited me to be alone—quite alone. Having neither wish nor power to force my way through a mass so close-packed, my station was on the farthest confines, where, indeed, I might hear, but could see little.

"Mademoiselle is not well placed," said a voice at my elbow. Who dared accost me, a being in a mood so little social? I turned, rather to repel than to reply. I saw a man—a burgher—an entire stranger, as I deemed him for one moment, but the next, recognised in him a certain tradesman—a bookseller, whose shop furnished the Rue Fossette with its books and stationery; a man notorious in our pensionnat for the excessive brittleness of his temper, and frequent snappishness of his manner, even to us, his principal customers: but whom, for my solitary self, I had ever been disposed to like, and had always found civil, sometimes kind; once, in aiding me about some troublesome little exchange of foreign money, he had done me a service. He was an intelligent man; under his asperity, he was a good-hearted man; the thought had sometimes crossed me, that a part of his nature bore affinity to a part of M. Emanuel's (whom he knew well, and whom I had often seen sitting on Miret's counter, turning over the current month's publications); and it was in this affinity I read the explanation of that conciliatory feeling with which I instinctively regarded him.

Strange to say, this man knew me under my straw-hat and closely-folded shawl; and, though I deprecated the effort, he insisted on making a way for me through the crowd, and finding me a better situation. He carried his disinterested civility further; and, from some quarter, procured me a chair. Once and again, I have found that the most cross-grained are by no means the worst of mankind; nor the humblest in station, the least polished in feeling. This man, in his courtesy, seemed to find nothing strange in my being here alone; only a reason for extending to me, as far as he could, a retiring, yet efficient attention. Having secured me a place and a seat, he withdrew without asking a question, without obtruding a remark, without adding a superfluous word. No wonder that Professor Emanuel

Villette

liked to take his cigar and his lounge, and to read his feuilleton in M. Miret's shop — the two must have suited.

I had not been seated five minutes, ere I became aware that chance and my worthy burgher friend had brought me once more within view of a familiar and domestic group. Right before me sat the Brettons and de Bassompierres. Within reach of my hand — had I chosen to extend it — sat a figure like a fairy-queen, whose array, lilies and their leaves seemed to have suggested; whatever was not spotless white, being forest-green. My godmother, too, sat so near, that, had I leaned forward, my breath might have stirred the ribbon of her bonnet. They were too near; having been just recognised by a comparative stranger, I felt uneasy at this close vicinage of intimate acquaintance.

It made me quite start when Mrs. Bretton, turning to Mr. Home, and speaking out of a kind impulse of memory, said, — "I wonder what my steady little Lucy would say to all this if she were here? I wish we had brought her, she would have enjoyed it much."

"So she would, so she would, in her grave sensible fashion; it is a pity but we had asked her," rejoined the kind gentleman; and added, "I like to see her so quietly pleased; so little moved, yet so content."

Dear were they both to me, dear are they to this day in their remembered benevolence. Little knew they the rack of pain which had driven Lucy almost into fever, and brought her out, guideless and reckless, urged and drugged to the brink of frenzy. I had half a mind to bend over the elders' shoulders, and answer their goodness with the thanks of my eyes. M. de Bassompierre did not well know me, but I knew him, and honoured and admired his nature, with all its plain sincerity, its warm affection, and unconscious enthusiasm. Possibly I might have spoken, but just then Graham turned; he turned with one of his stately firm movements, so different from those, of a sharp-tempered under-sized man: there was behind him a throng, a hundred ranks deep; there were thousands to meet his eye and divide its scrutiny — why then did he concentrate all on me — oppressing me with the whole force of that full, blue, steadfast orb? Why, if he would look, did not one glance satisfy him? why did he turn on his chair, rest his elbow on its back, and study me leisurely? He could not see my face, I held it down; surely, he could not recognise me: I stooped, I turned, I would not be known. He rose, by some means he contrived to approach, in two minutes he would have had my secret: my identity would have been grasped between his, never tyrannous, but always powerful hands. There was but one way to evade or to check him. I implied, by a sort of supplicatory gesture, that it was my prayer to be let alone; after that, had he persisted, he would perhaps have seen the spectacle of Lucy incensed: not all that was grand, or good, or kind in him (and Lucy felt the full amount) should have kept her quite tame, or absolutely inoffensive and shadowlike. He looked, but he desisted. He shook his handsome head, but he was mute. He resumed his seat, nor did he again turn or disturb me by a glance, except indeed for one single instant, when a look, rather solicitous than curious, stole my way—speaking what somehow stilled my heart like "the south-wind quieting the earth." Graham's thoughts of me were not entirely those of a frozen indifference, after all. I believe in that goodly mansion, his heart, he kept one little place under the sky-lights where Lucy might have entertainment, if she chose to call. It was not so handsome as the chambers where he lodged his male friends; it was not like the hall where he accommodated his philanthropy, or the library where he treasured his science, still less did it resemble the pavilion where his marriage feast was splendidly spread; yet, gradually, by long and equal kindness, he proved to me that he kept one little closet, over the door of which was written "Lucy's Room." I kept a place for him, too—a place of which I never took the measure, either by rule or compass: I think it was like the tent of Peri-Banou. All my life long I carried it folded in the hollow of my hand yet, released from that hold and constriction, I know not but its innate capacity for expanse might have magnified it into a tabernacle for a host.

Forbearing as he was to-night, I could not stay in this proximity; this dangerous place and seat must be given up: I watched my opportunity, rose, and stole away. He might think, he might even believe that Lucy was contained within that shawl, and sheltered under that hat; he never could be certain, for he did not see my face.

Surely the spirit of restlessness was by this time appeased? Had I not had enough of adventure? Did I not begin to flag, quail, and wish for safety under a roof? Not so. I still loathed my bed in the school dormitory more than words can express: I clung to whatever could distract thought. Somehow I felt, too, that the night's drama was but begun, that the prologue was scarce spoken: throughout this woody and turfy theatre reigned a shadow of mystery; actors and incidents unlooked-for, waited behind the scenes: I thought so foreboding told me as much.

Straying at random, obeying the push of every chance elbow, I was brought to a quarter where trees planted in clusters, or towering singly, broke up somewhat the dense packing of the crowd, and gave it a more scattered character. These confines were far from the music, and somewhat aloof even from the lamps, but there was sound enough to soothe, and with that full, high moon, lamps were scarce needed. Here had chiefly settled family-groups, burgher-parents; some of them, late as was the hour, actually surrounded by their children, with whom it had not been thought advisable to venture into the closer throng.

Three fine tall trees growing close, almost twined stem within stem, lifted a thick canopy of shade above a green knoll, crowned with a seat—a seat which might have held several, yet it seemed abandoned to one, the remaining members of the fortunate party in possession of this site standing dutifully round; yet, amongst this reverend circle was a lady, holding by the hand a little girl.

When I caught sight of this little girl, she was twisting herself round on her heel, swinging from her conductress's hand, flinging herself from side to side with wanton and fantastic gyrations. These perverse movements arrested my attention, they struck me as of a character fearfully familiar. On close inspection, no less so appeared the child's equipment; the lilac silk pelisse, the small swansdown boa, the white bonnet— the whole holiday toilette, in short, was the gala garb of a cherub but too well known, of that tadpole, Désirée Beck—and Désirée Beck it was—she, or an imp in her likeness.

I might have taken this discovery as a thunder-clap, but such hyperbole would have been premature; discovery was destined to rise more than one degree, ere it reached its climax.

On whose hand could the amiable Désirée swing thus selfishly, whose glove could she tear thus recklessly, whose arm thus strain with impunity, or on the borders of whose dress thus turn and trample insolently, if not the hand, glove, arm, and robe of her lady-mother? And there, in an Indian shawl and a pale-green crape bonnet—there, fresh, portly, blithe, and pleasant—there stood Madame Beck.

Curious! I had certainly deemed Madame in her bed, and Désirée in her crib, at this blessed minute, sleeping, both of them, the sleep of the just, within the sacred walls, amidst the profound seclusion of the Rue Fossette. Most certainly also they did not picture "Meess Lucie" otherwise engaged; and here we all three were taking our "ébats" in the fête-blazing park at midnight!

The fact was, Madame was only acting according to her quite justifiable wont. I remembered now I had heard it said among the teachers—though without at the time particularly noticing the gossip—that often, when we thought Madame in her chamber, sleeping, she was gone, full-dressed, to take her pleasure at operas, or plays, or balls. Madame had no sort of taste for a monastic life, and took care—largely, though discreetly—to season her existence with a relish of the world.

Half a dozen gentlemen of her friends stood about her. Amongst these, I was not slow to recognise two or three. There was her brother, M. Victor Kint; there was another person, moustached and with long hair—a calm, taciturn man, but whose traits bore a stamp and a semblance I could not mark unmoved. Amidst reserve and phlegm, amidst contrasts of character and of countenance, something there still was which recalled a face—mobile, fervent, feeling—a face changeable, now clouded, and now alight—a face from my world taken away, for my eyes lost, but where my best spring-hours of life had alternated in shadow and in glow; that face, where I had often seen movements so near the signs of genius—that why there did not shine fully out the undoubted fire, the thing, the spirit, and the secret itself—I could never tell. Yes—this Josef Emanuel—this man of peace—reminded me of his ardent brother.

Besides Messieurs Victor and Josef, I knew another of this party. This third person stood behind and in the shade, his attitude too was stooping, yet his dress and bald white head made him the most conspicuous figure of the group. He was an ecclesiastic: he was Père Silas. Do not fancy, reader, that there was any inconsistency in the priest's presence at this fête. This was not considered a show of Vanity Fair, but a commemoration of patriotic sacrifice. The Church patronised it, even with ostentation. There were troops of priests in the park that night.

Père Silas stooped over the seat with its single occupant, the rustic bench and that which sat upon it: a strange mass it was—bearing no shape, yet magnificent. You saw, indeed, the outline of a face, and features, but these were so cadaverous and so strangely placed, you could almost have fancied a head severed from its trunk, and flung at random on a pile of rich merchandise. The distant lamp-rays glanced on clear pendants, on broad rings; neither the chasteness of moonlight, nor the distance of the torches, could quite subdue the gorgeous dyes of the drapery. Hail, Madame Walravens! I think you looked more witch-like than ever. And presently the good lady proved that

Villette

she was indeed no corpse or ghost, but a harsh and hardy old woman; for, upon some aggravation in the clamorous petition of Désirée Beck to her mother, to go to the kiosk and take sweetmeats, the hunchback suddenly fetched her a resounding rap with her gold-knobbed cane.

There, then, were Madame Walravens, Madame Beck, Père Silas — the whole conjuration, the secret junta. The sight of them thus assembled did me good. I cannot say that I felt weak before them, or abashed, or dismayed. They outnumbered me, and I was worsted and under their feet; but, as yet, I was not dead.

CHAPTER XXXIX.
OLD AND NEW ACQUAINTANCE.

Fascinated as by a basilisk with three heads, I could not leave this clique; the ground near them seemed to hold my feet. The canopy of entwined trees held out shadow, the night whispered a pledge of protection, and an officious lamp flashed just one beam to show me an obscure, safe seat, and then vanished. Let me now briefly tell the reader all that, during the past dark fortnight, I have been silently gathering from Rumour, respecting the origin and the object of M. Emanuel's departure. The tale is short, and not new: its alpha is Mammon, and its omega Interest.

If Madame Walravens was hideous as a Hindoo idol, she seemed also to possess, in the estimation of these her votaries, an idol's consequence. The fact was, she had been rich — very rich; and though, for the present, without the command of money, she was likely one day to be rich again. At Basseterre, in Guadaloupe, she possessed a large estate, received in dowry on her marriage sixty years ago, sequestered since her husband's failure; but now, it was supposed, cleared of claim, and, if duly looked after by a competent agent of integrity, considered capable of being made, in a few years, largely productive.

Père Silas took an interest in this prospective improvement for the sake of religion and the church, whereof Magliore Walravens was a devout daughter. Madame Beck, distantly related to the hunchback and knowing her to be without family of her own, had long brooded over contingencies with a mother's calculating forethought, and, harshly treated as she was by Madame Walravens, never ceased to court her for interest's sake. Madame Beck and the priest were thus, for money reasons, equally and sincerely interested in the nursing of the West Indian estate.

But the distance was great, and the climate hazardous. The competent and upright agent wanted, must be a devoted man. Just such a man had Madame Walravens retained for twenty years in her service, blighting his life, and then living on him, like an old fungus; such a man had Père Silas trained, taught, and bound to him by the ties of gratitude, habit, and belief. Such a man Madame Beck knew, and could in some measure influence. "My pupil," said Père Silas, "if he remains in Europe, runs risk of apostacy, for he has become entangled with a heretic." Madame Beck made also her private comment, and preferred in her own breast her secret reason for desiring expatriation. The thing she could not obtain, she desired not another to win: rather would she destroy it. As to Madame Walravens, she wanted her money and her land, and knew Paul, if he liked, could make the best and faithfullest steward: so the three self-seekers banded and beset the one unselfish. They reasoned, they appealed, they implored; on his mercy they cast themselves, into his hands they confidingly thrust their interests. They asked but two or three years of devotion—after that, he should live for himself: one of the number, perhaps, wished that in the meantime he might die.

No living being ever humbly laid his advantage at M. Emanuel's feet, or confidingly put it into his hands, that he spurned the trust or repulsed the repository. What might be his private pain or inward reluctance to leave Europe—what his calculations for his own future—none asked, or knew, or reported. All this was a blank to me. His conferences with his confessor I might guess; the part duty and religion were made to play in the persuasions used, I might conjecture. He was gone, and had made no sign. There my knowledge closed.

With my head bent, and my forehead resting on my hands, I sat amidst grouped tree-stems and branching brushwood. Whatever talk passed amongst my neighbours, I might hear, if I would; I was near enough; but for some time, there was scarce motive to attend. They gossiped about the dresses, the music, the illuminations, the fine night. I listened to hear them say, "It is calm weather for his voyage; the Antigua" (his ship) "will sail prosperously." No such remark fell; neither the Antigua, nor her course, nor her passenger were named.

Perhaps the light chat scarcely interested old Madame Walravens more than it did me; she appeared restless, turning her head now to this side, now that, looking through the trees, and among the crowd, as if expectant of an arrival and impatient of delay. "Où sont-ils? Pourquoi ne viennent-ils?" I heard her mutter more than once; and at last, as if determined to have an answer to her question—which hitherto none seemed to mind, she spoke aloud this phrase—a phrase brief enough, simple enough, but it sent a shock through me—"Messieurs et mesdames," said she, "où donc est Justine Marie?"

"Justine Marie!" What was this? Justine Marie—the dead nun—where was she? Why, in her grave, Madame Walravens— what can you want with her? You shall go to her, but she shall not come to you.

Thus I should have answered, had the response lain with me, but nobody seemed to be of my mind; nobody seemed surprised, startled, or at a loss. The quietest commonplace answer met the strange, the dead-disturbing, the Witch-of-Endor query of the hunchback.

"Justine Marie," said one, "is coming; she is in the kiosk; she will be here presently."

Out of this question and reply sprang a change in the chat—chat it still remained, easy, desultory, familiar gossip. Hint, allusion, comment, went round the circle, but all so broken, so dependent on references to persons not named, or circumstances not defined, that listen as intently as I would—and I did listen now with a fated interest—I could make out no more than that some scheme was on foot, in which this ghostly Justine Marie—dead or alive—was concerned. This family-junta seemed grasping at her somehow, for some reason; there seemed question of a marriage, of a fortune—for whom I could not quite make out—perhaps for Victor Kint, perhaps for Josef Emanuel—both were bachelors. Once I thought the hints and jests rained upon a young fair-haired foreigner of the party, whom they called Heinrich Mühler. Amidst all the badinage, Madame Walravens still obtruded from time to time, hoarse, cross-grained speeches; her impatience being diverted only by an implacable surveillance of Désirée, who could not stir but the old woman menaced her with her staff.

"La voilà!" suddenly cried one of the gentlemen, "voilà Justine Marie qui arrive!"

This moment was for me peculiar. I called up to memory the pictured nun on the panel; present to my mind was the sad love-story; I saw in thought the vision of the garret, the apparition of the alley, the strange birth of the berceau; I underwent a presentiment of discovery, a strong conviction of coming disclosure. Ah! when imagination once runs riot where do we stop? What winter tree so bare and branchless—what way-side, hedge-munching animal so humble, that Fancy, a passing cloud, and a struggling moonbeam, will not clothe it in spirituality, and make of it a phantom?

With solemn force pressed on my heart, the expectation of mystery breaking up: hitherto I had seen this spectre only through a glass darkly; now was I to behold it face to face. I leaned forward; I looked.

"She comes!" cried Josef Emanuel.

Villette

The circle opened as if opening to admit a new and welcome member. At this instant a torch chanced to be carried past; its blaze aided the pale moon in doing justice to the crisis, in lighting to perfection the dénouement pressing on. Surely those near me must have felt some little of the anxiety I felt, in degree so unmeted. Of that group the coolest must have "held his breath for a time!" As for me, my life stood still.

It is over. The moment and the nun are come. The crisis and the revelation are passed by.

The flambeau glares still within a yard, held up in a park-keeper's hand; its long eager tongue of flame almost licks the figure of the Expected—there—where she stands full in my sight. What is she like? What does she wear? How does she look? Who is she?

There are many masks in the park to-night, and as the hour wears late, so strange a feeling of revelry and mystery begins to spread abroad, that scarce would you discredit me, reader, were I to say that she is like the nun of the attic, that she wears black skirts and white head-clothes, that she looks the resurrection of the flesh, and that she is a risen ghost.

All falsities—all figments! We will not deal in this gear. Let us be honest, and cut, as heretofore, from the homely web of truth.

Homely, though, is an ill-chosen word. What I see is not precisely homely. A girl of Villette stands there—a girl fresh from her pensionnat. She is very comely, with the beauty indigenous to this country. She looks well-nourished, fair, and fat of flesh. Her cheeks are round, her eyes good; her hair is abundant. She is handsomely dressed. She is not alone; her escort consists of three persons—two being elderly; these she addresses as "Mon Oncle" and "Ma Tante." She laughs, she chats; good-humoured, buxom, and blooming, she looks, at all points, the bourgeoise belle.

"So much for Justine Marie;" so much for ghosts and mystery: not that this last was solved—this girl certainly is not my nun: what I saw in the garret and garden must have been taller by a span.

We have looked at the city belle; we have cursorily glanced at the respectable old uncle and aunt. Have we a stray glance to give to the third member of this company? Can we spare him a moment's notice? We ought to distinguish him so far, reader; he has claims on us; we do not now meet him for the first time. I clasped my hands very hard, and I drew my breath very deep: I held in the cry, I devoured the ejaculation, I forbade the start, I spoke and I stirred no more than a stone; but I knew what I looked on; through the dimness left in my eyes by many nights' weeping, I knew him. They said he was to sail by the Antigua. Madame Beck said so. She lied, or she had uttered what was once truth, and failed to contradict it when it became false. The Antigua was gone, and there stood Paul Emanuel.

Was I glad? A huge load left me. Was it a fact to warrant joy? I know not. Ask first what were the circumstances attendant on this respite? How far did this delay concern me? Were there not those whom it might touch more nearly?

After all, who may this young girl, this Justine Marie, be? Not a stranger, reader; she is known to me by sight; she visits at the Rue Fossette: she is often of Madame Beck's Sunday parties. She is a relation of both the Becks and Walravens; she derives her baptismal name from the sainted nun who would have been her aunt had she lived; her patronymic is Sauveur; she is an heiress and an orphan, and M. Emanuel is her guardian; some say her godfather.

The family junta wish this heiress to be married to one of their band—which is it? Vital question—which is it?

I felt very glad now, that the drug administered in the sweet draught had filled me with a possession which made bed and chamber intolerable. I always, through my whole life, liked to penetrate to the real truth; I like seeking the goddess in her temple, and handling the veil, and daring the dread glance. O Titaness among deities! the covered outline of thine aspect sickens often through its uncertainty, but define to us one trait, show us one lineament, clear in awful sincerity; we may gasp in untold terror, but with that gasp we drink in a breath of thy divinity; our heart shakes, and its currents sway like rivers lifted by earthquake, but we have swallowed strength. To see and know the worst is to take from Fear her main advantage.

The Walravens' party, augmented in numbers, now became very gay. The gentlemen fetched refreshments from the kiosk, all sat down on the turf under the trees; they drank healths and sentiments; they laughed, they jested. M. Emanuel underwent some raillery, half good-humoured, half, I thought, malicious, especially on Madame Beck's part. I soon gathered that his voyage had been temporarily deferred of his own will, without the concurrence, even against the advice, of his friends; he had

Villette

let the Antigua go, and had taken his berth in the Paul et Virginie, appointed to sail a fortnight later. It was his reason for this resolve which they teased him to assign, and which he would only vaguely indicate as "the settlement of a little piece of business which he had set his heart upon." What was this business? Nobody knew. Yes, there was one who seemed partly, at least, in his confidence; a meaning look passed between him and Justine Marie. "La petite va m'aider—n'est-ce pas?" said he. The answer was prompt enough, God knows!

"Mais oui, je vous aiderai de tout mon cœur. Vous ferez de moi tout ce que vous voudrez, mon parrain."

And this dear "parrain" took her hand and lifted it to his grateful lips. Upon which demonstration, I saw the light-complexioned young Teuton, Heinrich Mühler, grow restless, as if he did not like it. He even grumbled a few words, whereat M. Emanuel actually laughed in his face, and with the ruthless triumph of the assured conqueror, he drew his ward nearer to him.

M. Emanuel was indeed very joyous that night. He seemed not one whit subdued by the change of scene and action impending. He was the true life of the party; a little despotic, perhaps, determined to be chief in mirth, as well as in labour, yet from moment to moment proving indisputably his right of leadership. His was the wittiest word, the pleasantest anecdote, the frankest laugh. Restlessly active, after his manner, he multiplied himself to wait on all; but oh! I saw which was his favourite. I saw at whose feet he lay on the turf, I saw whom he folded carefully from the night air, whom he tended, watched, and cherished as the apple of his eye.

Still, hint and raillery flew thick, and still I gathered that while M. Paul should be absent, working for others, these others, not quite ungrateful, would guard for him the treasure he left in Europe. Let him bring them an Indian fortune: they would give him in return a young bride and a rich inheritance. As for the saintly consecration, the vow of constancy, that was forgotten: the blooming and charming Present prevailed over the Past; and, at length, his nun was indeed buried.

Thus it must be. The revelation was indeed come. Presentiment had not been mistaken in her impulse: there is a kind of presentiment which never is mistaken; it was I who had for a moment miscalculated; not seeing the true bearing of the oracle, I had thought she muttered of vision when, in truth, her prediction touched reality.

I might have paused longer upon what I saw; I might have deliberated ere I drew inferences. Some, perhaps, would have held the premises doubtful, the proofs insufficient; some slow sceptics would have incredulously examined ere they conclusively accepted the project of a marriage between a poor and unselfish man of forty, and his wealthy ward of eighteen; but far from me such shifts and palliatives, far from me such temporary evasion of the actual, such coward fleeing from the dread, the swift-footed, the all-overtaking Fact, such feeble suspense of submission to her the sole sovereign, such paltering and faltering resistance to the Power whose errand is to march conquering and to conquer, such traitor defection from the TRUTH.

No. I hastened to accept the whole plan. I extended my grasp and took it all in. I gathered it to me with a sort of rage of haste, and folded it round me, as the soldier struck on the field folds his colours about his breast. I invoked Conviction to nail upon me the certainty, abhorred while embraced, to fix it with the strongest spikes her strongest strokes could drive; and when the iron had entered well my soul, I stood up, as I thought, renovated.

In my infatuation, I said, "Truth, you are a good mistress to your faithful servants! While a Lie pressed me, how I suffered! Even when the Falsehood was still sweet, still flattering to the fancy, and warm to the feelings, it wasted me with hourly torment. The persuasion that affection was won could not be divorced from the dread that, by another turn of the wheel, it might be lost. Truth stripped away Falsehood, and Flattery, and Expectancy, and here I stand—free!"

Nothing remained now but to take my freedom to my chamber, to carry it with me to my bed and see what I could make of it. The play was not yet, indeed, quite played out. I might have waited and watched longer that love-scene under the trees, that sylvan courtship. Had there been nothing of love in the demonstration, my Fancy in this hour was so generous, so creative, she could have modelled for it the most salient lineaments, and given it the deepest life and highest colour of passion. But I would not look; I had fixed my resolve, but I would not violate my nature. And then—something tore me so cruelly under my shawl, something so dug into my side, a vulture so strong in beak and talon, I must be alone to grapple with it. I think I never felt jealousy till now. This was not like enduring the endearments of Dr. John and Paulina, against which while I sealed my eyes and my ears, while I withdrew thence my thoughts, my sense of harmony still acknowledged

Villette

in it a charm. This was an outrage. The love born of beauty was not mine; I had nothing in common with it: I could not dare to meddle with it, but another love, venturing diffidently into life after long acquaintance, furnace-tried by pain, stamped by constancy, consolidated by affection's pure and durable alloy, submitted by intellect to intellect's own tests, and finally wrought up, by his own process, to his own unflawed completeness, this Love that laughed at Passion, his fast frenzies and his hot and hurried extinction, in this Love I had a vested interest; and whatever tended either to its culture or its destruction, I could not view impassibly.

I turned from the group of trees and the "merrie companie" in its shade. Midnight was long past; the concert was over, the crowds were thinning. I followed the ebb. Leaving the radiant park and well-lit Haute-Ville (still well lit, this it seems was to be a "nuit blanche" in Villette), I sought the dim lower quarter.

Dim I should not say, for the beauty of moonlight — forgotten in the park — here once more flowed in upon perception. High she rode, and calm and stainlessly she shone. The music and the mirth of the fête, the fire and bright hues of those lamps had out-done and out-shone her for an hour, but now, again, her glory and her silence triumphed. The rival lamps were dying: she held her course like a white fate. Drum, trumpet, bugle, had uttered their clangour, and were forgotten; with pencil-ray she wrote on heaven and on earth records for archives everlasting. She and those stars seemed to me at once the types and witnesses of truth all regnant. The night-sky lit her reign: like its slow-wheeling progress, advanced her victory — that onward movement which has been, and is, and will be from eternity to eternity.

These oil-twinkling streets are very still: I like them for their lowliness and peace. Homeward-bound burghers pass me now and then, but these companies are pedestrians, make little noise, and are soon gone. So well do I love Villette under her present aspect, not willingly would I re-enter under a roof, but that I am bent on pursuing my strange adventure to a successful close, and quietly regaining my bed in the great dormitory, before Madame Beck comes home.

Only one street lies between me and the Rue Fossette; as I enter it, for the first time, the sound of a carriage tears up the deep peace of this quarter. It comes this way — comes very fast. How loud sounds its rattle on the paved path! The street is narrow, and I keep carefully to the causeway. The carriage thunders past, but what do I see, or fancy I see, as it rushes by?

Surely something white fluttered from that window — surely a hand waved a handkerchief. Was that signal meant for me? Am I known? Who could recognise me? That is not M. de Bassompierre's carriage, nor Mrs. Bretton's; and besides, neither the Hôtel Crécy nor the château of La Terrasse lies in that direction. Well, I have no time for conjecture; I must hurry home.

Gaining the Rue Fossette, reaching the pensionnat, all there was still; no fiacre had yet arrived with Madame and Désirée. I had left the great door ajar; should I find it thus? Perhaps the wind or some other accident may have thrown it to with sufficient force to start the spring-bolt? In that case, hopeless became admission; my adventure must issue in catastrophe. I lightly pushed the heavy leaf; would it yield?

Yes. As soundless, as unresisting, as if some propitious genius had waited on a sesame-charm, in the vestibule within. Entering with bated breath, quietly making all fast, shoelessly mounting the staircase, I sought the dormitory, and reached my couch.

Ay! I reached it, and once more drew a free inspiration. The next moment, I almost shrieked — almost, but not quite, thank Heaven!

Throughout the dormitory, throughout the house, there reigned at this hour the stillness of death. All slept, and in such hush, it seemed that none dreamed. Stretched on the nineteen beds lay nineteen forms, at full-length and motionless. On mine — the twentieth couch — nothing ought to have lain: I had left it void, and void should have found it. What, then; do I see between the half-drawn curtains? What dark, usurping shape, supine, long, and strange? Is it a robber who has made his way through the open street-door, and lies there in wait? It looks very black, I think it looks — not human. Can it be a wandering dog that has come in from the street and crept and nestled hither? Will it spring, will it leap out if I approach? Approach I must. Courage! One step! —

My head reeled, for by the faint night-lamp, I saw stretched on my bed the old phantom — the NUN.

A cry at this moment might have ruined me. Be the spectacle what it might, I could afford neither consternation, scream, nor swoon. Besides, I was not overcome. Tempered by late incidents, my nerves disdained hysteria. Warm from illuminations, and music, and thronging thousands, thoroughly

Villette

lashed up by a new scourge, I defied spectra. In a moment, without exclamation, I had rushed on the haunted couch; nothing leaped out, or sprung, or stirred; all the movement was mine, so was all the life, the reality, the substance, the force; as my instinct felt. I tore her up—the incubus! I held her on high—the goblin! I shook her loose—the mystery! And down she fell—down all around me—down in shreds and fragments—and I trode upon her.

Here again—behold the branchless tree, the unstabled Rosinante; the film of cloud, the flicker of moonshine. The long nun proved a long bolster dressed in a long black stole, and artfully invested with a white veil. The garments in very truth, strange as it may seem, were genuine nun's garments, and by some hand they had been disposed with a view to illusion. Whence came these vestments? Who contrived this artifice? These questions still remained. To the head-bandage was pinned a slip of paper: it bore in pencil these mocking words—

"The nun of the attic bequeaths to Lucy Snowe her wardrobe. She will be seen in the Rue Fossette no more."

And what and who was she that had haunted me? She, I had actually seen three times. Not a woman of my acquaintance had the stature of that ghost. She was not of a female height. Not to any man I knew could the machination, for a moment, be attributed.

Still mystified beyond expression, but as thoroughly, as suddenly, relieved from all sense of the spectral and unearthly; scorning also to wear out my brain with the fret of a trivial though insoluble riddle, I just bundled together stole, veil, and bandages, thrust them beneath my pillow, lay down, listened till I heard the wheels of Madame's home-returning fiacre, then turned, and worn out by many nights' vigils, conquered, too, perhaps, by the now reacting narcotic, I deeply slept.

CHAPTER XL.

THE HAPPY PAIR.

The day succeeding this remarkable Midsummer night, proved no common day. I do not mean that it brought signs in heaven above, or portents on the earth beneath; nor do I allude to meteorological phenomena, to storm, flood, or whirlwind. On the contrary: the sun rose jocund, with a July face. Morning decked her beauty with rubies, and so filled her lap with roses, that they fell from her in showers, making her path blush: the Hours woke fresh as nymphs, and emptying on the early hills their dew-vials, they stepped out dismantled of vapour: shadowless, azure, and glorious, they led the sun's steeds on a burning and unclouded course.

In short, it was as fine a day as the finest summer could boast; but I doubt whether I was not the sole inhabitant of the Rue Fossette, who cared or remembered to note this pleasant fact. Another thought busied all other heads; a thought, indeed, which had its share in my meditations; but this master consideration, not possessing for me so entire a novelty, so overwhelming a suddenness, especially so dense a mystery, as it offered to the majority of my co-speculators thereon, left me somewhat more open than the rest to any collateral observation or impression.

Still, while walking in the garden, feeling the sunshine, and marking the blooming and growing plants, I pondered the same subject the whole house discussed.

What subject?

Merely this. When matins came to be said, there was a place vacant in the first rank of boarders. When breakfast was served, there remained a coffee-cup unclaimed. When the housemaid made the beds, she found in one, a bolster laid lengthwise, clad in a cap and night-gown; and when Ginevra Fanshawe's music-mistress came early, as usual, to give the morning lesson, that accomplished and promising young person, her pupil, failed utterly to be forthcoming.

High and low was Miss Fanshawe sought; through length and breadth was the house ransacked; vainly; not a trace, not an indication, not so much as a scrap of a billet rewarded the search; the nymph was vanished, engulfed in the past night, like a shooting star swallowed up by darkness.

Villette

Deep was the dismay of surveillante teachers, deeper the horror of the defaulting directress. Never had I seen Madame Beck so pale or so appalled. Here was a blow struck at her tender part, her weak side; here was damage done to her interest. How, too, had the untoward event happened? By what outlet had the fugitive taken wing? Not a casement was found unfastened, not a pane of glass broken; all the doors were bolted secure. Never to this day has Madame Beck obtained satisfaction on this point, nor indeed has anybody else concerned, save and excepting one, Lucy Snowe, who could not forget how, to facilitate a certain enterprise, a certain great door had been drawn softly to its lintel, closed, indeed, but neither bolted nor secure. The thundering carriage-and-pair encountered were now likewise recalled, as well as that puzzling signal, the waved handkerchief.

From these premises, and one or two others, inaccessible to any but myself, I could draw but one inference. It was a case of elopement. Morally certain on this head, and seeing Madame Beck's profound embarrassment, I at last communicated my conviction. Having alluded to M. de Hamal's suit, I found, as I expected, that Madame Beck was perfectly au fait to that affair. She had long since discussed it with Mrs. Cholmondeley, and laid her own responsibility in the business on that lady's shoulders. To Mrs. Cholmondeley and M. de Bassompierre she now had recourse.

We found that the Hôtel Crécy was already alive to what had happened. Ginevra had written to her cousin Paulina, vaguely signifying hymeneal intentions; communications had been received from the family of de Hamal; M. de Bassompierre was on the track of the fugitives. He overtook them too late.

In the course of the week, the post brought me a note. I may as well transcribe it; it contains explanation on more than one point: —

'DEAR OLD TIM "(short for Timon), — " I am off you see — gone like a shot. Alfred and I intended to be married in this way almost from the first; we never meant to be spliced in the humdrum way of other people; Alfred has too much spirit for that, and so have I — Dieu merci! Do you know, Alfred, who used to call you 'the dragon,' has seen so much of you during the last few months, that he begins to feel quite friendly towards you. He hopes you won't miss him now that he has gone; he begs to apologize for any little trouble he may have given you. He is afraid he rather inconvenienced you once when he came upon you in the grenier, just as you were reading a letter seemingly of the most special interest; but he could not resist the temptation to give you a start, you appeared so wonderfully taken up with your correspondent. En revanche, he says you once frightened him by rushing in for a dress or a shawl, or some other chiffon, at the moment when he had struck a light, and was going to take a quiet whiff of his cigar, while waiting for me.

"Do you begin to comprehend by this time that M. le Comte de Hamal was the nun of the attic, and that he came to see your humble servant? I will tell you how he managed it. You know he has the entrée of the Athénée, where two or three of his nephews, the sons of his eldest sister, Madame de Melcy, are students. You know the court of the Athénée is on the other side of the high wall bounding your walk, the allée défendue. Alfred can climb as well as he can dance or fence: his amusement was to make the escalade of our pensionnat by mounting, first the wall; then—by the aid of that high tree overspreading the grand berceau, and resting some of its boughs on the roof of the lower buildings of our premises—he managed to scale the first classe and the grand salle. One night, by the way, he fell out of this tree, tore down some of the branches, nearly broke his own neck, and after all, in running away, got a terrible fright, and was nearly caught by two people, Madame Beck and M. Emanuel, he thinks, walking in the alley. From the grande salle the ascent is not difficult to the highest block of building, finishing in the great garret. The skylight, you know, is, day and night, left half open for air; by the skylight he entered. Nearly a year ago I chanced to tell him our legend of the nun; that suggested his romantic idea of the spectral disguise, which I think you must allow he has very cleverly carried out.

"But for the nun's black gown and white veil, he would have been caught again and again both by you and that tiger-Jesuit, M. Paul. He thinks you both capital ghost-seers, and very brave. What I wonder at is, rather your secretiveness than your courage. How could you endure the visitations of that long spectre, time after time, without crying out, telling everybody, and rousing the whole house and neighbourhood?

"Oh, and how did you like the nun as a bed-fellow? I dressed her up: didn't I do it well? Did you shriek when you saw her: I should have gone mad; but then you have such nerves!—real iron and bend-leather! I believe you feel nothing. You haven't the same sensitiveness that a person of my constitution has. You seem to me insensible both to pain and fear and grief. You are a real old Diogenes.

Villette

"Well, dear grandmother! and are you not mightily angry at my moonlight flitting and run away match? I assure you it is excellent fun, and I did it partly to spite that minx, Paulina, and that bear, Dr. John: to show them that, with all their airs, I could get married as well as they. M. de Bassompierre was at first in a strange fume with Alfred; he threatened a prosecution for 'détournement de mineur,' and I know not what; he was so abominably in earnest, that I found myself forced to do a little bit of the melodramatic—go down on my knees, sob, cry, drench three pocket-handkerchiefs. Of course, 'mon oncle' soon gave in; indeed, where was the use of making a fuss? I am married, and that's all about it. He still says our marriage is not legal, because I am not of age, forsooth! As if that made any difference! I am just as much married as if I were a hundred. However, we are to be married again, and I am to have a trousseau, and Mrs. Cholmondeley is going to superintend it; and there are some hopes that M. de Bassompierre will give me a decent portion, which will be very convenient, as dear Alfred has nothing but his nobility, native and hereditary, and his pay. I only wish uncle would do things unconditionally, in a generous, gentleman-like fashion; he is so disagreeable as to make the dowry depend on Alfred's giving his written promise that he will never touch cards or dice from the day it is paid down. They accuse my angel of a tendency to play: I don't know anything about that, but I do know he is a dear, adorable creature.

"I cannot sufficiently extol the genius with which de Hamal managed our flight. How clever in him to select the night of the fête, when Madame (for he knows her habits), as he said, would infallibly be absent at the concert in the park. I suppose you must have gone with her. I watched you rise and leave the dormitory about eleven o'clock. How you returned alone, and on foot, I cannot conjecture. That surely was you we met in the narrow old Rue St. Jean? Did you see me wave my handkerchief from the carriage window?

"Adieu! Rejoice in my good luck: congratulate me on my supreme happiness, and believe me, dear cynic and misanthrope, yours, in the best of health and spirits,

GINEVRA LAURA DE HAMAL,

née FANSHAWE.

"P.S.—Remember, I am a countess now. Papa, mamma, and the girls at home, will be delighted to hear that. 'My daughter the Countess!' 'My sister the Countess!' Bravo! Sounds rather better than Mrs. John Bretton, hein?"

In winding up Mistress Fanshawe's memoirs, the reader will no doubt expect to hear that she came finally to bitter expiation of her youthful levities. Of course, a large share of suffering lies in reserve for her future.

A few words will embody my farther knowledge respecting her.

I saw her towards the close of her honeymoon. She called on Madame Beck, and sent for me into the salon. She rushed into my arms laughing. She looked very blooming and beautiful: her curls were longer, her cheeks rosier than ever: her white bonnet and her Flanders veil, her orange-flowers and her bride's dress, became her mightily.

"I have got my portion!" she cried at once; (Ginevra ever stuck to the substantial; I always thought there was a good trading element in her composition, much as she scorned the "bourgeoise;") "and uncle de Bassompierre is quite reconciled. I don't mind his calling Alfred a 'nincompoop'—that's only his coarse Scotch breeding; and I believe Paulina envies me, and Dr. John is wild with jealousy—fit to blow his brains out—and I'm so happy! I really think I've hardly anything left to wish for— unless it be a carriage and an hotel, and, oh! I—must introduce you to 'mon mari.' Alfred, come here!"

And Alfred appeared from the inner salon, where he was talking to Madame Beck, receiving the blended felicitations and reprimands of that lady. I was presented under my various names: the Dragon, Diogenes, and Timon. The young Colonel was very polite. He made me a prettily-turned, neatly-worded apology, about the ghost-visits, &c., concluding with saying that "the best excuse for all his iniquities stood there!" pointing to his bride.

And then the bride sent him back to Madame Beck, and she took me to herself, and proceeded literally to suffocate me with her unrestrained spirits, her girlish, giddy, wild nonsense. She showed her ring exultingly; she called herself Madame la Comtesse de Hamal, and asked how it sounded, a score of times. I said very little. I gave her only the crust and rind of my nature. No matter she expected of me nothing better—she knew me too well to look for compliments—my dry gibes pleased her well enough and the more impassible and prosaic my mien, the more merrily she laughed.

Villette

Soon after his marriage, M. de Hamal was persuaded to leave the army as the surest way of weaning him from certain unprofitable associates and habits; a post of attaché was procured for him, and he and his young wife went abroad. I thought she would forget me now, but she did not. For many years, she kept up a capricious, fitful sort of correspondence. During the first year or two, it was only of herself and Alfred she wrote; then, Alfred faded in the background; herself and a certain, new comer prevailed; one Alfred Fanshawe de Bassompierre de Hamal began to reign in his father's stead. There were great boastings about this personage, extravagant amplifications upon miracles of precocity, mixed with vehement objurgations against the phlegmatic incredulity with which I received them. I didn't know "what it was to be a mother;" "unfeeling thing that I was, the sensibilities of the maternal heart were Greek and Hebrew to me," and so on. In due course of nature this young gentleman took his degrees in teething, measles, hooping-cough: that was a terrible time for me—the mamma's letters became a perfect shout of affliction; never woman was so put upon by calamity: never human being stood in such need of sympathy. I was frightened at first, and wrote back pathetically; but I soon found out there was more cry than wool in the business, and relapsed into my natural cruel insensibility. As to the youthful sufferer, he weathered each storm like a hero. Five times was that youth "in articulo mortis," and five times did he miraculously revive.

In the course of years there arose ominous murmurings against Alfred the First; M. de Bassompierre had to be appealed to, debts had to be paid, some of them of that dismal and dingy order called "debts of honour;" ignoble plaints and difficulties became frequent. Under every cloud, no matter what its nature, Ginevra, as of old, called out lustily for sympathy and aid. She had no notion of meeting any distress single-handed. In some shape, from some quarter or other, she was pretty sure to obtain her will, and so she got on—fighting the battle of life by proxy, and, on the whole, suffering as little as any human being I have ever known.

CHAPTER XLI.

FAUBOURG CLOTILDE.

Must I, ere I close, render some account of that Freedom and Renovation which I won on the fête-night? Must I tell how I and the two stalwart companions I brought home from the illuminated park bore the test of intimate acquaintance?

I tried them the very next day. They had boasted their strength loudly when they reclaimed me from love and its bondage, but upon my demanding deeds, not words, some evidence of better comfort, some experience of a relieved life — Freedom excused himself, as for the present impoverished and disabled to assist; and Renovation never spoke; he had died in the night suddenly.

I had nothing left for it then but to trust secretly that conjecture might have hurried me too fast and too far, to sustain the oppressive hour by reminders of the distorting and discolouring magic of jealousy. After a short and vain struggle, I found myself brought back captive to the old rack of suspense, tied down and strained anew.

Shall I yet see him before he goes? Will he bear me in mind? Does he purpose to come? Will this day — will the next hour bring him? or must I again assay that corroding pain of long attent — that rude agony of rupture at the close, that mute, mortal wrench, which, in at once uprooting hope and doubt, shakes life; while the hand that does the violence cannot be caressed to pity, because absence interposes her barrier!

It was the Feast of the Assumption; no school was held. The boarders and teachers, after attending mass in the morning, were gone a long walk into the country to take their goûter, or afternoon meal, at some farm-house. I did not go with them, for now but two days remained ere the Paul et Virginie must sail, and I was clinging to my last chance, as the living waif of a wreck clings to his last raft or cable.

There was some joiners' work to do in the first classe, some bench or desk to repair; holidays were often turned to account for the performance of these operations, which could not be executed when the rooms were filled with pupils. As I sat solitary, purposing to adjourn to the garden and leave the coast clear, but too listless to fulfil my own intent, I heard the workmen coming.

Villette

Foreign artisans and servants do everything by couples: I believe it would take two Labassecourien carpenters to drive a nail. While tying on my bonnet, which had hitherto hung by its ribbons from my idle hand, I vaguely and momentarily wondered to hear the step of but one "ouvrier." I noted, too—as captives in dungeons find sometimes dreary leisure to note the merest trifles—that this man wore shoes, and not sabots: I concluded that it must be the master-carpenter, coming to inspect before he sent his journeymen. I threw round me my scarf. He advanced; he opened the door; my back was towards it; I felt a little thrill—a curious sensation, too quick and transient to be analyzed. I turned, I stood in the supposed master-artisan's presence: looking towards the door-way, I saw it filled with a figure, and my eyes printed upon my brain the picture of M. Paul.

Hundreds of the prayers with which we weary Heaven bring to the suppliant no fulfilment. Once haply in life, one golden gift falls prone in the lap—one boon full and bright, perfect from Fruition's mint.

M. Emanuel wore the dress in which he probably purposed to travel—a surtout, guarded with velvet; I thought him prepared for instant departure, and yet I had understood that two days were yet to run before the ship sailed. He looked well and cheerful. He looked kind and benign: he came in with eagerness; he was close to me in one second; he was all amity. It might be his bridegroom mood which thus brightened him. Whatever the cause, I could not meet his sunshine with cloud. If this were my last moment with him, I would not waste it in forced, unnatural distance. I loved him well—too well not to smite out of my path even Jealousy herself, when she would have obstructed a kind farewell. A cordial word from his lips, or a gentle look from his eyes, would do me good, for all the span of life that remained to me; it would be comfort in the last strait of loneliness; I would take it—I would taste the elixir, and pride should not spill the cup.

The interview would be short, of course: he would say to me just what he had said to each of the assembled pupils; he would take and hold my hand two minutes; he would touch my cheek with his lips for the first, last, only time—and then—no more. Then, indeed, the final parting, then the wide separation, the great gulf I could not pass to go to him—across which, haply, he would not glance, to remember me.

He took my hand in one of his, with the other he put back my bonnet; he looked into my face, his luminous smile went out, his lips expressed something almost like the wordless language of a mother who finds a child greatly and unexpectedly changed, broken with illness, or worn out by want. A check supervened.

"Paul, Paul!" said a woman's hurried voice behind, "Paul, come into the salon; I have yet a great many things to say to you—conversation for the whole day—and so has Victor; and Josef is here. Come Paul, come to your friends."

Madame Beck, brought to the spot by vigilance or an inscrutable instinct, pressed so near, she almost thrust herself between me and M. Emanuel.

"Come, Paul!" she reiterated, her eye grazing me with its hard ray like a steel stylet. She pushed against her kinsman. I thought he receded; I thought he would go. Pierced deeper than I could endure, made now to feel what defied suppression, I cried—

"My heart will break!"

What I felt seemed literal heart-break; but the seal of another fountain yielded under the strain: one breath from M. Paul, the whisper, "Trust me!" lifted a load, opened an outlet. With many a deep sob, with thrilling, with icy shiver, with strong trembling, and yet with relief—I wept.

"Leave her to me; it is a crisis: I will give her a cordial, and it will pass," said the calm Madame Beck.

To be left to her and her cordial seemed to me something like being left to the poisoner and her bowl. When M. Paul answered deeply, harshly, and briefly—

"Laissez-moi!" in the grim sound I felt a music strange, strong, but life-giving.

"Laissez-moi!" he repeated, his nostrils opening, and his facial muscles all quivering as he spoke.

"But this will never do," said Madame, with sternness. More sternly rejoined her kinsman—

"Sortez d'ici!"

"I will send for Père Silas: on the spot I will send for him," she threatened pertinaciously.

Villette

"Femme!" cried the Professor, not now in his deep tones, but in his highest and most excited key, "Femme! sortez à l'instant!"

He was roused, and I loved him in his wrath with a passion beyond what I had yet felt.

"What you do is wrong," pursued Madame; "it is an act characteristic of men of your unreliable, imaginative temperament; a step impulsive, injudicious, inconsistent—a proceeding vexatious, and not estimable in the view of persons of steadier and more resolute character."

"You know not what I have of steady and resolute in me," said he, "but you shall see; the event shall teach you. Modeste," he continued less fiercely, "be gentle, be pitying, be a woman; look at this poor face, and relent. You know I am your friend, and the friend of your friends; in spite of your taunts, you well and deeply know I may be trusted. Of sacrificing myself I made no difficulty but my heart is pained by what I see; it must have and give solace. Leave me!"

This time, in the "leave me" there was an intonation so bitter and so imperative, I wondered that even Madame Beck herself could for one moment delay obedience; but she stood firm; she gazed upon him dauntless; she met his eye, forbidding and fixed as stone. She was opening her lips to retort; I saw over all M. Paul's face a quick rising light and fire; I can hardly tell how he managed the movement; it did not seem violent; it kept the form of courtesy; he gave his hand; it scarce touched her I thought; she ran, she whirled from the room; she was gone, and the door shut, in one second.

The flash of passion was all over very soon. He smiled as he told me to wipe my eyes; he waited quietly till I was calm, dropping from time to time a stilling, solacing word. Ere long I sat beside him once more myself—re-assured, not desperate, nor yet desolate; not friendless, not hopeless, not sick of life, and seeking death.

"It made you very sad then to lose your friend?" said he.

"It kills me to be forgotten, Monsieur," I said. "All these weary days I have not heard from you one word, and I was crushed with the possibility, growing to certainty, that you would depart without saying farewell!"

"Must I tell you what I told Modeste Beck—that you do not know me? Must I show and teach you my character? You will have proof that I can be a firm friend? Without clear proof this hand will not lie still in mine, it will not trust my shoulder as a safe stay? Good. The proof is ready. I come to justify myself."

"Say anything, teach anything, prove anything, Monsieur; I can listen now."

"Then, in the first place, you must go out with me a good distance into the town. I came on purpose to fetch you."

Without questioning his meaning, or sounding his plan, or offering the semblance of an objection, I re-tied my bonnet: I was ready.

The route he took was by the boulevards: he several times made me sit down on the seats stationed under the lime-trees; he did not ask if I was tired, but looked, and drew his own conclusions.

"All these weary days," said he, repeating my words, with a gentle, kindly mimicry of my voice and foreign accent, not new from his lips, and of which the playful banter never wounded, not even when coupled, as it often was, with the assertion, that however I might write his language, I spoke and always should speak it imperfectly and hesitatingly. "'All these weary days' I have not for one hour forgotten you. Faithful women err in this, that they think themselves the sole faithful of God's creatures. On a very fervent and living truth to myself, I, too, till lately scarce dared count, from any quarter; but——look at me."

I lifted my happy eyes: they were happy now, or they would have been no interpreters of my heart.

"Well," said he, after some seconds' scrutiny, "there is no denying that signature: Constancy wrote it: her pen is of iron. Was the record painful?"

"Severely painful," I said, with truth. "Withdraw her hand, Monsieur; I can bear its inscribing force no more."

"Elle est toute pâle," said he, speaking to himself; "cette figure-là me fait mal."

"Ah! I am not pleasant to look at——?"

I could not help saying this; the words came unbidden: I never remember the time when I had not a haunting dread of what might be the degree of my outward deficiency; this dread

Villette

pressed me at the moment with special force.

A great softness passed upon his countenance; his violet eyes grew suffused and glistening under their deep Spanish lashes: he started up; "Let us walk on."

"Do I displease your eyes much?" I took courage to urge: the point had its vital import for me.

He stopped, and gave me a short, strong answer; an answer which silenced, subdued, yet profoundly satisfied. Ever after that I knew what I was for him; and what I might be for the rest of the world, I ceased painfully to care. Was it weak to lay so much stress on an opinion about appearance? I fear it might be; I fear it was; but in that case I must avow no light share of weakness. I must own great fear of displeasing—a strong wish moderately to please M. Paul.

Whither we rambled, I scarce knew. Our walk was long, yet seemed short; the path was pleasant, the day lovely. M. Emanuel talked of his voyage—he thought of staying away three years. On his return from Guadaloupe, he looked forward to release from liabilities and a clear course; and what did I purpose doing in the interval of his absence? he asked. I had talked once, he reminded me, of trying to be independent and keeping a little school of my own: had I dropped the idea?

"Indeed, I had not: I was doing my best to save what would enable me to put it in practice."

"He did not like leaving me in the Rue Fossette; he feared I should miss him there too much—I should feel desolate—I should grow sad—?"

This was certain; but I promised to do my best to endure.

"Still," said he, speaking low, "there is another objection to your present residence. I should wish to write to you sometimes: it would not be well to have any uncertainty about the safe transmission of letters; and in the Rue Fossette—in short, our Catholic discipline in certain matters—though justifiable and expedient—might possibly, under peculiar circumstances, become liable to misapplication—perhaps abuse."

"But if you write," said I, "I must have your letters; and I will have them: ten directors, twenty directresses, shall not keep them from me. I am a Protestant: I will not bear that kind of discipline: Monsieur, I will not."

"Doucement—doucement," rejoined he; "we will contrive a plan; we have our resources: soyez tranquille."

So speaking, he paused.

We were now returning from the long walk. We had reached the middle of a clean Faubourg, where the houses were small, but looked pleasant. It was before the white door-step of a very neat abode that M. Paul had halted.

"I call here," said he.

He did not knock, but taking from his pocket a key, he opened and entered at once. Ushering me in, he shut the door behind us. No servant appeared. The vestibule was small, like the house, but freshly and tastefully painted; its vista closed in a French window with vines trained about the panes, tendrils, and green leaves kissing the glass. Silence reigned in this dwelling.

Opening an inner door, M. Paul disclosed a parlour, or salon—very tiny, but I thought, very pretty. Its delicate walls were tinged like a blush; its floor was waxed; a square of brilliant carpet covered its centre; its small round table shone like the mirror over its hearth; there was a little couch, a little chiffonnière, the half-open, crimson-silk door of which, showed porcelain on the shelves; there was a French clock, a lamp; there were ornaments in biscuit china; the recess of the single ample window was filled with a green stand, bearing three green flower-pots, each filled with a fine plant glowing in bloom; in one corner appeared a guéridon with a marble top, and upon it a work-box, and a glass filled with violets in water. The lattice of this room was open; the outer air breathing through, gave freshness, the sweet violets lent fragrance.

"Pretty, pretty place!" said I. M. Paul smiled to see me so pleased.

"Must we sit down here and wait?" I asked in a whisper, half awed by the deep pervading hush.

"We will first peep into one or two other nooks of this nutshell," he replied.

"Dare you take the freedom of going all over the house?" I inquired.

Villette

"Yes, I dare," said he, quietly.

He led the way. I was shown a little kitchen with a little stove and oven, with few but bright brasses, two chairs and a table. A small cupboard held a diminutive but commodious set of earthenware.

"There is a coffee service of china in the salon," said M. Paul, as I looked at the six green and white dinner-plates; the four dishes, the cups and jugs to match.

Conducted up the narrow but clean staircase, I was permitted a glimpse of two pretty cabinets of sleeping-rooms; finally, I was once more led below, and we halted with a certain ceremony before a larger door than had yet been opened.

Producing a second key, M. Emanuel adjusted it to the lock of this door. He opened, put me in before him.

"Voici!" he cried.

I found myself in a good-sized apartment, scrupulously clean, though bare, compared with those I had hitherto seen. The well-scoured boards were carpetless; it contained two rows of green benches and desks, with an alley down the centre, terminating in an estrade, a teacher's chair and table; behind them a tableau. On the walls hung two maps; in the windows flowered a few hardy plants; in short, here was a miniature classe—complete, neat, pleasant.

"It is a school then?" said I. "Who keeps it? I never heard of an establishment in this faubourg."

"Will you have the goodness to accept of a few prospectuses for distribution in behalf of a friend of mine?" asked he, taking from his surtout-pocket some quires of these documents, and putting them into my hand. I looked, I read—printed in fair characters:—

"Externat de demoiselles. Numéro 7, Faubourg Clotilde, Directrice, Mademoiselle Lucy Snowe."

And what did I say to M. Paul Emanuel?

Certain junctures of our lives must always be difficult of recall to memory. Certain points, crises, certain feelings, joys, griefs, and amazements, when reviewed, must strike us as things wildered and whirling, dim as a wheel fast spun.

I can no more remember the thoughts or the words of the ten minutes succeeding this disclosure, than I can retrace the experience of my earliest year of life: and yet the first thing distinct to me is the consciousness that I was speaking very fast, repeating over and over again:—

"Did you do this, M. Paul? Is this your house? Did you furnish it? Did you get these papers printed? Do you mean me? Am I the directress? Is there another Lucy Snowe? Tell me: say something."

But he would not speak. His pleased silence, his laughing down-look, his attitude, are visible to me now.

"How is it? I must know all—all," I cried.

The packet of papers fell on the floor. He had extended his hand, and I had fastened thereon, oblivious of all else.

"Ah! you said I had forgotten you all these weary days," said he. "Poor old Emanuel! These are the thanks he gets for trudging about three mortal weeks from house-painter to upholsterer, from cabinet-maker to charwoman. Lucy and Lucy's cot, the sole thoughts in his head!"

I hardly knew what to do. I first caressed the soft velvet on his cuff, and then. I stroked the hand it surrounded. It was his foresight, his goodness, his silent, strong, effective goodness, that overpowered me by their proved reality. It was the assurance of his sleepless interest which broke on me like a light from heaven; it was his—I will dare to say it—his fond, tender look, which now shook me indescribably. In the midst of all I forced myself to look at the practical.

"The trouble!" I cried, "and the cost! Had you money, M. Paul?"

"Plenty of money!" said he heartily. "The disposal of my large teaching connection put me in possession of a handsome sum with part of it I determined to give myself the richest treat that I have known or shall know. I like this. I have reckoned on this hour day and night lately. I would not come near you, because I would not forestall it. Reserve is neither my virtue nor my vice. If I had put myself into your power, and you had begun with your questions of look and lip—Where have you been, M. Paul? What have you been doing? What is your mystery?—my solitary first and last secret would presently have unravelled itself in your lap. Now," he pursued, "you shall

Villette

live here and have a school; you shall employ yourself while I am away; you shall think of me sometimes; you shall mind your health and happiness for my sake, and when I come back—"

There he left a blank.

I promised to do all he told me. I promised to work hard and willingly. "I will be your faithful steward," I said; "I trust at your coming the account will be ready. Monsieur, monsieur, you are too good!"

In such inadequate language my feelings struggled for expression: they could not get it; speech, brittle and unmalleable, and cold as ice, dissolved or shivered in the effort. He watched me, still; he gently raised his hand to stroke my hair; it touched my lips in passing; I pressed it close, I paid it tribute. He was my king; royal for me had been that hand's bounty; to offer homage was both a joy and a duty.

The afternoon hours were over, and the stiller time of evening shaded the quiet faubourg. M. Paul claimed my hospitality; occupied and afoot since morning, he needed refreshment; he said I should offer him chocolate in my pretty gold and white china service. He went out and ordered what was needful from the restaurant; he placed the small guéridon and two chairs in the balcony outside the French window under the screening vines. With what shy joy I accepted my part as hostess, arranged the salver, served the benefactor-guest.

This balcony was in the rear of the house, the gardens of the faubourg were round us, fields extended beyond. The air was still, mild, and fresh. Above the poplars, the laurels, the cypresses, and the roses, looked up a moon so lovely and so halcyon, the heart trembled under her smile; a star shone subject beside her, with the unemulous ray of pure love. In a large garden near us, a jet rose from a well, and a pale statue leaned over the play of waters.

M. Paul talked to me. His voice was so modulated that it mixed harmonious with the silver whisper, the gush, the musical sigh, in which light breeze, fountain and foliage intoned their lulling vesper:

Happy hour—stay one moment! droop those plumes, rest those wings; incline to mine that brow of Heaven! White Angel! let thy light linger; leave its reflection on succeeding clouds; bequeath its cheer to that time which needs a ray in retrospect!

Our meal was simple: the chocolate, the rolls, the plate of fresh summer fruit, cherries and strawberries bedded in green leaves formed the whole: but it was what we both liked better than a feast, and I took a delight inexpressible in tending M. Paul. I asked him whether his friends, Père Silas and Madame Beck, knew what he had done—whether they had seen my house?

"Mon amie," said he, "none knows what I have done save you and myself: the pleasure is consecrated to us two, unshared and unprofaned. To speak truth, there has been to me in this matter a refinement of enjoyment I would not make vulgar by communication. Besides" (smiling) "I wanted to prove to Miss Lucy that I could keep a secret. How often has she taunted me with lack of dignified reserve and needful caution! How many times has she saucily insinuated that all my affairs are the secret of Polichinelle!"

This was true enough: I had not spared him on this point, nor perhaps on any other that was assailable. Magnificent-minded, grand-hearted, dear, faulty little man! You deserved candour, and from me always had it.

Continuing my queries, I asked to whom the house belonged, who was my landlord, the amount of my rent. He instantly gave me these particulars in writing; he had foreseen and prepared all things.

The house was not M. Paul's—that I guessed: he was hardly the man to become a proprietor; I more than suspected in him a lamentable absence of the saving faculty; he could get, but not keep; he needed a treasurer. The tenement, then, belonged to a citizen in the Basse-Ville—a man of substance, M. Paul said; he startled me by adding: "a friend of yours, Miss Lucy, a person who has a most respectful regard for you." And, to my pleasant surprise, I found the landlord was none other than M. Miret, the short-tempered and kind-hearted bookseller, who had so kindly found me a seat that eventful night in the park. It seems M. Miret was, in his station, rich, as well as much respected, and possessed several houses in this faubourg; the rent was moderate, scarce half of what it would have been for a house of equal size nearer the centre of Villette.

"And then," observed M. Paul, "should fortune not favour you, though I think she will, I have the satisfaction to think you are in good hands; M. Miret will not be extortionate: the first year's rent you have already in your savings; afterwards Miss Lucy must trust God, and herself. But now, what will you do for

Villette

pupils?"

"I must distribute my prospectuses."

"Right! By way of losing no time, I gave one to M. Miret yesterday. Should you object to beginning with three petite bourgeoises, the Demoiselles Miret? They are at your service."

"Monsieur, you forget nothing; you are wonderful. Object? It would become me indeed to object! I suppose I hardly expect at the outset to number aristocrats in my little day-school; I care not if they never come. I shall be proud to receive M. Miret's daughters."

"Besides these," pursued he, "another pupil offers, who will come daily to take lessons in English; and as she is rich, she will pay handsomely. I mean my god-daughter and ward, Justine Marie Sauveur."

What is in a name? — what in three words? Till this moment I had listened with living joy — I had answered with gleeful quickness; a name froze me; three words struck me mute. The effect could not be hidden, and indeed I scarce tried to hide it.

"What now?" said M. Paul.

"Nothing."

"Nothing! Your countenance changes: your colour and your very eyes fade. Nothing! You must be ill; you have some suffering; tell me what."

I had nothing to tell.

He drew his chair nearer. He did not grow vexed, though I continued silent and icy. He tried to win a word; he entreated with perseverance, he waited with patience.

"Justine Marie is a good girl," said he, "docile and amiable; not quick — but you will like her."

"I think not. I think she must not come here."

Such was my speech.

"Do you wish to puzzle me? Do you know her? But, in truth, there is something. Again you are pale as that statue. Rely on Paul Carlos; tell him the grief."

His chair touched mine; his hand, quietly advanced, turned me towards him.

"Do you know Marie Justine?" said he again.

The name re-pronounced by his lips overcame me unaccountably. It did not prostrate—no, it stirred me up, running with haste and heat through my veins—recalling an hour of quick pain, many days and nights of heart-sickness. Near me as he now sat, strongly and closely as he had long twined his life in mine—far as had progressed, and near as was achieved our minds' and affections' assimilation—the very suggestion of interference, of heart-separation, could be heard only with a fermenting excitement, an impetuous throe, a disdainful resolve, an ire, a resistance of which no human eye or cheek could hide the flame, nor any truth-accustomed human tongue curb the cry.

"I want to tell you something," I said: "I want to tell you all."

"Speak, Lucy; come near; speak. Who prizes you, if I do not? Who is your friend, if not Emanuel? Speak!"

I spoke. All escaped from my lips. I lacked not words now; fast I narrated; fluent I told my tale; it streamed on my tongue. I went back to the night in the park; I mentioned the medicated draught—why it was given—its goading effect—how it had torn rest from under my head, shaken me from my couch, carried me abroad with the lure of a vivid yet solemn fancy—a summer-night solitude on turf, under trees, near a deep, cool lakelet. I told the scene realized; the crowd, the masques, the music, the lamps, the splendours, the guns booming afar, the bells sounding on high. All I had encountered I detailed, all I had recognised, heard, and seen; how I had beheld and watched himself: how I listened, how much heard, what conjectured; the whole history, in brief, summoned to his confidence, rushed thither, truthful, literal, ardent, bitter.

Still as I narrated, instead of checking, he incited me to proceed, he spurred me by the gesture, the smile, the half-word. Before I had half done, he held both my hands, he consulted my eyes with a most piercing glance: there was something in his face which tended neither to calm nor to put me down; he forgot his own doctrine, he forsook his own system of repression when I most challenged its exercise. I think I deserved strong reproof; but when have we our deserts? I merited severity; he looked indulgence. To my very self I seemed imperious and unreasonable, for I forbade Justine Marie my door and roof; he smiled, betraying delight. Warm, jealous, and haughty, I knew not till now that my nature had such a mood: he gathered me near his heart. I was full of faults; he took them and me all home. For the moment of utmost mutiny, he reserved the one deep spell of peace. These words caressed my ear:—

"Lucy, take my love. One day share my life. Be my dearest, first on earth."

We walked back to the Rue Fossette by moonlight—such moonlight as fell on Eden—shining through the shades of the Great Garden, and haply gilding a path glorious for a step divine—a Presence nameless. Once in their lives some men and women go back to these first fresh days of our great Sire and Mother—taste that grand morning's dew—bathe in its sunrise.

In the course of the walk I was told how Justine Marie Sauveur had always been regarded with the affection proper to a daughter—how, with M. Paul's consent, she had been affianced for months to one Heinrich Mühler, a wealthy young German merchant, and was to be married in the course of a year. Some of M. Emanuel's relations and connections would, indeed, it seems, have liked him to marry her, with a view to securing her fortune in the family; but to himself the scheme was repugnant, and the idea totally inadmissible.

We reached Madame Beck's door. Jean Baptiste's clock tolled nine. At this hour, in this house, eighteen months since, had this man at my side bent before me, looked into my face and eyes, and arbitered my destiny. This very evening he had again stooped, gazed, and decreed. How different the look—how far otherwise the fate!

He deemed me born under his star: he seemed to have spread over me its beam like a banner. Once—unknown, and unloved, I held him harsh and strange; the low stature, the wiry make, the angles, the darkness, the manner, displeased me. Now, penetrated with his influence, and living by his affection, having his worth by intellect, and his goodness by heart—I preferred him before all humanity.

We parted: he gave me his pledge, and then his farewell. We parted: the next day—he sailed.

CHAPTER XLII.

FINIS.

Man cannot prophesy. Love is no oracle. Fear sometimes imagines a vain thing. Those years of absence! How had I sickened over their anticipation! The woe they must bring seemed certain as death. I knew the nature of their course: I never had doubt how it would harrow as it went. The juggernaut on his car towered there a grim load. Seeing him draw nigh, burying his broad wheels in the oppressed soil—I, the prostrate votary—felt beforehand the annihilating craunch.

Strange to say—strange, yet true, and owning many parallels in life's experience—that anticipatory craunch proved all—yes—nearly all the torture. The great Juggernaut, in his great chariot, drew on lofty, loud, and sullen. He passed quietly, like a shadow sweeping the sky, at noon. Nothing but a chilling dimness was seen or felt. I looked up. Chariot and demon charioteer were gone by; the votary still lived.

M. Emanuel was away three years. Reader, they were the three happiest years of my life. Do you scout the paradox? Listen. I commenced my school; I worked—I worked hard. I deemed myself the steward of his property, and determined, God willing, to render a good account. Pupils came—burghers at first—a higher class ere long. About the middle of the second year an unexpected chance threw into my hands an additional hundred pounds: one day I received from England a letter containing that sum. It came from Mr. Marchmont, the cousin and heir of my dear and dead mistress. He was just recovering from a dangerous illness; the money was a peace-offering to his conscience, reproaching him in the matter of, I know not what, papers or memoranda found after his kinswoman's death—naming or recommending Lucy Snowe. Mrs. Barrett had given him my address. How far his conscience had been sinned against, I never inquired. I asked no questions, but took the cash and made it useful.

With this hundred pounds I ventured to take the house adjoining mine. I would not leave that which M. Paul had chosen, in which he had left, and where he expected again to find me. My externat became a pensionnat; that also prospered.

The secret of my success did not lie so much in myself, in any endowment, any power of mine, as in a new state of circumstances, a wonderfully changed life, a relieved heart. The spring which moved my energies lay far away beyond seas, in an Indian isle. At parting, I had been left a legacy; such a thought for the present, such a hope for the future, such a motive for a persevering, a laborious, an enterprising, a patient and a brave course — I could not flag. Few things shook me now; few things had importance to vex, intimidate, or depress me: most things pleased — mere trifles had a charm.

Do not think that this genial flame sustained itself, or lived wholly on a bequeathed hope or a parting promise. A generous provider supplied bounteous fuel. I was spared all chill, all stint; I was not suffered to fear penury; I was not tried with suspense. By every vessel he wrote; he wrote as he gave and as he loved, in full-handed, full-hearted plenitude. He wrote because he liked to write; he did not abridge, because he cared not to abridge. He sat down, he took pen and paper, because he loved Lucy and had much to say to her; because he was faithful and thoughtful, because he was tender and true. There was no sham and no cheat, and no hollow unreal in him. Apology never dropped her slippery oil on his lips — never proffered, by his pen, her coward feints and paltry nullities: he would give neither a stone, nor an excuse — neither a scorpion; nor a disappointment; his letters were real food that nourished, living water that refreshed.

And was I grateful? God knows! I believe that scarce a living being so remembered, so sustained, dealt with in kind so constant, honourable and noble, could be otherwise than grateful to the death.

Adherent to his own religion (in him was not the stuff of which is made the facile apostate), he freely left me my pure faith. He did not tease nor tempt. He said: —

"Remain a Protestant. My little English Puritan, I love Protestantism in you. I own its severe charm. There is something in its ritual I cannot receive myself, but it is the sole creed for 'Lucy.'"

All Rome could not put into him bigotry, nor the Propaganda itself make him a real Jesuit. He was born honest, and not false — artless, and not cunning — a freeman, and not a slave. His tenderness had rendered him ductile in a priest's hands, his affection, his devotedness, his sincere pious enthusiasm blinded his kind eyes sometimes, made him abandon justice to himself to do the work of craft, and serve the ends of selfishness; but these are faults so rare to find, so costly to their owner to indulge, we scarce know whether they will not one day be reckoned amongst the jewels.

And now the three years are past: M. Emanuel's return is fixed. It is Autumn; he is to be with me ere the mists of November come. My school flourishes, my house is ready: I have made him a little library, filled its shelves with the books he left in my care: I have cultivated out of love for him (I was naturally no florist) the plants he preferred, and some of them are yet in bloom. I thought I loved him when he went away; I love him now in another degree: he is more my own.

The sun passes the equinox; the days shorten, the leaves grow sere; but—he is coming.

Frosts appear at night; November has sent his fogs in advance; the wind takes its autumn moan; but—he is coming.

The skies hang full and dark—a wrack sails from the west; the clouds cast themselves into strange forms—arches and broad radiations; there rise resplendent mornings—glorious, royal, purple as monarch in his state; the heavens are one flame; so wild are they, they rival battle at its thickest—so bloody, they shame Victory in her pride. I know some signs of the sky; I have noted them ever since childhood. God watch that sail! Oh! guard it!

The wind shifts to the west. Peace, peace, Banshee—"keening" at every window! It will rise—it will swell—it shrieks out long: wander as I may through the house this night, I cannot lull the blast. The advancing hours make it strong: by midnight, all sleepless watchers hear and fear a wild south-west storm. That storm roared frenzied, for seven days. It did not cease till the Atlantic was strewn with wrecks: it did not lull till the deeps had gorged their full of sustenance. Not till the destroying angel of tempest had achieved his perfect work, would he fold the wings whose waft was thunder—the tremor of whose plumes was storm.

Peace, be still! Oh! a thousand weepers, praying in agony on waiting shores, listened for that voice, but it was not uttered—not uttered till; when the hush came, some could not feel it: till, when the sun returned, his light was night to some!

Here pause: pause at once. There is enough said. Trouble no quiet, kind heart; leave sunny imaginations hope. Let it be theirs to conceive the delight of joy born again fresh out of great terror, the rapture of rescue from peril, the wondrous reprieve from dread, the fruition of return. Let them picture union and a happy succeeding life.

Madame Beck prospered all the days of her life; so did Père Silas; Madame Walravens fulfilled her ninetieth year before she died. Farewell.

THE END.

The House of the Seven Gables

By Nathaniel Hawthorne

PREFACE.

When a writer calls his work a Romance, it need hardly be observed that he wishes to claim a certain latitude, both as to its fashion and material, which he would not have felt himself entitled to assume had he professed to be writing a Novel. The latter form of composition is presumed to aim at a very minute fidelity, not merely to the possible, but to the probable and ordinary course of man's experience. The former—while, as a work of art, it must rigidly subject itself to laws, and while it sins unpardonably so far as it may swerve aside from the truth of the human heart—has fairly a right to present that truth under circumstances, to a great extent, of the writer's own choosing or creation. If he think fit, also, he may so manage his atmospherical medium as to bring out or mellow the lights and deepen and enrich the shadows of the picture. He will be wise, no doubt, to make a very moderate use of the privileges here stated, and, especially, to mingle the Marvelous rather as a slight, delicate, and evanescent flavor, than as any portion of the actual substance of the dish offered to the public. He can hardly be said, however, to commit a literary crime even if he disregard this caution.

In the present work, the author has proposed to himself—but with what success, fortunately, it is not for him to judge—to keep undeviatingly within his immunities. The point of view in which this tale comes under the Romantic definition lies in the attempt to connect a bygone time with the very present that is flitting away from us. It is a legend prolonging itself, from an epoch now gray in the distance, down into our own broad daylight, and bringing along with it some of its legendary mist, which the reader, according to his pleasure, may either disregard, or allow it to float almost imperceptibly about the characters and events for the sake of a picturesque effect. The narrative, it may be, is woven of so humble a texture as to require this advantage, and, at the same time, to render it the more difficult of attainment.

Many writers lay very great stress upon some definite moral purpose, at which they profess to aim their works. Not to be

The House of the Seven Gables

deficient in this particular, the author has provided himself with a moral,—the truth, namely, that the wrong-doing of one generation lives into the successive ones, and, divesting itself of every temporary advantage, becomes a pure and uncontrollable mischief; and he would feel it a singular gratification if this romance might effectually convince mankind—or, indeed, any one man—of the folly of tumbling down an avalanche of ill-gotten gold, or real estate, on the heads of an unfortunate posterity, thereby to maim and crush them, until the accumulated mass shall be scattered abroad in its original atoms. In good faith, however, he is not sufficiently imaginative to flatter himself with the slightest hope of this kind. When romances do really teach anything, or produce any effective operation, it is usually through a far more subtle process than the ostensible one. The author has considered it hardly worth his while, therefore, relentlessly to impale the story with its moral as with an iron rod,—or, rather, as by sticking a pin through a butterfly,—thus at once depriving it of life, and causing it to stiffen in an ungainly and unnatural attitude. A high truth, indeed, fairly, finely, and skilfully wrought out, brightening at every step, and crowning the final development of a work of fiction, may add an artistic glory, but is never any truer, and seldom any more evident, at the last page than at the first.

The reader may perhaps choose to assign an actual locality to the imaginary events of this narrative. If permitted by the historical connection,—which, though slight, was essential to his plan,—the author would very willingly have avoided anything of this nature. Not to speak of other objections, it exposes the romance to an inflexible and exceedingly dangerous species of criticism, by bringing his fancy-pictures almost into positive contact with the realities of the moment. It has been no part of his object, however, to describe local manners, nor in any way to meddle with the characteristics of a community for whom he cherishes a proper respect and a natural regard. He trusts not to be considered as unpardonably offending by laying out a street that infringes upon nobody's private rights, and appropriating a lot of land which had no visible owner, and building a house of materials long in use for constructing castles in the air. The personages of the tale—though they give themselves out to be of ancient stability and considerable prominence—are really of the author's own making, or at all events, of his own mixing; their virtues can shed no lustre, nor their defects redound, in the remotest degree, to the discredit of the venerable town of which they profess to be inhabitants. He would be glad, therefore, if—especially in the quarter to which he alludes—the book may be read strictly as a Romance, having a great deal more to do with the clouds overhead than with any portion of the actual soil of the County of Essex.

LENOX, January 27, 1851.

I.
The Old Pyncheon Family

Halfway down a by-street of one of our New England towns stands a rusty wooden house, with seven acutely peaked gables, facing towards various points of the compass, and a huge, clustered chimney in the midst. The street is Pyncheon Street; the house is the old Pyncheon House; and an elm-tree, of wide circumference, rooted before the door, is familiar to every town-born child by the title of the Pyncheon Elm. On my occasional visits to the town aforesaid, I seldom failed to turn down Pyncheon Street, for the sake of passing through the shadow of these two antiquities,—the great elm-tree and the weather-beaten edifice.

The aspect of the venerable mansion has always affected me like a human countenance, bearing the traces not merely of outward storm and sunshine, but expressive also, of the long lapse of mortal life, and accompanying vicissitudes that have passed within. Were these to be worthily recounted, they would form a narrative of no small interest and instruction, and possessing, moreover, a certain remarkable unity, which might almost seem the result of artistic arrangement. But the story would include a chain of events extending over the better part of two centuries, and, written out with reasonable amplitude, would fill a bigger folio volume, or a longer series of duodecimos, than could prudently be appropriated to the annals of all New England during a similar period. It consequently becomes imperative to make short work with most of the traditionary lore of which the old Pyncheon House, otherwise known as the House of the Seven Gables, has been the theme. With a brief sketch, therefore, of the circumstances amid which the foundation of the house was laid, and a rapid glimpse at its quaint exterior, as it grew black in the prevalent east wind,—pointing, too, here and there, at some spot of more verdant mossiness on its roof and walls,—we shall commence the real action of our tale at an epoch not very remote from the present day. Still, there will be a connection with the long past— a reference to forgotten events and personages, and to manners, feelings, and opinions, almost or wholly obsolete—which, if adequately translated to the reader, would serve to illustrate how much of old material goes to make up the freshest novelty of human life. Hence, too, might be drawn a weighty lesson from the little-regarded truth, that the act of the passing generation is the germ which may and must produce good or evil fruit in a far-distant time; that, together with the seed of the merely temporary crop, which mortals term expediency, they inevitably sow the acorns of a more enduring growth, which may darkly overshadow their posterity.

The House of the Seven Gables

The House of the Seven Gables, antique as it now looks, was not the first habitation erected by civilized man on precisely the same spot of ground. Pyncheon Street formerly bore the humbler appellation of Maule's Lane, from the name of the original occupant of the soil, before whose cottage-door it was a cow-path. A natural spring of soft and pleasant water—a rare treasure on the sea-girt peninsula where the Puritan settlement was made—had early induced Matthew Maule to build a hut, shaggy with thatch, at this point, although somewhat too remote from what was then the centre of the village. In the growth of the town, however, after some thirty or forty years, the site covered by this rude hovel had become exceedingly desirable in the eyes of a prominent and powerful personage, who asserted plausible claims to the proprietorship of this and a large adjacent tract of land, on the strength of a grant from the legislature. Colonel Pyncheon, the claimant, as we gather from whatever traits of him are preserved, was characterized by an iron energy of purpose. Matthew Maule, on the other hand, though an obscure man, was stubborn in the defence of what he considered his right; and, for several years, he succeeded in protecting the acre or two of earth which, with his own toil, he had hewn out of the primeval forest, to be his garden ground and homestead. No written record of this dispute is known to be in existence. Our acquaintance with the whole subject is derived chiefly from tradition. It would be bold, therefore, and possibly unjust, to venture a decisive opinion as to its merits; although it appears to have been at least a matter of doubt, whether Colonel Pyncheon's claim were not unduly stretched, in order to make it cover the small metes and bounds of Matthew Maule. What greatly strengthens such a suspicion is the fact that this controversy between two ill-matched antagonists—at a period, moreover, laud it as we may, when personal influence had far more weight than now—remained for years undecided, and came to a close only with the death of the party occupying the disputed soil. The mode of his death, too, affects the mind differently, in our day, from what it did a century and a half ago. It was a death that blasted with strange horror the humble name of the dweller in the cottage, and made it seem almost a religious act to drive the plough over the little area of his habitation, and obliterate his place and memory from among men.

Old Matthew Maule, in a word, was executed for the crime of witchcraft. He was one of the martyrs to that terrible delusion, which should teach us, among its other morals, that the influential classes, and those who take upon themselves to be leaders of the people, are fully liable to all the passionate error that has ever characterized the maddest mob. Clergymen, judges, statesmen,—the wisest, calmest, holiest persons of their day stood in the inner circle round about the gallows, loudest to applaud the work of blood, latest to confess themselves miserably deceived. If any one part of their proceedings can be said to deserve less blame than another, it was the singular indiscrimination with which they persecuted, not merely the poor and aged, as in former judicial massacres, but people of all ranks; their own equals, brethren, and wives. Amid the disorder of such various ruin, it is not strange that a man of inconsiderable note, like Maule, should have trodden the martyr's path to the hill of execution almost unremarked in the throng of his fellow sufferers. But, in after days, when the frenzy of that hideous epoch had subsided, it was remembered how loudly Colonel Pyncheon had joined in the general cry, to purge the land from witchcraft; nor did it fail to be whispered, that there was an invidious acrimony in the zeal with which he had sought the condemnation of Matthew Maule. It was well known that the victim had recognized the bitterness of personal enmity in his persecutor's conduct towards him, and that he declared himself hunted to death for his spoil. At the moment of execution — with the halter about his neck, and while Colonel Pyncheon sat on horseback, grimly gazing at the scene Maule had addressed him from the scaffold, and uttered a prophecy, of which history, as well as fireside tradition, has preserved the very words. "God," said the dying man, pointing his finger, with a ghastly look, at the undismayed countenance of his enemy, — "God will give him blood to drink!"

After the reputed wizard's death, his humble homestead had fallen an easy spoil into Colonel Pyncheon's grasp. When it was understood, however, that the Colonel intended to erect a family mansion — spacious, ponderously framed of oaken timber, and calculated to endure for many generations of his posterity over the spot first covered by the log-built hut of Matthew Maule, there was much shaking of the head among the village gossips. Without absolutely expressing a doubt whether the stalwart Puritan had acted as a man of conscience and integrity throughout the proceedings which have been sketched, they, nevertheless, hinted that he was about to build his house over an unquiet grave. His home would include the home of the dead and buried wizard, and would thus afford the ghost of the latter a kind of privilege to haunt its new apartments, and the chambers into which future bridegrooms were to lead their brides, and where children of the Pyncheon blood were to be born. The terror and ugliness of Maule's crime, and the wretchedness of his punishment, would darken the freshly plastered walls, and infect them early with the scent of an old and melancholy house. Why, then, — while so much of the soil around him was bestrewn with the virgin forest leaves, — why should Colonel Pyncheon prefer a site that had already been accurst?

But the Puritan soldier and magistrate was not a man to be turned aside from his well-considered scheme, either by dread of the wizard's ghost, or by flimsy sentimentalities of any kind, however specious. Had he been told of a bad air, it might have moved him somewhat; but he was ready to encounter an evil spirit on his own ground. Endowed with commonsense, as massive and hard as blocks of granite, fastened together by stern rigidity of purpose, as with iron clamps, he followed out his original design, probably without so much as imagining an objection to it. On the score of delicacy, or any scrupulousness which a finer sensibility might have taught him, the Colonel, like most of his breed and generation, was impenetrable. He therefore dug his cellar, and laid the deep foundations of his mansion, on the square of earth whence Matthew Maule, forty years before, had first swept away the fallen leaves. It was a curious, and, as some people thought, an ominous fact, that, very soon after the workmen began their operations, the spring of water, above mentioned, entirely lost the deliciousness of its pristine quality. Whether its sources were disturbed by the depth of the new cellar, or whatever subtler cause might lurk at the bottom, it is certain that the water of Maule's Well, as it continued to be called, grew hard and brackish. Even such we find it now; and any old woman of the neighborhood will certify that it is productive of intestinal mischief to those who quench their thirst there.

The reader may deem it singular that the head carpenter of the new edifice was no other than the son of the very man from whose dead gripe the property of the soil had been wrested. Not improbably he was the best workman of his time; or, perhaps, the Colonel thought it expedient, or was impelled by some better feeling, thus openly to cast aside all animosity against the race of his fallen antagonist. Nor was it out of keeping with the general coarseness and matter-of-fact character of the age, that the son should be willing to earn an honest penny, or, rather, a weighty amount of sterling pounds, from the purse of his father's deadly enemy. At all events, Thomas Maule became the architect of the House of the Seven Gables, and performed his duty so faithfully that the timber framework fastened by his hands still holds together.

Thus the great house was built. Familiar as it stands in the writer's recollection,—for it has been an object of curiosity with him from boyhood, both as a specimen of the best and stateliest architecture of a longpast epoch, and as the scene of events more full of human interest, perhaps, than those of a gray feudal castle,—familiar as it stands, in its rusty old age, it is therefore only the more difficult to imagine the bright novelty with which it first caught the sunshine. The impression of its actual state, at this distance of a hundred and sixty years, darkens inevitably through the picture which we would fain give of its appearance on the morning when the Puritan magnate bade all the town to be his guests. A ceremony of consecration, festive as well as religious, was now to be performed. A prayer and discourse from the Rev. Mr. Higginson, and the outpouring of a psalm from the general throat of the community, was to be made acceptable to the grosser sense by ale, cider, wine, and brandy, in copious effusion, and, as some authorities aver, by an ox, roasted whole, or at least, by the weight and substance of an ox, in more manageable joints and sirloins. The carcass of a deer, shot within twenty miles, had supplied material for the vast circumference of a pasty. A codfish of sixty pounds, caught in the bay, had been dissolved into the rich liquid of a chowder. The chimney of the new house, in short, belching forth its kitchen smoke, impregnated the whole air with the scent of meats, fowls, and fishes, spicily concocted with odoriferous herbs, and onions in abundance. The mere smell of such festivity, making its way to everybody's nostrils, was at once an invitation and an appetite.

Maule's Lane, or Pyncheon Street, as it were now more decorous to call it, was thronged, at the appointed hour, as with a congregation on its way to church. All, as they approached, looked upward at the imposing edifice, which was henceforth to assume its rank among the habitations of mankind. There it rose, a little withdrawn from the line of the street, but in pride, not modesty. Its whole visible exterior was ornamented with quaint figures, conceived in the grotesqueness of a Gothic fancy, and drawn or stamped in the glittering plaster, composed of lime, pebbles, and bits of glass, with which the woodwork of the walls was overspread. On every side the seven gables pointed sharply towards the sky, and presented the aspect of a whole sisterhood of edifices, breathing through the spiracles of one great chimney. The many lattices, with their small, diamond-shaped panes, admitted the sunlight into hall and chamber, while, nevertheless, the second story, projecting far over the base, and itself retiring beneath the third, threw a shadowy and thoughtful gloom into the lower rooms. Carved globes of wood were affixed under the jutting stories. Little spiral rods of iron beautified each of the seven peaks. On the triangular portion of the gable, that fronted next the street, was a dial, put up that very morning, and on which the sun was still marking the passage of the first bright hour in a history that was not destined to be all so bright. All around were scattered shavings, chips, shingles, and broken halves of bricks; these, together with the lately turned earth, on which the grass had not begun to grow, contributed to the impression of strangeness and novelty proper to a house that had yet its place to make among men's daily interests.

The principal entrance, which had almost the breadth of a church-door, was in the angle between the two front gables, and was covered by an open porch, with benches beneath its shelter. Under this arched doorway, scraping their feet on the unworn threshold, now trod the clergymen, the elders, the magistrates, the deacons, and whatever of aristocracy there was in town or county. Thither, too, thronged the plebeian classes as freely as

The House of the Seven Gables

their betters, and in larger number. Just within the entrance, however, stood two serving-men, pointing some of the guests to the neighborhood of the kitchen and ushering others into the statelier rooms,—hospitable alike to all, but still with a scrutinizing regard to the high or low degree of each. Velvet garments sombre but rich, stiffly plaited ruffs and bands, embroidered gloves, venerable beards, the mien and countenance of authority, made it easy to distinguish the gentleman of worship, at that period, from the tradesman, with his plodding air, or the laborer, in his leathern jerkin, stealing awe-stricken into the house which he had perhaps helped to build.

One inauspicious circumstance there was, which awakened a hardly concealed displeasure in the breasts of a few of the more punctilious visitors. The founder of this stately mansion—a gentleman noted for the square and ponderous courtesy of his demeanor, ought surely to have stood in his own hall, and to have offered the first welcome to so many eminent personages as here presented themselves in honor of his solemn festival. He was as yet invisible; the most favored of the guests had not beheld him. This sluggishness on Colonel Pyncheon's part became still more unaccountable, when the second dignitary of the province made his appearance, and found no more ceremonious a reception. The lieutenant-governor, although his visit was one of the anticipated glories of the day, had alighted from his horse, and assisted his lady from her side-saddle, and crossed the Colonel's threshold, without other greeting than that of the principal domestic.

This person—a gray-headed man, of quiet and most respectful deportment—found it necessary to explain that his master still remained in his study, or private apartment; on entering which, an hour before, he had expressed a wish on no account to be disturbed.

"Do not you see, fellow," said the high-sheriff of the county, taking the servant aside, "that this is no less a man than the lieutenant-governor? Summon Colonel Pyncheon at once! I know that he received letters from England this morning; and, in the perusal and consideration of them, an hour may have passed away without his noticing it. But he will be ill-pleased, I judge, if you suffer him to neglect the courtesy due to one of our chief rulers, and who may be said to represent King William, in the absence of the governor himself. Call your master instantly."

"Nay, please your worship," answered the man, in much perplexity, but with a backwardness that strikingly indicated the hard and severe character of Colonel Pyncheon's domestic rule; "my master's orders were exceeding strict; and, as your worship knows, he permits of no discretion in the obedience of those who owe him service. Let who list open yonder door; I dare not, though the governor's own voice should bid me do it!"

"Pooh, pooh, master high sheriff!" cried the lieutenant-governor, who had overheard the foregoing discussion, and felt himself high enough in station to play a little with his dignity. "I will take the matter into my own hands. It is time that the good Colonel came forth to greet his friends; else we shall be apt to suspect that he has taken a sip too much of his Canary wine, in his extreme deliberation which cask it were best to broach in honor of the day! But since he is so much behindhand, I will give him a remembrancer myself!"

Accordingly, with such a tramp of his ponderous riding-boots as might of itself have been audible in the remotest of the seven gables, he advanced to the door, which the servant pointed out, and made its new panels reecho with a loud, free knock. Then, looking round, with a smile, to the spectators, he awaited a response. As none came, however, he knocked again, but with the same unsatisfactory result as at first. And now, being a trifle choleric in his temperament, the lieutenant-governor uplifted the heavy hilt of his sword, wherewith he so beat and banged upon the door, that, as some of the bystanders whispered, the racket might have disturbed the dead. Be that as it might, it seemed to produce no awakening effect on Colonel Pyncheon. When the sound subsided, the silence through the house was deep, dreary, and oppressive, notwithstanding that the tongues of many of the guests had already been loosened by a surreptitious cup or two of wine or spirits.

"Strange, forsooth! — very strange!" cried the lieutenant-governor, whose smile was changed to a frown. "But seeing that our host sets us the good example of forgetting ceremony, I shall likewise throw it aside, and make free to intrude on his privacy."

He tried the door, which yielded to his hand, and was flung wide open by a sudden gust of wind that passed, as with a loud sigh, from the outermost portal through all the passages and apartments of the new house. It rustled the silken garments of the ladies, and waved the long curls of the gentlemen's wigs, and shook the window-hangings and the curtains of the bedchambers; causing everywhere a singular stir, which yet was more like a hush. A shadow of awe and half-fearful anticipation — nobody knew wherefore, nor of what — had all at once fallen over the company.

They thronged, however, to the now open door, pressing the lieutenant-governor, in the eagerness of their curiosity, into the room in advance of them. At the first glimpse they beheld nothing extraordinary: a handsomely furnished room, of moderate size, somewhat darkened by curtains; books arranged on shelves; a large map on the wall, and likewise a portrait of

The House of the Seven Gables

Colonel Pyncheon, beneath which sat the original Colonel himself, in an oaken elbow-chair, with a pen in his hand. Letters, parchments, and blank sheets of paper were on the table before him. He appeared to gaze at the curious crowd, in front of which stood the lieutenant-governor; and there was a frown on his dark and massive countenance, as if sternly resentful of the boldness that had impelled them into his private retirement.

A little boy — the Colonel's grandchild, and the only human being that ever dared to be familiar with him — now made his way among the guests, and ran towards the seated figure; then pausing halfway, he began to shriek with terror. The company, tremulous as the leaves of a tree, when all are shaking together, drew nearer, and perceived that there was an unnatural distortion in the fixedness of Colonel Pyncheon's stare; that there was blood on his ruff, and that his hoary beard was saturated with it. It was too late to give assistance. The iron-hearted Puritan, the relentless persecutor, the grasping and strong-willed man was dead! Dead, in his new house! There is a tradition, only worth alluding to as lending a tinge of superstitious awe to a scene perhaps gloomy enough without it, that a voice spoke loudly among the guests, the tones of which were like those of old Matthew Maule, the executed wizard, — "God hath given him blood to drink!"

Thus early had that one guest, — the only guest who is certain, at one time or another, to find his way into every human dwelling, — thus early had Death stepped across the threshold of the House of the Seven Gables!

Colonel Pyncheon's sudden and mysterious end made a vast deal of noise in its day. There were many rumors, some of which have vaguely drifted down to the present time, how that appearances indicated violence; that there were the marks of fingers on his throat, and the print of a bloody hand on his plaited ruff; and that his peaked beard was dishevelled, as if it had been fiercely clutched and pulled. It was averred, likewise, that the lattice window, near the Colonel's chair, was open; and that, only a few minutes before the fatal occurrence, the figure of a man had been seen clambering over the garden fence, in the rear of the house. But it were folly to lay any stress on stories of this kind, which are sure to spring up around such an event as that now related, and which, as in the present case, sometimes prolong themselves for ages afterwards, like the toadstools that indicate where the fallen and buried trunk of a tree has long since mouldered into the earth. For our own part, we allow them just as little credence as to that other fable of the skeleton hand which the lieutenant-governor was said to have seen at the Colonel's throat, but which vanished away, as he advanced farther into the room. Certain it is, however, that there was a great consultation and dispute of doctors over the dead body. One, — John Swinnerton by name, — who appears to have been a man of eminence, upheld it, if we have rightly understood his terms of art, to be a case of apoplexy. His professional brethren, each for himself, adopted various hypotheses, more or less plausible, but all dressed out in a perplexing mystery of phrase, which, if it do not show a bewilderment of mind in these erudite physicians, certainly causes it in the unlearned peruser of their opinions. The coroner's jury sat upon the corpse, and, like sensible men, returned an unassailable verdict of "Sudden Death!"

It is indeed difficult to imagine that there could have been a serious suspicion of murder, or the slightest grounds for implicating any particular individual as the perpetrator. The rank, wealth, and eminent character of the deceased must have insured the strictest scrutiny into every ambiguous circumstance. As none such is on record, it is safe to assume that none existed. Tradition,—which sometimes brings down truth that history has let slip, but is oftener the wild babble of the time, such as was formerly spoken at the fireside and now congeals in newspapers,—tradition is responsible for all contrary averments. In Colonel Pyncheon's funeral sermon, which was printed, and is still extant, the Rev. Mr. Higginson enumerates, among the many felicities of his distinguished parishioner's earthly career, the happy seasonableness of his death. His duties all performed,—the highest prosperity attained,—his race and future generations fixed on a stable basis, and with a stately roof to shelter them for centuries to come,—what other upward step remained for this good man to take, save the final step from earth to the golden gate of heaven! The pious clergyman surely would not have uttered words like these had he in the least suspected that the Colonel had been thrust into the other world with the clutch of violence upon his throat.

The family of Colonel Pyncheon, at the epoch of his death, seemed destined to as fortunate a permanence as can anywise consist with the inherent instability of human affairs. It might fairly be anticipated that the progress of time would rather increase and ripen their prosperity, than wear away and destroy it. For, not only had his son and heir come into immediate enjoyment of a rich estate, but there was a claim through an Indian deed, confirmed by a subsequent grant of the General Court, to a vast and as yet unexplored and unmeasured tract of Eastern lands. These possessions—for as such they might almost certainly be reckoned—comprised the greater part of what is now known as Waldo County, in the state of Maine, and were more extensive than many a dukedom, or even a reigning prince's territory, on European soil. When the pathless forest that still covered this wild principality should give place—as it inevitably must, though perhaps not till ages hence—to the golden fertility of human culture, it would be the source of incalculable wealth to the Pyncheon blood. Had the Colonel survived only a few weeks longer, it is probable that his great political influence, and powerful connections at home and abroad, would have consummated all that was necessary to render the claim available. But, in spite of good Mr. Higginson's congratulatory eloquence, this appeared to be the one thing which Colonel Pyncheon, provident and sagacious as he was, had allowed to go at loose ends. So far as the prospective territory was concerned, he unquestionably died too soon. His son lacked not merely the father's eminent position, but the talent and force of character to achieve it: he could, therefore, effect nothing by dint of political interest; and the bare justice or legality of the claim was not so apparent, after the Colonel's decease, as it had been pronounced in his lifetime. Some connecting link had slipped out of the evidence, and could not anywhere be found.

Efforts, it is true, were made by the Pyncheons, not only then, but at various periods for nearly a hundred years afterwards, to obtain what they stubbornly persisted in deeming their right. But, in course of time, the territory was partly regranted to more favored individuals, and partly cleared and occupied by actual settlers. These last, if they ever heard of the Pyncheon title, would have laughed at the idea of any man's asserting a right—on the strength of mouldy parchments, signed with the faded autographs of governors and legislators long dead and forgotten—to the lands which they or their fathers had wrested from the wild hand of nature by their own sturdy toil. This impalpable claim, therefore, resulted in nothing more solid than to cherish, from generation to generation, an absurd delusion of family importance, which all along characterized the Pyncheons. It caused the poorest member of the race to feel as if he inherited a kind of nobility, and might yet come into the possession of princely wealth to support it. In the better specimens of the breed, this peculiarity threw an ideal grace over the hard material of human life, without stealing away any truly valuable quality. In the baser sort, its effect was to increase the liability to sluggishness and dependence, and induce the victim of a shadowy hope to remit all self-effort, while awaiting the realization of his dreams. Years and years after their claim had passed out of the public memory, the Pyncheons were accustomed to consult the Colonel's ancient map, which had been projected while Waldo County was still an unbroken wilderness. Where the old land surveyor had put down woods, lakes, and rivers, they marked out the cleared spaces, and dotted the villages and towns, and calculated the progressively increasing value of the territory, as if there were yet a prospect of its ultimately forming a princedom for themselves.

In almost every generation, nevertheless, there happened to be some one descendant of the family gifted with a portion of the hard, keen sense, and practical energy, that had so remarkably distinguished the original founder. His character, indeed, might be traced all the way down, as distinctly as if the Colonel himself, a little diluted, had been gifted with a sort of intermittent immortality on earth. At two or three epochs, when the fortunes of the family were low, this representative of hereditary qualities had made his appearance, and caused the traditionary gossips of the town to whisper among themselves, "Here is the old Pyncheon come again! Now the Seven Gables will be new-shingled!" From father to son, they clung to the ancestral house with singular tenacity of home attachment. For various reasons, however, and from impressions often too vaguely founded to be put on paper, the writer cherishes the belief that many, if not most, of the successive proprietors of this estate were troubled with doubts as to their moral right to hold it. Of their legal tenure there could be no question; but old Matthew Maule, it is to be feared, trode downward from his own age to a far later one, planting a heavy footstep, all the way, on the conscience of a Pyncheon. If so, we are left to dispose of the awful query, whether each inheritor of the property—conscious of wrong, and failing to rectify it—did not commit anew the great guilt of his ancestor, and incur all its original responsibilities. And supposing such to be the case, would it not be a far truer mode of expression to say of the Pyncheon family, that they inherited a great misfortune, than the reverse?

We have already hinted that it is not our purpose to trace down the history of the Pyncheon family, in its unbroken connection with the House of the Seven Gables; nor to show, as in a magic picture, how the rustiness and infirmity of age gathered over the venerable house itself. As regards its interior life, a large, dim looking-glass used to hang in one of the rooms, and was fabled to contain within its depths all the shapes that had ever been reflected there,—the old Colonel himself, and his many descendants, some in the garb of antique babyhood, and others in the bloom of feminine beauty or manly prime, or saddened with the wrinkles of frosty age. Had we the secret of that mirror, we would gladly sit down before it, and transfer its revelations to our page. But there was a story, for which it is difficult to conceive any foundation, that the posterity of Matthew Maule had some connection with the mystery of the looking-glass, and that, by what appears to have been a sort of mesmeric process, they could make its inner region all alive with the departed Pyncheons; not as they had shown themselves to the world, nor in their better and happier hours, but as doing over again some deed of sin, or in the crisis of life's bitterest sorrow. The popular imagination, indeed, long kept itself busy with the affair of the old Puritan Pyncheon and the wizard Maule; the curse which the latter flung from his scaffold was remembered, with the very important addition, that it had become a part of the Pyncheon inheritance. If one of the family did but gurgle in his throat, a bystander would be likely enough to whisper, between jest and earnest, "He has Maule's blood to drink!" The sudden death of a Pyncheon, about a hundred years ago, with circumstances very similar to what have been related of the Colonel's exit, was held as giving additional probability to the received opinion on this topic. It was considered, moreover, an ugly and ominous circumstance, that Colonel Pyncheon's picture—in obedience, it was said, to a provision of his will—remained affixed to the wall of the room in which he died. Those stern, immitigable features seemed to symbolize an evil influence, and so darkly to mingle the shadow of their presence with the sunshine of the passing hour, that no good thoughts or purposes could ever spring up and blossom there. To the thoughtful mind there will be no tinge of superstition in what we figuratively express, by affirming that the ghost of a dead progenitor—perhaps as a portion of his own punishment—is often doomed to become the Evil Genius of his family.

The Pyncheons, in brief, lived along, for the better part of two centuries, with perhaps less of outward vicissitude than has attended most other New England families during the same period of time. Possessing very distinctive traits of their own, they nevertheless took the general characteristics of the little community in which they dwelt; a town noted for its frugal, discreet, well-ordered, and home-loving inhabitants, as well as for the somewhat confined scope of its sympathies; but in which, be it said, there are odder individuals, and, now and then, stranger occurrences, than one meets with almost anywhere else. During the Revolution, the Pyncheon of that epoch, adopting the royal side, became a refugee; but repented, and made his reappearance, just at the point of time to preserve the House of the Seven Gables from confiscation. For the last seventy years the most noted event in the Pyncheon annals had been likewise the heaviest calamity that ever befell the race; no less than the violent death—for so it was adjudged—of one member of the family by the criminal act of another. Certain circumstances attending this fatal occurrence had brought the deed irresistibly home to a nephew of the deceased Pyncheon. The young man was tried and convicted of the crime; but either the circumstantial nature of the evidence, and possibly some lurking doubts in the breast of the executive, or, lastly—an argument of greater weight in a republic than it could have been under a monarchy,—the high respectability and political influence of the criminal's connections, had availed to mitigate his doom from death to perpetual imprisonment. This sad affair had chanced about thirty years before the action of our story commences. Latterly, there were rumors (which few believed, and only one or two felt greatly interested in) that this long-buried man was likely, for some reason or other, to be summoned forth from his living tomb.

It is essential to say a few words respecting the victim of this now almost forgotten murder. He was an old bachelor, and possessed of great wealth, in addition to the house and real estate which constituted what remained of the ancient Pyncheon property. Being of an eccentric and melancholy turn of mind, and greatly given to rummaging old records and hearkening to old traditions, he had brought himself, it is averred, to the conclusion that Matthew Maule, the wizard, had been foully wronged out of his homestead, if not out of his life. Such being the case, and he, the old bachelor, in possession of the ill-gotten spoil,—with the black stain of blood sunken deep into it, and still to be scented by conscientious nostrils,—the question occurred, whether it were not imperative upon him, even at this late hour, to make restitution to Maule's posterity. To a man living so much in the past, and so little in the present, as the secluded and antiquarian old bachelor, a century and a half seemed not so vast a period as to obviate the propriety of substituting right for wrong. It was the belief of those who knew him best, that he would positively have taken the very singular step of giving up the House of the Seven Gables to the representative of Matthew Maule, but for the unspeakable tumult which a suspicion of the old gentleman's project awakened among his Pyncheon relatives. Their exertions had the effect of suspending his purpose; but it was feared that he would perform, after death, by the operation of his last will, what he had so hardly been prevented from doing in his proper lifetime. But there is no one thing which men so rarely do, whatever the provocation or inducement, as to bequeath patrimonial property away from their own blood. They may love other individuals far better than their relatives,—they may even cherish dislike, or positive hatred, to the latter; but yet, in view of death, the strong prejudice of propinquity revives, and impels the testator to send down his estate in the line marked out by custom so immemorial that it looks like nature. In all the Pyncheons, this feeling had the energy of disease. It was too powerful for the conscientious scruples of the old bachelor; at whose death, accordingly, the mansion-house, together with most of his other riches, passed into the possession of his next legal representative.

This was a nephew, the cousin of the miserable young man who had been convicted of the uncle's murder. The new heir, up to the period of his accession, was reckoned rather a dissipated youth, but had at once reformed, and made himself an exceedingly respectable member of society. In fact, he showed more of the Pyncheon quality, and had won higher eminence in the world, than any of his race since the time of the original Puritan. Applying himself in earlier manhood to the study of the law, and having a natural tendency towards office, he had attained, many years ago, to a judicial situation in some inferior court, which gave him for life the very desirable and imposing title of judge. Later, he had engaged in politics, and served a part of two terms in Congress, besides making a considerable figure in both branches of the State legislature. Judge Pyncheon was unquestionably an honor to his race. He had built himself a country-seat within a few miles of his native town, and there spent such portions of his time as could be spared from public service in the display of every grace and virtue—as a newspaper phrased it, on the eve of an election—befitting the Christian, the good citizen, the horticulturist, and the gentleman.

There were few of the Pyncheons left to sun themselves in the glow of the Judge's prosperity. In respect to natural increase, the breed had not thriven; it appeared rather to be dying out. The only members of the family known to be extant were, first, the Judge himself, and a single surviving son, who was now travelling in Europe; next, the thirty years' prisoner, already alluded to, and a sister of the latter, who occupied, in an extremely retired manner, the House of the Seven Gables, in which she had a life-estate by the will of the old bachelor. She was understood to be wretchedly poor, and seemed to make it her choice to remain so; inasmuch as her affluent cousin, the Judge, had repeatedly offered her all the comforts of life, either in the old mansion or his own modern residence. The last and youngest Pyncheon was a little country-girl of seventeen, the daughter of another of the Judge's cousins, who had married a young woman of no family or property, and died early and in poor circumstances. His widow had recently taken another husband.

As for Matthew Maule's posterity, it was supposed now to be extinct. For a very long period after the witchcraft delusion, however, the Maules had continued to inhabit the town where their progenitor had suffered so unjust a death. To all appearance, they were a quiet, honest, well-meaning race of people, cherishing no malice against individuals or the public for the wrong which had been done them; or if, at their own fireside, they transmitted from father to child any hostile recollection of the wizard's fate and their lost patrimony, it was never acted upon, nor openly expressed. Nor would it have been singular had they ceased to remember that the House of the Seven Gables was resting its heavy framework on a foundation that was rightfully their own. There is something so massive, stable, and almost irresistibly imposing in the exterior presentment of established rank and great possessions, that their very existence seems to give them a right to exist; at least, so excellent a counterfeit of right, that few poor and humble men have moral force enough to question it, even in their secret minds. Such is the case now, after so many ancient prejudices have been overthrown; and it was far more so in ante-Revolutionary days, when the aristocracy could venture to be proud, and the low were content to be abased. Thus the Maules, at all events, kept their resentments within their own breasts. They were generally poverty-stricken; always plebeian and obscure; working with unsuccessful diligence at handicrafts; laboring on the wharves, or following the sea, as sailors before the mast; living here and there about the town, in hired tenements, and coming finally to the almshouse as the natural home of their old age. At last, after creeping, as it were, for such a length of time along the utmost verge of the opaque puddle of obscurity, they had taken that downright plunge which, sooner or later, is the destiny of all families, whether princely or plebeian. For thirty years past, neither town-record, nor gravestone, nor the directory, nor the knowledge or memory of man, bore any trace of Matthew Maule's descendants. His blood might possibly exist elsewhere; here, where its lowly current could be traced so far back, it had ceased to keep an onward course.

So long as any of the race were to be found, they had been marked out from other men — not strikingly, nor as with a sharp line, but with an effect that was felt rather than spoken of — by an hereditary character of reserve. Their companions, or those who endeavored to become such, grew conscious of a circle round about the Maules, within the sanctity or the spell of which, in spite of an exterior of sufficient frankness and good-fellowship, it was impossible for any man to step. It was this indefinable peculiarity, perhaps, that, by insulating them from human aid, kept them always so unfortunate in life. It certainly operated to prolong in their case, and to confirm to them as their only inheritance, those feelings of repugnance and superstitious terror with which the people of the town, even after awakening from their frenzy, continued to regard the memory of the reputed witches. The mantle, or rather the ragged cloak, of old Matthew Maule had fallen upon his children. They were half believed to inherit mysterious attributes; the family eye was said to possess strange power. Among other good-for-nothing properties and privileges, one was especially assigned them, — that of exercising an influence over people's dreams. The Pyncheons, if all stories were true, haughtily as they bore themselves in the noonday streets of their native town, were no better than bond-servants to these plebeian Maules, on entering the topsy-turvy commonwealth of sleep. Modern psychology, it may be, will endeavor to reduce these alleged necromancies within a system, instead of rejecting them as altogether fabulous.

A descriptive paragraph or two, treating of the seven-gabled mansion in its more recent aspect, will bring this preliminary chapter to a close. The street in which it upreared its venerable peaks has long ceased to be a fashionable quarter of the town; so that, though the old edifice was surrounded by habitations of modern date, they were mostly small, built entirely of wood, and typical of the most plodding uniformity of common life. Doubtless, however, the whole story of human existence may be latent in each of them, but with no picturesqueness, externally, that can attract the imagination or sympathy to seek it there. But as for the old structure of our story, its white-oak frame, and its boards, shingles, and crumbling plaster, and even the huge, clustered chimney in the midst, seemed to constitute only the least and meanest part of its reality. So much of mankind's varied experience had passed there,—so much had been suffered, and something, too, enjoyed,—that the very timbers were oozy, as with the moisture of a heart. It was itself like a great human heart, with a life of its own, and full of rich and sombre reminiscences.

The deep projection of the second story gave the house such a meditative look, that you could not pass it without the idea that it had secrets to keep, and an eventful history to moralize upon. In front, just on the edge of the unpaved sidewalk, grew the Pyncheon Elm, which, in reference to such trees as one usually meets with, might well be termed gigantic. It had been planted by a great-grandson of the first Pyncheon, and, though now four-score years of age, or perhaps nearer a hundred, was still in its strong and broad maturity, throwing its shadow from side to side of the street, overtopping the seven gables, and sweeping the whole black roof with its pendant foliage. It gave beauty to the old edifice, and seemed to make it a part of nature. The street having been widened about forty years ago, the front gable was now precisely on a line with it. On either side extended a ruinous wooden fence of open lattice-work, through which could be seen a grassy yard, and, especially in the angles of the building, an enormous fertility of burdocks, with leaves, it is hardly an exaggeration to say, two or three feet long. Behind the house there appeared to be a garden, which undoubtedly had once been extensive, but was now infringed upon by other enclosures, or shut in by habitations and outbuildings that stood on another street. It would be an omission, trifling, indeed, but unpardonable, were we to forget the green moss that had long since gathered over the projections of the windows, and on the slopes of the roof nor must we fail to direct the reader's eye to a crop, not of weeds, but flower-shrubs, which were growing aloft in the air, not a great way from the chimney, in the nook between two of the gables. They were called Alice's Posies. The tradition was, that a certain Alice Pyncheon had flung up the seeds, in sport, and that the dust of the street and the decay of the roof gradually formed a kind of soil for them, out of which they grew, when Alice had long been in her grave. However the flowers might have come there, it was both sad and sweet to observe how Nature adopted to herself this desolate, decaying, gusty, rusty old house of the Pyncheon family; and how the ever-returning Summer did her best to gladden it with tender beauty, and grew melancholy in the effort.

There is one other feature, very essential to be noticed, but which, we greatly fear, may damage any picturesque and romantic impression which we have been willing to throw over our sketch of this respectable edifice. In the front gable, under the impending brow of the second story, and contiguous to the street, was a shop-door, divided horizontally in the midst, and with a window for its upper segment, such as is often seen in dwellings of a somewhat ancient date. This same shop-door had been a subject of no slight mortification to the present occupant of the august Pyncheon House, as well as to some of her predecessors. The matter is disagreeably delicate to handle; but, since the reader must needs be let into the secret, he will please to understand, that, about a century ago, the head of the Pyncheons found himself involved in serious financial difficulties. The fellow (gentleman, as he styled himself) can hardly have been other than a spurious interloper; for, instead of seeking office from the king or the royal governor, or urging his hereditary claim to Eastern lands, he bethought himself of no better avenue to wealth than by cutting a shop-door through the side of his ancestral residence. It was the custom of the time, indeed, for merchants to store their goods and transact business in their own dwellings. But there was something pitifully small in this old Pyncheon's mode of setting about his commercial operations; it was whispered, that, with his own hands, all beruffled as they were, he used to give change for a shilling, and would turn a half-penny twice over, to make sure that it was a good one. Beyond all question, he had the blood of a petty huckster in his veins, through whatever channel it may have found its way there.

Immediately on his death, the shop-door had been locked, bolted, and barred, and, down to the period of our story, had probably never once been opened. The old counter, shelves, and other fixtures of the little shop remained just as he had left them. It used to be affirmed, that the dead shop-keeper, in a white wig, a faded velvet coat, an apron at his waist, and his ruffles carefully turned back from his wrists, might be seen through the chinks of the shutters, any night of the year, ransacking his till, or poring over the dingy pages of his day-book. From the look of unutterable woe upon his face, it appeared to be his doom to spend eternity in a vain effort to make his accounts balance.

And now—in a very humble way, as will be seen—we proceed to open our narrative.

II.

The Little Shop-Window

It still lacked half an hour of sunrise, when Miss Hepzibah Pyncheon—we will not say awoke, it being doubtful whether the poor lady had so much as closed her eyes during the brief night of midsummer—but, at all events, arose from her solitary pillow, and began what it would be mockery to term the adornment of her person. Far from us be the indecorum of assisting, even in imagination, at a maiden lady's toilet! Our story must therefore await Miss Hepzibah at the threshold of her chamber; only presuming, meanwhile, to note some of the heavy sighs that labored from her bosom, with little restraint as to their lugubrious depth and volume of sound, inasmuch as they could be audible to nobody save a disembodied listener like ourself. The Old Maid was alone in the old house. Alone, except for a certain respectable and orderly young man, an artist in the daguerreotype line, who, for about three months back, had been a lodger in a remote gable,—quite a house by itself, indeed,—with locks, bolts, and oaken bars on all the intervening doors. Inaudible, consequently, were poor Miss Hepzibah's gusty sighs. Inaudible the creaking joints of her stiffened knees, as she knelt down by the bedside. And inaudible, too, by mortal ear, but heard with all-comprehending love and pity in the farthest heaven, that almost agony of prayer—now whispered, now a groan, now a struggling silence—wherewith she besought the Divine assistance through the day! Evidently, this is to be a day of more than ordinary trial to Miss Hepzibah, who, for above a quarter of a century gone by, has dwelt in strict seclusion, taking no part in the business of life, and just as little in its intercourse and pleasures. Not with such fervor prays the torpid recluse, looking forward to the cold, sunless, stagnant calm of a day that is to be like innumerable yesterdays.

The maiden lady's devotions are concluded. Will she now issue forth over the threshold of our story? Not yet, by many moments. First, every drawer in the tall, old-fashioned bureau is to be opened, with difficulty, and with a succession of spasmodic jerks then, all must close again, with the same fidgety reluctance. There is a rustling of stiff silks; a tread of backward and forward footsteps to and fro across the chamber. We suspect Miss Hepzibah, moreover, of taking a step upward into a chair, in order to give heedful regard to her appearance on all sides, and at full length, in the oval, dingy-framed toilet-glass, that hangs above her table. Truly! well, indeed! who would have thought it! Is all this precious time to be lavished on the matutinal repair and beautifying of an elderly person, who never goes abroad, whom nobody ever visits, and from whom, when she shall have done her utmost, it were the best charity to turn one's eyes another way?

Now she is almost ready. Let us pardon her one other pause; for it is given to the sole sentiment, or, we might better say,—heightened and rendered intense, as it has been, by sorrow and seclusion,—to the strong passion of her life. We heard the turning of a key in a small lock; she has opened a secret drawer of an escritoire, and is probably looking at a certain miniature, done in Malbone's most perfect style, and representing a face worthy of no less delicate a pencil. It was once our good fortune to see this picture. It is a likeness of a young man, in a silken dressing-gown of an old fashion, the soft richness of which is well adapted to the countenance of reverie, with its full, tender lips, and beautiful eyes, that seem to indicate not so much capacity of thought, as gentle and voluptuous emotion. Of the possessor of such features we shall have a right to ask nothing, except that he would take the rude world easily, and make himself happy in it. Can it have been an early lover of Miss Hepzibah? No; she never had a lover—poor thing, how could she?—nor ever knew, by her own experience, what love technically means. And yet, her undying faith and trust, her fresh remembrance, and continual devotedness towards the original of that miniature, have been the only substance for her heart to feed upon.

She seems to have put aside the miniature, and is standing again before the toilet-glass. There are tears to be wiped off. A few more footsteps to and fro; and here, at last,—with another pitiful sigh, like a gust of chill, damp wind out of a long-closed vault, the door of which has accidentally been set, ajar—here comes Miss Hepzibah Pyncheon! Forth she steps into the dusky, time-darkened passage; a tall figure, clad in black silk, with a long and shrunken waist, feeling her way towards the stairs like a near-sighted person, as in truth she is.

The sun, meanwhile, if not already above the horizon, was ascending nearer and nearer to its verge. A few clouds, floating high upward, caught some of the earliest light, and threw down its golden gleam on the windows of all the houses in the street, not forgetting the House of the Seven Gables, which—many such sunrises as it had witnessed—looked cheerfully at the present one. The reflected radiance served to show, pretty distinctly, the aspect and arrangement of the room which Hepzibah entered, after descending the stairs. It was a low-studded room, with a beam across the ceiling, panelled with dark wood, and having a large chimney-piece, set round with pictured tiles, but now closed by an iron fire-board, through which ran the funnel of a modern stove. There was a carpet on the floor, originally of rich texture, but so worn and faded in these latter years that its once brilliant figure had quite vanished into one indistinguishable hue. In the way of furniture, there were two tables: one, constructed with perplexing intricacy and exhibiting as many feet as a centipede; the other, most delicately wrought, with four long and slender legs, so apparently frail that it was almost incredible what a length of time the ancient tea-table had stood upon them. Half a dozen chairs stood about the room, straight and stiff, and so ingeniously contrived for the discomfort of the human person that they were irksome even to sight, and conveyed the ugliest possible idea of the state of society to which they could have been adapted. One exception there was, however, in a very antique elbow-chair, with a high back, carved elaborately in oak, and a roomy depth within its arms, that made up, by its spacious comprehensiveness, for the lack of any of those artistic curves which abound in a modern chair.

As for ornamental articles of furniture, we recollect but two, if such they may be called. One was a map of the Pyncheon territory at the eastward, not engraved, but the handiwork of some skilful old draughtsman, and grotesquely illuminated with pictures of Indians and wild beasts, among which was seen a lion; the natural history of the region being as little known as its geography, which was put down most fantastically awry. The other adornment was the portrait of old Colonel Pyncheon, at two thirds length, representing the stern features of a Puritanic-looking personage, in a skull-cap, with a laced band and a grizzly beard; holding a Bible with one hand, and in the other uplifting an iron sword-hilt. The latter object, being more successfully depicted by the artist, stood out in far greater prominence than the sacred volume. Face to face with this picture, on entering the apartment, Miss Hepzibah Pyncheon came to a pause; regarding it with a singular scowl, a strange contortion of the brow, which, by people who did not know her, would probably have been interpreted as an expression of bitter anger and ill-will. But it was no such thing. She, in fact, felt a reverence for the pictured visage, of which only a far-descended and time-stricken virgin could be susceptible; and this forbidding scowl was the innocent result of her near-sightedness, and an effort so to concentrate her powers of vision as to substitute a firm outline of the object instead of a vague one.

We must linger a moment on this unfortunate expression of poor Hepzibah's brow. Her scowl,—as the world, or such part of it as sometimes caught a transitory glimpse of her at the window, wickedly persisted in calling it,—her scowl had done Miss Hepzibah a very ill office, in establishing her character as an ill-tempered old maid; nor does it appear improbable that, by often gazing at herself in a dim looking-glass, and perpetually encountering her own frown with its ghostly sphere, she had been led to interpret the expression almost as unjustly as the world did. "How miserably cross I look!" she must often have whispered to herself; and ultimately have fancied herself so, by a sense of inevitable doom. But her heart never frowned. It was naturally tender, sensitive, and full of little tremors and palpitations; all of which weaknesses it retained, while her visage was growing so perversely stern, and even fierce. Nor had Hepzibah ever any hardihood, except what came from the very warmest nook in her affections.

All this time, however, we are loitering faintheartedly on the threshold of our story. In very truth, we have an invincible reluctance to disclose what Miss Hepzibah Pyncheon was about to do.

It has already been observed, that, in the basement story of the gable fronting on the street, an unworthy ancestor, nearly a century ago, had fitted up a shop. Ever since the old gentleman retired from trade, and fell asleep under his coffin-lid, not only the shop-door, but the inner arrangements, had been suffered to remain unchanged; while the dust of ages gathered inch-deep over the shelves and counter, and partly filled an old pair of scales, as if it were of value enough to be weighed. It treasured itself up, too, in the half-open till, where there still lingered a base sixpence, worth neither more nor less than the hereditary pride which had here been put to shame. Such had been the state and condition of the little shop in old Hepzibah's childhood, when she and her brother used to play at hide-and-seek in its forsaken precincts. So it had remained, until within a few days past.

But now, though the shop-window was still closely curtained from the public gaze, a remarkable change had taken place in its interior. The rich and heavy festoons of cobweb, which it had cost a long ancestral succession of spiders their life's labor to spin and weave, had been carefully brushed away from the ceiling. The counter, shelves, and floor had all been scoured, and the latter was overstrewn with fresh blue sand. The brown scales, too, had evidently undergone rigid discipline, in an unavailing effort to rub off the rust, which, alas! had eaten through and through their substance. Neither was the little old shop any longer empty of merchantable goods. A curious eye, privileged to take an account of stock and investigate behind the counter, would have discovered a barrel, yea, two or three barrels and half ditto,—one containing flour, another apples, and a third, perhaps, Indian meal. There was likewise a square box of pine-wood, full of soap in bars; also, another of the same size, in which were tallow candles, ten to the pound. A small stock of brown sugar, some white beans and split peas, and a few other commodities of low price, and such as are constantly in demand, made up the bulkier portion of the merchandise. It might have been taken for a ghostly or phantasmagoric reflection of the old shop-keeper Pyncheon's shabbily provided shelves, save that some of the articles were of a description and outward form which could hardly have been known in his day. For instance, there was a glass pickle-jar, filled with fragments of Gibraltar rock; not, indeed, splinters of the veritable stone foundation of the famous fortress, but bits of delectable candy, neatly done up in white paper. Jim Crow, moreover, was seen executing his world-renowned dance, in gingerbread. A party of leaden dragoons were galloping along one of the shelves, in equipments and uniform of modern cut; and there were some sugar figures, with no strong resemblance to the humanity of any epoch, but less unsatisfactorily representing our own fashions than those of a hundred years ago. Another phenomenon, still more strikingly modern, was a package of lucifer matches, which, in old times, would have been thought actually to borrow their instantaneous flame from the nether fires of Tophet.

In short, to bring the matter at once to a point, it was incontrovertibly evident that somebody had taken the shop and fixtures of the long-retired and forgotten Mr. Pyncheon, and was about to renew the enterprise of that departed worthy, with a different set of customers. Who could this bold adventurer be? And, of all places in the world, why had he chosen the House of the Seven Gables as the scene of his commercial speculations?

We return to the elderly maiden. She at length withdrew her eyes from the dark countenance of the Colonel's portrait, heaved a sigh,—indeed, her breast was a very cave of Aolus that morning,—and stept across the room on tiptoe, as is the customary gait of elderly women. Passing through an intervening passage, she opened a door that communicated with the shop, just now so elaborately described. Owing to the projection of the upper story—and still more to the thick shadow of the Pyncheon Elm, which stood almost directly in front of the gable—the twilight, here, was still as much akin to night as morning. Another heavy sigh from Miss Hepzibah! After a moment's pause on the threshold, peering towards the window with her near-sighted scowl, as if frowning down some bitter enemy, she suddenly projected herself into the shop. The haste, and, as it were, the galvanic impulse of the movement, were really quite startling.

Nervously—in a sort of frenzy, we might almost say—she began to busy herself in arranging some children's playthings, and other little wares, on the shelves and at the shop-window. In the aspect of this dark-arrayed, pale-faced, ladylike old figure there was a deeply tragic character that contrasted irreconcilably with the ludicrous pettiness of her employment. It seemed a queer anomaly, that so gaunt and dismal a personage should take a toy in hand; a miracle, that the toy did not vanish in her grasp; a miserably absurd idea, that she should go on perplexing her stiff and sombre intellect with the question how to tempt little boys into her premises! Yet such is undoubtedly her object. Now she places a gingerbread elephant against the window, but with so tremulous a touch that it tumbles upon the floor, with the dismemberment of three legs and its trunk; it has ceased to be an elephant, and has become a few bits of musty gingerbread. There, again, she has upset a tumbler of marbles, all of which roll different ways, and each individual marble, devil-directed, into the most difficult obscurity that it can find. Heaven help our poor old Hepzibah, and forgive us for taking a ludicrous view of her position! As her rigid and rusty frame goes down upon its hands and knees, in quest of the absconding marbles, we positively feel so much the more inclined to shed tears of sympathy, from the very fact that we must needs turn aside and laugh at her. For here, — and if we fail to impress it suitably upon the reader, it is our own fault, not that of the theme, here is one of the truest points of melancholy interest that occur in ordinary life. It was the final throe of what called itself old gentility. A lady — who had fed herself from childhood with the shadowy food of aristocratic reminiscences, and whose religion it was that a lady's hand soils itself irremediably by doing aught for bread, — this born lady, after sixty years of narrowing means, is fain to step down from her pedestal of imaginary rank. Poverty, treading closely at her heels for a lifetime, has come up with her at last. She must earn her own food, or starve! And we have stolen upon Miss Hepzibah Pyncheon, too irreverently, at the instant of time when the patrician lady is to be transformed into the plebeian woman.

In this republican country, amid the fluctuating waves of our social life, somebody is always at the drowning-point. The tragedy is enacted with as continual a repetition as that of a popular drama on a holiday, and, nevertheless, is felt as deeply, perhaps, as when an hereditary noble sinks below his order. More deeply; since, with us, rank is the grosser substance of wealth and a splendid establishment, and has no spiritual existence after the death of these, but dies hopelessly along with them. And, therefore, since we have been unfortunate enough to introduce our heroine at so inauspicious a juncture, we would entreat for a mood of due solemnity in the spectators of her fate. Let us behold, in poor Hepzibah, the immemorial, lady — two hundred years old, on this side of the water, and thrice as many on the other, — with her antique portraits, pedigrees, coats of arms, records and traditions, and her claim, as joint heiress, to that princely territory at the eastward, no longer a wilderness, but a populous fertility, — born, too, in Pyncheon Street, under the Pyncheon Elm, and in the Pyncheon House, where she has spent all her days, — reduced. Now, in that very house, to be the hucksteress of a cent-shop.

This business of setting up a petty shop is almost the only resource of women, in circumstances at all similar to those of our unfortunate recluse. With her near-sightedness, and those tremulous fingers of hers, at once inflexible and delicate, she could not be a seamstress; although her sampler, of fifty years gone by, exhibited some of the most recondite specimens of ornamental needlework. A school for little children had been often in her thoughts; and, at one time, she had begun a review of her early studies in the New England Primer, with a view to prepare herself for the office of instructress. But the love of children had never been quickened in Hepzibah's heart, and was now torpid, if not extinct; she watched the little people of the neighborhood from her chamber-window, and doubted whether she could tolerate a more intimate acquaintance with them. Besides, in our day, the very ABC has become a science greatly too abstruse to be any longer taught by pointing a pin from letter to letter. A modern child could teach old Hepzibah more than old Hepzibah could teach the child. So — with many a cold, deep heart-quake at the idea of at last coming into sordid contact with the world, from which she had so long kept aloof, while every added day of seclusion had rolled another stone against the cavern door of her hermitage — the poor thing bethought herself of the ancient shop-window, the rusty scales, and dusty till. She might have held back a little longer; but another circumstance, not yet hinted at, had somewhat hastened her decision. Her humble preparations, therefore, were duly made, and the enterprise was now to be commenced. Nor was she entitled to complain of any remarkable singularity in her fate; for, in the town of her nativity, we might point to several little shops of a similar description, some of them in houses as ancient as that of the Seven Gables; and one or two, it may be, where a decayed gentlewoman stands behind the counter, as grim an image of family pride as Miss Hepzibah Pyncheon herself.

It was overpoweringly ridiculous, — we must honestly confess it, — the deportment of the maiden lady while setting her shop in order for the public eye. She stole on tiptoe to the window, as cautiously as if she conceived some bloody-minded villain to be watching behind the elm-tree, with intent to take her life. Stretching out her long, lank arm, she put a paper of pearl-buttons, a jew's-harp, or whatever the small article might be, in its destined place, and straightway vanished back into the dusk, as if the world need never hope for another glimpse of her. It might have been fancied, indeed, that she expected to minister to the wants of the community unseen, like a disembodied divinity or enchantress, holding forth her bargains to the reverential and awe-stricken purchaser in an invisible hand. But Hepzibah had no such flattering dream. She was well aware that she must ultimately come forward, and stand revealed in her proper individuality; but, like other sensitive persons, she could not bear to be observed in the gradual process, and chose rather to flash forth on the world's astonished gaze at once.

The inevitable moment was not much longer to be delayed. The sunshine might now be seen stealing down the front of the opposite house, from the windows of which came a reflected gleam, struggling through the boughs of the elm-tree, and enlightening the interior of the shop more distinctly than heretofore. The town appeared to be waking up. A baker's cart had already rattled through the street, chasing away the latest vestige of night's sanctity with the jingle-jangle of its dissonant bells. A milkman was distributing the contents of his cans from door to door; and the harsh peal of a fisherman's conch shell was heard far off, around the corner. None of these tokens escaped Hepzibah's notice. The moment had arrived. To delay longer would be only to lengthen out her misery. Nothing remained, except to take down the bar from the shop-door, leaving the entrance free—more than free—welcome, as if all were household friends—to every passer-by, whose eyes might be attracted by the commodities at the window. This last act Hepzibah now performed, letting the bar fall with what smote upon her excited nerves as a most astounding clatter. Then—as if the only barrier betwixt herself and the world had been thrown down, and a flood of evil consequences would come tumbling through the gap—she fled into the inner parlor, threw herself into the ancestral elbow-chair, and wept.

Our miserable old Hepzibah! It is a heavy annoyance to a writer, who endeavors to represent nature, its various attitudes and circumstances, in a reasonably correct outline and true coloring, that so much of the mean and ludicrous should be hopelessly mixed up with the purest pathos which life anywhere supplies to him. What tragic dignity, for example, can be wrought into a scene like this! How can we elevate our history of retribution for the sin of long ago, when, as one of our most prominent figures, we are compelled to introduce—not a young and lovely woman, nor even the stately remains of beauty, storm-shattered by affliction—but a gaunt, sallow, rusty-jointed maiden, in a long-waisted silk gown, and with the strange horror of a turban on her head! Her visage is not even ugly. It is redeemed from insignificance only by the contraction of her eyebrows into a near-sighted scowl. And, finally, her great life-trial seems to be, that, after sixty years of idleness, she finds it convenient to earn comfortable bread by setting up a shop in a small way. Nevertheless, if we look through all the heroic fortunes of mankind, we shall find this same entanglement of something mean and trivial with whatever is noblest in joy or sorrow. Life is made up of marble and mud. And, without all the deeper trust in a comprehensive sympathy above us, we might hence be led to suspect the insult of a sneer, as well as an immitigable frown, on the iron countenance of fate. What is called poetic insight is the gift of discerning, in this sphere of strangely mingled elements, the beauty and the majesty which are compelled to assume a garb so sordid.

III.

The First Customer

Miss Hepzibah Pyncheon sat in the oaken elbow-chair, with her hands over her face, giving way to that heavy down-sinking of the heart which most persons have experienced, when the image of hope itself seems ponderously moulded of lead, on the eve of an enterprise at once doubtful and momentous. She was suddenly startled by the tinkling alarum—high, sharp, and irregular—of a little bell. The maiden lady arose upon her feet, as pale as a ghost at cock-crow; for she was an enslaved spirit, and this the talisman to which she owed obedience. This little bell,—to speak in plainer terms,—being fastened over the shop-door, was so contrived as to vibrate by means of a steel spring, and thus convey notice to the inner regions of the house when any customer should cross the threshold. Its ugly and spiteful little din (heard now for the first time, perhaps, since Hepzibah's periwigged predecessor had retired from trade) at once set every nerve of her body in responsive and tumultuous vibration. The crisis was upon her! Her first customer was at the door!

Without giving herself time for a second thought, she rushed into the shop, pale, wild, desperate in gesture and expression, scowling portentously, and looking far better qualified to do fierce battle with a housebreaker than to stand smiling behind the counter, bartering small wares for a copper recompense. Any ordinary customer, indeed, would have turned his back and fled. And yet there was nothing fierce in Hepzibah's poor old heart; nor had she, at the moment, a single bitter thought against the world at large, or one individual man or woman. She wished them all well, but wished, too, that she herself were done with them, and in her quiet grave.

The applicant, by this time, stood within the doorway. Coming freshly, as he did, out of the morning light, he appeared to have brought some of its cheery influences into the shop along with him. It was a slender young man, not more than one or two and twenty years old, with rather a grave and thoughtful expression for his years, but likewise a springy alacrity and vigor. These qualities were not only perceptible, physically, in his make and motions, but made themselves felt almost immediately in his character. A brown beard, not too silken in its texture, fringed his chin, but as yet without completely hiding it; he wore a short mustache, too, and his dark, high-featured countenance looked all the better for these natural ornaments. As for his dress, it was of the simplest kind; a summer sack of cheap and ordinary material, thin checkered pantaloons, and a straw hat, by no means of the finest braid. Oak Hall might have supplied his entire equipment. He was chiefly marked as a gentleman — if such, indeed, he made any claim to be — by the rather remarkable whiteness and nicety of his clean linen.

He met the scowl of old Hepzibah without apparent alarm, as having heretofore encountered it and found it harmless.

"So, my dear Miss Pyncheon," said the daguerreotypist, — for it was that sole other occupant of the seven-gabled mansion, — "I am glad to see that you have not shrunk from your good purpose. I merely look in to offer my best wishes, and to ask if I can assist you any further in your preparations."

People in difficulty and distress, or in any manner at odds with the world, can endure a vast amount of harsh treatment, and perhaps be only the stronger for it; whereas they give way at once before the simplest expression of what they perceive to be genuine sympathy. So it proved with poor Hepzibah; for, when she saw the young man's smile, — looking so much the brighter on a thoughtful face, — and heard his kindly tone, she broke first into a hysteric giggle and then began to sob.

"Ah, Mr. Holgrave," cried she, as soon as she could speak, "I never can go through with it! Never, never, never! I wish I were dead, and in the old family tomb, with all my forefathers! With my father, and my mother, and my sister! Yes, and with my brother, who had far better find me there than here! The world is too chill and hard, — and I am too old, and too feeble, and too hopeless!"

"Oh, believe me, Miss Hepzibah," said the young man quietly, "these feelings will not trouble you any longer, after you are once fairly in the midst of your enterprise. They are unavoidable at this moment, standing, as you do, on the outer verge of your long seclusion, and peopling the world with ugly shapes, which you will soon find to be as unreal as the giants and ogres of a child's story-book. I find nothing so singular in life, as that everything appears to lose its substance the instant one actually grapples with it. So it will be with what you think so terrible."

"But I am a woman!" said Hepzibah piteously. "I was going to say, a lady, — but I consider that as past."

"Well; no matter if it be past!" answered the artist, a strange gleam of half-hidden sarcasm flashing through the kindliness of his manner. "Let it go! You are the better without it. I speak frankly, my dear Miss Pyncheon! — for are we not friends? I look upon this as one of the fortunate days of your life. It ends an epoch and begins one. Hitherto, the life-blood has been gradually chilling in your veins as you sat aloof, within your circle of gentility, while the rest of the world was fighting out its battle with one kind of necessity or another. Henceforth, you will at least have the sense of healthy and natural effort for a purpose, and of lending your strength be it great or small—to the united struggle of mankind. This is success,—all the success that anybody meets with!"

"It is natural enough, Mr. Holgrave, that you should have ideas like these," rejoined Hepzibah, drawing up her gaunt figure with slightly offended dignity. "You are a man, a young man, and brought up, I suppose, as almost everybody is nowadays, with a view to seeking your fortune. But I was born a lady, and have always lived one; no matter in what narrowness of means, always a lady."

"But I was not born a gentleman; neither have I lived like one," said Holgrave, slightly smiling; "so, my dear madam, you will hardly expect me to sympathize with sensibilities of this kind; though, unless I deceive myself, I have some imperfect comprehension of them. These names of gentleman and lady had a meaning, in the past history of the world, and conferred privileges, desirable or otherwise, on those entitled to bear them. In the present—and still more in the future condition of society-they imply, not privilege, but restriction!"

"These are new notions," said the old gentlewoman, shaking her head. "I shall never understand them; neither do I wish it."

"We will cease to speak of them, then," replied the artist, with a friendlier smile than his last one, "and I will leave you to feel whether it is not better to be a true woman than a lady. Do you really think, Miss Hepzibah, that any lady of your family has ever done a more heroic thing, since this house was built, than you are performing in it to-day? Never; and if the Pyncheons had always acted so nobly, I doubt whether an old wizard Maule's anathema, of which you told me once, would have had much weight with Providence against them."

"Ah!—no, no!" said Hepzibah, not displeased at this allusion to the sombre dignity of an inherited curse. "If old Maule's ghost, or a descendant of his, could see me behind the counter to-day, he would call it the fulfillment of his worst wishes. But I thank you for your kindness, Mr. Holgrave, and will do my utmost to be a good shop-keeper."

"Pray do" said Holgrave, "and let me have the pleasure of being your first customer. I am about taking a walk to the seashore, before going to my rooms, where I misuse Heaven's blessed sunshine by tracing out human features through its agency. A few of those biscuits, dipt in sea-water, will be just what I need for breakfast. What is the price of half a dozen?"

"Let me be a lady a moment longer," replied Hepzibah, with a manner of antique stateliness to which a melancholy smile lent a kind of grace. She put the biscuits into his hand, but rejected the compensation. "A Pyncheon must not, at all events under her forefathers' roof, receive money for a morsel of bread from her only friend!"

Holgrave took his departure, leaving her, for the moment, with spirits not quite so much depressed. Soon, however, they had subsided nearly to their former dead level. With a beating heart, she listened to the footsteps of early passengers, which now began to be frequent along the street. Once or twice they seemed to linger; these strangers, or neighbors, as the case might be, were looking at the display of toys and petty commodities in Hepzibah's shop-window. She was doubly tortured; in part, with a sense of overwhelming shame that strange and unloving eyes should have the privilege of gazing, and partly because the idea occurred to her, with ridiculous importunity, that the window was not arranged so skilfully, nor nearly to so much advantage, as it might have been. It seemed as if the whole fortune or failure of her shop might depend on the display of a different set of articles, or substituting a fairer apple for one which appeared to be specked. So she made the change, and straightway fancied that everything was spoiled by it; not recognizing that it was the nervousness of the juncture, and her own native squeamishness as an old maid, that wrought all the seeming mischief.

Anon, there was an encounter, just at the door-step, betwixt two laboring men, as their rough voices denoted them to be. After some slight talk about their own affairs, one of them chanced to notice the shop-window, and directed the other's attention to it.

"See here!" cried he; "what do you think of this? Trade seems to be looking up in Pyncheon Street!"

"Well, well, this is a sight, to be sure!" exclaimed the other. "In the old Pyncheon House, and underneath the Pyncheon Elm! Who would have thought it? Old Maid Pyncheon is setting up a cent-shop!"

"Will she make it go, think you, Dixey?" said his friend. "I don't call it a very good stand. There's another shop just round the corner."

"Make it go!" cried Dixey, with a most contemptuous expression, as if the very idea were impossible to be conceived. "Not a bit of it! Why, her face—I've seen it, for I dug her garden for her one year—her face is enough to frighten the Old Nick himself, if he had ever so great a mind to trade with her. People can't stand it, I tell you! She scowls dreadfully, reason or none,

The House of the Seven Gables

out of pure ugliness of temper."

"Well, that's not so much matter," remarked the other man. "These sour-tempered folks are mostly handy at business, and know pretty well what they are about. But, as you say, I don't think she'll do much. This business of keeping cent-shops is overdone, like all other kinds of trade, handicraft, and bodily labor. I know it, to my cost! My wife kept a cent-shop three months, and lost five dollars on her outlay."

"Poor business!" responded Dixey, in a tone as if he were shaking his head,—"poor business."

For some reason or other, not very easy to analyze, there had hardly been so bitter a pang in all her previous misery about the matter as what thrilled Hepzibah's heart on overhearing the above conversation. The testimony in regard to her scowl was frightfully important; it seemed to hold up her image wholly relieved from the false light of her self-partialities, and so hideous that she dared not look at it. She was absurdly hurt, moreover, by the slight and idle effect that her setting up shop—an event of such breathless interest to herself—appeared to have upon the public, of which these two men were the nearest representatives. A glance; a passing word or two; a coarse laugh; and she was doubtless forgotten before they turned the corner. They cared nothing for her dignity, and just as little for her degradation. Then, also, the augury of ill-success, uttered from the sure wisdom of experience, fell upon her half-dead hope like a clod into a grave. The man's wife had already tried the same experiment, and failed! How could the born lady—the recluse of half a lifetime, utterly unpractised in the world, at sixty years of age,—how could she ever dream of succeeding, when the hard, vulgar, keen, busy, hackneyed New England woman had lost five dollars on her little outlay! Success presented itself as an impossibility, and the hope of it as a wild hallucination.

Some malevolent spirit, doing his utmost to drive Hepzibah mad, unrolled before her imagination a kind of panorama, representing the great thoroughfare of a city all astir with customers. So many and so magnificent shops as there were! Groceries, toy-shops, drygoods stores, with their immense panes of plate-glass, their gorgeous fixtures, their vast and complete assortments of merchandise, in which fortunes had been invested; and those noble mirrors at the farther end of each establishment, doubling all this wealth by a brightly burnished vista of unrealities! On one side of the street this splendid bazaar, with a multitude of perfumed and glossy salesmen, smirking, smiling, bowing, and measuring out the goods. On the other, the dusky old House of the Seven Gables, with the antiquated shop-window under its projecting story, and Hepzibah herself, in a gown of rusty black silk, behind the counter, scowling at the world as it went by! This mighty contrast thrust itself forward as a fair expression of the odds against which she was to begin her struggle for a subsistence. Success? Preposterous! She would never think of it again! The house might just as well be buried in an eternal fog while all other houses had the sunshine on them; for not a foot would ever cross the threshold, nor a hand so much as try the door!

But, at this instant, the shop-bell, right over her head, tinkled as if it were bewitched. The old gentlewoman's heart seemed to be attached to the same steel spring, for it went through a series of sharp jerks, in unison with the sound. The door was thrust open, although no human form was perceptible on the other side of the half-window. Hepzibah, nevertheless, stood at a gaze, with her hands clasped, looking very much as if she had summoned up an evil spirit, and were afraid, yet resolved, to hazard the encounter.

"Heaven help me!" she groaned mentally. "Now is my hour of need!"

The door, which moved with difficulty on its creaking and rusty hinges, being forced quite open, a square and sturdy little urchin became apparent, with cheeks as red as an apple. He was clad rather shabbily (but, as it seemed, more owing to his mother's carelessness than his father's poverty), in a blue apron, very wide and short trousers, shoes somewhat out at the toes, and a chip hat, with the frizzles of his curly hair sticking through its crevices. A book and a small slate, under his arm, indicated that he was on his way to school. He stared at Hepzibah a moment, as an elder customer than himself would have been likely enough to do, not knowing what to make of the tragic attitude and queer scowl wherewith she regarded him.

"Well, child," said she, taking heart at sight of a personage so little formidable, — "well, my child, what did you wish for?"

"That Jim Crow there in the window," answered the urchin, holding out a cent, and pointing to the gingerbread figure that had attracted his notice, as he loitered along to school; "the one that has not a broken foot."

So Hepzibah put forth her lank arm, and, taking the effigy from the shop-window, delivered it to her first customer.

"No matter for the money," said she, giving him a little push towards the door; for her old gentility was contumaciously squeamish at sight of the copper coin, and, besides, it seemed such pitiful meanness to take the child's pocket-money in exchange for a bit of stale gingerbread. "No matter for the cent.

534

The House of the Seven Gables

You are welcome to Jim Crow."

The child, staring with round eyes at this instance of liberality, wholly unprecedented in his large experience of cent-shops, took the man of gingerbread, and quitted the premises. No sooner had he reached the sidewalk (little cannibal that he was!) than Jim Crow's head was in his mouth. As he had not been careful to shut the door, Hepzibah was at the pains of closing it after him, with a pettish ejaculation or two about the troublesomeness of young people, and particularly of small boys. She had just placed another representative of the renowned Jim Crow at the window, when again the shop-bell tinkled clamorously, and again the door being thrust open, with its characteristic jerk and jar, disclosed the same sturdy little urchin who, precisely two minutes ago, had made his exit. The crumbs and discoloration of the cannibal feast, as yet hardly consummated, were exceedingly visible about his mouth.

"What is it now, child?" asked the maiden lady rather impatiently; "did you come back to shut the door?"

"No," answered the urchin, pointing to the figure that had just been put up; "I want that other Jim Crow."

"Well, here it is for you," said Hepzibah, reaching it down; but recognizing that this pertinacious customer would not quit her on any other terms, so long as she had a gingerbread figure in her shop, she partly drew back her extended hand, "Where is the cent?"

The little boy had the cent ready, but, like a true-born Yankee, would have preferred the better bargain to the worse. Looking somewhat chagrined, he put the coin into Hepzibah's hand, and departed, sending the second Jim Crow in quest of the former one. The new shop-keeper dropped the first solid result of her commercial enterprise into the till. It was done! The sordid stain of that copper coin could never be washed away from her palm. The little schoolboy, aided by the impish figure of the negro dancer, had wrought an irreparable ruin. The structure of ancient aristocracy had been demolished by him, even as if his childish gripe had torn down the seven-gabled mansion. Now let Hepzibah turn the old Pyncheon portraits with their faces to the wall, and take the map of her Eastern territory to kindle the kitchen fire, and blow up the flame with the empty breath of her ancestral traditions! What had she to do with ancestry? Nothing; no more than with posterity! No lady, now, but simply Hepzibah Pyncheon, a forlorn old maid, and keeper of a cent-shop!

Nevertheless, even while she paraded these ideas somewhat ostentatiously through her mind, it is altogether surprising what a calmness had come over her. The anxiety and misgivings which had tormented her, whether asleep or in melancholy daydreams, ever since her project began to take an aspect of solidity, had now vanished quite away. She felt the novelty of her position, indeed, but no longer with disturbance or affright. Now and then, there came a thrill of almost youthful enjoyment. It was the invigorating breath of a fresh outward atmosphere, after the long torpor and monotonous seclusion of her life. So wholesome is effort! So miraculous the strength that we do not know of! The healthiest glow that Hepzibah had known for years had come now in the dreaded crisis, when, for the first time, she had put forth her hand to help herself. The little circlet of the schoolboy's copper coin — dim and lustreless though it was, with the small services which it had been doing here and there about the world — had proved a talisman, fragrant with good, and deserving to be set in gold and worn next her heart. It was as potent, and perhaps endowed with the same kind of efficacy, as a galvanic ring! Hepzibah, at all events, was indebted to its subtile operation both in body and spirit; so much the more, as it inspired her with energy to get some breakfast, at which, still the better to keep up her courage, she allowed herself an extra spoonful in her infusion of black tea.

Her introductory day of shop-keeping did not run on, however, without many and serious interruptions of this mood of cheerful vigor. As a general rule, Providence seldom vouchsafes to mortals any more than just that degree of encouragement which suffices to keep them at a reasonably full exertion of their powers. In the case of our old gentlewoman, after the excitement of new effort had subsided, the despondency of her whole life threatened, ever and anon, to return. It was like the heavy mass of clouds which we may often see obscuring the sky, and making a gray twilight everywhere, until, towards nightfall, it yields temporarily to a glimpse of sunshine. But, always, the envious cloud strives to gather again across the streak of celestial azure.

Customers came in, as the forenoon advanced, but rather slowly; in some cases, too, it must be owned, with little satisfaction either to themselves or Miss Hepzibah; nor, on the whole, with an aggregate of very rich emolument to the till. A little girl, sent by her mother to match a skein of cotton thread, of a peculiar hue, took one that the near-sighted old lady pronounced extremely like, but soon came running back, with a blunt and cross message, that it would not do, and, besides, was very rotten! Then, there was a pale, care-wrinkled woman, not old but haggard, and already with streaks of gray among her hair, like silver ribbons; one of those women, naturally delicate, whom you at once recognize as worn to death by a brute — probably a drunken brute — of a husband, and at least nine children. She wanted a few pounds of flour, and offered the money, which the decayed gentlewoman silently rejected, and gave the poor soul better measure than if she had taken it.

Shortly afterwards, a man in a blue cotton frock, much soiled, came in and bought a pipe, filling the whole shop, meanwhile, with the hot odor of strong drink, not only exhaled in the torrid atmosphere of his breath, but oozing out of his entire system, like an inflammable gas. It was impressed on Hepzibah's mind that this was the husband of the care-wrinkled woman. He asked for a paper of tobacco; and as she had neglected to provide herself with the article, her brutal customer dashed down his newly-bought pipe and left the shop, muttering some unintelligible words, which had the tone and bitterness of a curse. Hereupon Hepzibah threw up her eyes, unintentionally scowling in the face of Providence!

No less than five persons, during the forenoon, inquired for ginger-beer, or root-beer, or any drink of a similar brewage, and, obtaining nothing of the kind, went off in an exceedingly bad humor. Three of them left the door open, and the other two pulled it so spitefully in going out that the little bell played the very deuce with Hepzibah's nerves. A round, bustling, fire-ruddy housewife of the neighborhood burst breathless into the shop, fiercely demanding yeast; and when the poor gentlewoman, with her cold shyness of manner, gave her hot customer to understand that she did not keep the article, this very capable housewife took upon herself to administer a regular rebuke.

"A cent-shop, and no yeast!" quoth she; "That will never do! Who ever heard of such a thing? Your loaf will never rise, no more than mine will to-day. You had better shut up shop at once."

"Well," said Hepzibah, heaving a deep sigh, "perhaps I had!"

Several times, moreover, besides the above instance, her lady-like sensibilities were seriously infringed upon by the familiar, if not rude, tone with which people addressed her. They evidently considered themselves not merely her equals, but her patrons and superiors. Now, Hepzibah had unconsciously flattered herself with the idea that there would be a gleam or halo, of some kind or other, about her person, which would insure an obeisance to her sterling gentility, or, at least, a tacit recognition of it. On the other hand, nothing tortured her more intolerably than when this recognition was too prominently expressed. To one or two rather officious offers of sympathy, her responses were little short of acrimonious; and, we regret to say, Hepzibah was thrown into a positively unchristian state of mind by the suspicion that one of her customers was drawn to the shop, not by any real need of the article which she pretended to seek, but by a wicked wish to stare at her. The vulgar creature was determined to see for herself what sort of a figure a mildewed piece of aristocracy, after wasting all the bloom and much of the decline of her life apart from the world, would cut behind a counter. In this particular case, however mechanical and innocuous it might be at other times, Hepzibah's contortion of brow served her in good stead.

"I never was so frightened in my life!" said the curious customer, in describing the incident to one of her acquaintances. "She's a real old vixen, take my word of it! She says little, to be sure; but if you could only see the mischief in her eye!"

On the whole, therefore, her new experience led our decayed gentlewoman to very disagreeable conclusions as to the temper and manners of what she termed the lower classes, whom heretofore she had looked down upon with a gentle and pitying complaisance, as herself occupying a sphere of unquestionable superiority. But, unfortunately, she had likewise to struggle against a bitter emotion of a directly opposite kind: a sentiment of virulence, we mean, towards the idle aristocracy to which it had so recently been her pride to belong. When a lady, in a delicate and costly summer garb, with a floating veil and gracefully swaying gown, and, altogether, an ethereal lightness that made you look at her beautifully slippered feet, to see whether she trod on the dust or floated in the air,—when such a vision happened to pass through this retired street, leaving it tenderly and delusively fragrant with her passage, as if a bouquet of tea-roses had been borne along,—then again, it is to be feared, old Hepzibah's scowl could no longer vindicate itself entirely on the plea of near-sightedness.

"For what end," thought she, giving vent to that feeling of hostility which is the only real abasement of the poor in presence of the rich,—"for what good end, in the wisdom of Providence, does that woman live? Must the whole world toil, that the palms of her hands may be kept white and delicate?"

Then, ashamed and penitent, she hid her face.

"May God forgive me!" said she.

Doubtless, God did forgive her. But, taking the inward and outward history of the first half-day into consideration, Hepzibah began to fear that the shop would prove her ruin in a moral and religious point of view, without contributing very essentially towards even her temporal welfare.

IV.
A Day Behind the Counter

Towards noon, Hepzibah saw an elderly gentleman, large and portly, and of remarkably dignified demeanor, passing slowly along on the opposite side of the white and dusty street. On coming within the shadow of the Pyncheon Elm, he stopt, and (taking off his hat, meanwhile, to wipe the perspiration from his brow) seemed to scrutinize, with especial interest, the dilapidated and rusty-visaged House of the Seven Gables. He himself, in a very different style, was as well worth looking at as the house. No better model need be sought, nor could have been found, of a very high order of respectability, which, by some indescribable magic, not merely expressed itself in his looks and gestures, but even governed the fashion of his garments, and rendered them all proper and essential to the man. Without appearing to differ, in any tangible way, from other people's clothes, there was yet a wide and rich gravity about them that must have been a characteristic of the wearer, since it could not be defined as pertaining either to the cut or material. His gold-headed cane, too, — a serviceable staff, of dark polished wood, — had similar traits, and, had it chosen to take a walk by itself, would have been recognized anywhere as a tolerably adequate representative of its master. This character — which showed itself so strikingly in everything about him, and the effect of which we seek to convey to the reader — went no deeper than his station, habits of life, and external circumstances. One perceived him to be a personage of marked influence and authority; and, especially, you could feel just as certain that he was opulent as if he had exhibited his bank account, or as if you had seen him touching the twigs of the Pyncheon Elm, and, Midas-like, transmuting them to gold.

In his youth, he had probably been considered a handsome man; at his present age, his brow was too heavy, his temples too bare, his remaining hair too gray, his eye too cold, his lips too closely compressed, to bear any relation to mere personal beauty. He would have made a good and massive portrait; better now, perhaps, than at any previous period of his life, although his look might grow positively harsh in the process of being fixed upon the canvas. The artist would have found it desirable to study his face, and prove its capacity for varied expression; to darken it with a frown, — to kindle it up with a smile.

While the elderly gentleman stood looking at the Pyncheon House, both the frown and the smile passed successively over his countenance. His eye rested on the shop-window, and putting up a pair of gold-bowed spectacles, which he held in his hand, he minutely surveyed Hepzibah's little arrangement of toys and commodities. At first it seemed not to please him,—nay, to cause him exceeding displeasure,—and yet, the very next moment, he smiled. While the latter expression was yet on his lips, he caught a glimpse of Hepzibah, who had involuntarily bent forward to the window; and then the smile changed from acrid and disagreeable to the sunniest complacency and benevolence. He bowed, with a happy mixture of dignity and courteous kindliness, and pursued his way.

"There he is!" said Hepzibah to herself, gulping down a very bitter emotion, and, since she could not rid herself of it, trying to drive it back into her heart. "What does he think of it, I wonder? Does it please him? Ah! he is looking back!"

The gentleman had paused in the street, and turned himself half about, still with his eyes fixed on the shop-window. In fact, he wheeled wholly round, and commenced a step or two, as if designing to enter the shop; but, as it chanced, his purpose was anticipated by Hepzibah's first customer, the little cannibal of Jim Crow, who, staring up at the window, was irresistibly attracted by an elephant of gingerbread. What a grand appetite had this small urchin!—Two Jim Crows immediately after breakfast!—and now an elephant, as a preliminary whet before dinner. By the time this latter purchase was completed, the elderly gentleman had resumed his way, and turned the street corner.

"Take it as you like, Cousin Jaffrey," muttered the maiden lady, as she drew back, after cautiously thrusting out her head, and looking up and down the street,—"Take it as you like! You have seen my little shop-window. Well!—what have you to say? —is not the Pyncheon House my own, while I'm alive?"

After this incident, Hepzibah retreated to the back parlor, where she at first caught up a half-finished stocking, and began knitting at it with nervous and irregular jerks; but quickly finding herself at odds with the stitches, she threw it aside, and walked hurriedly about the room. At length she paused before the portrait of the stern old Puritan, her ancestor, and the founder of the house. In one sense, this picture had almost faded into the canvas, and hidden itself behind the duskiness of age; in another, she could not but fancy that it had been growing more prominent and strikingly expressive, ever since her earliest familiarity with it as a child. For, while the physical outline and substance were darkening away from the beholder's eye, the bold, hard, and, at the same time, indirect character of the man seemed to be brought out in a kind of spiritual relief. Such an effect may occasionally be observed in pictures of antique date. They acquire a look which an artist (if he have anything like the complacency of artists nowadays) would never dream of presenting to a patron as his own characteristic expression, but which, nevertheless, we at once recognize as reflecting the unlovely truth of a human soul. In such cases, the painter's deep conception of his subject's inward traits has wrought itself into the essence of the picture, and is seen after the superficial coloring has been rubbed off by time.

While gazing at the portrait, Hepzibah trembled under its eye. Her hereditary reverence made her afraid to judge the character of the original so harshly as a perception of the truth compelled her to do. But still she gazed, because the face of the picture enabled her — at least, she fancied so — to read more accurately, and to a greater depth, the face which she had just seen in the street.

"This is the very man!" murmured she to herself. "Let Jaffrey Pyncheon smile as he will, there is that look beneath! Put on him a skull-cap, and a band, and a black cloak, and a Bible in one hand and a sword in the other, — then let Jaffrey smile as he might, — nobody would doubt that it was the old Pyncheon come again. He has proved himself the very man to build up a new house! Perhaps, too, to draw down a new curse!"

Thus did Hepzibah bewilder herself with these fantasies of the old time. She had dwelt too much alone, — too long in the Pyncheon House, — until her very brain was impregnated with the dry-rot of its timbers. She needed a walk along the noonday street to keep her sane.

By the spell of contrast, another portrait rose up before her, painted with more daring flattery than any artist would have ventured upon, but yet so delicately touched that the likeness remained perfect. Malbone's miniature, though from the same original, was far inferior to Hepzibah's air-drawn picture, at which affection and sorrowful remembrance wrought together. Soft, mildly, and cheerfully contemplative, with full, red lips, just on the verge of a smile, which the eyes seemed to herald by a gentle kindling-up of their orbs! Feminine traits, moulded inseparably with those of the other sex! The miniature, likewise, had this last peculiarity; so that you inevitably thought of the original as resembling his mother, and she a lovely and lovable woman, with perhaps some beautiful infirmity of character, that made it all the pleasanter to know and easier to love her.

"Yes," thought Hepzibah, with grief of which it was only the more tolerable portion that welled up from her heart to her eyelids, "they persecuted his mother in him! He never was a Pyncheon!"

But here the shop-bell rang; it was like a sound from a remote distance, — so far had Hepzibah descended into the sepulchral depths of her reminiscences. On entering the shop, she found an old man there, a humble resident of Pyncheon

Street, and whom, for a great many years past, she had suffered to be a kind of familiar of the house. He was an immemorial personage, who seemed always to have had a white head and wrinkles, and never to have possessed but a single tooth, and that a half-decayed one, in the front of the upper jaw. Well advanced as Hepzibah was, she could not remember when Uncle Venner, as the neighborhood called him, had not gone up and down the street, stooping a little and drawing his feet heavily over the gravel or pavement. But still there was something tough and vigorous about him, that not only kept him in daily breath, but enabled him to fill a place which would else have been vacant in the apparently crowded world. To go of errands with his slow and shuffling gait, which made you doubt how he ever was to arrive anywhere; to saw a small household's foot or two of firewood, or knock to pieces an old barrel, or split up a pine board for kindling-stuff; in summer, to dig the few yards of garden ground appertaining to a low-rented tenement, and share the produce of his labor at the halves; in winter, to shovel away the snow from the sidewalk, or open paths to the woodshed, or along the clothes-line; such were some of the essential offices which Uncle Venner performed among at least a score of families. Within that circle, he claimed the same sort of privilege, and probably felt as much warmth of interest, as a clergyman does in the range of his parishioners. Not that he laid claim to the tithe pig; but, as an analogous mode of reverence, he went his rounds, every morning, to gather up the crumbs of the table and overflowings of the dinner-pot, as food for a pig of his own.

In his younger days—for, after all, there was a dim tradition that he had been, not young, but younger—Uncle Venner was commonly regarded as rather deficient, than otherwise, in his wits. In truth he had virtually pleaded guilty to the charge, by scarcely aiming at such success as other men seek, and by taking only that humble and modest part in the intercourse of life which belongs to the alleged deficiency. But now, in his extreme old age,—whether it were that his long and hard experience had actually brightened him, or that his decaying judgment rendered him less capable of fairly measuring himself,—the venerable man made pretensions to no little wisdom, and really enjoyed the credit of it. There was likewise, at times, a vein of something like poetry in him; it was the moss or wall-flower of his mind in its small dilapidation, and gave a charm to what might have been vulgar and commonplace in his earlier and middle life. Hepzibah had a regard for him, because his name was ancient in the town and had formerly been respectable. It was a still better reason for awarding him a species of familiar reverence that Uncle Venner was himself the most ancient existence, whether of man or thing, in Pyncheon Street, except the House of the Seven Gables, and perhaps the elm that overshadowed it.

This patriarch now presented himself before Hepzibah, clad in an old blue coat, which had a fashionable air, and must have accrued to him from the cast-off wardrobe of some dashing clerk. As for his trousers, they were of tow-cloth, very short in the legs, and bagging down strangely in the rear, but yet having a suitableness to his figure which his other garment entirely lacked. His hat had relation to no other part of his dress, and but very little to the head that wore it. Thus Uncle Venner was a miscellaneous old gentleman, partly himself, but, in good measure, somebody else; patched together, too, of different epochs; an epitome of times and fashions.

"So, you have really begun trade," said he, — "really begun trade! Well, I'm glad to see it. Young people should never live idle in the world, nor old ones neither, unless when the rheumatize gets hold of them. It has given me warning already; and in two or three years longer, I shall think of putting aside business and retiring to my farm. That's yonder, — the great brick house, you know, — the workhouse, most folks call it; but I mean to do my work first, and go there to be idle and enjoy myself. And I'm glad to see you beginning to do your work, Miss Hepzibah!"

"Thank you, Uncle Venner" said Hepzibah, smiling; for she always felt kindly towards the simple and talkative old man. Had he been an old woman, she might probably have repelled the freedom, which she now took in good part. "It is time for me to begin work, indeed! Or, to speak the truth, I have just begun when I ought to be giving it up."

"Oh, never say that, Miss Hepzibah!" answered the old man. "You are a young woman yet. Why, I hardly thought myself younger than I am now, it seems so little while ago since I used to see you playing about the door of the old house, quite a small child! Oftener, though, you used to be sitting at the threshold, and looking gravely into the street; for you had always a grave kind of way with you, — a grown-up air, when you were only the height of my knee. It seems as if I saw you now; and your grandfather with his red cloak, and his white wig, and his cocked hat, and his cane, coming out of the house, and stepping so grandly up the street! Those old gentlemen that grew up before the Revolution used to put on grand airs. In my young days, the great man of the town was commonly called King; and his wife, not Queen to be sure, but Lady. Nowadays, a man would not dare to be called King; and if he feels himself a little above common folks, he only stoops so much the lower to them. I met your cousin, the Judge, ten minutes ago; and, in my old tow-cloth trousers, as you see, the Judge raised his hat to me, I do believe! At any rate, the Judge bowed and smiled!"

"Yes," said Hepzibah, with something bitter stealing unawares into her tone; "my cousin Jaffrey is thought to have a very pleasant smile!"

"And so he has" replied Uncle Venner. "And that's rather remarkable in a Pyncheon; for, begging your pardon, Miss Hepzibah, they never had the name of being an easy and agreeable set of folks. There was no getting close to them. But Now, Miss Hepzibah, if an old man may be bold to ask, why don't Judge Pyncheon, with his great means, step forward, and tell his cousin to shut up her little shop at once? It's for your credit to be doing something, but it's not for the Judge's credit to let you!"

"We won't talk of this, if you please, Uncle Venner," said Hepzibah coldly. "I ought to say, however, that, if I choose to earn bread for myself, it is not Judge Pyncheon's fault. Neither will he deserve the blame," added she more kindly, remembering Uncle Venner's privileges of age and humble familiarity, "if I should, by and by, find it convenient to retire with you to your farm."

"And it's no bad place, either, that farm of mine!" cried the old man cheerily, as if there were something positively delightful in the prospect. "No bad place is the great brick farm-house, especially for them that will find a good many old cronies there, as will be my case. I quite long to be among them, sometimes, of the winter evenings; for it is but dull business for a lonesome elderly man, like me, to be nodding, by the hour together, with no company but his air-tight stove. Summer or winter, there's a great deal to be said in favor of my farm! And, take it in the autumn, what can be pleasanter than to spend a whole day on the sunny side of a barn or a wood-pile, chatting with somebody as old as one's self; or, perhaps, idling away the time with a natural-born simpleton, who knows how to be idle, because even our busy Yankees never have found out how to put him to any use? Upon my word, Miss Hepzibah, I doubt whether I've ever been so comfortable as I mean to be at my farm, which most folks call the workhouse. But you,—you're a young woman yet,—you never need go there! Something still better will turn up for you. I'm sure of it!"

Hepzibah fancied that there was something peculiar in her venerable friend's look and tone; insomuch, that she gazed into his face with considerable earnestness, endeavoring to discover what secret meaning, if any, might be lurking there. Individuals whose affairs have reached an utterly desperate crisis almost invariably keep themselves alive with hopes, so much the more airily magnificent as they have the less of solid matter within their grasp whereof to mould any judicious and moderate expectation of good. Thus, all the while Hepzibah was perfecting the scheme of her little shop, she had cherished an unacknowledged idea that some harlequin trick of fortune would intervene in her favor. For example, an uncle—who had sailed for India fifty years before, and never been heard of since — might yet return, and adopt her to be the comfort of his very extreme and decrepit age, and adorn her with pearls, diamonds, and Oriental shawls and turbans, and make her the ultimate heiress of his unreckonable riches. Or the member of Parliament, now at the head of the English branch of the family, — with which the elder stock, on this side of the Atlantic, had held little or no intercourse for the last two centuries, — this eminent gentleman might invite Hepzibah to quit the ruinous House of the Seven Gables, and come over to dwell with her kindred at Pyncheon Hall. But, for reasons the most imperative, she could not yield to his request. It was more probable, therefore, that the descendants of a Pyncheon who had emigrated to Virginia, in some past generation, and became a great planter there, — hearing of Hepzibah's destitution, and impelled by the splendid generosity of character with which their Virginian mixture must have enriched the New England blood, — would send her a remittance of a thousand dollars, with a hint of repeating the favor annually. Or, — and, surely, anything so undeniably just could not be beyond the limits of reasonable anticipation, — the great claim to the heritage of Waldo County might finally be decided in favor of the Pyncheons; so that, instead of keeping a cent-shop, Hepzibah would build a palace, and look down from its highest tower on hill, dale, forest, field, and town, as her own share of the ancestral territory.

These were some of the fantasies which she had long dreamed about; and, aided by these, Uncle Venner's casual attempt at encouragement kindled a strange festal glory in the poor, bare, melancholy chambers of her brain, as if that inner world were suddenly lighted up with gas. But either he knew nothing of her castles in the air, — as how should he? — or else her earnest scowl disturbed his recollection, as it might a more courageous man's. Instead of pursuing any weightier topic, Uncle Venner was pleased to favor Hepzibah with some sage counsel in her shop-keeping capacity.

"Give no credit!" — these were some of his golden maxims, — "Never take paper-money. Look well to your change! Ring the silver on the four-pound weight! Shove back all English half-pence and base copper tokens, such as are very plenty about town! At your leisure hours, knit children's woollen socks and mittens! Brew your own yeast, and make your own ginger-beer!"

And while Hepzibah was doing her utmost to digest the hard little pellets of his already uttered wisdom, he gave vent to his final, and what he declared to be his all-important advice, as follows: —

"Put on a bright face for your customers, and smile

pleasantly as you hand them what they ask for! A stale article, if you dip it in a good, warm, sunny smile, will go off better than a fresh one that you've scowled upon."

To this last apothegm poor Hepzibah responded with a sigh so deep and heavy that it almost rustled Uncle Venner quite away, like a withered leaf,—as he was,—before an autumnal gale. Recovering himself, however, he bent forward, and, with a good deal of feeling in his ancient visage, beckoned her nearer to him.

"When do you expect him home?" whispered he.

"Whom do you mean?" asked Hepzibah, turning pale.

"Ah!—You don't love to talk about it," said Uncle Venner. "Well, well! we'll say no more, though there's word of it all over town. I remember him, Miss Hepzibah, before he could run alone!"

During the remainder of the day, poor Hepzibah acquitted herself even less creditably, as a shop-keeper, than in her earlier efforts. She appeared to be walking in a dream; or, more truly, the vivid life and reality assumed by her emotions made all outward occurrences unsubstantial, like the teasing phantasms of a half-conscious slumber. She still responded, mechanically, to the frequent summons of the shop-bell, and, at the demand of her customers, went prying with vague eyes about the shop, proffering them one article after another, and thrusting aside—perversely, as most of them supposed—the identical thing they asked for. There is sad confusion, indeed, when the spirit thus flits away into the past, or into the more awful future, or, in any manner, steps across the spaceless boundary betwixt its own region and the actual world; where the body remains to guide itself as best it may, with little more than the mechanism of animal life. It is like death, without death's quiet privilege,—its freedom from mortal care. Worst of all, when the actual duties are comprised in such petty details as now vexed the brooding soul of the old gentlewoman. As the animosity of fate would have it, there was a great influx of custom in the course of the afternoon. Hepzibah blundered to and fro about her small place of business, committing the most unheard-of errors: now stringing up twelve, and now seven, tallow-candles, instead of ten to the pound; selling ginger for Scotch snuff, pins for needles, and needles for pins; misreckoning her change, sometimes to the public detriment, and much oftener to her own; and thus she went on, doing her utmost to bring chaos back again, until, at the close of the day's labor, to her inexplicable astonishment, she found the money-drawer almost destitute of coin. After all her painful traffic, the whole proceeds were perhaps half a dozen coppers, and a questionable ninepence which ultimately proved to be copper likewise.

The House of the Seven Gables

At this price, or at whatever price, she rejoiced that the day had reached its end. Never before had she had such a sense of the intolerable length of time that creeps between dawn and sunset, and of the miserable irksomeness of having aught to do, and of the better wisdom that it would be to lie down at once, in sullen resignation, and let life, and its toils and vexations, trample over one's prostrate body as they may! Hepzibah's final operation was with the little devourer of Jim Crow and the elephant, who now proposed to eat a camel. In her bewilderment, she offered him first a wooden dragoon, and next a handful of marbles; neither of which being adapted to his else omnivorous appetite, she hastily held out her whole remaining stock of natural history in gingerbread, and huddled the small customer out of the shop. She then muffled the bell in an unfinished stocking, and put up the oaken bar across the door.

During the latter process, an omnibus came to a stand-still under the branches of the elm-tree. Hepzibah's heart was in her mouth. Remote and dusky, and with no sunshine on all the intervening space, was that region of the Past whence her only guest might be expected to arrive! Was she to meet him now?

Somebody, at all events, was passing from the farthest interior of the omnibus towards its entrance. A gentleman alighted; but it was only to offer his hand to a young girl whose slender figure, nowise needing such assistance, now lightly descended the steps, and made an airy little jump from the final one to the sidewalk. She rewarded her cavalier with a smile, the cheery glow of which was seen reflected on his own face as he reentered the vehicle. The girl then turned towards the House of the Seven Gables, to the door of which, meanwhile,—not the shop-door, but the antique portal,—the omnibus-man had carried a light trunk and a bandbox. First giving a sharp rap of the old iron knocker, he left his passenger and her luggage at the door-step, and departed.

"Who can it be?" thought Hepzibah, who had been screwing her visual organs into the acutest focus of which they were capable. "The girl must have mistaken the house." She stole softly into the hall, and, herself invisible, gazed through the dusty side-lights of the portal at the young, blooming, and very cheerful face which presented itself for admittance into the gloomy old mansion. It was a face to which almost any door would have opened of its own accord.

The young girl, so fresh, so unconventional, and yet so orderly and obedient to common rules, as you at once recognized her to be, was widely in contrast, at that moment, with everything about her. The sordid and ugly luxuriance of gigantic weeds that grew in the angle of the house, and the heavy projection that overshadowed her, and the time-worn framework of the door,—none of these things belonged to her sphere. But, even as a ray of sunshine, fall into what dismal place it may, instantaneously creates for itself a propriety in being there, so did it seem altogether fit that the girl should be standing at the threshold. It was no less evidently proper that the door should swing open to admit her. The maiden lady herself, sternly inhospitable in her first purposes, soon began to feel that the door ought to be shoved back, and the rusty key be turned in the reluctant lock.

"Can it be Phœbe?" questioned she within herself. "It must be little Phœbe; for it can be nobody else,—and there is a look of her father about her, too! But what does she want here? And how like a country cousin, to come down upon a poor body in this way, without so much as a day's notice, or asking whether she would be welcome! Well; she must have a night's lodging, I suppose; and to-morrow the child shall go back to her mother."

Phœbe, it must be understood, was that one little offshoot of the Pyncheon race to whom we have already referred, as a native of a rural part of New England, where the old fashions and feelings of relationship are still partially kept up. In her own circle, it was regarded as by no means improper for kinsfolk to visit one another without invitation, or preliminary and ceremonious warning. Yet, in consideration of Miss Hepzibah's recluse way of life, a letter had actually been written and despatched, conveying information of Phœbe's projected visit. This epistle, for three or four days past, had been in the pocket of the penny-postman, who, happening to have no other business in Pyncheon Street, had not yet made it convenient to call at the House of the Seven Gables.

"No—she can stay only one night," said Hepzibah, unbolting the door. "If Clifford were to find her here, it might disturb him!"

V.
May and November

    Phœbe Pyncheon slept, on the night of her arrival, in a chamber that looked down on the garden of the old house. It fronted towards the east, so that at a very seasonable hour a glow of crimson light came flooding through the window, and bathed the dingy ceiling and paper-hangings in its own hue. There were curtains to Phœbe's bed; a dark, antique canopy, and ponderous festoons of a stuff which had been rich, and even magnificent, in its time; but which now brooded over the girl like a cloud, making a night in that one corner, while elsewhere it was beginning to be day. The morning light, however, soon stole into the aperture at the foot of the bed, betwixt those faded curtains. Finding the new guest there,— with a bloom on her cheeks like the morning's own, and a gentle stir of departing slumber in her limbs, as when an early breeze moves the foliage,— the dawn kissed her brow. It was the caress which a dewy maiden—such as the Dawn is, immortally—gives to her sleeping sister, partly from the impulse of irresistible fondness, and partly as a pretty hint that it is time now to unclose her eyes.

    At the touch of those lips of light, Phœbe quietly awoke, and, for a moment, did not recognize where she was, nor how those heavy curtains chanced to be festooned around her. Nothing, indeed, was absolutely plain to her, except that it was now early morning, and that, whatever might happen next, it was proper, first of all, to get up and say her prayers. She was the more inclined to devotion from the grim aspect of the chamber and its furniture, especially the tall, stiff chairs; one of which stood close by her bedside, and looked as if some old-fashioned personage had been sitting there all night, and had vanished only just in season to escape discovery.

    When Phœbe was quite dressed, she peeped out of the window, and saw a rosebush in the garden. Being a very tall one, and of luxuriant growth, it had been propped up against the side of the house, and was literally covered with a rare and very beautiful species of white rose. A large portion of them, as the girl afterwards discovered, had blight or mildew at their hearts; but, viewed at a fair distance, the whole rosebush looked as if it had been brought from Eden that very summer, together with the mould in which it grew. The truth was, nevertheless, that it had been planted by Alice Pyncheon,—she was Phœbe's great-great-grand-aunt,—in soil which, reckoning only its cultivation as a garden-plat, was now unctuous with nearly two hundred years of vegetable decay. Growing as they did, however, out of the old earth, the flowers still sent a fresh and sweet incense up to their Creator; nor could it have been the less pure and acceptable because Phœbe's young breath mingled with it, as the fragrance floated past the window. Hastening down the creaking and carpetless staircase, she found her way into the garden, gathered some of the most perfect of the roses, and brought them to her chamber.

Little Phœbe was one of those persons who possess, as their exclusive patrimony, the gift of practical arrangement. It is a kind of natural magic that enables these favored ones to bring out the hidden capabilities of things around them; and particularly to give a look of comfort and habitableness to any place which, for however brief a period, may happen to be their home. A wild hut of underbrush, tossed together by wayfarers through the primitive forest, would acquire the home aspect by one night's lodging of such a woman, and would retain it long after her quiet figure had disappeared into the surrounding shade. No less a portion of such homely witchcraft was requisite to reclaim, as it were, Phœbe's waste, cheerless, and dusky chamber, which had been untenanted so long—except by spiders, and mice, and rats, and ghosts—that it was all overgrown with the desolation which watches to obliterate every trace of man's happier hours. What was precisely Phœbe's process we find it impossible to say. She appeared to have no preliminary design, but gave a touch here and another there; brought some articles of furniture to light and dragged others into the shadow; looped up or let down a window-curtain; and, in the course of half an hour, had fully succeeded in throwing a kindly and hospitable smile over the apartment. No longer ago than the night before, it had resembled nothing so much as the old maid's heart; for there was neither sunshine nor household fire in one nor the other, and, save for ghosts and ghostly reminiscences, not a guest, for many years gone by, had entered the heart or the chamber.

There was still another peculiarity of this inscrutable charm. The bedchamber, no doubt, was a chamber of very great and varied experience, as a scene of human life: the joy of bridal nights had throbbed itself away here; new immortals had first drawn earthly breath here; and here old people had died. But—whether it were the white roses, or whatever the subtle influence might be—a person of delicate instinct would have known at once that it was now a maiden's bedchamber, and had been purified of all former evil and sorrow by her sweet breath and happy thoughts. Her dreams of the past night, being such cheerful ones, had exorcised the gloom, and now haunted the chamber in its stead.

After arranging matters to her satisfaction, Phœbe emerged from her chamber, with a purpose to descend again into the garden. Besides the rosebush, she had observed several other species of flowers growing there in a wilderness of neglect, and obstructing one another's development (as is often the parallel case in human society) by their uneducated entanglement and confusion. At the head of the stairs, however, she met Hepzibah, who, it being still early, invited her into a room which she would probably have called her boudoir, had her education embraced any such French phrase. It was strewn about with a few old books, and a work-basket, and a dusty writing-desk; and had, on one side, a large black article of furniture, of very strange appearance, which the old gentlewoman told Phœbe was a harpsichord. It looked more like a coffin than anything else; and, indeed,—not having been played upon, or opened, for years,—there must have been a vast deal of dead music in it, stifled for want of air. Human finger was hardly known to have touched its chords since the days of Alice Pyncheon, who had learned the sweet accomplishment of melody in Europe.

Hepzibah bade her young guest sit down, and, herself taking a chair near by, looked as earnestly at Phœbe's trim little figure as if she expected to see right into its springs and motive secrets.

"Cousin Phœbe," said she, at last, "I really can't see my way clear to keep you with me."

These words, however, had not the inhospitable bluntness with which they may strike the reader; for the two relatives, in a talk before bedtime, had arrived at a certain degree of mutual understanding. Hepzibah knew enough to enable her to appreciate the circumstances (resulting from the second marriage of the girl's mother) which made it desirable for Phœbe to establish herself in another home. Nor did she misinterpret Phœbe's character, and the genial activity pervading it,—one of the most valuable traits of the true New England woman,—which had impelled her forth, as might be said, to seek her fortune, but with a self-respecting purpose to confer as much benefit as she could anywise receive. As one of her nearest kindred, she had naturally betaken herself to Hepzibah, with no idea of forcing herself on her cousin's protection, but only for a visit of a week or two, which might be indefinitely extended, should it prove for the happiness of both.

To Hepzibah's blunt observation, therefore, Phœbe replied as frankly, and more cheerfully.

"Dear cousin, I cannot tell how it will be," said she. "But I really think we may suit one another much better than you suppose."

"You are a nice girl,—I see it plainly," continued Hepzibah; "and it is not any question as to that point which makes me hesitate. But, Phœbe, this house of mine is but a melancholy place for a young person to be in. It lets in the wind and rain, and the snow, too, in the garret and upper chambers, in wintertime, but it never lets in the sunshine. And as for myself, you see what I am,—a dismal and lonesome old woman (for I begin to call myself old, Phœbe), whose temper, I am afraid, is none of the best, and whose spirits are as bad as can be! I cannot make your life pleasant, Cousin Phœbe, neither can I so much as give you bread to eat."

"You will find me a cheerful little body" answered Phœbe, smiling, and yet with a kind of gentle dignity, "and I mean to earn my bread. You know I have not been brought up a Pyncheon. A girl learns many things in a New England village."

"Ah! Phœbe," said Hepzibah, sighing, "your knowledge would do but little for you here! And then it is a wretched thought that you should fling away your young days in a place like this. Those cheeks would not be so rosy after a month or two. Look at my face!" and, indeed, the contrast was very striking,—"you see how pale I am! It is my idea that the dust and continual decay of these old houses are unwholesome for the lungs."

"There is the garden,—the flowers to be taken care of," observed Phœbe. "I should keep myself healthy with exercise in the open air."

"And, after all, child," exclaimed Hepzibah, suddenly rising, as if to dismiss the subject, "it is not for me to say who shall be a guest or inhabitant of the old Pyncheon House. Its master is coming."

"Do you mean Judge Pyncheon?" asked Phœbe in surprise.

"Judge Pyncheon!" answered her cousin angrily. "He will hardly cross the threshold while I live! No, no! But, Phœbe, you shall see the face of him I speak of."

She went in quest of the miniature already described, and returned with it in her hand. Giving it to Phœbe, she watched her features narrowly, and with a certain jealousy as to the mode in which the girl would show herself affected by the picture.

"How do you like the face?" asked Hepzibah.

"It is handsome!—it is very beautiful!" said Phœbe admiringly. "It is as sweet a face as a man's can be, or ought to be. It has something of a child's expression,—and yet not childish,—only one feels so very kindly towards him! He ought never to suffer anything. One would bear much for the sake of sparing him toil or sorrow. Who is it, Cousin Hepzibah?"

"Did you never hear," whispered her cousin, bending towards her, "of Clifford Pyncheon?"

"Never. I thought there were no Pyncheons left, except yourself and our cousin Jaffrey," answered Phœbe. "And yet I seem to have heard the name of Clifford Pyncheon. Yes!—from my father or my mother; but has he not been a long while dead?"

"Well, well, child, perhaps he has!" said Hepzibah with a sad, hollow laugh; "but, in old houses like this, you know, dead people are very apt to come back again! We shall see. And, Cousin Phœbe, since, after all that I have said, your courage does not fail you, we will not part so soon. You are welcome, my child, for the present, to such a home as your kinswoman can offer you."

With this measured, but not exactly cold assurance of a hospitable purpose, Hepzibah kissed her cheek.

They now went below stairs, where Phœbe—not so much assuming the office as attracting it to herself, by the magnetism of innate fitness—took the most active part in preparing breakfast. The mistress of the house, meanwhile, as is usual with persons of her stiff and unmalleable cast, stood mostly aside; willing to lend her aid, yet conscious that her natural inaptitude would be likely to impede the business in hand. Phœbe and the fire that boiled the teakettle were equally bright, cheerful, and efficient, in their respective offices. Hepzibah gazed forth from her habitual sluggishness, the necessary result of long solitude, as from another sphere. She could not help being interested, however, and even amused, at the readiness with which her new inmate adapted herself to the circumstances, and brought the house, moreover, and all its rusty old appliances, into a suitableness for her purposes. Whatever she did, too, was done without conscious effort, and with frequent outbreaks of song, which were exceedingly pleasant to the ear. This natural tunefulness made Phœbe seem like a bird in a shadowy tree; or conveyed the idea that the stream of life warbled through her heart as a brook sometimes warbles through a pleasant little dell. It betokened the cheeriness of an active temperament, finding joy in its activity, and, therefore, rendering it beautiful; it was a New England trait,—the stern old stuff of Puritanism with a gold thread in the web.

Hepzibah brought out some old silver spoons with the family crest upon them, and a china tea-set painted over with grotesque figures of man, bird, and beast, in as grotesque a landscape. These pictured people were odd humorists, in a world of their own,—a world of vivid brilliancy, so far as color went, and still unfaded, although the teapot and small cups were as ancient as the custom itself of tea-drinking.

"Your great-great-great-great-grandmother had these cups, when she was married," said Hepzibah to Phœbe. "She was a Davenport, of a good family. They were almost the first teacups ever seen in the colony; and if one of them were to be broken, my heart would break with it. But it is nonsense to speak so about a brittle teacup, when I remember what my heart has gone through without breaking."

The cups—not having been used, perhaps, since Hepzibah's youth—had contracted no small burden of dust, which Phœbe washed away with so much care and delicacy as to satisfy even the proprietor of this invaluable china.

"What a nice little housewife you are!" exclaimed the latter, smiling, and at the same time frowning so prodigiously that the smile was sunshine under a thunder-cloud. "Do you do other things as well? Are you as good at your book as you are at washing teacups?"

"Not quite, I am afraid," said Phœbe, laughing at the form of Hepzibah's question. "But I was schoolmistress for the little children in our district last summer, and might have been so still."

"Ah! 'tis all very well!" observed the maiden lady, drawing herself up. "But these things must have come to you with your mother's blood. I never knew a Pyncheon that had any turn for them."

It is very queer, but not the less true, that people are generally quite as vain, or even more so, of their deficiencies than of their available gifts; as was Hepzibah of this native inapplicability, so to speak, of the Pyncheons to any useful purpose. She regarded it as an hereditary trait; and so, perhaps, it was, but unfortunately a morbid one, such as is often generated in families that remain long above the surface of society.

Before they left the breakfast-table, the shop-bell rang sharply, and Hepzibah set down the remnant of her final cup of tea, with a look of sallow despair that was truly piteous to behold. In cases of distasteful occupation, the second day is generally worse than the first. We return to the rack with all the soreness of the preceding torture in our limbs. At all events, Hepzibah had fully satisfied herself of the impossibility of ever becoming wonted to this peevishly obstreperous little bell. Ring as often as it might, the sound always smote upon her nervous system rudely and suddenly. And especially now, while, with her crested teaspoons and antique china, she was flattering herself with ideas of gentility, she felt an unspeakable disinclination to confront a customer.

"Do not trouble yourself, dear cousin!" cried Phœbe, starting lightly up. "I am shop-keeper to-day."

"You, child!" exclaimed Hepzibah. "What can a little country girl know of such matters?"

"Oh, I have done all the shopping for the family at our village store," said Phœbe. "And I have had a table at a fancy fair, and made better sales than anybody. These things are not to be learnt; they depend upon a knack that comes, I suppose," added she, smiling, "with one's mother's blood. You shall see that I am as nice a little saleswoman as I am a housewife!"

The old gentlewoman stole behind Phœbe, and peeped from the passageway into the shop, to note how she would manage her undertaking. It was a case of some intricacy. A very ancient woman, in a white short gown and a green petticoat, with a string of gold beads about her neck, and what looked like a nightcap on her head, had brought a quantity of yarn to barter for the commodities of the shop. She was probably the very last person in town who still kept the time-honored spinning-wheel in constant revolution. It was worth while to hear the croaking and hollow tones of the old lady, and the pleasant voice of Phœbe, mingling in one twisted thread of talk; and still better to contrast their figures,—so light and bloomy,—so decrepit and dusky,—with only the counter betwixt them, in one sense, but more than threescore years, in another. As for the bargain, it was wrinkled slyness and craft pitted against native truth and sagacity.

"Was not that well done?" asked Phœbe, laughing, when the customer was gone.

"Nicely done, indeed, child!" answered Hepzibah. "I could not have gone through with it nearly so well. As you say, it must be a knack that belongs to you on the mother's side."

It is a very genuine admiration, that with which persons too shy or too awkward to take a due part in the bustling world regard the real actors in life's stirring scenes; so genuine, in fact, that the former are usually fain to make it palatable to their self-love, by assuming that these active and forcible qualities are incompatible with others, which they choose to deem higher and more important. Thus, Hepzibah was well content to acknowledge Phœbe's vastly superior gifts as a shop-keeper; she listened, with compliant ear, to her suggestion of various methods whereby the influx of trade might be increased, and rendered profitable, without a hazardous outlay of capital. She consented that the village maiden should manufacture yeast, both liquid and in cakes; and should brew a certain kind of beer, nectareous to the palate, and of rare stomachic virtues; and, moreover, should bake and exhibit for sale some little spice-cakes, which whosoever tasted would longingly desire to taste again. All such proofs of a ready mind and skilful handiwork were highly acceptable to the aristocratic hucksteress, so long as she could murmur to herself with a grim smile, and a half-natural sigh, and a sentiment of mixed wonder, pity, and growing affection: —

"What a nice little body she is! If she only could be a lady; too — but that's impossible! Phœbe is no Pyncheon. She takes everything from her mother!"

As to Phœbe's not being a lady, or whether she were a lady or no, it was a point, perhaps, difficult to decide, but which could hardly have come up for judgment at all in any fair and healthy mind. Out of New England, it would be impossible to meet with a person combining so many ladylike attributes with so many others that form no necessary (if compatible) part of the character. She shocked no canon of taste; she was admirably in keeping with herself, and never jarred against surrounding circumstances. Her figure, to be sure, — so small as to be almost childlike, and so elastic that motion seemed as easy or easier to it than rest, would hardly have suited one's idea of a countess. Neither did her face — with the brown ringlets on either side, and the slightly piquant nose, and the wholesome bloom, and the clear shade of tan, and the half dozen freckles, friendly remembrances of the April sun and breeze — precisely give us a right to call her beautiful. But there was both lustre and depth in her eyes. She was very pretty; as graceful as a bird, and graceful much in the same way; as pleasant about the house as a gleam of sunshine falling on the floor through a shadow of twinkling leaves, or as a ray of firelight that dances on the wall while evening is drawing nigh. Instead of discussing her claim to rank among ladies, it would be preferable to regard Phœbe as the example of feminine grace and availability combined, in a state of society, if there were any such, where ladies did not exist. There it should be woman's office to move in the midst of practical affairs, and to gild them all, the very homeliest, — were it even the scouring of pots and kettles, — with an atmosphere of loveliness and joy.

Such was the sphere of Phœbe. To find the born and educated lady, on the other hand, we need look no farther than Hepzibah, our forlorn old maid, in her rustling and rusty silks, with her deeply cherished and ridiculous consciousness of long descent, her shadowy claims to princely territory, and, in the way of accomplishment, her recollections, it may be, of having formerly thrummed on a harpsichord, and walked a minuet, and worked an antique tapestry-stitch on her sampler. It was a

The House of the Seven Gables

fair parallel between new Plebeianism and old Gentility.

It really seemed as if the battered visage of the House of the Seven Gables, black and heavy-browed as it still certainly looked, must have shown a kind of cheerfulness glimmering through its dusky windows as Phœbe passed to and fro in the interior. Otherwise, it is impossible to explain how the people of the neighborhood so soon became aware of the girl's presence. There was a great run of custom, setting steadily in, from about ten o'clock until towards noon,—relaxing, somewhat, at dinnertime, but recommencing in the afternoon, and, finally, dying away a half an hour or so before the long day's sunset. One of the stanchest patrons was little Ned Higgins, the devourer of Jim Crow and the elephant, who to-day signalized his omnivorous prowess by swallowing two dromedaries and a locomotive. Phœbe laughed, as she summed up her aggregate of sales upon the slate; while Hepzibah, first drawing on a pair of silk gloves, reckoned over the sordid accumulation of copper coin, not without silver intermixed, that had jingled into the till.

"We must renew our stock, Cousin Hepzibah!" cried the little saleswoman. "The gingerbread figures are all gone, and so are those Dutch wooden milkmaids, and most of our other playthings. There has been constant inquiry for cheap raisins, and a great cry for whistles, and trumpets, and jew's-harps; and at least a dozen little boys have asked for molasses-candy. And we must contrive to get a peck of russet apples, late in the season as it is. But, dear cousin, what an enormous heap of copper! Positively a copper mountain!"

"Well done! well done! well done!" quoth Uncle Venner, who had taken occasion to shuffle in and out of the shop several times in the course of the day. "Here's a girl that will never end her days at my farm! Bless my eyes, what a brisk little soul!"

"Yes, Phœbe is a nice girl!" said Hepzibah, with a scowl of austere approbation. "But, Uncle Venner, you have known the family a great many years. Can you tell me whether there ever was a Pyncheon whom she takes after?"

"I don't believe there ever was," answered the venerable man. "At any rate, it never was my luck to see her like among them, nor, for that matter, anywhere else. I've seen a great deal of the world, not only in people's kitchens and back-yards but at the street-corners, and on the wharves, and in other places where my business calls me; and I'm free to say, Miss Hepzibah, that I never knew a human creature do her work so much like one of God's angels as this child Phœbe does!"

Uncle Venner's eulogium, if it appear rather too high-strained for the person and occasion, had, nevertheless, a sense in which it was both subtile and true. There was a spiritual quality in Phœbe's activity. The life of the long and busy day—spent in occupations that might so easily have taken a squalid and ugly aspect—had been made pleasant, and even lovely, by the spontaneous grace with which these homely duties seemed to bloom out of her character; so that labor, while she dealt with it, had the easy and flexible charm of play. Angels do not toil, but let their good works grow out of them; and so did Phœbe.

The two relatives—the young maid and the old one—found time before nightfall, in the intervals of trade, to make rapid advances towards affection and confidence. A recluse, like Hepzibah, usually displays remarkable frankness, and at least temporary affability, on being absolutely cornered, and brought to the point of personal intercourse; like the angel whom Jacob wrestled with, she is ready to bless you when once overcome.

The old gentlewoman took a dreary and proud satisfaction in leading Phœbe from room to room of the house, and recounting the traditions with which, as we may say, the walls were lugubriously frescoed. She showed the indentations made by the lieutenant-governor's sword-hilt in the door-panels of the apartment where old Colonel Pyncheon, a dead host, had received his affrighted visitors with an awful frown. The dusky terror of that frown, Hepzibah observed, was thought to be lingering ever since in the passageway. She bade Phœbe step into one of the tall chairs, and inspect the ancient map of the Pyncheon territory at the eastward. In a tract of land on which she laid her finger, there existed a silver mine, the locality of which was precisely pointed out in some memoranda of Colonel Pyncheon himself, but only to be made known when the family claim should be recognized by government. Thus it was for the interest of all New England that the Pyncheons should have justice done them. She told, too, how that there was undoubtedly an immense treasure of English guineas hidden somewhere about the house, or in the cellar, or possibly in the garden.

"If you should happen to find it, Phœbe," said Hepzibah, glancing aside at her with a grim yet kindly smile, "we will tie up the shop-bell for good and all!"

"Yes, dear cousin," answered Phœbe; "but, in the mean time, I hear somebody ringing it!"

When the customer was gone, Hepzibah talked rather vaguely, and at great length, about a certain Alice Pyncheon, who had been exceedingly beautiful and accomplished in her lifetime, a hundred years ago. The fragrance of her rich and delightful character still lingered about the place where she had lived, as a dried rose-bud scents the drawer where it has withered and perished. This lovely Alice had met with some great and mysterious calamity, and had grown thin and white,

The House of the Seven Gables

and gradually faded out of the world. But, even now, she was supposed to haunt the House of the Seven Gables, and, a great many times, — especially when one of the Pyncheons was to die, — she had been heard playing sadly and beautifully on the harpsichord. One of these tunes, just as it had sounded from her spiritual touch, had been written down by an amateur of music; it was so exquisitely mournful that nobody, to this day, could bear to hear it played, unless when a great sorrow had made them know the still profounder sweetness of it.

"Was it the same harpsichord that you showed me?" inquired Phœbe.

"The very same," said Hepzibah. "It was Alice Pyncheon's harpsichord. When I was learning music, my father would never let me open it. So, as I could only play on my teacher's instrument, I have forgotten all my music long ago."

Leaving these antique themes, the old lady began to talk about the daguerreotypist, whom, as he seemed to be a well-meaning and orderly young man, and in narrow circumstances, she had permitted to take up his residence in one of the seven gables. But, on seeing more of Mr. Holgrave, she hardly knew what to make of him. He had the strangest companions imaginable; men with long beards, and dressed in linen blouses, and other such new-fangled and ill-fitting garments; reformers, temperance lecturers, and all manner of cross-looking philanthropists; community-men, and come-outers, as Hepzibah believed, who acknowledged no law, and ate no solid food, but lived on the scent of other people's cookery, and turned up their noses at the fare. As for the daguerreotypist, she had read a paragraph in a penny paper, the other day, accusing him of making a speech full of wild and disorganizing matter, at a meeting of his banditti-like associates. For her own part, she had reason to believe that he practised animal magnetism, and, if such things were in fashion nowadays, should be apt to suspect him of studying the Black Art up there in his lonesome chamber.

"But, dear cousin," said Phœbe, "if the young man is so dangerous, why do you let him stay? If he does nothing worse, he may set the house on fire!"

"Why, sometimes," answered Hepzibah, "I have seriously made it a question, whether I ought not to send him away. But, with all his oddities, he is a quiet kind of a person, and has such a way of taking hold of one's mind, that, without exactly liking him (for I don't know enough of the young man), I should be sorry to lose sight of him entirely. A woman clings to slight acquaintances when she lives so much alone as I do."

"But if Mr. Holgrave is a lawless person!" remonstrated

Phœbe, a part of whose essence it was to keep within the limits of law.

"Oh!" said Hepzibah carelessly, — for, formal as she was, still, in her life's experience, she had gnashed her teeth against human law, — "I suppose he has a law of his own!"

VI.
Maule's Well

After an early tea, the little country-girl strayed into the garden. The enclosure had formerly been very extensive, but was now contracted within small compass, and hemmed about, partly by high wooden fences, and partly by the outbuildings of houses that stood on another street. In its centre was a grass-plat, surrounding a ruinous little structure, which showed just enough of its original design to indicate that it had once been a summer-house. A hop-vine, springing from last year's root, was beginning to clamber over it, but would be long in covering the roof with its green mantle. Three of the seven gables either fronted or looked sideways, with a dark solemnity of aspect, down into the garden.

The black, rich soil had fed itself with the decay of a long period of time; such as fallen leaves, the petals of flowers, and the stalks and seed-vessels of vagrant and lawless plants, more useful after their death than ever while flaunting in the sun. The evil of these departed years would naturally have sprung up again, in such rank weeds (symbolic of the transmitted vices of society) as are always prone to root themselves about human dwellings. Phœbe saw, however, that their growth must have been checked by a degree of careful labor, bestowed daily and systematically on the garden. The white double rosebush had evidently been propped up anew against the house since the commencement of the season; and a pear-tree and three damson-trees, which, except a row of currant-bushes, constituted the only varieties of fruit, bore marks of the recent amputation of several superfluous or defective limbs. There were also a few species of antique and hereditary flowers, in no very flourishing condition, but scrupulously weeded; as if some person, either out of love or curiosity, had been anxious to bring them to such perfection as they were capable of attaining. The remainder of the garden presented a well-selected assortment of esculent vegetables, in a praiseworthy state of advancement. Summer squashes almost in their golden blossom; cucumbers, now evincing a tendency to spread away from the main stock, and ramble far and wide; two or three rows of string-beans and as many more that were about to festoon themselves on poles; tomatoes, occupying a site so sheltered and sunny that the plants were already gigantic, and promised an early and abundant harvest.

Phœbe wondered whose care and toil it could have been that had planted these vegetables, and kept the soil so clean and orderly. Not surely her cousin Hepzibah's, who had no taste nor spirits for the lady-like employment of cultivating flowers, and — with her recluse habits, and tendency to shelter herself within the dismal shadow of the house—would hardly have come forth under the speck of open sky to weed and hoe among the fraternity of beans and squashes.

It being her first day of complete estrangement from rural objects, Phœbe found an unexpected charm in this little nook of grass, and foliage, and aristocratic flowers, and plebeian vegetables. The eye of Heaven seemed to look down into it pleasantly, and with a peculiar smile, as if glad to perceive that nature, elsewhere overwhelmed, and driven out of the dusty town, had here been able to retain a breathing-place. The spot acquired a somewhat wilder grace, and yet a very gentle one, from the fact that a pair of robins had built their nest in the pear-tree, and were making themselves exceedingly busy and happy in the dark intricacy of its boughs. Bees, too,—strange to say,—had thought it worth their while to come hither, possibly from the range of hives beside some farm-house miles away. How many aerial voyages might they have made, in quest of honey, or honey-laden, betwixt dawn and sunset! Yet, late as it now was, there still arose a pleasant hum out of one or two of the squash-blossoms, in the depths of which these bees were plying their golden labor. There was one other object in the garden which Nature might fairly claim as her inalienable property, in spite of whatever man could do to render it his own. This was a fountain, set round with a rim of old mossy stones, and paved, in its bed, with what appeared to be a sort of mosaic-work of variously colored pebbles. The play and slight agitation of the water, in its upward gush, wrought magically with these variegated pebbles, and made a continually shifting apparition of quaint figures, vanishing too suddenly to be definable. Thence, swelling over the rim of moss-grown stones, the water stole away under the fence, through what we regret to call a gutter, rather than a channel. Nor must we forget to mention a hen-coop of very reverend antiquity that stood in the farther corner of the garden, not a great way from the fountain. It now contained only Chanticleer, his two wives, and a solitary chicken. All of them were pure specimens of a breed which had been transmitted down as an heirloom in the Pyncheon family, and were said, while in their prime, to have attained almost the size of turkeys, and, on the score of delicate flesh, to be fit for a prince's table. In proof of the authenticity of this legendary renown, Hepzibah could have exhibited the shell of a great egg, which an ostrich need hardly have been ashamed of. Be that as it might, the hens were now scarcely larger than pigeons, and had a queer, rusty, withered aspect, and a gouty kind of movement, and a sleepy and melancholy tone throughout all the variations of their clucking and cackling. It was evident that the race had degenerated, like many a noble race besides, in consequence of too strict a watchfulness to keep it pure. These feathered people had existed too long in their distinct variety; a fact of which the present representatives, judging by their lugubrious deportment, seemed to be aware. They kept

The House of the Seven Gables

themselves alive, unquestionably, and laid now and then an egg, and hatched a chicken; not for any pleasure of their own, but that the world might not absolutely lose what had once been so admirable a breed of fowls. The distinguishing mark of the hens was a crest of lamentably scanty growth, in these latter days, but so oddly and wickedly analogous to Hepzibah's turban, that Phœbe—to the poignant distress of her conscience, but inevitably—was led to fancy a general resemblance betwixt these forlorn bipeds and her respectable relative.

The girl ran into the house to get some crumbs of bread, cold potatoes, and other such scraps as were suitable to the accommodating appetite of fowls. Returning, she gave a peculiar call, which they seemed to recognize. The chicken crept through the pales of the coop and ran, with some show of liveliness, to her feet; while Chanticleer and the ladies of his household regarded her with queer, sidelong glances, and then croaked one to another, as if communicating their sage opinions of her character. So wise, as well as antique, was their aspect, as to give color to the idea, not merely that they were the descendants of a time-honored race, but that they had existed, in their individual capacity, ever since the House of the Seven Gables was founded, and were somehow mixed up with its destiny. They were a species of tutelary sprite, or Banshee; although winged and feathered differently from most other guardian angels.

"Here, you odd little chicken!" said Phœbe; "here are some nice crumbs for you!"

The chicken, hereupon, though almost as venerable in appearance as its mother—possessing, indeed, the whole antiquity of its progenitors in miniature,—mustered vivacity enough to flutter upward and alight on Phœbe's shoulder.

"That little fowl pays you a high compliment!" said a voice behind Phœbe.

Turning quickly, she was surprised at sight of a young man, who had found access into the garden by a door opening out of another gable than that whence she had emerged. He held a hoe in his hand, and, while Phœbe was gone in quest of the crumbs, had begun to busy himself with drawing up fresh earth about the roots of the tomatoes.

"The chicken really treats you like an old acquaintance," continued he in a quiet way, while a smile made his face pleasanter than Phœbe at first fancied it. "Those venerable personages in the coop, too, seem very affably disposed. You are lucky to be in their good graces so soon! They have known me much longer, but never honor me with any familiarity, though hardly a day passes without my bringing them food.

Miss Hepzibah, I suppose, will interweave the fact with her other traditions, and set it down that the fowls know you to be a Pyncheon!"

"The secret is," said Phœbe, smiling, "that I have learned how to talk with hens and chickens."

"Ah, but these hens," answered the young man,—"these hens of aristocratic lineage would scorn to understand the vulgar language of a barn-yard fowl. I prefer to think—and so would Miss Hepzibah—that they recognize the family tone. For you are a Pyncheon?"

"My name is Phœbe Pyncheon," said the girl, with a manner of some reserve; for she was aware that her new acquaintance could be no other than the daguerreotypist, of whose lawless propensities the old maid had given her a disagreeable idea. "I did not know that my cousin Hepzibah's garden was under another person's care."

"Yes," said Holgrave, "I dig, and hoe, and weed, in this black old earth, for the sake of refreshing myself with what little nature and simplicity may be left in it, after men have so long sown and reaped here. I turn up the earth by way of pastime. My sober occupation, so far as I have any, is with a lighter material. In short, I make pictures out of sunshine; and, not to be too much dazzled with my own trade, I have prevailed with Miss Hepzibah to let me lodge in one of these dusky gables. It is like a bandage over one's eyes, to come into it. But would you like to see a specimen of my productions?"

"A daguerreotype likeness, do you mean?" asked Phœbe with less reserve; for, in spite of prejudice, her own youthfulness sprang forward to meet his. "I don't much like pictures of that sort,—they are so hard and stern; besides dodging away from the eye, and trying to escape altogether. They are conscious of looking very unamiable, I suppose, and therefore hate to be seen."

"If you would permit me," said the artist, looking at Phœbe, "I should like to try whether the daguerreotype can bring out disagreeable traits on a perfectly amiable face. But there certainly is truth in what you have said. Most of my likenesses do look unamiable; but the very sufficient reason, I fancy, is, because the originals are so. There is a wonderful insight in Heaven's broad and simple sunshine. While we give it credit only for depicting the merest surface, it actually brings out the secret character with a truth that no painter would ever venture upon, even could he detect it. There is, at least, no flattery in my humble line of art. Now, here is a likeness which I have taken over and over again, and still with no better result. Yet the original wears, to common eyes, a very different expression. It would gratify me to have your judgment on this character."

He exhibited a daguerreotype miniature in a morocco case. Phœbe merely glanced at it, and gave it back.

"I know the face," she replied; "for its stern eye has been following me about all day. It is my Puritan ancestor, who hangs yonder in the parlor. To be sure, you have found some way of copying the portrait without its black velvet cap and gray beard, and have given him a modern coat and satin cravat, instead of his cloak and band. I don't think him improved by your alterations."

"You would have seen other differences had you looked a little longer," said Holgrave, laughing, yet apparently much struck. "I can assure you that this is a modern face, and one which you will very probably meet. Now, the remarkable point is, that the original wears, to the world's eye,—and, for aught I know, to his most intimate friends,—an exceedingly pleasant countenance, indicative of benevolence, openness of heart, sunny good-humor, and other praiseworthy qualities of that cast. The sun, as you see, tells quite another story, and will not be coaxed out of it, after half a dozen patient attempts on my part. Here we have the man, sly, subtle, hard, imperious, and, withal, cold as ice. Look at that eye! Would you like to be at its mercy? At that mouth! Could it ever smile? And yet, if you could only see the benign smile of the original! It is so much the more unfortunate, as he is a public character of some eminence, and the likeness was intended to be engraved."

"Well, I don't wish to see it any more," observed Phœbe, turning away her eyes. "It is certainly very like the old portrait. But my cousin Hepzibah has another picture,—a miniature. If the original is still in the world, I think he might defy the sun to make him look stern and hard."

"You have seen that picture, then!" exclaimed the artist, with an expression of much interest. "I never did, but have a great curiosity to do so. And you judge favorably of the face?"

"There never was a sweeter one," said Phœbe. "It is almost too soft and gentle for a man's."

"Is there nothing wild in the eye?" continued Holgrave, so earnestly that it embarrassed Phœbe, as did also the quiet freedom with which he presumed on their so recent acquaintance. "Is there nothing dark or sinister anywhere? Could you not conceive the original to have been guilty of a great crime?"

"It is nonsense," said Phœbe a little impatiently, "for us to talk about a picture which you have never seen. You mistake it for some other. A crime, indeed! Since you are a friend of my cousin Hepzibah's, you should ask her to show you the picture."

"It will suit my purpose still better to see the original," replied the daguerreotypist coolly. "As to his character, we need not discuss its points; they have already been settled by a competent tribunal, or one which called itself competent. But, stay! Do not go yet, if you please! I have a proposition to make you."

Phœbe was on the point of retreating, but turned back, with some hesitation; for she did not exactly comprehend his manner, although, on better observation, its feature seemed rather to be lack of ceremony than any approach to offensive rudeness. There was an odd kind of authority, too, in what he now proceeded to say, rather as if the garden were his own than a place to which he was admitted merely by Hepzibah's courtesy.

"If agreeable to you," he observed, "it would give me pleasure to turn over these flowers, and those ancient and respectable fowls, to your care. Coming fresh from country air and occupations, you will soon feel the need of some such out-of-door employment. My own sphere does not so much lie among flowers. You can trim and tend them, therefore, as you please; and I will ask only the least trifle of a blossom, now and then, in exchange for all the good, honest kitchen vegetables with which I propose to enrich Miss Hepzibah's table. So we will be fellow-laborers, somewhat on the community system."

Silently, and rather surprised at her own compliance, Phœbe accordingly betook herself to weeding a flower-bed, but busied herself still more with cogitations respecting this young man, with whom she so unexpectedly found herself on terms approaching to familiarity. She did not altogether like him. His character perplexed the little country-girl, as it might a more practised observer; for, while the tone of his conversation had generally been playful, the impression left on her mind was that of gravity, and, except as his youth modified it, almost sternness. She rebelled, as it were, against a certain magnetic element in the artist's nature, which he exercised towards her, possibly without being conscious of it.

After a little while, the twilight, deepened by the shadows of the fruit-trees and the surrounding buildings, threw an obscurity over the garden.

"There," said Holgrave, "it is time to give over work! That last stroke of the hoe has cut off a beanstalk. Good-night, Miss Phœbe Pyncheon! Any bright day, if you will put one of those rosebuds in your hair, and come to my rooms in Central Street, I will seize the purest ray of sunshine, and make a picture of the flower and its wearer." He retired towards his own solitary gable, but turned his head, on reaching the door, and called to Phœbe, with a tone which certainly had laughter in it, yet which seemed to be more than half in earnest.

"Be careful not to drink at Maule's well!" said he. "Neither drink nor bathe your face in it!"

"Maule's well!" answered Phœbe. "Is that it with the rim of mossy stones? I have no thought of drinking there,—but why not?"

"Oh," rejoined the daguerreotypist, "because, like an old lady's cup of tea, it is water bewitched!"

He vanished; and Phœbe, lingering a moment, saw a glimmering light, and then the steady beam of a lamp, in a chamber of the gable. On returning into Hepzibah's apartment of the house, she found the low-studded parlor so dim and dusky that her eyes could not penetrate the interior. She was indistinctly aware, however, that the gaunt figure of the old gentlewoman was sitting in one of the straight-backed chairs, a little withdrawn from the window, the faint gleam of which showed the blanched paleness of her cheek, turned sideways towards a corner.

"Shall I light a lamp, Cousin Hepzibah?" she asked.

"Do, if you please, my dear child," answered Hepzibah. "But put it on the table in the corner of the passage. My eyes are weak; and I can seldom bear the lamplight on them."

What an instrument is the human voice! How wonderfully responsive to every emotion of the human soul! In Hepzibah's tone, at that moment, there was a certain rich depth and moisture, as if the words, commonplace as they were, had been steeped in the warmth of her heart. Again, while lighting the lamp in the kitchen, Phœbe fancied that her cousin spoke to her.

"In a moment, cousin!" answered the girl. "These matches just glimmer, and go out."

But, instead of a response from Hepzibah, she seemed to hear the murmur of an unknown voice. It was strangely indistinct, however, and less like articulate words than an unshaped sound, such as would be the utterance of feeling and sympathy, rather than of the intellect. So vague was it, that its impression or echo in Phœbe's mind was that of unreality. She concluded that she must have mistaken some other sound for that of the human voice; or else that it was altogether in her fancy.

She set the lighted lamp in the passage, and again entered the parlor. Hepzibah's form, though its sable outline mingled with the dusk, was now less imperfectly visible. In the remoter parts of the room, however, its walls being so ill adapted to reflect light, there was nearly the same obscurity as before.

"Cousin," said Phœbe, "did you speak to me just now?"

"No, child!" replied Hepzibah.

Fewer words than before, but with the same mysterious music in them! Mellow, melancholy, yet not mournful, the tone seemed to gush up out of the deep well of Hepzibah's heart, all steeped in its profoundest emotion. There was a tremor in it, too, that—as all strong feeling is electric—partly communicated itself to Phœbe. The girl sat silently for a moment. But soon, her senses being very acute, she became conscious of an irregular respiration in an obscure corner of the room. Her physical organization, moreover, being at once delicate and healthy, gave her a perception, operating with almost the effect of a spiritual medium, that somebody was near at hand.

"My dear cousin," asked she, overcoming an indefinable reluctance, "is there not some one in the room with us?"

"Phœbe, my dear little girl," said Hepzibah, after a moment's pause, "you were up betimes, and have been busy all day. Pray go to bed; for I am sure you must need rest. I will sit in the parlor awhile, and collect my thoughts. It has been my custom for more years, child, than you have lived!" While thus dismissing her, the maiden lady stept forward, kissed Phœbe, and pressed her to her heart, which beat against the girl's bosom with a strong, high, and tumultuous swell. How came there to be so much love in this desolate old heart, that it could afford to well over thus abundantly?

"Goodnight, cousin," said Phœbe, strangely affected by Hepzibah's manner. "If you begin to love me, I am glad!"

She retired to her chamber, but did not soon fall asleep, nor then very profoundly. At some uncertain period in the depths of night, and, as it were, through the thin veil of a dream, she was conscious of a footstep mounting the stairs heavily, but not with force and decision. The voice of Hepzibah, with a hush through it, was going up along with the footsteps; and, again, responsive to her cousin's voice, Phœbe heard that strange, vague murmur, which might be likened to an indistinct shadow of human utterance.

VII.

The Guest

When Phœbe awoke,—which she did with the early twittering of the conjugal couple of robins in the pear-tree,—she heard movements below stairs, and, hastening down, found Hepzibah already in the kitchen. She stood by a window, holding a book in close contiguity to her nose, as if with the hope of gaining an olfactory acquaintance with its contents, since her imperfect vision made it not very easy to read them. If any volume could have manifested its essential wisdom in the mode suggested, it would certainly have been the one now in Hepzibah's hand; and the kitchen, in such an event, would forthwith have streamed with the fragrance of venison, turkeys, capons, larded partridges, puddings, cakes, and Christmas pies, in all manner of elaborate mixture and concoction. It was a cookery book, full of innumerable old fashions of English dishes, and illustrated with engravings, which represented the arrangements of the table at such banquets as it might have befitted a nobleman to give in the great hall of his castle. And, amid these rich and potent devices of the culinary art (not one of which, probably, had been tested, within the memory of any man's grandfather), poor Hepzibah was seeking for some nimble little titbit, which, with what skill she had, and such materials as were at hand, she might toss up for breakfast.

Soon, with a deep sigh, she put aside the savory volume, and inquired of Phœbe whether old Speckle, as she called one of the hens, had laid an egg the preceding day. Phœbe ran to see, but returned without the expected treasure in her hand. At that instant, however, the blast of a fish-dealer's conch was heard, announcing his approach along the street. With energetic raps at the shop-window, Hepzibah summoned the man in, and made purchase of what he warranted as the finest mackerel in his cart, and as fat a one as ever he felt with his finger so early in the season. Requesting Phœbe to roast some coffee,—which she casually observed was the real Mocha, and so long kept that each of the small berries ought to be worth its weight in gold,—the maiden lady heaped fuel into the vast receptacle of the ancient fireplace in such quantity as soon to drive the lingering dusk out of the kitchen. The country-girl, willing to give her utmost assistance, proposed to make an Indian cake, after her mother's peculiar method, of easy manufacture, and which she could vouch for as possessing a richness, and, if rightly prepared, a delicacy, unequalled by any other mode of breakfast-cake. Hepzibah gladly assenting, the kitchen was soon the scene of savory preparation. Perchance, amid their proper element of smoke, which eddied forth from the ill-constructed chimney, the ghosts of departed cook-maids looked wonderingly on, or peeped down the great breadth of the flue, despising the simplicity of the projected meal, yet ineffectually pining to thrust their shadowy hands into each inchoate dish. The half-starved rats, at any rate, stole visibly out of their hiding-places, and sat on their hind-legs, snuffing the fumy atmosphere, and wistfully awaiting an opportunity to nibble.

    Hepzibah had no natural turn for cookery, and, to say the truth, had fairly incurred her present meagreness by often choosing to go without her dinner rather than be attendant on the rotation of the spit, or ebullition of the pot. Her zeal over the fire, therefore, was quite an heroic test of sentiment. It was touching, and positively worthy of tears (if Phœbe, the only spectator, except the rats and ghosts aforesaid, had not been better employed than in shedding them), to see her rake out a bed of fresh and glowing coals, and proceed to broil the mackerel. Her usually pale cheeks were all ablaze with heat and hurry. She watched the fish with as much tender care and minuteness of attention as if,—we know not how to express it otherwise,—as if her own heart were on the gridiron, and her immortal happiness were involved in its being done precisely to a turn!

    Life, within doors, has few pleasanter prospects than a neatly arranged and well-provisioned breakfast-table. We come to it freshly, in the dewy youth of the day, and when our spiritual and sensual elements are in better accord than at a later period; so that the material delights of the morning meal are capable of being fully enjoyed, without any very grievous reproaches, whether gastric or conscientious, for yielding even a trifle overmuch to the animal department of our nature. The thoughts, too, that run around the ring of familiar guests have a piquancy and mirthfulness, and oftentimes a vivid truth, which more rarely find their way into the elaborate intercourse of dinner. Hepzibah's small and ancient table, supported on its slender and graceful legs, and covered with a cloth of the richest damask, looked worthy to be the scene and centre of one of the cheerfullest of parties. The vapor of the broiled fish arose like incense from the shrine of a barbarian idol, while the fragrance of the Mocha might have gratified the nostrils of a tutelary Lar, or whatever power has scope over a modern breakfast-table. Phœbe's Indian cakes were the sweetest offering of all,—in their hue befitting the rustic altars of the innocent and golden age,— or, so brightly yellow were they, resembling some of the bread which was changed to glistening gold when Midas tried to eat it. The butter must not be forgotten,—butter which Phœbe herself had churned, in her own rural home, and brought it to her cousin as a propitiatory gift,—smelling of clover-blossoms, and diffusing the charm of pastoral scenery through the dark-panelled parlor. All this, with the quaint gorgeousness of the old china cups and saucers, and the crested spoons, and a silver cream-jug (Hepzibah's only other article of plate, and shaped like the rudest porringer), set out a board at which the stateliest of old Colonel Pyncheon's guests need not have scorned to take his place. But the Puritan's face scowled down out of the picture, as if nothing on the table pleased his appetite.

By way of contributing what grace she could, Phœbe gathered some roses and a few other flowers, possessing either scent or beauty, and arranged them in a glass pitcher, which, having long ago lost its handle, was so much the fitter for a flower-vase. The early sunshine—as fresh as that which peeped into Eve's bower while she and Adam sat at breakfast there—came twinkling through the branches of the pear-tree, and fell quite across the table. All was now ready. There were chairs and plates for three. A chair and plate for Hepzibah,—the same for Phœbe,—but what other guest did her cousin look for?

Throughout this preparation there had been a constant tremor in Hepzibah's frame; an agitation so powerful that Phœbe could see the quivering of her gaunt shadow, as thrown by the firelight on the kitchen wall, or by the sunshine on the parlor floor. Its manifestations were so various, and agreed so little with one another, that the girl knew not what to make of it. Sometimes it seemed an ecstasy of delight and happiness. At such moments, Hepzibah would fling out her arms, and infold Phœbe in them, and kiss her cheek as tenderly as ever her mother had; she appeared to do so by an inevitable impulse, and as if her bosom were oppressed with tenderness, of which she must needs pour out a little, in order to gain breathing-room. The next moment, without any visible cause for the change, her unwonted joy shrank back, appalled, as it were, and clothed itself in mourning; or it ran and hid itself, so to speak, in the dungeon of her heart, where it had long lain chained, while a cold, spectral sorrow took the place of the imprisoned joy, that was afraid to be enfranchised,—a sorrow as black as that was bright. She often broke into a little, nervous, hysteric laugh, more touching than any tears could be; and forthwith, as if to try which was the most touching, a gush of tears would follow; or perhaps the laughter and tears came both at once, and surrounded our poor Hepzibah, in a moral sense, with a kind of pale, dim rainbow. Towards Phœbe, as we have said, she was affectionate,—far tenderer than ever before, in their brief acquaintance, except for that one kiss on the preceding night,—yet with a continually recurring pettishness and irritability. She would speak sharply to her; then, throwing aside all the starched reserve of her ordinary manner, ask pardon, and the next instant renew the just-forgiven injury.

At last, when their mutual labor was all finished, she took Phœbe's hand in her own trembling one.

"Bear with me, my dear child," she cried; "for truly my heart is full to the brim! Bear with me; for I love you, Phœbe, though I speak so roughly. Think nothing of it, dearest child! By and by, I shall be kind, and only kind!"

"My dearest cousin, cannot you tell me what has happened?" asked Phœbe, with a sunny and tearful sympathy. "What is it that moves you so?"

"Hush! hush! He is coming!" whispered Hepzibah, hastily wiping her eyes. "Let him see you first, Phœbe; for you are young and rosy, and cannot help letting a smile break out whether or no. He always liked bright faces! And mine is old now, and the tears are hardly dry on it. He never could abide tears. There; draw the curtain a little, so that the shadow may fall across his side of the table! But let there be a good deal of sunshine, too; for he never was fond of gloom, as some people are. He has had but little sunshine in his life, — poor Clifford, — and, oh, what a black shadow. Poor, poor Clifford!"

Thus murmuring in an undertone, as if speaking rather to her own heart than to Phœbe, the old gentlewoman stepped on tiptoe about the room, making such arrangements as suggested themselves at the crisis.

Meanwhile there was a step in the passage-way, above stairs. Phœbe recognized it as the same which had passed upward, as through her dream, in the night-time. The approaching guest, whoever it might be, appeared to pause at the head of the staircase; he paused twice or thrice in the descent; he paused again at the foot. Each time, the delay seemed to be without purpose, but rather from a forgetfulness of the purpose which had set him in motion, or as if the person's feet came involuntarily to a stand-still because the motive-power was too feeble to sustain his progress. Finally, he made a long pause at the threshold of the parlor. He took hold of the knob of the door; then loosened his grasp without opening it. Hepzibah, her hands convulsively clasped, stood gazing at the entrance.

"Dear Cousin Hepzibah, pray don't look so!" said Phœbe, trembling; for her cousin's emotion, and this mysteriously reluctant step, made her feel as if a ghost were coming into the room. "You really frighten me! Is something awful going to happen?"

"Hush!" whispered Hepzibah. "Be cheerful! whatever may happen, be nothing but cheerful!"

The final pause at the threshold proved so long, that Hepzibah, unable to endure the suspense, rushed forward, threw open the door, and led in the stranger by the hand. At the first glance, Phœbe saw an elderly personage, in an old-fashioned dressing-gown of faded damask, and wearing his gray or almost white hair of an unusual length. It quite overshadowed his forehead, except when he thrust it back, and stared vaguely about the room. After a very brief inspection of his face, it was easy to conceive that his footstep must necessarily be such an one as that which, slowly and with as indefinite an aim as a child's first journey across a floor, had just brought him hitherward. Yet there were no tokens that his physical strength might not have sufficed for a free and determined gait. It was the spirit of the man that could not walk. The expression of his countenance—while, notwithstanding it had the light of reason in it—seemed to waver, and glimmer, and nearly to die away, and feebly to recover itself again. It was like a flame which we see twinkling among half-extinguished embers; we gaze at it more intently than if it were a positive blaze, gushing vividly upward,—more intently, but with a certain impatience, as if it ought either to kindle itself into satisfactory splendor, or be at once extinguished.

For an instant after entering the room, the guest stood still, retaining Hepzibah's hand instinctively, as a child does that of the grown person who guides it. He saw Phœbe, however, and caught an illumination from her youthful and pleasant aspect, which, indeed, threw a cheerfulness about the parlor, like the circle of reflected brilliancy around the glass vase of flowers that was standing in the sunshine. He made a salutation, or, to speak nearer the truth, an ill-defined, abortive attempt at curtsy. Imperfect as it was, however, it conveyed an idea, or, at least, gave a hint, of indescribable grace, such as no practised art of external manners could have attained. It was too slight to seize upon at the instant; yet, as recollected afterwards, seemed to transfigure the whole man.

"Dear Clifford," said Hepzibah, in the tone with which one soothes a wayward infant, "this is our cousin Phœbe,—little Phœbe Pyncheon,—Arthur's only child, you know. She has come from the country to stay with us awhile; for our old house has grown to be very lonely now."

"Phœbe—Phœbe Pyncheon?—Phœbe?" repeated the guest, with a strange, sluggish, ill-defined utterance. "Arthur's child! Ah, I forget! No matter. She is very welcome!"

"Come, dear Clifford, take this chair," said Hepzibah, leading him to his place. "Pray, Phœbe, lower the curtain a very little more. Now let us begin breakfast."

The guest seated himself in the place assigned him, and looked strangely around. He was evidently trying to grapple with the present scene, and bring it home to his mind with a more satisfactory distinctness. He desired to be certain, at least, that he was here, in the low-studded, cross-beamed, oaken-panelled parlor, and not in some other spot, which had stereotyped itself into his senses. But the effort was too great to be sustained with more than a fragmentary success.

Continually, as we may express it, he faded away out of his place; or, in other words, his mind and consciousness took their departure, leaving his wasted, gray, and melancholy figure—a substantial emptiness, a material ghost—to occupy his seat at table. Again, after a blank moment, there would be a flickering taper-gleam in his eyeballs. It betokened that his spiritual part had returned, and was doing its best to kindle the heart's household fire, and light up intellectual lamps in the dark and ruinous mansion, where it was doomed to be a forlorn inhabitant.

At one of these moments of less torpid, yet still imperfect animation, Phœbe became convinced of what she had at first rejected as too extravagant and startling an idea. She saw that the person before her must have been the original of the beautiful miniature in her cousin Hepzibah's possession. Indeed, with a feminine eye for costume, she had at once identified the damask dressing-gown, which enveloped him, as the same in figure, material, and fashion, with that so elaborately represented in the picture. This old, faded garment, with all its pristine brilliancy extinct, seemed, in some indescribable way, to translate the wearer's untold misfortune, and make it perceptible to the beholder's eye. It was the better to be discerned, by this exterior type, how worn and old were the soul's more immediate garments; that form and countenance, the beauty and grace of which had almost transcended the skill of the most exquisite of artists. It could the more adequately be known that the soul of the man must have suffered some miserable wrong, from its earthly experience. There he seemed to sit, with a dim veil of decay and ruin betwixt him and the world, but through which, at flitting intervals, might be caught the same expression, so refined, so softly imaginative, which Malbone—venturing a happy touch, with suspended breath—had imparted to the miniature! There had been something so innately characteristic in this look, that all the dusky years, and the burden of unfit calamity which had fallen upon him, did not suffice utterly to destroy it.

Hepzibah had now poured out a cup of deliciously fragrant coffee, and presented it to her guest. As his eyes met hers, he seemed bewildered and disquieted.

"Is this you, Hepzibah?" he murmured sadly; then, more apart, and perhaps unconscious that he was overheard, "How changed! how changed! And is she angry with me? Why does she bend her brow so?"

Poor Hepzibah! It was that wretched scowl which time and her near-sightedness, and the fret of inward discomfort, had rendered so habitual that any vehemence of mood invariably evoked it. But at the indistinct murmur of his words her whole face grew tender, and even lovely, with sorrowful affection; the harshness of her features disappeared, as it were, behind the warm and misty glow.

"Angry!" she repeated; "angry with you, Clifford!"

Her tone, as she uttered the exclamation, had a plaintive and really exquisite melody thrilling through it, yet without subduing a certain something which an obtuse auditor might still have mistaken for asperity. It was as if some transcendent musician should draw a soul-thrilling sweetness out of a cracked instrument, which makes its physical imperfection heard in the midst of ethereal harmony,—so deep was the sensibility that found an organ in Hepzibah's voice!

"There is nothing but love here, Clifford," she added,—"nothing but love! You are at home!"

The guest responded to her tone by a smile, which did not half light up his face. Feeble as it was, however, and gone in a moment, it had a charm of wonderful beauty. It was followed by a coarser expression; or one that had the effect of coarseness on the fine mould and outline of his countenance, because there was nothing intellectual to temper it. It was a look of appetite. He ate food with what might almost be termed voracity; and seemed to forget himself, Hepzibah, the young girl, and everything else around him, in the sensual enjoyment which the bountifully spread table afforded. In his natural system, though high-wrought and delicately refined, a sensibility to the delights of the palate was probably inherent. It would have been kept in check, however, and even converted into an accomplishment, and one of the thousand modes of intellectual culture, had his more ethereal characteristics retained their vigor. But as it existed now, the effect was painful and made Phœbe droop her eyes.

In a little while the guest became sensible of the fragrance of the yet untasted coffee. He quaffed it eagerly. The subtle essence acted on him like a charmed draught, and caused the opaque substance of his animal being to grow transparent, or, at least, translucent; so that a spiritual gleam was transmitted through it, with a clearer lustre than hitherto.

"More, more!" he cried, with nervous haste in his utterance, as if anxious to retain his grasp of what sought to escape him. "This is what I need! Give me more!"

Under this delicate and powerful influence he sat more erect, and looked out from his eyes with a glance that took note of what it rested on. It was not so much that his expression grew more intellectual; this, though it had its share, was not the most peculiar effect. Neither was what we call the moral nature so forcibly awakened as to present itself in remarkable prominence. But a certain fine temper of being was now not brought out in full relief, but changeably and imperfectly betrayed, of which it was the function to deal with all beautiful and enjoyable things. In a character where it should exist as the chief attribute, it would bestow on its possessor an exquisite taste, and an enviable susceptibility of happiness. Beauty would be his life; his aspirations would all tend toward it; and, allowing his frame and physical organs to be in consonance, his own developments would likewise be beautiful. Such a man should have nothing to do with sorrow; nothing with strife; nothing with the martyrdom which, in an infinite variety of shapes, awaits those who have the heart, and will, and conscience, to fight a battle with the world. To these heroic tempers, such martyrdom is the richest meed in the world's gift. To the individual before us, it could only be a grief, intense in due proportion with the severity of the infliction. He had no right to be a martyr; and, beholding him so fit to be happy and so feeble for all other purposes, a generous, strong, and noble spirit would, methinks, have been ready to sacrifice what little enjoyment it might have planned for itself,—it would have flung down the hopes, so paltry in its regard,—if thereby the wintry blasts of our rude sphere might come tempered to such a man.

Not to speak it harshly or scornfully, it seemed Clifford's nature to be a Sybarite. It was perceptible, even there, in the dark old parlor, in the inevitable polarity with which his eyes were attracted towards the quivering play of sunbeams through the shadowy foliage. It was seen in his appreciating notice of the vase of flowers, the scent of which he inhaled with a zest almost peculiar to a physical organization so refined that spiritual ingredients are moulded in with it. It was betrayed in the unconscious smile with which he regarded Phœbe, whose fresh and maidenly figure was both sunshine and flowers,—their essence, in a prettier and more agreeable mode of manifestation. Not less evident was this love and necessity for the Beautiful, in the instinctive caution with which, even so soon, his eyes turned away from his hostess, and wandered to any quarter rather than come back. It was Hepzibah's misfortune,—not Clifford's fault. How could he,—so yellow as she was, so wrinkled, so sad of mien, with that odd uncouthness of a turban on her head, and that most perverse of scowls contorting her brow,—how could he love to gaze at her? But, did he owe her no affection for so much as she had silently given? He owed her nothing. A nature like Clifford's can contract no debts of that kind. It is—we say it without censure, nor in diminution of the claim which it indefeasibly possesses on beings of another mould—it is always selfish in its essence; and we must give it leave to be so, and heap up our heroic and disinterested love upon it so much the more, without a recompense. Poor Hepzibah knew this truth, or, at least, acted on the instinct of it. So long estranged from what was lovely as Clifford had been, she rejoiced—rejoiced, though with a present sigh, and a secret purpose to shed tears in her own chamber that he had brighter objects now before his eyes than her aged and uncomely features. They never possessed a charm; and if they had, the canker of her grief for him would long since have destroyed it.

The guest leaned back in his chair. Mingled in his countenance with a dreamy delight, there was a troubled look of effort and unrest. He was seeking to make himself more fully sensible of the scene around him; or, perhaps, dreading it to be a dream, or a play of imagination, was vexing the fair moment with a struggle for some added brilliancy and more durable illusion.

"How pleasant!—How delightful!" he murmured, but not as if addressing any one. "Will it last? How balmy the atmosphere through that open window! An open window! How beautiful that play of sunshine! Those flowers, how very fragrant! That young girl's face, how cheerful, how blooming!—a flower with the dew on it, and sunbeams in the dew-drops! Ah! this must be all a dream! A dream! A dream! But it has quite hidden the four stone walls!"

Then his face darkened, as if the shadow of a cavern or a dungeon had come over it; there was no more light in its expression than might have come through the iron grates of a prison-window—still lessening, too, as if he were sinking farther into the depths. Phœbe (being of that quickness and activity of temperament that she seldom long refrained from taking a part, and generally a good one, in what was going forward) now felt herself moved to address the stranger.

"Here is a new kind of rose, which I found this morning in the garden," said she, choosing a small crimson one from among the flowers in the vase. "There will be but five or six on the bush this season. This is the most perfect of them all; not a speck of blight or mildew in it. And how sweet it is!—sweet like no other rose! One can never forget that scent!"

"Ah!—let me see!—let me hold it!" cried the guest, eagerly seizing the flower, which, by the spell peculiar to remembered odors, brought innumerable associations along with the fragrance that it exhaled. "Thank you! This has done me good. I remember how I used to prize this flower,—long ago, I suppose, very long ago!—or was it only yesterday? It makes me feel young again! Am I young? Either this remembrance is singularly distinct, or this consciousness strangely dim! But how kind of the fair young girl! Thank you! Thank you!"

The favorable excitement derived from this little crimson rose afforded Clifford the brightest moment which he enjoyed at the breakfast-table. It might have lasted longer, but that his eyes happened, soon afterwards, to rest on the face of the old Puritan, who, out of his dingy frame and lustreless canvas, was looking down on the scene like a ghost, and a most ill-tempered and ungenial one. The guest made an impatient gesture of the hand, and addressed Hepzibah with what might easily be recognized as the licensed irritability of a petted member of the family.

"Hepzibah! — Hepzibah!" cried he with no little force and distinctness, "why do you keep that odious picture on the wall? Yes, yes! — that is precisely your taste! I have told you, a thousand times, that it was the evil genius of the house! — my evil genius particularly! Take it down, at once!"

"Dear Clifford," said Hepzibah sadly, "you know it cannot be!"

"Then, at all events," continued he, still speaking with some energy, "pray cover it with a crimson curtain, broad enough to hang in folds, and with a golden border and tassels. I cannot bear it! It must not stare me in the face!"

"Yes, dear Clifford, the picture shall be covered," said Hepzibah soothingly. "There is a crimson curtain in a trunk above stairs, — a little faded and moth-eaten, I'm afraid, — but Phœbe and I will do wonders with it."

"This very day, remember" said he; and then added, in a low, self-communing voice, "Why should we live in this dismal house at all? Why not go to the South of France? — to Italy? — Paris, Naples, Venice, Rome? Hepzibah will say we have not the means. A droll idea that!"

He smiled to himself, and threw a glance of fine sarcastic meaning towards Hepzibah.

But the several moods of feeling, faintly as they were marked, through which he had passed, occurring in so brief an interval of time, had evidently wearied the stranger. He was probably accustomed to a sad monotony of life, not so much flowing in a stream, however sluggish, as stagnating in a pool around his feet. A slumberous veil diffused itself over his countenance, and had an effect, morally speaking, on its naturally delicate and elegant outline, like that which a brooding mist, with no sunshine in it, throws over the features of a landscape. He appeared to become grosser, — almost cloddish. If aught of interest or beauty — even ruined beauty — had heretofore been visible in this man, the beholder might now begin to doubt it, and to accuse his own imagination of deluding him with whatever grace had flickered over that visage, and whatever exquisite lustre had gleamed in those filmy eyes.

Before he had quite sunken away, however, the sharp and peevish tinkle of the shop-bell made itself audible. Striking most disagreeably on Clifford's auditory organs and the characteristic sensibility of his nerves, it caused him to start upright out of his chair.

"Good heavens, Hepzibah! what horrible disturbance have we now in the house?" cried he, wreaking his resentful impatience — as a matter of course, and a custom of old — on the one person in the world that loved him. "I have never heard such a hateful clamor! Why do you permit it? In the name of all dissonance, what can it be?"

It was very remarkable into what prominent relief — even as if a dim picture should leap suddenly from its canvas — Clifford's character was thrown by this apparently trifling annoyance. The secret was, that an individual of his temper can always be pricked more acutely through his sense of the beautiful and harmonious than through his heart. It is even possible — for similar cases have often happened — that if Clifford, in his foregoing life, had enjoyed the means of cultivating his taste to its utmost perfectibility, that subtle attribute might, before this period, have completely eaten out or filed away his affections. Shall we venture to pronounce, therefore, that his long and black calamity may not have had a redeeming drop of mercy at the bottom?

"Dear Clifford, I wish I could keep the sound from your ears," said Hepzibah, patiently, but reddening with a painful suffusion of shame. "It is very disagreeable even to me. But, do you know, Clifford, I have something to tell you? This ugly noise, — pray run, Phœbe, and see who is there! — this naughty little tinkle is nothing but our shop-bell!"

"Shop-bell!" repeated Clifford, with a bewildered stare.

"Yes, our shop-bell," said Hepzibah, a certain natural dignity, mingled with deep emotion, now asserting itself in her manner. "For you must know, dearest Clifford, that we are very poor. And there was no other resource, but either to accept assistance from a hand that I would push aside (and so would you!) were it to offer bread when we were dying for it, — no help, save from him, or else to earn our subsistence with my own hands! Alone, I might have been content to starve. But you were to be given back to me! Do you think, then, dear Clifford," added she, with a wretched smile, "that I have brought an irretrievable disgrace on the old house, by opening a little shop in the front gable? Our great-great-grandfather did the same, when there was far less need! Are you ashamed of me?"

The House of the Seven Gables

"Shame! Disgrace! Do you speak these words to me, Hepzibah?" said Clifford,—not angrily, however; for when a man's spirit has been thoroughly crushed, he may be peevish at small offences, but never resentful of great ones. So he spoke with only a grieved emotion. "It was not kind to say so, Hepzibah! What shame can befall me now?"

And then the unnerved man—he that had been born for enjoyment, but had met a doom so very wretched—burst into a woman's passion of tears. It was but of brief continuance, however; soon leaving him in a quiescent, and, to judge by his countenance, not an uncomfortable state. From this mood, too, he partially rallied for an instant, and looked at Hepzibah with a smile, the keen, half-derisory purport of which was a puzzle to her.

"Are we so very poor, Hepzibah?" said he.

Finally, his chair being deep and softly cushioned, Clifford fell asleep. Hearing the more regular rise and fall of his breath (which, however, even then, instead of being strong and full, had a feeble kind of tremor, corresponding with the lack of vigor in his character),—hearing these tokens of settled slumber, Hepzibah seized the opportunity to peruse his face more attentively than she had yet dared to do. Her heart melted away in tears; her profoundest spirit sent forth a moaning voice, low, gentle, but inexpressibly sad. In this depth of grief and pity she felt that there was no irreverence in gazing at his altered, aged, faded, ruined face. But no sooner was she a little relieved than her conscience smote her for gazing curiously at him, now that he was so changed; and, turning hastily away, Hepzibah let down the curtain over the sunny window, and left Clifford to slumber there.

VIII.
The Pyncheon of To-day

Phœbe, on entering the shop, beheld there the already familiar face of the little devourer—if we can reckon his mighty deeds aright—of Jim Crow, the elephant, the camel, the dromedaries, and the locomotive. Having expended his private fortune, on the two preceding days, in the purchase of the above unheard-of luxuries, the young gentleman's present errand was on the part of his mother, in quest of three eggs and half a pound of raisins. These articles Phœbe accordingly supplied, and, as a mark of gratitude for his previous patronage, and a slight super-added morsel after breakfast, put likewise into his hand a whale! The great fish, reversing his experience with the prophet of Nineveh, immediately began his progress down the same red pathway of fate whither so varied a caravan had preceded him. This remarkable urchin, in truth, was the very emblem of old Father Time, both in respect of his all-devouring appetite for men and things, and because he, as well as Time, after ingulfing thus much of creation, looked almost as youthful as if he had been just that moment made.

After partly closing the door, the child turned back, and mumbled something to Phœbe, which, as the whale was but half disposed of, she could not perfectly understand.

"What did you say, my little fellow?" asked she.

"Mother wants to know" repeated Ned Higgins more distinctly, "how Old Maid Pyncheon's brother does? Folks say he has got home."

"My cousin Hepzibah's brother?" exclaimed Phœbe, surprised at this sudden explanation of the relationship between Hepzibah and her guest. "Her brother! And where can he have been?"

The little boy only put his thumb to his broad snub-nose, with that look of shrewdness which a child, spending much of his time in the street, so soon learns to throw over his features, however unintelligent in themselves. Then as Phœbe continued to gaze at him, without answering his mother's message, he took his departure.

As the child went down the steps, a gentleman ascended them, and made his entrance into the shop. It was the portly, and, had it possessed the advantage of a little more height, would have been the stately figure of a man considerably in the decline of life, dressed in a black suit of some thin stuff, resembling broadcloth as closely as possible. A gold-headed cane, of rare Oriental wood, added materially to the high respectability of his aspect, as did also a neckcloth of the utmost snowy purity, and the conscientious polish of his boots. His dark, square countenance, with its almost shaggy depth of eyebrows, was naturally impressive, and would, perhaps, have been rather stern, had not the gentleman considerately taken upon himself to mitigate the harsh effect by a look of exceeding good-humor and benevolence. Owing, however, to a somewhat massive accumulation of animal substance about the lower region of his face, the look was, perhaps, unctuous rather than spiritual, and had, so to speak, a kind of fleshly effulgence, not altogether so satisfactory as he doubtless intended it to be. A susceptible observer, at any rate, might have regarded it as affording very little evidence of the general benignity of soul whereof it purported to be the outward reflection. And if the observer chanced to be ill-natured, as well as acute and susceptible, he would probably suspect that the smile on the gentleman's face was a good deal akin to the shine on his boots, and that each must have cost him and his boot-black, respectively, a good deal of hard labor to bring out and preserve them.

As the stranger entered the little shop, where the projection of the second story and the thick foliage of the elm-tree, as well as the commodities at the window, created a sort of gray medium, his smile grew as intense as if he had set his heart on counteracting the whole gloom of the atmosphere (besides any moral gloom pertaining to Hepzibah and her inmates) by the unassisted light of his countenance. On perceiving a young rose-bud of a girl, instead of the gaunt presence of the old maid, a look of surprise was manifest. He at first knit his brows; then smiled with more unctuous benignity than ever.

"Ah, I see how it is!" said he in a deep voice,—a voice which, had it come from the throat of an uncultivated man, would have been gruff, but, by dint of careful training, was now sufficiently agreeable,—"I was not aware that Miss Hepzibah Pyncheon had commenced business under such favorable auspices. You are her assistant, I suppose?"

"I certainly am," answered Phœbe, and added, with a little air of lady-like assumption (for, civil as the gentleman was, he evidently took her to be a young person serving for wages), "I am a cousin of Miss Hepzibah, on a visit to her."

"Her cousin?—and from the country? Pray pardon me, then," said the gentleman, bowing and smiling, as Phœbe never had been bowed to nor smiled on before; "in that case, we must be better acquainted; for, unless I am sadly mistaken, you are my own little kinswoman likewise! Let me see,—Mary?—Dolly? —Phœbe?—yes, Phœbe is the name! Is it possible that you are Phœbe Pyncheon, only child of my dear cousin and classmate,

The House of the Seven Gables

Arthur? Ah, I see your father now, about your mouth! Yes, yes! we must be better acquainted! I am your kinsman, my dear. Surely you must have heard of Judge Pyncheon?"

As Phœbe curtsied in reply, the Judge bent forward, with the pardonable and even praiseworthy purpose—considering the nearness of blood and the difference of age—of bestowing on his young relative a kiss of acknowledged kindred and natural affection. Unfortunately (without design, or only with such instinctive design as gives no account of itself to the intellect) Phœbe, just at the critical moment, drew back; so that her highly respectable kinsman, with his body bent over the counter and his lips protruded, was betrayed into the rather absurd predicament of kissing the empty air. It was a modern parallel to the case of Ixion embracing a cloud, and was so much the more ridiculous as the Judge prided himself on eschewing all airy matter, and never mistaking a shadow for a substance. The truth was,—and it is Phœbe's only excuse,—that, although Judge Pyncheon's glowing benignity might not be absolutely unpleasant to the feminine beholder, with the width of a street, or even an ordinary-sized room, interposed between, yet it became quite too intense, when this dark, full-fed physiognomy (so roughly bearded, too, that no razor could ever make it smooth) sought to bring itself into actual contact with the object of its regards. The man, the sex, somehow or other, was entirely too prominent in the Judge's demonstrations of that sort. Phœbe's eyes sank, and, without knowing why, she felt herself blushing deeply under his look. Yet she had been kissed before, and without any particular squeamishness, by perhaps half a dozen different cousins, younger as well as older than this dark-browned, grisly-bearded, white-neck-clothed, and unctuously-benevolent Judge! Then, why not by him?

On raising her eyes, Phœbe was startled by the change in Judge Pyncheon's face. It was quite as striking, allowing for the difference of scale, as that betwixt a landscape under a broad sunshine and just before a thunder-storm; not that it had the passionate intensity of the latter aspect, but was cold, hard, immitigable, like a day-long brooding cloud.

"Dear me! what is to be done now?" thought the country-girl to herself. "He looks as if there were nothing softer in him than a rock, nor milder than the east wind! I meant no harm! Since he is really my cousin, I would have let him kiss me, if I could!"

Then, all at once, it struck Phœbe that this very Judge Pyncheon was the original of the miniature which the daguerreotypist had shown her in the garden, and that the hard, stern, relentless look, now on his face, was the same that the sun had so inflexibly persisted in bringing out. Was it, therefore, no momentary mood, but, however skilfully concealed, the settled temper of his life? And not merely so, but was it hereditary in him, and transmitted down, as a precious heirloom, from that bearded ancestor, in whose picture both the expression and, to a singular degree, the features of the modern Judge were shown as by a kind of prophecy? A deeper philosopher than Phœbe might have found something very terrible in this idea. It implied that the weaknesses and defects, the bad passions, the mean tendencies, and the moral diseases which lead to crime are handed down from one generation to another, by a far surer process of transmission than human law has been able to establish in respect to the riches and honors which it seeks to entail upon posterity.

But, as it happened, scarcely had Phœbe's eyes rested again on the Judge's countenance than all its ugly sternness vanished; and she found herself quite overpowered by the sultry, dog-day heat, as it were, of benevolence, which this excellent man diffused out of his great heart into the surrounding atmosphere, — very much like a serpent, which, as a preliminary to fascination, is said to fill the air with his peculiar odor.

"I like that, Cousin Phœbe!" cried he, with an emphatic nod of approbation. "I like it much, my little cousin! You are a good child, and know how to take care of yourself. A young girl — especially if she be a very pretty one — can never be too chary of her lips."

"Indeed, sir," said Phœbe, trying to laugh the matter off, "I did not mean to be unkind."

Nevertheless, whether or no it were entirely owing to the inauspicious commencement of their acquaintance, she still acted under a certain reserve, which was by no means customary to her frank and genial nature. The fantasy would not quit her, that the original Puritan, of whom she had heard so many sombre traditions, — the progenitor of the whole race of New England Pyncheons, the founder of the House of the Seven Gables, and who had died so strangely in it, — had now stepped into the shop. In these days of off-hand equipment, the matter was easily enough arranged. On his arrival from the other world, he had merely found it necessary to spend a quarter of an hour at a barber's, who had trimmed down the Puritan's full beard into a pair of grizzled whiskers, then, patronizing a ready-made clothing establishment, he had exchanged his velvet doublet and sable cloak, with the richly worked band under his chin, for a white collar and cravat, coat, vest, and pantaloons; and lastly, putting aside his steel-hilted broadsword to take up a gold-headed cane, the Colonel Pyncheon of two centuries ago steps forward as the Judge of the passing moment!

Of course, Phœbe was far too sensible a girl to entertain this idea in any other way than as matter for a smile. Possibly, also, could the two personages have stood together before her eye, many points of difference would have been perceptible, and perhaps only a general resemblance. The long lapse of intervening years, in a climate so unlike that which had fostered the ancestral Englishman, must inevitably have wrought important changes in the physical system of his descendant. The Judge's volume of muscle could hardly be the same as the Colonel's; there was undoubtedly less beef in him. Though looked upon as a weighty man among his contemporaries in respect of animal substance, and as favored with a remarkable degree of fundamental development, well adapting him for the judicial bench, we conceive that the modern Judge Pyncheon, if weighed in the same balance with his ancestor, would have required at least an old-fashioned fifty-six to keep the scale in equilibrio. Then the Judge's face had lost the ruddy English hue that showed its warmth through all the duskiness of the Colonel's weather-beaten cheek, and had taken a sallow shade, the established complexion of his countrymen. If we mistake not, moreover, a certain quality of nervousness had become more or less manifest, even in so solid a specimen of Puritan descent as the gentleman now under discussion. As one of its effects, it bestowed on his countenance a quicker mobility than the old Englishman's had possessed, and keener vivacity, but at the expense of a sturdier something, on which these acute endowments seemed to act like dissolving acids. This process, for aught we know, may belong to the great system of human progress, which, with every ascending footstep, as it diminishes the necessity for animal force, may be destined gradually to spiritualize us, by refining away our grosser attributes of body. If so, Judge Pyncheon could endure a century or two more of such refinement as well as most other men.

The similarity, intellectual and moral, between the Judge and his ancestor appears to have been at least as strong as the resemblance of mien and feature would afford reason to anticipate. In old Colonel Pyncheon's funeral discourse the clergyman absolutely canonized his deceased parishioner, and opening, as it were, a vista through the roof of the church, and thence through the firmament above, showed him seated, harp in hand, among the crowned choristers of the spiritual world. On his tombstone, too, the record is highly eulogistic; nor does history, so far as he holds a place upon its page, assail the consistency and uprightness of his character. So also, as regards the Judge Pyncheon of to-day, neither clergyman, nor legal critic, nor inscriber of tombstones, nor historian of general or local politics, would venture a word against this eminent person's sincerity as a Christian, or respectability as a man, or integrity as a judge, or courage and faithfulness as the often-tried representative of his political party. But, besides these cold, formal, and empty words of the chisel that inscribes, the voice that speaks, and the pen that writes, for the public eye and for distant time,—and which inevitably lose much of their truth and freedom by the fatal consciousness of so doing,—there were traditions about the ancestor, and private diurnal gossip about the Judge, remarkably accordant in their testimony. It is often instructive to take the woman's, the private and domestic, view of a public man; nor can anything be more curious than the vast discrepancy between portraits intended for engraving and the pencil-sketches that pass from hand to hand behind the original's back.

For example: tradition affirmed that the Puritan had been greedy of wealth; the Judge, too, with all the show of liberal expenditure, was said to be as close-fisted as if his gripe were of iron. The ancestor had clothed himself in a grim assumption of kindliness, a rough heartiness of word and manner, which most people took to be the genuine warmth of nature, making its way through the thick and inflexible hide of a manly character. His descendant, in compliance with the requirements of a nicer age, had etherealized this rude benevolence into that broad benignity of smile wherewith he shone like a noonday sun along the streets, or glowed like a household fire in the drawing-rooms of his private acquaintance. The Puritan—if not belied by some singular stories, murmured, even at this day, under the narrator's breath—had fallen into certain transgressions to which men of his great animal development, whatever their faith or principles, must continue liable, until they put off impurity, along with the gross earthly substance that involves it. We must not stain our page with any contemporary scandal, to a similar purport, that may have been whispered against the Judge. The Puritan, again, an autocrat in his own household, had worn out three wives, and, merely by the remorseless weight and hardness of his character in the conjugal relation, had sent them, one after another, broken-hearted, to their graves. Here the parallel, in some sort, fails. The Judge had wedded but a single wife, and lost her in the third or fourth year of their marriage. There was a fable, however,—for such we choose to consider it, though, not impossibly, typical of Judge Pyncheon's marital deportment,—that the lady got her death-blow in the honeymoon, and never smiled again, because her husband compelled her to serve him with coffee every morning at his bedside, in token of fealty to her liege-lord and master.

But it is too fruitful a subject, this of hereditary resemblances,—the frequent recurrence of which, in a direct line, is truly unaccountable, when we consider how large an accumulation of ancestry lies behind every man at the distance of one or two centuries. We shall only add, therefore, that the Puritan—so, at least, says chimney-corner tradition, which often preserves traits of character with marvellous fidelity—was bold, imperious, relentless, crafty; laying his purposes deep, and following them out with an inveteracy of pursuit that knew neither rest nor conscience; trampling on the weak, and, when

The House of the Seven Gables

essential to his ends, doing his utmost to beat down the strong. Whether the Judge in any degree resembled him, the further progress of our narrative may show.

Scarcely any of the items in the above-drawn parallel occurred to Phœbe, whose country birth and residence, in truth, had left her pitifully ignorant of most of the family traditions, which lingered, like cobwebs and incrustations of smoke, about the rooms and chimney-corners of the House of the Seven Gables. Yet there was a circumstance, very trifling in itself, which impressed her with an odd degree of horror. She had heard of the anathema flung by Maule, the executed wizard, against Colonel Pyncheon and his posterity,—that God would give them blood to drink,—and likewise of the popular notion, that this miraculous blood might now and then be heard gurgling in their throats. The latter scandal—as became a person of sense, and, more especially, a member of the Pyncheon family—Phœbe had set down for the absurdity which it unquestionably was. But ancient superstitions, after being steeped in human hearts and embodied in human breath, and passing from lip to ear in manifold repetition, through a series of generations, become imbued with an effect of homely truth. The smoke of the domestic hearth has scented them through and through. By long transmission among household facts, they grow to look like them, and have such a familiar way of making themselves at home that their influence is usually greater than we suspect. Thus it happened, that when Phœbe heard a certain noise in Judge Pyncheon's throat,—rather habitual with him, not altogether voluntary, yet indicative of nothing, unless it were a slight bronchial complaint, or, as some people hinted, an apoplectic symptom,—when the girl heard this queer and awkward ingurgitation (which the writer never did hear, and therefore cannot describe), she very foolishly started, and clasped her hands.

Of course, it was exceedingly ridiculous in Phœbe to be discomposed by such a trifle, and still more unpardonable to show her discomposure to the individual most concerned in it. But the incident chimed in so oddly with her previous fancies about the Colonel and the Judge, that, for the moment, it seemed quite to mingle their identity.

"What is the matter with you, young woman?" said Judge Pyncheon, giving her one of his harsh looks. "Are you afraid of anything?"

"Oh, nothing, sir—nothing in the world!" answered Phœbe, with a little laugh of vexation at herself. "But perhaps you wish to speak with my cousin Hepzibah. Shall I call her?"

"Stay a moment, if you please," said the Judge, again beaming sunshine out of his face. "You seem to be a little nervous this morning. The town air, Cousin Phœbe, does not agree with your good, wholesome country habits. Or has anything happened to disturb you?—anything remarkable in Cousin Hepzibah's family?— An arrival, eh? I thought so! No wonder you are out of sorts, my little cousin. To be an inmate with such a guest may well startle an innocent young girl!"

"You quite puzzle me, sir," replied Phœbe, gazing inquiringly at the Judge. "There is no frightful guest in the house, but only a poor, gentle, childlike man, whom I believe to be Cousin Hepzibah's brother. I am afraid (but you, sir, will know better than I) that he is not quite in his sound senses; but so mild and quiet he seems to be, that a mother might trust her baby with him; and I think he would play with the baby as if he were only a few years older than itself. He startle me!—Oh, no indeed!"

"I rejoice to hear so favorable and so ingenuous an account of my cousin Clifford," said the benevolent Judge. "Many years ago, when we were boys and young men together, I had a great affection for him, and still feel a tender interest in all his concerns. You say, Cousin Phœbe, he appears to be weak minded. Heaven grant him at least enough of intellect to repent of his past sins!"

"Nobody, I fancy," observed Phœbe, "can have fewer to repent of."

"And is it possible, my dear," rejoined the Judge, with a commiserating look, "that you have never heard of Clifford Pyncheon?—that you know nothing of his history? Well, it is all right; and your mother has shown a very proper regard for the good name of the family with which she connected herself. Believe the best you can of this unfortunate person, and hope the best! It is a rule which Christians should always follow, in their judgments of one another; and especially is it right and wise among near relatives, whose characters have necessarily a degree of mutual dependence. But is Clifford in the parlor? I will just step in and see."

"Perhaps, sir, I had better call my cousin Hepzibah," said Phœbe; hardly knowing, however, whether she ought to obstruct the entrance of so affectionate a kinsman into the private regions of the house. "Her brother seemed to be just falling asleep after breakfast; and I am sure she would not like him to be disturbed. Pray, sir, let me give her notice!"

But the Judge showed a singular determination to enter unannounced; and as Phœbe, with the vivacity of a person whose movements unconsciously answer to her thoughts, had stepped towards the door, he used little or no ceremony in putting her aside.

The House of the Seven Gables

"No, no, Miss Phœbe!" said Judge Pyncheon in a voice as deep as a thunder-growl, and with a frown as black as the cloud whence it issues. "Stay you here! I know the house, and know my cousin Hepzibah, and know her brother Clifford likewise. — nor need my little country cousin put herself to the trouble of announcing me!" — in these latter words, by the bye, there were symptoms of a change from his sudden harshness into his previous benignity of manner. "I am at home here, Phœbe, you must recollect, and you are the stranger. I will just step in, therefore, and see for myself how Clifford is, and assure him and Hepzibah of my kindly feelings and best wishes. It is right, at this juncture, that they should both hear from my own lips how much I desire to serve them. Ha! here is Hepzibah herself!"

Such was the case. The vibrations of the Judge's voice had reached the old gentlewoman in the parlor, where she sat, with face averted, waiting on her brother's slumber. She now issued forth, as would appear, to defend the entrance, looking, we must needs say, amazingly like the dragon which, in fairy tales, is wont to be the guardian over an enchanted beauty. The habitual scowl of her brow was undeniably too fierce, at this moment, to pass itself off on the innocent score of near-sightedness; and it was bent on Judge Pyncheon in a way that seemed to confound, if not alarm him, so inadequately had he estimated the moral force of a deeply grounded antipathy. She made a repelling gesture with her hand, and stood a perfect picture of prohibition, at full length, in the dark frame of the doorway. But we must betray Hepzibah's secret, and confess that the native timorousness of her character even now developed itself in a quick tremor, which, to her own perception, set each of her joints at variance with its fellows.

Possibly, the Judge was aware how little true hardihood lay behind Hepzibah's formidable front. At any rate, being a gentleman of steady nerves, he soon recovered himself, and failed not to approach his cousin with outstretched hand; adopting the sensible precaution, however, to cover his advance with a smile, so broad and sultry, that, had it been only half as warm as it looked, a trellis of grapes might at once have turned purple under its summer-like exposure. It may have been his purpose, indeed, to melt poor Hepzibah on the spot, as if she were a figure of yellow wax.

"Hepzibah, my beloved cousin, I am rejoiced!" exclaimed the Judge most emphatically. "Now, at length, you have something to live for. Yes, and all of us, let me say, your friends and kindred, have more to live for than we had yesterday. I have lost no time in hastening to offer any assistance in my power towards making Clifford comfortable. He belongs to us all. I know how much he requires, — how much he used to require, — with his delicate taste, and his love of the beautiful. Anything in my house, — pictures, books, wine, luxuries of the table,—he may command them all! It would afford me most heartfelt gratification to see him! Shall I step in, this moment?"

"No," replied Hepzibah, her voice quivering too painfully to allow of many words. "He cannot see visitors!"

"A visitor, my dear cousin!—do you call me so?" cried the Judge, whose sensibility, it seems, was hurt by the coldness of the phrase. "Nay, then, let me be Clifford's host, and your own likewise. Come at once to my house. The country air, and all the conveniences,—I may say luxuries,—that I have gathered about me, will do wonders for him. And you and I, dear Hepzibah, will consult together, and watch together, and labor together, to make our dear Clifford happy. Come! why should we make more words about what is both a duty and a pleasure on my part? Come to me at once!"

On hearing these so hospitable offers, and such generous recognition of the claims of kindred, Phœbe felt very much in the mood of running up to Judge Pyncheon, and giving him, of her own accord, the kiss from which she had so recently shrunk away. It was quite otherwise with Hepzibah; the Judge's smile seemed to operate on her acerbity of heart like sunshine upon vinegar, making it ten times sourer than ever.

"Clifford," said she,—still too agitated to utter more than an abrupt sentence,—"Clifford has a home here!"

"May Heaven forgive you, Hepzibah," said Judge Pyncheon, —reverently lifting his eyes towards that high court of equity to which he appealed,—"if you suffer any ancient prejudice or animosity to weigh with you in this matter. I stand here with an open heart, willing and anxious to receive yourself and Clifford into it. Do not refuse my good offices,—my earnest propositions for your welfare! They are such, in all respects, as it behooves your nearest kinsman to make. It will be a heavy responsibility, cousin, if you confine your brother to this dismal house and stifled air, when the delightful freedom of my country-seat is at his command."

"It would never suit Clifford," said Hepzibah, as briefly as before.

"Woman!" broke forth the Judge, giving way to his resentment, "what is the meaning of all this? Have you other resources? Nay, I suspected as much! Take care, Hepzibah, take care! Clifford is on the brink of as black a ruin as ever befell him yet! But why do I talk with you, woman as you are? Make way! —I must see Clifford!"

Hepzibah spread out her gaunt figure across the door, and

The House of the Seven Gables

seemed really to increase in bulk; looking the more terrible, also, because there was so much terror and agitation in her heart. But Judge Pyncheon's evident purpose of forcing a passage was interrupted by a voice from the inner room; a weak, tremulous, wailing voice, indicating helpless alarm, with no more energy for self-defence than belongs to a frightened infant.

"Hepzibah, Hepzibah!" cried the voice; "go down on your knees to him! Kiss his feet! Entreat him not to come in! Oh, let him have mercy on me! Mercy! mercy!"

For the instant, it appeared doubtful whether it were not the Judge's resolute purpose to set Hepzibah aside, and step across the threshold into the parlor, whence issued that broken and miserable murmur of entreaty. It was not pity that restrained him, for, at the first sound of the enfeebled voice, a red fire kindled in his eyes, and he made a quick pace forward, with something inexpressibly fierce and grim darkening forth, as it were, out of the whole man. To know Judge Pyncheon was to see him at that moment. After such a revelation, let him smile with what sultriness he would, he could much sooner turn grapes purple, or pumpkins yellow, than melt the iron-branded impression out of the beholder's memory. And it rendered his aspect not the less, but more frightful, that it seemed not to express wrath or hatred, but a certain hot fellness of purpose, which annihilated everything but itself.

Yet, after all, are we not slandering an excellent and amiable man? Look at the Judge now! He is apparently conscious of having erred, in too energetically pressing his deeds of loving-kindness on persons unable to appreciate them. He will await their better mood, and hold himself as ready to assist them then as at this moment. As he draws back from the door, an all-comprehensive benignity blazes from his visage, indicating that he gathers Hepzibah, little Phœbe, and the invisible Clifford, all three, together with the whole world besides, into his immense heart, and gives them a warm bath in its flood of affection.

"You do me great wrong, dear Cousin Hepzibah!" said he, first kindly offering her his hand, and then drawing on his glove preparatory to departure. "Very great wrong! But I forgive it, and will study to make you think better of me. Of course, our poor Clifford being in so unhappy a state of mind, I cannot think of urging an interview at present. But I shall watch over his welfare as if he were my own beloved brother; nor do I at all despair, my dear cousin, of constraining both him and you to acknowledge your injustice. When that shall happen, I desire no other revenge than your acceptance of the best offices in my power to do you."

With a bow to Hepzibah, and a degree of paternal benevolence in his parting nod to Phœbe, the Judge left the shop, and went smiling along the street. As is customary with the rich, when they aim at the honors of a republic, he apologized, as it were, to the people, for his wealth, prosperity, and elevated station, by a free and hearty manner towards those who knew him; putting off the more of his dignity in due proportion with the humbleness of the man whom he saluted, and thereby proving a haughty consciousness of his advantages as irrefragably as if he had marched forth preceded by a troop of lackeys to clear the way. On this particular forenoon, so excessive was the warmth of Judge Pyncheon's kindly aspect, that (such, at least, was the rumor about town) an extra passage of the water-carts was found essential, in order to lay the dust occasioned by so much extra sunshine!

No sooner had he disappeared than Hepzibah grew deadly white, and, staggering towards Phœbe, let her head fall on the young girl's shoulder.

"O Phœbe!" murmured she, "that man has been the horror of my life! Shall I never, never have the courage, — will my voice never cease from trembling long enough to let me tell him what he is?"

"Is he so very wicked?" asked Phœbe. "Yet his offers were surely kind!"

"Do not speak of them, — he has a heart of iron!" rejoined Hepzibah. "Go, now, and talk to Clifford! Amuse and keep him quiet! It would disturb him wretchedly to see me so agitated as I am. There, go, dear child, and I will try to look after the shop."

Phœbe went accordingly, but perplexed herself, meanwhile, with queries as to the purport of the scene which she had just witnessed, and also whether judges, clergymen, and other characters of that eminent stamp and respectability, could really, in any single instance, be otherwise than just and upright men. A doubt of this nature has a most disturbing influence, and, if shown to be a fact, comes with fearful and startling effect on minds of the trim, orderly, and limit-loving class, in which we find our little country-girl. Dispositions more boldly speculative may derive a stern enjoyment from the discovery, since there must be evil in the world, that a high man is as likely to grasp his share of it as a low one. A wider scope of view, and a deeper insight, may see rank, dignity, and station, all proved illusory, so far as regards their claim to human reverence, and yet not feel as if the universe were thereby tumbled headlong into chaos. But Phœbe, in order to keep the universe in its old place, was fain to smother, in some degree, her own intuitions as to Judge Pyncheon's character. And as for her cousin's testimony in disparagement of it, she concluded that Hepzibah's judgment was embittered by one of those family feuds which render hatred the more deadly by the dead and corrupted love that they intermingle with its native poison.

IX.
Clifford and Phœbe

Truly was there something high, generous, and noble in the native composition of our poor old Hepzibah! Or else,—and it was quite as probably the case,—she had been enriched by poverty, developed by sorrow, elevated by the strong and solitary affection of her life, and thus endowed with heroism, which never could have characterized her in what are called happier circumstances. Through dreary years Hepzibah had looked forward—for the most part despairingly, never with any confidence of hope, but always with the feeling that it was her brightest possibility—to the very position in which she now found herself. In her own behalf, she had asked nothing of Providence but the opportunity of devoting herself to this brother, whom she had so loved,—so admired for what he was, or might have been,—and to whom she had kept her faith, alone of all the world, wholly, unfalteringly, at every instant, and throughout life. And here, in his late decline, the lost one had come back out of his long and strange misfortune, and was thrown on her sympathy, as it seemed, not merely for the bread of his physical existence, but for everything that should keep him morally alive. She had responded to the call. She had come forward,—our poor, gaunt Hepzibah, in her rusty silks, with her rigid joints, and the sad perversity of her scowl,—ready to do her utmost; and with affection enough, if that were all, to do a hundred times as much! There could be few more tearful sights,—and Heaven forgive us if a smile insist on mingling with our conception of it!—few sights with truer pathos in them, than Hepzibah presented on that first afternoon.

How patiently did she endeavor to wrap Clifford up in her great, warm love, and make it all the world to him, so that he should retain no torturing sense of the coldness and dreariness without! Her little efforts to amuse him! How pitiful, yet magnanimous, they were!

Remembering his early love of poetry and fiction, she unlocked a bookcase, and took down several books that had been excellent reading in their day. There was a volume of Pope, with the Rape of the Lock in it, and another of the Tatler, and an odd one of Dryden's Miscellanies, all with tarnished gilding on their covers, and thoughts of tarnished brilliancy inside. They had no success with Clifford. These, and all such writers of society, whose new works glow like the rich texture of a just-woven carpet, must be content to relinquish their charm, for every reader, after an age or two, and could hardly be supposed to retain any portion of it for a mind that had utterly lost its estimate of modes and manners. Hepzibah then took up Rasselas, and began to read of the Happy Valley, with a vague idea that some secret of a contented life had there been elaborated, which might at least serve Clifford and herself for this one day. But the Happy Valley had a cloud over it. Hepzibah troubled her auditor, moreover, by innumerable sins of emphasis, which he seemed to detect, without any reference to the meaning; nor, in fact, did he appear to take much note of the sense of what she read, but evidently felt the tedium of the lecture, without harvesting its profit. His sister's voice, too, naturally harsh, had, in the course of her sorrowful lifetime, contracted a kind of croak, which, when it once gets into the human throat, is as ineradicable as sin. In both sexes, occasionally, this lifelong croak, accompanying each word of joy or sorrow, is one of the symptoms of a settled melancholy; and wherever it occurs, the whole history of misfortune is conveyed in its slightest accent. The effect is as if the voice had been dyed black; or, — if we must use a more moderate simile, — this miserable croak, running through all the variations of the voice, is like a black silken thread, on which the crystal beads of speech are strung, and whence they take their hue. Such voices have put on mourning for dead hopes; and they ought to die and be buried along with them!

Discerning that Clifford was not gladdened by her efforts, Hepzibah searched about the house for the means of more exhilarating pastime. At one time, her eyes chanced to rest on Alice Pyncheon's harpsichord. It was a moment of great peril; for, — despite the traditionary awe that had gathered over this instrument of music, and the dirges which spiritual fingers were said to play on it, — the devoted sister had solemn thoughts of thrumming on its chords for Clifford's benefit, and accompanying the performance with her voice. Poor Clifford! Poor Hepzibah! Poor harpsichord! All three would have been miserable together. By some good agency, — possibly, by the unrecognized interposition of the long-buried Alice herself, — the threatening calamity was averted.

But the worst of all — the hardest stroke of fate for Hepzibah to endure, and perhaps for Clifford, too was his invincible distaste for her appearance. Her features, never the most agreeable, and now harsh with age and grief, and resentment against the world for his sake; her dress, and especially her turban; the queer and quaint manners, which had unconsciously grown upon her in solitude, — such being the poor gentlewoman's outward characteristics, it is no great marvel, although the mournfullest of pities, that the instinctive lover of the Beautiful was fain to turn away his eyes. There was no help for it. It would be the latest impulse to die within him. In his last extremity, the expiring breath stealing faintly through Clifford's lips, he would doubtless press Hepzibah's hand, in fervent recognition of all her lavished love, and close his eyes, — but not so much to die, as to be constrained to look no longer on her face! Poor Hepzibah! She took counsel with herself what might be done, and thought of putting ribbons on her turban; but, by the instant rush of several guardian angels, was withheld from an experiment that could hardly have proved less than fatal to the beloved object of her anxiety.

To be brief, besides Hepzibah's disadvantages of person, there was an uncouthness pervading all her deeds; a clumsy something, that could but ill adapt itself for use, and not at all for ornament. She was a grief to Clifford, and she knew it. In this extremity, the antiquated virgin turned to Phœbe. No grovelling jealousy was in her heart. Had it pleased Heaven to crown the heroic fidelity of her life by making her personally the medium of Clifford's happiness, it would have rewarded her for all the past, by a joy with no bright tints, indeed, but deep and true, and worth a thousand gayer ecstasies. This could not be. She therefore turned to Phœbe, and resigned the task into the young girl's hands. The latter took it up cheerfully, as she did everything, but with no sense of a mission to perform, and succeeding all the better for that same simplicity.

By the involuntary effect of a genial temperament, Phœbe soon grew to be absolutely essential to the daily comfort, if not the daily life, of her two forlorn companions. The grime and sordidness of the House of the Seven Gables seemed to have vanished since her appearance there; the gnawing tooth of the dry-rot was stayed among the old timbers of its skeleton frame; the dust had ceased to settle down so densely, from the antique ceilings, upon the floors and furniture of the rooms below, — or, at any rate, there was a little housewife, as light-footed as the breeze that sweeps a garden walk, gliding hither and thither to brush it all away. The shadows of gloomy events that haunted the else lonely and desolate apartments; the heavy, breathless scent which death had left in more than one of the bedchambers, ever since his visits of long ago, — these were less powerful than the purifying influence scattered throughout the atmosphere of the household by the presence of one youthful, fresh, and thoroughly wholesome heart. There was no morbidness in Phœbe; if there had been, the old Pyncheon House was the very locality to ripen it into incurable disease. But now her spirit resembled, in its potency, a minute quantity of ottar of rose in one of Hepzibah's huge, iron-bound trunks, diffusing its fragrance through the various articles of linen and wrought-lace, kerchiefs, caps, stockings, folded dresses, gloves, and whatever else was treasured there. As every article in the great trunk was the sweeter for the rose-scent, so did all the thoughts and emotions of Hepzibah and Clifford, sombre as they might seem, acquire a subtle attribute of happiness from Phœbe's intermixture with them. Her activity of body, intellect, and heart impelled her continually to perform the ordinary little toils that offered themselves around her, and to think the thought proper for the moment, and to sympathize, — now with the twittering gayety of the robins in the pear-tree, and now to such a depth as she could with Hepzibah's dark anxiety, or the vague moan of her brother. This facile adaptation was at once the symptom of perfect health and its best preservative.

A nature like Phœbe's has invariably its due influence, but is seldom regarded with due honor. Its spiritual force, however, may be partially estimated by the fact of her having found a place for herself, amid circumstances so stern as those which surrounded the mistress of the house; and also by the effect which she produced on a character of so much more mass than her own. For the gaunt, bony frame and limbs of Hepzibah, as compared with the tiny lightsomeness of Phœbe's figure, were perhaps in some fit proportion with the moral weight and substance, respectively, of the woman and the girl.

To the guest,—to Hepzibah's brother,—or Cousin Clifford, as Phœbe now began to call him,—she was especially necessary. Not that he could ever be said to converse with her, or often manifest, in any other very definite mode, his sense of a charm in her society. But if she were a long while absent he became pettish and nervously restless, pacing the room to and fro with the uncertainty that characterized all his movements; or else would sit broodingly in his great chair, resting his head on his hands, and evincing life only by an electric sparkle of ill-humor, whenever Hepzibah endeavored to arouse him. Phœbe's presence, and the contiguity of her fresh life to his blighted one, was usually all that he required. Indeed, such was the native gush and play of her spirit, that she was seldom perfectly quiet and undemonstrative, any more than a fountain ever ceases to dimple and warble with its flow. She possessed the gift of song, and that, too, so naturally, that you would as little think of inquiring whence she had caught it, or what master had taught her, as of asking the same questions about a bird, in whose small strain of music we recognize the voice of the Creator as distinctly as in the loudest accents of his thunder. So long as Phœbe sang, she might stray at her own will about the house. Clifford was content, whether the sweet, airy homeliness of her tones came down from the upper chambers, or along the passageway from the shop, or was sprinkled through the foliage of the pear-tree, inward from the garden, with the twinkling sunbeams. He would sit quietly, with a gentle pleasure gleaming over his face, brighter now, and now a little dimmer, as the song happened to float near him, or was more remotely heard. It pleased him best, however, when she sat on a low footstool at his knee.

It is perhaps remarkable, considering her temperament, that Phœbe oftener chose a strain of pathos than of gayety. But the young and happy are not ill pleased to temper their life with a transparent shadow. The deepest pathos of Phœbe's voice and song, moreover, came sifted through the golden texture of a cheery spirit, and was somehow so interfused with the quality thence acquired, that one's heart felt all the lighter for having wept at it. Broad mirth, in the sacred presence of dark misfortune, would have jarred harshly and irreverently with the solemn symphony that rolled its undertone through Hepzibah's and her brother's life. Therefore, it was well that Phœbe so often chose sad themes, and not amiss that they ceased to be so sad while she was singing them.

Becoming habituated to her companionship, Clifford readily showed how capable of imbibing pleasant tints and gleams of cheerful light from all quarters his nature must originally have been. He grew youthful while she sat by him. A beauty,—not precisely real, even in its utmost manifestation, and which a painter would have watched long to seize and fix upon his canvas, and, after all, in vain,—beauty, nevertheless, that was not a mere dream, would sometimes play upon and illuminate his face. It did more than to illuminate; it transfigured him with an expression that could only be interpreted as the glow of an exquisite and happy spirit. That gray hair, and those furrows,—with their record of infinite sorrow so deeply written across his brow, and so compressed, as with a futile effort to crowd in all the tale, that the whole inscription was made illegible,—these, for the moment, vanished. An eye at once tender and acute might have beheld in the man some shadow of what he was meant to be. Anon, as age came stealing, like a sad twilight, back over his figure, you would have felt tempted to hold an argument with Destiny, and affirm, that either this being should not have been made mortal, or mortal existence should have been tempered to his qualities. There seemed no necessity for his having drawn breath at all; the world never wanted him; but, as he had breathed, it ought always to have been the balmiest of summer air. The same perplexity will invariably haunt us with regard to natures that tend to feed exclusively upon the Beautiful, let their earthly fate be as lenient as it may.

Phœbe, it is probable, had but a very imperfect comprehension of the character over which she had thrown so beneficent a spell. Nor was it necessary. The fire upon the hearth can gladden a whole semicircle of faces round about it, but need not know the individuality of one among them all. Indeed, there was something too fine and delicate in Clifford's traits to be perfectly appreciated by one whose sphere lay so much in the Actual as Phœbe's did. For Clifford, however, the reality, and simplicity, and thorough homeliness of the girl's nature were as powerful a charm as any that she possessed. Beauty, it is true, and beauty almost perfect in its own style, was indispensable. Had Phœbe been coarse in feature, shaped clumsily, of a harsh voice, and uncouthly mannered, she might have been rich with all good gifts, beneath this unfortunate exterior, and still, so long as she wore the guise of woman, she would have shocked Clifford, and depressed him by her lack of beauty. But nothing more beautiful—nothing prettier, at least—

was ever made than Phœbe. And, therefore, to this man,—whose whole poor and impalpable enjoyment of existence heretofore, and until both his heart and fancy died within him, had been a dream,—whose images of women had more and more lost their warmth and substance, and been frozen, like the pictures of secluded artists, into the chillest ideality,—to him, this little figure of the cheeriest household life was just what he required to bring him back into the breathing world. Persons who have wandered, or been expelled, out of the common track of things, even were it for a better system, desire nothing so much as to be led back. They shiver in their loneliness, be it on a mountain-top or in a dungeon. Now, Phœbe's presence made a home about her,—that very sphere which the outcast, the prisoner, the potentate,—the wretch beneath mankind, the wretch aside from it, or the wretch above it,—instinctively pines after,—a home! She was real! Holding her hand, you felt something; a tender something; a substance, and a warm one: and so long as you should feel its grasp, soft as it was, you might be certain that your place was good in the whole sympathetic chain of human nature. The world was no longer a delusion.

By looking a little further in this direction, we might suggest an explanation of an often-suggested mystery. Why are poets so apt to choose their mates, not for any similarity of poetic endowment, but for qualities which might make the happiness of the rudest handicraftsman as well as that of the ideal craftsman of the spirit? Because, probably, at his highest elevation, the poet needs no human intercourse; but he finds it dreary to descend, and be a stranger.

There was something very beautiful in the relation that grew up between this pair, so closely and constantly linked together, yet with such a waste of gloomy and mysterious years from his birthday to hers. On Clifford's part it was the feeling of a man naturally endowed with the liveliest sensibility to feminine influence, but who had never quaffed the cup of passionate love, and knew that it was now too late. He knew it, with the instinctive delicacy that had survived his intellectual decay. Thus, his sentiment for Phœbe, without being paternal, was not less chaste than if she had been his daughter. He was a man, it is true, and recognized her as a woman. She was his only representative of womankind. He took unfailing note of every charm that appertained to her sex, and saw the ripeness of her lips, and the virginal development of her bosom. All her little womanly ways, budding out of her like blossoms on a young fruit-tree, had their effect on him, and sometimes caused his very heart to tingle with the keenest thrills of pleasure. At such moments,—for the effect was seldom more than momentary,—the half-torpid man would be full of harmonious life, just as a long-silent harp is full of sound, when the musician's fingers sweep across it. But, after all, it seemed rather a perception, or a sympathy, than a sentiment belonging to himself as an individual. He read Phœbe as he would a sweet and simple story; he listened to her as if she were a verse of household poetry, which God, in requital of his bleak and dismal lot, had permitted some angel, that most pitied him, to warble through the house. She was not an actual fact for him, but the interpretation of all that he lacked on earth brought warmly home to his conception; so that this mere symbol, or life-like picture, had almost the comfort of reality.

But we strive in vain to put the idea into words. No adequate expression of the beauty and profound pathos with which it impresses us is attainable. This being, made only for happiness, and heretofore so miserably failing to be happy,—his tendencies so hideously thwarted, that, some unknown time ago, the delicate springs of his character, never morally or intellectually strong, had given way, and he was now imbecile,—this poor, forlorn voyager from the Islands of the Blest, in a frail bark, on a tempestuous sea, had been flung, by the last mountain-wave of his shipwreck, into a quiet harbor. There, as he lay more than half lifeless on the strand, the fragrance of an earthly rose-bud had come to his nostrils, and, as odors will, had summoned up reminiscences or visions of all the living and breathing beauty amid which he should have had his home. With his native susceptibility of happy influences, he inhales the slight, ethereal rapture into his soul, and expires!

And how did Phœbe regard Clifford? The girl's was not one of those natures which are most attracted by what is strange and exceptional in human character. The path which would best have suited her was the well-worn track of ordinary life; the companions in whom she would most have delighted were such as one encounters at every turn. The mystery which enveloped Clifford, so far as it affected her at all, was an annoyance, rather than the piquant charm which many women might have found in it. Still, her native kindliness was brought strongly into play, not by what was darkly picturesque in his situation, nor so much, even, by the finer graces of his character, as by the simple appeal of a heart so forlorn as his to one so full of genuine sympathy as hers. She gave him an affectionate regard, because he needed so much love, and seemed to have received so little. With a ready tact, the result of ever-active and wholesome sensibility, she discerned what was good for him, and did it. Whatever was morbid in his mind and experience she ignored; and thereby kept their intercourse healthy, by the incautious, but, as it were, heaven-directed freedom of her whole conduct. The sick in mind, and, perhaps, in body, are rendered more darkly and hopelessly so by the manifold reflection of their disease, mirrored back from all quarters in the deportment of those about them; they are compelled to inhale the poison of their own breath, in infinite repetition. But Phœbe afforded her poor patient a supply of purer air. She impregnated it, too, not with a wild-flower scent,—for wildness was no trait of hers,—but with the perfume of garden-roses, pinks, and other blossoms of much sweetness, which nature and man have consented together in making grow from summer to summer, and from century to century. Such a flower was Phœbe in her relation with Clifford, and such the delight that he inhaled from her.

Yet, it must be said, her petals sometimes drooped a little, in consequence of the heavy atmosphere about her. She grew more thoughtful than heretofore. Looking aside at Clifford's face, and seeing the dim, unsatisfactory elegance and the intellect almost quenched, she would try to inquire what had been his life. Was he always thus? Had this veil been over him from his birth?— this veil, under which far more of his spirit was hidden than revealed, and through which he so imperfectly discerned the actual world,—or was its gray texture woven of some dark calamity? Phœbe loved no riddles, and would have been glad to escape the perplexity of this one. Nevertheless, there was so far a good result of her meditations on Clifford's character, that, when her involuntary conjectures, together with the tendency of every strange circumstance to tell its own story, had gradually taught her the fact, it had no terrible effect upon her. Let the world have done him what vast wrong it might, she knew Cousin Clifford too well—or fancied so—ever to shudder at the touch of his thin, delicate fingers.

Within a few days after the appearance of this remarkable inmate, the routine of life had established itself with a good deal of uniformity in the old house of our narrative. In the morning, very shortly after breakfast, it was Clifford's custom to fall asleep in his chair; nor, unless accidentally disturbed, would he emerge from a dense cloud of slumber or the thinner mists that flitted to and fro, until well towards noonday. These hours of drowsihead were the season of the old gentlewoman's attendance on her brother, while Phœbe took charge of the shop; an arrangement which the public speedily understood, and evinced their decided preference of the younger shopwoman by the multiplicity of their calls during her administration of affairs. Dinner over, Hepzibah took her knitting-work,—a long stocking of gray yarn, for her brother's winter wear,—and with a sigh, and a scowl of affectionate farewell to Clifford, and a gesture enjoining watchfulness on Phœbe, went to take her seat behind the counter. It was now the young girl's turn to be the nurse,—the guardian, the playmate, —or whatever is the fitter phrase,—of the gray-haired man.

X.

The Pyncheon Garden

Clifford, except for Phœbe's more active instigation would ordinarily have yielded to the torpor which had crept through all his modes of being, and which sluggishly counselled him to sit in his morning chair till eventide. But the girl seldom failed to propose a removal to the garden, where Uncle Venner and the daguerreotypist had made such repairs on the roof of the ruinous arbor, or summer-house, that it was now a sufficient shelter from sunshine and casual showers. The hop-vine, too, had begun to grow luxuriantly over the sides of the little edifice, and made an interior of verdant seclusion, with innumerable peeps and glimpses into the wider solitude of the garden.

Here, sometimes, in this green play-place of flickering light, Phœbe read to Clifford. Her acquaintance, the artist, who appeared to have a literary turn, had supplied her with works of fiction, in pamphlet form,—and a few volumes of poetry, in altogether a different style and taste from those which Hepzibah selected for his amusement. Small thanks were due to the books, however, if the girl's readings were in any degree more successful than her elderly cousin's. Phœbe's voice had always a pretty music in it, and could either enliven Clifford by its sparkle and gayety of tone, or soothe him by a continued flow of pebbly and brook-like cadences. But the fictions—in which the country-girl, unused to works of that nature, often became deeply absorbed—interested her strange auditor very little, or not at all. Pictures of life, scenes of passion or sentiment, wit, humor, and pathos, were all thrown away, or worse than thrown away, on Clifford; either because he lacked an experience by which to test their truth, or because his own griefs were a touch-stone of reality that few feigned emotions could withstand. When Phœbe broke into a peal of merry laughter at what she read, he would now and then laugh for sympathy, but oftener respond with a troubled, questioning look. If a tear—a maiden's sunshiny tear over imaginary woe—dropped upon some melancholy page, Clifford either took it as a token of actual calamity, or else grew peevish, and angrily motioned her to close the volume. And wisely too! Is not the world sad enough, in genuine earnest, without making a pastime of mock sorrows?

With poetry it was rather better. He delighted in the swell and subsidence of the rhythm, and the happily recurring rhyme. Nor was Clifford incapable of feeling the sentiment of poetry,—not, perhaps, where it was highest or deepest, but where it was most flitting and ethereal. It was impossible to foretell in what exquisite verse the awakening spell might lurk; but, on raising her eyes from the page to Clifford's face, Phœbe would be made aware, by the light breaking through it, that a more delicate intelligence than her own had caught a lambent flame from what she read. One glow of this kind, however, was often the precursor of gloom for many hours afterward; because, when the glow left him, he seemed conscious of a missing sense and power, and groped about for them, as if a blind man should go seeking his lost eyesight.

It pleased him more, and was better for his inward welfare, that Phœbe should talk, and make passing occurrences vivid to his mind by her accompanying description and remarks. The life of the garden offered topics enough for such discourse as suited Clifford best. He never failed to inquire what flowers had bloomed since yesterday. His feeling for flowers was very exquisite, and seemed not so much a taste as an emotion; he was fond of sitting with one in his hand, intently observing it, and looking from its petals into Phœbe's face, as if the garden flower were the sister of the household maiden. Not merely was there a delight in the flower's perfume, or pleasure in its beautiful form, and the delicacy or brightness of its hue; but Clifford's enjoyment was accompanied with a perception of life, character, and individuality, that made him love these blossoms of the garden, as if they were endowed with sentiment and intelligence. This affection and sympathy for flowers is almost exclusively a woman's trait. Men, if endowed with it by nature, soon lose, forget, and learn to despise it, in their contact with coarser things than flowers. Clifford, too, had long forgotten it; but found it again now, as he slowly revived from the chill torpor of his life.

It is wonderful how many pleasant incidents continually came to pass in that secluded garden-spot when once Phœbe had set herself to look for them. She had seen or heard a bee there, on the first day of her acquaintance with the place. And often, — almost continually, indeed, — since then, the bees kept coming thither, Heaven knows why, or by what pertinacious desire, for far-fetched sweets, when, no doubt, there were broad clover-fields, and all kinds of garden growth, much nearer home than this. Thither the bees came, however, and plunged into the squash-blossoms, as if there were no other squash-vines within a long day's flight, or as if the soil of Hepzibah's garden gave its productions just the very quality which these laborious little wizards wanted, in order to impart the Hymettus odor to their whole hive of New England honey. When Clifford heard their sunny, buzzing murmur, in the heart of the great yellow blossoms, he looked about him with a joyful sense of warmth, and blue sky, and green grass, and of God's free air in the whole height from earth to heaven. After all, there need be no question why the bees came to that one green nook in the dusty town. God sent them thither to gladden our poor Clifford. They brought the rich summer with them, in requital of a little honey.

The House of the Seven Gables

When the bean-vines began to flower on the poles, there was one particular variety which bore a vivid scarlet blossom. The daguerreotypist had found these beans in a garret, over one of the seven gables, treasured up in an old chest of drawers by some horticultural Pyncheon of days gone by, who doubtless meant to sow them the next summer, but was himself first sown in Death's garden-ground. By way of testing whether there were still a living germ in such ancient seeds, Holgrave had planted some of them; and the result of his experiment was a splendid row of bean-vines, clambering, early, to the full height of the poles, and arraying them, from top to bottom, in a spiral profusion of red blossoms. And, ever since the unfolding of the first bud, a multitude of humming-birds had been attracted thither. At times, it seemed as if for every one of the hundred blossoms there was one of these tiniest fowls of the air,—a thumb's bigness of burnished plumage, hovering and vibrating about the bean-poles. It was with indescribable interest, and even more than childish delight, that Clifford watched the humming-birds. He used to thrust his head softly out of the arbor to see them the better; all the while, too, motioning Phœbe to be quiet, and snatching glimpses of the smile upon her face, so as to heap his enjoyment up the higher with her sympathy. He had not merely grown young;—he was a child again.

Hepzibah, whenever she happened to witness one of these fits of miniature enthusiasm, would shake her head, with a strange mingling of the mother and sister, and of pleasure and sadness, in her aspect. She said that it had always been thus with Clifford when the humming-birds came,—always, from his babyhood,—and that his delight in them had been one of the earliest tokens by which he showed his love for beautiful things. And it was a wonderful coincidence, the good lady thought, that the artist should have planted these scarlet-flowering beans—which the humming-birds sought far and wide, and which had not grown in the Pyncheon garden before for forty years—on the very summer of Clifford's return.

Then would the tears stand in poor Hepzibah's eyes, or overflow them with a too abundant gush, so that she was fain to betake herself into some corner, lest Clifford should espy her agitation. Indeed, all the enjoyments of this period were provocative of tears. Coming so late as it did, it was a kind of Indian summer, with a mist in its balmiest sunshine, and decay and death in its gaudiest delight. The more Clifford seemed to taste the happiness of a child, the sadder was the difference to be recognized. With a mysterious and terrible Past, which had annihilated his memory, and a blank Future before him, he had only this visionary and impalpable Now, which, if you once look closely at it, is nothing. He himself, as was perceptible by many symptoms, lay darkly behind his pleasure, and knew it to be a baby-play, which he was to toy and trifle with, instead of thoroughly believing. Clifford saw, it may be, in the mirror of his deeper consciousness, that he was an example and representative of that great class of people whom an inexplicable Providence is continually putting at cross-purposes with the world: breaking what seems its own promise in their nature; withholding their proper food, and setting poison before them for a banquet; and thus—when it might so easily, as one would think, have been adjusted otherwise—making their existence a strangeness, a solitude, and torment. All his life long, he had been learning how to be wretched, as one learns a foreign tongue; and now, with the lesson thoroughly by heart, he could with difficulty comprehend his little airy happiness. Frequently there was a dim shadow of doubt in his eyes. "Take my hand, Phœbe," he would say, "and pinch it hard with your little fingers! Give me a rose, that I may press its thorns, and prove myself awake by the sharp touch of pain!" Evidently, he desired this prick of a trifling anguish, in order to assure himself, by that quality which he best knew to be real, that the garden, and the seven weather-beaten gables, and Hepzibah's scowl, and Phœbe's smile, were real likewise. Without this signet in his flesh, he could have attributed no more substance to them than to the empty confusion of imaginary scenes with which he had fed his spirit, until even that poor sustenance was exhausted.

The author needs great faith in his reader's sympathy; else he must hesitate to give details so minute, and incidents apparently so trifling, as are essential to make up the idea of this garden-life. It was the Eden of a thunder-smitten Adam, who had fled for refuge thither out of the same dreary and perilous wilderness into which the original Adam was expelled.

One of the available means of amusement, of which Phœbe made the most in Clifford's behalf, was that feathered society, the hens, a breed of whom, as we have already said, was an immemorial heirloom in the Pyncheon family. In compliance with a whim of Clifford, as it troubled him to see them in confinement, they had been set at liberty, and now roamed at will about the garden; doing some little mischief, but hindered from escape by buildings on three sides, and the difficult peaks of a wooden fence on the other. They spent much of their abundant leisure on the margin of Maule's well, which was haunted by a kind of snail, evidently a titbit to their palates; and the brackish water itself, however nauseous to the rest of the world, was so greatly esteemed by these fowls, that they might be seen tasting, turning up their heads, and smacking their bills, with precisely the air of wine-bibbers round a probationary cask. Their generally quiet, yet often brisk, and constantly diversified talk, one to another, or sometimes in soliloquy,—as they scratched worms out of the rich, black soil, or pecked at such plants as suited their taste,—had such a domestic tone, that it was almost a wonder why you could not establish a regular interchange of ideas about household matters, human and gallinaceous. All hens are well worth studying for the piquancy and rich variety of their manners; but by no possibility can there have been other fowls of such odd appearance and deportment as these ancestral ones. They probably embodied the traditional peculiarities of their whole line of progenitors, derived through an unbroken succession of eggs; or else this individual Chanticleer and his two wives had grown to be humorists, and a little crack-brained withal, on account of their solitary way of life, and out of sympathy for Hepzibah, their lady-patroness.

Queer, indeed, they looked! Chanticleer himself, though stalking on two stilt-like legs, with the dignity of interminable descent in all his gestures, was hardly bigger than an ordinary partridge; his two wives were about the size of quails; and as for the one chicken, it looked small enough to be still in the egg, and, at the same time, sufficiently old, withered, wizened, and experienced, to have been founder of the antiquated race. Instead of being the youngest of the family, it rather seemed to have aggregated into itself the ages, not only of these living specimens of the breed, but of all its forefathers and foremothers, whose united excellences and oddities were squeezed into its little body. Its mother evidently regarded it as the one chicken of the world, and as necessary, in fact, to the world's continuance, or, at any rate, to the equilibrium of the present system of affairs, whether in church or state. No lesser sense of the infant fowl's importance could have justified, even in a mother's eyes, the perseverance with which she watched over its safety, ruffling her small person to twice its proper size, and flying in everybody's face that so much as looked towards her hopeful progeny. No lower estimate could have vindicated the indefatigable zeal with which she scratched, and her unscrupulousness in digging up the choicest flower or vegetable, for the sake of the fat earthworm at its root. Her nervous cluck, when the chicken happened to be hidden in the long grass or under the squash-leaves; her gentle croak of satisfaction, while sure of it beneath her wing; her note of ill-concealed fear and obstreperous defiance, when she saw her arch-enemy, a neighbor's cat, on the top of the high fence,—one or other of these sounds was to be heard at almost every moment of the day. By degrees, the observer came to feel nearly as much interest in this chicken of illustrious race as the mother-hen did.

Phœbe, after getting well acquainted with the old hen, was sometimes permitted to take the chicken in her hand, which was quite capable of grasping its cubic inch or two of body. While she curiously examined its hereditary marks,—the peculiar speckle of its plumage, the funny tuft on its head, and a knob on each of its legs,—the little biped, as she insisted, kept giving her a sagacious wink. The daguerreotypist once whispered her that these marks betokened the oddities of the Pyncheon family, and that the chicken itself was a symbol of the life of the old house, embodying its interpretation, likewise, although an unintelligible one, as such clews generally are. It was a feathered riddle; a mystery hatched out of an egg, and just as mysterious as if the egg had been addle!

The second of Chanticleer's two wives, ever since Phœbe's arrival, had been in a state of heavy despondency, caused, as it afterwards appeared, by her inability to lay an egg. One day, however, by her self-important gait, the sideways turn of her head, and the cock of her eye, as she pried into one and another nook of the garden, — croaking to herself, all the while, with inexpressible complacency, — it was made evident that this identical hen, much as mankind undervalued her, carried something about her person the worth of which was not to be estimated either in gold or precious stones. Shortly after, there was a prodigious cackling and gratulation of Chanticleer and all his family, including the wizened chicken, who appeared to understand the matter quite as well as did his sire, his mother, or his aunt. That afternoon Phœbe found a diminutive egg, — not in the regular nest, it was far too precious to be trusted there, — but cunningly hidden under the currant-bushes, on some dry stalks of last year's grass. Hepzibah, on learning the fact, took possession of the egg and appropriated it to Clifford's breakfast, on account of a certain delicacy of flavor, for which, as she affirmed, these eggs had always been famous. Thus unscrupulously did the old gentlewoman sacrifice the continuance, perhaps, of an ancient feathered race, with no better end than to supply her brother with a dainty that hardly filled the bowl of a tea-spoon! It must have been in reference to this outrage that Chanticleer, the next day, accompanied by the bereaved mother of the egg, took his post in front of Phœbe and Clifford, and delivered himself of a harangue that might have proved as long as his own pedigree, but for a fit of merriment on Phœbe's part. Hereupon, the offended fowl stalked away on his long stilts, and utterly withdrew his notice from Phœbe and the rest of human nature, until she made her peace with an offering of spice-cake, which, next to snails, was the delicacy most in favor with his aristocratic taste.

We linger too long, no doubt, beside this paltry rivulet of life that flowed through the garden of the Pyncheon House. But we deem it pardonable to record these mean incidents and poor delights, because they proved so greatly to Clifford's benefit. They had the earth-smell in them, and contributed to give him health and substance. Some of his occupations wrought less desirably upon him. He had a singular propensity, for example, to hang over Maule's well, and look at the constantly shifting phantasmagoria of figures produced by the agitation of the water over the mosaic-work of colored pebbles at the bottom. He said that faces looked upward to him there, — beautiful faces, arrayed in bewitching smiles, — each momentary face so fair and rosy, and every smile so sunny, that he felt wronged at its departure, until the same flitting witchcraft made a new one. But sometimes he would suddenly cry out, "The dark face gazes at me!" and be miserable the whole day afterwards. Phœbe, when she hung over the fountain by Clifford's side, could see nothing of all this, — neither the beauty nor the ugliness, — but only the colored pebbles, looking as if the gush of the waters shook and disarranged them. And the dark face, that so troubled Clifford, was no more than the shadow thrown from a branch of one of the damson-trees, and breaking the inner light of Maule's well. The truth was, however, that his fancy — reviving faster than his will and judgment, and always stronger than they — created shapes of loveliness that were symbolic of his native character, and now and then a stern and dreadful shape that typified his fate.

On Sundays, after Phœbe had been at church, — for the girl had a church-going conscience, and would hardly have been at ease had she missed either prayer, singing, sermon, or benediction, — after church-time, therefore, there was, ordinarily, a sober little festival in the garden. In addition to Clifford, Hepzibah, and Phœbe, two guests made up the company. One was the artist Holgrave, who, in spite of his consociation with reformers, and his other queer and questionable traits, continued to hold an elevated place in Hepzibah's regard. The other, we are almost ashamed to say, was the venerable Uncle Venner, in a clean shirt, and a broadcloth coat, more respectable than his ordinary wear, inasmuch as it was neatly patched on each elbow, and might be called an entire garment, except for a slight inequality in the length of its skirts. Clifford, on several occasions, had seemed to enjoy the old man's intercourse, for the sake of his mellow, cheerful vein, which was like the sweet flavor of a frost-bitten apple, such as one picks up under the tree in December. A man at the very lowest point of the social scale was easier and more agreeable for the fallen gentleman to encounter than a person at any of the intermediate degrees; and, moreover, as Clifford's young manhood had been lost, he was fond of feeling himself comparatively youthful, now, in apposition with the patriarchal age of Uncle Venner. In fact, it was sometimes observable that Clifford half wilfully hid from himself the consciousness of being stricken in years, and cherished visions of an earthly future still before him; visions, however, too indistinctly drawn to be followed by disappointment — though, doubtless, by depression — when any casual incident or recollection made him sensible of the withered leaf.

So this oddly composed little social party used to assemble under the ruinous arbor. Hepzibah — stately as ever at heart, and yielding not an inch of her old gentility, but resting upon it so much the more, as justifying a princess-like condescension — exhibited a not ungraceful hospitality. She talked kindly to the vagrant artist, and took sage counsel—lady as she was—with the wood-sawyer, the messenger of everybody's petty errands, the patched philosopher. And Uncle Venner, who had studied the world at street-corners, and other posts equally well adapted for just observation, was as ready to give out his wisdom as a town-pump to give water.

"Miss Hepzibah, ma'am," said he once, after they had all been cheerful together, "I really enjoy these quiet little meetings of a Sabbath afternoon. They are very much like what I expect to have after I retire to my farm!"

"Uncle Venner" observed Clifford in a drowsy, inward tone, "is always talking about his farm. But I have a better scheme for him, by and by. We shall see!"

"Ah, Mr. Clifford Pyncheon!" said the man of patches, "you may scheme for me as much as you please; but I'm not going to give up this one scheme of my own, even if I never bring it really to pass. It does seem to me that men make a wonderful mistake in trying to heap up property upon property. If I had done so, I should feel as if Providence was not bound to take care of me; and, at all events, the city wouldn't be! I'm one of those people who think that infinity is big enough for us all—and eternity long enough."

"Why, so they are, Uncle Venner," remarked Phœbe after a pause; for she had been trying to fathom the profundity and appositeness of this concluding apothegm. "But for this short life of ours, one would like a house and a moderate garden-spot of one's own."

"It appears to me," said the daguerreotypist, smiling, "that Uncle Venner has the principles of Fourier at the bottom of his wisdom; only they have not quite so much distinctness in his mind as in that of the systematizing Frenchman."

"Come, Phœbe," said Hepzibah, "it is time to bring the currants."

And then, while the yellow richness of the declining sunshine still fell into the open space of the garden, Phœbe brought out a loaf of bread and a china bowl of currants, freshly gathered from the bushes, and crushed with sugar. These, with water,—but not from the fountain of ill omen, close at hand,—constituted all the entertainment. Meanwhile, Holgrave took some pains to establish an intercourse with Clifford, actuated, it might seem, entirely by an impulse of kindliness, in order that the present hour might be cheerfuller than most which the poor recluse had spent, or was destined yet to spend. Nevertheless, in the artist's deep, thoughtful, all-observant eyes, there was, now and then, an expression, not sinister, but questionable; as if he had some other interest in the scene than a stranger, a youthful and unconnected adventurer, might be supposed to have. With great mobility of outward mood, however, he applied himself to the task of enlivening the party; and with so much success, that even dark-hued Hepzibah threw off one tint of melancholy, and made what shift she could with the remaining portion. Phœbe said to herself,—"How pleasant he can be!" As for Uncle Venner, as a mark of friendship and approbation, he readily consented to afford the young man his countenance in the way of his profession,—not metaphorically, be it understood, but literally, by allowing a daguerreotype of his face, so familiar to the town, to be exhibited at the entrance of Holgrave's studio.

Clifford, as the company partook of their little banquet, grew to be the gayest of them all. Either it was one of those up-quivering flashes of the spirit, to which minds in an abnormal state are liable, or else the artist had subtly touched some chord that made musical vibration. Indeed, what with the pleasant summer evening, and the sympathy of this little circle of not unkindly souls, it was perhaps natural that a character so susceptible as Clifford's should become animated, and show itself readily responsive to what was said around him. But he gave out his own thoughts, likewise, with an airy and fanciful glow; so that they glistened, as it were, through the arbor, and made their escape among the interstices of the foliage. He had been as cheerful, no doubt, while alone with Phœbe, but never with such tokens of acute, although partial intelligence.

But, as the sunlight left the peaks of the Seven Gables, so did the excitement fade out of Clifford's eyes. He gazed vaguely and mournfully about him, as if he missed something precious, and missed it the more drearily for not knowing precisely what it was.

"I want my happiness!" at last he murmured hoarsely and indistinctly, hardly shaping out the words. "Many, many years have I waited for it! It is late! It is late! I want my happiness!"

Alas, poor Clifford! You are old, and worn with troubles that ought never to have befallen you. You are partly crazy and partly imbecile; a ruin, a failure, as almost everybody is,—though some in less degree, or less perceptibly, than their fellows. Fate has no happiness in store for you; unless your quiet home in the old family residence with the faithful Hepzibah, and your long summer afternoons with Phœbe, and these Sabbath festivals with Uncle Venner and the daguerreotypist, deserve to be called happiness! Why not? If not the thing itself, it is marvellously like it, and the more so for that ethereal and intangible quality which causes it all to vanish at too close an introspection. Take it, therefore, while you may. Murmur not,—question not,—but make the most of it!

XI.
The Arched Window

From the inertness, or what we may term the vegetative character, of his ordinary mood, Clifford would perhaps have been content to spend one day after another, interminably,—or, at least, throughout the summer-time,—in just the kind of life described in the preceding pages. Fancying, however, that it might be for his benefit occasionally to diversify the scene, Phœbe sometimes suggested that he should look out upon the life of the street. For this purpose, they used to mount the staircase together, to the second story of the house, where, at the termination of a wide entry, there was an arched window, of uncommonly large dimensions, shaded by a pair of curtains. It opened above the porch, where there had formerly been a balcony, the balustrade of which had long since gone to decay, and been removed. At this arched window, throwing it open, but keeping himself in comparative obscurity by means of the curtain, Clifford had an opportunity of witnessing such a portion of the great world's movement as might be supposed to roll through one of the retired streets of a not very populous city. But he and Phœbe made a sight as well worth seeing as any that the city could exhibit. The pale, gray, childish, aged, melancholy, yet often simply cheerful, and sometimes delicately intelligent aspect of Clifford, peering from behind the faded crimson of the curtain,—watching the monotony of every-day occurrences with a kind of inconsequential interest and earnestness, and, at every petty throb of his sensibility, turning for sympathy to the eyes of the bright young girl!

If once he were fairly seated at the window, even Pyncheon Street would hardly be so dull and lonely but that, somewhere or other along its extent, Clifford might discover matter to occupy his eye, and titillate, if not engross, his observation. Things familiar to the youngest child that had begun its outlook at existence seemed strange to him. A cab; an omnibus, with its populous interior, dropping here and there a passenger, and picking up another, and thus typifying that vast rolling vehicle, the world, the end of whose journey is everywhere and nowhere; these objects he followed eagerly with his eyes, but forgot them before the dust raised by the horses and wheels had settled along their track. As regarded novelties (among which cabs and omnibuses were to be reckoned), his mind appeared to have lost its proper gripe and retentiveness. Twice or thrice, for example, during the sunny hours of the day, a water-cart went along by the Pyncheon House, leaving a broad wake of moistened earth, instead of the white dust that had risen at a lady's lightest footfall; it was like a summer shower, which the city authorities had caught and tamed, and compelled it into the commonest routine of their convenience. With the water-cart Clifford could never grow familiar; it always affected him with just the same surprise as at first. His mind took an apparently sharp impression from it, but lost the recollection of this perambulatory shower, before its next reappearance, as completely as did the street itself, along which the heat so quickly strewed white dust again. It was the same with the railroad. Clifford could hear the obstreperous howl of the steam-devil, and, by leaning a little way from the arched window, could catch a glimpse of the trains of cars, flashing a brief transit across the extremity of the street. The idea of terrible energy thus forced upon him was new at every recurrence, and seemed to affect him as disagreeably, and with almost as much surprise, the hundredth time as the first.

Nothing gives a sadder sense of decay than this loss or suspension of the power to deal with unaccustomed things, and to keep up with the swiftness of the passing moment. It can merely be a suspended animation; for, were the power actually to perish, there would be little use of immortality. We are less than ghosts, for the time being, whenever this calamity befalls us.

Clifford was indeed the most inveterate of conservatives. All the antique fashions of the street were dear to him; even such as were characterized by a rudeness that would naturally have annoyed his fastidious senses. He loved the old rumbling and jolting carts, the former track of which he still found in his long-buried remembrance, as the observer of to-day finds the wheel-tracks of ancient vehicles in Herculaneum. The butcher's cart, with its snowy canopy, was an acceptable object; so was the fish-cart, heralded by its horn; so, likewise, was the countryman's cart of vegetables, plodding from door to door, with long pauses of the patient horse, while his owner drove a trade in turnips, carrots, summer-squashes, string-beans, green peas, and new potatoes, with half the housewives of the neighborhood. The baker's cart, with the harsh music of its bells, had a pleasant effect on Clifford, because, as few things else did, it jingled the very dissonance of yore. One afternoon a scissor-grinder chanced to set his wheel a-going under the Pyncheon Elm, and just in front of the arched window. Children came running with their mothers' scissors, or the carving-knife, or the paternal razor, or anything else that lacked an edge (except, indeed, poor Clifford's wits), that the grinder might apply the article to his magic wheel, and give it back as good as new. Round went the busily revolving machinery, kept in motion by the scissor-grinder's foot, and wore away the hard steel against the hard stone, whence issued an intense and spiteful prolongation of a hiss as fierce as those emitted by Satan and his compeers in Pandemonium, though squeezed into smaller compass. It was an ugly, little, venomous serpent of a noise, as ever did petty violence to human ears. But Clifford listened with rapturous delight. The sound, however disagreeable, had very brisk life in it, and, together with the circle of curious children watching the revolutions of the wheel, appeared to give him a more vivid sense of active, bustling, and sunshiny existence than he had attained in almost any other way. Nevertheless, its charm lay chiefly in the past; for the scissor-grinder's wheel had hissed in his childish ears.

He sometimes made doleful complaint that there were no stage-coaches nowadays. And he asked in an injured tone what had become of all those old square-topped chaises, with wings sticking out on either side, that used to be drawn by a plough-horse, and driven by a farmer's wife and daughter, peddling whortle-berries and blackberries about the town. Their disappearance made him doubt, he said, whether the berries had not left off growing in the broad pastures and along the shady country lanes.

But anything that appealed to the sense of beauty, in however humble a way, did not require to be recommended by these old associations. This was observable when one of those Italian boys (who are rather a modern feature of our streets) came along with his barrel-organ, and stopped under the wide and cool shadows of the elm. With his quick professional eye he took note of the two faces watching him from the arched window, and, opening his instrument, began to scatter its melodies abroad. He had a monkey on his shoulder, dressed in a Highland plaid; and, to complete the sum of splendid attractions wherewith he presented himself to the public, there was a company of little figures, whose sphere and habitation was in the mahogany case of his organ, and whose principle of life was the music which the Italian made it his business to grind out. In all their variety of occupation, — the cobbler, the blacksmith, the soldier, the lady with her fan, the toper with his bottle, the milk-maid sitting by her cow — this fortunate little society might truly be said to enjoy a harmonious existence, and to make life literally a dance. The Italian turned a crank; and, behold! every one of these small individuals started into the most curious vivacity. The cobbler wrought upon a shoe; the blacksmith hammered his iron, the soldier waved his glittering blade; the lady raised a tiny breeze with her fan; the jolly toper swigged lustily at his bottle; a scholar opened his book with eager thirst for knowledge, and turned his head to and fro along the page; the milkmaid energetically drained her cow; and a miser counted gold into his strong-box, — all at the same turning of a crank. Yes; and, moved by the self-same impulse, a lover saluted his mistress on her lips! Possibly some cynic, at once merry and bitter, had desired to signify, in this pantomimic scene, that we mortals, whatever our business or amusement, — however serious, however trifling, — all dance to one identical tune, and, in spite of our ridiculous activity, bring nothing finally to pass. For the most remarkable aspect of the affair was, that, at the cessation of the music, everybody was petrified at once, from the most extravagant life into a dead torpor. Neither was the cobbler's shoe finished, nor the blacksmith's iron shaped out; nor was there a drop less of brandy in the toper's bottle, nor a drop more of milk in the milkmaid's pail, nor one additional coin in the miser's strong-box, nor was the scholar a page deeper in his book. All were precisely in the same condition as before they made themselves so ridiculous by their haste to toil, to enjoy, to accumulate gold, and to become wise. Saddest of all, moreover, the lover was none the happier for the maiden's granted kiss! But, rather than swallow this last too acrid ingredient, we reject the whole moral of the show.

The monkey, meanwhile, with a thick tail curling out into preposterous prolixity from beneath his tartans, took his station at the Italian's feet. He turned a wrinkled and abominable little visage to every passer-by, and to the circle of children that soon gathered round, and to Hepzibah's shop-door, and upward to the arched window, whence Phœbe and Clifford were looking down. Every moment, also, he took off his Highland bonnet, and performed a bow and scrape. Sometimes, moreover, he made personal application to individuals, holding out his small black palm, and otherwise plainly signifying his excessive desire for whatever filthy lucre might happen to be in anybody's pocket. The mean and low, yet strangely man-like expression of his wilted countenance; the prying and crafty glance, that showed him ready to gripe at every miserable advantage; his enormous tail (too enormous to be decently concealed under his gabardine), and the deviltry of nature which it betokened,—take this monkey just as he was, in short, and you could desire no better image of the Mammon of copper coin, symbolizing the grossest form of the love of money. Neither was there any possibility of satisfying the covetous little devil. Phœbe threw down a whole handful of cents, which he picked up with joyless eagerness, handed them over to the Italian for safekeeping, and immediately recommenced a series of pantomimic petitions for more.

Doubtless, more than one New-Englander—or, let him be of what country he might, it is as likely to be the case—passed by, and threw a look at the monkey, and went on, without imagining how nearly his own moral condition was here exemplified. Clifford, however, was a being of another order. He had taken childish delight in the music, and smiled, too, at the figures which it set in motion. But, after looking awhile at the long-tailed imp, he was so shocked by his horrible ugliness, spiritual as well as physical, that he actually began to shed tears; a weakness which men of merely delicate endowments, and destitute of the fiercer, deeper, and more tragic power of laughter, can hardly avoid, when the worst and meanest aspect of life happens to be presented to them.

Pyncheon Street was sometimes enlivened by spectacles of more imposing pretensions than the above, and which brought the multitude along with them. With a shivering repugnance at the idea of personal contact with the world, a powerful impulse still seized on Clifford, whenever the rush and roar of the human tide grew strongly audible to him. This was made evident, one day, when a political procession, with hundreds of flaunting banners, and drums, fifes, clarions, and cymbals, reverberating between the rows of buildings, marched all through town, and trailed its length of trampling footsteps, and most infrequent uproar, past the ordinarily quiet House of the Seven Gables. As a mere object of sight, nothing is more deficient in picturesque features than a procession seen in its passage through narrow streets. The spectator feels it to be fool's play, when he can distinguish the tedious commonplace of each man's visage, with the perspiration and weary self-importance on it, and the very cut of his pantaloons, and the stiffness or laxity of his shirt-collar, and the dust on the back of his black coat. In order to become majestic, it should be viewed from some vantage point, as it rolls its slow and long array through the centre of a wide plain, or the stateliest public square of a city; for then, by its remoteness, it melts all the petty personalities, of which it is made up, into one broad mass of existence,—one great life,—one collected body of mankind, with a vast, homogeneous spirit animating it. But, on the other hand, if an impressible person, standing alone over the brink of one of these processions, should behold it, not in its atoms, but in its aggregate,—as a mighty river of life, massive in its tide, and black with mystery, and, out of its depths, calling to the kindred depth within him,—then the contiguity would add to the effect. It might so fascinate him that he would hardly be restrained from plunging into the surging stream of human sympathies.

So it proved with Clifford. He shuddered; he grew pale; he threw an appealing look at Hepzibah and Phœbe, who were with him at the window. They comprehended nothing of his emotions, and supposed him merely disturbed by the unaccustomed tumult. At last, with tremulous limbs, he started up, set his foot on the window-sill, and in an instant more would have been in the unguarded balcony. As it was, the whole procession might have seen him, a wild, haggard figure, his gray locks floating in the wind that waved their banners; a lonely being, estranged from his race, but now feeling himself man again, by virtue of the irrepressible instinct that possessed him. Had Clifford attained the balcony, he would probably have leaped into the street; but whether impelled by the species of terror that sometimes urges its victim over the very precipice which he shrinks from, or by a natural magnetism, tending towards the great centre of humanity, it were not easy to decide. Both impulses might have wrought on him at once.

But his companions, affrighted by his gesture,—which was that of a man hurried away in spite of himself,—seized Clifford's garment and held him back. Hepzibah shrieked.

The House of the Seven Gables

Phœbe, to whom all extravagance was a horror, burst into sobs and tears.

"Clifford, Clifford! are you crazy?" cried his sister.

"I hardly know, Hepzibah," said Clifford, drawing a long breath. "Fear nothing, — it is over now, — but had I taken that plunge, and survived it, methinks it would have made me another man!"

Possibly, in some sense, Clifford may have been right. He needed a shock; or perhaps he required to take a deep, deep plunge into the ocean of human life, and to sink down and be covered by its profoundness, and then to emerge, sobered, invigorated, restored to the world and to himself. Perhaps again, he required nothing less than the great final remedy — death!

A similar yearning to renew the broken links of brotherhood with his kind sometimes showed itself in a milder form; and once it was made beautiful by the religion that lay even deeper than itself. In the incident now to be sketched, there was a touching recognition, on Clifford's part, of God's care and love towards him, — towards this poor, forsaken man, who, if any mortal could, might have been pardoned for regarding himself as thrown aside, forgotten, and left to be the sport of some fiend, whose playfulness was an ecstasy of mischief.

It was the Sabbath morning; one of those bright, calm Sabbaths, with its own hallowed atmosphere, when Heaven seems to diffuse itself over the earth's face in a solemn smile, no less sweet than solemn. On such a Sabbath morn, were we pure enough to be its medium, we should be conscious of the earth's natural worship ascending through our frames, on whatever spot of ground we stood. The church-bells, with various tones, but all in harmony, were calling out and responding to one another, — "It is the Sabbath! — The Sabbath! — Yea; the Sabbath!" — and over the whole city the bells scattered the blessed sounds, now slowly, now with livelier joy, now one bell alone, now all the bells together, crying earnestly, — "It is the Sabbath!" — and flinging their accents afar off, to melt into the air and pervade it with the holy word. The air with God's sweetest and tenderest sunshine in it, was meet for mankind to breathe into their hearts, and send it forth again as the utterance of prayer.

Clifford sat at the window with Hepzibah, watching the neighbors as they stepped into the street. All of them, however unspiritual on other days, were transfigured by the Sabbath influence; so that their very garments — whether it were an old man's decent coat well brushed for the thousandth time, or a little boy's first sack and trousers finished yesterday by his mother's needle — had somewhat of the quality of ascension-robes. Forth, likewise, from the portal of the old house stepped Phœbe, putting up her small green sunshade, and throwing upward a glance and smile of parting kindness to the faces at the arched window. In her aspect there was a familiar gladness, and a holiness that you could play with, and yet reverence it as much as ever. She was like a prayer, offered up in the homeliest beauty of one's mother-tongue. Fresh was Phœbe, moreover, and airy and sweet in her apparel; as if nothing that she wore — neither her gown, nor her small straw bonnet, nor her little kerchief, any more than her snowy stockings — had ever been put on before; or, if worn, were all the fresher for it, and with a fragrance as if they had lain among the rosebuds.

The girl waved her hand to Hepzibah and Clifford, and went up the street; a religion in herself, warm, simple, true, with a substance that could walk on earth, and a spirit that was capable of heaven.

"Hepzibah," asked Clifford, after watching Phœbe to the corner, "do you never go to church?"

"No, Clifford!" she replied, — "not these many, many years!"

"Were I to be there," he rejoined, "it seems to me that I could pray once more, when so many human souls were praying all around me!"

She looked into Clifford's face, and beheld there a soft natural effusion; for his heart gushed out, as it were, and ran over at his eyes, in delightful reverence for God, and kindly affection for his human brethren. The emotion communicated itself to Hepzibah. She yearned to take him by the hand, and go and kneel down, they two together, — both so long separate from the world, and, as she now recognized, scarcely friends with Him above, — to kneel down among the people, and be reconciled to God and man at once.

"Dear brother," said she earnestly, "let us go! We belong nowhere. We have not a foot of space in any church to kneel upon; but let us go to some place of worship, even if we stand in the broad aisle. Poor and forsaken as we are, some pew-door will be opened to us!"

So Hepzibah and her brother made themselves, ready — as ready as they could in the best of their old-fashioned garments, which had hung on pegs, or been laid away in trunks, so long that the dampness and mouldy smell of the past was on them, — made themselves ready, in their faded bettermost, to go to church. They descended the staircase together, — gaunt, sallow Hepzibah, and pale, emaciated, age-stricken Clifford! They

The House of the Seven Gables

pulled open the front door, and stepped across the threshold, and felt, both of them, as if they were standing in the presence of the whole world, and with mankind's great and terrible eye on them alone. The eye of their Father seemed to be withdrawn, and gave them no encouragement. The warm sunny air of the street made them shiver. Their hearts quaked within them at the idea of taking one step farther.

"It cannot be, Hepzibah!—it is too late," said Clifford with deep sadness. "We are ghosts! We have no right among human beings,—no right anywhere but in this old house, which has a curse on it, and which, therefore, we are doomed to haunt! And, besides," he continued, with a fastidious sensibility, inalienably characteristic of the man, "it would not be fit nor beautiful to go! It is an ugly thought that I should be frightful to my fellow-beings, and that children would cling to their mothers' gowns at sight of me!"

They shrank back into the dusky passage-way, and closed the door. But, going up the staircase again, they found the whole interior of the house tenfold more dismal, and the air closer and heavier, for the glimpse and breath of freedom which they had just snatched. They could not flee; their jailer had but left the door ajar in mockery, and stood behind it to watch them stealing out. At the threshold, they felt his pitiless gripe upon them. For, what other dungeon is so dark as one's own heart! What jailer so inexorable as one's self!

But it would be no fair picture of Clifford's state of mind were we to represent him as continually or prevailingly wretched. On the contrary, there was no other man in the city, we are bold to affirm, of so much as half his years, who enjoyed so many lightsome and griefless moments as himself. He had no burden of care upon him; there were none of those questions and contingencies with the future to be settled which wear away all other lives, and render them not worth having by the very process of providing for their support. In this respect he was a child,—a child for the whole term of his existence, be it long or short. Indeed, his life seemed to be standing still at a period little in advance of childhood, and to cluster all his reminiscences about that epoch; just as, after the torpor of a heavy blow, the sufferer's reviving consciousness goes back to a moment considerably behind the accident that stupefied him. He sometimes told Phœbe and Hepzibah his dreams, in which he invariably played the part of a child, or a very young man. So vivid were they, in his relation of them, that he once held a dispute with his sister as to the particular figure or print of a chintz morning-dress which he had seen their mother wear, in the dream of the preceding night. Hepzibah, piquing herself on a woman's accuracy in such matters, held it to be slightly different from what Clifford described; but, producing the very gown from an old trunk, it proved to be identical with his remembrance of it. Had Clifford, every time that he emerged out of dreams so lifelike, undergone the torture of transformation from a boy into an old and broken man, the daily recurrence of the shock would have been too much to bear. It would have caused an acute agony to thrill from the morning twilight, all the day through, until bedtime; and even then would have mingled a dull, inscrutable pain and pallid hue of misfortune with the visionary bloom and adolescence of his slumber. But the nightly moonshine interwove itself with the morning mist, and enveloped him as in a robe, which he hugged about his person, and seldom let realities pierce through; he was not often quite awake, but slept open-eyed, and perhaps fancied himself most dreaming then.

Thus, lingering always so near his childhood, he had sympathies with children, and kept his heart the fresher thereby, like a reservoir into which rivulets were pouring not far from the fountain-head. Though prevented, by a subtile sense of propriety, from desiring to associate with them, he loved few things better than to look out of the arched window and see a little girl driving her hoop along the sidewalk, or schoolboys at a game of ball. Their voices, also, were very pleasant to him, heard at a distance, all swarming and intermingling together as flies do in a sunny room.

Clifford would, doubtless, have been glad to share their sports. One afternoon he was seized with an irresistible desire to blow soap-bubbles; an amusement, as Hepzibah told Phœbe apart, that had been a favorite one with her brother when they were both children. Behold him, therefore, at the arched window, with an earthen pipe in his mouth! Behold him, with his gray hair, and a wan, unreal smile over his countenance, where still hovered a beautiful grace, which his worst enemy must have acknowledged to be spiritual and immortal, since it had survived so long! Behold him, scattering airy spheres abroad from the window into the street! Little impalpable worlds were those soap-bubbles, with the big world depicted, in hues bright as imagination, on the nothing of their surface. It was curious to see how the passers-by regarded these brilliant fantasies, as they came floating down, and made the dull atmosphere imaginative about them. Some stopped to gaze, and perhaps, carried a pleasant recollection of the bubbles onward as far as the street-corner; some looked angrily upward, as if poor Clifford wronged them by setting an image of beauty afloat so near their dusty pathway. A great many put out their fingers or their walking-sticks to touch, withal; and were perversely gratified, no doubt, when the bubble, with all its pictured earth and sky scene, vanished as if it had never been.

At length, just as an elderly gentleman of very dignified presence happened to be passing, a large bubble sailed majestically down, and burst right against his nose! He looked

The House of the Seven Gables

up,—at first with a stern, keen glance, which penetrated at once into the obscurity behind the arched window,—then with a smile which might be conceived as diffusing a dog-day sultriness for the space of several yards about him.

"Aha, Cousin Clifford!" cried Judge Pyncheon. "What! Still blowing soap-bubbles!"

The tone seemed as if meant to be kind and soothing, but yet had a bitterness of sarcasm in it. As for Clifford, an absolute palsy of fear came over him. Apart from any definite cause of dread which his past experience might have given him, he felt that native and original horror of the excellent Judge which is proper to a weak, delicate, and apprehensive character in the presence of massive strength. Strength is incomprehensible by weakness, and, therefore, the more terrible. There is no greater bugbear than a strong-willed relative in the circle of his own connections.

XII.
The Daguerreotypist

It must not be supposed that the life of a personage naturally so active as Phœbe could be wholly confined within the precincts of the old Pyncheon House. Clifford's demands upon her time were usually satisfied, in those long days, considerably earlier than sunset. Quiet as his daily existence seemed, it nevertheless drained all the resources by which he lived. It was not physical exercise that overwearied him, — for except that he sometimes wrought a little with a hoe, or paced the garden-walk, or, in rainy weather, traversed a large unoccupied room, — it was his tendency to remain only too quiescent, as regarded any toil of the limbs and muscles. But, either there was a smouldering fire within him that consumed his vital energy, or the monotony that would have dragged itself with benumbing effect over a mind differently situated was no monotony to Clifford. Possibly, he was in a state of second growth and recovery, and was constantly assimilating nutriment for his spirit and intellect from sights, sounds, and events which passed as a perfect void to persons more practised with the world. As all is activity and vicissitude to the new mind of a child, so might it be, likewise, to a mind that had undergone a kind of new creation, after its long-suspended life.

Be the cause what it might, Clifford commonly retired to rest, thoroughly exhausted, while the sunbeams were still melting through his window-curtains, or were thrown with late lustre on the chamber wall. And while he thus slept early, as other children do, and dreamed of childhood, Phœbe was free to follow her own tastes for the remainder of the day and evening.

This was a freedom essential to the health even of a character so little susceptible of morbid influences as that of Phœbe. The old house, as we have already said, had both the dry-rot and the damp-rot in its walls; it was not good to breathe no other atmosphere than that. Hepzibah, though she had her valuable and redeeming traits, had grown to be a kind of lunatic by imprisoning herself so long in one place, with no other company than a single series of ideas, and but one affection, and one bitter sense of wrong. Clifford, the reader may perhaps imagine, was too inert to operate morally on his fellow-creatures, however intimate and exclusive their relations with him. But the sympathy or magnetism among human beings is more subtle and universal than we think; it exists, indeed, among different classes of organized life, and vibrates from one to another. A flower, for instance, as Phœbe herself observed, always began to droop sooner in Clifford's hand, or Hepzibah's, than in her own; and by the same law, converting her whole daily life into a flower fragrance for these two sickly spirits, the blooming girl must inevitably droop and fade much sooner than if worn on a younger and happier breast. Unless she had now and then indulged her brisk impulses, and breathed rural air in a suburban walk, or ocean breezes along the shore, — had occasionally obeyed the impulse of Nature, in New England girls, by attending a metaphysical or philosophical lecture, or viewing a seven-mile panorama, or listening to a concert, — had gone shopping about the city, ransacking entire depots of splendid merchandise, and bringing home a ribbon, — had employed, likewise, a little time to read the Bible in her chamber, and had stolen a little more to think of her mother and her native place — unless for such moral medicines as the above, we should soon have beheld our poor Phœbe grow thin and put on a bleached, unwholesome aspect, and assume strange, shy ways, prophetic of old-maidenhood and a cheerless future.

Even as it was, a change grew visible; a change partly to be regretted, although whatever charm it infringed upon was repaired by another, perhaps more precious. She was not so constantly gay, but had her moods of thought, which Clifford, on the whole, liked better than her former phase of unmingled cheerfulness; because now she understood him better and more delicately, and sometimes even interpreted him to himself. Her eyes looked larger, and darker, and deeper; so deep, at some silent moments, that they seemed like Artesian wells, down, down, into the infinite. She was less girlish than when we first beheld her alighting from the omnibus; less girlish, but more a woman.

The only youthful mind with which Phœbe had an opportunity of frequent intercourse was that of the daguerreotypist. Inevitably, by the pressure of the seclusion about them, they had been brought into habits of some familiarity. Had they met under different circumstances, neither of these young persons would have been likely to bestow much thought upon the other, unless, indeed, their extreme dissimilarity should have proved a principle of mutual attraction. Both, it is true, were characters proper to New England life, and possessing a common ground, therefore, in their more external developments; but as unlike, in their respective interiors, as if their native climes had been at world-wide distance. During the early part of their acquaintance, Phœbe had held back rather more than was customary with her frank and simple manners from Holgrave's not very marked advances. Nor was she yet satisfied that she knew him well, although they almost daily met and talked together, in a kind, friendly, and what seemed to be a familiar way.

The artist, in a desultory manner, had imparted to Phœbe something of his history. Young as he was, and had his career terminated at the point already attained, there had been enough of incident to fill, very creditably, an autobiographic volume. A romance on the plan of Gil Blas, adapted to American society and manners, would cease to be a romance. The experience of many individuals among us, who think it hardly worth the telling, would equal the vicissitudes of the Spaniard's earlier life; while their ultimate success, or the point whither they tend, may be incomparably higher than any that a novelist would imagine for his hero. Holgrave, as he told Phœbe somewhat proudly, could not boast of his origin, unless as being exceedingly humble, nor of his education, except that it had been the scantiest possible, and obtained by a few winter-months' attendance at a district school. Left early to his own guidance, he had begun to be self-dependent while yet a boy; and it was a condition aptly suited to his natural force of will. Though now but twenty-two years old (lacking some months, which are years in such a life), he had already been, first, a country schoolmaster; next, a salesman in a country store; and, either at the same time or afterwards, the political editor of a country newspaper. He had subsequently travelled New England and the Middle States, as a peddler, in the employment of a Connecticut manufactory of cologne-water and other essences. In an episodical way he had studied and practised dentistry, and with very flattering success, especially in many of the factory-towns along our inland streams. As a supernumerary official, of some kind or other, aboard a packet-ship, he had visited Europe, and found means, before his return, to see Italy, and part of France and Germany. At a later period he had spent some months in a community of Fourierists. Still more recently he had been a public lecturer on Mesmerism, for which science (as he assured Phœbe, and, indeed, satisfactorily proved, by putting Chanticleer, who happened to be scratching near by, to sleep) he had very remarkable endowments.

His present phase, as a daguerreotypist, was of no more importance in his own view, nor likely to be more permanent, than any of the preceding ones. It had been taken up with the careless alacrity of an adventurer, who had his bread to earn. It would be thrown aside as carelessly, whenever he should choose to earn his bread by some other equally digressive means. But what was most remarkable, and, perhaps, showed a more than common poise in the young man, was the fact that, amid all these personal vicissitudes, he had never lost his identity. Homeless as he had been,—continually changing his whereabout, and, therefore, responsible neither to public opinion nor to individuals,—putting off one exterior, and snatching up another, to be soon shifted for a third,—he had never violated the innermost man, but had carried his conscience along with him. It was impossible to know Holgrave without recognizing this to be the fact. Hepzibah had seen it. Phœbe soon saw it likewise, and gave him the sort of confidence which such a certainty inspires. She was startled, however, and sometimes repelled,—not by any doubt of his integrity to whatever law he acknowledged, but by a sense that his law differed from her own. He made her uneasy, and seemed to unsettle everything around her, by his lack of reverence for what was fixed, unless, at a moment's warning, it could establish its right to hold its ground.

Then, moreover, she scarcely thought him affectionate in his nature. He was too calm and cool an observer. Phœbe felt his eye, often; his heart, seldom or never. He took a certain kind of interest in Hepzibah and her brother, and Phœbe herself. He studied them attentively, and allowed no slightest circumstance of their individualities to escape him. He was ready to do them whatever good he might; but, after all, he never exactly made common cause with them, nor gave any reliable evidence that he loved them better in proportion as he knew them more. In his relations with them, he seemed to be in quest of mental food, not heart-sustenance. Phœbe could not conceive what interested him so much in her friends and herself, intellectually, since he cared nothing for them, or, comparatively, so little, as objects of human affection.

Always, in his interviews with Phœbe, the artist made especial inquiry as to the welfare of Clifford, whom, except at the Sunday festival, he seldom saw.

"Does he still seem happy?" he asked one day.

"As happy as a child," answered Phœbe; "but—like a child, too—very easily disturbed."

"How disturbed?" inquired Holgrave. "By things without, or by thoughts within?"

"I cannot see his thoughts! How should I?" replied Phœbe with simple piquancy. "Very often his humor changes without any reason that can be guessed at, just as a cloud comes over the sun. Latterly, since I have begun to know him better, I feel it to be not quite right to look closely into his moods. He has had such a great sorrow, that his heart is made all solemn and sacred by it. When he is cheerful,—when the sun shines into his mind,—then I venture to peep in, just as far as the light reaches, but no further. It is holy ground where the shadow falls!"

"How prettily you express this sentiment!" said the artist. "I can understand the feeling, without possessing it. Had I your opportunities, no scruples would prevent me from fathoming Clifford to the full depth of my plummet-line!"

"How strange that you should wish it!" remarked Phœbe involuntarily. "What is Cousin Clifford to you?"

"Oh, nothing,—of course, nothing!" answered Holgrave with a smile. "Only this is such an odd and incomprehensible world! The more I look at it, the more it puzzles me, and I begin to suspect that a man's bewilderment is the measure of his wisdom. Men and women, and children, too, are such strange creatures, that one never can be certain that he really knows them; nor ever guess what they have been from what he sees them to be now. Judge Pyncheon! Clifford! What a complex riddle—a complexity of complexities—do they present! It requires intuitive sympathy, like a young girl's, to solve it. A mere observer, like myself (who never have any intuitions, and am, at best, only subtile and acute), is pretty certain to go astray."

The artist now turned the conversation to themes less dark than that which they had touched upon. Phœbe and he were young together; nor had Holgrave, in his premature experience of life, wasted entirely that beautiful spirit of youth, which, gushing forth from one small heart and fancy, may diffuse itself over the universe, making it all as bright as on the first day of creation. Man's own youth is the world's youth; at least, he feels as if it were, and imagines that the earth's granite substance is something not yet hardened, and which he can mould into whatever shape he likes. So it was with Holgrave. He could talk sagely about the world's old age, but never actually believed what he said; he was a young man still, and therefore looked upon the world—that gray-bearded and wrinkled profligate, decrepit, without being venerable—as a tender stripling, capable of being improved into all that it ought to be, but scarcely yet had shown the remotest promise of becoming. He had that sense, or inward prophecy,—which a young man had better never have been born than not to have, and a mature man had better die at once than utterly to relinquish,—that we are not doomed to creep on forever in the old bad way, but that, this very now, there are the harbingers abroad of a golden era, to be accomplished in his own lifetime. It seemed to Holgrave, —as doubtless it has seemed to the hopeful of every century since the epoch of Adam's grandchildren,—that in this age, more than ever before, the moss-grown and rotten Past is to be torn down, and lifeless institutions to be thrust out of the way, and their dead corpses buried, and everything to begin anew.

As to the main point,—may we never live to doubt it!—as to the better centuries that are coming, the artist was surely right. His error lay in supposing that this age, more than any past or future one, is destined to see the tattered garments of Antiquity exchanged for a new suit, instead of gradually renewing themselves by patchwork; in applying his own little life-span as the measure of an interminable achievement; and, more than all, in fancying that it mattered anything to the great end in view whether he himself should contend for it or against it. Yet it was well for him to think so. This enthusiasm, infusing itself through the calmness of his character, and thus taking an aspect of settled thought and wisdom, would serve to keep his youth pure, and make his aspirations high. And when, with the years settling down more weightily upon him, his early faith should be modified by inevitable experience, it would be with no harsh and sudden revolution of his sentiments. He would still have faith in man's brightening destiny, and perhaps love him all the better, as he should recognize his helplessness in his own behalf; and the haughty faith, with which he began life, would be well bartered for a far humbler one at its close, in discerning that man's best directed effort accomplishes a kind of dream, while God is the sole worker of realities.

Holgrave had read very little, and that little in passing through the thoroughfare of life, where the mystic language of his books was necessarily mixed up with the babble of the multitude, so that both one and the other were apt to lose any sense that might have been properly their own. He considered himself a thinker, and was certainly of a thoughtful turn, but, with his own path to discover, had perhaps hardly yet reached the point where an educated man begins to think. The true value of his character lay in that deep consciousness of inward strength, which made all his past vicissitudes seem merely like a change of garments; in that enthusiasm, so quiet that he scarcely knew of its existence, but which gave a warmth to everything that he laid his hand on; in that personal ambition, hidden—from his own as well as other eyes—among his more generous impulses, but in which lurked a certain efficacy, that might solidify him from a theorist into the champion of some practicable cause. Altogether in his culture and want of culture, —in his crude, wild, and misty philosophy, and the practical experience that counteracted some of its tendencies; in his magnanimous zeal for man's welfare, and his recklessness of whatever the ages had established in man's behalf; in his faith, and in his infidelity; in what he had, and in what he lacked,—the artist might fitly enough stand forth as the representative of many compeers in his native land.

His career it would be difficult to prefigure. There appeared to be qualities in Holgrave, such as, in a country where everything is free to the hand that can grasp it, could hardly fail to put some of the world's prizes within his reach. But these matters are delightfully uncertain. At almost every step in life, we meet with young men of just about Holgrave's age, for whom we anticipate wonderful things, but of whom, even after much and careful inquiry, we never happen to hear another word. The effervescence of youth and passion, and the fresh gloss of the intellect and imagination, endow them with a false brilliancy, which makes fools of themselves and other people. Like certain chintzes, calicoes, and ginghams, they show finely in their first newness, but cannot stand the sun and rain, and assume a very sober aspect after washing-day.

But our business is with Holgrave as we find him on this particular afternoon, and in the arbor of the Pyncheon garden. In that point of view, it was a pleasant sight to behold this young man, with so much faith in himself, and so fair an appearance of admirable powers, — so little harmed, too, by the many tests that had tried his metal, — it was pleasant to see him in his kindly intercourse with Phœbe. Her thought had scarcely done him justice when it pronounced him cold; or, if so, he had grown warmer now. Without such purpose on her part, and unconsciously on his, she made the House of the Seven Gables like a home to him, and the garden a familiar precinct. With the insight on which he prided himself, he fancied that he could look through Phœbe, and all around her, and could read her off like a page of a child's story-book. But these transparent natures are often deceptive in their depth; those pebbles at the bottom of the fountain are farther from us than we think. Thus the artist, whatever he might judge of Phœbe's capacity, was beguiled, by some silent charm of hers, to talk freely of what he dreamed of doing in the world. He poured himself out as to another self. Very possibly, he forgot Phœbe while he talked to her, and was moved only by the inevitable tendency of thought, when rendered sympathetic by enthusiasm and emotion, to flow into the first safe reservoir which it finds. But, had you peeped at them through the chinks of the garden-fence, the young man's earnestness and heightened color might have led you to suppose that he was making love to the young girl!

At length, something was said by Holgrave that made it apposite for Phœbe to inquire what had first brought him acquainted with her cousin Hepzibah, and why he now chose to lodge in the desolate old Pyncheon House. Without directly answering her, he turned from the Future, which had heretofore been the theme of his discourse, and began to speak of the influences of the Past. One subject, indeed, is but the reverberation of the other.

"Shall we never, never get rid of this Past?" cried he, keeping up the earnest tone of his preceding conversation. "It lies upon the Present like a giant's dead body! In fact, the case is just as if a young giant were compelled to waste all his strength in carrying about the corpse of the old giant, his grandfather, who died a long while ago, and only needs to be decently buried. Just think a moment, and it will startle you to see what slaves we are to bygone times, — to Death, if we give the matter the right word!"

"But I do not see it," observed Phœbe.

"For example, then," continued Holgrave: "a dead man, if he happens to have made a will, disposes of wealth no longer his own; or, if he die intestate, it is distributed in accordance with the notions of men much longer dead than he. A dead man sits on all our judgment-seats; and living judges do but search out and repeat his decisions. We read in dead men's books! We laugh at dead men's jokes, and cry at dead men's pathos! We are sick of dead men's diseases, physical and moral, and die of the same remedies with which dead doctors killed their patients! We worship the living Deity according to dead men's forms and creeds. Whatever we seek to do, of our own free motion, a dead man's icy hand obstructs us! Turn our eyes to what point we may, a dead man's white, immitigable face encounters them, and freezes our very heart! And we must be dead ourselves before we can begin to have our proper influence on our own world, which will then be no longer our world, but the world of another generation, with which we shall have no shadow of a right to interfere. I ought to have said, too, that we live in dead men's houses; as, for instance, in this of the Seven Gables!"

"And why not," said Phœbe, "so long as we can be comfortable in them?"

"But we shall live to see the day, I trust," went on the artist, "when no man shall build his house for posterity. Why should he? He might just as reasonably order a durable suit of clothes, — leather, or guttapercha, or whatever else lasts longest, — so that his great-grandchildren should have the benefit of them, and cut precisely the same figure in the world that he himself does. If each generation were allowed and expected to build its own houses, that single change, comparatively unimportant in itself, would imply almost every reform which society is now suffering for. I doubt whether even our public edifices — our capitols, state-houses, court-houses, city-hall, and churches, — ought to be built of such permanent materials as stone or brick. It were better that they should crumble to ruin once in twenty years, or thereabouts, as a hint to the people to examine into and reform the institutions which they symbolize."

"How you hate everything old!" said Phœbe in dismay. "It makes me dizzy to think of such a shifting world!"

"I certainly love nothing mouldy," answered Holgrave. "Now, this old Pyncheon House! Is it a wholesome place to live in, with its black shingles, and the green moss that shows how damp they are? — its dark, low-studded rooms — its grime and sordidness, which are the crystallization on its walls of the human breath, that has been drawn and exhaled here in discontent and anguish? The house ought to be purified with fire, — purified till only its ashes remain!"

"Then why do you live in it?" asked Phœbe, a little piqued.

"Oh, I am pursuing my studies here; not in books, however," replied Holgrave. "The house, in my view, is expressive of that odious and abominable Past, with all its bad influences, against which I have just been declaiming. I dwell in it for a while, that I may know the better how to hate it. By the bye, did you ever hear the story of Maule, the wizard, and what happened between him and your immeasurably great-grandfather?"

"Yes, indeed!" said Phœbe; "I heard it long ago, from my father, and two or three times from my cousin Hepzibah, in the month that I have been here. She seems to think that all the calamities of the Pyncheons began from that quarrel with the wizard, as you call him. And you, Mr. Holgrave look as if you thought so too! How singular that you should believe what is so very absurd, when you reject many things that are a great deal worthier of credit!"

"I do believe it," said the artist seriously; "not as a superstition, however, but as proved by unquestionable facts, and as exemplifying a theory. Now, see: under those seven gables, at which we now look up, — and which old Colonel Pyncheon meant to be the house of his descendants, in prosperity and happiness, down to an epoch far beyond the present, — under that roof, through a portion of three centuries, there has been perpetual remorse of conscience, a constantly defeated hope, strife amongst kindred, various misery, a strange form of death, dark suspicion, unspeakable disgrace, — all, or most of which calamity I have the means of tracing to the old Puritan's inordinate desire to plant and endow a family. To plant a family! This idea is at the bottom of most of the wrong and mischief which men do. The truth is, that, once in every half-century, at longest, a family should be merged into the great, obscure mass of humanity, and forget all about its ancestors. Human blood, in order to keep its freshness, should run in hidden streams, as the water of an aqueduct is conveyed in subterranean pipes. In the family existence of these Pyncheons, for instance, — forgive me Phœbe, but I cannot think of you as one of them, — in their brief New England pedigree, there has been time enough to infect them all with one kind of lunacy or another."

"You speak very unceremoniously of my kindred," said Phœbe, debating with herself whether she ought to take offence.

"I speak true thoughts to a true mind!" answered Holgrave, with a vehemence which Phœbe had not before witnessed in him. "The truth is as I say! Furthermore, the original perpetrator and father of this mischief appears to have perpetuated himself, and still walks the street, — at least, his very image, in mind and body, — with the fairest prospect of transmitting to posterity as rich and as wretched an inheritance as he has received! Do you remember the daguerreotype, and its resemblance to the old portrait?"

"How strangely in earnest you are!" exclaimed Phœbe, looking at him with surprise and perplexity; half alarmed and partly inclined to laugh. "You talk of the lunacy of the Pyncheons; is it contagious?"

"I understand you!" said the artist, coloring and laughing. "I believe I am a little mad. This subject has taken hold of my mind with the strangest tenacity of clutch since I have lodged in yonder old gable. As one method of throwing it off, I have put an incident of the Pyncheon family history, with which I happen to be acquainted, into the form of a legend, and mean to publish it in a magazine."

"Do you write for the magazines?" inquired Phœbe.

"Is it possible you did not know it?" cried Holgrave. "Well, such is literary fame! Yes. Miss Phœbe Pyncheon, among the multitude of my marvellous gifts I have that of writing stories; and my name has figured, I can assure you, on the covers of Graham and Godey, making as respectable an appearance, for aught I could see, as any of the canonized bead-roll with which it was associated. In the humorous line, I am thought to have a very pretty way with me; and as for pathos, I am as provocative of tears as an onion. But shall I read you my story?"

"Yes, if it is not very long," said Phœbe, — and added laughingly, — "nor very dull."

As this latter point was one which the daguerreotypist could not decide for himself, he forthwith produced his roll of manuscript, and, while the late sunbeams gilded the seven gables, began to read.

XIII.
Alice Pyncheon

There was a message brought, one day, from the worshipful Gervayse Pyncheon to young Matthew Maule, the carpenter, desiring his immediate presence at the House of the Seven Gables.

"And what does your master want with me?" said the carpenter to Mr. Pyncheon's black servant. "Does the house need any repair? Well it may, by this time; and no blame to my father who built it, neither! I was reading the old Colonel's tombstone, no longer ago than last Sabbath; and, reckoning from that date, the house has stood seven-and-thirty years. No wonder if there should be a job to do on the roof."

"Don't know what massa wants," answered Scipio. "The house is a berry good house, and old Colonel Pyncheon think so too, I reckon;—else why the old man haunt it so, and frighten a poor nigga, As he does?"

"Well, well, friend Scipio; let your master know that I'm coming," said the carpenter with a laugh. "For a fair, workmanlike job, he'll find me his man. And so the house is haunted, is it? It will take a tighter workman than I am to keep the spirits out of the Seven Gables. Even if the Colonel would be quiet," he added, muttering to himself, "my old grandfather, the wizard, will be pretty sure to stick to the Pyncheons as long as their walls hold together."

"What's that you mutter to yourself, Matthew Maule?" asked Scipio. "And what for do you look so black at me?"

"No matter, darky," said the carpenter. "Do you think nobody is to look black but yourself? Go tell your master I'm coming; and if you happen to see Mistress Alice, his daughter, give Matthew Maule's humble respects to her. She has brought a fair face from Italy,—fair, and gentle, and proud,—has that same Alice Pyncheon!"

"He talk of Mistress Alice!" cried Scipio, as he returned from his errand. "The low carpenter-man! He no business so much as to look at her a great way off!"

This young Matthew Maule, the carpenter, it must be observed, was a person little understood, and not very generally liked, in the town where he resided; not that anything could be alleged against his integrity, or his skill and diligence in the handicraft which he exercised. The aversion (as it might justly be called) with which many persons regarded him was partly

The House of the Seven Gables

the result of his own character and deportment, and partly an inheritance.

He was the grandson of a former Matthew Maule, one of the early settlers of the town, and who had been a famous and terrible wizard in his day. This old reprobate was one of the sufferers when Cotton Mather, and his brother ministers, and the learned judges, and other wise men, and Sir William Phipps, the sagacious governor, made such laudable efforts to weaken the great enemy of souls, by sending a multitude of his adherents up the rocky pathway of Gallows Hill. Since those days, no doubt, it had grown to be suspected that, in consequence of an unfortunate overdoing of a work praiseworthy in itself, the proceedings against the witches had proved far less acceptable to the Beneficent Father than to that very Arch Enemy whom they were intended to distress and utterly overwhelm. It is not the less certain, however, that awe and terror brooded over the memories of those who died for this horrible crime of witchcraft. Their graves, in the crevices of the rocks, were supposed to be incapable of retaining the occupants who had been so hastily thrust into them. Old Matthew Maule, especially, was known to have as little hesitation or difficulty in rising out of his grave as an ordinary man in getting out of bed, and was as often seen at midnight as living people at noonday. This pestilent wizard (in whom his just punishment seemed to have wrought no manner of amendment) had an inveterate habit of haunting a certain mansion, styled the House of the Seven Gables, against the owner of which he pretended to hold an unsettled claim for ground-rent. The ghost, it appears, — with the pertinacity which was one of his distinguishing characteristics while alive, — insisted that he was the rightful proprietor of the site upon which the house stood. His terms were, that either the aforesaid ground-rent, from the day when the cellar began to be dug, should be paid down, or the mansion itself given up; else he, the ghostly creditor, would have his finger in all the affairs of the Pyncheons, and make everything go wrong with them, though it should be a thousand years after his death. It was a wild story, perhaps, but seemed not altogether so incredible to those who could remember what an inflexibly obstinate old fellow this wizard Maule had been.

Now, the wizard's grandson, the young Matthew Maule of our story, was popularly supposed to have inherited some of his ancestor's questionable traits. It is wonderful how many absurdities were promulgated in reference to the young man. He was fabled, for example, to have a strange power of getting into people's dreams, and regulating matters there according to his own fancy, pretty much like the stage-manager of a theatre. There was a great deal of talk among the neighbors, particularly the petticoated ones, about what they called the witchcraft of Maule's eye. Some said that he could look into people's minds;

others, that, by the marvellous power of this eye, he could draw people into his own mind, or send them, if he pleased, to do errands to his grandfather, in the spiritual world; others, again, that it was what is termed an Evil Eye, and possessed the valuable faculty of blighting corn, and drying children into mummies with the heartburn. But, after all, what worked most to the young carpenter's disadvantage was, first, the reserve and sternness of his natural disposition, and next, the fact of his not being a church-communicant, and the suspicion of his holding heretical tenets in matters of religion and polity.

After receiving Mr. Pyncheon's message, the carpenter merely tarried to finish a small job, which he happened to have in hand, and then took his way towards the House of the Seven Gables. This noted edifice, though its style might be getting a little out of fashion, was still as respectable a family residence as that of any gentleman in town. The present owner, Gervayse Pyncheon, was said to have contracted a dislike to the house, in consequence of a shock to his sensibility, in early childhood, from the sudden death of his grandfather. In the very act of running to climb Colonel Pyncheon's knee, the boy had discovered the old Puritan to be a corpse. On arriving at manhood, Mr. Pyncheon had visited England, where he married a lady of fortune, and had subsequently spent many years, partly in the mother country, and partly in various cities on the continent of Europe. During this period, the family mansion had been consigned to the charge of a kinsman, who was allowed to make it his home for the time being, in consideration of keeping the premises in thorough repair. So faithfully had this contract been fulfilled, that now, as the carpenter approached the house, his practised eye could detect nothing to criticise in its condition. The peaks of the seven gables rose up sharply; the shingled roof looked thoroughly water-tight; and the glittering plaster-work entirely covered the exterior walls, and sparkled in the October sun, as if it had been new only a week ago.

The house had that pleasant aspect of life which is like the cheery expression of comfortable activity in the human countenance. You could see, at once, that there was the stir of a large family within it. A huge load of oak-wood was passing through the gateway, towards the outbuildings in the rear; the fat cook—or probably it might be the housekeeper—stood at the side door, bargaining for some turkeys and poultry which a countryman had brought for sale. Now and then a maid-servant, neatly dressed, and now the shining sable face of a slave, might be seen bustling across the windows, in the lower part of the house. At an open window of a room in the second story, hanging over some pots of beautiful and delicate flowers, —exotics, but which had never known a more genial sunshine than that of the New England autumn,—was the figure of a young lady, an exotic, like the flowers, and beautiful and delicate as they. Her presence imparted an indescribable grace and faint witchery to the whole edifice. In other respects, it was a substantial, jolly-looking mansion, and seemed fit to be the residence of a patriarch, who might establish his own headquarters in the front gable and assign one of the remainder to each of his six children, while the great chimney in the centre should symbolize the old fellow's hospitable heart, which kept them all warm, and made a great whole of the seven smaller ones.

There was a vertical sundial on the front gable; and as the carpenter passed beneath it, he looked up and noted the hour.

"Three o'clock!" said he to himself. "My father told me that dial was put up only an hour before the old Colonel's death. How truly it has kept time these seven-and-thirty years past! The shadow creeps and creeps, and is always looking over the shoulder of the sunshine!"

It might have befitted a craftsman, like Matthew Maule, on being sent for to a gentleman's house, to go to the back door, where servants and work-people were usually admitted; or at least to the side entrance, where the better class of tradesmen made application. But the carpenter had a great deal of pride and stiffness in his nature; and, at this moment, moreover, his heart was bitter with the sense of hereditary wrong, because he considered the great Pyncheon House to be standing on soil which should have been his own. On this very site, beside a spring of delicious water, his grandfather had felled the pine-trees and built a cottage, in which children had been born to him; and it was only from a dead man's stiffened fingers that Colonel Pyncheon had wrested away the title-deeds. So young Maule went straight to the principal entrance, beneath a portal of carved oak, and gave such a peal of the iron knocker that you would have imagined the stern old wizard himself to be standing at the threshold.

Black Scipio answered the summons in a prodigious hurry; but showed the whites of his eyes, in amazement on beholding only the carpenter.

"Lord-a-mercy, what a great man he be, this carpenter fellow!" mumbled Scipio, down in his throat. "Anybody think he beat on the door with his biggest hammer!"

"Here I am!" said Maule sternly. "Show me the way to your master's parlor."

As he stept into the house, a note of sweet and melancholy music thrilled and vibrated along the passage-way, proceeding from one of the rooms above stairs. It was the harpsichord which Alice Pyncheon had brought with her from beyond the sea. The fair Alice bestowed most of her maiden leisure between flowers and music, although the former were apt to droop, and the melodies were often sad. She was of foreign education, and could not take kindly to the New England modes of life, in which nothing beautiful had ever been developed.

As Mr. Pyncheon had been impatiently awaiting Maule's arrival, black Scipio, of course, lost no time in ushering the carpenter into his master's presence. The room in which this gentleman sat was a parlor of moderate size, looking out upon the garden of the house, and having its windows partly shadowed by the foliage of fruit-trees. It was Mr. Pyncheon's peculiar apartment, and was provided with furniture, in an elegant and costly style, principally from Paris; the floor (which was unusual at that day) being covered with a carpet, so skilfully and richly wrought that it seemed to glow as with living flowers. In one corner stood a marble woman, to whom her own beauty was the sole and sufficient garment. Some pictures—that looked old, and had a mellow tinge diffused through all their artful splendor—hung on the walls. Near the fireplace was a large and very beautiful cabinet of ebony, inlaid with ivory; a piece of antique furniture, which Mr. Pyncheon had bought in Venice, and which he used as the treasure-place for medals, ancient coins, and whatever small and valuable curiosities he had picked up on his travels. Through all this variety of decoration, however, the room showed its original characteristics; its low stud, its cross-beam, its chimney-piece, with the old-fashioned Dutch tiles; so that it was the emblem of a mind industriously stored with foreign ideas, and elaborated into artificial refinement, but neither larger, nor, in its proper self, more elegant than before.

There were two objects that appeared rather out of place in this very handsomely furnished room. One was a large map, or surveyor's plan, of a tract of land, which looked as if it had been drawn a good many years ago, and was now dingy with smoke, and soiled, here and there, with the touch of fingers. The other was a portrait of a stern old man, in a Puritan garb, painted roughly, but with a bold effect, and a remarkably strong expression of character.

At a small table, before a fire of English sea-coal, sat Mr. Pyncheon, sipping coffee, which had grown to be a very favorite beverage with him in France. He was a middle-aged and really handsome man, with a wig flowing down upon his shoulders; his coat was of blue velvet, with lace on the borders and at the button-holes; and the firelight glistened on the spacious breadth of his waistcoat, which was flowered all over with gold. On the entrance of Scipio, ushering in the carpenter, Mr. Pyncheon turned partly round, but resumed his former position, and proceeded deliberately to finish his cup of coffee, without immediate notice of the guest whom he had summoned to his presence. It was not that he intended any rudeness or improper neglect,—which, indeed, he would have blushed to be guilty of,—but it never occurred to him that a person in Maule's station had a claim on his courtesy, or would trouble himself about it one way or the other.

The carpenter, however, stepped at once to the hearth, and turned himself about, so as to look Mr. Pyncheon in the face.

"You sent for me," said he. "Be pleased to explain your business, that I may go back to my own affairs."

"Ah! excuse me," said Mr. Pyncheon quietly. "I did not mean to tax your time without a recompense. Your name, I think, is Maule,—Thomas or Matthew Maule,—a son or grandson of the builder of this house?"

"Matthew Maule," replied the carpenter,—"son of him who built the house,—grandson of the rightful proprietor of the soil."

"I know the dispute to which you allude," observed Mr. Pyncheon with undisturbed equanimity. "I am well aware that my grandfather was compelled to resort to a suit at law, in order to establish his claim to the foundation-site of this edifice. We will not, if you please, renew the discussion. The matter was settled at the time, and by the competent authorities,—equitably, it is to be presumed,—and, at all events, irrevocably. Yet, singularly enough, there is an incidental reference to this very subject in what I am now about to say to you. And this same inveterate grudge,—excuse me, I mean no offence,—this irritability, which you have just shown, is not entirely aside from the matter."

"If you can find anything for your purpose, Mr. Pyncheon," said the carpenter, "in a man's natural resentment for the wrongs done to his blood, you are welcome to it."

"I take you at your word, Goodman Maule," said the owner of the Seven Gables, with a smile, "and will proceed to suggest a mode in which your hereditary resentments—justifiable or otherwise—may have had a bearing on my affairs. You have heard, I suppose, that the Pyncheon family, ever since my grandfather's days, have been prosecuting a still unsettled claim to a very large extent of territory at the Eastward?"

"Often," replied Maule,—and it is said that a smile came over his face,—"very often,—from my father!"

"This claim," continued Mr. Pyncheon, after pausing a

moment, as if to consider what the carpenter's smile might mean, "appeared to be on the very verge of a settlement and full allowance, at the period of my grandfather's decease. It was well known, to those in his confidence, that he anticipated neither difficulty nor delay. Now, Colonel Pyncheon, I need hardly say, was a practical man, well acquainted with public and private business, and not at all the person to cherish ill-founded hopes, or to attempt the following out of an impracticable scheme. It is obvious to conclude, therefore, that he had grounds, not apparent to his heirs, for his confident anticipation of success in the matter of this Eastern claim. In a word, I believe,—and my legal advisers coincide in the belief, which, moreover, is authorized, to a certain extent, by the family traditions,—that my grandfather was in possession of some deed, or other document, essential to this claim, but which has since disappeared."

"Very likely," said Matthew Maule,—and again, it is said, there was a dark smile on his face,—"but what can a poor carpenter have to do with the grand affairs of the Pyncheon family?"

"Perhaps nothing," returned Mr. Pyncheon, "possibly much!"

Here ensued a great many words between Matthew Maule and the proprietor of the Seven Gables, on the subject which the latter had thus broached. It seems (although Mr. Pyncheon had some hesitation in referring to stories so exceedingly absurd in their aspect) that the popular belief pointed to some mysterious connection and dependence, existing between the family of the Maules and these vast unrealized possessions of the Pyncheons. It was an ordinary saying that the old wizard, hanged though he was, had obtained the best end of the bargain in his contest with Colonel Pyncheon; inasmuch as he had got possession of the great Eastern claim, in exchange for an acre or two of garden-ground. A very aged woman, recently dead, had often used the metaphorical expression, in her fireside talk, that miles and miles of the Pyncheon lands had been shovelled into Maule's grave; which, by the bye, was but a very shallow nook, between two rocks, near the summit of Gallows' Hill. Again, when the lawyers were making inquiry for the missing document, it was a by-word that it would never be found, unless in the wizard's skeleton hand. So much weight had the shrewd lawyers assigned to these fables, that (but Mr. Pyncheon did not see fit to inform the carpenter of the fact) they had secretly caused the wizard's grave to be searched. Nothing was discovered, however, except that, unaccountably, the right hand of the skeleton was gone.

Now, what was unquestionably important, a portion of these popular rumors could be traced, though rather doubtfully

The House of the Seven Gables

and indistinctly, to chance words and obscure hints of the executed wizard's son, and the father of this present Matthew Maule. And here Mr. Pyncheon could bring an item of his own personal evidence into play. Though but a child at the time, he either remembered or fancied that Matthew's father had had some job to perform on the day before, or possibly the very morning of the Colonel's decease, in the private room where he and the carpenter were at this moment talking. Certain papers belonging to Colonel Pyncheon, as his grandson distinctly recollected, had been spread out on the table.

Matthew Maule understood the insinuated suspicion.

"My father," he said,—but still there was that dark smile, making a riddle of his countenance,—"my father was an honester man than the bloody old Colonel! Not to get his rights back again would he have carried off one of those papers!"

"I shall not bandy words with you," observed the foreign-bred Mr. Pyncheon, with haughty composure. "Nor will it become me to resent any rudeness towards either my grandfather or myself. A gentleman, before seeking intercourse with a person of your station and habits, will first consider whether the urgency of the end may compensate for the disagreeableness of the means. It does so in the present instance."

He then renewed the conversation, and made great pecuniary offers to the carpenter, in case the latter should give information leading to the discovery of the lost document, and the consequent success of the Eastern claim. For a long time Matthew Maule is said to have turned a cold ear to these propositions. At last, however, with a strange kind of laugh, he inquired whether Mr. Pyncheon would make over to him the old wizard's homestead-ground, together with the House of the Seven Gables, now standing on it, in requital of the documentary evidence so urgently required.

The wild, chimney-corner legend (which, without copying all its extravagances, my narrative essentially follows) here gives an account of some very strange behavior on the part of Colonel Pyncheon's portrait. This picture, it must be understood, was supposed to be so intimately connected with the fate of the house, and so magically built into its walls, that, if once it should be removed, that very instant the whole edifice would come thundering down in a heap of dusty ruin. All through the foregoing conversation between Mr. Pyncheon and the carpenter, the portrait had been frowning, clenching its fist, and giving many such proofs of excessive discomposure, but without attracting the notice of either of the two colloquists. And finally, at Matthew Maule's audacious suggestion of a transfer of the seven-gabled structure, the ghostly portrait is averred to have lost all patience, and to have shown itself on the point of descending bodily from its frame. But such incredible incidents are merely to be mentioned aside.

"Give up this house!" exclaimed Mr. Pyncheon, in amazement at the proposal. "Were I to do so, my grandfather would not rest quiet in his grave!"

"He never has, if all stories are true," remarked the carpenter composedly. "But that matter concerns his grandson more than it does Matthew Maule. I have no other terms to propose."

Impossible as he at first thought it to comply with Maule's conditions, still, on a second glance, Mr. Pyncheon was of opinion that they might at least be made matter of discussion. He himself had no personal attachment for the house, nor any pleasant associations connected with his childish residence in it. On the contrary, after seven-and-thirty years, the presence of his dead grandfather seemed still to pervade it, as on that morning when the affrighted boy had beheld him, with so ghastly an aspect, stiffening in his chair. His long abode in foreign parts, moreover, and familiarity with many of the castles and ancestral halls of England, and the marble palaces of Italy, had caused him to look contemptuously at the House of the Seven Gables, whether in point of splendor or convenience. It was a mansion exceedingly inadequate to the style of living which it would be incumbent on Mr. Pyncheon to support, after realizing his territorial rights. His steward might deign to occupy it, but never, certainly, the great landed proprietor himself. In the event of success, indeed, it was his purpose to return to England; nor, to say the truth, would he recently have quitted that more congenial home, had not his own fortune, as well as his deceased wife's, begun to give symptoms of exhaustion. The Eastern claim once fairly settled, and put upon the firm basis of actual possession, Mr. Pyncheon's property — to be measured by miles, not acres — would be worth an earldom, and would reasonably entitle him to solicit, or enable him to purchase, that elevated dignity from the British monarch. Lord Pyncheon! — or the Earl of Waldo! — how could such a magnate be expected to contract his grandeur within the pitiful compass of seven shingled gables?

In short, on an enlarged view of the business, the carpenter's terms appeared so ridiculously easy that Mr. Pyncheon could scarcely forbear laughing in his face. He was quite ashamed, after the foregoing reflections, to propose any diminution of so moderate a recompense for the immense service to be rendered.

"I consent to your proposition, Maule!" cried he. "Put me in possession of the document essential to establish my rights, and the House of the Seven Gables is your own!"

According to some versions of the story, a regular contract to the above effect was drawn up by a lawyer, and signed and sealed in the presence of witnesses. Others say that Matthew Maule was contented with a private written agreement, in which Mr. Pyncheon pledged his honor and integrity to the fulfillment of the terms concluded upon. The gentleman then ordered wine, which he and the carpenter drank together, in confirmation of their bargain. During the whole preceding discussion and subsequent formalities, the old Puritan's portrait seems to have persisted in its shadowy gestures of disapproval; but without effect, except that, as Mr. Pyncheon set down the emptied glass, he thought he beheld his grandfather frown.

"This sherry is too potent a wine for me; it has affected my brain already," he observed, after a somewhat startled look at the picture. "On returning to Europe, I shall confine myself to the more delicate vintages of Italy and France, the best of which will not bear transportation."

"My Lord Pyncheon may drink what wine he will, and wherever he pleases," replied the carpenter, as if he had been privy to Mr. Pyncheon's ambitious projects. "But first, sir, if you desire tidings of this lost document, I must crave the favor of a little talk with your fair daughter Alice."

"You are mad, Maule!" exclaimed Mr. Pyncheon haughtily; and now, at last, there was anger mixed up with his pride. "What can my daughter have to do with a business like this?"

Indeed, at this new demand on the carpenter's part, the proprietor of the Seven Gables was even more thunder-struck than at the cool proposition to surrender his house. There was, at least, an assignable motive for the first stipulation; there appeared to be none whatever for the last. Nevertheless, Matthew Maule sturdily insisted on the young lady being summoned, and even gave her father to understand, in a mysterious kind of explanation,—which made the matter considerably darker than it looked before,—that the only chance of acquiring the requisite knowledge was through the clear, crystal medium of a pure and virgin intelligence, like that of the fair Alice. Not to encumber our story with Mr. Pyncheon's scruples, whether of conscience, pride, or fatherly affection, he at length ordered his daughter to be called. He well knew that she was in her chamber, and engaged in no occupation that could not readily be laid aside; for, as it happened, ever since Alice's name had been spoken, both her father and the carpenter had heard the sad and sweet music of her harpsichord, and the airier melancholy of her accompanying voice.

So Alice Pyncheon was summoned, and appeared. A portrait of this young lady, painted by a Venetian artist, and left by her father in England, is said to have fallen into the hands of the present Duke of Devonshire, and to be now preserved at Chatsworth; not on account of any associations with the original, but for its value as a picture, and the high character of beauty in the countenance. If ever there was a lady born, and set apart from the world's vulgar mass by a certain gentle and cold stateliness, it was this very Alice Pyncheon. Yet there was the womanly mixture in her; the tenderness, or, at least, the tender capabilities. For the sake of that redeeming quality, a man of generous nature would have forgiven all her pride, and have been content, almost, to lie down in her path, and let Alice set her slender foot upon his heart. All that he would have required was simply the acknowledgment that he was indeed a man, and a fellow-being, moulded of the same elements as she.

As Alice came into the room, her eyes fell upon the carpenter, who was standing near its centre, clad in green woollen jacket, a pair of loose breeches, open at the knees, and with a long pocket for his rule, the end of which protruded; it was as proper a mark of the artisan's calling as Mr. Pyncheon's full-dress sword of that gentleman's aristocratic pretensions. A glow of artistic approval brightened over Alice Pyncheon's face; she was struck with admiration—which she made no attempt to conceal—of the remarkable comeliness, strength, and energy of Maule's figure. But that admiring glance (which most other men, perhaps, would have cherished as a sweet recollection all through life) the carpenter never forgave. It must have been the devil himself that made Maule so subtile in his preception.

"Does the girl look at me as if I were a brute beast?" thought he, setting his teeth. "She shall know whether I have a human spirit; and the worse for her, if it prove stronger than her own!"

"My father, you sent for me," said Alice, in her sweet and harp-like voice. "But, if you have business with this young man, pray let me go again. You know I do not love this room, in spite of that Claude, with which you try to bring back sunny recollections."

"Stay a moment, young lady, if you please!" said Matthew Maule. "My business with your father is over. With yourself, it is now to begin!"

Alice looked towards her father, in surprise and inquiry.

"Yes, Alice," said Mr. Pyncheon, with some disturbance and confusion. "This young man—his name is Matthew Maule—professes, so far as I can understand him, to be able to discover, through your means, a certain paper or parchment, which was missing long before your birth. The importance of the document in question renders it advisable to neglect no possible, even if improbable, method of regaining it. You will therefore oblige me, my dear Alice, by answering this person's inquiries, and complying with his lawful and reasonable requests, so far as they may appear to have the aforesaid object in view. As I shall remain in the room, you need apprehend no rude nor unbecoming deportment, on the young man's part; and, at your slightest wish, of course, the investigation, or whatever we may call it, shall immediately be broken off."

"Mistress Alice Pyncheon," remarked Matthew Maule, with the utmost deference, but yet a half-hidden sarcasm in his look and tone, "will no doubt feel herself quite safe in her father's presence, and under his all-sufficient protection."

"I certainly shall entertain no manner of apprehension, with my father at hand," said Alice with maidenly dignity. "Neither do I conceive that a lady, while true to herself, can have aught to fear from whomsoever, or in any circumstances!"

Poor Alice! By what unhappy impulse did she thus put herself at once on terms of defiance against a strength which she could not estimate?

"Then, Mistress Alice," said Matthew Maule, handing a chair, — gracefully enough, for a craftsman, "will it please you only to sit down, and do me the favor (though altogether beyond a poor carpenter's deserts) to fix your eyes on mine!"

Alice complied, She was very proud. Setting aside all advantages of rank, this fair girl deemed herself conscious of a power — combined of beauty, high, unsullied purity, and the preservative force of womanhood — that could make her sphere impenetrable, unless betrayed by treachery within. She instinctively knew, it may be, that some sinister or evil potency was now striving to pass her barriers; nor would she decline the contest. So Alice put woman's might against man's might; a match not often equal on the part of woman.

Her father meanwhile had turned away, and seemed absorbed in the contemplation of a landscape by Claude, where a shadowy and sun-streaked vista penetrated so remotely into an ancient wood, that it would have been no wonder if his fancy had lost itself in the picture's bewildering depths. But, in truth, the picture was no more to him at that moment than the blank wall against which it hung. His mind was haunted with the many and strange tales which he had heard, attributing mysterious if not supernatural endowments to these Maules, as well the grandson here present as his two immediate ancestors. Mr. Pyncheon's long residence abroad, and intercourse with men of wit and fashion, — courtiers, worldlings, and free-thinkers, — had done much towards obliterating the grim Puritan superstitions, which no man of New England birth at that early period could entirely escape. But, on the other hand, had not a whole community believed Maule's grandfather to be a wizard? Had not the crime been proved? Had not the wizard died for it? Had he not bequeathed a legacy of hatred against the Pyncheons to this only grandson, who, as it appeared, was now about to exercise a subtle influence over the daughter of his enemy's house? Might not this influence be the same that was called witchcraft?

Turning half around, he caught a glimpse of Maule's figure in the looking-glass. At some paces from Alice, with his arms uplifted in the air, the carpenter made a gesture as if directing downward a slow, ponderous, and invisible weight upon the maiden.

"Stay, Maule!" exclaimed Mr. Pyncheon, stepping forward. "I forbid your proceeding further!"

"Pray, my dear father, do not interrupt the young man," said Alice, without changing her position. "His efforts, I assure you, will prove very harmless."

Again Mr. Pyncheon turned his eyes towards the Claude. It was then his daughter's will, in opposition to his own, that the experiment should be fully tried. Henceforth, therefore, he did but consent, not urge it. And was it not for her sake far more than for his own that he desired its success? That lost parchment once restored, the beautiful Alice Pyncheon, with the rich dowry which he could then bestow, might wed an English duke or a German reigning-prince, instead of some New England clergyman or lawyer! At the thought, the ambitious father almost consented, in his heart, that, if the devil's power were needed to the accomplishment of this great object, Maule might evoke him. Alice's own purity would be her safeguard.

With his mind full of imaginary magnificence, Mr. Pyncheon heard a half-uttered exclamation from his daughter. It was very faint and low; so indistinct that there seemed but half a will to shape out the words, and too undefined a purport to be intelligible. Yet it was a call for help! — his conscience never doubted it; — and, little more than a whisper to his ear, it was a dismal shriek, and long reechoed so, in the region round his heart! But this time the father did not turn.

After a further interval, Maule spoke.

"Behold your daughter," said he.

Mr. Pyncheon came hastily forward. The carpenter was standing erect in front of Alice's chair, and pointing his finger towards the maiden with an expression of triumphant power, the limits of which could not be defined, as, indeed, its scope

The House of the Seven Gables

stretched vaguely towards the unseen and the infinite. Alice sat in an attitude of profound repose, with the long brown lashes drooping over her eyes.

"There she is!" said the carpenter. "Speak to her!"

"Alice! My daughter!" exclaimed Mr. Pyncheon. "My own Alice!"

She did not stir.

"Louder!" said Maule, smiling.

"Alice! Awake!" cried her father. "It troubles me to see you thus! Awake!"

He spoke loudly, with terror in his voice, and close to that delicate ear which had always been so sensitive to every discord. But the sound evidently reached her not. It is indescribable what a sense of remote, dim, unattainable distance betwixt himself and Alice was impressed on the father by this impossibility of reaching her with his voice.

"Best touch her!" said Matthew Maule "Shake the girl, and roughly, too! My hands are hardened with too much use of axe, saw, and plane,—else I might help you!"

Mr. Pyncheon took her hand, and pressed it with the earnestness of startled emotion. He kissed her, with so great a heart-throb in the kiss, that he thought she must needs feel it. Then, in a gust of anger at her insensibility, he shook her maiden form with a violence which, the next moment, it affrighted him to remember. He withdrew his encircling arms, and Alice—whose figure, though flexible, had been wholly impassive—relapsed into the same attitude as before these attempts to arouse her. Maule having shifted his position, her face was turned towards him slightly, but with what seemed to be a reference of her very slumber to his guidance.

Then it was a strange sight to behold how the man of conventionalities shook the powder out of his periwig; how the reserved and stately gentleman forgot his dignity; how the gold-embroidered waistcoat flickered and glistened in the firelight with the convulsion of rage, terror, and sorrow in the human heart that was beating under it.

"Villain!" cried Mr. Pyncheon, shaking his clenched fist at Maule. "You and the fiend together have robbed me of my daughter. Give her back, spawn of the old wizard, or you shall climb Gallows Hill in your grandfather's footsteps!"

"Softly, Mr. Pyncheon!" said the carpenter with scornful composure. "Softly, an' it please your worship, else you will spoil those rich lace-ruffles at your wrists! Is it my crime if you have sold your daughter for the mere hope of getting a sheet of yellow parchment into your clutch? There sits Mistress Alice quietly asleep. Now let Matthew Maule try whether she be as proud as the carpenter found her awhile since."

He spoke, and Alice responded, with a soft, subdued, inward acquiescence, and a bending of her form towards him, like the flame of a torch when it indicates a gentle draught of air. He beckoned with his hand, and, rising from her chair,—blindly, but undoubtingly, as tending to her sure and inevitable centre,—the proud Alice approached him. He waved her back, and, retreating, Alice sank again into her seat.

"She is mine!" said Matthew Maule. "Mine, by the right of the strongest spirit!"

In the further progress of the legend, there is a long, grotesque, and occasionally awe-striking account of the carpenter's incantations (if so they are to be called), with a view of discovering the lost document. It appears to have been his object to convert the mind of Alice into a kind of telescopic medium, through which Mr. Pyncheon and himself might obtain a glimpse into the spiritual world. He succeeded, accordingly, in holding an imperfect sort of intercourse, at one remove, with the departed personages in whose custody the so much valued secret had been carried beyond the precincts of earth. During her trance, Alice described three figures as being present to her spiritualized perception. One was an aged, dignified, stern-looking gentleman, clad as for a solemn festival in grave and costly attire, but with a great blood-stain on his richly wrought band; the second, an aged man, meanly dressed, with a dark and malign countenance, and a broken halter about his neck; the third, a person not so advanced in life as the former two, but beyond the middle age, wearing a coarse woollen tunic and leather breeches, and with a carpenter's rule sticking out of his side pocket. These three visionary characters possessed a mutual knowledge of the missing document. One of them, in truth,—it was he with the blood-stain on his band,—seemed, unless his gestures were misunderstood, to hold the parchment in his immediate keeping, but was prevented by his two partners in the mystery from disburdening himself of the trust. Finally, when he showed a purpose of shouting forth the secret loudly enough to be heard from his own sphere into that of mortals, his companions struggled with him, and pressed their hands over his mouth; and forthwith—whether that he were choked by it, or that the secret itself was of a crimson hue—there was a fresh flow of blood upon his band. Upon this, the two meanly dressed figures mocked and jeered at the much-abashed old dignitary, and pointed their fingers at the stain.

At this juncture, Maule turned to Mr. Pyncheon.

"It will never be allowed," said he. "The custody of this secret, that would so enrich his heirs, makes part of your grandfather's retribution. He must choke with it until it is no longer of any value. And keep you the House of the Seven Gables! It is too dear bought an inheritance, and too heavy with the curse upon it, to be shifted yet awhile from the Colonel's posterity."

Mr. Pyncheon tried to speak, but—what with fear and passion—could make only a gurgling murmur in his throat. The carpenter smiled.

"Aha, worshipful sir!—so you have old Maule's blood to drink!" said he jeeringly.

"Fiend in man's shape! why dost thou keep dominion over my child?" cried Mr. Pyncheon, when his choked utterance could make way. "Give me back my daughter. Then go thy ways; and may we never meet again!"

"Your daughter!" said Matthew Maule. "Why, she is fairly mine! Nevertheless, not to be too hard with fair Mistress Alice, I will leave her in your keeping; but I do not warrant you that she shall never have occasion to remember Maule, the carpenter."

He waved his hands with an upward motion; and, after a few repetitions of similar gestures, the beautiful Alice Pyncheon awoke from her strange trance. She awoke without the slightest recollection of her visionary experience; but as one losing herself in a momentary reverie, and returning to the consciousness of actual life, in almost as brief an interval as the down-sinking flame of the hearth should quiver again up the chimney. On recognizing Matthew Maule, she assumed an air of somewhat cold but gentle dignity, the rather, as there was a certain peculiar smile on the carpenter's visage that stirred the native pride of the fair Alice. So ended, for that time, the quest for the lost title-deed of the Pyncheon territory at the Eastward; nor, though often subsequently renewed, has it ever yet befallen a Pyncheon to set his eye upon that parchment.

But, alas for the beautiful, the gentle, yet too haughty Alice! A power that she little dreamed of had laid its grasp upon her maiden soul. A will, most unlike her own, constrained her to do its grotesque and fantastic bidding. Her father as it proved, had martyred his poor child to an inordinate desire for measuring his land by miles instead of acres. And, therefore, while Alice Pyncheon lived, she was Maule's slave, in a bondage more humiliating, a thousand-fold, than that which binds its chain around the body. Seated by his humble fireside, Maule had but to wave his hand; and, wherever the proud lady chanced to be, — whether in her chamber, or entertaining her father's stately guests, or worshipping at church, — whatever her place or occupation, her spirit passed from beneath her own control, and bowed itself to Maule. "Alice, laugh!" — the carpenter, beside his hearth, would say; or perhaps intensely will it, without a spoken word. And, even were it prayer-time, or at a funeral, Alice must break into wild laughter. "Alice, be sad!" — and, at the instant, down would come her tears, quenching all the mirth of those around her like sudden rain upon a bonfire. "Alice, dance." — and dance she would, not in such court-like measures as she had learned abroad, but some high-paced jig, or hop-skip rigadoon, befitting the brisk lasses at a rustic merry-making. It seemed to be Maule's impulse, not to ruin Alice, nor to visit her with any black or gigantic mischief, which would have crowned her sorrows with the grace of tragedy, but to wreak a low, ungenerous scorn upon her. Thus all the dignity of life was lost. She felt herself too much abased, and longed to change natures with some worm!

One evening, at a bridal party (but not her own; for, so lost from self-control, she would have deemed it sin to marry), poor Alice was beckoned forth by her unseen despot, and constrained, in her gossamer white dress and satin slippers, to hasten along the street to the mean dwelling of a laboring-man. There was laughter and good cheer within; for Matthew Maule, that night, was to wed the laborer's daughter, and had summoned proud Alice Pyncheon to wait upon his bride. And so she did; and when the twain were one, Alice awoke out of her enchanted sleep. Yet, no longer proud, — humbly, and with a smile all steeped in sadness, — she kissed Maule's wife, and went her way. It was an inclement night; the southeast wind drove the mingled snow and rain into her thinly sheltered bosom; her satin slippers were wet through and through, as she trod the muddy sidewalks. The next day a cold; soon, a settled cough; anon, a hectic cheek, a wasted form, that sat beside the harpsichord, and filled the house with music! Music in which a strain of the heavenly choristers was echoed! Oh; joy! For Alice had borne her last humiliation! Oh, greater joy! For Alice was penitent of her one earthly sin, and proud no more!

The Pyncheons made a great funeral for Alice. The kith and kin were there, and the whole respectability of the town besides. But, last in the procession, came Matthew Maule, gnashing his teeth, as if he would have bitten his own heart in twain, — the darkest and wofullest man that ever walked behind a corpse! He meant to humble Alice, not to kill her; but he had taken a woman's delicate soul into his rude gripe, to play with — and she was dead!

XIV.
Phœbe's Good-Bye

Holgrave, plunging into his tale with the energy and absorption natural to a young author, had given a good deal of action to the parts capable of being developed and exemplified in that manner. He now observed that a certain remarkable drowsiness (wholly unlike that with which the reader possibly feels himself affected) had been flung over the senses of his auditress. It was the effect, unquestionably, of the mystic gesticulations by which he had sought to bring bodily before Phœbe's perception the figure of the mesmerizing carpenter. With the lids drooping over her eyes, — now lifted for an instant, and drawn down again as with leaden weights, — she leaned slightly towards him, and seemed almost to regulate her breath by his. Holgrave gazed at her, as he rolled up his manuscript, and recognized an incipient stage of that curious psychological condition which, as he had himself told Phœbe, he possessed more than an ordinary faculty of producing. A veil was beginning to be muffled about her, in which she could behold only him, and live only in his thoughts and emotions. His glance, as he fastened it on the young girl, grew involuntarily more concentrated; in his attitude there was the consciousness of power, investing his hardly mature figure with a dignity that did not belong to its physical manifestation. It was evident, that, with but one wave of his hand and a corresponding effort of his will, he could complete his mastery over Phœbe's yet free and virgin spirit: he could establish an influence over this good, pure, and simple child, as dangerous, and perhaps as disastrous, as that which the carpenter of his legend had acquired and exercised over the ill-fated Alice.

To a disposition like Holgrave's, at once speculative and active, there is no temptation so great as the opportunity of acquiring empire over the human spirit; nor any idea more seductive to a young man than to become the arbiter of a young girl's destiny. Let us, therefore, — whatever his defects of nature and education, and in spite of his scorn for creeds and institutions, — concede to the daguerreotypist the rare and high quality of reverence for another's individuality. Let us allow him integrity, also, forever after to be confided in; since he forbade himself to twine that one link more which might have rendered his spell over Phœbe indissoluble.

He made a slight gesture upward with his hand.

"You really mortify me, my dear Miss Phœbe!" he exclaimed, smiling half-sarcastically at her. "My poor story, it is but too evident, will never do for Godey or Graham! Only think of your falling asleep at what I hoped the newspaper critics would pronounce a most brilliant, powerful, imaginative, pathetic, and original winding up! Well, the manuscript must serve to light lamps with;—if, indeed, being so imbued with my gentle dulness, it is any longer capable of flame!"

"Me asleep! How can you say so?" answered Phœbe, as unconscious of the crisis through which she had passed as an infant of the precipice to the verge of which it has rolled. "No, no! I consider myself as having been very attentive; and, though I don't remember the incidents quite distinctly, yet I have an impression of a vast deal of trouble and calamity,—so, no doubt, the story will prove exceedingly attractive."

By this time the sun had gone down, and was tinting the clouds towards the zenith with those bright hues which are not seen there until some time after sunset, and when the horizon has quite lost its richer brilliancy. The moon, too, which had long been climbing overhead, and unobtrusively melting its disk into the azure,—like an ambitious demagogue, who hides his aspiring purpose by assuming the prevalent hue of popular sentiment,—now began to shine out, broad and oval, in its middle pathway. These silvery beams were already powerful enough to change the character of the lingering daylight. They softened and embellished the aspect of the old house; although the shadows fell deeper into the angles of its many gables, and lay brooding under the projecting story, and within the half-open door. With the lapse of every moment, the garden grew more picturesque; the fruit-trees, shrubbery, and flower-bushes had a dark obscurity among them. The commonplace characteristics—which, at noontide, it seemed to have taken a century of sordid life to accumulate—were now transfigured by a charm of romance. A hundred mysterious years were whispering among the leaves, whenever the slight sea-breeze found its way thither and stirred them. Through the foliage that roofed the little summer-house the moonlight flickered to and fro, and fell silvery white on the dark floor, the table, and the circular bench, with a continual shift and play, according as the chinks and wayward crevices among the twigs admitted or shut out the glimmer.

So sweetly cool was the atmosphere, after all the feverish day, that the summer eve might be fancied as sprinkling dews and liquid moonlight, with a dash of icy temper in them, out of a silver vase. Here and there, a few drops of this freshness were scattered on a human heart, and gave it youth again, and sympathy with the eternal youth of nature. The artist chanced to be one on whom the reviving influence fell. It made him feel—what he sometimes almost forgot, thrust so early as he had been into the rude struggle of man with man—how youthful he still was.

"It seems to me," he observed, "that I never watched the

The House of the Seven Gables

coming of so beautiful an eve, and never felt anything so very much like happiness as at this moment. After all, what a good world we live in! How good, and beautiful! How young it is, too, with nothing really rotten or age-worn in it! This old house, for example, which sometimes has positively oppressed my breath with its smell of decaying timber! And this garden, where the black mould always clings to my spade, as if I were a sexton delving in a graveyard! Could I keep the feeling that now possesses me, the garden would every day be virgin soil, with the earth's first freshness in the flavor of its beans and squashes; and the house!—it would be like a bower in Eden, blossoming with the earliest roses that God ever made. Moonlight, and the sentiment in man's heart responsive to it, are the greatest of renovators and reformers. And all other reform and renovation, I suppose, will prove to be no better than moonshine!"

"I have been happier than I am now; at least, much gayer," said Phœbe thoughtfully. "Yet I am sensible of a great charm in this brightening moonlight; and I love to watch how the day, tired as it is, lags away reluctantly, and hates to be called yesterday so soon. I never cared much about moonlight before. What is there, I wonder, so beautiful in it, to-night?"

"And you have never felt it before?" inquired the artist, looking earnestly at the girl through the twilight.

"Never," answered Phœbe; "and life does not look the same, now that I have felt it so. It seems as if I had looked at everything, hitherto, in broad daylight, or else in the ruddy light of a cheerful fire, glimmering and dancing through a room. Ah, poor me!" she added, with a half-melancholy laugh. "I shall never be so merry as before I knew Cousin Hepzibah and poor Cousin Clifford. I have grown a great deal older, in this little time. Older, and, I hope, wiser, and,—not exactly sadder,—but, certainly, with not half so much lightness in my spirits! I have given them my sunshine, and have been glad to give it; but, of course, I cannot both give and keep it. They are welcome, notwithstanding!"

"You have lost nothing, Phœbe, worth keeping, nor which it was possible to keep," said Holgrave after a pause. "Our first youth is of no value; for we are never conscious of it until after it is gone. But sometimes—always, I suspect, unless one is exceedingly unfortunate—there comes a sense of second youth, gushing out of the heart's joy at being in love; or, possibly, it may come to crown some other grand festival in life, if any other such there be. This bemoaning of one's self (as you do now) over the first, careless, shallow gayety of youth departed, and this profound happiness at youth regained,—so much deeper and richer than that we lost,—are essential to the soul's development. In some cases, the two states come almost simultaneously, and mingle the sadness and the rapture in one mysterious emotion."

"I hardly think I understand you," said Phœbe.

"No wonder," replied Holgrave, smiling; "for I have told you a secret which I hardly began to know before I found myself giving it utterance. Remember it, however; and when the truth becomes clear to you, then think of this moonlight scene!"

"It is entirely moonlight now, except only a little flush of faint crimson, upward from the west, between those buildings," remarked Phœbe. "I must go in. Cousin Hepzibah is not quick at figures, and will give herself a headache over the day's accounts, unless I help her."

But Holgrave detained her a little longer.

"Miss Hepzibah tells me," observed he, "that you return to the country in a few days."

"Yes, but only for a little while," answered Phœbe; "for I look upon this as my present home. I go to make a few arrangements, and to take a more deliberate leave of my mother and friends. It is pleasant to live where one is much desired and very useful; and I think I may have the satisfaction of feeling myself so here."

"You surely may, and more than you imagine," said the artist. "Whatever health, comfort, and natural life exists in the house is embodied in your person. These blessings came along with you, and will vanish when you leave the threshold. Miss Hepzibah, by secluding herself from society, has lost all true relation with it, and is, in fact, dead; although she galvanizes herself into a semblance of life, and stands behind her counter, afflicting the world with a greatly-to-be-deprecated scowl. Your poor cousin Clifford is another dead and long-buried person, on whom the governor and council have wrought a necromantic miracle. I should not wonder if he were to crumble away, some morning, after you are gone, and nothing be seen of him more, except a heap of dust. Miss Hepzibah, at any rate, will lose what little flexibility she has. They both exist by you."

"I should be very sorry to think so," answered Phœbe gravely. "But it is true that my small abilities were precisely what they needed; and I have a real interest in their welfare,— an odd kind of motherly sentiment,— which I wish you would not laugh at! And let me tell you frankly, Mr. Holgrave, I am sometimes puzzled to know whether you wish them well or ill."

"Undoubtedly," said the daguerreotypist, "I do feel an

The House of the Seven Gables

interest in this antiquated, poverty-stricken old maiden lady, and this degraded and shattered gentleman,—this abortive lover of the beautiful. A kindly interest, too, helpless old children that they are! But you have no conception what a different kind of heart mine is from your own. It is not my impulse, as regards these two individuals, either to help or hinder; but to look on, to analyze, to explain matters to myself, and to comprehend the drama which, for almost two hundred years, has been dragging its slow length over the ground where you and I now tread. If permitted to witness the close, I doubt not to derive a moral satisfaction from it, go matters how they may. There is a conviction within me that the end draws nigh. But, though Providence sent you hither to help, and sends me only as a privileged and meet spectator, I pledge myself to lend these unfortunate beings whatever aid I can!"

"I wish you would speak more plainly," cried Phœbe, perplexed and displeased; "and, above all, that you would feel more like a Christian and a human being! How is it possible to see people in distress without desiring, more than anything else, to help and comfort them? You talk as if this old house were a theatre; and you seem to look at Hepzibah's and Clifford's misfortunes, and those of generations before them, as a tragedy, such as I have seen acted in the hall of a country hotel, only the present one appears to be played exclusively for your amusement. I do not like this. The play costs the performers too much, and the audience is too cold-hearted."

"You are severe," said Holgrave, compelled to recognize a degree of truth in the piquant sketch of his own mood.

"And then," continued Phœbe, "what can you mean by your conviction, which you tell me of, that the end is drawing near? Do you know of any new trouble hanging over my poor relatives? If so, tell me at once, and I will not leave them!"

"Forgive me, Phœbe!" said the daguerreotypist, holding out his hand, to which the girl was constrained to yield her own. "I am somewhat of a mystic, it must be confessed. The tendency is in my blood, together with the faculty of mesmerism, which might have brought me to Gallows Hill, in the good old times of witchcraft. Believe me, if I were really aware of any secret, the disclosure of which would benefit your friends,—who are my own friends, likewise,—you should learn it before we part. But I have no such knowledge."

"You hold something back!" said Phœbe.

"Nothing,—no secrets but my own," answered Holgrave. "I can perceive, indeed, that Judge Pyncheon still keeps his eye on Clifford, in whose ruin he had so large a share. His motives and intentions, however are a mystery to me. He is a determined and relentless man, with the genuine character of an inquisitor; and had he any object to gain by putting Clifford to the rack, I verily believe that he would wrench his joints from their sockets, in order to accomplish it. But, so wealthy and eminent as he is, — so powerful in his own strength, and in the support of society on all sides, — what can Judge Pyncheon have to hope or fear from the imbecile, branded, half-torpid Clifford?"

"Yet," urged Phœbe, "you did speak as if misfortune were impending!"

"Oh, that was because I am morbid!" replied the artist. "My mind has a twist aside, like almost everybody's mind, except your own. Moreover, it is so strange to find myself an inmate of this old Pyncheon House, and sitting in this old garden — (hark, how Maule's well is murmuring!) — that, were it only for this one circumstance, I cannot help fancying that Destiny is arranging its fifth act for a catastrophe."

"There!" cried Phœbe with renewed vexation; for she was by nature as hostile to mystery as the sunshine to a dark corner. "You puzzle me more than ever!"

"Then let us part friends!" said Holgrave, pressing her hand. "Or, if not friends, let us part before you entirely hate me. You, who love everybody else in the world!"

"Good-by, then," said Phœbe frankly. "I do not mean to be angry a great while, and should be sorry to have you think so. There has Cousin Hepzibah been standing in the shadow of the doorway, this quarter of an hour past! She thinks I stay too long in the damp garden. So, good-night, and good-by."

On the second morning thereafter, Phœbe might have been seen, in her straw bonnet, with a shawl on one arm and a little carpet-bag on the other, bidding adieu to Hepzibah and Cousin Clifford. She was to take a seat in the next train of cars, which would transport her to within half a dozen miles of her country village.

The tears were in Phœbe's eyes; a smile, dewy with affectionate regret, was glimmering around her pleasant mouth. She wondered how it came to pass, that her life of a few weeks, here in this heavy-hearted old mansion, had taken such hold of her, and so melted into her associations, as now to seem a more important centre-point of remembrance than all which had gone before. How had Hepzibah — grim, silent, and irresponsive to her overflow of cordial sentiment — contrived to win so much love? And Clifford, — in his abortive decay, with the mystery of fearful crime upon him, and the close prison-atmosphere yet lurking in his breath, — how had he transformed himself into the

The House of the Seven Gables

simplest child, whom Phœbe felt bound to watch over, and be, as it were, the providence of his unconsidered hours! Everything, at that instant of farewell, stood out prominently to her view. Look where she would, lay her hand on what she might, the object responded to her consciousness, as if a moist human heart were in it.

She peeped from the window into the garden, and felt herself more regretful at leaving this spot of black earth, vitiated with such an age-long growth of weeds, than joyful at the idea of again scenting her pine forests and fresh clover-fields. She called Chanticleer, his two wives, and the venerable chicken, and threw them some crumbs of bread from the breakfast-table. These being hastily gobbled up, the chicken spread its wings, and alighted close by Phœbe on the window-sill, where it looked gravely into her face and vented its emotions in a croak. Phœbe bade it be a good old chicken during her absence, and promised to bring it a little bag of buckwheat.

"Ah, Phœbe!" remarked Hepzibah, "you do not smile so naturally as when you came to us! Then, the smile chose to shine out; now, you choose it should. It is well that you are going back, for a little while, into your native air. There has been too much weight on your spirits. The house is too gloomy and lonesome; the shop is full of vexations; and as for me, I have no faculty of making things look brighter than they are. Dear Clifford has been your only comfort!"

"Come hither, Phœbe," suddenly cried her cousin Clifford, who had said very little all the morning. "Close!—closer!—and look me in the face!"

Phœbe put one of her small hands on each elbow of his chair, and leaned her face towards him, so that he might peruse it as carefully as he would. It is probable that the latent emotions of this parting hour had revived, in some degree, his bedimmed and enfeebled faculties. At any rate, Phœbe soon felt that, if not the profound insight of a seer, yet a more than feminine delicacy of appreciation, was making her heart the subject of its regard. A moment before, she had known nothing which she would have sought to hide. Now, as if some secret were hinted to her own consciousness through the medium of another's perception, she was fain to let her eyelids droop beneath Clifford's gaze. A blush, too,—the redder, because she strove hard to keep it down,—ascended bigger and higher, in a tide of fitful progress, until even her brow was all suffused with it.

"It is enough, Phœbe," said Clifford, with a melancholy smile. "When I first saw you, you were the prettiest little maiden in the world; and now you have deepened into beauty. Girlhood has passed into womanhood; the bud is a bloom! Go, now — I feel lonelier than I did."

Phœbe took leave of the desolate couple, and passed through the shop, twinkling her eyelids to shake off a dew-drop; for — considering how brief her absence was to be, and therefore the folly of being cast down about it — she would not so far acknowledge her tears as to dry them with her handkerchief. On the doorstep, she met the little urchin whose marvellous feats of gastronomy have been recorded in the earlier pages of our narrative. She took from the window some specimen or other of natural history, — her eyes being too dim with moisture to inform her accurately whether it was a rabbit or a hippopotamus, — put it into the child's hand as a parting gift, and went her way. Old Uncle Venner was just coming out of his door, with a wood-horse and saw on his shoulder; and, trudging along the street, he scrupled not to keep company with Phœbe, so far as their paths lay together; nor, in spite of his patched coat and rusty beaver, and the curious fashion of his tow-cloth trousers, could she find it in her heart to outwalk him.

"We shall miss you, next Sabbath afternoon," observed the street philosopher. "It is unaccountable how little while it takes some folks to grow just as natural to a man as his own breath; and, begging your pardon, Miss Phœbe (though there can be no offence in an old man's saying it), that's just what you've grown to me! My years have been a great many, and your life is but just beginning; and yet, you are somehow as familiar to me as if I had found you at my mother's door, and you had blossomed, like a running vine, all along my pathway since. Come back soon, or I shall be gone to my farm; for I begin to find these wood-sawing jobs a little too tough for my back-ache."

"Very soon, Uncle Venner," replied Phœbe.

"And let it be all the sooner, Phœbe, for the sake of those poor souls yonder," continued her companion. "They can never do without you, now, — never, Phœbe; never — no more than if one of God's angels had been living with them, and making their dismal house pleasant and comfortable! Don't it seem to you they'd be in a sad case, if, some pleasant summer morning like this, the angel should spread his wings, and fly to the place he came from? Well, just so they feel, now that you're going home by the railroad! They can't bear it, Miss Phœbe; so be sure to come back!"

"I am no angel, Uncle Venner," said Phœbe, smiling, as she offered him her hand at the street-corner. "But, I suppose, people never feel so much like angels as when they are doing what little good they may. So I shall certainly come back!"

Thus parted the old man and the rosy girl; and Phœbe took the wings of the morning, and was soon flitting almost as

The House of the Seven Gables

rapidly away as if endowed with the aerial locomotion of the angels to whom Uncle Venner had so graciously compared her.

XV.

The Scowl and Smile

Several days passed over the Seven Gables, heavily and drearily enough. In fact (not to attribute the whole gloom of sky and earth to the one inauspicious circumstance of Phœbe's departure), an easterly storm had set in, and indefatigably apply itself to the task of making the black roof and walls of the old house look more cheerless than ever before. Yet was the outside not half so cheerless as the interior. Poor Clifford was cut off, at once, from all his scanty resources of enjoyment. Phœbe was not there; nor did the sunshine fall upon the floor. The garden, with its muddy walks, and the chill, dripping foliage of its summer-house, was an image to be shuddered at. Nothing flourished in the cold, moist, pitiless atmosphere, drifting with the brackish scud of sea-breezes, except the moss along the joints of the shingle-roof, and the great bunch of weeds, that had lately been suffering from drought, in the angle between the two front gables.

As for Hepzibah, she seemed not merely possessed with the east wind, but to be, in her very person, only another phase of this gray and sullen spell of weather; the East-Wind itself, grim and disconsolate, in a rusty black silk gown, and with a turban of cloud-wreaths on its head. The custom of the shop fell off, because a story got abroad that she soured her small beer and other damageable commodities, by scowling on them. It is, perhaps, true that the public had something reasonably to complain of in her deportment; but towards Clifford she was neither ill-tempered nor unkind, nor felt less warmth of heart than always, had it been possible to make it reach him. The inutility of her best efforts, however, palsied the poor old gentlewoman. She could do little else than sit silently in a corner of the room, when the wet pear-tree branches, sweeping across the small windows, created a noonday dusk, which Hepzibah unconsciously darkened with her woe-begone aspect. It was no fault of Hepzibah's. Everything—even the old chairs and tables, that had known what weather was for three or four such lifetimes as her own—looked as damp and chill as if the present were their worst experience. The picture of the Puritan Colonel shivered on the wall. The house itself shivered, from every attic of its seven gables down to the great kitchen fireplace, which served all the better as an emblem of the mansion's heart, because, though built for warmth, it was now so comfortless and empty.

Hepzibah attempted to enliven matters by a fire in the parlor. But the storm demon kept watch above, and, whenever a flame was kindled, drove the smoke back again, choking the chimney's sooty throat with its own breath. Nevertheless,

The House of the Seven Gables

during four days of this miserable storm, Clifford wrapt himself in an old cloak, and occupied his customary chair. On the morning of the fifth, when summoned to breakfast, he responded only by a broken-hearted murmur, expressive of a determination not to leave his bed. His sister made no attempt to change his purpose. In fact, entirely as she loved him, Hepzibah could hardly have borne any longer the wretched duty—so impracticable by her few and rigid faculties—of seeking pastime for a still sensitive, but ruined mind, critical and fastidious, without force or volition. It was at least something short of positive despair, that to-day she might sit shivering alone, and not suffer continually a new grief, and unreasonable pang of remorse, at every fitful sigh of her fellow sufferer.

But Clifford, it seemed, though he did not make his appearance below stairs, had, after all, bestirred himself in quest of amusement. In the course of the forenoon, Hepzibah heard a note of music, which (there being no other tuneful contrivance in the House of the Seven Gables) she knew must proceed from Alice Pyncheon's harpsichord. She was aware that Clifford, in his youth, had possessed a cultivated taste for music, and a considerable degree of skill in its practice. It was difficult, however, to conceive of his retaining an accomplishment to which daily exercise is so essential, in the measure indicated by the sweet, airy, and delicate, though most melancholy strain, that now stole upon her ear. Nor was it less marvellous that the long-silent instrument should be capable of so much melody. Hepzibah involuntarily thought of the ghostly harmonies, prelusive of death in the family, which were attributed to the legendary Alice. But it was, perhaps, proof of the agency of other than spiritual fingers, that, after a few touches, the chords seemed to snap asunder with their own vibrations, and the music ceased.

But a harsher sound succeeded to the mysterious notes; nor was the easterly day fated to pass without an event sufficient in itself to poison, for Hepzibah and Clifford, the balmiest air that ever brought the humming-birds along with it. The final echoes of Alice Pyncheon's performance (or Clifford's, if his we must consider it) were driven away by no less vulgar a dissonance than the ringing of the shop-bell. A foot was heard scraping itself on the threshold, and thence somewhat ponderously stepping on the floor. Hepzibah delayed a moment, while muffling herself in a faded shawl, which had been her defensive armor in a forty years' warfare against the east wind. A characteristic sound, however,—neither a cough nor a hem, but a kind of rumbling and reverberating spasm in somebody's capacious depth of chest;—impelled her to hurry forward, with that aspect of fierce faint-heartedness so common to women in cases of perilous emergency. Few of her sex, on such occasions, have ever looked so terrible as our poor scowling Hepzibah. But the visitor quietly closed the shop-door behind him, stood up his umbrella against the counter, and turned a visage of composed benignity, to meet the alarm and anger which his appearance had excited.

Hepzibah's presentiment had not deceived her. It was no other than Judge Pyncheon, who, after in vain trying the front door, had now effected his entrance into the shop.

"How do you do, Cousin Hepzibah?—and how does this most inclement weather affect our poor Clifford?" began the Judge; and wonderful it seemed, indeed, that the easterly storm was not put to shame, or, at any rate, a little mollified, by the genial benevolence of his smile. "I could not rest without calling to ask, once more, whether I can in any manner promote his comfort, or your own."

"You can do nothing," said Hepzibah, controlling her agitation as well as she could. "I devote myself to Clifford. He has every comfort which his situation admits of."

"But allow me to suggest, dear cousin," rejoined the Judge, "you err,—in all affection and kindness, no doubt, and with the very best intentions,—but you do err, nevertheless, in keeping your brother so secluded. Why insulate him thus from all sympathy and kindness? Clifford, alas! has had too much of solitude. Now let him try society,—the society, that is to say, of kindred and old friends. Let me, for instance, but see Clifford, and I will answer for the good effect of the interview."

"You cannot see him," answered Hepzibah. "Clifford has kept his bed since yesterday."

"What! How! Is he ill?" exclaimed Judge Pyncheon, starting with what seemed to be angry alarm; for the very frown of the old Puritan darkened through the room as he spoke. "Nay, then, I must and will see him! What if he should die?"

"He is in no danger of death," said Hepzibah,—and added, with bitterness that she could repress no longer, "none; unless he shall be persecuted to death, now, by the same man who long ago attempted it!"

"Cousin Hepzibah," said the Judge, with an impressive earnestness of manner, which grew even to tearful pathos as he proceeded, "is it possible that you do not perceive how unjust, how unkind, how unchristian, is this constant, this long-continued bitterness against me, for a part which I was constrained by duty and conscience, by the force of law, and at my own peril, to act? What did I do, in detriment to Clifford, which it was possible to leave undone? How could you, his sister,—if, for your never-ending sorrow, as it has been for mine, you had known what I did,—have, shown greater tenderness? And do you think, cousin, that it has cost me no pang?—that it has left no anguish in my bosom, from that day to this, amidst all the prosperity with which Heaven has blessed me?—or that I do not now rejoice, when it is deemed consistent with the dues of public justice and the welfare of society that this dear kinsman, this early friend, this nature so delicately and beautifully constituted,—so unfortunate, let us pronounce him, and forbear to say, so guilty,—that our own Clifford, in fine, should be given back to life, and its possibilities of enjoyment? Ah, you little know me, Cousin Hepzibah! You little know this heart! It now throbs at the thought of meeting him! There lives not the human being (except yourself,—and you not more than I) who has shed so many tears for Clifford's calamity. You behold some of them now. There is none who would so delight to promote his happiness! Try me, Hepzibah!—try me, Cousin! —try the man whom you have treated as your enemy and Clifford's!—try Jaffrey Pyncheon, and you shall find him true, to the heart's core!"

"In the name of Heaven," cried Hepzibah, provoked only to intenser indignation by this outgush of the inestimable tenderness of a stern nature,—"in God's name, whom you insult, and whose power I could almost question, since he hears you utter so many false words without palsying your tongue,— give over, I beseech you, this loathsome pretence of affection for your victim! You hate him! Say so, like a man! You cherish, at this moment, some black purpose against him in your heart! Speak it out, at once!—or, if you hope so to promote it better, hide it till you can triumph in its success! But never speak again of your love for my poor brother. I cannot bear it! It will drive me beyond a woman's decency! It will drive me mad! Forbear! Not another word! It will make me spurn you!"

For once, Hepzibah's wrath had given her courage. She had spoken. But, after all, was this unconquerable distrust of Judge Pyncheon's integrity, and this utter denial, apparently, of his claim to stand in the ring of human sympathies,—were they founded in any just perception of his character, or merely the offspring of a woman's unreasonable prejudice, deduced from nothing?

The Judge, beyond all question, was a man of eminent respectability. The church acknowledged it; the state acknowledged it. It was denied by nobody. In all the very extensive sphere of those who knew him, whether in his public or private capacities, there was not an individual—except Hepzibah, and some lawless mystic, like the daguerreotypist, and, possibly, a few political opponents—who would have dreamed of seriously disputing his claim to a high and honorable place in the world's regard. Nor (we must do him the further justice to say) did Judge Pyncheon himself, probably, entertain many or very frequent doubts, that his enviable reputation accorded with his deserts. His conscience, therefore, usually considered the surest witness to a man's integrity, — his conscience, unless it might be for the little space of five minutes in the twenty-four hours, or, now and then, some black day in the whole year's circle, — his conscience bore an accordant testimony with the world's laudatory voice. And yet, strong as this evidence may seem to be, we should hesitate to peril our own conscience on the assertion, that the Judge and the consenting world were right, and that poor Hepzibah with her solitary prejudice was wrong. Hidden from mankind, — forgotten by himself, or buried so deeply under a sculptured and ornamented pile of ostentatious deeds that his daily life could take no note of it, — there may have lurked some evil and unsightly thing. Nay, we could almost venture to say, further, that a daily guilt might have been acted by him, continually renewed, and reddening forth afresh, like the miraculous blood-stain of a murder, without his necessarily and at every moment being aware of it.

Men of strong minds, great force of character, and a hard texture of the sensibilities, are very capable of falling into mistakes of this kind. They are ordinarily men to whom forms are of paramount importance. Their field of action lies among the external phenomena of life. They possess vast ability in grasping, and arranging, and appropriating to themselves, the big, heavy, solid unrealities, such as gold, landed estate, offices of trust and emolument, and public honors. With these materials, and with deeds of goodly aspect, done in the public eye, an individual of this class builds up, as it were, a tall and stately edifice, which, in the view of other people, and ultimately in his own view, is no other than the man's character, or the man himself. Behold, therefore, a palace! Its splendid halls and suites of spacious apartments are floored with a mosaic-work of costly marbles; its windows, the whole height of each room, admit the sunshine through the most transparent of plate-glass; its high cornices are gilded, and its ceilings gorgeously painted; and a lofty dome — through which, from the central pavement, you may gaze up to the sky, as with no obstructing medium between — surmounts the whole. With what fairer and nobler emblem could any man desire to shadow forth his character? Ah! but in some low and obscure nook, — some narrow closet on the ground-floor, shut, locked and bolted, and the key flung away, — or beneath the marble pavement, in a stagnant water-puddle, with the richest pattern of mosaic-work above, — may lie a corpse, half decayed, and still decaying, and diffusing its death-scent all through the palace! The inhabitant will not be conscious of it, for it has long been his daily breath! Neither will the visitors, for they smell only the rich odors which the master sedulously scatters through the palace, and the incense which they bring, and delight to burn before him! Now and then, perchance, comes in a seer, before whose sadly gifted eye the whole structure melts into thin air, leaving only the hidden nook, the bolted closet, with the cobwebs festooned over its forgotten door, or the deadly hole under the pavement, and the decaying corpse within. Here, then, we are to seek the true emblem of the man's character, and of the deed that gives whatever reality it possesses to his life. And, beneath the show of a marble palace, that pool of stagnant water, foul with many impurities, and, perhaps, tinged with blood,—that secret abomination, above which, possibly, he may say his prayers, without remembering it,—is this man's miserable soul!

To apply this train of remark somewhat more closely to Judge Pyncheon. We might say (without in the least imputing crime to a personage of his eminent respectability) that there was enough of splendid rubbish in his life to cover up and paralyze a more active and subtle conscience than the Judge was ever troubled with. The purity of his judicial character, while on the bench; the faithfulness of his public service in subsequent capacities; his devotedness to his party, and the rigid consistency with which he had adhered to its principles, or, at all events, kept pace with its organized movements; his remarkable zeal as president of a Bible society; his unimpeachable integrity as treasurer of a widow's and orphan's fund; his benefits to horticulture, by producing two much esteemed varieties of the pear and to agriculture, through the agency of the famous Pyncheon bull; the cleanliness of his moral deportment, for a great many years past; the severity with which he had frowned upon, and finally cast off, an expensive and dissipated son, delaying forgiveness until within the final quarter of an hour of the young man's life; his prayers at morning and eventide, and graces at meal-time; his efforts in furtherance of the temperance cause; his confining himself, since the last attack of the gout, to five diurnal glasses of old sherry wine; the snowy whiteness of his linen, the polish of his boots, the handsomeness of his gold-headed cane, the square and roomy fashion of his coat, and the fineness of its material, and, in general, the studied propriety of his dress and equipment; the scrupulousness with which he paid public notice, in the street, by a bow, a lifting of the hat, a nod, or a motion of the hand, to all and sundry of his acquaintances, rich or poor; the smile of broad benevolence wherewith he made it a point to gladden the whole world,—what room could possibly be found for darker traits in a portrait made up of lineaments like these? This proper face was what he beheld in the looking-glass. This admirably arranged life was what he was conscious of in the progress of every day. Then might not he claim to be its result and sum, and say to himself and the community, "Behold Judge Pyncheon there"?

And allowing that, many, many years ago, in his early and

reckless youth, he had committed some one wrong act,—or that, even now, the inevitable force of circumstances should occasionally make him do one questionable deed among a thousand praiseworthy, or, at least, blameless ones,—would you characterize the Judge by that one necessary deed, and that half-forgotten act, and let it overshadow the fair aspect of a lifetime? What is there so ponderous in evil, that a thumb's bigness of it should outweigh the mass of things not evil which were heaped into the other scale! This scale and balance system is a favorite one with people of Judge Pyncheon's brotherhood. A hard, cold man, thus unfortunately situated, seldom or never looking inward, and resolutely taking his idea of himself from what purports to be his image as reflected in the mirror of public opinion, can scarcely arrive at true self-knowledge, except through loss of property and reputation. Sickness will not always help him do it; not always the death-hour!

But our affair now is with Judge Pyncheon as he stood confronting the fierce outbreak of Hepzibah's wrath. Without premeditation, to her own surprise, and indeed terror, she had given vent, for once, to the inveteracy of her resentment, cherished against this kinsman for thirty years.

Thus far the Judge's countenance had expressed mild forbearance,—grave and almost gentle deprecation of his cousin's unbecoming violence,—free and Christian-like forgiveness of the wrong inflicted by her words. But when those words were irrevocably spoken, his look assumed sternness, the sense of power, and immitigable resolve; and this with so natural and imperceptible a change, that it seemed as if the iron man had stood there from the first, and the meek man not at all. The effect was as when the light, vapory clouds, with their soft coloring, suddenly vanish from the stony brow of a precipitous mountain, and leave there the frown which you at once feel to be eternal. Hepzibah almost adopted the insane belief that it was her old Puritan ancestor, and not the modern Judge, on whom she had just been wreaking the bitterness of her heart. Never did a man show stronger proof of the lineage attributed to him than Judge Pyncheon, at this crisis, by his unmistakable resemblance to the picture in the inner room.

"Cousin Hepzibah," said he very calmly, "it is time to have done with this."

"With all my heart!" answered she. "Then, why do you persecute us any longer? Leave poor Clifford and me in peace. Neither of us desires anything better!"

"It is my purpose to see Clifford before I leave this house," continued the Judge. "Do not act like a madwoman, Hepzibah! I am his only friend, and an all-powerful one. Has it never occurred to you,—are you so blind as not to have seen,—that,

The House of the Seven Gables

without not merely my consent, but my efforts, my representations, the exertion of my whole influence, political, official, personal, Clifford would never have been what you call free? Did you think his release a triumph over me? Not so, my good cousin; not so, by any means! The furthest possible from that! No; but it was the accomplishment of a purpose long entertained on my part. I set him free!"

"You!" answered Hepzibah. "I never will believe it! He owed his dungeon to you; his freedom to God's providence!"

"I set him free!" reaffirmed Judge Pyncheon, with the calmest composure. "And I came hither now to decide whether he shall retain his freedom. It will depend upon himself. For this purpose, I must see him."

"Never! — it would drive him mad!" exclaimed Hepzibah, but with an irresoluteness sufficiently perceptible to the keen eye of the Judge; for, without the slightest faith in his good intentions, she knew not whether there was most to dread in yielding or resistance. "And why should you wish to see this wretched, broken man, who retains hardly a fraction of his intellect, and will hide even that from an eye which has no love in it?"

"He shall see love enough in mine, if that be all!" said the Judge, with well-grounded confidence in the benignity of his aspect. "But, Cousin Hepzibah, you confess a great deal, and very much to the purpose. Now, listen, and I will frankly explain my reasons for insisting on this interview. At the death, thirty years since, of our uncle Jaffrey, it was found, — I know not whether the circumstance ever attracted much of your attention, among the sadder interests that clustered round that event, — but it was found that his visible estate, of every kind, fell far short of any estimate ever made of it. He was supposed to be immensely rich. Nobody doubted that he stood among the weightiest men of his day. It was one of his eccentricities, however, — and not altogether a folly, neither, — to conceal the amount of his property by making distant and foreign investments, perhaps under other names than his own, and by various means, familiar enough to capitalists, but unnecessary here to be specified. By Uncle Jaffrey's last will and testament, as you are aware, his entire property was bequeathed to me, with the single exception of a life interest to yourself in this old family mansion, and the strip of patrimonial estate remaining attached to it."

"And do you seek to deprive us of that?" asked Hepzibah, unable to restrain her bitter contempt. "Is this your price for ceasing to persecute poor Clifford?"

"Certainly not, my dear cousin!" answered the Judge,

smiling benevolently. "On the contrary, as you must do me the justice to own, I have constantly expressed my readiness to double or treble your resources, whenever you should make up your mind to accept any kindness of that nature at the hands of your kinsman. No, no! But here lies the gist of the matter. Of my uncle's unquestionably great estate, as I have said, not the half—no, not one third, as I am fully convinced—was apparent after his death. Now, I have the best possible reasons for believing that your brother Clifford can give me a clew to the recovery of the remainder."

"Clifford!—Clifford know of any hidden wealth? Clifford have it in his power to make you rich?" cried the old gentlewoman, affected with a sense of something like ridicule at the idea. "Impossible! You deceive yourself! It is really a thing to laugh at!"

"It is as certain as that I stand here!" said Judge Pyncheon, striking his gold-headed cane on the floor, and at the same time stamping his foot, as if to express his conviction the more forcibly by the whole emphasis of his substantial person. "Clifford told me so himself!"

"No, no!" exclaimed Hepzibah incredulously. "You are dreaming, Cousin Jaffrey."

"I do not belong to the dreaming class of men," said the Judge quietly. "Some months before my uncle's death, Clifford boasted to me of the possession of the secret of incalculable wealth. His purpose was to taunt me, and excite my curiosity. I know it well. But, from a pretty distinct recollection of the particulars of our conversation, I am thoroughly convinced that there was truth in what he said. Clifford, at this moment, if he chooses,—and choose he must!—can inform me where to find the schedule, the documents, the evidences, in whatever shape they exist, of the vast amount of Uncle Jaffrey's missing property. He has the secret. His boast was no idle word. It had a directness, an emphasis, a particularity, that showed a backbone of solid meaning within the mystery of his expression."

"But what could have been Clifford's object," asked Hepzibah, "in concealing it so long?"

"It was one of the bad impulses of our fallen nature," replied the Judge, turning up his eyes. "He looked upon me as his enemy. He considered me as the cause of his overwhelming disgrace, his imminent peril of death, his irretrievable ruin. There was no great probability, therefore, of his volunteering information, out of his dungeon, that should elevate me still higher on the ladder of prosperity. But the moment has now come when he must give up his secret."

"And what if he should refuse?" inquired Hepzibah. "Or, — as I steadfastly believe, — what if he has no knowledge of this wealth?"

"My dear cousin," said Judge Pyncheon, with a quietude which he had the power of making more formidable than any violence, "since your brother's return, I have taken the precaution (a highly proper one in the near kinsman and natural guardian of an individual so situated) to have his deportment and habits constantly and carefully overlooked. Your neighbors have been eye-witnesses to whatever has passed in the garden. The butcher, the baker, the fish-monger, some of the customers of your shop, and many a prying old woman, have told me several of the secrets of your interior. A still larger circle — I myself, among the rest — can testify to his extravagances at the arched window. Thousands beheld him, a week or two ago, on the point of flinging himself thence into the street. From all this testimony, I am led to apprehend — reluctantly, and with deep grief — that Clifford's misfortunes have so affected his intellect, never very strong, that he cannot safely remain at large. The alternative, you must be aware, — and its adoption will depend entirely on the decision which I am now about to make, — the alternative is his confinement, probably for the remainder of his life, in a public asylum for persons in his unfortunate state of mind."

"You cannot mean it!" shrieked Hepzibah.

"Should my cousin Clifford," continued Judge Pyncheon, wholly undisturbed, "from mere malice, and hatred of one whose interests ought naturally to be dear to him, — a mode of passion that, as often as any other, indicates mental disease, — should he refuse me the information so important to myself, and which he assuredly possesses, I shall consider it the one needed jot of evidence to satisfy my mind of his insanity. And, once sure of the course pointed out by conscience, you know me too well, Cousin Hepzibah, to entertain a doubt that I shall pursue it."

"O Jaffrey, — Cousin Jaffrey," cried Hepzibah mournfully, not passionately, "it is you that are diseased in mind, not Clifford! You have forgotten that a woman was your mother! — that you have had sisters, brothers, children of your own! — or that there ever was affection between man and man, or pity from one man to another, in this miserable world! Else, how could you have dreamed of this? You are not young, Cousin Jaffrey! — no, nor middle-aged, — but already an old man! The hair is white upon your head! How many years have you to live? Are you not rich enough for that little time? Shall you be hungry, — shall you lack clothes, or a roof to shelter you, — between this point and the grave? No! but, with the half of what you now possess, you could revel in costly food and wines, and build a house twice as splendid as you now inhabit, and make a far greater show to the world,—and yet leave riches to your only son, to make him bless the hour of your death! Then, why should you do this cruel, cruel thing?—so mad a thing, that I know not whether to call it wicked! Alas, Cousin Jaffrey, this hard and grasping spirit has run in our blood these two hundred years. You are but doing over again, in another shape, what your ancestor before you did, and sending down to your posterity the curse inherited from him!"

"Talk sense, Hepzibah, for Heaven's sake!" exclaimed the Judge, with the impatience natural to a reasonable man, on hearing anything so utterly absurd as the above, in a discussion about matters of business. "I have told you my determination. I am not apt to change. Clifford must give up his secret, or take the consequences. And let him decide quickly; for I have several affairs to attend to this morning, and an important dinner engagement with some political friends."

"Clifford has no secret!" answered Hepzibah. "And God will not let you do the thing you meditate!"

"We shall see," said the unmoved Judge. "Meanwhile, choose whether you will summon Clifford, and allow this business to be amicably settled by an interview between two kinsmen, or drive me to harsher measures, which I should be most happy to feel myself justified in avoiding. The responsibility is altogether on your part."

"You are stronger than I," said Hepzibah, after a brief consideration; "and you have no pity in your strength! Clifford is not now insane; but the interview which you insist upon may go far to make him so. Nevertheless, knowing you as I do, I believe it to be my best course to allow you to judge for yourself as to the improbability of his possessing any valuable secret. I will call Clifford. Be merciful in your dealings with him!—be far more merciful than your heart bids you be!—for God is looking at you, Jaffrey Pyncheon!"

The Judge followed his cousin from the shop, where the foregoing conversation had passed, into the parlor, and flung himself heavily into the great ancestral chair. Many a former Pyncheon had found repose in its capacious arms: rosy children, after their sports; young men, dreamy with love; grown men, weary with cares; old men, burdened with winters,—they had mused, and slumbered, and departed to a yet profounder sleep. It had been a long tradition, though a doubtful one, that this was the very chair, seated in which the earliest of the Judge's New England forefathers—he whose picture still hung upon the wall—had given a dead man's silent and stern reception to the throng of distinguished guests. From that hour of evil omen until the present, it may be,—though we know not the secret of

The House of the Seven Gables

his heart,—but it may be that no wearier and sadder man had ever sunk into the chair than this same Judge Pyncheon, whom we have just beheld so immitigably hard and resolute. Surely, it must have been at no slight cost that he had thus fortified his soul with iron. Such calmness is a mightier effort than the violence of weaker men. And there was yet a heavy task for him to do. Was it a little matter—a trifle to be prepared for in a single moment, and to be rested from in another moment,—that he must now, after thirty years, encounter a kinsman risen from a living tomb, and wrench a secret from him, or else consign him to a living tomb again?

"Did you speak?" asked Hepzibah, looking in from the threshold of the parlor; for she imagined that the Judge had uttered some sound which she was anxious to interpret as a relenting impulse. "I thought you called me back."

"No, no" gruffly answered Judge Pyncheon with a harsh frown, while his brow grew almost a black purple, in the shadow of the room. "Why should I call you back? Time flies! Bid Clifford come to me!"

The Judge had taken his watch from his vest pocket and now held it in his hand, measuring the interval which was to ensue before the appearance of Clifford.

XVI.

Clifford's Chamber

Never had the old house appeared so dismal to poor Hepzibah as when she departed on that wretched errand. There was a strange aspect in it. As she trode along the foot-worn passages, and opened one crazy door after another, and ascended the creaking staircase, she gazed wistfully and fearfully around. It would have been no marvel, to her excited mind, if, behind or beside her, there had been the rustle of dead people's garments, or pale visages awaiting her on the landing-place above. Her nerves were set all ajar by the scene of passion and terror through which she had just struggled. Her colloquy with Judge Pyncheon, who so perfectly represented the person and attributes of the founder of the family, had called back the dreary past. It weighed upon her heart. Whatever she had heard, from legendary aunts and grandmothers, concerning the good or evil fortunes of the Pyncheons,—stories which had heretofore been kept warm in her remembrance by the chimney-corner glow that was associated with them,—now recurred to her, sombre, ghastly, cold, like most passages of family history, when brooded over in melancholy mood. The whole seemed little else but a series of calamity, reproducing itself in successive generations, with one general hue, and varying in little, save the outline. But Hepzibah now felt as if the Judge, and Clifford, and herself,—they three together,—were on the point of adding another incident to the annals of the house, with a bolder relief of wrong and sorrow, which would cause it to stand out from all the rest. Thus it is that the grief of the passing moment takes upon itself an individuality, and a character of climax, which it is destined to lose after a while, and to fade into the dark gray tissue common to the grave or glad events of many years ago. It is but for a moment, comparatively, that anything looks strange or startling,—a truth that has the bitter and the sweet in it.

But Hepzibah could not rid herself of the sense of something unprecedented at that instant passing and soon to be accomplished. Her nerves were in a shake. Instinctively she paused before the arched window, and looked out upon the street, in order to seize its permanent objects with her mental grasp, and thus to steady herself from the reel and vibration which affected her more immediate sphere. It brought her up, as we may say, with a kind of shock, when she beheld everything under the same appearance as the day before, and numberless preceding days, except for the difference between sunshine and sullen storm. Her eyes travelled along the street, from doorstep to doorstep, noting the wet sidewalks, with here and there a puddle in hollows that had been imperceptible until filled with water. She screwed her dim optics to their acutest point, in the hope of making out, with greater distinctness, a

The House of the Seven Gables

certain window, where she half saw, half guessed, that a tailor's seamstress was sitting at her work. Hepzibah flung herself upon that unknown woman's companionship, even thus far off. Then she was attracted by a chaise rapidly passing, and watched its moist and glistening top, and its splashing wheels, until it had turned the corner, and refused to carry any further her idly trifling, because appalled and overburdened, mind. When the vehicle had disappeared, she allowed herself still another loitering moment; for the patched figure of good Uncle Venner was now visible, coming slowly from the head of the street downward, with a rheumatic limp, because the east wind had got into his joints. Hepzibah wished that he would pass yet more slowly, and befriend her shivering solitude a little longer. Anything that would take her out of the grievous present, and interpose human beings betwixt herself and what was nearest to her, — whatever would defer for an instant the inevitable errand on which she was bound, — all such impediments were welcome. Next to the lightest heart, the heaviest is apt to be most playful.

Hepzibah had little hardihood for her own proper pain, and far less for what she must inflict on Clifford. Of so slight a nature, and so shattered by his previous calamities, it could not well be short of utter ruin to bring him face to face with the hard, relentless man who had been his evil destiny through life. Even had there been no bitter recollections, nor any hostile interest now at stake between them, the mere natural repugnance of the more sensitive system to the massive, weighty, and unimpressible one, must, in itself, have been disastrous to the former. It would be like flinging a porcelain vase, with already a crack in it, against a granite column. Never before had Hepzibah so adequately estimated the powerful character of her cousin Jaffrey, — powerful by intellect, energy of will, the long habit of acting among men, and, as she believed, by his unscrupulous pursuit of selfish ends through evil means. It did but increase the difficulty that Judge Pyncheon was under a delusion as to the secret which he supposed Clifford to possess. Men of his strength of purpose and customary sagacity, if they chance to adopt a mistaken opinion in practical matters, so wedge it and fasten it among things known to be true, that to wrench it out of their minds is hardly less difficult than pulling up an oak. Thus, as the Judge required an impossibility of Clifford, the latter, as he could not perform it, must needs perish. For what, in the grasp of a man like this, was to become of Clifford's soft poetic nature, that never should have had a task more stubborn than to set a life of beautiful enjoyment to the flow and rhythm of musical cadences! Indeed, what had become of it already? Broken! Blighted! All but annihilated! Soon to be wholly so!

For a moment, the thought crossed Hepzibah's mind, whether Clifford might not really have such knowledge of their

The House of the Seven Gables

deceased uncle's vanished estate as the Judge imputed to him. She remembered some vague intimations, on her brother's part, which—if the supposition were not essentially preposterous—might have been so interpreted. There had been schemes of travel and residence abroad, day-dreams of brilliant life at home, and splendid castles in the air, which it would have required boundless wealth to build and realize. Had this wealth been in her power, how gladly would Hepzibah have bestowed it all upon her iron-hearted kinsman, to buy for Clifford the freedom and seclusion of the desolate old house! But she believed that her brother's schemes were as destitute of actual substance and purpose as a child's pictures of its future life, while sitting in a little chair by its mother's knee. Clifford had none but shadowy gold at his command; and it was not the stuff to satisfy Judge Pyncheon!

Was there no help in their extremity? It seemed strange that there should be none, with a city round about her. It would be so easy to throw up the window, and send forth a shriek, at the strange agony of which everybody would come hastening to the rescue, well understanding it to be the cry of a human soul, at some dreadful crisis! But how wild, how almost laughable, the fatality,—and yet how continually it comes to pass, thought Hepzibah, in this dull delirium of a world,—that whosoever, and with however kindly a purpose, should come to help, they would be sure to help the strongest side! Might and wrong combined, like iron magnetized, are endowed with irresistible attraction. There would be Judge Pyncheon,—a person eminent in the public view, of high station and great wealth, a philanthropist, a member of Congress and of the church, and intimately associated with whatever else bestows good name,—so imposing, in these advantageous lights, that Hepzibah herself could hardly help shrinking from her own conclusions as to his hollow integrity. The Judge, on one side! And who, on the other? The guilty Clifford! Once a byword! Now, an indistinctly remembered ignominy!

Nevertheless, in spite of this perception that the Judge would draw all human aid to his own behalf, Hepzibah was so unaccustomed to act for herself, that the least word of counsel would have swayed her to any mode of action. Little Phœbe Pyncheon would at once have lighted up the whole scene, if not by any available suggestion, yet simply by the warm vivacity of her character. The idea of the artist occurred to Hepzibah. Young and unknown, mere vagrant adventurer as he was, she had been conscious of a force in Holgrave which might well adapt him to be the champion of a crisis. With this thought in her mind, she unbolted a door, cobwebbed and long disused, but which had served as a former medium of communication between her own part of the house and the gable where the wandering daguerreotypist had now established his temporary home. He was not there. A book, face downward, on the table, a roll of manuscript, a half-written sheet, a newspaper, some tools of his present occupation, and several rejected daguerreotypes, conveyed an impression as if he were close at hand. But, at this period of the day, as Hepzibah might have anticipated, the artist was at his public rooms. With an impulse of idle curiosity, that flickered among her heavy thoughts, she looked at one of the daguerreotypes, and beheld Judge Pyncheon frowning at her. Fate stared her in the face. She turned back from her fruitless quest, with a heartsinking sense of disappointment. In all her years of seclusion, she had never felt, as now, what it was to be alone. It seemed as if the house stood in a desert, or, by some spell, was made invisible to those who dwelt around, or passed beside it; so that any mode of misfortune, miserable accident, or crime might happen in it without the possibility of aid. In her grief and wounded pride, Hepzibah had spent her life in divesting herself of friends; she had wilfully cast off the support which God has ordained his creatures to need from one another; and it was now her punishment, that Clifford and herself would fall the easier victims to their kindred enemy.

Returning to the arched window, she lifted her eyes,— scowling, poor, dim-sighted Hepzibah, in the face of Heaven!— and strove hard to send up a prayer through the dense gray pavement of clouds. Those mists had gathered, as if to symbolize a great, brooding mass of human trouble, doubt, confusion, and chill indifference, between earth and the better regions. Her faith was too weak; the prayer too heavy to be thus uplifted. It fell back, a lump of lead, upon her heart. It smote her with the wretched conviction that Providence intermeddled not in these petty wrongs of one individual to his fellow, nor had any balm for these little agonies of a solitary soul; but shed its justice, and its mercy, in a broad, sunlike sweep, over half the universe at once. Its vastness made it nothing. But Hepzibah did not see that, just as there comes a warm sunbeam into every cottage window, so comes a lovebeam of God's care and pity for every separate need.

At last, finding no other pretext for deferring the torture that she was to inflict on Clifford,—her reluctance to which was the true cause of her loitering at the window, her search for the artist, and even her abortive prayer,—dreading, also, to hear the stern voice of Judge Pyncheon from below stairs, chiding her delay,—she crept slowly, a pale, grief-stricken figure, a dismal shape of woman, with almost torpid limbs, slowly to her brother's door, and knocked!

There was no reply.

And how should there have been? Her hand, tremulous with the shrinking purpose which directed it, had smitten so feebly against the door that the sound could hardly have gone inward. She knocked again. Still no response! Nor was it to be wondered at. She had struck with the entire force of her heart's vibration, communicating, by some subtle magnetism, her own terror to the summons. Clifford would turn his face to the pillow, and cover his head beneath the bedclothes, like a startled child at midnight. She knocked a third time, three regular strokes, gentle, but perfectly distinct, and with meaning in them; for, modulate it with what cautious art we will, the hand cannot help playing some tune of what we feel upon the senseless wood.

Clifford returned no answer.

"Clifford! Dear brother!" said Hepzibah. "Shall I come in?"

A silence.

Two or three times, and more, Hepzibah repeated his name, without result; till, thinking her brother's sleep unwontedly profound, she undid the door, and entering, found the chamber vacant. How could he have come forth, and when, without her knowledge? Was it possible that, in spite of the stormy day, and worn out with the irksomeness within doors he had betaken himself to his customary haunt in the garden, and was now shivering under the cheerless shelter of the summer-house? She hastily threw up a window, thrust forth her turbaned head and the half of her gaunt figure, and searched the whole garden through, as completely as her dim vision would allow. She could see the interior of the summer-house, and its circular seat, kept moist by the droppings of the roof. It had no occupant. Clifford was not thereabouts; unless, indeed, he had crept for concealment (as, for a moment, Hepzibah fancied might be the case) into a great, wet mass of tangled and broad-leaved shadow, where the squash-vines were clambering tumultuously upon an old wooden framework, set casually aslant against the fence. This could not be, however; he was not there; for, while Hepzibah was looking, a strange grimalkin stole forth from the very spot, and picked his way across the garden. Twice he paused to snuff the air, and then anew directed his course towards the parlor window. Whether it was only on account of the stealthy, prying manner common to the race, or that this cat seemed to have more than ordinary mischief in his thoughts, the old gentlewoman, in spite of her much perplexity, felt an impulse to drive the animal away, and accordingly flung down a window stick. The cat stared up at her, like a detected thief or murderer, and, the next instant, took to flight. No other living creature was visible in the garden. Chanticleer and his family had either not left their roost, disheartened by the interminable rain, or had done the next wisest thing, by seasonably returning to it. Hepzibah closed the window.

But where was Clifford? Could it be that, aware of the presence of his Evil Destiny, he had crept silently down the staircase, while the Judge and Hepzibah stood talking in the shop, and had softly undone the fastenings of the outer door, and made his escape into the street? With that thought, she seemed to behold his gray, wrinkled, yet childlike aspect, in the old-fashioned garments which he wore about the house; a figure such as one sometimes imagines himself to be, with the world's eye upon him, in a troubled dream. This figure of her wretched brother would go wandering through the city, attracting all eyes, and everybody's wonder and repugnance, like a ghost, the more to be shuddered at because visible at noontide. To incur the ridicule of the younger crowd, that knew him not,—the harsher scorn and indignation of a few old men, who might recall his once familiar features! To be the sport of boys, who, when old enough to run about the streets, have no more reverence for what is beautiful and holy, nor pity for what is sad,—no more sense of sacred misery, sanctifying the human shape in which it embodies itself,—than if Satan were the father of them all! Goaded by their taunts, their loud, shrill cries, and cruel laughter,—insulted by the filth of the public ways, which they would fling upon him,—or, as it might well be, distracted by the mere strangeness of his situation, though nobody should afflict him with so much as a thoughtless word,—what wonder if Clifford were to break into some wild extravagance which was certain to be interpreted as lunacy? Thus Judge Pyncheon's fiendish scheme would be ready accomplished to his hands!

Then Hepzibah reflected that the town was almost completely water-girdled. The wharves stretched out towards the centre of the harbor, and, in this inclement weather, were deserted by the ordinary throng of merchants, laborers, and sea-faring men; each wharf a solitude, with the vessels moored stem and stern, along its misty length. Should her brother's aimless footsteps stray thitherward, and he but bend, one moment, over the deep, black tide, would he not bethink himself that here was the sure refuge within his reach, and that, with a single step, or the slightest overbalance of his body, he might be forever beyond his kinsman's gripe? Oh, the temptation! To make of his ponderous sorrow a security! To sink, with its leaden weight upon him, and never rise again!

The horror of this last conception was too much for Hepzibah. Even Jaffrey Pyncheon must help her now! She hastened down the staircase, shrieking as she went.

"Clifford is gone!" she cried. "I cannot find my brother. Help, Jaffrey Pyncheon! Some harm will happen to him!"

She threw open the parlor-door. But, what with the shade of branches across the windows, and the smoke-blackened ceiling, and the dark oak-panelling of the walls, there was hardly so much daylight in the room that Hepzibah's imperfect sight could accurately distinguish the Judge's figure. She was certain, however, that she saw him sitting in the ancestral arm-chair, near the centre of the floor, with his face somewhat averted, and looking towards a window. So firm and quiet is the nervous system of such men as Judge Pyncheon, that he had perhaps stirred not more than once since her departure, but, in the hard composure of his temperament, retained the position into which accident had thrown him.

"I tell you, Jaffrey," cried Hepzibah impatiently, as she turned from the parlor-door to search other rooms, "my brother is not in his chamber! You must help me seek him!"

But Judge Pyncheon was not the man to let himself be startled from an easy-chair with haste ill-befitting either the dignity of his character or his broad personal basis, by the alarm of an hysteric woman. Yet, considering his own interest in the matter, he might have bestirred himself with a little more alacrity.

"Do you hear me, Jaffrey Pyncheon?" screamed Hepzibah, as she again approached the parlor-door, after an ineffectual search elsewhere. "Clifford is gone."

At this instant, on the threshold of the parlor, emerging from within, appeared Clifford himself! His face was preternaturally pale; so deadly white, indeed, that, through all the glimmering indistinctness of the passageway, Hepzibah could discern his features, as if a light fell on them alone. Their vivid and wild expression seemed likewise sufficient to illuminate them; it was an expression of scorn and mockery, coinciding with the emotions indicated by his gesture. As Clifford stood on the threshold, partly turning back, he pointed his finger within the parlor, and shook it slowly as though he would have summoned, not Hepzibah alone, but the whole world, to gaze at some object inconceivably ridiculous. This action, so ill-timed and extravagant,—accompanied, too, with a look that showed more like joy than any other kind of excitement,—compelled Hepzibah to dread that her stern kinsman's ominous visit had driven her poor brother to absolute insanity. Nor could she otherwise account for the Judge's quiescent mood than by supposing him craftily on the watch, while Clifford developed these symptoms of a distracted mind.

"Be quiet, Clifford!" whispered his sister, raising her hand to impress caution. "Oh, for Heaven's sake, be quiet!"

"Let him be quiet! What can he do better?" answered Clifford, with a still wilder gesture, pointing into the room which he had just quitted. "As for us, Hepzibah, we can dance now!—we can sing, laugh, play, do what we will! The weight is gone, Hepzibah! It is gone off this weary old world, and we may be as light-hearted as little Phœbe herself."

And, in accordance with his words, he began to laugh, still pointing his finger at the object, invisible to Hepzibah, within the parlor. She was seized with a sudden intuition of some horrible thing. She thrust herself past Clifford, and disappeared into the room; but almost immediately returned, with a cry choking in her throat. Gazing at her brother with an affrighted glance of inquiry, she beheld him all in a tremor and a quake, from head to foot, while, amid these commoted elements of passion or alarm, still flickered his gusty mirth.

"My God! what is to become of us?" gasped Hepzibah.

"Come!" said Clifford in a tone of brief decision, most unlike what was usual with him. "We stay here too long! Let us leave the old house to our cousin Jaffrey! He will take good care of it!"

Hepzibah now noticed that Clifford had on a cloak,—a garment of long ago,—in which he had constantly muffled himself during these days of easterly storm. He beckoned with his hand, and intimated, so far as she could comprehend him, his purpose that they should go together from the house. There are chaotic, blind, or drunken moments, in the lives of persons who lack real force of character,—moments of test, in which courage would most assert itself,—but where these individuals, if left to themselves, stagger aimlessly along, or follow implicitly whatever guidance may befall them, even if it be a child's. No matter how preposterous or insane, a purpose is a Godsend to them. Hepzibah had reached this point. Unaccustomed to action or responsibility,—full of horror at what she had seen, and afraid to inquire, or almost to imagine, how it had come to pass,—affrighted at the fatality which seemed to pursue her brother,—stupefied by the dim, thick, stifling atmosphere of dread which filled the house as with a death-smell, and obliterated all definiteness of thought,—she yielded without a question, and on the instant, to the will which Clifford expressed. For herself, she was like a person in a dream, when the will always sleeps. Clifford, ordinarily so destitute of this faculty, had found it in the tension of the crisis.

"Why do you delay so?" cried he sharply. "Put on your cloak and hood, or whatever it pleases you to wear! No matter what; you cannot look beautiful nor brilliant, my poor Hepzibah! Take your purse, with money in it, and come along!"

Hepzibah obeyed these instructions, as if nothing else were to be done or thought of. She began to wonder, it is true, why she did not wake up, and at what still more intolerable pitch of dizzy trouble her spirit would struggle out of the maze, and make her conscious that nothing of all this had actually happened. Of course it was not real; no such black, easterly day as this had yet begun to be; Judge Pyncheon had not talked with, her. Clifford had not laughed, pointed, beckoned her away with him; but she had merely been afflicted—as lonely sleepers often are—with a great deal of unreasonable misery, in a morning dream!

"Now—now—I shall certainly awake!" thought Hepzibah, as she went to and fro, making her little preparations. "I can bear it no longer I must wake up now!"

But it came not, that awakening moment! It came not, even when, just before they left the house, Clifford stole to the parlor-door, and made a parting obeisance to the sole occupant of the room.

"What an absurd figure the old fellow cuts now!" whispered he to Hepzibah. "Just when he fancied he had me completely under his thumb! Come, come; make haste! or he will start up, like Giant Despair in pursuit of Christian and Hopeful, and catch us yet!"

As they passed into the street, Clifford directed Hepzibah's attention to something on one of the posts of the front door. It was merely the initials of his own name, which, with somewhat of his characteristic grace about the forms of the letters, he had cut there when a boy. The brother and sister departed, and left Judge Pyncheon sitting in the old home of his forefathers, all by himself; so heavy and lumpish that we can liken him to nothing better than a defunct nightmare, which had perished in the midst of its wickedness, and left its flabby corpse on the breast of the tormented one, to be gotten rid of as it might!

XVII.
The Flight of Two Owls

Summer as it was, the east wind set poor Hepzibah's few remaining teeth chattering in her head, as she and Clifford faced it, on their way up Pyncheon Street, and towards the centre of the town. Not merely was it the shiver which this pitiless blast brought to her frame (although her feet and hands, especially, had never seemed so death-a-cold as now), but there was a moral sensation, mingling itself with the physical chill, and causing her to shake more in spirit than in body. The world's broad, bleak atmosphere was all so comfortless! Such, indeed, is the impression which it makes on every new adventurer, even if he plunge into it while the warmest tide of life is bubbling through his veins. What, then, must it have been to Hepzibah and Clifford,—so time-stricken as they were, yet so like children in their inexperience,—as they left the doorstep, and passed from beneath the wide shelter of the Pyncheon Elm! They were wandering all abroad, on precisely such a pilgrimage as a child often meditates, to the world's end, with perhaps a sixpence and a biscuit in his pocket. In Hepzibah's mind, there was the wretched consciousness of being adrift. She had lost the faculty of self-guidance; but, in view of the difficulties around her, felt it hardly worth an effort to regain it, and was, moreover, incapable of making one.

As they proceeded on their strange expedition, she now and then cast a look sidelong at Clifford, and could not but observe that he was possessed and swayed by a powerful excitement. It was this, indeed, that gave him the control which he had at once, and so irresistibly, established over his movements. It not a little resembled the exhilaration of wine. Or, it might more fancifully be compared to a joyous piece of music, played with wild vivacity, but upon a disordered instrument. As the cracked jarring note might always be heard, and as it jarred loudest amidst the loftiest exultation of the melody, so was there a continual quake through Clifford, causing him most to quiver while he wore a triumphant smile, and seemed almost under a necessity to skip in his gait.

They met few people abroad, even on passing from the retired neighborhood of the House of the Seven Gables into what was ordinarily the more thronged and busier portion of the town. Glistening sidewalks, with little pools of rain, here and there, along their unequal surface; umbrellas displayed ostentatiously in the shop-windows, as if the life of trade had concentrated itself in that one article; wet leaves of the horse-chestnut or elm-trees, torn off untimely by the blast and scattered along the public way; an unsightly accumulation of mud in the middle of the street, which perversely grew the more unclean for its long and laborious washing,—these were the more definable points of a very sombre picture. In the way of movement and human life, there was the hasty rattle of a cab or coach, its driver protected by a waterproof cap over his head and shoulders; the forlorn figure of an old man, who seemed to have crept out of some subterranean sewer, and was stooping along the kennel, and poking the wet rubbish with a stick, in quest of rusty nails; a merchant or two, at the door of the post-office, together with an editor and a miscellaneous politician, awaiting a dilatory mail; a few visages of retired sea-captains at the window of an insurance office, looking out vacantly at the vacant street, blaspheming at the weather, and fretting at the dearth as well of public news as local gossip. What a treasure-trove to these venerable quidnuncs, could they have guessed the secret which Hepzibah and Clifford were carrying along with them! But their two figures attracted hardly so much notice as that of a young girl, who passed at the same instant, and happened to raise her skirt a trifle too high above her ankles. Had it been a sunny and cheerful day, they could hardly have gone through the streets without making themselves obnoxious to remark. Now, probably, they were felt to be in keeping with the dismal and bitter weather, and therefore did not stand out in strong relief, as if the sun were shining on them, but melted into the gray gloom and were forgotten as soon as gone.

Poor Hepzibah! Could she have understood this fact, it would have brought her some little comfort; for, to all her other troubles,—strange to say!—there was added the womanish and old-maiden-like misery arising from a sense of unseemliness in her attire. Thus, she was fain to shrink deeper into herself, as it were, as if in the hope of making people suppose that here was only a cloak and hood, threadbare and woefully faded, taking an airing in the midst of the storm, without any wearer!

As they went on, the feeling of indistinctness and unreality kept dimly hovering round about her, and so diffusing itself into her system that one of her hands was hardly palpable to the touch of the other. Any certainty would have been preferable to this. She whispered to herself, again and again, "Am I awake?—Am I awake?" and sometimes exposed her face to the chill spatter of the wind, for the sake of its rude assurance that she was. Whether it was Clifford's purpose, or only chance, had led them thither, they now found themselves passing beneath the arched entrance of a large structure of gray stone. Within, there was a spacious breadth, and an airy height from floor to roof, now partially filled with smoke and steam, which eddied voluminously upward and formed a mimic cloud-region over their heads. A train of cars was just ready for a start; the locomotive was fretting and fuming, like a steed impatient for a headlong rush; and the bell rang out its hasty peal, so well expressing the brief summons which life vouchsafes to us in its hurried career. Without question or delay,—with the irresistible

The House of the Seven Gables

decision, if not rather to be called recklessness, which had so strangely taken possession of him, and through him of Hepzibah,—Clifford impelled her towards the cars, and assisted her to enter. The signal was given; the engine puffed forth its short, quick breaths; the train began its movement; and, along with a hundred other passengers, these two unwonted travellers sped onward like the wind.

At last, therefore, and after so long estrangement from everything that the world acted or enjoyed, they had been drawn into the great current of human life, and were swept away with it, as by the suction of fate itself.

Still haunted with the idea that not one of the past incidents, inclusive of Judge Pyncheon's visit, could be real, the recluse of the Seven Gables murmured in her brother's ear,—

"Clifford! Clifford! Is not this a dream?"

"A dream, Hepzibah!" repeated he, almost laughing in her face. "On the contrary, I have never been awake before!"

Meanwhile, looking from the window, they could see the world racing past them. At one moment, they were rattling through a solitude; the next, a village had grown up around them; a few breaths more, and it had vanished, as if swallowed by an earthquake. The spires of meeting-houses seemed set adrift from their foundations; the broad-based hills glided away. Everything was unfixed from its age-long rest, and moving at whirlwind speed in a direction opposite to their own.

Within the car there was the usual interior life of the railroad, offering little to the observation of other passengers, but full of novelty for this pair of strangely enfranchised prisoners. It was novelty enough, indeed, that there were fifty human beings in close relation with them, under one long and narrow roof, and drawn onward by the same mighty influence that had taken their two selves into its grasp. It seemed marvellous how all these people could remain so quietly in their seats, while so much noisy strength was at work in their behalf. Some, with tickets in their hats (long travellers these, before whom lay a hundred miles of railroad), had plunged into the English scenery and adventures of pamphlet novels, and were keeping company with dukes and earls. Others, whose briefer span forbade their devoting themselves to studies so abstruse, beguiled the little tedium of the way with penny-papers. A party of girls, and one young man, on opposite sides of the car, found huge amusement in a game of ball. They tossed it to and fro, with peals of laughter that might be measured by mile-lengths; for, faster than the nimble ball could fly, the merry players fled unconsciously along, leaving the trail of their mirth afar behind, and ending their game under another sky than had witnessed its commencement. Boys, with apples, cakes, candy, and rolls of variously tinctured lozenges,—merchandise that reminded Hepzibah of her deserted shop,—appeared at each momentary stopping-place, doing up their business in a hurry, or breaking it short off, lest the market should ravish them away with it. New people continually entered. Old acquaintances— for such they soon grew to be, in this rapid current of affairs— continually departed. Here and there, amid the rumble and the tumult, sat one asleep. Sleep; sport; business; graver or lighter study; and the common and inevitable movement onward! It was life itself!

Clifford's naturally poignant sympathies were all aroused. He caught the color of what was passing about him, and threw it back more vividly than he received it, but mixed, nevertheless, with a lurid and portentous hue. Hepzibah, on the other hand, felt herself more apart from human kind than even in the seclusion which she had just quitted.

"You are not happy, Hepzibah!" said Clifford, apart, in a tone of reproach. "You are thinking of that dismal old house, and of Cousin Jaffrey"—here came the quake through him,— "and of Cousin Jaffrey sitting there, all by himself! Take my advice,—follow my example,—and let such things slip aside. Here we are, in the world, Hepzibah!—in the midst of life!—in the throng of our fellow beings! Let you and I be happy! As happy as that youth and those pretty girls, at their game of ball!"

"Happy—" thought Hepzibah, bitterly conscious, at the word, of her dull and heavy heart, with the frozen pain in it,— "happy. He is mad already; and, if I could once feel myself broad awake, I should go mad too!"

If a fixed idea be madness, she was perhaps not remote from it. Fast and far as they had rattled and clattered along the iron track, they might just as well, as regarded Hepzibah's mental images, have been passing up and down Pyncheon Street. With miles and miles of varied scenery between, there was no scene for her save the seven old gable-peaks, with their moss, and the tuft of weeds in one of the angles, and the shop-window, and a customer shaking the door, and compelling the little bell to jingle fiercely, but without disturbing Judge Pyncheon! This one old house was everywhere! It transported its great, lumbering bulk with more than railroad speed, and set itself phlegmatically down on whatever spot she glanced at. The quality of Hepzibah's mind was too unmalleable to take new impressions so readily as Clifford's. He had a winged nature; she was rather of the vegetable kind, and could hardly be kept long alive, if drawn up by the roots. Thus it happened that the relation heretofore existing between her brother and herself was changed. At home, she was his guardian; here, Clifford had become hers, and seemed to comprehend whatever belonged to their new position with a singular rapidity of intelligence. He had been startled into manhood and intellectual vigor; or, at least, into a condition that resembled them, though it might be both diseased and transitory.

The conductor now applied for their tickets; and Clifford, who had made himself the purse-bearer, put a bank-note into his hand, as he had observed others do.

"For the lady and yourself?" asked the conductor. "And how far?"

"As far as that will carry us," said Clifford. "It is no great matter. We are riding for pleasure merely."

"You choose a strange day for it, sir!" remarked a gimlet-eyed old gentleman on the other side of the car, looking at Clifford and his companion, as if curious to make them out. "The best chance of pleasure, in an easterly rain, I take it, is in a man's own house, with a nice little fire in the chimney."

"I cannot precisely agree with you," said Clifford, courteously bowing to the old gentleman, and at once taking up the clew of conversation which the latter had proffered. "It had just occurred to me, on the contrary, that this admirable invention of the railroad — with the vast and inevitable improvements to be looked for, both as to speed and convenience — is destined to do away with those stale ideas of home and fireside, and substitute something better."

"In the name of common-sense," asked the old gentleman rather testily, "what can be better for a man than his own parlor and chimney-corner?"

"These things have not the merit which many good people attribute to them," replied Clifford. "They may be said, in few and pithy words, to have ill served a poor purpose. My impression is, that our wonderfully increased and still increasing facilities of locomotion are destined to bring us around again to the nomadic state. You are aware, my dear sir, — you must have observed it in your own experience, — that all human progress is in a circle; or, to use a more accurate and beautiful figure, in an ascending spiral curve. While we fancy ourselves going straight forward, and attaining, at every step, an entirely new position of affairs, we do actually return to something long ago tried and abandoned, but which we now find etherealized, refined, and perfected to its ideal. The past is but a coarse and sensual prophecy of the present and the future. To apply this truth to the topic now under discussion. In the early epochs of our race, men dwelt in temporary huts, of bowers of branches, as easily constructed as a bird's-nest, and which they built,—if it should be called building, when such sweet homes of a summer solstice rather grew than were made with hands,—which Nature, we will say, assisted them to rear where fruit abounded, where fish and game were plentiful, or, most especially, where the sense of beauty was to be gratified by a lovelier shade than elsewhere, and a more exquisite arrangement of lake, wood, and hill. This life possessed a charm which, ever since man quitted it, has vanished from existence. And it typified something better than itself. It had its drawbacks; such as hunger and thirst, inclement weather, hot sunshine, and weary and foot-blistering marches over barren and ugly tracts, that lay between the sites desirable for their fertility and beauty. But in our ascending spiral, we escape all this. These railroads—could but the whistle be made musical, and the rumble and the jar got rid of—are positively the greatest blessing that the ages have wrought out for us. They give us wings; they annihilate the toil and dust of pilgrimage; they spiritualize travel! Transition being so facile, what can be any man's inducement to tarry in one spot? Why, therefore, should he build a more cumbrous habitation than can readily be carried off with him? Why should he make himself a prisoner for life in brick, and stone, and old worm-eaten timber, when he may just as easily dwell, in one sense, nowhere,—in a better sense, wherever the fit and beautiful shall offer him a home?"

Clifford's countenance glowed, as he divulged this theory; a youthful character shone out from within, converting the wrinkles and pallid duskiness of age into an almost transparent mask. The merry girls let their ball drop upon the floor, and gazed at him. They said to themselves, perhaps, that, before his hair was gray and the crow's-feet tracked his temples, this now decaying man must have stamped the impress of his features on many a woman's heart. But, alas! no woman's eye had seen his face while it was beautiful.

"I should scarcely call it an improved state of things," observed Clifford's new acquaintance, "to live everywhere and nowhere!"

"Would you not?" exclaimed Clifford, with singular energy. "It is as clear to me as sunshine,—were there any in the sky,—that the greatest possible stumbling-blocks in the path of human happiness and improvement are these heaps of bricks and stones, consolidated with mortar, or hewn timber, fastened together with spike-nails, which men painfully contrive for their own torment, and call them house and home! The soul needs air; a wide sweep and frequent change of it. Morbid influences, in a thousand-fold variety, gather about hearths, and pollute the life of households. There is no such unwholesome atmosphere as that of an old home, rendered poisonous by one's defunct forefathers and relatives. I speak of what I know. There is a certain house within my familiar recollection,—one of those peaked-gable (there are seven of them), projecting-storied edifices, such as you occasionally see in our older towns,—a rusty, crazy, creaky, dry-rotted, dingy, dark, and miserable old dungeon, with an arched window over the porch, and a little shop-door on one side, and a great, melancholy elm before it! Now, sir, whenever my thoughts recur to this seven-gabled mansion (the fact is so very curious that I must needs mention it), immediately I have a vision or image of an elderly man, of remarkably stern countenance, sitting in an oaken elbow-chair, dead, stone-dead, with an ugly flow of blood upon his shirt-bosom! Dead, but with open eyes! He taints the whole house, as I remember it. I could never flourish there, nor be happy, nor do nor enjoy what God meant me to do and enjoy."

His face darkened, and seemed to contract, and shrivel itself up, and wither into age.

"Never, sir!" he repeated. "I could never draw cheerful breath there!"

"I should think not," said the old gentleman, eyeing Clifford earnestly, and rather apprehensively. "I should conceive not, sir, with that notion in your head!"

"Surely not," continued Clifford; "and it were a relief to me if that house could be torn down, or burnt up, and so the earth be rid of it, and grass be sown abundantly over its foundation. Not that I should ever visit its site again! for, sir, the farther I get away from it, the more does the joy, the lightsome freshness, the heart-leap, the intellectual dance, the youth, in short,—yes, my youth, my youth!—the more does it come back to me. No longer ago than this morning, I was old. I remember looking in the glass, and wondering at my own gray hair, and the wrinkles, many and deep, right across my brow, and the furrows down my cheeks, and the prodigious trampling of crow's-feet about my temples! It was too soon! I could not bear it! Age had no right to come! I had not lived! But now do I look old? If so, my aspect belies me strangely; for—a great weight being off my mind—I feel in the very heyday of my youth, with the world and my best days before me!"

"I trust you may find it so," said the old gentleman, who seemed rather embarrassed, and desirous of avoiding the observation which Clifford's wild talk drew on them both. "You have my best wishes for it."

"For Heaven's sake, dear Clifford, be quiet!" whispered his sister. "They think you mad."

"Be quiet yourself, Hepzibah!" returned her brother. "No

matter what they think! I am not mad. For the first time in thirty years my thoughts gush up and find words ready for them. I must talk, and I will!"

He turned again towards the old gentleman, and renewed the conversation.

"Yes, my dear sir," said he, "it is my firm belief and hope that these terms of roof and hearth-stone, which have so long been held to embody something sacred, are soon to pass out of men's daily use, and be forgotten. Just imagine, for a moment, how much of human evil will crumble away, with this one change! What we call real estate—the solid ground to build a house on—is the broad foundation on which nearly all the guilt of this world rests. A man will commit almost any wrong,—he will heap up an immense pile of wickedness, as hard as granite, and which will weigh as heavily upon his soul, to eternal ages, —only to build a great, gloomy, dark-chambered mansion, for himself to die in, and for his posterity to be miserable in. He lays his own dead corpse beneath the underpinning, as one may say, and hangs his frowning picture on the wall, and, after thus converting himself into an evil destiny, expects his remotest great-grandchildren to be happy there. I do not speak wildly. I have just such a house in my mind's eye!"

"Then, sir," said the old gentleman, getting anxious to drop the subject, "you are not to blame for leaving it."

"Within the lifetime of the child already born," Clifford went on, "all this will be done away. The world is growing too ethereal and spiritual to bear these enormities a great while longer. To me, though, for a considerable period of time, I have lived chiefly in retirement, and know less of such things than most men,—even to me, the harbingers of a better era are unmistakable. Mesmerism, now! Will that effect nothing, think you, towards purging away the grossness out of human life?"

"All a humbug!" growled the old gentleman.

"These rapping spirits, that little Phœbe told us of, the other day," said Clifford,—"what are these but the messengers of the spiritual world, knocking at the door of substance? And it shall be flung wide open!"

"A humbug, again!" cried the old gentleman, growing more and more testy at these glimpses of Clifford's metaphysics. "I should like to rap with a good stick on the empty pates of the dolts who circulate such nonsense!"

"Then there is electricity,—the demon, the angel, the mighty physical power, the all-pervading intelligence!" exclaimed

The House of the Seven Gables

Clifford. "Is that a humbug, too? Is it a fact—or have I dreamt it—that, by means of electricity, the world of matter has become a great nerve, vibrating thousands of miles in a breathless point of time? Rather, the round globe is a vast head, a brain, instinct with intelligence! Or, shall we say, it is itself a thought, nothing but thought, and no longer the substance which we deemed it!"

"If you mean the telegraph," said the old gentleman, glancing his eye toward its wire, alongside the rail-track, "it is an excellent thing,—that is, of course, if the speculators in cotton and politics don't get possession of it. A great thing, indeed, sir, particularly as regards the detection of bank-robbers and murderers."

"I don't quite like it, in that point of view," replied Clifford. "A bank-robber, and what you call a murderer, likewise, has his rights, which men of enlightened humanity and conscience should regard in so much the more liberal spirit, because the bulk of society is prone to controvert their existence. An almost spiritual medium, like the electric telegraph, should be consecrated to high, deep, joyful, and holy missions. Lovers, day by day—hour by hour, if so often moved to do it,—might send their heart-throbs from Maine to Florida, with some such words as these 'I love you forever!'—'My heart runs over with love!'—'I love you more than I can!' and, again, at the next message 'I have lived an hour longer, and love you twice as much!' Or, when a good man has departed, his distant friend should be conscious of an electric thrill, as from the world of happy spirits, telling him 'Your dear friend is in bliss!' Or, to an absent husband, should come tidings thus 'An immortal being, of whom you are the father, has this moment come from God!' and immediately its little voice would seem to have reached so far, and to be echoing in his heart. But for these poor rogues, the bank-robbers,—who, after all, are about as honest as nine people in ten, except that they disregard certain formalities, and prefer to transact business at midnight rather than 'Change-hours,—and for these murderers, as you phrase it, who are often excusable in the motives of their deed, and deserve to be ranked among public benefactors, if we consider only its result,—for unfortunate individuals like these, I really cannot applaud the enlistment of an immaterial and miraculous power in the universal world-hunt at their heels!"

"You can't, hey?" cried the old gentleman, with a hard look.

"Positively, no!" answered Clifford. "It puts them too miserably at disadvantage. For example, sir, in a dark, low, cross-beamed, panelled room of an old house, let us suppose a dead man, sitting in an arm-chair, with a blood-stain on his shirt-bosom,—and let us add to our hypothesis another man, issuing from the house, which he feels to be over-filled with the dead man's presence,—and let us lastly imagine him fleeing,

Heaven knows whither, at the speed of a hurricane, by railroad! Now, sir, if the fugitive alight in some distant town, and find all the people babbling about that self-same dead man, whom he has fled so far to avoid the sight and thought of, will you not allow that his natural rights have been infringed? He has been deprived of his city of refuge, and, in my humble opinion, has suffered infinite wrong!"

"You are a strange man; Sir!" said the old gentleman, bringing his gimlet-eye to a point on Clifford, as if determined to bore right into him. "I can't see through you!"

"No, I'll be bound you can't!" cried Clifford, laughing. "And yet, my dear sir, I am as transparent as the water of Maule's well! But come, Hepzibah! We have flown far enough for once. Let us alight, as the birds do, and perch ourselves on the nearest twig, and consult wither we shall fly next!"

Just then, as it happened, the train reached a solitary way-station. Taking advantage of the brief pause, Clifford left the car, and drew Hepzibah along with him. A moment afterwards, the train — with all the life of its interior, amid which Clifford had made himself so conspicuous an object — was gliding away in the distance, and rapidly lessening to a point which, in another moment, vanished. The world had fled away from these two wanderers. They gazed drearily about them. At a little distance stood a wooden church, black with age, and in a dismal state of ruin and decay, with broken windows, a great rift through the main body of the edifice, and a rafter dangling from the top of the square tower. Farther off was a farm-house, in the old style, as venerably black as the church, with a roof sloping downward from the three-story peak, to within a man's height of the ground. It seemed uninhabited. There were the relics of a wood-pile, indeed, near the door, but with grass sprouting up among the chips and scattered logs. The small rain-drops came down aslant; the wind was not turbulent, but sullen, and full of chilly moisture.

Clifford shivered from head to foot. The wild effervescence of his mood — which had so readily supplied thoughts, fantasies, and a strange aptitude of words, and impelled him to talk from the mere necessity of giving vent to this bubbling-up gush of ideas had entirely subsided. A powerful excitement had given him energy and vivacity. Its operation over, he forthwith began to sink.

"You must take the lead now, Hepzibah!" murmured he, with a torpid and reluctant utterance. "Do with me as you will!" She knelt down upon the platform where they were standing and lifted her clasped hands to the sky. The dull, gray weight of clouds made it invisible; but it was no hour for disbelief, — no juncture this to question that there was a sky above, and an

Almighty Father looking from it!

"O God!" — ejaculated poor, gaunt Hepzibah, — then paused a moment, to consider what her prayer should be, — "O God, — our Father, — are we not thy children? Have mercy on us!"

XVIII.
Governor Pyncheon

Judge Pyncheon, while his two relatives have fled away with such ill-considered haste, still sits in the old parlor, keeping house, as the familiar phrase is, in the absence of its ordinary occupants. To him, and to the venerable House of the Seven Gables, does our story now betake itself, like an owl, bewildered in the daylight, and hastening back to his hollow tree.

The Judge has not shifted his position for a long while now. He has not stirred hand or foot, nor withdrawn his eyes so much as a hair's-breadth from their fixed gaze towards the corner of the room, since the footsteps of Hepzibah and Clifford creaked along the passage, and the outer door was closed cautiously behind their exit. He holds his watch in his left hand, but clutched in such a manner that you cannot see the dial-plate. How profound a fit of meditation! Or, supposing him asleep, how infantile a quietude of conscience, and what wholesome order in the gastric region, are betokened by slumber so entirely undisturbed with starts, cramp, twitches, muttered dreamtalk, trumpet-blasts through the nasal organ, or any slightest irregularity of breath! You must hold your own breath, to satisfy yourself whether he breathes at all. It is quite inaudible. You hear the ticking of his watch; his breath you do not hear. A most refreshing slumber, doubtless! And yet, the Judge cannot be asleep. His eyes are open! A veteran politician, such as he, would never fall asleep with wide-open eyes, lest some enemy or mischief-maker, taking him thus at unawares, should peep through these windows into his consciousness, and make strange discoveries among the reminiscences, projects, hopes, apprehensions, weaknesses, and strong points, which he has heretofore shared with nobody. A cautious man is proverbially said to sleep with one eye open. That may be wisdom. But not with both; for this were heedlessness! No, no! Judge Pyncheon cannot be asleep.

It is odd, however, that a gentleman so burdened with engagements, — and noted, too, for punctuality, — should linger thus in an old lonely mansion, which he has never seemed very fond of visiting. The oaken chair, to be sure, may tempt him with its roominess. It is, indeed, a spacious, and, allowing for the rude age that fashioned it, a moderately easy seat, with capacity enough, at all events, and offering no restraint to the Judge's breadth of beam. A bigger man might find ample accommodation in it. His ancestor, now pictured upon the wall, with all his English beef about him, used hardly to present a front extending from elbow to elbow of this chair, or a base that would cover its whole cushion. But there are better chairs than this,—mahogany, black walnut, rosewood, spring-seated and damask-cushioned, with varied slopes, and innumerable artifices to make them easy, and obviate the irksomeness of too tame an ease,—a score of such might be at Judge Pyncheon's service. Yes! in a score of drawing-rooms he would be more than welcome. Mamma would advance to meet him, with outstretched hand; the virgin daughter, elderly as he has now got to be,—an old widower, as he smilingly describes himself,—would shake up the cushion for the Judge, and do her pretty utmost to make him comfortable. For the Judge is a prosperous man. He cherishes his schemes, moreover, like other people, and reasonably brighter than most others; or did so, at least, as he lay abed this morning, in an agreeable half-drowse, planning the business of the day, and speculating on the probabilities of the next fifteen years. With his firm health, and the little inroad that age has made upon him, fifteen years or twenty—yes, or perhaps five-and-twenty!—are no more than he may fairly call his own. Five-and-twenty years for the enjoyment of his real estate in town and country, his railroad, bank, and insurance shares, his United States stock,—his wealth, in short, however invested, now in possession, or soon to be acquired; together with the public honors that have fallen upon him, and the weightier ones that are yet to fall! It is good! It is excellent! It is enough!

Still lingering in the old chair! If the Judge has a little time to throw away, why does not he visit the insurance office, as is his frequent custom, and sit awhile in one of their leathern-cushioned arm-chairs, listening to the gossip of the day, and dropping some deeply designed chance-word, which will be certain to become the gossip of to-morrow. And have not the bank directors a meeting at which it was the Judge's purpose to be present, and his office to preside? Indeed they have; and the hour is noted on a card, which is, or ought to be, in Judge Pyncheon's right vest-pocket. Let him go thither, and loll at ease upon his moneybags! He has lounged long enough in the old chair!

This was to have been such a busy day. In the first place, the interview with Clifford. Half an hour, by the Judge's reckoning, was to suffice for that; it would probably be less, but—taking into consideration that Hepzibah was first to be dealt with, and that these women are apt to make many words where a few would do much better—it might be safest to allow half an hour. Half an hour? Why, Judge, it is already two hours, by your own undeviatingly accurate chronometer. Glance your eye down at it and see! Ah; he will not give himself the trouble either to bend his head, or elevate his hand, so as to bring the faithful time-keeper within his range of vision! Time, all at once, appears to have become a matter of no moment with the Judge!

And has he forgotten all the other items of his memoranda?

Clifford's affair arranged, he was to meet a State Street broker, who has undertaken to procure a heavy percentage, and the best of paper, for a few loose thousands which the Judge happens to have by him, uninvested. The wrinkled note-shaver will have taken his railroad trip in vain. Half an hour later, in the street next to this, there was to be an auction of real estate, including a portion of the old Pyncheon property, originally belonging to Maule's garden ground. It has been alienated from the Pyncheons these four-score years; but the Judge had kept it in his eye, and had set his heart on reannexing it to the small demesne still left around the Seven Gables; and now, during this odd fit of oblivion, the fatal hammer must have fallen, and transferred our ancient patrimony to some alien possessor. Possibly, indeed, the sale may have been postponed till fairer weather. If so, will the Judge make it convenient to be present, and favor the auctioneer with his bid, on the proximate occasion?

The next affair was to buy a horse for his own driving. The one heretofore his favorite stumbled, this very morning, on the road to town, and must be at once discarded. Judge Pyncheon's neck is too precious to be risked on such a contingency as a stumbling steed. Should all the above business be seasonably got through with, he might attend the meeting of a charitable society; the very name of which, however, in the multiplicity of his benevolence, is quite forgotten; so that this engagement may pass unfulfilled, and no great harm done. And if he have time, amid the press of more urgent matters, he must take measures for the renewal of Mrs. Pyncheon's tombstone, which, the sexton tells him, has fallen on its marble face, and is cracked quite in twain. She was a praiseworthy woman enough, thinks the Judge, in spite of her nervousness, and the tears that she was so oozy with, and her foolish behavior about the coffee; and as she took her departure so seasonably, he will not grudge the second tombstone. It is better, at least, than if she had never needed any! The next item on his list was to give orders for some fruit-trees, of a rare variety, to be deliverable at his country-seat in the ensuing autumn. Yes, buy them, by all means; and may the peaches be luscious in your mouth, Judge Pyncheon! After this comes something more important. A committee of his political party has besought him for a hundred or two of dollars, in addition to his previous disbursements, towards carrying on the fall campaign. The Judge is a patriot; the fate of the country is staked on the November election; and besides, as will be shadowed forth in another paragraph, he has no trifling stake of his own in the same great game. He will do what the committee asks; nay, he will be liberal beyond their expectations; they shall have a check for five hundred dollars, and more anon, if it be needed. What next? A decayed widow, whose husband was Judge Pyncheon's early friend, has laid her case of destitution before him, in a very moving letter. She and her fair daughter have scarcely bread to eat. He partly intends to call on her to-day,—perhaps so—perhaps not,—accordingly as he may happen to have leisure, and a small bank-note.

Another business, which, however, he puts no great weight on (it is well, you know, to be heedful, but not over-anxious, as respects one's personal health),—another business, then, was to consult his family physician. About what, for Heaven's sake? Why, it is rather difficult to describe the symptoms. A mere dimness of sight and dizziness of brain, was it?—or disagreeable choking, or stifling, or gurgling, or bubbling, in the region of the thorax, as the anatomists say?—or was it a pretty severe throbbing and kicking of the heart, rather creditable to him than otherwise, as showing that the organ had not been left out of the Judge's physical contrivance? No matter what it was. The doctor probably would smile at the statement of such trifles to his professional ear; the Judge would smile in his turn; and meeting one another's eyes, they would enjoy a hearty laugh together! But a fig for medical advice. The Judge will never need it.

Pray, pray, Judge Pyncheon, look at your watch, Now! What—not a glance! It is within ten minutes of the dinner hour! It surely cannot have slipped your memory that the dinner of to-day is to be the most important, in its consequences, of all the dinners you ever ate. Yes, precisely the most important; although, in the course of your somewhat eminent career, you have been placed high towards the head of the table, at splendid banquets, and have poured out your festive eloquence to ears yet echoing with Webster's mighty organ-tones. No public dinner this, however. It is merely a gathering of some dozen or so of friends from several districts of the State; men of distinguished character and influence, assembling, almost casually, at the house of a common friend, likewise distinguished, who will make them welcome to a little better than his ordinary fare. Nothing in the way of French cookery, but an excellent dinner, nevertheless. Real turtle, we understand, and salmon, tautog, canvas-backs, pig, English mutton, good roast beef, or dainties of that serious kind, fit for substantial country gentlemen, as these honorable persons mostly are. The delicacies of the season, in short, and flavored by a brand of old Madeira which has been the pride of many seasons. It is the Juno brand; a glorious wine, fragrant, and full of gentle might; a bottled-up happiness, put by for use; a golden liquid, worth more than liquid gold; so rare and admirable, that veteran wine-bibbers count it among their epochs to have tasted it! It drives away the heart-ache, and substitutes no head-ache! Could the Judge but quaff a glass, it might enable him to shake off the unaccountable lethargy which (for the ten intervening minutes, and five to boot, are already past) has made him such a laggard at this momentous dinner. It would all but revive a dead man! Would you like to sip it now, Judge Pyncheon?

Alas, this dinner. Have you really forgotten its true object? Then let us whisper it, that you may start at once out of the oaken chair, which really seems to be enchanted, like the one in Comus, or that in which Moll Pitcher imprisoned your own grandfather. But ambition is a talisman more powerful than witchcraft. Start up, then, and, hurrying through the streets, burst in upon the company, that they may begin before the fish is spoiled! They wait for you; and it is little for your interest that they should wait. These gentlemen — need you be told it? — have assembled, not without purpose, from every quarter of the State. They are practised politicians, every man of them, and skilled to adjust those preliminary measures which steal from the people, without its knowledge, the power of choosing its own rulers. The popular voice, at the next gubernatorial election, though loud as thunder, will be really but an echo of what these gentlemen shall speak, under their breath, at your friend's festive board. They meet to decide upon their candidate. This little knot of subtle schemers will control the convention, and, through it, dictate to the party. And what worthier candidate, — more wise and learned, more noted for philanthropic liberality, truer to safe principles, tried oftener by public trusts, more spotless in private character, with a larger stake in the common welfare, and deeper grounded, by hereditary descent, in the faith and practice of the Puritans, — what man can be presented for the suffrage of the people, so eminently combining all these claims to the chief-rulership as Judge Pyncheon here before us?

Make haste, then! Do your part! The meed for which you have toiled, and fought, and climbed, and crept, is ready for your grasp! Be present at this dinner! — drink a glass or two of that noble wine! — make your pledges in as low a whisper as you will! — and you rise up from table virtually governor of the glorious old State! Governor Pyncheon of Massachusetts!

And is there no potent and exhilarating cordial in a certainty like this? It has been the grand purpose of half your lifetime to obtain it. Now, when there needs little more than to signify your acceptance, why do you sit so lumpishly in your great-great-grandfather's oaken chair, as if preferring it to the gubernatorial one? We have all heard of King Log; but, in these jostling times, one of that royal kindred will hardly win the race for an elective chief-magistracy.

Well; it is absolutely too late for dinner! Turtle, salmon, tautog, woodcock, boiled turkey, South-Down mutton, pig, roast-beef, have vanished, or exist only in fragments, with lukewarm potatoes, and gravies crusted over with cold fat. The Judge, had he done nothing else, would have achieved wonders with his knife and fork. It was he, you know, of whom it used to be said, in reference to his ogre-like appetite, that his Creator made him a great animal, but that the dinner-hour made him a

The House of the Seven Gables

great beast. Persons of his large sensual endowments must claim indulgence, at their feeding-time. But, for once, the Judge is entirely too late for dinner! Too late, we fear, even to join the party at their wine! The guests are warm and merry; they have given up the Judge; and, concluding that the Free-Soilers have him, they will fix upon another candidate. Were our friend now to stalk in among them, with that wide-open stare, at once wild and stolid, his ungenial presence would be apt to change their cheer. Neither would it be seemly in Judge Pyncheon, generally so scrupulous in his attire, to show himself at a dinner-table with that crimson stain upon his shirt-bosom. By the bye, how came it there? It is an ugly sight, at any rate; and the wisest way for the Judge is to button his coat closely over his breast, and, taking his horse and chaise from the livery stable, to make all speed to his own house. There, after a glass of brandy and water, and a mutton-chop, a beefsteak, a broiled fowl, or some such hasty little dinner and supper all in one, he had better spend the evening by the fireside. He must toast his slippers a long while, in order to get rid of the chilliness which the air of this vile old house has sent curdling through his veins.

Up, therefore, Judge Pyncheon, up! You have lost a day. But to-morrow will be here anon. Will you rise, betimes, and make the most of it? To-morrow. To-morrow! To-morrow. We, that are alive, may rise betimes to-morrow. As for him that has died to-day, his morrow will be the resurrection morn.

Meanwhile the twilight is glooming upward out of the corners of the room. The shadows of the tall furniture grow deeper, and at first become more definite; then, spreading wider, they lose their distinctness of outline in the dark gray tide of oblivion, as it were, that creeps slowly over the various objects, and the one human figure sitting in the midst of them. The gloom has not entered from without; it has brooded here all day, and now, taking its own inevitable time, will possess itself of everything. The Judge's face, indeed, rigid and singularly white, refuses to melt into this universal solvent. Fainter and fainter grows the light. It is as if another double-handful of darkness had been scattered through the air. Now it is no longer gray, but sable. There is still a faint appearance at the window; neither a glow, nor a gleam, nor a glimmer, — any phrase of light would express something far brighter than this doubtful perception, or sense, rather, that there is a window there. Has it yet vanished? No! — yes! — not quite! And there is still the swarthy whiteness, — we shall venture to marry these ill-agreeing words, — the swarthy whiteness of Judge Pyncheon's face. The features are all gone: there is only the paleness of them left. And how looks it now? There is no window! There is no face! An infinite, inscrutable blackness has annihilated sight! Where is our universe? All crumbled away from us; and we, adrift in chaos, may hearken to the gusts of homeless wind, that go sighing and murmuring about in quest of what was once a world!

Is there no other sound? One other, and a fearful one. It is the ticking of the Judge's watch, which, ever since Hepzibah left the room in search of Clifford, he has been holding in his hand. Be the cause what it may, this little, quiet, never-ceasing throb of Time's pulse, repeating its small strokes with such busy regularity, in Judge Pyncheon's motionless hand, has an effect of terror, which we do not find in any other accompaniment of the scene.

But, listen! That puff of the breeze was louder. It had a tone unlike the dreary and sullen one which has bemoaned itself, and afflicted all mankind with miserable sympathy, for five days past. The wind has veered about! It now comes boisterously from the northwest, and, taking hold of the aged framework of the Seven Gables, gives it a shake, like a wrestler that would try strength with his antagonist. Another and another sturdy tussle with the blast! The old house creaks again, and makes a vociferous but somewhat unintelligible bellowing in its sooty throat (the big flue, we mean, of its wide chimney), partly in complaint at the rude wind, but rather, as befits their century and a half of hostile intimacy, in tough defiance. A rumbling kind of a bluster roars behind the fire-board. A door has slammed above stairs. A window, perhaps, has been left open, or else is driven in by an unruly gust. It is not to be conceived, before-hand, what wonderful wind-instruments are these old timber mansions, and how haunted with the strangest noises, which immediately begin to sing, and sigh, and sob, and shriek,—and to smite with sledge-hammers, airy but ponderous, in some distant chamber,—and to tread along the entries as with stately footsteps, and rustle up and down the staircase, as with silks miraculously stiff,—whenever the gale catches the house with a window open, and gets fairly into it. Would that we were not an attendant spirit here! It is too awful! This clamor of the wind through the lonely house; the Judge's quietude, as he sits invisible; and that pertinacious ticking of his watch!

As regards Judge Pyncheon's invisibility, however, that matter will soon be remedied. The northwest wind has swept the sky clear. The window is distinctly seen. Through its panes, moreover, we dimly catch the sweep of the dark, clustering foliage outside, fluttering with a constant irregularity of movement, and letting in a peep of starlight, now here, now there. Oftener than any other object, these glimpses illuminate the Judge's face. But here comes more effectual light. Observe that silvery dance upon the upper branches of the pear-tree, and now a little lower, and now on the whole mass of boughs, while, through their shifting intricacies, the moonbeams fall aslant into the room. They play over the Judge's figure and show that he has not stirred throughout the hours of darkness.

The House of the Seven Gables

They follow the shadows, in changeful sport, across his unchanging features. They gleam upon his watch. His grasp conceals the dial-plate,—but we know that the faithful hands have met; for one of the city clocks tells midnight.

A man of sturdy understanding, like Judge Pyncheon, cares no more for twelve o'clock at night than for the corresponding hour of noon. However just the parallel drawn, in some of the preceding pages, between his Puritan ancestor and himself, it fails in this point. The Pyncheon of two centuries ago, in common with most of his contemporaries, professed his full belief in spiritual ministrations, although reckoning them chiefly of a malignant character. The Pyncheon of to-night, who sits in yonder arm-chair, believes in no such nonsense. Such, at least, was his creed, some few hours since. His hair will not bristle, therefore, at the stories which—in times when chimney-corners had benches in them, where old people sat poking into the ashes of the past, and raking out traditions like live coals—used to be told about this very room of his ancestral house. In fact, these tales are too absurd to bristle even childhood's hair. What sense, meaning, or moral, for example, such as even ghost-stories should be susceptible of, can be traced in the ridiculous legend, that, at midnight, all the dead Pyncheons are bound to assemble in this parlor? And, pray, for what? Why, to see whether the portrait of their ancestor still keeps its place upon the wall, in compliance with his testamentary directions! Is it worth while to come out of their graves for that?

We are tempted to make a little sport with the idea. Ghost-stories are hardly to be treated seriously any longer. The family-party of the defunct Pyncheons, we presume, goes off in this wise.

First comes the ancestor himself, in his black cloak, steeple-hat, and trunk-breeches, girt about the waist with a leathern belt, in which hangs his steel-hilted sword; he has a long staff in his hand, such as gentlemen in advanced life used to carry, as much for the dignity of the thing as for the support to be derived from it. He looks up at the portrait; a thing of no substance, gazing at its own painted image! All is safe. The picture is still there. The purpose of his brain has been kept sacred thus long after the man himself has sprouted up in graveyard grass. See! he lifts his ineffectual hand, and tries the frame. All safe! But is that a smile?—is it not, rather a frown of deadly import, that darkens over the shadow of his features? The stout Colonel is dissatisfied! So decided is his look of discontent as to impart additional distinctness to his features; through which, nevertheless, the moonlight passes, and flickers on the wall beyond. Something has strangely vexed the ancestor! With a grim shake of the head, he turns away. Here come other Pyncheons, the whole tribe, in their half a dozen generations, jostling and elbowing one another, to reach the picture. We behold aged men and grandames, a clergyman with the Puritanic stiffness still in his garb and mien, and a red-coated officer of the old French war; and there comes the shop-keeping Pyncheon of a century ago, with the ruffles turned back from his wrists; and there the periwigged and brocaded gentleman of the artist's legend, with the beautiful and pensive Alice, who brings no pride out of her virgin grave. All try the picture-frame. What do these ghostly people seek? A mother lifts her child, that his little hands may touch it! There is evidently a mystery about the picture, that perplexes these poor Pyncheons when they ought to be at rest. In a corner, meanwhile, stands the figure of an elderly man, in a leathern jerkin and breeches, with a carpenter's rule sticking out of his side pocket; he points his finger at the bearded Colonel and his descendants, nodding, jeering, mocking, and finally bursting into obstreperous, though inaudible laughter.

Indulging our fancy in this freak, we have partly lost the power of restraint and guidance. We distinguish an unlooked-for figure in our visionary scene. Among those ancestral people there is a young man, dressed in the very fashion of to-day: he wears a dark frock-coat, almost destitute of skirts, gray pantaloons, gaiter boots of patent leather, and has a finely wrought gold chain across his breast, and a little silver-headed whalebone stick in his hand. Were we to meet this figure at noonday, we should greet him as young Jaffrey Pyncheon, the Judge's only surviving child, who has been spending the last two years in foreign travel. If still in life, how comes his shadow hither? If dead, what a misfortune! The old Pyncheon property, together with the great estate acquired by the young man's father, would devolve on whom? On poor, foolish Clifford, gaunt Hepzibah, and rustic little Phœbe! But another and a greater marvel greets us! Can we believe our eyes? A stout, elderly gentleman has made his appearance; he has an aspect of eminent respectability, wears a black coat and pantaloons, of roomy width, and might be pronounced scrupulously neat in his attire, but for a broad crimson stain across his snowy neckcloth and down his shirt-bosom. Is it the Judge, or no? How can it be Judge Pyncheon? We discern his figure, as plainly as the flickering moonbeams can show us anything, still seated in the oaken chair! Be the apparition whose it may, it advances to the picture, seems to seize the frame, tries to peep behind it, and turns away, with a frown as black as the ancestral one.

The fantastic scene just hinted at must by no means be considered as forming an actual portion of our story. We were betrayed into this brief extravagance by the quiver of the moonbeams; they dance hand-in-hand with shadows, and are reflected in the looking-glass, which, you are aware, is always a kind of window or doorway into the spiritual world. We needed relief, moreover, from our too long and exclusive contemplation of that figure in the chair. This wild wind, too,

The House of the Seven Gables

has tossed our thoughts into strange confusion, but without tearing them away from their one determined centre. Yonder leaden Judge sits immovably upon our soul. Will he never stir again? We shall go mad unless he stirs! You may the better estimate his quietude by the fearlessness of a little mouse, which sits on its hind legs, in a streak of moonlight, close by Judge Pyncheon's foot, and seems to meditate a journey of exploration over this great black bulk. Ha! what has startled the nimble little mouse? It is the visage of grimalkin, outside of the window, where he appears to have posted himself for a deliberate watch. This grimalkin has a very ugly look. Is it a cat watching for a mouse, or the devil for a human soul? Would we could scare him from the window!

Thank Heaven, the night is well-nigh past! The moonbeams have no longer so silvery a gleam, nor contrast so strongly with the blackness of the shadows among which they fall. They are paler now; the shadows look gray, not black. The boisterous wind is hushed. What is the hour? Ah! the watch has at last ceased to tick; for the Judge's forgetful fingers neglected to wind it up, as usual, at ten o'clock, being half an hour or so before his ordinary bedtime,—and it has run down, for the first time in five years. But the great world-clock of Time still keeps its beat. The dreary night—for, oh, how dreary seems its haunted waste, behind us!—gives place to a fresh, transparent, cloudless morn. Blessed, blessed radiance! The daybeam—even what little of it finds its way into this always dusky parlor—seems part of the universal benediction, annulling evil, and rendering all goodness possible, and happiness attainable. Will Judge Pyncheon now rise up from his chair? Will he go forth, and receive the early sunbeams on his brow? Will he begin this new day,—which God has smiled upon, and blessed, and given to mankind,—will he begin it with better purposes than the many that have been spent amiss? Or are all the deep-laid schemes of yesterday as stubborn in his heart, and as busy in his brain, as ever?

In this latter case, there is much to do. Will the Judge still insist with Hepzibah on the interview with Clifford? Will he buy a safe, elderly gentleman's horse? Will he persuade the purchaser of the old Pyncheon property to relinquish the bargain in his favor? Will he see his family physician, and obtain a medicine that shall preserve him, to be an honor and blessing to his race, until the utmost term of patriarchal longevity? Will Judge Pyncheon, above all, make due apologies to that company of honorable friends, and satisfy them that his absence from the festive board was unavoidable, and so fully retrieve himself in their good opinion that he shall yet be Governor of Massachusetts? And all these great purposes accomplished, will he walk the streets again, with that dog-day smile of elaborate benevolence, sultry enough to tempt flies to come and buzz in it? Or will he, after the tomb-like seclusion of the past day and night, go forth a humbled and repentant man, sorrowful, gentle, seeking no profit, shrinking from worldly honor, hardly daring to love God, but bold to love his fellow man, and to do him what good he may? Will he bear about with him, — no odious grin of feigned benignity, insolent in its pretence, and loathsome in its falsehood, — but the tender sadness of a contrite heart, broken, at last, beneath its own weight of sin? For it is our belief, whatever show of honor he may have piled upon it, that there was heavy sin at the base of this man's being.

Rise up, Judge Pyncheon! The morning sunshine glimmers through the foliage, and, beautiful and holy as it is, shuns not to kindle up your face. Rise up, thou subtle, worldly, selfish, iron-hearted hypocrite, and make thy choice whether still to be subtle, worldly, selfish, iron-hearted, and hypocritical, or to tear these sins out of thy nature, though they bring the lifeblood with them! The Avenger is upon thee! Rise up, before it be too late!

What! Thou art not stirred by this last appeal? No, not a jot! And there we see a fly, — one of your common house-flies, such as are always buzzing on the window-pane, — which has smelt out Governor Pyncheon, and alights, now on his forehead, now on his chin, and now, Heaven help us! is creeping over the bridge of his nose, towards the would-be chief-magistrate's wide-open eyes! Canst thou not brush the fly away? Art thou too sluggish? Thou man, that hadst so many busy projects yesterday! Art thou too weak, that wast so powerful? Not brush away a fly? Nay, then, we give thee up!

And hark! the shop-bell rings. After hours like these latter ones, through which we have borne our heavy tale, it is good to be made sensible that there is a living world, and that even this old, lonely mansion retains some manner of connection with it. We breathe more freely, emerging from Judge Pyncheon's presence into the street before the Seven Gables.

XIX.
Alice's Posies

Uncle Venner, trundling a wheelbarrow, was the earliest person stirring in the neighborhood the day after the storm.

Pyncheon Street, in front of the House of the Seven Gables, was a far pleasanter scene than a by-lane, confined by shabby fences, and bordered with wooden dwellings of the meaner class, could reasonably be expected to present. Nature made sweet amends, that morning, for the five unkindly days which had preceded it. It would have been enough to live for, merely to look up at the wide benediction of the sky, or as much of it as was visible between the houses, genial once more with sunshine. Every object was agreeable, whether to be gazed at in the breadth, or examined more minutely. Such, for example, were the well-washed pebbles and gravel of the sidewalk; even the sky-reflecting pools in the centre of the street; and the grass, now freshly verdant, that crept along the base of the fences, on the other side of which, if one peeped over, was seen the multifarious growth of gardens. Vegetable productions, of whatever kind, seemed more than negatively happy, in the juicy warmth and abundance of their life. The Pyncheon Elm, throughout its great circumference, was all alive, and full of the morning sun and a sweet-tempered little breeze, which lingered within this verdant sphere, and set a thousand leafy tongues a-whispering all at once. This aged tree appeared to have suffered nothing from the gale. It had kept its boughs unshattered, and its full complement of leaves; and the whole in perfect verdure, except a single branch, that, by the earlier change with which the elm-tree sometimes prophesies the autumn, had been transmuted to bright gold. It was like the golden branch that gained Aeneas and the Sibyl admittance into Hades.

This one mystic branch hung down before the main entrance of the Seven Gables, so nigh the ground that any passer-by might have stood on tiptoe and plucked it off. Presented at the door, it would have been a symbol of his right to enter, and be made acquainted with all the secrets of the house. So little faith is due to external appearance, that there was really an inviting aspect over the venerable edifice, conveying an idea that its history must be a decorous and happy one, and such as would be delightful for a fireside tale. Its windows gleamed cheerfully in the slanting sunlight. The lines and tufts of green moss, here and there, seemed pledges of familiarity and sisterhood with Nature; as if this human dwelling-place, being of such old date, had established its prescriptive title among primeval oaks and whatever other objects, by virtue of their long continuance, have acquired a gracious right to be. A person of imaginative temperament, while passing by the house, would turn, once and again, and peruse it well: its many peaks, consenting together in the clustered chimney; the deep projection over its basement-story; the arched window, imparting a look, if not of grandeur, yet of antique gentility, to the broken portal over which it opened; the luxuriance of gigantic burdocks, near the threshold; he would note all these characteristics, and be conscious of something deeper than he saw. He would conceive the mansion to have been the residence of the stubborn old Puritan, Integrity, who, dying in some forgotten generation, had left a blessing in all its rooms and chambers, the efficacy of which was to be seen in the religion, honesty, moderate competence, or upright poverty and solid happiness, of his descendants, to this day.

One object, above all others, would take root in the imaginative observer's memory. It was the great tuft of flowers, — weeds, you would have called them, only a week ago, — the tuft of crimson-spotted flowers, in the angle between the two front gables. The old people used to give them the name of Alice's Posies, in remembrance of fair Alice Pyncheon, who was believed to have brought their seeds from Italy. They were flaunting in rich beauty and full bloom to-day, and seemed, as it were, a mystic expression that something within the house was consummated.

It was but little after sunrise, when Uncle Venner made his appearance, as aforesaid, impelling a wheelbarrow along the street. He was going his matutinal rounds to collect cabbage-leaves, turnip-tops, potato-skins, and the miscellaneous refuse of the dinner-pot, which the thrifty housewives of the neighborhood were accustomed to put aside, as fit only to feed a pig. Uncle Venner's pig was fed entirely, and kept in prime order, on these eleemosynary contributions; insomuch that the patched philosopher used to promise that, before retiring to his farm, he would make a feast of the portly grunter, and invite all his neighbors to partake of the joints and spare-ribs which they had helped to fatten. Miss Hepzibah Pyncheon's housekeeping had so greatly improved, since Clifford became a member of the family, that her share of the banquet would have been no lean one; and Uncle Venner, accordingly, was a good deal disappointed not to find the large earthen pan, full of fragmentary eatables, that ordinarily awaited his coming at the back doorstep of the Seven Gables.

"I never knew Miss Hepzibah so forgetful before," said the patriarch to himself. "She must have had a dinner yesterday, — no question of that! She always has one, nowadays. So where's the pot-liquor and potato-skins, I ask? Shall I knock, and see if she's stirring yet? No, no, — 'twon't do! If little Phœbe was about the house, I should not mind knocking; but Miss Hepzibah, likely as not, would scowl down at me out of the window, and look cross, even if she felt pleasantly. So, I'll come back at noon."

With these reflections, the old man was shutting the gate of the little back-yard. Creaking on its hinges, however, like every other gate and door about the premises, the sound reached the ears of the occupant of the northern gable, one of the windows of which had a side-view towards the gate.

"Good-morning, Uncle Venner!" said the daguerreotypist, leaning out of the window. "Do you hear nobody stirring?"

"Not a soul," said the man of patches. "But that's no wonder. 'Tis barely half an hour past sunrise, yet. But I'm really glad to see you, Mr. Holgrave! There's a strange, lonesome look about this side of the house; so that my heart misgave me, somehow or other, and I felt as if there was nobody alive in it. The front of the house looks a good deal cheerier; and Alice's Posies are blooming there beautifully; and if I were a young man, Mr. Holgrave, my sweetheart should have one of those flowers in her bosom, though I risked my neck climbing for it! Well, and did the wind keep you awake last night?"

"It did, indeed!" answered the artist, smiling. "If I were a believer in ghosts,—and I don't quite know whether I am or not,—I should have concluded that all the old Pyncheons were running riot in the lower rooms, especially in Miss Hepzibah's part of the house. But it is very quiet now."

"Yes, Miss Hepzibah will be apt to over-sleep herself, after being disturbed, all night, with the racket," said Uncle Venner. "But it would be odd, now, wouldn't it, if the Judge had taken both his cousins into the country along with him? I saw him go into the shop yesterday."

"At what hour?" inquired Holgrave.

"Oh, along in the forenoon," said the old man. "Well, well! I must go my rounds, and so must my wheelbarrow. But I'll be back here at dinner-time; for my pig likes a dinner as well as a breakfast. No meal-time, and no sort of victuals, ever seems to come amiss to my pig. Good morning to you! And, Mr. Holgrave, if I were a young man, like you, I'd get one of Alice's Posies, and keep it in water till Phœbe comes back."

"I have heard," said the daguerreotypist, as he drew in his head, "that the water of Maule's well suits those flowers best."

Here the conversation ceased, and Uncle Venner went on his way. For half an hour longer, nothing disturbed the repose of the Seven Gables; nor was there any visitor, except a carrier-boy, who, as he passed the front doorstep, threw down one of his newspapers; for Hepzibah, of late, had regularly taken it in. After a while, there came a fat woman, making prodigious speed, and stumbling as she ran up the steps of the shop-door. Her face glowed with fire-heat, and, it being a pretty warm morning, she bubbled and hissed, as it were, as if all a-fry with chimney-warmth, and summer-warmth, and the warmth of her own corpulent velocity. She tried the shop-door; it was fast. She tried it again, with so angry a jar that the bell tinkled angrily back at her.

"The deuce take Old Maid Pyncheon!" muttered the irascible housewife. "Think of her pretending to set up a cent-shop, and then lying abed till noon! These are what she calls gentlefolk's airs, I suppose! But I'll either start her ladyship, or break the door down!"

She shook it accordingly, and the bell, having a spiteful little temper of its own, rang obstreperously, making its remonstrances heard,—not, indeed, by the ears for which they were intended,—but by a good lady on the opposite side of the street. She opened the window, and addressed the impatient applicant.

"You'll find nobody there, Mrs. Gubbins."

"But I must and will find somebody here!" cried Mrs. Gubbins, inflicting another outrage on the bell. "I want a half-pound of pork, to fry some first-rate flounders for Mr. Gubbins's breakfast; and, lady or not, Old Maid Pyncheon shall get up and serve me with it!"

"But do hear reason, Mrs. Gubbins!" responded the lady opposite. "She, and her brother too, have both gone to their cousin's, Judge Pyncheon's at his country-seat. There's not a soul in the house, but that young daguerreotype-man that sleeps in the north gable. I saw old Hepzibah and Clifford go away yesterday; and a queer couple of ducks they were, paddling through the mud-puddles! They're gone, I'll assure you."

"And how do you know they're gone to the Judge's?" asked Mrs. Gubbins. "He's a rich man; and there's been a quarrel between him and Hepzibah this many a day, because he won't give her a living. That's the main reason of her setting up a cent-shop."

"I know that well enough," said the neighbor. "But they're gone,—that's one thing certain. And who but a blood relation, that couldn't help himself, I ask you, would take in that awful-tempered old maid, and that dreadful Clifford? That's it, you may be sure."

The House of the Seven Gables

Mrs. Gubbins took her departure, still brimming over with hot wrath against the absent Hepzibah. For another half-hour, or, perhaps, considerably more, there was almost as much quiet on the outside of the house as within. The elm, however, made a pleasant, cheerful, sunny sigh, responsive to the breeze that was elsewhere imperceptible; a swarm of insects buzzed merrily under its drooping shadow, and became specks of light whenever they darted into the sunshine; a locust sang, once or twice, in some inscrutable seclusion of the tree; and a solitary little bird, with plumage of pale gold, came and hovered about Alice's Posies.

At last our small acquaintance, Ned Higgins, trudged up the street, on his way to school; and happening, for the first time in a fortnight, to be the possessor of a cent, he could by no means get past the shop-door of the Seven Gables. But it would not open. Again and again, however, and half a dozen other agains, with the inexorable pertinacity of a child intent upon some object important to itself, did he renew his efforts for admittance. He had, doubtless, set his heart upon an elephant; or, possibly, with Hamlet, he meant to eat a crocodile. In response to his more violent attacks, the bell gave, now and then, a moderate tinkle, but could not be stirred into clamor by any exertion of the little fellow's childish and tiptoe strength. Holding by the door-handle, he peeped through a crevice of the curtain, and saw that the inner door, communicating with the passage towards the parlor, was closed.

"Miss Pyncheon!" screamed the child, rapping on the window-pane, "I want an elephant!"

There being no answer to several repetitions of the summons, Ned began to grow impatient; and his little pot of passion quickly boiling over, he picked up a stone, with a naughty purpose to fling it through the window; at the same time blubbering and sputtering with wrath. A man—one of two who happened to be passing by—caught the urchin's arm.

"What's the trouble, old gentleman?" he asked.

"I want old Hepzibah, or Phœbe, or any of them!" answered Ned, sobbing. "They won't open the door; and I can't get my elephant!"

"Go to school, you little scamp!" said the man. "There's another cent-shop round the corner. 'Tis very strange, Dixey," added he to his companion, "what's become of all these Pyncheon's! Smith, the livery-stable keeper, tells me Judge Pyncheon put his horse up yesterday, to stand till after dinner, and has not taken him away yet. And one of the Judge's hired men has been in, this morning, to make inquiry about him. He's a kind of person, they say, that seldom breaks his habits, or stays out o' nights."

"Oh, he'll turn up safe enough!" said Dixey. "And as for Old Maid Pyncheon, take my word for it, she has run in debt, and gone off from her creditors. I foretold, you remember, the first morning she set up shop, that her devilish scowl would frighten away customers. They couldn't stand it!"

"I never thought she'd make it go," remarked his friend. "This business of cent-shops is overdone among the women-folks. My wife tried it, and lost five dollars on her outlay!"

"Poor business!" said Dixey, shaking his head. "Poor business!"

In the course of the morning, there were various other attempts to open a communication with the supposed inhabitants of this silent and impenetrable mansion. The man of root-beer came, in his neatly painted wagon, with a couple of dozen full bottles, to be exchanged for empty ones; the baker, with a lot of crackers which Hepzibah had ordered for her retail custom; the butcher, with a nice titbit which he fancied she would be eager to secure for Clifford. Had any observer of these proceedings been aware of the fearful secret hidden within the house, it would have affected him with a singular shape and modification of horror, to see the current of human life making this small eddy hereabouts,—whirling sticks, straws and all such trifles, round and round, right over the black depth where a dead corpse lay unseen!

The butcher was so much in earnest with his sweetbread of lamb, or whatever the dainty might be, that he tried every accessible door of the Seven Gables, and at length came round again to the shop, where he ordinarily found admittance.

"It's a nice article, and I know the old lady would jump at it," said he to himself. "She can't be gone away! In fifteen years that I have driven my cart through Pyncheon Street, I've never known her to be away from home; though often enough, to be sure, a man might knock all day without bringing her to the door. But that was when she'd only herself to provide for."

Peeping through the same crevice of the curtain where, only a little while before, the urchin of elephantine appetite had peeped, the butcher beheld the inner door, not closed, as the child had seen it, but ajar, and almost wide open. However it might have happened, it was the fact. Through the passage-way there was a dark vista into the lighter but still obscure interior of the parlor. It appeared to the butcher that he could pretty clearly discern what seemed to be the stalwart legs, clad in black pantaloons, of a man sitting in a large oaken chair, the back of which concealed all the remainder of his figure. This contemptuous tranquillity on the part of an occupant of the house, in response to the butcher's indefatigable efforts to attract notice, so piqued the man of flesh that he determined to withdraw.

"So," thought he, "there sits Old Maid Pyncheon's bloody brother, while I've been giving myself all this trouble! Why, if a hog hadn't more manners, I'd stick him! I call it demeaning a man's business to trade with such people; and from this time forth, if they want a sausage or an ounce of liver, they shall run after the cart for it!"

He tossed the titbit angrily into his cart, and drove off in a pet.

Not a great while afterwards there was a sound of music turning the corner and approaching down the street, with several intervals of silence, and then a renewed and nearer outbreak of brisk melody. A mob of children was seen moving onward, or stopping, in unison with the sound, which appeared to proceed from the centre of the throng; so that they were loosely bound together by slender strains of harmony, and drawn along captive; with ever and anon an accession of some little fellow in an apron and straw-hat, capering forth from door or gateway. Arriving under the shadow of the Pyncheon Elm, it proved to be the Italian boy, who, with his monkey and show of puppets, had once before played his hurdy-gurdy beneath the arched window. The pleasant face of Phœbe—and doubtless, too, the liberal recompense which she had flung him—still dwelt in his remembrance. His expressive features kindled up, as he recognized the spot where this trifling incident of his erratic life had chanced. He entered the neglected yard (now wilder than ever, with its growth of hog-weed and burdock), stationed himself on the doorstep of the main entrance, and, opening his show-box, began to play. Each individual of the automatic community forthwith set to work, according to his or her proper vocation: the monkey, taking off his Highland bonnet, bowed and scraped to the by-standers most obsequiously, with ever an observant eye to pick up a stray cent; and the young foreigner himself, as he turned the crank of his machine, glanced upward to the arched window, expectant of a presence that would make his music the livelier and sweeter. The throng of children stood near; some on the sidewalk; some within the yard; two or three establishing themselves on the very door-step; and one squatting on the threshold. Meanwhile, the locust kept singing in the great old Pyncheon Elm.

"I don't hear anybody in the house," said one of the children to another. "The monkey won't pick up anything here."

"There is somebody at home," affirmed the urchin on the threshold. "I heard a step!"

Still the young Italian's eye turned sidelong upward; and it really seemed as if the touch of genuine, though slight and almost playful, emotion communicated a juicier sweetness to the dry, mechanical process of his minstrelsy. These wanderers are readily responsive to any natural kindness — be it no more than a smile, or a word itself not understood, but only a warmth in it — which befalls them on the roadside of life. They remember these things, because they are the little enchantments which, for the instant, — for the space that reflects a landscape in a soap-bubble, — build up a home about them. Therefore, the Italian boy would not be discouraged by the heavy silence with which the old house seemed resolute to clog the vivacity of his instrument. He persisted in his melodious appeals; he still looked upward, trusting that his dark, alien countenance would soon be brightened by Phœbe's sunny aspect. Neither could he be willing to depart without again beholding Clifford, whose sensibility, like Phœbe's smile, had talked a kind of heart's language to the foreigner. He repeated all his music over and over again, until his auditors were getting weary. So were the little wooden people in his show-box, and the monkey most of all. There was no response, save the singing of the locust.

"No children live in this house," said a schoolboy, at last. "Nobody lives here but an old maid and an old man. You'll get nothing here! Why don't you go along?"

"You fool, you, why do you tell him?" whispered a shrewd little Yankee, caring nothing for the music, but a good deal for the cheap rate at which it was had. "Let him play as he likes! If there's nobody to pay him, that's his own lookout!"

Once more, however, the Italian ran over his round of melodies. To the common observer — who could understand nothing of the case, except the music and the sunshine on the hither side of the door — it might have been amusing to watch the pertinacity of the street-performer. Will he succeed at last? Will that stubborn door be suddenly flung open? Will a group of joyous children, the young ones of the house, come dancing, shouting, laughing, into the open air, and cluster round the show-box, looking with eager merriment at the puppets, and tossing each a copper for long-tailed Mammon, the monkey, to pick up?

But to us, who know the inner heart of the Seven Gables as well as its exterior face, there is a ghastly effect in this repetition of light popular tunes at its door-step. It would be an ugly business, indeed, if Judge Pyncheon (who would not have cared a fig for Paganini's fiddle in his most harmonious mood) should make his appearance at the door, with a bloody shirt-bosom,

The House of the Seven Gables

and a grim frown on his swarthily white visage, and motion the foreign vagabond away! Was ever before such a grinding out of jigs and waltzes, where nobody was in the cue to dance? Yes, very often. This contrast, or intermingling of tragedy with mirth, happens daily, hourly, momently. The gloomy and desolate old house, deserted of life, and with awful Death sitting sternly in its solitude, was the emblem of many a human heart, which, nevertheless, is compelled to hear the thrill and echo of the world's gayety around it.

Before the conclusion of the Italian's performance, a couple of men happened to be passing, On their way to dinner. "I say, you young French fellow!" called out one of them,—"come away from that doorstep, and go somewhere else with your nonsense! The Pyncheon family live there; and they are in great trouble, just about this time. They don't feel musical to-day. It is reported all over town that Judge Pyncheon, who owns the house, has been murdered; and the city marshal is going to look into the matter. So be off with you, at once!"

As the Italian shouldered his hurdy-gurdy, he saw on the doorstep a card, which had been covered, all the morning, by the newspaper that the carrier had flung upon it, but was now shuffled into sight. He picked it up, and perceiving something written in pencil, gave it to the man to read. In fact, it was an engraved card of Judge Pyncheon's with certain pencilled memoranda on the back, referring to various businesses which it had been his purpose to transact during the preceding day. It formed a prospective epitome of the day's history; only that affairs had not turned out altogether in accordance with the programme. The card must have been lost from the Judge's vest-pocket in his preliminary attempt to gain access by the main entrance of the house. Though well soaked with rain, it was still partially legible.

"Look here; Dixey!" cried the man. "This has something to do with Judge Pyncheon. See!—here's his name printed on it; and here, I suppose, is some of his handwriting."

"Let's go to the city marshal with it!" said Dixey. "It may give him just the clew he wants. After all," whispered he in his companion's ear, "it would be no wonder if the Judge has gone into that door and never come out again! A certain cousin of his may have been at his old tricks. And Old Maid Pyncheon having got herself in debt by the cent-shop,—and the Judge's pocket-book being well filled,—and bad blood amongst them already! Put all these things together and see what they make!"

"Hush, hush!" whispered the other. "It seems like a sin to be the first to speak of such a thing. But I think, with you, that we had better go to the city marshal."

707

"Yes, yes!" said Dixey. "Well! — I always said there was something devilish in that woman's scowl!"

The men wheeled about, accordingly, and retraced their steps up the street. The Italian, also, made the best of his way off, with a parting glance up at the arched window. As for the children, they took to their heels, with one accord, and scampered as if some giant or ogre were in pursuit, until, at a good distance from the house, they stopped as suddenly and simultaneously as they had set out. Their susceptible nerves took an indefinite alarm from what they had overheard. Looking back at the grotesque peaks and shadowy angles of the old mansion, they fancied a gloom diffused about it which no brightness of the sunshine could dispel. An imaginary Hepzibah scowled and shook her finger at them, from several windows at the same moment. An imaginary Clifford — for (and it would have deeply wounded him to know it) he had always been a horror to these small people — stood behind the unreal Hepzibah, making awful gestures, in a faded dressing-gown. Children are even more apt, if possible, than grown people, to catch the contagion of a panic terror. For the rest of the day, the more timid went whole streets about, for the sake of avoiding the Seven Gables; while the bolder signalized their hardihood by challenging their comrades to race past the mansion at full speed.

It could not have been more than half an hour after the disappearance of the Italian boy, with his unseasonable melodies, when a cab drove down the street. It stopped beneath the Pyncheon Elm; the cabman took a trunk, a canvas bag, and a bandbox, from the top of his vehicle, and deposited them on the doorstep of the old house; a straw bonnet, and then the pretty figure of a young girl, came into view from the interior of the cab. It was Phœbe! Though not altogether so blooming as when she first tripped into our story, — for, in the few intervening weeks, her experiences had made her graver, more womanly, and deeper-eyed, in token of a heart that had begun to suspect its depths, — still there was the quiet glow of natural sunshine over her. Neither had she forfeited her proper gift of making things look real, rather than fantastic, within her sphere. Yet we feel it to be a questionable venture, even for Phœbe, at this juncture, to cross the threshold of the Seven Gables. Is her healthful presence potent enough to chase away the crowd of pale, hideous, and sinful phantoms, that have gained admittance there since her departure? Or will she, likewise, fade, sicken, sadden, and grow into deformity, and be only another pallid phantom, to glide noiselessly up and down the stairs, and affright children as she pauses at the window?

At least, we would gladly forewarn the unsuspecting girl that there is nothing in human shape or substance to receive her, unless it be the figure of Judge Pyncheon, who — wretched spectacle that he is, and frightful in our remembrance, since our night-long vigil with him! — still keeps his place in the oaken chair.

Phœbe first tried the shop-door. It did not yield to her hand; and the white curtain, drawn across the window which formed the upper section of the door, struck her quick perceptive faculty as something unusual. Without making another effort to enter here, she betook herself to the great portal, under the arched window. Finding it fastened, she knocked. A reverberation came from the emptiness within. She knocked again, and a third time; and, listening intently, fancied that the floor creaked, as if Hepzibah were coming, with her ordinary tiptoe movement, to admit her. But so dead a silence ensued upon this imaginary sound, that she began to question whether she might not have mistaken the house, familiar as she thought herself with its exterior.

Her notice was now attracted by a child's voice, at some distance. It appeared to call her name. Looking in the direction whence it proceeded, Phœbe saw little Ned Higgins, a good way down the street, stamping, shaking his head violently, making deprecatory gestures with both hands, and shouting to her at mouth-wide screech.

"No, no, Phœbe!" he screamed. "Don't you go in! There's something wicked there! Don't — don't — don't go in!"

But, as the little personage could not be induced to approach near enough to explain himself, Phœbe concluded that he had been frightened, on some of his visits to the shop, by her cousin Hepzibah; for the good lady's manifestations, in truth, ran about an equal chance of scaring children out of their wits, or compelling them to unseemly laughter. Still, she felt the more, for this incident, how unaccountably silent and impenetrable the house had become. As her next resort, Phœbe made her way into the garden, where on so warm and bright a day as the present, she had little doubt of finding Clifford, and perhaps Hepzibah also, idling away the noontide in the shadow of the arbor. Immediately on her entering the garden gate, the family of hens half ran, half flew to meet her; while a strange grimalkin, which was prowling under the parlor window, took to his heels, clambered hastily over the fence, and vanished. The arbor was vacant, and its floor, table, and circular bench were still damp, and bestrewn with twigs and the disarray of the past storm. The growth of the garden seemed to have got quite out of bounds; the weeds had taken advantage of Phœbe's absence, and the long-continued rain, to run rampant over the flowers and kitchen-vegetables. Maule's well had overflowed its stone border, and made a pool of formidable breadth in that corner of the garden.

The impression of the whole scene was that of a spot where no human foot had left its print for many preceding days, — probably not since Phœbe's departure, — for she saw a side-comb of her own under the table of the arbor, where it must have fallen on the last afternoon when she and Clifford sat there.

The girl knew that her two relatives were capable of far greater oddities than that of shutting themselves up in their old house, as they appeared now to have done. Nevertheless, with indistinct misgivings of something amiss, and apprehensions to which she could not give shape, she approached the door that formed the customary communication between the house and garden. It was secured within, like the two which she had already tried. She knocked, however; and immediately, as if the application had been expected, the door was drawn open, by a considerable exertion of some unseen person's strength, not wide, but far enough to afford her a sidelong entrance. As Hepzibah, in order not to expose herself to inspection from without, invariably opened a door in this manner, Phœbe necessarily concluded that it was her cousin who now admitted her.

Without hesitation, therefore, she stepped across the threshold, and had no sooner entered than the door closed behind her.

XX.
The Flower of Eden

Phœbe, coming so suddenly from the sunny daylight, was altogether bedimmed in such density of shadow as lurked in most of the passages of the old house. She was not at first aware by whom she had been admitted. Before her eyes had adapted themselves to the obscurity, a hand grasped her own with a firm but gentle and warm pressure, thus imparting a welcome which caused her heart to leap and thrill with an indefinable shiver of enjoyment. She felt herself drawn along, not towards the parlor, but into a large and unoccupied apartment, which had formerly been the grand reception-room of the Seven Gables. The sunshine came freely into all the uncurtained windows of this room, and fell upon the dusty floor; so that Phœbe now clearly saw—what, indeed, had been no secret, after the encounter of a warm hand with hers—that it was not Hepzibah nor Clifford, but Holgrave, to whom she owed her reception. The subtile, intuitive communication, or, rather, the vague and formless impression of something to be told, had made her yield unresistingly to his impulse. Without taking away her hand, she looked eagerly in his face, not quick to forebode evil, but unavoidably conscious that the state of the family had changed since her departure, and therefore anxious for an explanation.

The artist looked paler than ordinary; there was a thoughtful and severe contraction of his forehead, tracing a deep, vertical line between the eyebrows. His smile, however, was full of genuine warmth, and had in it a joy, by far the most vivid expression that Phœbe had ever witnessed, shining out of the New England reserve with which Holgrave habitually masked whatever lay near his heart. It was the look wherewith a man, brooding alone over some fearful object, in a dreary forest or illimitable desert, would recognize the familiar aspect of his dearest friend, bringing up all the peaceful ideas that belong to home, and the gentle current of every-day affairs. And yet, as he felt the necessity of responding to her look of inquiry, the smile disappeared.

"I ought not to rejoice that you have come, Phœbe," said he. "We meet at a strange moment!"

"What has happened!" she exclaimed. "Why is the house so deserted? Where are Hepzibah and Clifford?"

"Gone! I cannot imagine where they are!" answered Holgrave. "We are alone in the house!"

"Hepzibah and Clifford gone?" cried Phœbe. "It is not

possible! And why have you brought me into this room, instead of the parlor? Ah, something terrible has happened! I must run and see!"

"No, no, Phœbe!" said Holgrave holding her back. "It is as I have told you. They are gone, and I know not whither. A terrible event has, indeed happened, but not to them, nor, as I undoubtingly believe, through any agency of theirs. If I read your character rightly, Phœbe," he continued, fixing his eyes on hers with stern anxiety, intermixed with tenderness, "gentle as you are, and seeming to have your sphere among common things, you yet possess remarkable strength. You have wonderful poise, and a faculty which, when tested, will prove itself capable of dealing with matters that fall far out of the ordinary rule."

"Oh, no, I am very weak!" replied Phœbe, trembling. "But tell me what has happened!"

"You are strong!" persisted Holgrave. "You must be both strong and wise; for I am all astray, and need your counsel. It may be you can suggest the one right thing to do!"

"Tell me! — tell me!" said Phœbe, all in a tremble. "It oppresses, — it terrifies me, — this mystery! Anything else I can bear!"

The artist hesitated. Notwithstanding what he had just said, and most sincerely, in regard to the self-balancing power with which Phœbe impressed him, it still seemed almost wicked to bring the awful secret of yesterday to her knowledge. It was like dragging a hideous shape of death into the cleanly and cheerful space before a household fire, where it would present all the uglier aspect, amid the decorousness of everything about it. Yet it could not be concealed from her; she must needs know it.

"Phœbe," said he, "do you remember this?" He put into her hand a daguerreotype; the same that he had shown her at their first interview in the garden, and which so strikingly brought out the hard and relentless traits of the original.

"What has this to do with Hepzibah and Clifford?" asked Phœbe, with impatient surprise that Holgrave should so trifle with her at such a moment. "It is Judge Pyncheon! You have shown it to me before!"

"But here is the same face, taken within this half-hour" said the artist, presenting her with another miniature. "I had just finished it when I heard you at the door."

"This is death!" shuddered Phœbe, turning very pale.

The House of the Seven Gables

"Judge Pyncheon dead!"

"Such as there represented," said Holgrave, "he sits in the next room. The Judge is dead, and Clifford and Hepzibah have vanished! I know no more. All beyond is conjecture. On returning to my solitary chamber, last evening, I noticed no light, either in the parlor, or Hepzibah's room, or Clifford's; no stir nor footstep about the house. This morning, there was the same death-like quiet. From my window, I overheard the testimony of a neighbor, that your relatives were seen leaving the house in the midst of yesterday's storm. A rumor reached me, too, of Judge Pyncheon being missed. A feeling which I cannot describe—an indefinite sense of some catastrophe, or consummation—impelled me to make my way into this part of the house, where I discovered what you see. As a point of evidence that may be useful to Clifford, and also as a memorial valuable to myself,—for, Phœbe, there are hereditary reasons that connect me strangely with that man's fate,—I used the means at my disposal to preserve this pictorial record of Judge Pyncheon's death."

Even in her agitation, Phœbe could not help remarking the calmness of Holgrave's demeanor. He appeared, it is true, to feel the whole awfulness of the Judge's death, yet had received the fact into his mind without any mixture of surprise, but as an event preordained, happening inevitably, and so fitting itself into past occurrences that it could almost have been prophesied.

"Why have you not thrown open the doors, and called in witnesses?" inquired she with a painful shudder. "It is terrible to be here alone!"

"But Clifford!" suggested the artist. "Clifford and Hepzibah! We must consider what is best to be done in their behalf. It is a wretched fatality that they should have disappeared! Their flight will throw the worst coloring over this event of which it is susceptible. Yet how easy is the explanation, to those who know them! Bewildered and terror-stricken by the similarity of this death to a former one, which was attended with such disastrous consequences to Clifford, they have had no idea but of removing themselves from the scene. How miserably unfortunate! Had Hepzibah but shrieked aloud,—had Clifford flung wide the door, and proclaimed Judge Pyncheon's death,—it would have been, however awful in itself, an event fruitful of good consequences to them. As I view it, it would have gone far towards obliterating the black stain on Clifford's character."

"And how," asked Phœbe, "could any good come from what is so very dreadful?"

"Because," said the artist, "if the matter can be fairly considered and candidly interpreted, it must be evident that

Judge Pyncheon could not have come unfairly to his end. This mode of death had been an idiosyncrasy with his family, for generations past; not often occurring, indeed, but, when it does occur, usually attacking individuals about the Judge's time of life, and generally in the tension of some mental crisis, or, perhaps, in an access of wrath. Old Maule's prophecy was probably founded on a knowledge of this physical predisposition in the Pyncheon race. Now, there is a minute and almost exact similarity in the appearances connected with the death that occurred yesterday and those recorded of the death of Clifford's uncle thirty years ago. It is true, there was a certain arrangement of circumstances, unnecessary to be recounted, which made it possible nay, as men look at these things, probable, or even certain—that old Jaffrey Pyncheon came to a violent death, and by Clifford's hands."

"Whence came those circumstances?" exclaimed Phœbe. "He being innocent, as we know him to be!"

"They were arranged," said Holgrave,—"at least such has long been my conviction,—they were arranged after the uncle's death, and before it was made public, by the man who sits in yonder parlor. His own death, so like that former one, yet attended by none of those suspicious circumstances, seems the stroke of God upon him, at once a punishment for his wickedness, and making plain the innocence of Clifford. But this flight,—it distorts everything! He may be in concealment, near at hand. Could we but bring him back before the discovery of the Judge's death, the evil might be rectified."

"We must not hide this thing a moment longer!" said Phœbe. "It is dreadful to keep it so closely in our hearts. Clifford is innocent. God will make it manifest! Let us throw open the doors, and call all the neighborhood to see the truth!"

"You are right, Phœbe," rejoined Holgrave. "Doubtless you are right."

Yet the artist did not feel the horror, which was proper to Phœbe's sweet and order-loving character, at thus finding herself at issue with society, and brought in contact with an event that transcended ordinary rules. Neither was he in haste, like her, to betake himself within the precincts of common life. On the contrary, he gathered a wild enjoyment,—as it were, a flower of strange beauty, growing in a desolate spot, and blossoming in the wind,—such a flower of momentary happiness he gathered from his present position. It separated Phœbe and himself from the world, and bound them to each other, by their exclusive knowledge of Judge Pyncheon's mysterious death, and the counsel which they were forced to hold respecting it. The secret, so long as it should continue such, kept them within the circle of a spell, a solitude in the midst of men, a remoteness as entire as that of an island in mid-ocean; once divulged, the ocean would flow betwixt them, standing on its widely sundered shores. Meanwhile, all the circumstances of their situation seemed to draw them together; they were like two children who go hand in hand, pressing closely to one another's side, through a shadow-haunted passage. The image of awful Death, which filled the house, held them united by his stiffened grasp.

These influences hastened the development of emotions that might not otherwise have flowered so. Possibly, indeed, it had been Holgrave's purpose to let them die in their undeveloped germs. "Why do we delay so?" asked Phœbe. "This secret takes away my breath! Let us throw open the doors!"

"In all our lives there can never come another moment like this!" said Holgrave. "Phœbe, is it all terror? — nothing but terror? Are you conscious of no joy, as I am, that has made this the only point of life worth living for?"

"It seems a sin," replied Phœbe, trembling, "to think of joy at such a time!"

"Could you but know, Phœbe, how it was with me the hour before you came!" exclaimed the artist. "A dark, cold, miserable hour! The presence of yonder dead man threw a great black shadow over everything; he made the universe, so far as my perception could reach, a scene of guilt and of retribution more dreadful than the guilt. The sense of it took away my youth. I never hoped to feel young again! The world looked strange, wild, evil, hostile; my past life, so lonesome and dreary; my future, a shapeless gloom, which I must mould into gloomy shapes! But, Phœbe, you crossed the threshold; and hope, warmth, and joy came in with you! The black moment became at once a blissful one. It must not pass without the spoken word. I love you!"

"How can you love a simple girl like me?" asked Phœbe, compelled by his earnestness to speak. "You have many, many thoughts, with which I should try in vain to sympathize. And I, — I, too, — I have tendencies with which you would sympathize as little. That is less matter. But I have not scope enough to make you happy."

"You are my only possibility of happiness!" answered Holgrave. "I have no faith in it, except as you bestow it on me!"

"And then — I am afraid!" continued Phœbe, shrinking towards Holgrave, even while she told him so frankly the doubts with which he affected her. "You will lead me out of my own quiet path. You will make me strive to follow you where it is pathless. I cannot do so. It is not my nature. I shall sink down and perish!"

"Ah, Phœbe!" exclaimed Holgrave, with almost a sigh, and a smile that was burdened with thought.

"It will be far otherwise than as you forebode. The world owes all its onward impulses to men ill at ease. The happy man inevitably confines himself within ancient limits. I have a presentiment that, hereafter, it will be my lot to set out trees, to make fences,—perhaps, even, in due time, to build a house for another generation,—in a word, to conform myself to laws and the peaceful practice of society. Your poise will be more powerful than any oscillating tendency of mine."

"I would not have it so!" said Phœbe earnestly.

"Do you love me?" asked Holgrave. "If we love one another, the moment has room for nothing more. Let us pause upon it, and be satisfied. Do you love me, Phœbe?"

"You look into my heart," said she, letting her eyes drop. "You know I love you!"

And it was in this hour, so full of doubt and awe, that the one miracle was wrought, without which every human existence is a blank. The bliss which makes all things true, beautiful, and holy shone around this youth and maiden. They were conscious of nothing sad nor old. They transfigured the earth, and made it Eden again, and themselves the two first dwellers in it. The dead man, so close beside them, was forgotten. At such a crisis, there is no death; for immortality is revealed anew, and embraces everything in its hallowed atmosphere.

But how soon the heavy earth-dream settled down again!

"Hark!" whispered Phœbe. "Somebody is at the street door!"

"Now let us meet the world!" said Holgrave. "No doubt, the rumor of Judge Pyncheon's visit to this house, and the flight of Hepzibah and Clifford, is about to lead to the investigation of the premises. We have no way but to meet it. Let us open the door at once."

But, to their surprise, before they could reach the street door,—even before they quitted the room in which the foregoing interview had passed,—they heard footsteps in the farther passage. The door, therefore, which they supposed to be securely locked,—which Holgrave, indeed, had seen to be so, and at which Phœbe had vainly tried to enter,—must have been opened from without. The sound of footsteps was not harsh, bold, decided, and intrusive, as the gait of strangers would naturally be, making authoritative entrance into a dwelling where they knew themselves unwelcome. It was feeble, as of persons either weak or weary; there was the mingled murmur of two voices, familiar to both the listeners.

"Can it be?" whispered Holgrave.

"It is they!" answered Phœbe. "Thank God!—thank God!"

And then, as if in sympathy with Phœbe's whispered ejaculation, they heard Hepzibah's voice more distinctly.

"Thank God, my brother, we are at home!"

"Well!—Yes!—thank God!" responded Clifford. "A dreary home, Hepzibah! But you have done well to bring me hither! Stay! That parlor door is open. I cannot pass by it! Let me go and rest me in the arbor, where I used,—oh, very long ago, it seems to me, after what has befallen us,—where I used to be so happy with little Phœbe!"

But the house was not altogether so dreary as Clifford imagined it. They had not made many steps,—in truth, they were lingering in the entry, with the listlessness of an accomplished purpose, uncertain what to do next,—when Phœbe ran to meet them. On beholding her, Hepzibah burst into tears. With all her might, she had staggered onward beneath the burden of grief and responsibility, until now that it was safe to fling it down. Indeed, she had not energy to fling it down, but had ceased to uphold it, and suffered it to press her to the earth. Clifford appeared the stronger of the two.

"It is our own little Phœbe!—Ah! and Holgrave with, her" exclaimed he, with a glance of keen and delicate insight, and a smile, beautiful, kind, but melancholy. "I thought of you both, as we came down the street, and beheld Alice's Posies in full bloom. And so the flower of Eden has bloomed, likewise, in this old, darksome house to-day."

XXI.
The Departure

The sudden death of so prominent a member of the social world as the Honorable Judge Jaffrey Pyncheon created a sensation (at least, in the circles more immediately connected with the deceased) which had hardly quite subsided in a fortnight.

It may be remarked, however, that, of all the events which constitute a person's biography, there is scarcely one—none, certainly, of anything like a similar importance—to which the world so easily reconciles itself as to his death. In most other cases and contingencies, the individual is present among us, mixed up with the daily revolution of affairs, and affording a definite point for observation. At his decease, there is only a vacancy, and a momentary eddy,—very small, as compared with the apparent magnitude of the ingurgitated object,—and a bubble or two, ascending out of the black depth and bursting at the surface. As regarded Judge Pyncheon, it seemed probable, at first blush, that the mode of his final departure might give him a larger and longer posthumous vogue than ordinarily attends the memory of a distinguished man. But when it came to be understood, on the highest professional authority, that the event was a natural, and—except for some unimportant particulars, denoting a slight idiosyncrasy—by no means an unusual form of death, the public, with its customary alacrity, proceeded to forget that he had ever lived. In short, the honorable Judge was beginning to be a stale subject before half the country newspapers had found time to put their columns in mourning, and publish his exceedingly eulogistic obituary.

Nevertheless, creeping darkly through the places which this excellent person had haunted in his lifetime, there was a hidden stream of private talk, such as it would have shocked all decency to speak loudly at the street-corners. It is very singular, how the fact of a man's death often seems to give people a truer idea of his character, whether for good or evil, than they have ever possessed while he was living and acting among them. Death is so genuine a fact that it excludes falsehood, or betrays its emptiness; it is a touchstone that proves the gold, and dishonors the baser metal. Could the departed, whoever he may be, return in a week after his decease, he would almost invariably find himself at a higher or lower point than he had formerly occupied, on the scale of public appreciation. But the talk, or scandal, to which we now allude, had reference to matters of no less old a date than the supposed murder, thirty or forty years ago, of the late Judge Pyncheon's uncle. The medical opinion with regard to his own recent and regretted decease had almost entirely obviated the idea that a murder was

The House of the Seven Gables

committed in the former case. Yet, as the record showed, there were circumstances irrefragably indicating that some person had gained access to old Jaffrey Pyncheon's private apartments, at or near the moment of his death. His desk and private drawers, in a room contiguous to his bedchamber, had been ransacked; money and valuable articles were missing; there was a bloody hand-print on the old man's linen; and, by a powerfully welded chain of deductive evidence, the guilt of the robbery and apparent murder had been fixed on Clifford, then residing with his uncle in the House of the Seven Gables.

Whencesoever originating, there now arose a theory that undertook so to account for these circumstances as to exclude the idea of Clifford's agency. Many persons affirmed that the history and elucidation of the facts, long so mysterious, had been obtained by the daguerreotypist from one of those mesmerical seers who, nowadays, so strangely perplex the aspect of human affairs, and put everybody's natural vision to the blush, by the marvels which they see with their eyes shut.

According to this version of the story, Judge Pyncheon, exemplary as we have portrayed him in our narrative, was, in his youth, an apparently irreclaimable scapegrace. The brutish, the animal instincts, as is often the case, had been developed earlier than the intellectual qualities, and the force of character, for which he was afterwards remarkable. He had shown himself wild, dissipated, addicted to low pleasures, little short of ruffianly in his propensities, and recklessly expensive, with no other resources than the bounty of his uncle. This course of conduct had alienated the old bachelor's affection, once strongly fixed upon him. Now it is averred, — but whether on authority available in a court of justice, we do not pretend to have investigated, — that the young man was tempted by the devil, one night, to search his uncle's private drawers, to which he had unsuspected means of access. While thus criminally occupied, he was startled by the opening of the chamber-door. There stood old Jaffrey Pyncheon, in his nightclothes! The surprise of such a discovery, his agitation, alarm, and horror, brought on the crisis of a disorder to which the old bachelor had an hereditary liability; he seemed to choke with blood, and fell upon the floor, striking his temple a heavy blow against the corner of a table. What was to be done? The old man was surely dead! Assistance would come too late! What a misfortune, indeed, should it come too soon, since his reviving consciousness would bring the recollection of the ignominious offence which he had beheld his nephew in the very act of committing!

But he never did revive. With the cool hardihood that always pertained to him, the young man continued his search of the drawers, and found a will, of recent date, in favor of Clifford, — which he destroyed, — and an older one, in his own favor, which he suffered to remain. But before retiring, Jaffrey bethought himself of the evidence, in these ransacked drawers, that some one had visited the chamber with sinister purposes. Suspicion, unless averted, might fix upon the real offender. In the very presence of the dead man, therefore, he laid a scheme that should free himself at the expense of Clifford, his rival, for whose character he had at once a contempt and a repugnance. It is not probable, be it said, that he acted with any set purpose of involving Clifford in a charge of murder. Knowing that his uncle did not die by violence, it may not have occurred to him, in the hurry of the crisis, that such an inference might be drawn. But, when the affair took this darker aspect, Jaffrey's previous steps had already pledged him to those which remained. So craftily had he arranged the circumstances, that, at Clifford's trial, his cousin hardly found it necessary to swear to anything false, but only to withhold the one decisive explanation, by refraining to state what he had himself done and witnessed.

Thus Jaffrey Pyncheon's inward criminality, as regarded Clifford, was, indeed, black and damnable; while its mere outward show and positive commission was the smallest that could possibly consist with so great a sin. This is just the sort of guilt that a man of eminent respectability finds it easiest to dispose of. It was suffered to fade out of sight or be reckoned a venial matter, in the Honorable Judge Pyncheon's long subsequent survey of his own life. He shuffled it aside, among the forgotten and forgiven frailties of his youth, and seldom thought of it again.

We leave the Judge to his repose. He could not be styled fortunate at the hour of death. Unknowingly, he was a childless man, while striving to add more wealth to his only child's inheritance. Hardly a week after his decease, one of the Cunard steamers brought intelligence of the death, by cholera, of Judge Pyncheon's son, just at the point of embarkation for his native land. By this misfortune Clifford became rich; so did Hepzibah; so did our little village maiden, and, through her, that sworn foe of wealth and all manner of conservatism,—the wild reformer, —Holgrave!

It was now far too late in Clifford's life for the good opinion of society to be worth the trouble and anguish of a formal vindication. What he needed was the love of a very few; not the admiration, or even the respect, of the unknown many. The latter might probably have been won for him, had those on whom the guardianship of his welfare had fallen deemed it advisable to expose Clifford to a miserable resuscitation of past ideas, when the condition of whatever comfort he might expect lay in the calm of forgetfulness. After such wrong as he had suffered, there is no reparation. The pitiable mockery of it, which the world might have been ready enough to offer, coming so long after the agony had done its utmost work,

The House of the Seven Gables

would have been fit only to provoke bitterer laughter than poor Clifford was ever capable of. It is a truth (and it would be a very sad one but for the higher hopes which it suggests) that no great mistake, whether acted or endured, in our mortal sphere, is ever really set right. Time, the continual vicissitude of circumstances, and the invariable inopportunity of death, render it impossible. If, after long lapse of years, the right seems to be in our power, we find no niche to set it in. The better remedy is for the sufferer to pass on, and leave what he once thought his irreparable ruin far behind him.

The shock of Judge Pyncheon's death had a permanently invigorating and ultimately beneficial effect on Clifford. That strong and ponderous man had been Clifford's nightmare. There was no free breath to be drawn, within the sphere of so malevolent an influence. The first effect of freedom, as we have witnessed in Clifford's aimless flight, was a tremulous exhilaration. Subsiding from it, he did not sink into his former intellectual apathy. He never, it is true, attained to nearly the full measure of what might have been his faculties. But he recovered enough of them partially to light up his character, to display some outline of the marvellous grace that was abortive in it, and to make him the object of no less deep, although less melancholy interest than heretofore. He was evidently happy. Could we pause to give another picture of his daily life, with all the appliances now at command to gratify his instinct for the Beautiful, the garden scenes, that seemed so sweet to him, would look mean and trivial in comparison.

Very soon after their change of fortune, Clifford, Hepzibah, and little Phœbe, with the approval of the artist, concluded to remove from the dismal old House of the Seven Gables, and take up their abode, for the present, at the elegant country-seat of the late Judge Pyncheon. Chanticleer and his family had already been transported thither, where the two hens had forthwith begun an indefatigable process of egg-laying, with an evident design, as a matter of duty and conscience, to continue their illustrious breed under better auspices than for a century past. On the day set for their departure, the principal personages of our story, including good Uncle Venner, were assembled in the parlor.

"The country-house is certainly a very fine one, so far as the plan goes," observed Holgrave, as the party were discussing their future arrangements. "But I wonder that the late Judge—being so opulent, and with a reasonable prospect of transmitting his wealth to descendants of his own—should not have felt the propriety of embodying so excellent a piece of domestic architecture in stone, rather than in wood. Then, every generation of the family might have altered the interior, to suit its own taste and convenience; while the exterior, through the lapse of years, might have been adding venerableness to its original beauty, and thus giving that impression of permanence which I consider essential to the happiness of any one moment."

"Why," cried Phœbe, gazing into the artist's face with infinite amazement, "how wonderfully your ideas are changed! A house of stone, indeed! It is but two or three weeks ago that you seemed to wish people to live in something as fragile and temporary as a bird's-nest!"

"Ah, Phœbe, I told you how it would be!" said the artist, with a half-melancholy laugh. "You find me a conservative already! Little did I think ever to become one. It is especially unpardonable in this dwelling of so much hereditary misfortune, and under the eye of yonder portrait of a model conservative, who, in that very character, rendered himself so long the evil destiny of his race."

"That picture!" said Clifford, seeming to shrink from its stern glance. "Whenever I look at it, there is an old dreamy recollection haunting me, but keeping just beyond the grasp of my mind. Wealth, it seems to say!—boundless wealth!—unimaginable wealth! I could fancy that, when I was a child, or a youth, that portrait had spoken, and told me a rich secret, or had held forth its hand, with the written record of hidden opulence. But those old matters are so dim with me, nowadays! What could this dream have been?"

"Perhaps I can recall it," answered Holgrave. "See! There are a hundred chances to one that no person, unacquainted with the secret, would ever touch this spring."

"A secret spring!" cried Clifford. "Ah, I remember now! I did discover it, one summer afternoon, when I was idling and dreaming about the house, long, long ago. But the mystery escapes me."

The artist put his finger on the contrivance to which he had referred. In former days, the effect would probably have been to cause the picture to start forward. But, in so long a period of concealment, the machinery had been eaten through with rust; so that at Holgrave's pressure, the portrait, frame and all, tumbled suddenly from its position, and lay face downward on the floor. A recess in the wall was thus brought to light, in which lay an object so covered with a century's dust that it could not immediately be recognized as a folded sheet of parchment. Holgrave opened it, and displayed an ancient deed, signed with the hieroglyphics of several Indian sagamores, and conveying to Colonel Pyncheon and his heirs, forever, a vast extent of territory at the Eastward.

"This is the very parchment, the attempt to recover which

722

cost the beautiful Alice Pyncheon her happiness and life," said the artist, alluding to his legend. "It is what the Pyncheons sought in vain, while it was valuable; and now that they find the treasure, it has long been worthless."

"Poor Cousin Jaffrey! This is what deceived him," exclaimed Hepzibah. "When they were young together, Clifford probably made a kind of fairy-tale of this discovery. He was always dreaming hither and thither about the house, and lighting up its dark corners with beautiful stories. And poor Jaffrey, who took hold of everything as if it were real, thought my brother had found out his uncle's wealth. He died with this delusion in his mind!"

"But," said Phœbe, apart to Holgrave, "how came you to know the secret?"

"My dearest Phœbe," said Holgrave, "how will it please you to assume the name of Maule? As for the secret, it is the only inheritance that has come down to me from my ancestors. You should have known sooner (only that I was afraid of frightening you away) that, in this long drama of wrong and retribution, I represent the old wizard, and am probably as much a wizard as ever he was. The son of the executed Matthew Maule, while building this house, took the opportunity to construct that recess, and hide away the Indian deed, on which depended the immense land-claim of the Pyncheons. Thus they bartered their eastern territory for Maule's garden-ground."

"And now" said Uncle Venner "I suppose their whole claim is not worth one man's share in my farm yonder!"

"Uncle Venner," cried Phœbe, taking the patched philosopher's hand, "you must never talk any more about your farm! You shall never go there, as long as you live! There is a cottage in our new garden, — the prettiest little yellowish-brown cottage you ever saw; and the sweetest-looking place, for it looks just as if it were made of gingerbread, — and we are going to fit it up and furnish it, on purpose for you. And you shall do nothing but what you choose, and shall be as happy as the day is long, and shall keep Cousin Clifford in spirits with the wisdom and pleasantness which is always dropping from your lips!"

"Ah! my dear child," quoth good Uncle Venner, quite overcome, "if you were to speak to a young man as you do to an old one, his chance of keeping his heart another minute would not be worth one of the buttons on my waistcoat! And — soul alive! — that great sigh, which you made me heave, has burst off the very last of them! But, never mind! It was the happiest sigh I ever did heave; and it seems as if I must have drawn in a gulp of heavenly breath, to make it with. Well, well, Miss Phœbe!

They'll miss me in the gardens hereabouts, and round by the back doors; and Pyncheon Street, I'm afraid, will hardly look the same without old Uncle Venner, who remembers it with a mowing field on one side, and the garden of the Seven Gables on the other. But either I must go to your country-seat, or you must come to my farm,—that's one of two things certain; and I leave you to choose which!"

"Oh, come with us, by all means, Uncle Venner!" said Clifford, who had a remarkable enjoyment of the old man's mellow, quiet, and simple spirit. "I want you always to be within five minutes, saunter of my chair. You are the only philosopher I ever knew of whose wisdom has not a drop of bitter essence at the bottom!"

"Dear me!" cried Uncle Venner, beginning partly to realize what manner of man he was. "And yet folks used to set me down among the simple ones, in my younger days! But I suppose I am like a Roxbury russet,—a great deal the better, the longer I can be kept. Yes; and my words of wisdom, that you and Phœbe tell me of, are like the golden dandelions, which never grow in the hot months, but may be seen glistening among the withered grass, and under the dry leaves, sometimes as late as December. And you are welcome, friends, to my mess of dandelions, if there were twice as many!"

A plain, but handsome, dark-green barouche had now drawn up in front of the ruinous portal of the old mansion-house. The party came forth, and (with the exception of good Uncle Venner, who was to follow in a few days) proceeded to take their places. They were chatting and laughing very pleasantly together; and—as proves to be often the case, at moments when we ought to palpitate with sensibility—Clifford and Hepzibah bade a final farewell to the abode of their forefathers, with hardly more emotion than if they had made it their arrangement to return thither at tea-time. Several children were drawn to the spot by so unusual a spectacle as the barouche and pair of gray horses. Recognizing little Ned Higgins among them, Hepzibah put her hand into her pocket, and presented the urchin, her earliest and staunchest customer, with silver enough to people the Domdaniel cavern of his interior with as various a procession of quadrupeds as passed into the ark.

Two men were passing, just as the barouche drove off.

"Well, Dixey," said one of them, "what do you think of this? My wife kept a cent-shop three months, and lost five dollars on her outlay. Old Maid Pyncheon has been in trade just about as long, and rides off in her carriage with a couple of hundred thousand,—reckoning her share, and Clifford's, and Phœbe's,—and some say twice as much! If you choose to call it luck, it is all very well; but if we are to take it as the will of Providence, why, I can't exactly fathom it!"

"Pretty good business!" quoth the sagacious Dixey, — "pretty good business!"

Maule's well, all this time, though left in solitude, was throwing up a succession of kaleidoscopic pictures, in which a gifted eye might have seen foreshadowed the coming fortunes of Hepzibah and Clifford, and the descendant of the legendary wizard, and the village maiden, over whom he had thrown love's web of sorcery. The Pyncheon Elm, moreover, with what foliage the September gale had spared to it, whispered unintelligible prophecies. And wise Uncle Venner, passing slowly from the ruinous porch, seemed to hear a strain of music, and fancied that sweet Alice Pyncheon — after witnessing these deeds, this bygone woe and this present happiness, of her kindred mortals — had given one farewell touch of a spirit's joy upon her harpsichord, as she floated heavenward from the HOUSE OF THE SEVEN GABLES!